Stella Riley was born an[...] trained as a teacher in Lo[...] [...]ing up writing full time in 1983 when her first novel, *The Marigold Chain*, was published.

She lived for some time in Banbury where much of the action in *The Black Madonna* takes place.

The Black Madonna

Stella Riley

HEADLINE

First published in 1992
by HEADLINE BOOK PUBLISHING PLC

First published paperback in 1992
by HEADLINE BOOK PUBLISHING PLC

10 9 8 7 6 5 4 3 2 1

ISBN 0 7472 3857 X

Printed and bound in Great Britain by
HarperCollins Manufacturing, Glasgow

HEADLINE BOOK PUBLISHING PLC
Headline House
79 Great Titchfield Street
London W1P 7FN

For Mum, Dad and Terry,
all of whom have waited a long time

Genoa

February, 1636

'I am arm'd with more than complete
steel – the justice of my quarrel.'

Marlowe

Prologue

Beneath the richly painted ceiling of the Villa Falcieri's vast and opulent salon, four pairs of eyes dwelt with varying degrees of incredulity on the still, slight figure which faced them across several yards of gleaming marble floor. Vittorio Falcieri's normally inscrutable gaze held a glint of speculative interest – mixed, almost imperceptibly, with amusement; but two of his three sons bristled with such strong hostility that Vittorio could almost hear the blood pounding in their heads. His amusement deepened and acquired a touch of malice.

It would do his finicky, silken-clad brood no harm to wait. They were too cocksure, too spoiled by soft living; and much too eager to forget that their grandfather had started his life in the backstreets of Genoa. Now it was only Vittorio himself who recalled the tiny workshop in the Via Margarita that had been the foundation of the present Falcieri empire; and he wished his sons had just a tithe of the steel such memories engendered, and of which their cousin, standing alone in his shabby black amidst the chilly splendour, had in plenty.

It was evident in the cold quiet way he waited for an answer. Iron control – and something more. Something which Vittorio had never quite been able to name but which, even when the boy had first presented himself as a gaunt and travel-torn twelve-year-old, had whispered that this unknown nephew with the face of a hungry angel, incongruously set above a pair of imperfectly matched shoulders, had more strength of character in his little finger than all three of his own sons put together.

3

It was an unpalatable thought and one which laid new and bitter resentment over the old. For the boy was the son of Alessandro and Lucia: Alessandro, his bright and laughing elder brother – and Lucia Vitri, the girl whom he, Vittorio, had striven so long and hard to win, only to see her fall victim to Alessandro's charm and elope with him to England. And, as if this had not been hurt enough, they had taken with them the symbol of the Falcieri luck and left behind a void that no amount of carefully nurtured anger could ever quite fill.

It had been a black time but Vittorio had survived it. He'd married Lucia's sister, Mariana – always second best but a good woman for all that – and he'd prospered. And then, after a silence lasting fifteen years, had come the boy, bringing a tale of treachery and ruin, and his tiny sister, Gianetta, to tear at Vittorio's heart by looking at him with Lucia's eyes. Lucia, who was still more real to him than her sister had ever been and who it seemed had died in some French hovel after Alessandro had gone to a traitor's grave in England.

Ignoring the hiatus of impatience behind him, Vittorio laid his fingertips together and regarded his nephew thoughtfully. Eight years ago the boy had stared him in the eye and demanded nought save to be apprenticed to a master-goldsmith. Now, in much the same manner, he was calmly asking for a loan large enough to buy half of Genoa.

The apprenticeship, Vittorio had given him – binding him for seven years to Lorenzo Verga in the Via Margarita where he'd learned his own trade – and trying thereafter to ignore him. But little Gianetta he'd made into the daughter of his heart and, by installing her in his house and gratifying her every wish, effectively sundered her from her oddly disturbing brother. What the boy had made of this was impossible to tell; but as time wore on, Vittorio began to suspect that it was he himself who was the loser. For Alessandro had grounded his son well; at fifteen the lad had mastered all the techniques and, at eighteen, was crafting pieces so intricate that every goldsmith in Genoa was trying to buy his indentures. And thus, prompted by an emotion he was still reluctant to name, Vittorio had opened the door which led to the other Falcieri interests of money-lending and shipping . . . and then watched without surprise as his nephew developed a flair for finance that bade fair to outstrip his skill with the gold.

And that, of course, was why his request wasn't as ridiculous as it appeared. For if anyone ever had the will and power to succeed, it was the neat but threadbare young man in front of him.

'Don't I pay you enough to buy a decent coat?' he demanded abruptly. 'You dress like a lawyer's clerk.'

'I dress to suit my station,' came the pleasantly indifferent reply.

'Damn it – you're a Falcieri!'

'Del Santi,' added his youngest son, *sotto voce*.

'Del Santi,' nodded Vittorio, oblivious of levity.

'So.' His nephew's dark brows rose in faint but eloquent mockery. 'Do I shame you, signor?'

'Don't flatter yourself.' Vittorio scowled at him. 'What makes you think I'd lend you the price of a hair-cut – let alone a sum of this size?'

'Because you know I don't fail,' said the distant voice simply.

This was too much for his cousins. Carlo and Giuseppe burst into a torrent of impassioned speech and young Mario (who alone of the three had been born with a sense of humour) gave a long, appreciative whistle. Then Carlo's voice emerged triumphant.

'Arrogant upstart!' he spat. 'You've already wormed your way far enough into this family's intimate concerns to learn financial details that even I – the eldest son – don't know!'

The ghost of a sardonic smile touched the lean mouth but its owner said nothing. It was left to Vittorio to observe that, if Carlo had any interest in finance beyond having sufficient money to entertain his fine friends, it was the first he'd heard of it. Then, bidding him be silent or get out, he looked back at his nephew and said slowly, 'Now, Luciano . . . Let us know what we say. You are asking me for a family favour? A massive loan on no better security than my faith in your abilities?'

'Not at all,' came the cool reply. 'I am asking you to advance me fifty thousand in gold for a period of ten years, at a rate of interest in accordance with your normal transactions and to be repaid annually. Should I fail to meet this obligation, you are entitled to terminate our agreement and reclaim the whole. As to the matter of security . . .' He paused and, moving for the first time, produced from the folds of his cloak a narrow, irregular-shaped package. 'For security, I offer you this.'

Carlo sniggered: 'Some bauble you won in a dice game?'

With the unshakeable impassivity that had maddened Carlo for eight years, Luciano ignored him and crossed the room to lay the parcel before his uncle. 'I understand that you once held this in some esteem . . . but it is possible, I suppose, that you no longer care to have it.'

Vittorio reached out a hand but, even before he touched the package, knowledge of its contents rushed in upon him and he said hoarsely, 'You – you have it still?'

'Of course.' A vagrant smile flickered across the remote, finely boned face. 'Did you never suspect it?'

'You said everything was put under seal – confiscated by the English Crown. The house, land, money, papers . . . everything. I thought that this, too—' He broke off; and then, a surge of colour staining his skin, 'You deceived me!'

'No. You deceived yourself.'

The admission implicit in this speech caused Vittorio's flush to assume choleric proportions and prompted sixteen-year-old Mario to say quickly, 'Father? Won't you open the packet?'

'Yes,' drawled Carlo. 'By all means let us see if what our dear cousin offers us against three years' profit is worth it.'

There was a long pause and then Vittorio said quietly, 'It is worth it. He has brought the Black Madonna home.'

The effect of this announcement on Carlo and Giuseppe was not prodigious but Mario said eagerly, 'The Madonna? Truly? May we see it?'

And finally, with an odd reluctance, Vittorio took the parcel between his hands and slowly unwrapped it.

The Madonna was not large – nor did it possess any obvious feature to suggest that it was, in fact, a Madonna at all. There was no enamelling, no gilding, no jewels; only the slender form of a young girl, simply fashioned of dark, red-veined obsidian. Her hair was demurely covered, her hands clasped in the folds of her robe and her mouth curved in a sweet, secret smile.

For the first time in twenty years, Vittorio's eyes caressed the smooth glossy surface of the stone and marvelled afresh at the mystery of it. He was not a sentimental man and nowadays he had a house full of beautiful, expensive things; but not one of them held a fragment of the lure contained in this austere and probably valueless piece. All he knew of the lady was that she had been in his family for generations and had been treasured through years of obscurity and squalor since before the Falcieri had left their native village of Santi. He had been bred to revere her – as had Alessandro. But Alessandro had stolen her and, in doing so, brought about his own destruction. Or so Vittorio thought. Yet the wheel of Fate had ground on – and the Madonna was home at last.

'Is that it?' Carlo shattered the silence with three supremely disparaging syllables. 'How unspeakably dreary! It's no more than a crudely worked lump of stone.'

Vittorio came to his feet with a force that sent his chair grating back across the floor. For a long moment Carlo was subjected to a wave of intense, silent fury. Then, sweeping round to face his nephew, Vittorio said, 'And you? Do *you* see only a lump of stone?'

'No.' Luciano looked on the Madonna with hooded eyes. 'I see something which, once lost, I can never replace.'

Some of the wrath left Vittorio's face and he growled, 'Then you'd better be sure of what you do.'

'I am sure. I have had eight years in which to plan it.'

'And?'

'And I propose, signor, that we gamble.' Again that chilly, impersonal smile. 'You hold the Madonna and

7

advance me the money. If I use it successfully, you regain it in full and with interest. If not, you take what I have and keep her. Either way, you can't lose.'

'Very clever.'

'Not particularly. It's my only option.'

Unexpectedly, Vittorio laughed.

'You don't favour your father, do you? He hadn't a calculating bone in his body.'

Luciano replied with the merest suggestion of a shrug, a gesture he rarely permitted himself because it emphasised the slight deformity of his left shoulder. He said only, 'I have read *Il Principe*.'

'Machiavelli? Yes. You would. But there's more to this than a desire for your own enterprise. What is it? A girl?'

The black eyes filled with derision.

'Hardly.'

'Then what? I think even you will admit that I've a right to know.'

It was a long time before Luciano spoke and, when he did, each word arrived sheathed in ice.

'Revenge, signor. It is a matter of revenge. I am surprised that you did not guess it.'

'The authority of a King is the keystone which closeth up the arch of order and government – which, once shaken, all the frame falls together in a confused heap of foundation and battlement.'

Thomas Wentworth
Earl of Strafford

Merrie England

July 1639 to October 1640

Gather ye rosebuds while ye may,
Old Time is still a-flying:
And this same flower that smiles to-day,
To-morrow will be dying.

The glorious lamp of heaven, the sun,
The higher he's a-getting,
The sooner will his race be run,
And nearer he's to setting.

Robert Herrick

One

Merrie England

July 1639 to October 1640

One

Situated on a slight rise in the ground and shrouded on the north side by the gentle screen of ash and whitethorn that gave it its name, the modest gabled manor nestled peacefully like a jewel in its setting. It was built around a small but pleasant courtyard; a low, two-storeyed quadrangle of weathered amber and grey stone in which three styles of architecture blended into a mellow, stubbornly unmodernised whole.

Begun by Roger Maxwell in 1351, it had remained almost untouched until great-grandson Robert's timely switch on the eve of Bosworth Field resulted in the addition of a chapel and a gatehouse. Then, three decades on, Robert's son Piers saw the completion of an upper floor to the inner court. Succeeding Maxwells had continued to play a spasmodic part in the affairs of the nation and one, indeed, had gone to the stake under Catholic Mary; but in the last century, none of them had chosen to alter the structure of their dwelling. And now, in this shimmering July of 1639, when the creeper glowed against the stone and the small panes of Piers' lancet-tipped windows reflected the sky, it was the turn of Richard Maxwell to look on the irregular, unimposing house of his ancestors and, like them, to love it.

Soft air, heavy with the scent of roses and slumbrous with the humming of bees, drifted gently through the open window where, her embroidery forgotten in her lap, his wife Dorothy sat gazing dreamily into the garden below. Laughing, youthful voices rose and fell in the distance and she smiled a little. It was a perfect day.

Through the swaying fronds of the willow-tree, she caught a glimpse of rich mahogany hair and her glance quickened. Eden, eldest of her children, had been home for almost two weeks now, but each morning she still revelled in the knowledge of his presence as though it were new. After twenty months at the finest military academy in Europe, he had come back – no longer a boy and so like his father that at times it stopped her breath. It was not his looks, of course: those he had from her. But the quiet obstinacy, the sensitive, open mind, the ready laughter – these things he had from Richard. And Dorothy was well satisfied.

'What's the matter, Dolly? Afraid he'll vanish in a puff of smoke?'

She turned, smiling. 'No. I was just thinking.'

'Oh?' Brown-haired and in his mid-forties, Richard Maxwell was cast in a large mould. 'Of what?'

'Of how well he's turned out – and that having him home again will be good for Kate. The twins are too young to be company for her; and, as for Amy, well . . .'

'Yes.' A quiet laugh shook Richard's frame. 'With all due respect, there are times when I wonder how we came by Amy.'

'I know. She's too – too . . . too *everything* for a four-teen-year-old. And have you seen the way she's behaving with that nice boy Eden brought home with him? It's no wonder Kate finds her such a trial.'

'Chalk and cheese,' said Richard, his fingers lightly exploring her nape. 'They always were. Or can you possibly be intimating that young Cochrane has exposed a chink in Kate's armour?'

Dorothy looked up at him. 'Is it likely?'

'Not unless she's changed since yesterday,' he replied, and took the opportunity to kiss her.

A long moment later Dorothy freed herself to say as sternly as she was able, 'This won't do. The Langley children are in the garden with our brood and we are standing in the window.' She failed to subdue entirely the betraying quiver in her voice. 'Aged parents like us don't behave this way.'

'They do – but in the case of Gervase and Mary Langley, not usually with each other.' He grinned at her. 'And how can I settle into respectable middle age? Matrons with grown-up children are supposed to be plump and homely.'

'And middle-aged squires are supposed to fondle the dairy-maid and snore in front of the fire of an evening.'

'Oh? I could try if you like.' His fingers tightened on her shoulders. 'But not while you still look at me like that.'

She achieved a downcast sigh, 'I'm very sorry.'

He pulled her close again.

'Don't be sorry – just don't do it now. Or alternatively, let's move away from the window.'

On the smooth turf beyond the shrubbery a young gentleman sprawled gracefully on the grass with a volume of poetry while two others passed an idle hour at the butts. Only one of these held a bow; a fine-boned figure whose dark red hair fell in thick waves about his shoulders. Watched critically by the giant at his elbow, he shook back the fullness of his cambric shirt-sleeves, positioned another arrow and took careful aim. The sun burnished his head to living bronze and lent his arrow a transitory gleaming grace as it sped from the bow to land quivering in the mark.

There was silence. Then the giant turned a fair, perpetually ruffled head to encompass the lace-trimmed elegance of the man reclining on the grass a few feet away. 'Francis?'

Dark eyes were reluctantly raised from the page.

'Yes?'

'The devil's in it now. Our Eden has scored a bull's-eye.'

Mischievous amusement dispelled the languor and, tossing aside his book, Francis Langley came lightly to his feet.

'Well, it was bound to happen sooner or later. There's precious little he hasn't hit at some time or other . . . but never more than once, you'll have noticed.'

'Oh come, now!' protested the archer laughingly. 'It's an antiquated sport and I've little patience with it, but I'm no worse than you are at siege-craft or Ralph at mathematics.

13

And then, of course, you both have longer arms.'

Ralph Cochrane, second son of a baron and six feet three inches in his stockinged feet, bent a vivid blue gaze on his friend. 'Excuses, my midget. You'll be telling us next that your lack of effort at the butts is just a kindness to those of us who struggle to keep up with you at everything else.'

'Oh no.' The hazel eyes held a gleam oddly at variance with the meek tone. 'I wouldn't dare.'

'Very wise,' observed Francis, gently relieving him of the bow. He fitted an arrow, nocked and released it. 'Very wise.'

Eden Maxwell's gaze followed the arrow's flight and watched it split his own neatly in two.

'Ah well,' he sighed. 'At least I am spared the sin of pride.'

'Quite,' retorted Francis amicably. 'It's our function. But why the sudden interest in archery?'

'It's because,' confided Ralph, 'he's suddenly conscious of having spent eighteen months under Joachim Martin without learning to fire three arrows with any kind of consistency.'

Eden smiled and picked up his coat.

'Perhaps. Or perhaps I'm just wasting time while I may.'

A deep laugh shook Ralph's chest.

'Anyone would think it was *you* who was off to the wars. As it is, in a couple of weeks from now – while you've no more to worry you than whether to tumble the dairy-maid or the laundress – I'll be sitting in a filthy foreign ditch, desperately trying to remember how to set a damned mine. Think of that, children, and be glad neither of you is the younger son of a church-mouse peer!'

Francis raised faintly supercilious brows and flicked a speck of dust from his blue satin sleeve.

'It has yet to be announced,' he remarked lightly, 'but His Majesty is honouring my father with a viscountcy.'

Eden's eyes widened a trifle but before he could speak Ralph said trenchantly, 'I hope your family can afford it, then. It's all very well for the King to hand out titles as if they were pea-pods – *he* don't have the problem of main- taining 'em. And it's an expensive business, Francis, I can tell you! My father's so deep in debt to some scurvy Italian in the City that he don't even own his own breeches any more. Ship-money – feudal dues – piffling fines for infringements. There don't seem any end to it.'

'Firstly,' said Francis sweetly, 'I would remind you that none of this is new to us. There has been a peerage in my family since the time of Elizabeth. And secondly, I'd like to point out that the fines and dues you mention are all necessary. His Majesty has the Scots rebels to deal with.'

'Then he ought to call a Parliament,' came the swift retort. 'And who wants to fight the Scots, anyway? Not me! Not over a parcel of weasely bishops and the Lambeth Pope's new prayer book.'

'Dear me! Turning Calvinist, Ralph?'

'No. Nor Papist neither!'

'Then I suggest you moderate your tone and refer to Archbishop Laud by his proper title,' returned Francis coolly. 'As for the new book of prayer, if the King wishes the Scots to use it, they have no—'

'The King and the Scots signed a treaty more than a month ago and I wish that the two of you could do the same.' A little apart from them and apparently absorbed in fastening his coat, Eden spoke with quiet finality. 'If you care to find me when you've finished bickering, I'll be in the rose garden with the girls.' And he turned away towards the shrubbery.

He was quite prepared to leave them and, because they knew that he was, Ralph and Francis exchanged a glance of mutual resignation and abandoned their quarrel to follow him. Eden was the magnet which had begun their not always easy friendship and he was the thread by which it held. And despite his lack of the flamboyance which they had in abundance, where he led they usually followed.

They were very different, these three. Even in the mixed bag of Angers where Danes, Swedes, French, Germans and Scots all went to study the profession of arms, it had been hard to find a more dissimilar trio. Their only visible bond had been that of nationality and their other friendships overlapped scarcely at all. But Francis and Eden had taken with them the closeness born of long, childhood years and this, in time, Ralph Cochrane had come to share.

Without ever quite recognising the fact, Francis regarded Ralph as an interloper – and the fact that he was totally lacking the refinements of speech and manner befitting his estate was not calculated to help matters. Tall, dark and gracefully built, Francis had gone to Angers merely as a matter of form before joining his father at Court; and, inclined by temperament towards literature and art, he had an in-built distaste for those whose blunt-tongued cheerfulness, careless apparel and loud laughter all grated on his finer feelings. Ralph, Francis was convinced, *had* no finer feelings. And the army – where coarse jokes and ungentlemanly effort were doubtless appreciated – was the perfect setting for him.

Ralph would have been surprised had he known how much Francis thought about him, for he thought of Francis hardly at all; and though he was fully aware of that gentleman's strictures on his person, he inevitably digested them with tolerant amusement. Ralph might tease Francis about his wish to succeed without appearing to try, but he never pointed out that a good officer did not regard his men as so much dirt beneath his feet. By choice, Ralph would have tramped his father's cornfields rather than those of battle; but, since he must earn his living some other way, a soldier's life was probably as good as any – and at least offered prospects of amusement and good company.

Alone of the three, Eden Maxwell had gone to Angers with no preconceived plans for his future and found there the perfect, undreamed-of answer. The School of Arms offered instruction in every branch of modern warfare, and Eden absorbed it all like a sponge. From the physical skills of horsemanship and weaponry to the intricacies of tactics and strategy, it was all meat and drink to him. He pored over charts and battle-plans, spent hour upon greasy hour dismantling and reassembling pieces of artillery, and fell in love with mathematical calculation and the art of making and breaking ciphers. In these things where effort was pure pleasure, he shone; and even though languages did not come easily to him, he doggedly acquired a working knowledge of German and French. But dancing was a chore and archery had little practical use so he escaped them whenever he could and stubbornly reserved his energies for other things.

Fortunately, he never minded being a target for amusement and this was just as well for, between Ralph who was quite simply massive, and Francis whose lean elegance just reached six feet, he was made constantly aware of his shortcomings. Five feet eight inches in his boots and built in compact proportion, he had philosophically accepted that at the age of nineteen he was unlikely to grow any taller. He had also, rather less philosophically, come to the conclusion that dark red hair and hazel eyes were never going to exercise any immense fascination over the opposite sex. And this was a pity because in the last two years, Celia Langley had at some point ceased being merely Francis's plump and rather tiresome little sister and changed into the loveliest creature that Eden had ever seen.

Just now, their game of quoits abandoned and apparently forgotten, she was engaged in demonstrating the latest dance-steps for his sister, Amy . . . pivoting in a swirl of blood-red taffeta and talking all the time. Amy looked entranced and Eden, pausing in the shadow of the box-hedge, did not blame her.

'Oh bravo!' applauded Amy, as the full skirts swept the grass in a deep curtsy. 'I wish Mother would engage a dancing-master for *us* – don't you, Kate?'

Lying full length and face down, her weight resting ungenteelly on her elbows, Kate continued to peruse the litter of strange charts and diagrams in front of her. 'No.'

Celia gave her charming, silvery laugh and, tossing her dark curls, touched Amy's cheek with one careless finger. 'Well . . . perhaps I can teach you a little myself. Only you must promise not to grow any prettier – or you will be stealing all my admirers.'

And that, reflected Eden, was generous. Amy might be the accredited beauty of the family but she couldn't hold a candle to Celia. No one could.

Aware that Francis and Ralph had arrived at his shoulder, he strolled forward saying lightly, 'Grass-stains, Kate. Flossie will be after you again.'

Kate turned her head and peered at him out of wide cat's eyes. 'Your sash is twisted,' she informed him kindly. And returned to her charts.

Laughing a little, Ralph went to look over her shoulder. 'Is that my birth-chart?'

'It will be.'

'It looks decidedly complicated.'

'It is.'

'Ah. And will it be finished before I leave tomorrow?'

'Only,' sighed Kate, 'if I'm allowed to get on with it.'

Rising from her bench, Amy laid a coaxing hand on Ralph's sleeve. 'Leave her alone before she gets cross. She did mine last week and wouldn't even let me peep till it was finished.'

Ralph smiled indulgently. 'But was it worth waiting for?'

'Oh yes. I'm to marry young and be quite rich and maybe even go to Court.'

Looking down into her provocative face, Ralph could not help thinking that an early marriage was something Amy's parents might do well to arrange. Unlike Kate – who at sixteen was still flat as a board and about as coquettish as a hedgehog – Amy had already blossomed into a very tempting armful indeed and was eagerly testing the power of her dimples and long-lashed, dark grey eyes. In short, she was walking gunpowder and would need some watching if a match were not to be put to her outside wedlock.

Just now she was pouting up at him and asking, 'Must you *really* leave us tomorrow?'

'I really must. But I'll come back one day when you're a smart married lady decked in rubies and I'm a colonel with a hundred foreign orders on my chest.'

'And a romantic scar or two?' grinned Eden. 'But where will the rest of us be by then, I wonder?'

'That's easy.' Francis kicked a quoit aside and disposed himself on the grass. 'I'll be an acknowledged poet and you'll be a major in the Lifeguards. Celia will be a duchess and Kate . . .' He looked down with a hint of mischief on Kate's ferociously red and seemingly oblivious head. 'Kate will be so well known for her wit that she'll be able to be as rude as she likes to everyone. *Voilà!*'

'*Voilà*, indeed,' agreed Kate in the husky-sweet tone that usually heralded her more acid remarks. '*What* a good thing the Scots war didn't amount to much. Berwick-on-Tweed hasn't quite the same cachet as Whitehall, has it?'

'Father says it's quite barbarous.' Celia rose and shook out her skirts. 'But luckily he should be home quite soon now. No later, he hopes, than the beginning of next month.'

'Oh?' Eden's brows rose. 'Does he return before the King, then?'

'Not at all!' laughed Celia. 'He comes *with* the King – which is why he can't say exactly when—'

'But I thought the King was to attend the opening of the Estates in Edinburgh,' exclaimed Ralph. 'It was one of the terms of the peace, wasn't it? Is it in session already?'

Celia's sapphire gaze dwelt on him with a mixture of astonishment and affront. It was therefore left to Francis to say curtly, 'No. It's not.'

'Then what's the King coming home for? If he said he'd stay, it seems to me he ought to do it.'

'Possibly. But though you may be aware that the Scottish Church Assembly was ordered to rescind its illegal abolition of the episcopacy, what you may *not* know is that there were riots on the day the new Assembly was convened – during which His Majesty's own representative received some rather rough handling. Therefore—'

'Therefore,' interposed Ralph dryly, 'the King ain't about to chance *his* dignity in a like manner. I might have known.'

'And I,' snapped Francis, 'might have saved my breath.'

'Oh, do stop arguing!' cried Celia. 'It's all so tedious – and nothing whatever to do with us here. For my part, I'm delighted that the King's leaving Scotland for it means that, with Father coming home, Mother will be able to hold her house-party after all. I've been terrified it would

19

all come to nothing – the Great Tew set are to come, you know.'

Eden smiled at her. 'The Great Tew set of what?'

'Why Lord and Lady Falkland, of course – and Will Davenant and John Suckling and . . .' She stopped and stared at him in disbelief. 'Don't tell me you've never heard of the gatherings at Great Tew!'

'I'm afraid not,' said Eden meekly. 'Or, it seems, any of the people who attend them.'

'Philistine,' mourned Francis, his flash of temper gone. 'Great Tew is the home of Lucius Cary, Viscount Falkland – and Will Davenant is the Poet Laureate. He is also possibly the son of Shakespeare. I take it you *have* heard of Shakespeare?'

'Oh yes. Wasn't he the fellow who wrote that piece we saw at Oxford about the philosopher's stone?'

Francis groaned and shut his eyes.

Quite slowly, Kate turned her head and impaled her brother with a jade green stare. 'You mean *The Alchemist*, of course. But I suppose some people will believe anything.'

Eden grinned at her. 'Exactly. Well done, Kate.' And then, turning to Celia, 'That was Shakespeare, wasn't it?'

'No!' said Celia and her brother in unison.

'Oh.' Apparently crestfallen, Eden picked up a quoit and measured it in his hand. 'Then it must have been Ben Jonson,' he said. And sent the ring spinning to encircle the pin.

Despite its high trussed roof supported by crown-posts and grotesquely carved corbels, the Great Hall of Thorne Ash was well proportioned rather than vast and presented a comfortable, lived-in appearance. There were large pots of delphiniums and hollyhocks in the fireplace, bright cushions on the dark, high-backed settles and a gleaming array of fine but serviceable silver- and pewter-ware on the massive oak dresser. A long table, pitted from years of wear and flanked by benches, ran lengthways between the oriel window at the north end and the screened gallery at the south and was covered, except at meal times, by a glowing

Turkey carpet; and the long opposing walls boasted a pair of richly vibrant tapestries which Richard had bought from Mortlake only the year before.

Here, together with Goodwife Flossing the housekeeper (who had been born at Thorne Ash and was therefore much more than a servant) and Nathan Cresswell (a distant connection of Richard's who had been engaged as the children's tutor), the family gathered thrice daily – for breakfast at eight, dinner at two in the afternoon, and evening prayers immediately followed by supper. The latter was always a simple meal and consisted on this, the last evening of young Mr Cochrane's visit, of little more than boiled capon, marrow-bone pie and rice pudding. But it conformed – as did everything that left the kitchens – to Cook's creed of 'good, wholesome and plentiful'; and the pudding, made with cream, eggs, dates and fine sugar and served a day old, made such a deep impression on Ralph that he ate three helpings and then insisted on taking the recipe home to his mother.

This seemingly harmless request produced a mild furore as Amy, still determined to attract her god-like hero's attention, offered to write out the recipe herself and thus gave the twelve-year-old twins the opportunity they had been waiting for. Felix and Felicity had spent the greater part of the meal in discreet mimicry of Amy's languishing airs, and their swift denunciation of her handwriting was delivered with both flair and merciless truth. It also earned Felix a well-placed kick under the table.

'Ow!' He made a great show of rubbing his ankle. 'What did *I* do?'

Amy avoided Kate's eyes and smiled angelically. 'I don't know *what* you mean.'

'Peace, brats.' Richard rose and frowned with apparent severity on his three young offspring. 'Felix, Felicity – take yourselves off and get your horrible menagerie fed. And latch the cages properly this time. The ferret got out again last night and rampaged its way through the laundry. The next escape will result in dire reprisals. Now go.'

They went, unsuccessfully stifling their laughter. Richard

looked meditatively across at his wife. 'And they,' he said, 'definitely do *not* take after me. Now . . . the recipe. Perhaps, for the sake of Ralph's stomach, we ought to play safe and let Kate write it.'

'Oh, Father!' Amy's greatest talent was an ability to summon tears at will. '*I* want to do it!'

'And I,' said Kate, 'have a birth-chart to finish before the morning. If I may be excused?' Waiting only for her mother's reluctant nod, she crossed to the door and then, with a wicked slanting smile, turned to say, 'I'm sure Ralph won't mind being poisoned in a good cause.' And was gone.

Eden laughed and then, looking at his mother, said, 'Forget it. You might as well wish for the moon.'

Dorothy eyed him calmly. She had been wishing that her two elder daughters could somehow modify each other, make Amy less forward and Kate less retiring, and the expression on her first-born's face told her that he knew it perfectly well. Smiling a little, she said, 'You should do that for money. Otherwise you'll end up at the stake like great-grandfather Henry.' And then, 'Very well, Amy. Go with Flossie and see if you can coax Cook into parting with her secrets – and do *try* to write legibly for once.'

Belatedly recognising a strategic error, Amy hovered irresolutely for a moment before quitting the room with something approaching a flounce. Ralph heaved a sigh of relief.

But he had enjoyed his stay at Thorne Ash and later, sitting in the pleasant parlour where the last dying rays of evening sunshine still lingered, he found himself regretting that the future would offer him scant opportunity to repeat it. No special effort had been made to entertain him; just now, for example, Dorothy was busy with her embroidery and Richard was reviewing the farm accounts with Nathan Cresswell. But the Maxwells had succeeded in making him feel one of the family and he much preferred their unpretentious cheerfulness to the stiff formality of the Langley household. He had visited Far Flamstead only once – and that had been enough. The house might be elegantly built, tastefully furnished and equipped with every modern convenience, but he had thought it about as cosy as a mausoleum; worse still, its pristine neatness coupled with its mistress's chilly eye had made him nervous of sitting down and caused him to wonder if he shouldn't have left his boots at the door.

No such doubts would ever torment a visitor to Thorne Ash. Rambling and inconvenient as it undoubtedly was, it was a home; and Dorothy, with her tawny-green eyes and the incredible dark red hair which she had passed on to Eden, and rather less successfully to Kate, was both a charming hostess and exceptionally easy on the eye.

Kate . . . Too astute by half and with a trick of seeming to look straight into one. Ralph grinned at her oddness and said idly, 'Astrology's a strange interest for a young girl. Has Kate been studying it long?'

'Not very,' replied Dorothy, her head bent over her tambour-frame. 'A cousin of mine visited us in May and inadvertently began it. Before that it was bees.'

'Bees?' echoed Ralph.

'Bees.' Dorothy lifted her head and gave him her lovely smile. 'We got quite used to seeing Kate swathed in gauze – rather in the style of Banquo's ghost, you know. And the honey was delicious.'

'Ah.' Ralph was beginning to see. 'And before the bees?'

'The flageolet. Or was it moral philosophy? I'm afraid I lose track. But I *do* remember her taking up cookery, for it gave us all a sharp attack of colic. Kate, sadly, is not inclined towards the domestic pursuits.'

'So she forsook the kitchen in favour of learning how to fire a musket,' said Richard, looking wryly up from his books. 'The noise kept the hens from laying for a fortnight.' He waited for the laughter to subside and then added, 'We call them her Magnificent Obsessions. And since – thanks to Nathan – she's still managed to acquire all the more usual skills, we see no harm in them. No *real* harm, anyway.'

Mr Cresswell, an austere gentleman of some twenty-five summers, acknowledged this tribute with a thin smile and said, 'It is easy for a teacher to shine through a diligent pupil. But I am unhappily aware how little I have accomplished with Amy.'

'Quite. Fortunately, however, we don't expect miracles.' Richard closed the ledgers and stood up. 'That will do for tonight, I think. Thank you, Nathan.'

Inclining his head, Mr Cresswell gathered the books into a neat pile. 'Then I'll bid you goodnight, cousin.'

Dorothy looked at him kindly. 'Won't you sit with us a little?'

'Thank you, but no. I have Felix's essay to correct and some preparation for tomorrow's lessons still to do. We are studying the decline of Byzantium.' And on this sombre note, he bowed again and removed himself from the room.

There was a tiny pause before Dorothy said carefully, 'His . . . his devotion to duty is quite admirable, isn't it?'

'Admirable,' agreed Richard. 'It's just a pity he can't leaven it with a grain or two of humour. However. Rome – or even Byzantium – wasn't built in a day; and he's only been with us six years, after all.'

Eden grinned appreciatively but said, 'Why do you involve him in estate matters? You used always to prefer to act as your own steward.'

'And still do.' Richard seated himself beside his wife and folded his arms. 'I'm merely training Nathan to act in my stead – should the need arise.'

'You mean,' said his son slowly, 'if the King should call a Parliament. But after ten years, do you think it likely that he will?'

'I suspect the time is coming when he must. Since the City refused to help finance the recent unpleasantness in Scotland, His Majesty has been in the awkward position of relying on Catholic donations. An unpopular move and one which I doubt does much to ease the strain on the royal purse.'

'What strain?' asked Ralph, grimly. 'They say the revenue from the Court of Wards alone is stupendous.'

'It is. Iniquitous systems generally pay well.' Richard's smile was edged with irony. 'But Crown revenue has been declining for years and what there is costs a great deal to collect – mainly because it passes through too many grasping hands en route to the exchequer. Also, His Majesty is committed to a number of expensive schemes; the rebuilding of St Paul's; the enlargement of his deer park at Richmond; the founding of a royal art collection. He can't, I suspect, afford the Scots as well.'

'Then it's a pity he don't leave 'em alone,' growled Ralph. 'If he *must* have a war, let him help the Dutch fight the Dons.'

'He can't,' said Richard. 'Without a policy of neutrality towards Spain, the gold trade would cease. Neither can he risk stirring up the Emperor Ferdinand and the whole of the Holy Roman Empire to get young Rupert out of prison. It's a cleft stick, Ralph. We can't afford a skirmish or two in Scotland – let alone a proper war.'

'All right.' Ralph shifted restlessly. 'But where's his excuse for persecuting the likes of Prynne and Bastwicke? And how d'you justify him imposing illegal taxes?'

'Prynne and his friends should have stuck to shouting "No bishops" and refrained from attacking the Queen,' came the patient reply. 'As for illegal taxes . . . I presume you're talking about ship-money. And all I can do is remind you that it's been levied before and that the Navy has to be funded somehow.'

'You mean you *agree* with it?'

'I don't agree with any tax that hasn't been sanctioned by Parliament. I do, however, accept that the old system of placing the whole burden on the coastal towns was unjust.'

'Do we pay it?' It was Eden who spoke.

'Since John Hampden lost his case against it in the courts – yes.'

Ralph gave a bark of derisive laughter. 'My father held back too – and suddenly found himself fined for infringing the forest laws. God! What's happening to this country? It comes to something when the only ones left to mind their own business are the damned Papists.'

Eden frowned slightly. 'Aren't you getting a bit carried away?'

'No. It's just that *I* have an opinion – which is more, I sometimes think, than *you* do.'

25

Dorothy's eyes widened a little and she stopped sewing.

Eden, however, merely raised his brows and said calmly, 'You're entitled to think what you like. I just wish, occasionally, that you wouldn't do it with your stomach.'

Ralph glared at him and then grinned. 'Meaning?'

'Meaning that, like you, I've been out of England for some time and so don't feel myself qualified to judge. While we were at Angers, Francis quoted his father and you yours – and, as far as I can see, you're both still doing it. Now the time may come when I echo mine; but meanwhile I'll keep my mouth shut and try to assess these things for myself.' Eden paused and looked companionably across at Richard. 'No disrespect intended.'

'I'm glad to hear it.'

'I thought you would be. Ah – and that reminds me. I've some other news for you. Guess who's being made a viscount?'

'Gervase Langley?' suggested Richard, not noticeably impressed. 'Well, well. I imagine that's one honour he could have done without. His present title's already enough to preserve him from knighthood fines – and the feudal dues of a viscountcy are likely to cripple him. Still, I expect Mary is pleased.'

'Knighthood fines?' said Eden. 'What are they?'

'The penalty for breaking a law passed over four hundred years ago,' replied Richard. 'How does the song go?

'Come all you farmers out of the country,
Carters, ploughmen, hedgers and all;
Honour invites you to delights,
Come to Court and be all made knights.'

'What he's trying to explain,' offered Dorothy, 'is that owners of freehold land worth more than forty pounds a year should have applied for knighthood at the coronation. And those who chose to remain mere gentlemen have to pay for the privilege.'

Eden looked at his father. 'Such as you?'

'Such as me. What are you thinking? That it's unfair?'

26

'Well, isn't it? What's the King trying to do?'

'Keep his head above water. Given the present tricky situation and no new revenues in ten years, what would you be trying to do?'

'Call Parliament,' said Eden trenchantly. 'And make a lasting peace with Scotland.'

Two

With only a few weeks between her lord's homecoming and the date set for his return to duty at Whitehall, the erstwhile Lady Langley – now created Viscountess Wroxton – wasted no time, and by the middle of August Far Flamstead was filled with a glittering and select company. Days were passed in riding, hawking, witty conversation and laughing dalliance in the gardens; and in the evenings there was music, poetry, dining and dancing – and more dalliance, low-voiced and elegant in the golden pools of candlelight.

Often the Maxwells were bidden to join the festivities and Dorothy was able to look, with an interest wholly untouched by regret, on the world that she and Richard had long ago abandoned. And if she was human enough to enjoy the novelty of having Sir John Suckling lay his susceptible heart at her feet, it was largely because his sudden, lyrical devotion gave Richard new and thoroughly delightful dimensions to explore when they went home again. She did not and never could envy Lady Wroxton, whose elegant husband never teased or laughed, nor minded where she slept or with whom.

But, with one or two exceptions, the company was pleasant enough and it was impossible not to like Sir John or his friend Will Davenant, that 'Sweet Swan of Isis' who they said was old Will Shakespeare's bastard. Even more universally popular than these were Lord and Lady Falkland – he, grating of voice and jerky of movement and she serious and almost *religieuse,* but both of them intelligent, sensitive and kind. Richard was content to talk business with his old friend Lord Brooke; and when, as so often happened these days, business became politics, they were usually joined by the prim-mouthed lawyer, Mr Hyde, whose only claim to notice, so Mary said, was his friendship with Viscount Falkland.

The only fly in Dorothy's ointment was Kate. For instead of integrating herself with the other young people and learning to be at ease in their company, she was still freezing them with forbidding looks and monosyllabic replies. In short, the experiment of introducing her to society had so far been a dismal failure.

It had been a mistake, perhaps, to insist; and certainly the timing was unfortunate, colliding as it did with the harvest. Mary, naturally, wouldn't have thought of that. But at Thorne Ash there was no rigid division between gentleman and tenant, house and Home Farm; and Richard was as likely to be found with his coat off mending a fence as ordering his bailiff, Jacob Bennet, to see to it. The result was that – with the exception of Amy, who'd been born with an in-built horror of soiling her hands – the Maxwell children had always been encouraged to join the tenants in the fields for the fun of bringing the harvest home. And, more than any of them, Kate loved it; so much so that when Dorothy had suggested that she should forgo the pleasure for this one year, her response had been something approaching mutiny.

'You want me to sit in the house with my hands folded in my lap while Eden and the twins are out on the farm?' she had asked, aghast. 'You can't mean it!'

'Actually, I do,' replied her mother, not without sympathy. 'I know it's hard but it won't really hurt you to miss the hay-making just this once. And I don't think you'll enjoy going to Far Flamstead looking like a lobster.'

'I won't enjoy going to Far Flamstead at *all*!'

'How do you know? And at the moment I'm concerned with your skin and what the sun invariably does to it.'

Kate sighed. The twins became brown as gypsies and even Eden acquired a light tan. She just turned bright pink and peeled. She said, 'I'll wear a hat.'

'Also, your hands get covered in scratches and your fingernails end up looking as if the mice have been at them,' continued Dorothy flatly.

'And gloves.'

'Oh, Kate! However good your intentions, you'd drop them under the first bush and we both know it. I don't want to take a scarecrow with me.'

'I don't see why you want to take me at all. I shall hate it and probably make an utter fool of myself. Why don't you take Amy? She's cross as a crab at being left out and I daresay she'd get on a lot better with Celia and her friends than I should.'

'Amy,' said Dorothy patiently, 'is too young. You, on the other hand, are sixteen and just ripe for a little social polish. And as for coping with the people you'll meet – you'll find it's only a matter of practice. My own opinion is that you've character enough to cope with anything. And you're due a new interest. Astrology's palled somewhat, hasn't it?'

A reluctant smile dawned. 'Are you suggesting I look upon it as a new exercise?'

'As long as you open your mind, I don't care how you look at it. But I had hoped that you'd do it to please me.'

And that, of course, had been that.

Kate had stayed out of the sun and been plagued, instead, by Amy. But although Dorothy had had her way, very little seemed to be coming of it. And, as if that were not enough, Eden was showing an alarming tendency to gravitate towards Lettice Cary, Lady Falkland. It was not surprising; but Dorothy wished, for his own sake, that he would show a little more interest in the rest of the company.

Prompted gently to this end, Eden had merely grinned and said that he left the poets to those who appreciated them – namely herself and Francis. Further inquiries elicited the information that the sophisticated Court beauties were all either tedious or terrifying and that Lord George Goring, despite the graceful limp acquired at Breda, had a disappointing line in conversation.

'He talks,' said Eden simply, 'of taverns, boudoirs and

30

brothels. It's amusing enough in its way but not what I want to hear about.'

'Oh.' Dorothy stared at him, nonplussed. 'And what *did* you want to hear about?'

He raised faintly astonished brows. 'Cavalry tactics. The man's supposed to be a soldier, isn't he? And he's fought in the German wars – as Ralph is doing now – so I've a certain curiosity to know what it was like. You look disappointed. Are you?'

This might have been disconcerting had she not caught the familiar gleam in his eyes. 'No. Merely bewildered. Your father said I should be prepared for the petticoat phase and I am. It's just confusing to find it wasted.'

'Save it,' advised her unconventional son. 'Alternatively, you might comfort yourself with the thought that, though taverns and brothels hold no particular lure for me, I've nothing against boudoirs. It's simply that, unlike Lord George, I don't care to advertise my pleasures in discussion.'

'*Eden!*'

'Well?' The gleam became a singularly disarming smile. 'What is it now? Do you think I'm a rakehell?'

'No,' said Dorothy with strong feeling. 'I think you're outrageous.'

'I know.' Eden dropped a kiss on her cheek. 'But whose fault is that?'

Like Dorothy – but for very different reasons – Celia Langley also found herself watching Eden's progress through the bright, lazy days of August. He had changed, she decided; his silences were an enigma and his talk unexpected. Occasionally, she would catch his glance resting on her with an expression she half recognised but it always vanished before she could be sure. And that made him a challenge. It was just a pity that he cared so little for fashion and finery. He was invariably neat, of course; but beside Francis or charming, carefree Sir Hugo Verney, with their bright, beribboned silks, embroidered baldricks and carefully ordered curls, he appeared positively austere. His preference was for plainly cut coats of black or the darker shades of green and russet, and his only concession to

31

elegance was the beautiful lace of his wide, scalloped collars. He did not even curl his hair.

Once she tried teasing him about these things only to emerge feeling rather silly.

'I think,' had said Eden cheerfully, 'that it's better I stay as I am. For even if I managed to look like Francis, I doubt I could master all the necessary attendant graces . . . so the transformation would be rather pointless, wouldn't it? Like becoming a bird only to find one couldn't fly.'

'I don't understand,' Celia had said blankly. 'What are you now?'

He had smiled, then; that slow, infectious smile that made her strictures suddenly very trivial. 'I rather think, just at the moment . . . a red herring.'

After a conversation like this which always left her feeling that something important had eluded her, she turned with relief to the easy companionship of Sir Hugo Verney. Him, she understood; his mind and his values were hers also. And the undisguised admiration in his laughing brown eyes was both a balm and an invitation to the kind of pleasure that Eden never offered.

In the late afternoons it had become the generally accepted custom to gather in the serenity of the walled garden to savour the last of the sun's warmth. Someone usually brought a lute or guitar with them and the hour was passed in pleasant idleness. On one such day when the month was drawing to its close, the party was scattered in small groups around the garden. By the sundial, Lord George Goring was using his considerable charm in the seduction of lovely Anne Morton while, around the ornamental fishpond, Francis exchanged verses with Will Davenant, and Sir John Suckling amused Dorothy with flirtatious banter. Bored, irritable, and feeling at odds with the world, Kate sat on the periphery of a trio of the Queen's ladies, modishly gowned and chattering like magpies; and, at Celia's feet, Hugo Verney strummed lightly on a guitar and introduced her name into a dozen songs that had never held it before.

'Ask me no more where those stars light,
That downwards fall in dead of night:
In Celia's eyes they sit, and there,
Fixed become as in their sphere.'

Celia flushed, repressed a smile and shook her head at him. 'Shame on you! That isn't how Mr Carew wrote it.'

'Perhaps not. But it's how he *would* have written it, had he been sitting where I am now.'

A dimple peeped and was gone. 'And where is that, sir? On the spur of the moment?'

'Not at all, mistress. I am in the fields of Elysium when you are by.'

'And when I am not?'

Sir Hugo's teeth gleamed white against his meticulously trimmed moustache. 'Ah – then I am left desolate in the darkness of limbo. But I see you don't believe me. That is unkind.'

Celia frowned on him. 'And how can I believe you, pray? You are laughing at me.'

'Never!'

'But you are. I see it in your eyes.'

Even as she spoke, the brown gaze became unexpectedly solemn.

'And what would you wish to see there?'

Suddenly breathless, Celia said lightly, 'My goodness! What makes you suppose that I have a preference?'

'Nothing at all. I merely took the liberty of hoping that you had.'

She stared at him uncertainly. She had no way of knowing that careless, light-hearted Hugo Verney, who everyone said was never serious, was alarmed to find himself serious now and already regretting that he had allowed it to show. She did not know of his debts or that he was on the brink of contracting an eminently suitable alliance with a girl whose family would settle his obligations and of whom – until he had come to Far Flamstead – he had thought himself fond. And because she did not know, she said coquettishly, 'Then, sir, you take one liberty too many.'

'So it seems.' Irony rippled on the edge of his smile but he banished it and matched his tone to hers. 'Here's another. I take it with Will, there . . . and give it to you.

'The Lark now leaves his watery Nest
And climbing, shakes his dewy Wings;
He takes this Window for the East;
And to implore your Light, he Sings,
Awake, awake, the Morn will never rise,
For her Beauty's made pale beside Celia's eyes.'

There was a moment of glorious anticipation and then the voice of the Poet Laureate cut across it with perfectly dramatised agony. 'Why stop there? Why not just take out my bones and polish them? What,' demanded Will Davenant, 'have I ever done to deserve such torture?'

Over the scattered bubble of laughter, Lord George said, 'Not a thing, my dear. It's simply that we deem you great enough to rise above it.'

'And you're right.' There was laughter, too, in the poet's eyes. 'But why must it always be *my* verse that suffers?'

'It isn't.' His lordship limped gracefully into the centre of the turf and struck a pose. '*Prithee why so wan, fond poet? Prithee, why so pale? Will, if looking grim can't move 'em—*' And there he stopped, stepping smartly back to avoid the sparkling shower sent flying at him by Sir John Suckling.

This time even Kate was seen to smile.

Eden turned back from the genial raillery on the lawn to Lettice Cary, with whom he sat on a stone bench beside a bed of scarlet roses. 'Is it very bad of me to admit complete ignorance of either poem?'

'No – though I wouldn't admit it before John or Will, if I were you. Don't you like poetry?'

'Some of it. But I don't carry it in my head – and am finding it a temporary disadvantage.'

'You mean you are *allowing* it to be one. You have other talents. Use them.'

The hazel eyes registered amused astonishment. 'I might if I knew what they were. Enlighten me.'

'No.' She paused thoughtfully. 'I don't think I will. But when you learn to recognise them, I've a feeling that you'll become a force to be reckoned with.' For a moment the intense grey gaze absorbed him. And then, turning, 'Well, Francis. Has Will taught you the art of verse-drama yet?'

Resplendent in cornflower silk, Francis swept an accomplished bow and smiled on her. 'Not quite – but we persevere. I'd tell you about it save that our friend here would do us both the discourtesy of falling asleep.'

Eden grinned. 'Whatever makes you think that?'

'Experience,' retorted Francis. 'But it isn't your fault. And if my lady permits, I've come to bear you off to the mews. There's a new falcon I thought you might like to see.'

Lettice rose and shook out her skirts. 'By all means. It's time I sought the shade . . . and I think Mr Maxwell has earned some entertainment more suited to his taste.'

'Mr Maxwell,' said Eden gravely, 'has no complaints.'

The bird was a young peregrine falcon and beautiful. Gently but with confidence, Eden took her to his gauntleted wrist and stroked the gleaming, grey-barred plumage of her breast. Her huge dark-ringed eyes stared unwinkingly back at him and she sat motionless, the great talons fast in the leather glove. Eden held her gaze and murmured soothingly, as if forging a bond.

'She is not named,' said Francis at length. 'Have you any suggestions?'

Eden tore his eyes from the falcon and, reaching for her hood, slipped it deftly over her head. 'No.'

'No? That's a pity. I was rather relying on you.'

There was silence while Eden settled the bird back on her perch and fastened the jesses. Then he said, 'When will you fly her?'

'I shan't. But I thought that *you* might. Tomorrow.'

Something kindled in the hazel eyes and Eden drew a sharp breath, then closed his lips firmly.

Francis laughed. 'Well, why do you think I bought her? You know I haven't your gift with birds. And tomorrow, as I recall, is the day when you theoretically catch up with me for a few months.'

Eden flushed. It would be his twentieth birthday. He said, 'Francis, I—'

'Don't you like her?'

'I love her. You knew I would.'

'Then why,' asked Francis patiently, 'don't you give her a name?'

'I already have.' The reply came on a tiny choke of laughter. 'It came to me as soon as I saw her. I shall call her Jezebel.'

Straight-backed and silent, Kate watched her brother and Francis leave the garden and wished that she had been asked to go with them. She felt like a cat in a cage, a dry crust in a dish of marchpane; and somewhere at home, Felix and Felicity were riding high on a hay-cart, singing.

She had not wanted to come and it was no better than she had expected. She was here, corseted and dressed in her best watered silk, to acquire some poise; but if poise meant that one no longer looked as uncomfortable as one felt, she didn't think she had found much of it as yet. Not that she minded the dress; the colour of thick cream, it seemed to reduce the unfortunate fieriness of her hair and made a pleasant sighing sound when she walked. But the corset was pure penance. It constricted every breath and movement and made her itch; and all for nothing, since she was still virtually bereft of those particular assets the nasty thing was designed to emphasise.

It was all very provoking and she wished she was anywhere but here, having to listen to the silly gossip of the three ladies on her left. They had spent the last hour delicately shredding reputations, moving from one to the next with fluid ease. It seemed, for example, that the King had recalled from Ireland one Thomas Wentworth – a fact that Kate found mildly interesting since the gentleman was her favourite uncle's employer. What did *not* interest her, however, was hearing that Viscount Wentworth had apparently managed to get the Irish chancellor dismissed for abusing his office, whilst simultaneously conducting an adulterous liaison with the said chancellor's daughter-in-law. So Kate stifled a yawn, wondered if Uncle Ivo would presently appear at Thorne Ash . . . and debated various means of staying there herself on the morrow.

It was then, against all expectation, that her attention was first attracted and then caught fast by the arrival of a newcomer to the garden. A stranger dressed in rich, sable satin and with a massive emerald glinting on one long-fingered hand, who stood remote and silent beneath the riot of golden roses that covered the trellised entrance and surveyed the assembled company out of impassive, black eyes. A man whose masterly stillness seemed to breathe a sort of mocking challenge, wrapped round in ice and steel. Kate's gaze sharpened and she sat up. The latecomer had presence . . . and something more, something that could only be described as style.

He was not a big man – a little taller, perhaps, than Eden. And he was quite young. Thick, night-dark hair fell in heavy waves to a Mechlin lace collar and framed a face that was at once both remarkable and yet disturbingly familiar. It was a fine-boned, almost ascetic face that might – but for its complete lack of expression – have been sculpted from marble by some master hand. The cheekbones were high and well defined, the nose a perfect aquiline and the mouth shapely but hard. It was only the piercing dark eyes, glinting beneath heavy lids, that denied the illusion and transformed the mask into a severe but living beauty of flesh and blood and bone. He had, decided Kate critically, the face of a Renaissance angel . . . and then, with shock, realised that she had found the key to her odd sense of familiarity.

Shock was followed by dubious amusement – but not for long, for she became suddenly aware that a change was taking place in the atmosphere around her. Somehow, although she could have sworn he neither moved nor spoke, the stranger was slowly but surely commanding every eye; and, as he did so, the light-hearted chatter that had filled the evening air gradually withered and died. For a long, frozen moment there was silence, while some faces reflected Kate's own baffled but expectant interest and others a coldness ranging from disdain to dislike. And then, as if putting the upstart puppeteer in his place by showing that he too could pull strings, Lord George Goring turned his shoulder and in his light, carrying drawl, said, 'Time was when tradesmen and duns used the back door. Do you know, John, I believe I must have stayed abroad too long. The whole damned country's going to the dogs.'

There was a ripple of laughter to which, Kate noticed, Sir John Suckling did not contribute. She thought he looked oddly strained but no one else appeared to notice. They were all absorbed in awaiting the stranger's reply; and he, knowing it, seemed content to let them.

Without a flicker of expression, the black eyes passed over Lord George and conducted a leisurely appraisal of the company before capturing Anne Morton's soft blue gaze and holding it fast for a long, timeless moment. There was something almost indecent about that look, thought Kate; something that made the air crackle with tension and caused the silver ribbons on Mistress Morton's bodice to flutter a little. Then, just as a shiver of unrest began to pass through his audience, the stranger's face relaxed into a swift, heart-stopping smile and he made the lady a faultlessly extravagant bow. A spectral gasp filtered round the garden while, as if unable to help herself, Anne Morton blushed, smiled and inclined her corn-gold head. The gasp became a whisper and Lord George looked as though most of his suavity and wit had suddenly drained into his boots.

Someone laughed.

It was Kate; and the sound of it – husky, rich, and full of unmistakable amusement – surprised her as much as it did everybody else. The dark gentleman's tactics were superb, but she had not meant to make herself the centre of attention by applauding them. She found herself impaled on a blank, black stare; and, since there didn't seem to be anything else to do, she simply raised her brows and stared back. Fortunately, however, it did not last long. With one last intimate glance at Mistress Morton and a briefer, more mocking one, for Lord George, the stranger was gone –

plainly taking the lovely Anne's thoughts with him. And the garden erupted into a buzz of gossip.

Without a moment's hesitation, Kate turned to the trio of Court butterflies and unlocked her tongue.

'Excuse me,' she said baldly, 'but who was that gentleman?'

The three exchanged amused glances and then one of them said carelessly, 'That, my child, was no gentleman. It was merely an indication of how low the tide must be in Gervase Langley's coffers. In short, the man is a moneylender.'

'Oh.' Kate digested this for a moment and returned to her original point. 'But what's his name?'

'I haven't the remotest idea. Something quite unpronounceable, I imagine,' came the bored reply. 'In London they call him the Italian.'

Supper – an opulent meal that deserved a better title – was punctuated with the news that, having opened with the Bishop of Orkney's diplomatic repudiation of his own office, the Assembly of the Scots Kirk had gone on to confirm all the so-called illegal edicts passed in Glasgow, asserted its right to scrutinise the King's religious policy, and abolished the episcopacy again as contrary to God's law. My lord Traquair, having a most natural regard for his person, had bowed to the inevitable and accepted all these resolutions on behalf of his royal master.

Discussion of this grew heated when it became clear that not all those present considered the King ill used and badly served. In their usual insouciant way, Suckling and Davenant supported their host but, against them, Lords Brooke and Falkland, and also Richard Maxwell, maintained a limited sympathy with the Scots cause. And, amidst it all, Richard's daughter divided her attention between George Goring's attempts to recover Mistress Morton's wandering eye and the enigmatic, still silent presence at the other end of the table.

Further down the board, Eden was also toying absently with his food and contributing suspiciously little to the debate. Opposite him, Celia watched between demure lashes. Her dark hair, drawn up into a high knot, feathered her brow with tiny curls and fell in gleaming ringlets about her ears. A single strand of pearls encircled her throat and, from the low décolletage of her elaborate gown, her shoulders emerged white and enticingly soft. Rose-coloured silk rippled around her and revealed, through slashed sleeves, an exquisitely embroidered chemise. She looked radiantly beautiful; and she wondered if Eden was even faintly aware of her – or, if he was, if she would ever know it.

Then, entirely without warning, the golden-green eyes were looking directly into her own and she felt herself flushing. Her fingers tightened on the bone handle of her knife while the seconds stretched out to infinity. And finally, with the slow sweet charm that was always so unexpected, Eden smiled.

The moment was still with her later when the musicians struck up an air and he asked her to dance with him. It was the first time, Celia realised, that he had danced at all. She said so.

'Yes . . . well, there's a reason for that. But if I explain it now, you'll almost certainly refuse me.'

'But, if I dance with you, you'll tell me later?'

'I doubt,' said Eden, taking her hand in a light clasp, 'if I'll need to.'

This turned out to be perfectly true for, though he moved with the physical coordination of an athlete and therefore never actually trod on her feet, he proved lamentably unfamiliar with the figures of the dance. Torn between amusement and exasperation, Celia eyed him severely.

'Francis learned to dance at Angers. Why didn't you?'

'I'm afraid I avoided the classes.'

'Well, I hope you're sorry for it!'

'I'm beginning to be,' he said meekly. 'But don't judge me too harshly. You see, at Angers there wasn't any incentive.'

The sapphire eyes widened. 'And now there is?'

'Oh yes.' He sent her a glance brimming with mischief.

'I never much liked holding hands with Francis.'

Neither, just at that moment, did Kate. She would much have preferred to continue watching the *ménage-à-trois* instead of romping through a boisterous country dance. Not that it could be said that Francis romped; but the word seemed an adequate description of what she herself was doing. Moreover, the myriad of pins holding her hair were beginning to slip and she was getting tired of being asked to reveal the secrets of Ralph Cochrane's horoscope. She snatched at a hairpin that was threatening to drop down her neck and, when the dance brought her back to Francis, said rapidly, 'I'm not telling. And it's no use asking Eden because I wouldn't tell him either.'

'Killjoy.' Francis spun her under his arm, grinning. 'However, since you're so discreet, I might let you do mine. Before your enthusiasm wanes.'

'*My reputation, Iago, my reputation!*' She curtsied, cast him an oblique smile and prepared to pass on. 'But the word is ask – not let. And there's a price.'

Wisely, Francis waited until the dance was over before asking the obvious question and, when he did, Kate said simply, 'I want to know about that man who came today. The one over there in black.'

Francis glanced across the room and then, satirically, back at Kate. 'My dear child! Can it be you're smitten?'

'That,' she sighed, 'is a silly question and you know it.'

'Do I? I'm not entirely convinced of it. But I hope you're not. He's not at all suitable, you know . . . and I've always felt that your first infatuation, when it came, ought to be with me.'

'Have you?' Her brows rose. 'Well, I suppose anything is possible.'

He laughed. 'Clever Kate. Ambiguous as ever.'

'Only if you choose to think so.'

'And equipped with sharp claws.'

'Of course. They go with the rest of me.' She fixed him with a jewel-green stare. 'Is he really Italian?'

Francis sighed and gave up.

'He really is. He is also a goldsmith, a merchant and as

41

rich as Croesus – or so they say. Rich enough, at any rate, to be owed money by half the Court – not excluding the King. And that, of course, is why he's here. The only reason, I might add . . . but one powerful enough to take him anywhere he wishes to go.'

A slight frown creased Kate's brow but she said merely, 'And his name?'

'His name, I believe, is del Santi. And that, dear Kate, is really all I know. Will it do?'

'Will what do?' Eden materialised at Francis's side.

'Yes.' Forbidding green eyes met suddenly mischievous blue ones. 'It will. Thank you.'

It was a vain attempt and she knew it. Francis had always enjoyed baiting her. Turning to Eden, he said, 'I've been singing for my supper, so to speak. Kate has a new interest. I rather think she's discovering the more grown-up pursuits.'

Eden grinned at his sister. 'Are you?'

'Not the ones Francis means,' she said shortly. And then, by way of retaliation, 'Where's Celia?'

'Presiding over a duel of artistic compliments between Will Davenant and Hugo Verney.'

'And enjoying every minute of it,' drawled Francis, looking across the room. 'Aren't you at all tempted to join in?'

'Oh no.' An odd smile touched Eden's mouth. 'You should know by now that I don't play pointless games.'

Kate had stopped listening. Very close to where Celia sat with her swains, the man called del Santi was speaking to Gervase, Lord Wroxton – and seemingly making him twitch. This, after the information presented to her in the garden, was not especially surprising; but what she did not expect was the way he seemed almost to anticipate her gaze and turned to meet it. Kate had a sudden, confused awareness that the angel had not, as she had first thought, been created perfect – that his left shoulder was a fraction higher than his right – and then she forgot it as he stunned her with a slight, impassive bow of acknowledgement. For the first time in her life, she blushed and, infuriated by the fact, achieved without effort a brusquely flawless curtsy and an expression cold enough to make hell freeze. Then, without waiting for a reaction, she turned back to Eden and Francis.

Of course they had both seen. Francis looked smugly indulgent and Eden mildly hilarious. He said, 'Friend of yours, Kate?'

She shrugged. 'Ask Francis. He's full of opinions.'

This worked. Francis liked to win his points, not be awarded them. He said, provocatively, 'I am, of course – but your secrets are safe with me.'

'I'll remember that,' said Kate irritably, 'when I have any.'

'Peace, children.' Eden was used to their sparring. 'What I want to know is why I seem to feel I've seen that fellow before when I'm fairly sure I haven't.'

Kate looked up at him, grinning. 'Oh, but you have.'

'Yes? Where?'

'Work it out for yourself. And, if you can't – try asking Mother. She's probably noticed it too.'

By the time they left Far Flamstead, however, Eden had forgotten the matter and spent the journey home discussing field-drainage with his father. And Dorothy, looking thoughtfully at Kate, finally said, 'All right. I give in. If you want to send your excuses for tomorrow's hawking party, I won't say a word. Well?'

For a moment or two Kate looked faintly taken aback. Then, on a creditable note of indifference she said, 'Thank you. But I think I'll persevere, after all. And I'd quite like to see Eden fly the falcon Francis is giving him for his birthday. Yes.' She paused consideringly. 'I think I'll go.'

It was not a large cavalcade which Eden and Kate joined outside the mews at Far Flamstead next morning, most of the ladies and several of the gentlemen having baulked at the early start. But Francis was with it – and Celia, closely attended by Sir Hugo Verney; and even George Goring, despite the absence of Mistress Morton. So too was Signor del Santi, along with a colourful person whose exotic olive skin, scimitar-like nose and luxuriant black moustache paled into insignificance beside the ornately sheathed but purposeful-looking knife that was thrust through his sash.

'My God!' murmured Eden in Kate's ear. 'Is it a groom, a body-guard or an assassin?'

'Or all three. Perhaps it's an Italian custom,' suggested Kate. 'Tom had better be careful.'

Tom Tripp, whose father was head-groom at Thorne Ash – as once his grandfather had been – continued to settle Jezebel on Eden's wrist and grinned without looking up. He had gone bird's nesting with Eden and taught Kate to fire a pistol, so formality was neither necessary nor appropriate. He said laconically, 'So had he. He's in a Christian country now – not foreign parts. And he'd better keep his nasty heathen knife to hisself.'

Kate laughed and Eden said gently, 'I see. And you'll be telling him that, will you?'

'Aye – if needs be.' Tom finished adjusting the jesses and stepped back. 'She looks to be a lively 'un, Mr Eden. Best have a care wi' her this morning.'

'And every morning, I should think,' said Francis, joining them. 'Unnervingly unpredictable creatures, falcons. I can't imagine why you like them so much – or why *you*,' to Kate, 'aren't keeping a safe distance. Celia is. Like me, she's just along for the ride. Ah good, we seem to be off at last. Eden – that bird is fidgeting. It's not going to do anything tiresome, is it?'

'Only if you continue calling her "it",' responded Eden. 'She's a queen and knows it. I really can't thank you enough.'

'You can and you have. And before you become a bore, beloved, I shall depart and be sociable elsewhere. *A bientôt, enfants!*'

By the time they had left the tiny village of Farnborough behind them, Kate was tired of the sedate pace and pining for a gallop. She said so.

'Go, then,' said Eden. 'Francis will probably come with you.'

'No thank you. On that showy slug he's riding and with his determination to talk non-stop, he'll never keep up with me.'

This, Eden conceded silently, was perfectly true. Kate might not be as visually delightful in her old rust-coloured habit as was Celia in her expertly cut scarlet, but she rode as well as most men and a good deal better than some. He said, 'Take Tom, then. You may be glad of a chaperone.'

She laughed. '*Me?* You're mad. I'm not nearly pretty enough.' And, turning aside from the track, was off across the common in a swirl of dust.

'Well I'm damned!' exclaimed George Goring. And with a hearty 'View halloo!', was off in energetic pursuit.

Eden watched him go and dissolved into silent laughter. 'Nemesis taking up the gauntlet. Oh, *Kate!*'

They did not meet again until the party halted on the heights of Avon Dassett and Eden said mischievously, 'Well? Wishing you'd taken Tom after all?'

'I did at first – but it was all right after he stopped being silly and talking to me as if I were Celia.' She paused and gave a half-apologetic shrug. 'Actually, I quite like him. He reminds me a bit of Uncle Ivo.'

Eden looked at his lordship and thought he detected a certain brittle glassiness. 'You didn't, by any chance, tell him so?'

'Yes I did. Why not?'

'Oh l-lord!' came the unsteady reply. 'Go away. I can't stand it. And if I laugh any harder, Jezebel will do something t-tiresome.'

He waited until she had moved away and he could control his breathing. Then, with Tom Tripp at his side, he moved a little apart from the others and eased off the falcon's hood. She blinked and started to absorb the world out of great, black eyes. Very gently, Eden released the soft leather straps from his fist and waited.

Jezebel was in no hurry. She shifted a little on the glove to the music of the small bells on her legs and continued her measured stare. Finally she spread her wings and, with a power that jarred Eden's shoulder, rose swiftly to circle the air above. Smiling – and completely unaware that Celia, having decided to make Sir Hugo work a little harder, had ridden over to join him – Eden shaded his eyes against the light and followed Jezebel's progress as she climbed steadily up and up to become no more than a dark speck in the sky.

'Isn't she superb, Tom?' he murmured.

'Aye. She could be the best we've flown. Only you'd best start training her soon or—'

'Do you think,' interrupted Celia brightly, 'that we might ride?'

Eden started and his eyes left the sky. 'I'm sorry. Yes – of course. Shall we go to the beacon?'

'Why not?' Petulance vanished and she laughed. 'Race me!'

She was a competent rider but no more than that and her mare was no match for Eden's long-tailed grey. By the time she caught up with him, he had reined in and was facing her, smiling.

Flushed, breathless, and with her dark curls in charming disorder, she said plaintively, 'A gentleman would have let me win.'

'Oh?' Eden contemplated the elusive dimple by her mouth. 'And is that what you like? To be patronised?'

'That isn't patronage. It's gallantry.'

'Is it?' He appeared to consider the matter. 'Don't you find that rather confusing? For if I deceive you with courtesy, how are you to know when I'm sincere? And when I say you're the most beautiful girl I've ever seen, how are you to tell it from flattery?'

'By intuition,' began Celia firmly. And then, 'Oh! *Am* I?'

Eden bent to adjust his stirrup and arose faintly flushed. 'Knowing my graceless bluntness as you do, how can you doubt it? Shall we go? I'm not sure how easy it will be to bring Jezebel back . . . and I don't suppose you'll care for becoming food for the gossips.'

'Oh, *Eden!*' She gave a gay, rippling laugh. 'How can you be so ridiculous? I'm as safe with you as I would be with Francis.'

'Of course. But there is a difference.' His smile was slightly crooked. 'I am not your brother.'

Kate watched Celia's scarlet habit streaming in Eden's wake and then looked away, giving a mental shrug. If Eden didn't mind being picked up and put down as bait for Hugo Verney, it was entirely his own affair. Not that Kate had anything against Sir Hugo – quite the reverse. He was pleasant enough company; not exactly stimulating, but pleasant. Indeed, she was discovering that they all were, these witty, fashionable people she had expected to dislike. Mother had been right about that. Only Celia had not improved upon closer scrutiny; and someone really should have taught her not to jerk on her bridle like that. She was ruining that nice little mare's mouth.

'You find my servant interesting, Mistress Maxwell?'

The beautiful, faintly accented voice made Kate jump and snatch at her own reins before her head snapped round to meet the impersonal black gaze she had hitherto encountered only at a distance. It was no less unnerving close-to; more so, in fact. She swallowed and said weakly, 'Your servant?'

The man known to London as the Italian assented with the merest suggestion of a nod. 'Also myself, I suspect. But you were staring so hard at Selim just now that I felt impelled to ask why.'

Too late, Kate realised that she had indeed been staring – but not consciously. She also realised that he was never going to believe it. Recovering herself a little, she said, 'Yes . . . well in England our grooms don't commonly ride about armed to the teeth. Unless that pretty knife is a toy?'

'Far from it.' A wayward gleam lit the obsidian gaze. 'Would you care to inspect it?'

'No thank you.' She set her jaw and attacked. 'You know my name. I'm surprised.'

His brows rose and he said, with irritating urbanity, 'Yes? But then, you also know mine, do you not? And, by now, probably a good deal more.'

Kate found that she was beginning to feel foolish and suspected that he meant her to. She had laughed at him in the garden – thus somewhat spoiling his little spell – and he was taking his fee. They were right about him; he wasn't

47

a gentleman. She said, 'You take a lot for granted. But if the thought worries you, you should try to be less . . . theatrical.'

His smile was swift and cold. 'Nothing worries me, mistress.'

Kate believed him. She was also coming to see why he might find it handy to have his groom carry a knife.

'That's nice,' she said coolly. 'But, if that's so, why are we having this conversation?'

'You are not enjoying it?'

'Am I supposed to?'

'Of course. I'm giving you the chance to decide precisely why I intrigue you so.'

Kate shut her mouth and allowed her lungs time to reinflate. Then she said sweetly, 'Thank you – but I really don't need it. You see, it's your face.'

'My face?'

'Yes. We've a rather splendid picture of it at home.'

She had the mild satisfaction of seeing his eyes widen a trifle. He said, 'You fascinate me.'

'I thought I would.' She smiled on him, benignly. 'It's on the chapel ceiling. An extravagant but interesting interpretation of the Fall of Lucifer. You really ought to see it.'

Three

At the end of August, Lord and Lady Wroxton's glittering guests left Far Flamstead to go their various ways, and life returned to normal. Kate gave up astrology in favour of sketching – a pastime which somehow led her to spend long hours in the chapel. And if she was plagued by the knowledge that the face she drew was never quite the face in the frescoed ceiling, she did not show it and was able, in any case, to put the matter into simple perspective. Who, after all, would not be intrigued by the discovery that even Lucifer could laugh?

September came and went and then the first weeks of October. In Scotland, the young Earl of Montrose enraged his fellow Covenanters by criticising their infringements of the King's traditional rights, and in England there was general rejoicing when the fleet disobeyed orders and allowed the Dutch to devastate seventy-five Spanish ships in the Downs. Meanwhile, at Thorne Ash, the leaves turned rusty-brown and drifted from the trees while Eden spent a good deal of time riding with Celia Langley and a private concern festered in his mother's heart.

'Mary says she's taking Celia to join Gervase and Francis at Court for Christmas,' she told Richard late one night. 'That's good, isn't it?'

'It is if it will stop you worrying. Will it?'

'I don't know. It might.' She stirred restlessly. 'It wouldn't be so bad if I actually disliked Celia – but I don't. She's charming enough in her way and lively and beautiful. Isn't she?'

'Absolutely. But you don't want her for your daughter.'

'No. Do you think I'm uncharitable?'

'Not especially,' sighed Richard. 'Totally lacking in a sense of timing . . . but not uncharitable.'

A tremor of something that might have been laughter passed through the pliant body in his arms.

'After all it's not her fault she's grown up self-absorbed and without a trace of empathy.'

'Pot calling kettle,' said her husband gloomily. 'I must remember to warn Eden.'

This time there was no doubt at all about the laughter and Dorothy twined her arms about his neck. 'I'm sorry. Are you tired of waiting?'

There was a long silence.

Then, 'Aren't you?' asked Richard.

It would have surprised Dorothy to learn that Celia's self-absorption shielded her neither from knowing that Kate did not like her nor from noticing that, no matter how nice she was to Kate, all she ever got in return was a sort of off-hand courtesy. This rankled. Indeed, the only good thing to be said for it was that it kept Kate at home when she and Eden rode out together. But this – between the presence of Eden's groom and the horrible bird Francis had given him – was small comfort.

Out on the vale below Avon Dassett, Celia surveyed Jezebel with resentful suspicion. Even when she was hooded, the falcon's sheer size was worrying; but when, as now, Eden loosed the scarlet hood and removed it, the look in those huge, ringed eyes was frankly terrifying. It was undoubtedly a great pity that, with the house-party over and Francis gone to London, these rides were her only distraction.

The bird was in the air now, an upward-soaring, swiftly diminishing shape. Celia wished it would forget to come back. Cutting across some observation that Tom was making, she said impatiently, 'Oh – do come and ride, Eden! I'm chilled to the bone.'

He gave her a smile of rueful apology.

'I'm sorry. I'm a thoughtless oaf. I don't know why you bear with me.'

'No more do I.' She turned her mare towards the track and set off ahead of him. 'You certainly don't deserve that I should.'

Eden brought the Nomad up beside her. 'I know.'

She glanced sideways at him between her lashes. 'It appears to me that you often forget I'm here at all.'

'Then you misjudge me,' came the quiet reply. 'I never forget you for a minute.'

This, decided Celia, was better. It might have been more gracefully put . . . but, for Eden, it really wasn't bad. She smiled at him. 'No?'

'No. And I suspect that you know it very well.'

'My goodness! Do you think I've a crystal ball, sir? Or that I've nothing better to do with my time than wonder about you?'

Eden perceived that this was his cue to say something suitably gallant but did not know how. Instead he said simply, 'No. I don't imagine you think of me at all. But I wish that you would.'

Dimpling, she said, 'Then you will have to try harder, will you not?'

His hand came down over hers, checking the mare's pace along with that of the Nomad. 'And if I do?'

Faintly startled, Celia looked into intent hazel eyes from which all trace of levity had vanished, and was aware that things were moving too far and too fast. She liked Eden and, at times, was even attracted by him. But there was another who attracted her more – and even had there not been, Eden was not the husband she wanted, for he was untitled, unfashionable, and by far too blunt. On the other hand, it might be fun to teach him how the game of flirtation ought to be played.

Shrugging lightly, she said, 'How can I tell? At the moment you're in danger of having me think of you only as the person whose grip has bruised my wrist.'

Her hand was released on the instant and a hint of betraying colour mantled his cheek. He said, 'I beg your pardon. I didn't mean to hurt you. It's just that I . . . I can't find it in me to play games with you.'

51

'And who,' demanded Celia, thoroughly annoyed at having her mind read, 'suggested that you should? *I* certainly did not – any more than I've given you the right to ask me impertinent questions.'

For a long moment, Eden simply looked at her. Then, with a small rueful smile, he said, 'I seem to be making a lot of mistakes today. Perhaps we'd better turn back before I make any more. And, in any case, Tom will be waiting – for I doubt Jezebel will come to him if I'm not there.'

'Dear me!' came the withering response. 'Then we'd best go *immediately*, hadn't we? God forbid that we should keep your groom waiting – or that, just once in a while, you should fly that wretched bird without him.'

Frowning slightly, he turned his horse alongside hers. 'I don't think you quite understand. Tom isn't just a groom – he's a friend.'

Her brows soared. 'But he works in your stables.'

'So? I've known him all my life and he loves hawking as much as I do.' He met her blank stare thoughtfully. 'What's the matter? Don't you like him?'

'Don't be silly. He's a servant – aside from the fact that he puts himself forward too much, I've no feelings either way. Neither can I imagine why we're wasting time discussing him,' she shrugged. Then, deliberately summoning her most ravishing smile, 'I've something much more exciting to tell you. Father has promised that I may spend Christmas at Whitehall this year. Isn't that splendid?'

As she intended, a knife twisted in Eden's stomach and it was a moment before he could bring himself to reply. Then he said flatly, 'That rather depends on one's point of view, doesn't it? But I'm sure you'll be a great success . . . and of course I wish you every pleasure.'

It had been their last meeting but any residue of regret fell solely to Eden for, while gusty winds pounded the window-panes with sudden, heavy showers of rain, Celia was lost in an orgy of preparation and thought only of London.

It was not her first visit to the metropolis but it was to

be her first as an adult and, most exciting of all, she was to be presented at Court and become one of the cultured, glittering company that surrounded King Charles and his French Queen. The only fly in her ointment was that she was thrown suddenly and rather alarmingly into the company of her mother. As a child reared by a rapid succession of nursery-maids who, as she learned later, found more favour in the eyes of her father than those of her mother, Lady Wroxton had always been an elegant, remote figure; a creature of jewels and scented satin whose attention the little Celia had seldom been successful in capturing. And though she was now grown up enough to see past the glamour that had dazzled her childhood to the woman who had never been exactly beautiful and was now beginning to age, Mary was still the one person who could make Celia feel gauche. She was also the one person who ought surely to have loved her but somehow never had.

They left Far Flamstead a full week earlier than planned, before the persistently wet weather should turn the roads into quagmires and so prevent them from going at all. Celia glowed with anticipation and Lady Wroxton resigned herself to at least two days of unmitigated tedium and discomfort. But on the following day, when they were less than an hour from their destination, she finally summoned enough energy to ensure that her daughter understood exactly where her duty lay.

Settling her hands more deeply into her sable muff, she said with a distant smile, 'Well, my dear, I think it's time we had a little talk about your future. Reluctant as I am to mention so vulgar a matter, you can't be unaware that the cost of giving you this opportunity will not be small. And your father is not a rich man.'

'No,' agreed Celia, dutifully. 'I am very grateful to him – to you both.'

Lady Wroxton sighed and a trace of irritation appeared on her carefully painted face. 'I am relieved to hear it. You will therefore do your best not to disappoint us.'

'N-no, madam. But I don't quite—'

53

My lady Wroxton drew a long breath and abandoned subtlety.

'Celia. Why do you think you're going to Court?'

'To be presented to Their Majesties and to – to find a husband.'

'Quite. Most particularly the latter. What I am trying to make plain is that I expect you to marry well. A gentleman of breeding and . . . substance. Someone with the right connections and perhaps a position at Court. There is no reason why you should not aim high, my dear; in fact, there is every reason why you *should*. I trust I make myself clear?'

'Perfectly, madam.' Celia had never doubted that she would become a Countess at the very least. 'And I think I should like to live in London. The country is very dull.'

Satisfied, Lady Wroxton permitted herself a smile of approval. Never having taken the trouble to acquaint herself with the workings of her daughter's mind, it did not occur to her that, unlike Francis, Celia had very little idea of the deep financial waters in which her father was perpetually struggling – nor had ever contemplated the possibility that she might one day wish to marry a man who was not rich. And so her mother saw only the compliance of a properly reared girl and decided that it was quite unnecessary to broach the distasteful matter of the dowry. Relief warmed her smile and she said lightly, 'You're a sensible child – and a pretty one. I'm sure your father and I can rely on you to be a credit to us.'

The result of this was that mother and daughter arrived at the narrow house in the Strand in a state of rare mutual accord which enabled them to overlook the sad fact that there were none but servants to greet them. And when, on the following morning, Lord Wroxton deigned to favour his wife with a few minutes of his time, she was able to tell him that they need have no fears about Celia.

'She's more sense than I'd supposed, then,' was his lordship's reply. 'I'd begun to think her head was full of romantic flummery and that she was set on having young Maxwell.'

'That was nothing – merely a flirtation.'

Gervase laughed. 'I see. Trying out her claws, was she? Well, I can't blame her for that.'

'No. And we should not lose sight of the fact that Eden Maxwell is perfectly eligible. Not, I realise, the best we can hope for – but by no means contemptible,' said his wife coolly. 'He dresses deplorably, of course. But that is something which might be mended.'

My lord smothered a yawn.

'Yes . . . well, let's hope it doesn't come to that. If I'm to pay off that damned Italian, I need a son-in-law already in control of his fortune – not one who could wait twenty years to inherit.' He paused and then, anxiety creasing his brow, said abruptly, 'I don't like this debt, Mary. I wish I'd never let you talk me into it.'

'And how else, pray, are we to support the costs of our new title in addition to establishing Francis at Court and finding a match for Celia?'

'I don't know. But I don't like borrowing from foreigners. It leads to all sorts of trouble. I remember my cousin Giles being up to his neck in debt to one, years ago, and he never seemed free of worry till the day he died. I don't want to go the same way. And – say what you like – this bloody Italian's dangerous.'

'Oh, don't be such a weakling!' snapped Mary irritably. 'The man's a usurer, that's all. And if the King can borrow from him, why shouldn't we?'

'Because, unlike His Majesty, *we* can be bankrupted,' came the bitter reply. 'And I don't fancy spending the rest of my days in a French hovel. Particularly with you.'

The days became weeks, Christmas approached and Celia was in her element. Graciously welcomed by King Charles and Queen Henrietta Maria to their brilliant and elegant court at Whitehall, she rapidly renewed old acquaintances, made a host of new ones, and was soon engaged in a number of delicious flirtations – the most delicious of all being with Sir Hugo Verney.

But weaving in and out of the season's festivities was a thread that was not festive at all, and Celia found it dull.

There was always such talk, she decided, and it never amounted to anything. Last year everyone had talked of war with Scotland; now they talked of it again. They had even appointed a council to discuss it thrice weekly and there were rumours that a Parliament would be called to vote money for it. Celia dismissed it with a shrug and merely wished that the gentlemen were less prone to gather in corners debating the state of the northern defences and the purchase of arms from Hamburg.

She was rather more interested in Viscount Wentworth, a dark and grimly distinguished gentleman who had been recalled from Ireland to deal with the Scottish rebels and who, it was said, had contributed twenty thousand pounds from his own pocket in order to raise the army he thought necessary to do it. If this was so, he was duly rewarded, for the King promptly created him Earl of Strafford – an honour which, as far as Celia could see, neither lessened his grimness nor increased his popularity. The latter, according to Francis, was something to do with the new Earl's refusal to sacrifice Ireland to English profiteering and his ruthless determination to solve problems which the vacillating nature of the King's other ministers seemed only to aggravate. Francis, it appeared, approved wholeheartedly of my lord Strafford.

It was all much too serious for Celia, and she turned with relief to Sir Hugo – who never mentioned politics and kept her constantly amused. She found that she liked him even better than she remembered and was quite astonished how much his laughing glances and outrageous compliments contributed to her pleasure. He was not, of course, her only gallant, but he was most definitely the only one she really cared for.

Of her other admirers, most were Francis's friends: men like the Queen's Master of Horse, Harry Jermyn, and the Earl of Bristol's son, George Digby. All these she liked and had no wish to discourage. And then there was Cyrus Winter whose attentions she would willingly have dispensed with had she only known how. His cold grey eyes and prematurely silvered hair did not please her eye, and there was

56

something in his manner that disturbed her. But Mr Winter was no ordinary young man whose eagerness could be blunted by a snub. In fact, he was not young at all and seemed regrettably friendly with her mother. *How* friendly, Celia was by no means sure. As friendly, for example, as was her father with Sarah Davenport? Court life was a great eye-opener and not everything that one learned was pleasant.

Lady Wroxton watched her daughter's progress carefully and with rather more than usual interest. She had been surprised that Cyrus should notice the child . . . but not much, for unexpectedness was a habit with him. It was his main charm, thought Mary idly; and he was quite likely to cultivate Celia out of no more than a spirit of devilment. He had been her own lover now for almost a year and still, despite an increasingly jaded palate, she was reluctant to relinquish him. He was innovative in bed and amusing out of it – and he was rich enough to make their liaison extremely profitable to her. So when she saw Celia being cold to the point of rudeness, she was swift to deliver a reprimand – for though Cyrus was the last man on earth to give two straws for a chit of seventeen, he might just find the challenge of her dislike too piquant a temptation to resist. And Mary wanted no rivals at all – least of all her own daughter.

As she watched, it seemed that her instinct had been right, for tonight he had given the girl no more than a civil greeting. That was very satisfactory. Less so was the fact that, of the other gentlemen clustered about Celia, not one was worth more than three thousand a year, and Hugo Verney nothing at all. With Gervase developing a nervous tic over his indebtedness to the Italian, it was extremely provoking that his daughter seemed unable to attract even one man with a purse fat enough to remedy the situation.

A dark figure paused at her side and, turning, she found herself looking at Luciano del Santi. The aptness of his appearance gave her a slight jolt . . . but then, he was everywhere these days. A crow at the elbow of society, said

Gervase. And yet, thought Mary, despite that ill-formed shoulder of his, he was the only man she'd seen in a long time who just might prove an adequate replacement for Cyrus Winter. Certainly he was equally rich – and his coldness was intriguing. Her eyes narrowed appraisingly and a slow smile touched her mouth as she wondered how deep the chill went.

'You are often among us these days, sir,' she said lightly. 'I'm told that the King declares your financial advice to be quite . . . priceless.'

'Indeed?' The dark eyes told her nothing and the melodious voice was smooth as butter. 'How fortunate it is, then, that I find the honour of serving His Majesty sufficient reward.'

'Just so.' She suspected irony but could not be sure of it. 'They say you are a wizard.'

'Do they so?' His smile was sudden and dazzling. 'And is that all they say?'

She laughed, a rare thing for her, and said, 'You know it is not. And I suspect care very little for it or you'd not be here.'

He inclined his head in the oblique, almost imperceptible manner that was so peculiarly his own and said nothing.

'Why *do* you come, I wonder?'

'Is it not everyone's ambition to be accepted at Court?'

'Perhaps. But if that were all, you would take a little more care not to antagonise people . . . instead of being openly contemptuous of their good opinion.'

His glance swept the room. 'Should I not be contemptuous of it?'

She shrugged. 'You may think what you please. What you may *not* do is show it.'

'So.' A faint smile curled his mouth. 'You find me transparent. I congratulate you.'

This time the irony was unmistakable but Mary refused to let it annoy her. She said, 'You are too clever for your own good, signor, and you make enemies needlessly. Could you but bring yourself to be a trifle more conciliatory, there are those amongst us who would not find it difficult to . . . like you.'

Luciano del Santi's impersonal gaze rested on her calmly. 'Such as yourself, for example? Your ladyship does me too much honour. So much that I am almost tempted.'

'Only almost? That is scarcely flattering.'

'No. But you see, there is one small problem. I do not crawl.' He paused and then continued blandly, 'A mixed blessing, perhaps. If I were more compliant, something tells me that I should have been less fortunate in engaging your ladyship's . . . interest.'

Mary met the black eyes and, seeing the knowledge there, drew a long, slightly unsteady breath. Then, deciding to meet fire with fire, she said calmly, 'You, sir, are a bastard.'

'Yes.' He smiled with soft, malicious charm. 'I thought that was my main attraction.'

Whitehall was a gay, confident place that Christmas. The King forgot his need to economise and ordered a new set of tapestries from Mortlake; the Queen was pregnant again – by Harry Jermyn, said the scandal-mongers; and the masque of *Philogenes and the Furies*, with words by Will Davenant and decor by Mr Inigo Jones, promised spectacular entertainment.

It was on the evening that this was to be performed that Hugo Verney, overcome by an emotion that was entirely new to him, finally lost his head and, drawing Celia first into the semi-privacy of a curtained alcove and then into his arms, gave way to an impulse that was not new at all and kissed her. To his credit, he recovered himself almost immediately and stepped back, watchful and a little pale, with an apology already on his lips.

'Celia . . . I beg your pardon. That was inexcusable of me. Have I upset you? I didn't mean to.'

Flushed and thoroughly startled, Celia lost herself in a tangle of half sentences. She was not surprised that he had kissed her – only by how much she had liked it. And the result was utter confusion.

59

Hugo stared desperately at her downcast head. 'Oh hell!' he said. And then, very gently, 'I'm sorry – I really am. Can you believe that I meant no disrespect?'

'Yes.'

It was the merest whisper and it all but undid him. Celia, however, began to regain a little of her poise – though her colour was still high and she kept her eyes fixed on her hands. These were somewhat unsteady and, to hide the fact, she began toying with the bunches of ribbon on her blue satin bodice. A sweet expectancy was growing inside her and, when he showed no sign of adding to what he had said, she murmured, 'But I think, sir, that you are grown over-bold.' And waited hopefully.

'I know it,' came the wooden reply.

Surprised, she stole a quick look at him and wondered at the grimness of his expression. Then, happily misconstruing it, she said encouragingly, 'But perhaps I may forgive you . . . just this once.'

Unable for the first time he could remember to think of a single thing to say, Hugo drew a long breath and wished that the floor would open and swallow him up. It would be easier if she were angry; but, instead of rebuking him, she stood there looking as though she thought he was going to do something more than offer the very real apology that was all he had to give.

A stab of sudden comprehension tore through his chest.

That was it, of course. He had never spoken of his betrothal; when he was with Celia, it had always been something he preferred not to remember. And, unbelievably, it seemed that – despite the fact that it was common knowledge – no one else had told her either. She did not know. It was as simple as that. And, because she did not know, she was expecting him to talk of love.

He swallowed and forced himself to say flatly, 'I don't deserve that you should even speak to me again. It appears that . . . that I've deceived you.'

The beautiful eyes, filled with innocent inquiry, rose to meet his. 'Deceived me? But how?'

'Because there's something I should have told you myself – instead of just presuming you knew.'

A trickle of apprehension made its way down Celia's back, causing her smile to fade a little. 'Knew what? I'm afraid I don't understand. I thought—' She stopped, blushing afresh.

'I know. I know,' he said quickly. 'And God knows there's nothing I'd like more than to tell you how much I . . . than to tell you what I feel for you. But I don't have the right. I'm betrothed.'

There was a long silence. Finally, Celia said distantly, 'You're what?'

'I'm contracted to marry Lucy Marston. Her father's lands adjoin mine and it's been understood since we were children that one day we'd marry. Everyone knows of it . . . and I thought you did too.'

'No.' Celia held her head very high and concentrated hard on not allowing herself to feel faint. 'I – I didn't know. I suppose it's too late to – to felicitate you, isn't it?'

'Don't!' he said violently. 'Do you think I wouldn't sell my soul to be free? But souls, sadly, are not a saleable commodity . . . which is a pity since mine is the only thing I have that isn't already mortgaged.'

Still not fully understanding, a gleam of hope lit Celia's eyes and she said, 'If you d-don't wish to marry the lady – could you not b-break the contract?'

'Would that I could,' came the bitter reply. 'But the fact is that I've scarcely two pennies to rub together and a mountain of debts. Lucy is a considerable heiress; and I – God help me – have no choice but to marry money.'

'I see.' Disappointment formed a hard lump in Celia's throat and hurt pride made her want to hit back. 'She has my sympathy then – for it seems she's getting a poor bargain.'

'Probably. And I wish for all our sakes that things were different – but they're not. You must know, however, how deeply . . . how very deeply I care for you.'

'Of course.' She gave him a brittle smile. 'You've just demonstrated it, haven't you? And now I must go – for I promised to watch the masque with Lord Digby and I'd hate him to think I'd forgotten. I believe he pays cleverer compliments than any gentleman I know.'

'Does he?' Hugo followed her from the alcove, his heart like a leaden weight. 'And since you – more than any other lady I know – deserve them, no doubt he is sincere.'

'Yes,' she replied with savage bitterness. 'No doubt he is. And if he is not – who are you to cavil?'

The masque went well. The King played Philogenes with dignified restraint, the chorus of Beloved People praised him with gusto, and Inigo Jones's mechanical devices were truly spectacular. Or so everyone said. Celia thought it tedious and found that it quite failed to hold her attention.

With the turn of the year and quarter-day fast approaching, money continued to be a major preoccupation, and a strain of increased nervousness began to afflict those whose bonds were in the hands of the Italian. It was rumoured that each year in March, del Santi beggared four of his debtors by the simple means of recalling their bonds as they fell due. Certainly he had done so last year and possibly also the year before – although no one could recall precisely who had suffered on that occasion. There was therefore great speculation as to what 1640 would bring amongst those who were safe, and rising panic in those who were not.

Gervase Langley, Viscount Wroxton, was one of the latter, and morosely inclined to fear the worst. By the middle of January, his wife had reason to believe him safer than most, but it was naturally not possible to reassure him by explaining that, after several weeks of determined pursuit, she had finally succeeded in luring Luciano del Santi to lie with her. True, it had so far happened only once and not quite in the way she'd had in mind. But that was something that could be remedied; indeed, for the sake of her sanity, it had to be.

She had known many lovers but the Italian was like none of them. He had been rough and callous and she had revelled in it. There was fire beneath the ice. She knew that now. But it was a cold, white fire that left her seared and haunted . . . and feverishly desperate in case she could not lure him to her a second time.

But in the meantime she continued her desultory affair with Cyrus Winter. She no longer cared very much that it should last, but it soothed her, and one afternoon, almost out of habit, she tried touching him for a little money. However, instead of his usual mocking assent, he rolled back against the pillows and gave way to genuinely amused laughter.

She stared at him. 'What's so funny?'

'Why you, my dear. I don't know if it's monumental nerve that allows you to ask, or whether you're possessed of a naïvety I never suspected.'

'No doubt you intend to explain that remark.'

'If you insist.' He stretched out a lazy hand to brush the fading smudges beneath her breast where Luciano del Santi's fingers had been. 'I doubt you owe these to that ineffective husband of yours . . . and, indeed, I've a shrewd suspicion where you came by them. If I'm right, you've found richer prey than I.'

Mary frowned and jerked the sheet about her. 'How do you know?' she asked coolly.

'I didn't know. I guessed. Intimately acquainted with you as I am, it wasn't very difficult.'

'Thank you.' The complete indifference in his tone stung but she refused to let him see it. 'Are you jealous?'

'Never in this life, my dear – and certainly not on your account. No. If you wish to bed with something barely risen from the gutter, it is entirely your own affair. And please . . .' He laid a finger over her lips. 'Please don't trouble to defend him to me. You know exactly what he is – and therein lies his attraction. But in such a case – and particularly in *this* case – I don't think you can expect me to help finance your pleasures. Does your money-lender demand his pound of flesh? Or are you still too unsure of him to ask?' Her expression told him that he had hit home and he laughed again. 'I should have known. I only hope you're in no immediate need of the money.'

He was baiting her and she knew it, but the habit of confiding in him was long-established. Shrugging, she said, 'No more than usual. It's just that Gervase has some wild idea of paying off his bond in March. It's impossible, of course – but all this silly gossip has made him nervous.'

Cyrus Winter surveyed her with renewed and fascinated amusement. 'Are you telling me that your husband is in debt to your lover?'

'Yes. Surely you knew?'

'Not I, dear heart. But what a novel situation! You like to live dangerously, don't you?'

'I don't foresee any problem. You make too much of it.'

'And you've no imagination. But I don't want to alarm you.' He leaned back and, but for the watchful gleam in his eyes, appeared to be perfectly at ease. 'Suffice it to say that I might be persuaded to . . . smooth your path. Upon certain conditions, naturally.'

'Naturally.' Mary hid her surprise beneath a veil of arid mockery. 'And just what did you have in mind?'

'Nothing tremendously original, I'm afraid. It's simply that I believe it might amuse me to marry your daughter.'

The shock of it deprived her of breath. Then she said jerkily, 'There are times when I find your sense of humour misplaced.'

'I believe you. But, odd as it may seem, I am not joking.'

'Then you've lost your mind,' she snapped. 'How can I let you have Celia when for months you and I have – have . . .'

'My God – can there be a prude beneath that worldly exterior? Or does the delectable Celia know you're my mistress?'

'Of course she doesn't. But—'

'Then I don't see that the matter has any relevance.'

'But it – it's almost incestuous!'

'It is, isn't it?' he smiled. 'Come, Mary . . . don't you want me as your son-in-law? I could be very generous, you know.'

'You bastard!' Suddenly she was shaking with anger.

'You're only doing this out of spite because I've—'

'I'm not such a fool.'

'Then what can you want with a chit of seventeen? The Court will laugh itself silly and say you're in your dotage.'

'The Court may please itself.' He pulled her back into his arms. 'Give me Celia, my dear, and I'll see you're not the loser.'

'No.' She held him off. 'I'll not make us all a laughing-stock.'

'Will you not? Just consider how much easier it will be to attach your Italian when you no longer need raise the sordid matter of money.' An arrested expression crept into her eyes and, twining one hand into her hair, he ran the other down her body. 'Think about it, Mary.'

Wavering but derisive, she said, 'It's not like you to be so persuasive. You'll be saying next that you love the child.'

'Hardly. Like you, I love only myself. But Celia has looks and a hint of unawakened passion . . . a sufficient foundation, shall we say, for my expert moulding.' His mouth hovered over hers. 'And there is something so wickedly erotic about keeping these things in the family, isn't there? Who knows? We might all three end sharing a bed.'

Four

While Mary, Lady Wroxton was casting her bread upon the waters of Luciano del Santi's indifference and trying to school her daughter into a gradual appreciation of Cyrus Winter's manifold attractions, King Charles finally bowed to the inevitable and called his first Parliament for eleven years. He also received a new deputation of Scots Covenanters who made all the usual demands and were given the usual refusals . . . and then he wrote to his garrison in Edinburgh, ordering it to make ready to fire on the city should the command be issued.

Unrest, however, was no longer the sole prerogative of the Scots. In Huntingdon, a vicar complained that his once obedient flock now refused to take the sacrament at the altar rail because of the pattern set them by a pair of troublesome Puritans – and in Sudbury, the mayor locked a government official in a cage and allowed the townsfolk to pelt him with filth. Northumbrian Puritans encouraged the Scots to roam the borders, spying; opposition to ship-money was in evidence from Yorkshire to Devon, and the powerful Merchants Adventurers' company was up in arms over moves to provide work for English weavers by limiting the exportation of raw wool.

All in all, the spring was showing less than its traditional promise and, feeling that some demonstration of goodwill was called for, His Majesty decided to free two members of the 1629 Parliament who had been in prison ever since for refusing to pay fines imposed for their recalcitrant behaviour. Then, confident that the new Parliament would do his bidding all the quicker for knowing him already in a position of strength, he sent Strafford back to Ireland to recruit nine thousand men for use against the Scots.

In the rural fastness of northern Oxfordshire, Richard Maxwell was both more aware of the rumbling discontent than his sovereign and more in sympathy with it. He was not particularly worried to discover that, with his own seat already secure in the Upper House, the new Lord Wroxton was also vying with him for the right to represent the borough in the Commons by sponsoring a second candidate; but when he learned that Gervase had sent agents to suborn the county of behalf of his nominee, Richard was furious. Bribery in elections was not new, but he'd never previously encountered it for himself and he found the experience bitter.

'He's been told to secure the seat for the Crown,' he told his wife, 'and, typically, he's doing it with stealth and coin. But I'll see him damned first. And I'll take that seat if I have to break bread with every man in the Hundred who has a vote!'

Dorothy shook her head, laughingly. 'Then, since I've no wish to see your digestion utterly ruined, it's lucky that you won't have to, isn't it?'

Her faith, though unashamedly biased, was not misplaced, for Richard was widely known and well liked. The result was that Lord Wroxton's agents received some rather rough handling and his nominee less respect than derisory laughter. And, when the election was complete, Richard Maxwell was returned to Parliament by a margin that his lordship, had he been present, might have found humiliating.

Afterwards, whilst still exhibiting signs of too much bonhomie and beer, Richard smiled lazily at his wife and said, 'You'll come with me this time?'

'To London?' Dorothy leaned her chin on both palms and thought about it. At the time of the last Parliament, she'd considered the twins too young to be left. She said, 'And the children?'

'By all means, if you wish – and don't feel the need for a holiday from them. Certainly I'd thought to take Eden . . . and Kate too if you're to be there.'

'Mm. But you know, I think I'd as soon take them all. They're old enough to see the sights and this is as good an opportunity as any. Who knows when His Majesty will see fit to call another Parliament after this one?'

Richard grinned at her. 'Very true. So you'll come?'

'Yes, please . . . if your purse will stand the expense?' She twisted a curl round her finger and gave him a gentle, wide-eyed smile. 'After all, you can't expect me to visit London without doing a little shopping, can you?'

Things moved quickly after that for, with the opening of Parliament set for 13 April, there was a good deal to be done. Richard left for London during the last week in March in order to find suitable lodgings for his tribe, and Eden, on the excuse of preferring a swift ride with his father to a slow one beside the ancient family coach, went with him. Meanwhile, news of their forthcoming holiday produced whoops of delight from the twins, an immense list of her sartorial needs from Amy and, from Kate, an absence of comment that her mother found vaguely unnerving.

Once in London, Eden left his father to the business of house-hunting and took himself off to the Strand, ostensibly in search of Francis. He was admitted to Langley House after some delay by a flushed and dishevelled maid-servant who had plainly been engaged in some more pleasant occupation before being summoned by the door-bell. She informed him that Master Francis was at Court, Miss Celia laid down upon her bed with a sick headache, and my lady already busy with a visitor in the parlour.

'I see.' Eden swallowed his disappointment and said, 'Then, if I may trouble you for writing materials, I'd like to leave Master Francis a note.'

'Very good, sir. This way, if you please.' With ill-concealed resignation, she showed him through a curtained archway to a small chamber containing a fully-furnished writing-table and chair. 'Will there be anything else, sir?'

'I don't think so. And you needn't wait, for I can see myself out when I'm done.'

'Well, sir, if you're sure?' She was suddenly torn between her duty and her obvious desire to be off.

'Quite sure.' Grinning, he dug a sovereign from his pocket and passed it to her. 'I'll leave my letter here and you can make sure it's delivered for me.'

'Yes, sir. Thank you, sir,' she smiled, wooed as much by his charm as by his largesse. Then, bobbing a grateful curtsy, she was gone.

It was the work of but a few minutes to scrawl the half-dozen lines containing news of his arrival and that he could presently be found at the Lamb and Flag in Cannon Row. He was just folding his missive in preparation for sealing it when his attention was diverted by the sound of a door opening, followed by footsteps and a low, angry voice that belonged, unmistakably, to Lady Wroxton.

'How *dare* you walk out on me! I'm not some trollop to be treated so. Or do you think I am a toy to be picked up and put down at your whim?'

A brief pause succeeded her words and then a mellow, faintly accented voice said distantly, 'The whim, as I recall it, was yours. It is your misfortune that I do not share it.'

'You shared it well enough not so very long ago when you all but raped me on your own hearth!'

'An interesting statement – but incorrect on both counts. The truth, surely, is that you were devoured by a certain curiosity; and I, having nothing better to do at the time, satisfied it.'

Eden whistled silently and then winced as the sound of a violent slap reverberated around the hall. It was at this point that common sense warned him that it would be a major tactical error to advertise his presence and that his best course was to stay quietly where he was and hope to slip out unnoticed a little later.

'Get out!' ordered Mary, with uncaring shrillness. 'Get out and don't come back.'

'Willingly.'

'But don't think I've finished with you – because I haven't! Do you think I'll allow myself to be insulted by a – a filthy, hunchbacked little tradesman like you?'

'I didn't know,' remarked the infuriatingly cool voice, 'that it was possible to insult you. However . . . I would advise you to think very carefully before attempting to make an enemy of me. After all, your husband's bond is one of those which fall due at the end of this month, and I should be desolate to have to inconvenience you by recalling it.'

The silence that followed this bland threat was long and airless.

Christ! thought Eden. *It's that Italian fellow who keeps his own assassin. I wonder if Francis knows?*

'Just so,' said Luciano del Santi, mockingly. 'Of course, you may prefer to depend on seeing your daughter become Madam Winter in time to pay me . . . but personally I think you would be unwise. The gentleman will doubtless wish to have the knot tied before parting with his money, and Mistress Celia doesn't appear particularly eager to rush headlong to the altar. I sympathise with you. Life is made up of such petty complications. But it would be a mistake, after once angering me, to hope to appeal to my better nature. I'm afraid I don't have one.'

For quite a long time after the crisp footfalls had left the house and Lady Wroxton had fled up the stairs in an impassioned flurry of taffeta, Eden stayed where he was, frowning absently at his hands. And when he finally rose to leave, he strode uncaringly across the marble floor and let the front door slam behind him, his mind lost to every thought save one.

He did not see Francis that day but instead received a poetically conceived note full of witty excuses which he was not in the mood to appreciate. And that evening, finding that time was hanging unaccustomedly heavy on his hands, he was glad to fall in with his father's suggestion that they leave the Lamb and Flag behind them and sup in the convivial atmosphere of the Bear-at-the-Bridge-Foot.

The capons were juicy, the ale well brewed and the company noisy, cheerful and common; and if Richard noticed that his son and heir was a trifle distrait of manner, he elected not to mention it. They therefore left in quiet amity at a little before midnight and strolled back across London Bridge to look for a boat at the Old Swan stairs.

There was only one, its waterman drunk as a lord and singing. Richard, mindful of the tricky currents about the bridge, decided walking was preferable; Eden, mindful only of his own thoughts, nodded absently and followed his father up towards Thames Street. Richard smothered a sigh and wondered what Dolly expected him to do if Eden finally unlocked his tongue on the subject of Celia Langley.

They passed Doctor's Commons and then turned north through the labyrinthine alleyways of Bridewell in order to cross the Fleet. It was an insalubrious area and, fully alive to the possibility of robbery, Richard kept a watchful eye around them – which was how he came to notice the savage proceedings illuminated by fitful moonlight in a yard off to his left.

What was happening was happening in silence – largely due to the gag which had been stuffed into the victim's mouth while two pairs of hands held him roughly upright to receive the blows of a third. Richard broke his son's lethargy with one sharp stab of his elbow and then went plunging in at the assailants with a sort of flying dive that Eden, plunging swiftly in behind him, still found time to admire.

Dropped like a well-roasted chestnut while his captors met the unexpected attack, the victim slithered down the wall into an inert heap on the cobbles. His fall passed unheeded. Finding himself bereft of his cudgel without quite knowing how, the first man launched himself at Richard and collided with a fist that broke two teeth and loosened several others. Eden, meanwhile, in a series of flawlessly executed moves learned in the Hôtel de Cazenove (and a couple of effective but less genteel ones picked up in the taverns outside it), laid one man out cold against a water-butt and sent the other into staggering, retching retreat up the lane with Gap-Tooth in wise if unsteady pursuit.

Richard flexed the fingers of his right hand, winced and grinned companionably at his son. 'Well. It's nice to know that your time at Angers wasn't completely wasted.'

'And almost as comforting to discover you've still got the hardest fist in three counties,' retorted Eden peaceably.

Then, in a very different tone, 'The only satisfaction, I suspect, either one of us will get. Have you seen who we've rescued?'

Richard dropped on one knee and peered into the battered, unconscious face. 'Ah. Didn't I see him at Far Flamstead last summer? A money-lender, isn't he?'

'Amongst other things,' came the dry response. 'Aside from pegging him up on London Bridge, what do you suggest we do with him?'

Richard looked up, his brows lifting in mild surprise. 'You don't like him?'

'Does anyone?'

'I've no idea. But if they don't, one presumes they have cause. Have you?'

'Only indirectly. Not as much, shall we say, as whoever ordered this . . . but enough to understand why they might want to.' Eden bent to disentangle one wrist from the human wreckage on the cobbles. 'He's not dead, at any rate.'

'Nor even dying,' added a thread-like voice with commendable distinctness. 'Though I confess that it feels like it.'

Slowly and with extreme caution, Luciano del Santi opened his eyes on Richard's face and achieved the ghost of his usual sardonic smile. 'Ah. Mr Maxwell, I believe.'

'Yes – but never mind that now. I suspect that you need some rather prompt attention. If you'll tell us where your house is, we'll endeavour to get you there.'

'Cheapside.' The black eyes closed again, as if in an effort to conserve energy. 'The corner with Friday Street. It's too far.'

'Then where?'

'Malt Lane . . . near Blackfriars Stairs,' came the fading response. 'The sign of the Heart and Coin.'

Eden met his father's quizzical gaze with a carefully neutral one of his own. 'The Heart and Coin?' he said. 'It sounds like a bawdy-house.'

'The word,' said Luciano del Santi, 'is brothel. Don't be shy. Just knock three times and ask for Gwynneth.'

On the difficult but mercifully short journey to Malt Lane,

the Italian lapsed in and out of consciousness with a frequency that made his bearers greet the sign of the Heart and Coin with profound relief. It was a modest property but scrupulously maintained and looking more like a comfortable country inn than the stew they had expected. There were even newly planted window-boxes and some kind of creeper being lovingly trained around the open door. And inside, the cosy well-lit taproom was full of people.

The dark, beak-faced individual that Eden remembered from the hawking party was there, one hand resting on his knife and a nasty glint in his eye. In front of him and involved in heated discussion with each other were a slender, soberly dressed woman with the whitest skin Eden had ever seen and an expression of desperate anxiety, and a small dynamic personage who waved his arms wildly as he talked and still managed to look like a large brown nut with moustaches. Behind these three and collected into little tearful huddles, were the girls. Girls with skin of every shade from lustrous pearl to ebony, hair of gold and copper and jet . . . and apparently only one thing in common. They were all uniquely beautiful.

Eden found that his mouth was open, and resolutely shut it. Richard blinked and said something under his breath. Luciano del Santi opened his eyes, summoned his dwindling resources and said clearly, 'Pardon my intrusion . . . but if there is a chair, I believe these gentlemen would be glad to put me in it.' And promptly passed out again.

For thirty glorious seconds there was silence and then the occupants of the room surged forward on a tide of exclamation. Predictably, the man with the knife got there first by the simple expedient of brushing the others aside. Nor did he waste time talking, but merely removed his master from the hands of Richard and Eden and carried him easily inside to lay him carefully on the soft rug in front of the hearth.

The woman in grey, surrounded by the girls like a dove amongst humming-birds, followed, issuing a stream of lilting orders. 'Marie-Claude – pillows and blankets; Aysha – hot water and cloths; Catalina – salves and bandages;

Ghislaine – the best eau-de-vie from the cellar. Firuze and Zorah – stop crying and keep out of the way. Bridie – look after the gentlemen who were good enough to bring the master back to us.'

'*The master?*' thought Eden, hysterically. And then forgot all about it as his gaze was trapped by a pair of pansy-blue eyes, surrounded by shining red-gold curls.

'Please to be coming in, sirs,' invited Bridie appealingly and in a brogue as thick as butter. 'Sure, we were all that worried and himself gone off to the good-Lord-knows-where without Selim when we all know well what comes of it. But will you not come in and take a drop? For it's plain enough you've had to save himself from the heathen devils coming after him – and you with your good clothes all dirtied up.'

Under this gentle flow of chatter, Richard and Eden found themselves sitting on a cushioned settle while a dazzling blonde pressed glasses of brandy into their hands. Meanwhile, ousted from the hearth by the Welsh woman, the nut-brown rotundity poured Latin vitriol on the man called Selim.

'Rogue – idiot! Where is it you are 'iding when all zis is 'appening? I tell you! You 'ide in ze bed wiz Aysha. And if monsignor is killed, 'is blood it is on your 'ead! Ha! Of what use is zat pretty knife if you do not 'ave ze sense to stay wiz 'im? I sink you do not know 'ow to gut even ze fish!'

Selim looked scornfully down his magnificent nose. 'Take care, son of a donkey, that you do not choke on your own swollen tongue. Or that, one day, I do not cut it out.'

'*You?* Ha! Is joke. I spit!'

'Not in this house you won't!' snapped Gwynneth. 'And if you've nought better to do than deafen us with your chatter, you'd best take yourself back to Cheapside.'

The plump face settled into lines of pure affront. '*I* do not leave monsignor. I never desert 'im. Since 'e is sixteen years old in Genoa, I – Giacomo Federigo Arzini – am wiz 'im. I do everysing for 'im. I am valet, cook, friend—'

'Monkey,' said Selim. 'Fool.'

74

Giacomo ignored the interruption. 'I am 'is right 'and. I 'ave—'

'You've a bell in every tooth,' remarked Gwynneth firmly. 'And if you can't be quiet, I'll have Selim remove the clappers.'

The little man swelled with speechless indignation.

Selim gave a slow, wolfish smile and then stalked across the room to confront Richard. He said, 'You do to the *amir* much kindness. We do not forget. I make you a thousand thanks.'

A gleam of humour lurked in the grey eyes but Richard's tone was suitably grave as he said, 'It was nothing. Anyone would have done as much.'

'No.' The hawk face hardened. 'Sadly, this is not so. The *amir* has many enemies.'

'We know,' murmured Eden, the afternoon's scene still vivid in his mind.

'Ah.' Selim regarded him keenly for a moment and then turned back to Richard. 'You have seen the assailants, *hakim*?'

'I saw them. There were three. But even if I were to recognise them again – which is unlikely – I doubt it would help you. I imagine they were hired bravos. The sort that come six to a groat.'

'Perhaps,' suggested Eden gently, 'you should try asking your master for the name of the last person he offended.'

'You know something.' Selim's voice remained courteous but it was not a question.

'No. In fact I don't. But anyone may guess.'

It was fortunate, perhaps, that Gwynneth chose this moment to pause in her cautious examination of the unconscious man's ribs and sat back on her heels to look across at Selim. She said, 'There's some damage here but it will need a doctor to say how much. Certainly it's worse than last time and I don't like the look of him.'

'And that, as they say, adds insult to injury,' remarked Luciano del Santi from behind closed lids. 'But I forgive you. I'll even allow Selim to put me to bed. The only question is – whose?'

A sudden flush stained the lovely skin and Gwynneth lost her calm façade. 'You fool – you fool! Why do you do it? It's not the first time and it won't be the last. You promised not to stir after dark without Selim – you promised us all. One day they'll kill you.'

The Italian opened his eyes, his mouth twisting with wry amusement. 'No. Haven't you realised yet that the devil looks after his own? I'm indestructible.'

'Yes. You look it.'

He sighed. 'My looks again? You're unkind, *cara*. Don't cry.'

'I'm not crying! You think I'd waste my tears on you? You, who are stubborn and careless and too proud to tell us what it is you're trying to do?' She sniffed and cradled his hand in both of hers. 'Don't think I care what you do – I don't. But you might spare a thought for what's to become of the girls and me if you get your throat cut.'

A faint laugh, abruptly checked, caused him to close his eyes again until the pain receded and made Gwynneth reach for the brandy.

'Here,' she said roughly. 'Drink it all. You may as well be drunk as stupid.'

The fine-boned face lost some of its greyness and he was able, at length, to say mordantly, 'I'm glad you're enjoying yourself. I'd be sorry to suffer like this for nothing.'

Her eyes were bleak but she said, 'Ah – be quiet. Or, if you *must* talk, say thank you to the good gentlemen who saved your worthless life tonight.'

Luciano del Santi turned his head to locate Richard and Eden, his brow furrowed with the effort of it. Then he said, 'Forgive me. I thought you had gone.'

Richard crossed to his side, followed more slowly by Eden. 'Think nothing of it. The brandy is excellent, so I've no complaints. And I'm sure that – for other reasons entirely – my son has none either.' He paused briefly and then said, 'Tell me . . . does this kind of thing happen to you often?'

'Not often. Only when I grow careless.'

'Only when you go out without Selim, you mean,' said Gwynneth tartly. 'Why not tell the truth? There's scarcely one of those fine gentlemen of the Court who buy their dinners with your money who wouldn't stick a knife in your back given only the chance to do it.'

'You talk too much, *cara*.' The melodious voice was pleasantly final. 'There's no reason why Mr Maxwell should interest himself in my affairs.'

'None,' said Richard, 'save that I've already done so.'

'And thereby placed me under an obligation to you.'

'Are you suggesting that as my reason?'

The black eyes stared inscrutably back at him. 'No. I'm saying that if there is anything – either now or in the future – that I may do for you, you have but to name it.'

An arrested expression crossed Eden's face and he opened his mouth as if to speak, then thought better of it.

Richard said, 'I appreciate the offer and the fact that it is not lightly made. But not quite everything has to be paid for, signor.'

'I know it.' Luciano del Santi's smile was crooked but oddly infectious. 'But you must allow me to observe that you are the first Englishman I have met who knew it also.'

'If that's so, I can only deduce that your experience has been unfortunate. But it explains a lot.' Richard looked with some amusement at the hotch-potch of nationalities surrounding them and then, with none at all, at the man on the floor. 'But you've talked enough and we should go.'

The dark eyes closed again and the Italian gave no sign of having heard. Then, 'Thank you,' he said.

At the door, Eden felt a small soft hand slip into his own and looked down into Bridie's cheerfully admiring eyes. 'Come again, sir,' she said with sincerity. 'Please.'

On the following day, Eden was reunited with both Celia and Francis but found curiously little satisfaction in the event. Celia was distinctly irritable, absent of manner and plainly disinclined to talk. Francis, on the other hand, talked a good deal more than Eden thought necessary – mostly about Court fashions and who was sleeping with whom. Eden left without having said anything that he had meant to say and in a mood of restless depression. If Lord

Wroxton *was* facing financial ruin and Celia being steered into wealthy wedlock, no one was going to tell him of it – and it was not a matter about which he could well ask. And if he *did* ask and found it was true . . . what, in God's name, was he supposed to do then? Run off with Celia? Hardly. Blackmail Lady Wroxton over her affair with the Italian? Unthinkable. And the only thing left was to wait and see how events transpired – a course of action which accorded ill with his inclinations.

The result of all this was that he went back rather sooner than might have been expected to Blackfriars and the Heart and Coin. It was not, naturally, the first time he had visited a brothel. Eighteen months in Angers with Francis and Ralph had made sure of that. But it was the first time he had gone to one of his own volition and on the invitation, moreover, of a very pretty courtesan, so the occasion took on something of the flavour of an adventure. It was also, as it turned out, thoroughly enjoyable; and though Bridie could not banish his anxiety about Celia, she could and did rid him of his restlessness. That she also taught him quite a lot was something in the nature of a bonus.

The end of the week saw Richard and Eden established in a small but comfortable house near Old Palace Yard with a pleasant garden running down to the river. And two days later Dorothy arrived with Kate, Amy, Felix and Felicity, two personal maidservants, Eden's groom to act as general factotum, and a mountain of luggage. Richard laughed at his wife, swung her crazily off her feet and wondered if he shouldn't have leased a bigger house.

Kate, as usual, came straight to the point. 'How's Celia?' she asked Eden, without noticeable warmth. 'Still taking Whitehall by storm, I suppose?'

'As far as I know – yes.'

Her brows soared. 'You mean you haven't seen her?'

'Only once.' He hesitated and then, because he had to confide in someone, said, 'She wasn't herself at all. I heard . . . there was some talk about a wealthy marriage for her. But, if it's true, she didn't seem particularly happy about it.'

78

Kate sighed. Trust Eden to jump to the conclusion that Celia was being forced to the altar. She said, 'I don't suppose you've considered the fact that she's been in London for almost four months without becoming betrothed? That she may be tired of waiting for the talk to become reality?'

'No. And I'm fairly sure it's not that.' He looked at her, a slight frown in his eyes. 'Why do you dislike her, Kate?'

'I don't. I just can't see why you're so taken with her, that's all. As far as I'm concerned, she's no different from Amy. And one of those is enough in any family.'

'You don't really know her,' he said slowly.

'Perhaps not,' agreed Kate. 'But do you?'

This was such obvious provocation that Eden decided not to answer it. Instead, he said casually, 'I almost forgot. Father and I have been seeing something of that Italian fellow who was at Far Flamstead last summer.'

'Signor del Santi?' The green eyes sharpened. 'And how did that come about?'

'Someone decided to break a few of his bones. Fortunately – or unfortunately, depending on your point of view – Father and I happened to be passing and put a stop to it.' He paused to examine her face. 'By then, of course, they'd done a fairly good job on him. A sight that I'm sure some people would have paid money for.'

'Yes. Well, it sounds as though somebody did, doesn't it?' replied Kate prosaically. 'And I can't say I'm particularly surprised.'

Eden grinned at her. 'Nor was I. On the other hand, I *did* think of paying a call on him . . . just to ask after his health, you know.'

'And why,' she asked, 'should you want to do that?'

'That's my business. But I'll let you come with me if you like.'

'That's kind of you.'

'Isn't it?' He folded his arms and regarded her knowingly. 'And you may as well save that look of indifference for someone who's likely to be fooled by it, dear Kate. I know you too well.'

'And I suppose you think I'm dying to come?'

'Aren't you?'

'Maybe.' She held his gaze coolly for a moment and then dissolved into laughter. 'Actually, wild horses wouldn't stop me.'

On Monday 13 April, Richard Maxwell and several hundred other gentlemen presented themselves at Westminster Hall for the formal opening of Parliament. It was not a howling success. The King, whose slight stammer made public speaking something of a trial, delegated the task of making his policy known to Lord Keeper Finch – the tactless and conceited Speaker of the last Parliament, whose patronising and arrogant tone did little to promote goodwill. And, after listening to a catalogue of imperiously phrased demands ranging from subsidies to pay for subduing the Scots, to a retroactive bill granting His Majesty Tonnage and Poundage for the whole reign, no one was in the mood to wax patriotic over the Covenanters' alleged dealings with Louis of France. Neither were they noticeably appeased by the prospect of being permitted to lay their grievances before the King if they first took care of his finances. It was, as the member for Tavistock was heard to mutter, no more than a carrot; and none but the most reckless gambler in the House would have laid long odds on their chances of remaining in session for more than a matter of days once His Majesty had got what he wanted.

So as the week wore by and Richard listened with the rest to petitions about ship-money and religion and watched the member for Tavistock rise to the front rank of the King's critics, the arrest of an eminent Scots lord for treason took place amidst a positive fog of indifference. And, moved by a spirit of curiosity so intense that it faintly alarmed her, Kate Maxwell put on her second-best green velvet and went with her brother to call on a usurer.

They ended up taking Felix with them – for no better reason than, finding himself at a loose end and catching up with his elders about to depart for a destination they refused to disclose, Felix decided to enliven his morning by following them. He dodged in and out of doorways all the way to Westminster Stairs and then, realising that they were about to take to the water, abandoned discreet surveillance and jumped recklessly aboard the boat at the very moment that the waterman cast off. It was rather disappointing that neither Kate nor Eden showed any sign of surprise, but the reaction of the boatman more than made up for their indifference and Felix settled down to investigate the bilges feeling that his time hadn't been completely wasted.

They disembarked at Paul's Wharf. Eden asked the boatman if he'd care to return Felix whence he came and received a pungent refusal. And when even an offer to tie Felix to the seat failed to have any effect, Eden and Kate gave up and set off resignedly up Lambeth Hill with Felix marching cheerfully behind them, whistling.

It was when they were nearing the top of Old Change that Kate's nerve unexpectedly started to waver and she said, 'You know, I'm not sure this is a good idea. He'll find it odd enough that *you've* come – and at least you have an excuse, threadbare though it is.'

Eden accorded her a brief, slanting grin. 'Cold feet, Kate?'

'Certainly not. Just a trifle tepid. I think I'd forgotten what he's like and now I'm starting to remember. And then there's the question of how to explain Felix.'

'You can't. No one could.'

'Don't be flippant.' She eyed him severely. 'I suppose you *do* know what you're going to say?'

'Yes. I thought I'd tell him that you're tired of drawing the chapel ceiling and wanted to try from life.'

Kate's fingers closed hard over his arm and she stopped walking so abruptly that Felix cannoned into the back of them.

'How do you know what I've been drawing?' she demanded furiously. 'I don't show my sketches to *anyone*!'

'That bad, are they? Well, never mind. No one can be good at everything.'

Kate glared at him. 'I asked how you knew.'

'I expect Amy told him,' volunteered Felix obligingly. 'She told everyone else. Not that anybody found it in the least bit interesting.'

'Except you,' said Kate frigidly to Eden.

'Not even me,' he replied placidly. 'Or not until the other night when I suddenly realised where I'd seen Signor del Santi before . . . and why you'd suddenly developed a fascination for the Fall of Lucifer. Do you think we might go on? And if you're too chicken-hearted to come with me, you can always take Felix to the nearest pie shop. I shan't mind.'

'I know you won't,' came the astringent reply as they fell into step again. 'But if you think I'm going to miss the chance of finding out what you're up to, you're mistaken. I'll come. And if you don't feel you can depend on swearing Felix to secrecy, you'll just have to bribe him.'

'I don't mind being bribed,' said Felix hopefully from behind. 'Honest.'

'That's comforting,' said Eden. 'Perhaps you won't mind being knocked on the head either.'

The premises of Luciano del Santi lay on the corner of Friday Street and Cheapside and were not hard to find, for a large hanging sign proclaimed the owner's name in flowing Italianate script over a symbol that looked like a peculiarly convoluted knot. And below the sign, somewhat to Eden's surprise, was the entrance to what was very plainly a goldsmith's shop. Of course, it shouldn't have surprised him; most goldsmiths were money-lenders. But all money-lenders were not goldsmiths – and, as far as he could recall, no one had mentioned the fact that Signor del Santi was also, presumably, a craftsman.

The expressively blank gaze that Kate gave him told him that she felt the same. Felix, on the other hand, was suddenly enthusiastic. He always liked watching people work.

The door was flung open and Giacomo bounced through it. He seized Eden's hand, moustaches quivering, and kissed him on both cheeks.

'Come in, signor – come in! Welcome to the 'ouse of del Santi! Welcome, welcome. Monsignor, 'e will be so

82

'appy! I tell 'im you are 'ere *pronto*. And *la bella signorina*,' he said, releasing Eden in favour of Kate. '*Bellissima!* You are ze sister, no?'

'Yes,' said Kate, grinning and at the same time stepping back in case the little fellow embraced her again. Felix, she noticed, had put himself out of range and was wearing a look which defied anybody to kiss him. 'Yes, I'm Mr Maxwell's sister. And I too have some small acquaintance with Mr . . . with Signor del Santi. So we called to inquire after his health.'

'Is kind of you.' Giacomo beamed with gratification. 'I tell monsignor you are 'ere. 'E is in 'is workshop and 'e do not come out for heverybody – but for you 'e will come. *Scusi – momento!*'

'Workshop?' said Felix, on just the right note of appeal.

Giacomo stopped in his tracks and regarded the boy with benevolence. '*Sì*. You are interested? You like to see?'

'Well,' said Felix in the tone of one reluctant to give trouble but willing to be persuaded, 'it's just that I've never – *Ow!*'

Having discreetly trodden on his brother's foot, Eden smiled blandly at Giacomo and said, 'Another time, perhaps – if Signor del Santi permits. We've no wish to cause him any inconvenience.'

'Is not inconvenience – is pleasure!' cried Giacomo expansively. 'Please – you come. Monsignor will be so 'appy. You come.'

There was no help for it. They went, Felix clattering on in front at Giacomo's heels.

'Damn,' said Eden softly to Kate. 'Why didn't I drop him overboard while I had the chance?'

'No resolution,' she replied. 'But don't worry. You heard what the man said. "Monsignor will be so 'appy." '

Ahead of them, Giacomo had opened a door and embarked on a vivacious flow of Italian which was stemmed almost immediately by a brief and pungently delivered sentence in the same language. Kate and Eden exchanged glances and then, arriving in the doorway, looked past Giacomo to the scene within.

Luciano del Santi was in his shirt-sleeves, sitting at a large trestle on which reposed an impressive array of small tools. His concentrated gaze was wholly taken up with the gleaming object held in one long-fingered hand. In shape and size it resembled a goblet, being set upon a delicately slender stem; but the bowl was composed of intricately pierced lattice-work so fine that it gave the appearance of a spider's web spun in gold.

The clever hands stilled and, without haste, the Italian looked up at his visitors. The impassive black eyes held Kate's gaze for a couple of seconds and then he said, 'In a few minutes' time you will be welcome . . . but, until then, I would appreciate silence.' And turned coolly back to his work.

Somewhere at the back of her mind, Kate discovered the first twinges of respect. If the lovely thing in his hands was of his own creating, then there was more to this man than malicious wit. It did not, of course, make him any easier to like; but it did render him a grain or two less obnoxious.

Felix, meanwhile, had approached the table so stealthily that no one had noticed him doing it. And when Luciano del Santi finally set the piece down, it was Felix who was the first one to speak. He said, 'Did you make *all* of that?'

The Italian looked at him thoughtfully. 'Yes.'

'How long did it take?'

'In hours of work? I don't know. It isn't important. These things are finished in their own time.'

Felix nodded, apparently understanding this. 'And is it finished now?'

'Not quite. There are still some slightly roughened edges here – and here.' He lifted the goblet for Felix's inspection and pointed to it in various places. 'You see? These must be smoothed and polished. And then I shall engrave the base along this curvature here.'

'And then?' asked Felix. 'What is it?'

'What does it look like?'

'A wine-cup. But you can't drink out of that. It's got holes in it.'

Luciano del Santi reached to his left and picked up an object wrapped in a soft cloth. Then, opening it, he placed its contents gently inside the golden web of the goblet.

'So,' he said, apparently unaware of the faint breathiness that had suddenly afflicted Kate. 'The finest amber . . . I carved it myself. And the gold, you see, is no more than a shell.'

For probably the first time in his life, Felix took at least two minutes to decide what to say. The amber was beautiful and so thin that the light shone through it; and, set in its fragile tracery of gold, it glowed with almost uncanny life. And Felix, looking at it, was consumed of a sudden thirst for knowledge. Drawing a long breath, he stared the Italian straight in the eye and said, 'Can – can *anyone* learn to do that?'

'No.' The word was bland and unequivocal.

'Could *I*?'

There was a long pause. Then, 'If you mean, could you learn to work gold . . . yes. Perhaps. It is a skill and can therefore be taught. If, however, you are asking me if you can learn to be a master, then the answer is no. Master-goldsmiths are born, not made. And if you don't already have the ingredients within you, no one can put them there.'

Again and much to the surprise of Kate and Eden, Felix seemed to accept this without question. He just nodded slowly and said, 'Will you teach me?'

Luciano del Santi leaned his elbows on the trestle and regarded Felix steadily over his hands. 'No,' he said.

'Why not?'

'That's enough, Felix.' Eden stepped forward and dropped a hand on his young brother's shoulder. 'Signor del Santi has been more than patient – so just take no for an answer and stop haranguing him.'

Felix shook off Eden's hand and stood his ground. 'Why?' he said again.

For the first time since they had come in, a vagrant smile touched the sculpted face.

'Because I don't know anything about you,' came the

calm reply. 'Today you think you want to be a goldsmith. For all I know to the contrary, yesterday it may have been a soldier, and tomorrow a pastry-cook. I'm not inclined to waste my time.'

'All right.' The boy shook back a lock of unruly brown hair from his face and thought about it. 'I suppose that's fair. But if I prove I really mean it – *then* will you teach me?'

'Felix.' Eden was beginning to see a chasm yawning ahead. The Italian had been amazingly tolerant so far but it couldn't last. 'Felix . . . for God's sake, stop arguing.'

'I'm not arguing,' said Felix. 'I'm *inquiring*.'

Kate stared hard at the floor and tried to straighten out her face. Luciano del Santi startled them all by laughing.

'I don't see what's so funny,' Felix objected. 'I just want to know whether you'll ever agree to teach me – or whether you're just making excuses. Because if you *won't* teach me, I'll just have to find someone who will.'

Something in his voice broke through Kate's amusement and caused her to unlock her tongue. She said, 'Are you serious, Felix? Because if you are, you'll need Father's permission and a formal apprenticeship. You'd have to live away from home and sign away your life for years to – to someone like Signor del Santi. It's not something to be decided on a moment's impulse.'

'I don't care,' came the stubborn reply. 'I want to know how to make things like that . . . and I shan't change my mind, no matter *what* you think!'

Giacomo chuckled and said something in his own language. His master replied with what appeared to be dry humour and then relapsed into silence. Kate decided it was time she learned to speak Italian.

'Very well,' said Luciano del Santi, crisply. 'I'll make you no promises. Perhaps I'll teach you – perhaps not. We'll see. In the meantime you may have the freedom of my workshop. You may come here when you wish and pick up what knowledge you can by watching. I, myself, am not always here, but my assistant, Gino, will be pleased to answer your questions. If you care to wait for half an hour or so, you can meet him. But what you will *not* do is to touch anything at all without either his permission or mine. And if, in the end, I refuse to take you as a pupil, you will have to accept that I mean it and will not change my mind. Do I make myself quite clear?'

'Yes.' Felix flushed and grinned widely. 'Yes. Thank you.'

The Italian laid his fingers on the table-edge and rose from his stool with a caution which reminded Kate that he had been recently set upon in the street by a trio of hired ruffians. Strangely, she was conscious of a twinge of sympathy that had not been there when Eden had first told her of it and frowned, wondering why.

'Don't thank me,' he was saying to Felix. 'Just remember that I've promised you nothing. Yet. And now, Giacomo will give you a guided tour and introduce you to Gino when he comes, whilst I take your brother and sister upstairs for a little refreshment.' And without waiting for a reply, he crossed a little stiffly to Kate's side and offered his arm.

She took it, felt herself colouring and was annoyed. It was this, more than anything, that made her say abruptly, 'Why are you doing this for Felix?'

'Because he reminds Giacomo of someone.'

Kate shot him a suspicious glance. 'Who?'

He sighed and for a moment she thought he wasn't going to answer. Then, 'Me,' he said.

Effectively silenced and not daring, this time, to catch Eden's eye, Kate trod meekly up the stairs and into a light, spacious parlour. The Italian invited them to be seated, poured wine with his own hands and then joined them near the empty hearth. 'And now,' he said smoothly to Eden, 'you may tell me what I can do for you.'

Eden liked directness but this was disconcerting. He found himself saying that they had thought to visit the Gold-smith's Hall and merely called, in passing, to inquire after the signor's health.

Without changing his expression by a hair's breadth, the signor managed to convey total and satiric disbelief. It was a long time before he spoke and Kate began to share her brother's discomfort. More than anyone she had ever met, this man had the most infuriating knack of using silence as a weapon.

'My health – save for the temporary inconvenience of a couple of cracked ribs – is excellent,' he said at last. 'But you disappoint me, Mr Maxwell.'

'Do I?'

'Yes. I had thought you capable of coming to the point without feeling it necessary first to play social games.'

'Like Felix, you mean?' Eden grinned ruefully. The fellow was right, of course – but he himself was in a slight quandary. He had hoped for a few minutes away from Kate's sharp ears and it didn't look as if he was going to get it. Temporising, he said, 'You seem very sure that there *is* a point.'

'Naturally.' Luciano del Santi smiled coldly. 'You don't like me very much, Mr Maxwell, and you did all that could be expected of you the other evening. Therefore the obvious conclusion is that I owe you a favour and you have come to collect it.'

There was no answer to this. Eden turned his head and looked consideringly at Kate but, short of drenching her in malmsey, there seemed to be no way of shifting her. And, as if reading his thought, she said flatly, 'No. I'm staying exactly where I am. But I'm willing to be discreet.'

'You'd better be,' he returned briefly. And then, to the Italian, 'All right. It's perfectly true – I *do* want something. I'd like you to kindly refrain from terminating Gervase Langley – I mean Lord Wroxton's bond.'

Kate choked on her malmsey. Whatever else she had expected to hear, it certainly wasn't that. The two men ignored her, hazel eyes locked with black; and Luciano del Santi, as usual, appeared in no hurry to speak. Finally he said gently, 'And just what makes you suppose that I hold such a bond – let alone that I may have been considering recalling it?'

'I don't suppose – I know,' said Eden baldly. And then, deciding to live dangerously, 'Just as I've a shrewd suspicion to whom you owe those cracked ribs.'

This time the silence was airlessly unpleasant. Kate

looked uneasily from one to the other of them and tried, unsuccessfully, to understand what was going on.

'You appear to know a great deal, Mr Maxwell. I cannot help wondering how.'

'Purely by accident, I can assure you. But it's irrelevant, isn't it?'

'Hardly.' The hard mouth curled into something that was not quite a smile. '*Nam et ipsa scientia potestas est*. Or so I have always found.'

'I beg your pardon?' said Eden.

The dark eyes continued to impale him until Kate unexpectedly drew their fire.

'Knowledge itself is power,' she said helpfully. 'Francis Bacon – *Religious Meditations*.' And then, 'My brother dislikes quotations, Signor del Santi. They bring out the worst in him. You might find the fact useful for future reference.'

Against all expectation and entirely without warning, a very different and singularly infectious smile dawned.

'Not particularly, mistress. I automatically bring out the worst in almost everyone.'

Damn him! thought Kate, assuming her most wooden stare and ruthlessly ascribing the odd sensation in her chest to queasiness. *I wish he wouldn't do that.* Aloud, she said sweetly, 'Oh? And there I was thinking you had to work at it.'

Eden groaned. 'Pot calling kettle, Kate. So just drink your wine and be quiet.' Then, to the other man, 'Well? As a favour to me, will you continue to hold his lordship's bond past quarter-day?'

Luciano del Santi gave an almost imperceptible shrug and came to his feet. 'Why not? Though how grateful you will find him, I take leave to doubt.'

'Grateful? What do you mean?'

'Simply that I imagine you can have only one reason for making such a request of me.' A sudden glint lit the dark eyes. 'Or am I mistaken? It is less a desire to put his lordship under an obligation to you and more a question of freeing his daughter from the pressures which I suspect may be surrounding her?'

A hint of colour crept beneath Eden's skin and he said curtly, 'Possibly. But my reasons are my own business.'

'True. And, in either case, it's a neat strategy. But for one minor point, I would even be inclined to congratulate you.'

Eden rose to face him. 'Oh? And what is that?'

'Nothing that you will find in the least palatable, I am sure,' said the Italian dispassionately. 'It merely occurs to me that, in this particular case, you might be advised to heed the old maxim and take a long look at the mother before you think of marrying the daughter.'

His meaning was perfectly plain and a hard knot of anger formed in Eden's chest. Controlling his voice as best he could, he said, 'I'll try to believe that you mean well – but I find your suggestion both offensive and insulting. Celia is nothing like her mother.'

'As yet, not very much perhaps. But I'm just expressing an opinion. You don't have to agree – or even listen.'

'Then I'll do neither.'

'And that, if you ask me, is a pity,' remarked Kate to no one in particular. 'Because it's the most straightforward and sensible thing he's said today. Much as I hate to admit it.'

Five

For the first time in their marriage, Dorothy Maxwell was aware that Richard's attention was wholly absorbed by matters outside his family – and it worried her. He had sat in the House before and been much occupied by its business, but never to the degree where he could be oblivious to the peculiar pursuits of his children. But so it was now. He did not know that Amy had somehow acquired a secret supply of cosmetics and that, discovering them, Felicity had appeared in front of her mother's guests with her face inexpertly plastered in orris powder and carmine. Neither had he noticed that Felix was consumed of an inexplicable desire to become a goldsmith and was spending every waking moment in Luciano del Santi's establishment on Cheapside – accompanied, more often than not, by Kate on the pretext of learning Italian. He did not know and Dorothy did not tell him. She simply consigned Amy's illicit hoard to the kitchen fire, told Felix not to trouble his father with talk of apprenticeships just yet, and forbade Kate to set foot outside the house without her maid.

Less easy to deal with was the strange state of armed neutrality that seemed to exist these days between Eden and Kate, or the fact that Eden was dividing his time between Whitehall – whither he had been introduced by Francis – and somewhere unspecified that frequently kept him out half the night and into which his mother saw the wisdom of not inquiring too closely. Under normal circumstances she would have discussed it with Richard, but an unpleasant sense of foreboding told her that it was not the time; that he had greater and graver things on his mind.

She was right. Led by the member for Tavistock, one John Pym, the King's critics accused Lord Keeper Finch of breach of privilege during the last Parliament, demanded an inquiry into the imprisonment of Holles and Strode after the conclusion of the last Parliament, and began to re-examine the case of John Hampden – thus refuelling the fiery question of ship-money. Then, as April drifted into May, the Earl of Strafford returned from Ireland to oppose Mr Pym from the other side of the chessboard.

The Earl appealed to the Upper House and secured a majority in favour of voting subsidies to His Majesty before taking up the grievances of Parliament; Pym countered by demanding a consultation between both Houses – and, with the help of my lords Warwick, Saye and Brooke, neatly squashed potential dissent. Lord Keeper Finch, meanwhile, tried to unleash a storm by announcing that the Scots rebels had fired on Edinburgh Castle only to be hoist by his own petard when word came that, in fact, the reverse was true. That night the taverns of Westminster abounded with rowdiness and rumour – and a desire to burn Lambeth Palace and Archbishop Laud along with it before permitting him to wage his Papist war on the good Protestants north of the border.

Then, just as Richard started to wonder if the situation wasn't getting somewhat out of hand, a new and encouraging development took place. The King showed his first sign of weakness by having Secretary Vane offer to accept eight subsidies in place of the original twelve if only they were voted immediately. He would even, the Commons were told, go so far as to halt the present levy of ship-money. Scenting desperation, the House replied that it could not debate this proposal without first hearing the Privy Council's opinion on the legality of the said ship-money, at which point Secretary Vane offered complete abolition of the thrice-blasted ship-money if only the House would cease its delay and grant all twelve subsidies that very day. Mr Pym came slowly to his feet on a long, satisfied sigh and gently refused the bribe. Grievances first, he said; subsidies later. And to himself while the House roared its approval, 'Check!'

While all this was happening, four lesser gentlemen of the Court found themselves facing financial ruin. One retired to his crumbling manor, two fled their creditors to France and the fourth blew his head off with a cavalry pistol. My lord Wroxton was not one of them and was thus able to leave for a brief visit to Far Flamstead with a clear mind. And while the inevitable buzz of gossip echoed around the corridors of Whitehall, Luciano del Santi departed unobtrusively on his annual pilgrimage to Genoa and took the amber goblet with him. Felix, who had wanted to see the finished product, was disgruntled; Kate had no such excuse.

She found that she hardly saw anything of Eden these days and rather regretted it – both for the loss of their easy rapport and because she was necessarily thrown more into the company of her sisters. But they had quarrelled with unusual thoroughness on their return from Cheapside that day and, since she could not in all conscience retract what she had said about Celia, there was nothing for it but to wait for him to come round in his own good time.

But though she could not talk to Eden, she could and did talk to Francis – thus discovering that all was not well in the Langley household. With the laconic candour he always employed with Kate and, oddly enough, never with anyone else, he revealed that Celia was being sought in marriage by a Gentleman of Means and behaving like a chicken with its head cut off in consequence.

'Why?' asked Kate, bluntly. 'It sounds to me to be just what she always wanted.'

'Yes. A position at Court, influence and a husband with considerable style – who is also, with the possible exception of that Italian crook-back, the richest man in London.'

'He's not a crook-back,' said Kate without thinking.

The dark blue eyes gleamed with lazy amusement. 'Why, Kate . . . such passion! It won't do, you know.'

'Don't be ridiculous. It's just that he's been surprisingly good to Felix – and I dislike inaccurate and exaggerated statements.' Battening down her annoyance, she smiled at him. 'So what's wrong with this paragon of Celia's?'

'Something you might describe as a skeleton in his closet – and ours,' came the cryptic reply. 'And more than that, dearest Kate, it would be grossly improper of me to tell you. Except perhaps to add that although Celia's objections are not without foundation, our lady mother is not inclined to be sympathetic. The result is deadlock – and noisy, histrionic deadlock at that. Very wearing on the nerves.'

'Yes,' said Kate sardonically. 'It must be. So why don't you bestir yourself to talk some sense into one or other of them?'

Francis smiled slowly and with cheerful malice. 'Dear heart, I've done better than that. I've written to tell Father. Under the circumstances, that should do the trick. And in the meantime, we can all go a-Maying with a clear conscience.'

Richard Maxwell, had he been privileged to hear this remark, would have laughed. With May Day still a week away, he had arrived that morning in Westminster Hall along with his fellow members to find that Speaker Glanvil had mysteriously failed to appear. There was one obvious possibility that might account for this and, while they were grimly discussing it, the Usher of the Black Rod entered the chamber and confirmed their suspicions by announcing that His Majesty commanded their attendance in the Upper House. Dourly silent, they followed him; and there was the King with a prepared speech of some length, but which said neither more nor less than they had expected. It was not, he said, either the fault of the Upper House or his own that this Parliament had not come to a happy end – nor even that of the entire Commons – but only 'the malicious cunning of some few seditiously affected men'.

Richard glanced across at Pym and Hampden, their faces marked only with resolution, and then looked back to the small, neat figure who was slowly but surely coming to the point.

'As for the liberty of the people,' concluded Charles, in the measured tones that enabled him to control his stammer, 'no king in the world shall be more careful in the propriety of their goods, the liberty of their persons and true religion than I shall. And now, my lord Keeper, do as I have commanded you.'

There was silence as Finch stood up, as heavy a silence as Richard could ever remember. And then the words came.

'My lords – and you, the gentlemen of the House of Commons – the King's Majesty doth dissolve this Parliament.'

The breath that everyone seemed to have been holding released itself in a long sigh and Richard found himself thinking, 'That's that, then. Twenty-two days – and it's all over.'

John Hampden touched his arm. 'We can't give up now. There has to be a way forward. Will you join with those of us who are resolved to look for it?'

Richard thought about it. Pym he respected but could not like. Hampden was a different matter. He said logically, 'Why me?'

Hampden smiled. 'Because I take you for a man of sense, not easily carried away by high-flown words. I think we shall need such as you before we're done. And I don't ask you to commit yourself; simply to dine at my house tomorrow so that we may have the opportunity to understand each other.'

It was too reasonable an invitation to decline but, in the event, it came to nothing. For on the morning following the dissolution, John Hampden was arrested and committed to the Tower – along with John Pym, Walter Earle and my lords Saye, Brooke and Warwick. All had their lodgings searched for evidence of treasonable communication with the Scots and all were held for questioning before the Council on the matter of the King's rights in Parliament. Richard was suddenly angry; he was not, he decided, ready to go back to Thorne Ash just yet.

It was Felicity who woke first to the ghostly pre-dawn light of May Day and, shivering a little, clambered out of the big feather bed she shared with her sisters to throw back the shutters and open the window.

'Kate? Kate – do get up or we'll be late and miss all the fun.'

Kate opened sleepy eyes and raised a tousled red head. 'What time is it?'

'I don't know. But it's getting light and you know you have to go while the dew's still wet or it's not the same.'

'All right – I'm coming.' Kate's grin widened into a yawn and she dug an elbow into the mound that was Amy. 'If you want to bathe your face in the grass and so on, you'd better wake up.'

Amy grunted and burrowed deeper into the pillows.

Felicity pattered back across the boards and looked at Kate. She said, 'She takes absolutely ages to dress and we won't get out till noon. Help me?'

'Why not?' said Kate. And moving in perfect, practised unison, they flung back the covers and set about propelling Amy out of bed.

'Stop it!' she snapped furiously but without much hope of being heeded. And then, 'All right – all right! I'm awake and I'm up so there's no need to maul me. You're so rough!'

'And nasty and vulgar and childish,' said Kate. 'We know. And you're a delicate little blossom of the utmost refinement. We know that too.'

'She bruises very easily,' offered Felicity wisely. 'Or so she's always saying.'

'Well, I do!' Flushed with annoyance, Amy tugged the ribbons from her braids with unaccustomed vigour and began to unloose her hair. 'And I just wish you'd remember it because I don't want to end the day black and blue! Where's Meg with the water? If you want me to get ready quickly, you'll have to let her just help *me*. I need her to dress my hair.'

'Selfish cat,' muttered Felicity, fumbling with her own ribbons which had somehow tied themselves into a knot.

'No I'm not. It's just that *I* care what I look like.'

'And we don't?' Kate unfastened the drawstring of her night-rail and allowed it to slither to her feet. For a moment she stood still while the chilly air struck her skin and surveyed herself critically in the mirror. In four days' time she would be seventeen, and still there was scant sign of the voluptuous curves that everyone said were so necessary to beauty and which Amy, at just turned fifteen, already had in plenty. Then, with a shrug of resignation, she reached for the hairbrush and set about disentangling her hair. 'Or perhaps it's just that we've other uses for our energies.'

Amy wriggled out of her shift and smiled complacently. 'Yes? Well, under the circumstances I suppose you'd have to say that, wouldn't you? I mean, you still haven't got any figure to speak of – despite being so much older—'

Her words ended in a strangled gasp as Felicity hit her squarely in the back with a pillow.

'Shut up! Kate's got a perfectly good figure – and at least she's not fat like you!'

'I'm not fat!' Amy swept round, snatched up the pillow and hurled it at her younger sister, missing by a good yard. 'But it's not fashionable to be as thin as a rail. You have to have a bosom – and everything. And I've got one.'

'You certainly have,' said Kate, grinning. 'How can we miss it? But just put it away, like a good girl, and let's all stop bickering and get ourselves ready. Look – here's Meg with the water.'

'Mercy me – you're up! And there was I thinking I'd never rouse Miss Amy afore nine,' said the girl breathlessly as she heaved the great copper jug on to the wash-stand and poured water into the bowl. Scarcely a year older than Kate and as plump as Amy, Meg Bennet was possessed of a generously freckled nose and a pair of roguish dimples. Her father was bailiff at Thorne Ash and, like Tom Tripp (who had lately begun to pay her some interesting attention) she had grown up with the Maxwell children and so been the obvious choice when Dorothy decided that Kate, at least, was old enough to have her own maid. 'It's barely cock-crow. What wakened you all so early?'

'Felicity,' replied Kate dryly. 'She wants to weave a wreath of whitethorn and look for her true love.'

Felicity denied this with one unladylike word.

Kate laughed. 'My sentiments exactly. But the general opinion is that we'll change our minds. Meg already has, haven't you, Meg?'

Meg blushed and dimpled.

'*Have* you?' asked Felicity curiously. 'Really?'

'I might have,' came the prim reply, 'and then again I might not. You'll have to wait and see.'

'Do my hair now, Meg.' Amy turned from the wash-stand and dropped the towel carelessly on the floor. 'I want it twined with ribbons.'

'What for?' demanded Felicity. 'It'll look stupid with your riding-dress.'

'I'm not wearing my riding-dress. I'm going to wear my new blue silk,' replied Amy flatly. And then, 'Meg – is it really true about meeting your one true love on May morning?'

'So they say. But it don't happen till it's time – and I reckon this year's a bit soon for you, my duck.'

'So perhaps today will be Kate's turn,' giggled Felicity.

Amy opened her mouth and then, catching Felicity's eye, closed it again. She smiled at her reflection and decided that it wasn't really necessary to say anything at all.

By the time they arrived downstairs everyone else was already in the hall waiting to depart.

'At last!' said Felix, then, 'God's boots!' – before meeting his mother's gaze and adding quickly, 'Sorry. But why is Amy all prinked out like a candied tart?'

Dorothy looked at her daughters. Felicity and Kate were neatly and sensibly clad in their riding-dresses – Kate's a new velvet one in a becoming shade of moss and the only new garment in which she'd shown the slightest interest. Amy, on the other hand, was resplendent in cascading lace and silken flounces and sporting enough ribbons to encircle St Paul's cathedral.

'I don't know what you think you look like, Amy – but that dress is totally unsuitable for this morning. Why didn't you wear your blue broadcloth?'

'Because it's old – and I want to look pretty.'

'I see.' Dorothy looked inquiringly at Kate. 'I suppose neither you nor Meg bothered to try and talk her out of it?'

Kate grinned. 'What was the point?'

Dorothy's sigh acknowledged the truth of this. 'Very well. If Amy wants to try riding to Westminster Fields in a silk gown, she can – but perhaps it will teach her a valuable lesson. Let's go.'

The sun was up as they left Old Palace Yard and guided their horses through the network of streets, but as yet it was a pale thing that promised a lovely day but offered little warmth. There was also a light breeze which tugged playfully at Amy's ribbons and threatened to turn her skirt into a huge blue silk balloon. Eden watched her attempting to control this phenomenon with one hand whilst gripping her reins with the other and wondered if she would stay in the saddle long enough to get where they were going. His mouth twitched and, momentarily forgetting that he was annoyed with her, he sought Kate's eyes. They gleamed appreciatively back at him beneath expressively raised brows and he yielded to reluctant laughter. Kate was Kate . . . and the person who could stop her saying what she thought had yet to be born.

He said, 'If I didn't know better, I'd be tempted to ask if she's doing this for a wager.'

'No, no. She just likes to be noticed.'

He looked behind at the growing gaggle of apprentice lads, all tagging along in the hope of seeing Amy's garters.

'She should be pleased then. She's attracting more attention than a dancing bear.'

'Look on the bright side,' advised Kate. 'At least when she falls off there'll be no shortage of volunteers.'

The air grew warmer, the sky bluer and the whitethorn was a mass of fluffy waving blossoms.

'Oh – look!' cried Felicity. 'Isn't it pretty? Come on, Felix – I'll race you to that tree!'

'Oh look,' said Kate expressionlessly and looking in completely the other direction. 'It's Francis and Celia . . . and so on. What a surprise.'

In fact it was more of a surprise to Eden than she suspected, for he hadn't known that Francis intended to bring a party. But Goring was there and Sir John Suckling – and two ladies and a gentleman, all of whom Eden had seen before but could not name.

'Hail and well met!' drawled Francis. And then, to Dorothy, 'God's greetings, lady. I trust you enjoy your customary health?'

'Clumsy, dear boy – very clumsy. You should've said that you'd no need to ask after her health when her radiance dims the morning.' Suckling bowed over Dorothy's hand and raised it to his lips. 'And yet you wound me, madam. In truth, I believe I am cut to the quick.'

'Then you hide it very well,' came the amused reply.

'Ah, but appearances were ever deceptive. And I'm grieved that you should have come to London without sending word to your humble servant. Where have you been hiding yourself? And why haven't I seen you at Court?'

'We don't aspire to Court circles,' said Dorothy calmly. 'And since my husband sat in the late Parliament, I doubt we'd find this a good time to begin.'

Suckling's brows rose but he said airily enough, 'Nonsense, dear lady. I hope England's not so far gone yet that politics must come between friends. Come – let's leave these children to their own devices and discuss the matter.'

Amy watched her mother ride off with the Court gallant who hadn't so much as glanced in her own direction and was piqued. None of Francis's friends were taking any notice of her either . . . but that could be mended. She pulled off one of her gloves and let it fall with a distressful little cry. But the brief satisfaction of turning every head was swiftly cancelled out by the fact that not one face expressed admiration; and the smart lady beside Francis actually tittered.

Francis said feebly, 'Amy. It *is* Amy?'

'Yes,' said Kate lightly, whilst wishing the ground would swallow someone up – preferably Amy, who seemed quite unaware that she now looked as though she had been dragged through a bush. 'It's her day for being original.'

The other girl in Francis's party, a silver-fair beauty in

green, said, 'It's a very pretty dress . . . but perhaps not best suited for riding?'

'But the hairstyle, Venetia darling!' drawled the sophisticated lady who had laughed. And to Amy, 'Tell me, my dear, what do you call it! *Meule de foin aux rubans?*'

Amy's grasp of the French tongue was minimal. Kate's, on the other hand, was rather better, and she opened her mouth on an astringent retort – only to be forestalled by the man Francis had introduced as Kit Clifford and who was the fair girl's brother.

'No,' he said mildly. 'She calls it *Mode Naturel d'une Jeune Fille* – and it's strictly forbidden to *soignée* widows such as yourself, Louise.' Then, through the ripple of largely good-natured laughter, he met Kate's eye with the suggestion of a wink and added, 'Indeed, I'm sure it was charming before this devilish wind got at it – and I daresay a clever hand could soon put it right. Venetia?'

Five minutes later Amy was restored to a passable degree of neatness and they were all strolling companionably across the grass, leading their horses and pausing every now and then to gather boughs of May. Kate joined Venetia in bathing her face in the dew and was soon also responding to Kit's raillery as easily as she did to that of Francis. Eden, meanwhile, employed a dexterity of which he would have been incapable a bare six months earlier and extricated Celia deftly from the others.

She looked heavy-eyed and the faint droop of her lips wrung his heart so that he said without thinking, 'I love you so much. But you must already know that.'

Slowly, she raised her eyes to his face. For weeks, ever since the day Hugo Verney had left town to prepare for his wedding and all her hopes had finally been dashed, she had lived in a desert of loneliness and hurt. She had not felt loved by anyone – least of all by her short-tempered mother or the man who said he wanted to marry her. And now, here was Eden – whom she had always liked but almost forgotten – offering precisely the balm she so badly needed. Sparkling tears overflowed on to her lashes and she said, 'Do you? Do you *really*?'

101

'Of course.' Her reaction surprised him, for he had been blunt and he knew she scorned bluntness. He sought, as always, for something he could say that would please her and, not knowing that he had already found it, failed. 'If I thought there was the least chance for me, I'd have spoken to my father weeks ago and had him approach yours. But there isn't, is there?'

'I – I don't know,' she said helplessly. And meant it. He was different . . . and his difference had always both attracted and confused her. It did so now; but he said he loved her and she needed very badly to be loved. The only trouble was that she could not help wishing he were Hugo – or that Cyrus Winter was. She said softly, 'It's all so difficult. My – my mother has received a very flattering offer for my hand, you see. But though I know it's stupid of me to hesitate – for he can give me all I've ever wanted – I c-can't quite bring myself to agree. Do you see?'

'Perfectly,' said Eden. And he did – for Francis hadn't felt the same need to withhold the cream of the jest from Kate's brother as he had from Kate herself. He hadn't known that, far from appreciating the tale, Eden had found it made him feel sick. He said, 'It's Mr Winter, isn't it?'

She nodded. 'I – I'm not sure I l-like him . . . but Mother says I will when I know him better. I wish I knew what to do!'

'Go on saying no,' said Eden flatly. 'You can't marry a man you dislike just because he's rich – and no one should make you.'

'You don't know my mother.'

'Perhaps not. But doubtless your father does. In the meantime, you may rely on Francis. And there's always me.'

For the first time in a month, her spirits rose a little and she peeped coquettishly at him beneath her lashes. 'Always?'

'Always,' he said firmly. And then, less confidently, 'I know I oughtn't to ask . . . but is there – have you – do you care for anyone else?'

'N-no. No one,' she said. And thought, 'No one that I can have, at all events.'

'Well that's something.' He struggled to hide the bubble

of hope that was growing inside his chest. 'Then let me be your friend until you give me leave to become something more . . . and your friend still if you don't. Smile for me and let's go and watch the maypole-dancing with the others. It's too beautiful a day to be gloomy.'

If he had thought about it at all – which, of course, he didn't – he would have said that there could surely be none to disagree with this statement. He would have been wrong.

They were all sitting outside a small tavern, sipping ale and eating honey-cakes when the first small signs of dissent appeared. One moment tanned and rosy-cheeked girls in their Sunday-best gowns were dipping and weaving around a brightly beribboned maypole whilst Sir John Suckling roared out the words in time to the music with a gusto that might have surprised his sovereign; and the next, everything faltered to a halt under the stern gaze and fiery words of some half-dozen sober individuals in steeple-crowned hats.

Kate stared. She was familiar with the sight and sound of Puritans – living so close to zeal-famed Banbury, it was impossible not to be. And these men who ranted so glibly about 'heathen, idolatrous practices' and 'lewd ungodliness' were no different. She supposed she should have known that the merchants of London would find Puritanism as appealing as did the merchants of Banbury; it kept the apprentices' minds off sports and mummery and meant that everyone worked harder. But it did seem excessive to render their religious observances austere to the point of ugliness and to prohibit Sunday football which – barring a broken head or two – had been played harmlessly enough for generations. There was, Kate had often suspected, more than half a Puritan lurking inside Nathan Cresswell; *he* never approved of anything unless it was tedious or ugly.

'Damned poke-noses!' growled Sir John. 'There'll not be an ounce of pleasure left to any of us by the time they're done. Pity a few more of the Bible-canting miseries don't take themselves off to the Americas, that's what I say!'

'If the King hadn't stopped it, John Hampden would have gone five years ago – and taken that boorish cousin of his with him,' remarked Kit Clifford idly. 'What's the fellow's name – Cromwell, is it? Got a big nose and a noisy laugh. I can't think why His Majesty didn't let them go. Pity, if you ask me.'

Dorothy surveyed him quizzically. 'Because he lacks style?'

The grey eyes laughed disarmingly back at her. 'Why else, madam?'

At Francis's suggestion, they rose and left the inn before the Friday-faced gentlemen in black could completely cloud their day. And Kate, feeling Amy's eyes like knives in her back, found herself riding homeward beside the charming and insouciant Mr Clifford.

She said cautiously, 'Thank you for stopping Amy being made to look even more ridiculous than she already did. It was kind of you – and more than she deserved.'

'Think nothing of it. Venetia and I have younger sisters, too, so we know what it's like. And I suspect you'd have done just as well yourself – for all you were thoroughly annoyed with her.' He grinned. 'You aren't much alike, are you?'

'No,' agreed Kate calmly. 'But I don't count it very civil in you to mention it.'

His brows rose. 'Why not?'

'Because Amy is generally accepted to be the beauty of the family.'

'Is she?' he asked blankly. 'You surprise me.'

Kate began to wonder if Mr Clifford suffered from defective eyesight but, before she could ask, he completed her confusion by saying pleasantly, 'I don't mean to disparage her, of course. No one could deny that she's a pretty enough child . . . just a trifle insipid when seen beside you.' He paused and smiled apologetically. 'You'll have to forgive me. But I've always had a weakness for red hair.'

Kate closed her mouth, swallowed, and then said weakly, 'Colour-blind. I knew it.'

He laughed. 'Don't you believe me?'

'No. And if you'd been called carrot-top as often as I

have, you'd understand why. Mother has *red* hair – and Eden. Mine was a mistake.'

It took him a long time to master his mirth and when he finally did so it was to confound her still further by saying, 'I hope I'll have the chance to know you better. I think I might relish it. Do you suppose your lady mother would mind if Venetia and I were to call?'

The company parted at the Gate House and Kate rode home so deep in thought that she scarcely heard Amy's carping remarks on the subject of sisters who spoiled other people's chances. Admiration was an unknown quantity to her and, because it was, her strongest reaction was one of cynicism; but below that flowered a warm glow of pleasure – and it was really that, she realised, that she ought to mistrust most of all.

'After all, *I* saw him first!'

'I beg your pardon, Amy?' said Dorothy gently, bringing her horse up on the other side of Kate.

Amy flushed. 'I – nothing.'

'I'm glad to hear it.' Dorothy conducted a discreet appraisal of her eldest daughter and noted, with amusement, the unusual air of abstraction. It was high time, she thought; and a little masculine attention was probably just what Kate needed to make her take more trouble with herself. She said, 'A very pleasant morning. I liked Francis's young friends, didn't you?'

'Yes.' Kate bent to rearrange the boughs of whitethorn looped on her saddle. 'He – Mr Clifford – suggested that they might call on us.'

'Oh? Well I'm sure we'd all be very pleased to see them. Just as I, at this moment, would be very pleased to see Felix and Felicity. Eden – do you know where they've got to?'

'Mm? Oh, they rode on ahead,' replied Eden vaguely. 'They probably – or no. Here they come.'

'Mother, Eden! Come and see. Something's happening on the Surrey bank. Crowds of people all shouting – listen! You can hear from here!' cried the twins in excited and jumbled counterpoint.

Eden's gaze sharpened and the image of Celia faded from

his mind. He looked at his mother and said, 'They're right. Listen. It sounds like a riot.'

It was. Discontented dock-hands and sailors and young apprentices out for a spree had poured out of Southwark and Blackfriars towards the Archbishop's palace at Lambeth, shouting for the release of all their favourite preachers and that of my lord Warwick. The English fleet, they cried, was an object of scorn, trade was hampered, and Spanish Papists given too much freedom everywhere. Wisely, Archbishop Laud had removed himself as the mob approached, and so was not there to see them trying to break into his house. Then, suddenly, it was all over. The militia arrived to disperse the crowd and arrest the ringleaders and peace was restored. It was a sad end to May Day.

Sadder still was the case of the seaman who had tried to force the Archbishop's door with a crowbar and was duly condemned – incredibly – as a traitor. He was hung, drawn and quartered and his head fixed on a spike on London Bridge. He was nineteen years old.

Able to spend more time at home now that what people were already calling the 'Short Parliament' had been dissolved, Richard discussed the widespread grievances with his wife and eldest son. The most pressing of these was contained in the series of reforms currently being passed by the Convocation of the Clergy under the direction of Laud.

'As far as the Puritans are concerned, it's a red rag to a bull,' explained Richard. 'All learned professions, so we're told, are now required to swear not to subvert the ruling of the Church by "archbishops, bishops, deans and archdeacons etcetera, as it now stands established". Not surprisingly, they're calling it the Etcetera Oath and saying that, for aught anyone knows, it might be stretched to cover the Pope. Add to that the fact that the King is reviving the monopoly on white paper and preparing to levy a forced loan on the richest merchants in the City, whilst simultaneously considering the possibility of taking money from Spain in return for protecting their troop-ships from the Dutch, and you'll see why the populace is in uproar. And at the root of it all, as always, is His Majesty's determination to subdue the Scots.'

'At the head of an army?' asked Eden slowly.

'How else? Rumour has it that Strafford left eight thousand Irish troops ready to embark at a moment's notice. If that's true, all they need now is the money to pay them.'

In the week that followed, the lucrative business transaction which His Majesty had been contemplating with Spain was crushed by the disapproval of two of his nearer neighbours. Cardinal Richelieu contemptuously withdrew the French Ambassador; and the Dutch envoy pointed out that, if England assisted in the transportation of Spanish soldiers, Holland could no longer regard her as neutral. Faced with the alternative of fighting the Dutch, the King was forced regretfully to decline four million Spanish ducats. Instead, he seized the bullion deposited by the City merchants in the Mint and offered to pay them eight per cent for the use of it. He also announced his plans to debase all coinage below the value of a shilling.

While every merchant in London was busy convincing His Majesty of the folly of this move and finally, in desperation, promising him two hundred thousand pounds, Viscount Wroxton came wrathfully back from Far Flamstead to demand his wife's explanation of her marriage plans for their daughter. My lady replied at length, expounding her reasons first with deceptive cajolery and then with defensively hard-headed logic. Neither did her any good, her lord was adamant. He refused, he said bluntly, to be made the biggest marital joke since the Earl of Essex – and there wasn't enough money in the world to tempt him.

Mary passed from icy sarcasm to open derision and finally lost her temper. 'You're a fool, Gervase – and all this bleating about pride makes me sick! You *have* no pride. No, nor ever will have so long as we're forced to grovel about for every penny!'

'After twenty-two years of marriage to you, I am left with only shreds of self-respect,' he retorted, eyeing her with complete dislike. 'But at least I have some excuses. You, sadly, were born with the mind of a shopkeeper and the morals of a slut . . . and it's therefore a waste of time trying to explain that not quite everything in this life can be weighed and measured.'

'Dear God! You're living in a dream.'

'I think not. But let us return to the point. I will not sell Celia to your lover – and, if you continue to flout me or even to argue the matter further, I'll have you removed to Far Flamstead for the rest of your life.'

There could be no doubting that he meant it and for a moment she could only stare at him, white-faced with loathing. Then, 'And what, pray, am I to say to Cyrus?'

'Tell him to go to hell.'

'I see,' she said viciously. 'Then you'd better not come whining to me when the Italian beggars you – because the only help I'll give you is to help load the pistol!' And, turning on her heel, she swept through the house to vent her fury on Celia.

'Well, Mistress Stupidity – you've just kissed goodbye to a fortune and the only respectable offer it appears you'll ever get. I hope you're pleased with yourself and that you'll remain so when you're a dried-up, insignificant spinster living on your brother's charity! But you needn't think that your father and I can afford to keep you here in London, suitably dressed and seen in all the right places, because we can't. So tell your maid to pack. You leave for home on Friday.'

After she had gone, Celia continued to stare blindly at her reflection, torn between thankfulness and depression. Father had stepped between her and marriage to Cyrus Winter just as Francis had told her he would. She ought to be glad; perhaps some small part of her *was* glad. But she'd never before considered just what her situation would be afterwards – and now that her mother had put it into words for her, she saw that the prospect was bleak indeed.

She did not want to go home, to be forever mewed up in the country with scarcely any society and no one to dazzle or flirt with. Neither did she want to dwindle into an old maid while girls less beautiful than herself found husbands and regarded her with sympathetic superiority. She could not bear it. And at the back of her mind was the horrible suspicion that, though she could attract men, she could not inspire the sort of passion that resulted in marriage. Except, except, just possibly, with Eden.

Eden. His face swam into her mind's eye, blurred into that of Hugo Verney and then lingered till she banished it. No point in thinking of Hugo now; he was gone and had to be forgotten. It was Eden who had said he loved her and he who represented her only hope; and of course she was fond of him. But fond enough for marriage? questioned a tiny voice inside her head. Truly?

'Yes,' said Celia, aloud to her reflection. 'Easily.' Then, silently to herself, 'Oh God – let him only ask me and I swear I'll love him forever.'

If Eden was surprised to receive a note from his love asking him to meet her in secret amidst the bookstalls of Paternoster Row, his pleasure was more than enough to outweigh it, and he set off for the assignation with a heart full of hope. That she wanted to see him so urgently and in such a way could surely only mean one thing: but when one had wanted a girl as long and as much as he had wanted Celia – and with as little hope – the sudden change was almost terrifying.

'Oh God,' he prayed. 'Let her only say yes and I'll see that she never regrets it – never.'

He found her pretending to browse through a copy of Ben Jonson's *Volpone* whilst casting wary glances around her. Then she saw him and he was struck by the realisation that she didn't know what to say – any more than he did himself. So he gave her a slow, sweet smile and said neutrally, 'You wanted to see me?'

'I – yes.' She flushed and bent her head over the pages of the book, wondering how on earth she was to begin. 'I c-can't stay long. Someone might see. It's just that I wanted – I thought you should know that I – that I—'

'Yes?' said Eden, not daring to say more.

Her fingers clenched in frustration, crumpling the paper. Why wasn't he helping her? For if he had any sense at all, he must know perfectly well why she was here. She said carefully, 'I'm going home. Father's come back and – and saved me from the match mother wanted for me . . . but of course she's furious and she's sending me home in disgrace. I – I doubt I'll be permitted much freedom so we're unlikely to meet for a while. She's determined to punish me, you see.' She managed a small, unhappy smile. 'You're the only one who's been kind to me in such a long time . . . and I wanted to thank you and say g-goodbye.'

There was silence and she allowed her long lashes to veil her eyes, not daring to breathe and not knowing that Eden could not. Finally, when he still did not speak, a great wave of self-pity engulfed her and she said, on a genuine sob, 'Oh – what's the use? I should have known you d-didn't really mean what you said. I wish I were dead!'

'Don't!' Eden's arms ached to hold her but the place was too damnably public. He said, 'Don't ever wish that – I can't bear it. As for my loving you – how can you doubt it? Ever since I came back from Angers – well, I've thought of little but how very much I'd like to have you as my wife. You know that. You must always have known it.'

Quite slowly, she raised brilliant eyes to his face. 'How could I – when you've never said it?'

He stared at her, his face pale and set. 'Then let me say it now. I love you now and for my lifetime. Will you . . . will you give me leave to ask my father to call on yours?'

Celia waited, but only for a moment. 'Yes,' she said softly. 'Yes, dear Eden – I will.'

Six

'Father?' Eden stood just inside the door of the room that Richard had appropriated as some sort of office and looked at his father across the mountain of paperwork that littered the desk. 'Are you very busy?'

'Very,' grinned Richard, dropping a letter on to the heap. 'Come in.'

Eden closed the door and crossed slowly to the hearth to stare thoughtfully down at the empty fire-dogs. From behind his desk, Richard eyed him resignedly but made no attempt to hurry the process. Finally, Eden looked up and said, 'It's Celia. I expect you've guessed. I want to marry her.'

'Ah.' Richard leaned back in his chair. 'And she?'

'Feels the same.'

'I see. I suppose it would be stupid of me to ask if you've given the matter careful thought?'

'Yes.' A smile touched Eden's mouth.

'Or to point out that you're still quite young and have – as far as I know – little acquaintance with other young ladies?'

'I've met enough to know that Celia outshines them all.' It was said briskly but the hazel eyes softened. 'Are there objections? No. I don't mean that. Is it – would it be displeasing to you?'

Richard ran a quill through and through his fingers, frowning a little. 'I think the word is worrying.'

'Why?' Eden dropped neatly into a chair. 'I think I almost suspected as much – but why? I know it can't be money. Is it Celia herself?'

111

'Partly – or so your mother would say. And I usually find her views worthy of attention. But there's more to it than that. What, for example, are your opinions of the King's more recent and better-known policies?'

Eden blinked. 'Much the same as yours, I imagine.'

'Not good enough. Try again. What about the dissolution of Parliament before it had been in session a month? What about the forced loan from the City and the arrests of Mr Hampden and Lord Brooke? Should we have upset the Dutch by considering protection deals with Spain? Should Strafford be allowed to bring Irish troops into Scotland? Come to that, should we fight the Scots at all – let alone again? Think!'

'All right.' Eden sat up. 'Financial matters are a mess; our natural alliances ought to be Protestant rather than Catholic; the Scots are our countrymen, their church is their own affair and bishops have no place in civil government anyway. As for the Parliament – there's no point to it at all as long as it's only there to say "yes and amen" to the King's every wish . . . and it's been proved that this King has no intention of allowing it to do anything else. All of which suggests that either His Majesty doesn't know how much public opinion is against him – or he's too stubborn to care.'

'Thank you,' said Richard mildly. 'Now tell me what Francis's answer would have been.'

Eden drew a long breath and then loosed it.

'Roughly the opposite. All right. I take your point. But does it matter? Celia isn't Francis.'

'No. But she's as much a product of her upbringing as anyone else and she'll have absorbed the attitudes of her parents without necessarily even knowing it.' He paused and then said slowly, 'A marriage based on such disparate views hasn't the greatest chance of success at the best of times. And just now is *not* the best of times. A growing number of men are coming into open opposition to the King and the closure of Parliament has only aggravated matters. I'm not talking about the Puritans – they, like the poor, seem to have been with us always; but Pym and the

112

others mean business, and to a large extent I am with them. Consequently, the differences between Gervase Langley and myself are widening every day. Do you understand what I'm trying to say?'

'Yes. But I don't see why these things need come between Celia and myself.'

'Then you haven't looked ahead. For even if Gervase and I agree on this match – which I wouldn't have thought likely – something tells me that our other points of variance are going to multiply. And if I'm right, Celia could find herself caught between two stools and you'll have a wife who doesn't understand you.'

Eden came slowly to his feet. 'Are you telling me to forget her?'

'No – though I can't deny that I think it would be best. I'm just trying to open your eyes a little. Do you, for example, relish the prospect of acquiring Lady Wroxton as a mother-in-law?'

'Not particularly. But I'm prepared to put up with it.'

There was a moment's silence. Then Richard said flatly, 'Daughters are apt to resemble their mothers.'

Eden flinched. It was what the Italian had said – and Kate – and it was still a suggestion that he found it impossible to tolerate. Keeping his voice under rigid control, he said, 'I'll never believe it. I love Celia and I won't give her up for such reasons any more than I imagine you'd have given up Mother.'

And that, of course, was unanswerable.

'All right,' sighed Richard. 'I'll think about it. But you'd better be very sure that Celia understands what she's doing and that her feelings equal yours – because I know very well that your mother is going to require some convincing.'

Richard was right – she did. And he himself had too much wisdom and too many reservations of his own even to try. Instead, they talked late into the night, sharing their misgivings and regretting for the first time that they'd chosen to rear their children in an atmosphere of greater freedom than was usual in order to encourage them to think for themselves.

'It makes it rather difficult suddenly to start issuing vetoes,' said Dorothy gloomily. 'What are you going to do? Talk to Gervase and hope he refuses?'

'It may come to that, in the end. But first I intend to wait till you've spoken with Eden and formed your opinions of the strength of his affections. The trouble is that all our objections to Celia herself stem purely from instinct – and we could be wrong. Eden's not a fool and he must know her better than we do. He loves her, and if she loves him it could be the making of her.'

'*If* she does.' Dorothy leaned her head on his shoulder. 'I, personally, doubt it. And how will we ever know?'

She expressed this thought, albeit somewhat more delicately, on the following morning when she managed to isolate Eden after breakfast. His response, however, did little to reassure her. 'You've missed your cue,' he grinned. '*I'm* the one who's supposed to think myself lucky; *you're* supposed to think me so irresistible that no girl could possibly *not* love me!'

Dorothy did not smile. 'I'm sorry, but it's not a matter about which I feel able to be flippant. I want you to be happy. And I don't think you'll be happy with Celia.'

Amusement faded from his face and he said, 'Then you're mistaken. I can be happy with no one else.'

'You can't know that.'

'I can. But if you want to tell me what you've got against her, I'll listen.'

'With your mind already made up?'

'I can't help that,' he admitted. 'But it doesn't mean I can't try to appreciate your point of view.'

'That's generous of you.' The sudden flash of acidity was strongly reminiscent of Kate; but then she said more patiently, 'She's a lovely girl and I can understand you wanting her. But there's more to marriage than two bodies in a bed – and however much you may think you know of *her* mind, I suspect she hasn't the faintest idea of what goes on in yours.'

'She's known me all her life,' protested Eden.

'So? You can meet someone every day God sends and

114

never really know them – or be with someone for only an hour and know them utterly. I'm speaking of – of a meeting of minds. And I've a notion that yours and Celia's have scarcely passed within nodding distance. I'd be surprised, for example, if you've ever held a conversation that didn't revolve almost solely around Celia herself. Am I right?'

'No,' said Eden, irritably and without thought. 'But all you're really saying is that she isn't clever and that—'

'She could have a brain to rival Leonardo,' said Dorothy roundly, without pausing to absorb this interesting remark, 'and be no more suited to you than if she were a simpleton. The things that matter are perception and instinct and the ability to understand. Convince me that those things exist between you and Celia – on both sides and in equal measure – and I'll give you my blessing.'

'What you're saying is "Give me proof" – and I can't. No one could. But do you think I don't know what marriage should be – that I've learned nothing from seeing how it is between you and Father? And, having seen, do you think I'll be content with anything less?' He smiled suddenly and opened his hands in a gesture of appeal. 'No one can choose who they will love. And I love Celia.'

Dorothy looked back at him helplessly. But, before she could speak, the door opened on one of her maids.

'Please to excuse me, madam,' said the girl, 'but the master asked me to tell you as how my lord Wroxton has called and that he's wishful for you to join him in the parlour.'

Dorothy's eyes travelled to her son's face and rested there for a long moment before returning to the maid.

'Thank you, Nan. I'll be along in a minute.' And then, when they were alone again, 'Well . . . he hasn't wasted much time, has he?'

Eden looked slightly uncomfortable. 'Celia must have told him. You can't wonder at it. Her mother was intent on bundling her back to Far Flamstead tomorrow morning.'

'Was she?' The green eyes sharpened. 'Why?'

'Because Celia won't do as she's bid and marry some rich old man Lady Wroxton's found for her,' came the rapid

115

reply. 'Mother – I should think his lordship must be willing, shouldn't you? Otherwise he'd not be here. What will you say to him?'

'I don't know.' Dorothy moved towards the door. 'I don't know. And Gervase may just as easily have come to say he'll have none of the matter. It wouldn't surprise me if he did. You're hardly the match he was hoping for, after all.'

'Because I've no influence at Court?'

'No. Because you can't pay his debts,' she returned sardonically. And was gone.

Her hopes were soon dashed. My lord Wroxton was of a mind to put a spoke in his wife's wheel and make himself master in his own house. He cared little for Mary's infidelities so long as she was discreet, but her attempt to marry Celia to her lover was more than he could swallow. Consequently, when Celia informed him that he was to receive a call from Richard Maxwell on behalf of Eden, and Mary immediately said that such a match was out of the question, Gervase naturally gave his consent to it. And by the following morning he'd managed to convince himself that he hadn't done so *purely* in order to spite Mary – for the Maxwells were well connected and Eden heir to a snug property. It wasn't what he'd hoped for . . . but it began to seem eminently suitable.

While her parents were listening unwillingly to the simple pleasure emanating from Lord Wroxton, Kate and her maid delivered Felix to Cheapside en route for a shopping expedition with Venetia Clifford – only to be delayed by a cheerful scolding from Giacomo.

'Why you are not staying? You don't come so often no more and is not good. 'Ow I teach you to speak my language if you are coming and going so fast?'

Kate grinned. 'I'm sorry. I promise I'll come tomorrow. But this morning I have another engagement.'

'Ah?' His face creased and he waggled a gleeful finger. 'So! Ze wind 'e is blowing zis way! I see it all! You find a young man.'

'No. I do not find a young man.'

'*Si – si*. Is natural. I congratulate 'im. 'Ow 'e is fortunate. But for me, is great pity. My 'eart, 'e is broken. And
for you, Signorina Catarina, is also pity – maybe. Zese
Englishmen are cold, you know? And for you zis is waste.
Maybe you look for nice Italian boy, no?'

'No,' said Kate, trying not to laugh. 'Nor any boy at all,
I thank you. I'm going to meet a young lady.' And, seeing
the plump face settle into lines of sympathetic disapproval,
continued quickly, 'Tell me – how is Felix progressing?'

'Good,' came the reply. 'Gino, 'e say 'e think the signor
will be surprised.'

'That's nice.' She smiled blandly. 'And when is the
signor likely to return?'

Giacomo spread expressive hands. ''Oo can say? Maybe
two weeks, maybe three. Every year 'e go and 'e come back
but 'e don't say when. Sometimes is short time, sometimes
long.'

Kate filed this piece of information and tried to add to
it. 'No doubt he is visiting his family?'

'Is so,' nodded Giacomo. And immediately changed the
subject.

Walking thoughtfully down Cheapside a few minutes
later, Kate reflected that, for a man who liked talking as
much as Giacomo did, he could be remarkably unexpan-
sive. It wasn't the first time she had noticed it; it was,
however, the first time she'd wondered why.

Kate met her new friend beneath the porticoed entrance
of the Royal Exchange and found that her own lateness
was not the only change to the morning's plan. Mistress
Venetia had brought her brother with her. Kate wasn't
particularly surprised; and, catching the speculative gleam
in her maid's eye, realised that Meg wasn't either. The
novelty of being sought after was one thing, she decided;
but the expectations it raised in everyone else were quite
another. She didn't think she was ready for it. None of these
thoughts were apparent though as she said lightly, 'I'm sure
we'll find your advice invaluable, sir. But can you really
have any interest in haberdashers and drapers?'

117

The grey eyes twinkled. 'More – as I understand it – than *you* have.'

Meg turned a giggle into an unconvincing cough. Ignoring her, Kate said resignedly, 'I see someone's been telling tales. Francis, probably.'

'How did you guess?' grinned Kit. And then, flicking a coin into Meg's palm, 'Go and buy yourself something pretty. And, if your mistress will permit us, we'll see her safe home again.'

Kate's brows rose a little and then she decided that she could do without Meg following her about, jumping to silly conclusions. So she nodded her agreement, accompanied her friends into the colonnaded quadrangle of the Exchange and trod up the stairs to the hundred or so small shops that nestled above.

Mr Clifford, to whom May Day had brought a sort of revelation, followed the girls in and out of silk mercers and watched Kate stifling a yawn as Venetia debated the merits of various materials.

'I'll take the peach satin,' said Venetia at length. 'But you're more difficult, Kate. I wonder if we shouldn't go and try Bennett's in Paternoster Row?'

'Why?' Kate gestured to the half-dozen shades of green silk spread on the trestle in front of her. 'Any of these will do. Pick one.'

Venetia looked at her with mingled severity and frustration. 'Kate. I'll allow that clothes are not the only thing in life – but just occasionally one has to treat them as such. Like now. So will you please take an interest?'

'I am. I've taken an interest in each and every one of the hundred or so bolts of cloth we've seen so far.'

'And liked none of them,' said Kit cheerfully. 'Time *I* took a hand. Now, let's see . . .' And, under the gaze of the bemused shopkeeper, he embarked on a lightning tour of the shelves, pausing every now and then as something caught his fancy.

Kate and Venetia watched with growing amusement as the trestle began to groan beneath the weight of his selection. Then, abandoning the shelves, he began unrolling great swathes of material and draping them one after the other around Kate, absorbing the effect of each one and progressing to the next with a speed that soon had her gasping with laughter. Finally, he brushed aside a tangled heap of silks and velvets as if they were of no account whatsoever and spread just three out for Kate's inspection.

'There! Take any or all of 'em.'

Kate looked. A supple pale mint satin; glowing jade silk, shot with silver-grey; and a watered taffeta of the purest amber. Her eyes wandered consideringly from one to the other and then returned to Mr Clifford's face. She said, 'I don't know whether I'm impressed or alarmed. Venetia?'

'Both – but who cares? He's right. They're all perfect for you.'

'Yes,' said Kate. 'That's what I thought. So I suppose it behoves me to have them all.'

'Extravagant girl.' Kit shook his head reprovingly but his eyes teased her. 'What *is* your mother going to say?'

'Hallelujah?' suggested Kate. And then, with a sudden grin, 'After which I imagine she'll probably fall on your neck.'

In the event, Dorothy did neither, and although she made the Cliffords welcome and expressed pleasure over Kate's purchases, her manner was uncharacteristically distrait. Unable, for the time being, to ask what was wrong, Kate possessed her soul in patience until her friends took their leave and then said bluntly, 'Something's happened. What?'

Dorothy's hands lay loose in her lap and she leaned her head back against the chair, closing her eyes. Finally she said tonelessly, 'It rather appears that Eden is going to marry Celia Langley.'

Kate sat down with a bump. 'Oh God,' she said bitterly. 'How can he be so stupid? Is it definite?'

'Not yet – but it will be. Your father and Gervase have spent all the morning negotiating.'

'Then it can still be stopped, can't it? All Father has to do is be difficult.'

'Unfortunately,' said Dorothy, opening her eyes, 'it's not

119

that simple. You see, Eden's already spoken to Celia, and Gervase is treating it as a formal proposal. Besides which . . . Eden says he loves her. So for his sake it seems we'll have to put a brave face on it and welcome her into the family. *All* of us, Kate – including you. I know you don't like her – but you'll treat her as another sister and I as another daughter. And then, if she ever causes him a moment's disillusionment or misery, I'll personally wring her exquisite neck.'

There was a long silence. Then Kate said with artificial brightness, 'Well, I suppose it might have been worse. He could have picked a tight-lipped Puritan or a vulgar widow. And at least Amy will be pleased.'

May became June. Formal contracts of betrothal were drawn up between Eden Maxwell and Celia Margaret Langley; Cardinal Richelieu released the Elector Palatine from prison; and the Barbary pirates carried off some sixty Cornish men and women from Penzance. The King, meanwhile, continued to weaken the Channel guard in favour of preparing to make war on the Scots, and arrested several gentlemen who refused to raise local levies for the army. Of those levies already raised, many began to refuse orders from officers who were thought to be Papist – and in Dorset a Catholic lieutenant was stoned to death by his recruits. Wild-fire rumours spread amongst troops assembled at the ports that they were destined, not for Scotland, but for slavery in Barbados – thus causing most of them to vanish overnight. There were riots in Uttoxeter, Warwick, Leominster, Oxford and Cambridge and, across the border, the Estates declared that their government should henceforth be independent of both England and the King. Charles, however, remained calm and undismayed. He went hunting at Oatlands and worried less about the cauldron of discontent around him than about the Queen's approaching confinement.

'You'll fight, of course?' said Francis idly to Eden one afternoon towards the end of the month.

'Fight?' asked Eden vaguely.

'The Scots, you bufflehead! Everything's in good shape and the campaigning season is already with us – so all we're waiting for is the arrival of the royal infant and then His Majesty will no doubt march north.' Francis had been spending a good deal of time with Sir John Suckling and his small but splendidly equipped troop and was consequently beginning to see the projected war as a glorious excuse for panoply instead of the tedious and untidy business it had always seemed at Angers. 'I daresay you'd get a lieutenancy at the very least.'

'Possibly,' came the placid reply. 'But I shan't go.'

'What?' Francis's attention left the pair of buxom City wives he'd been ogling through the tavern window. 'Not go? Oh, of course. I forgot. The wedding's set for September, isn't it? And damned inconvenient it's likely to be. I wish you might have made it sooner.'

'So do I,' said Eden, with perfect truth. For a moment or two he contemplated telling Francis that, wedding or no wedding, he had no intention of fighting the Scots; then decided against it. 'You think this war is actually going to happen, then?'

'Well, considering that the Court and the Council have talked of nothing else for the last year or more—'

'Yes. That's just it. They've talked. But what else have they done? You can't go to war just on words, you know.' He stopped, his gaze held, as Francis's had been, by something on the other side of the glass. 'Well, well. Felix *will* be pleased.'

Francis looked and then turned indifferently back to his wine. 'So, I imagine, will the King.'

'Oh?'

'Yes. After all, what's the point in forcing a loan from the richest merchants in the City without Crook-back Luke?'

Returning home a little later, Eden met Kate on the stairs. They'd had little to say to each other since his betrothal, each tacitly avoiding the potential confrontation. But now Eden said briefly, 'He's back.'

Kate did not pretend to misunderstand him. 'I know. Felix is currently busy haranguing Father.'

'More fool him, then. It's a crazy scheme at best, so I don't see Father giving his consent.'

'Why not?' asked Kate astringently as she started to move on downwards. 'It's like murder. After the first time it doesn't seem so difficult.'

For two whole days Kate kept away from Cheapside. Then, on the third morning, her curiosity got the better of her and, taking Meg with her, she accompanied Felix on his daily pilgrimage.

'Has he decided yet whether or not he'll take you?' she asked.

'No. I've scarcely seen him,' came the gruff reply. 'He's hardly ever there and, when he's in, he stays out of the workshop. I suppose he's fussing round his stupid sister.'

'What?' Kate stared at him. 'Did you say his *sister*?'

'Yes.' Felix looked irritably back at her. 'He brought her back with him from Genoa, or so Gino says. I haven't seen her. I think she's sulking or something. At any rate, she does a lot of shouting and slamming doors when Mr Santi's about.' He paused. 'I don't know why you're looking so surprised. I told you about it, didn't I?'

'No. You didn't.'

'Didn't I? Oh. Well, perhaps it was Felicity I told,' he shrugged. 'It's not important, anyway. All *I* want is for Mr Santi to say he'll accept my indentures – because until he does that, Father won't even go and talk to him about it. And I'm fed up with waiting.'

'You still want it that much then?'

'Yes. More, I think.'

He said nothing more and, busy with her own thoughts, Kate did not ask him to. She had wanted to see Luciano del Santi again because she was curious about the mysterious annual visits he apparently paid to Genoa. But the notion of his possessing a sister who had the temerity to shout at him was even better. She hoped she would be privileged to see it.

She was. Giacomo let them in with rather less than his usual bonhomie and looked at Kate and Meg as if he

122

didn't know quite what to do with them – while, clearly audible from above, came a flood of shrilly impassioned Italian, spasmodically punctuated with the sound of breaking glass. Kate thought of the rare and expensive vessels in which, on her first visit, she'd been offered wine, and smiled sympathetically at Giacomo.

'A small domestic crisis, perhaps?'

'*Si*,' he said. And then, wincing at a particularly violent crash, 'No. Is Signorina Gianetta. She scream, she shout, she break everysing in ze 'ouse. And what she not break in ze salon, 'er maid Maria break in ze kitchen. Is enough! I go mad!'

'So long as she doesn't break everything in the workshop,' said Felix, single-mindedly. And he stalked off to check the matter out.

Kate was left looking at a decidedly frayed Giacomo. She knew it wasn't fair to aggravate matters by staying but she couldn't resist it. She said delicately, 'No doubt the signorina is worn down by the journey and feeling a trifle homesick. Perhaps a visitor might help?'

Giacomo ran his hands through his hair and didn't even pretend to be deceived. 'You want to see 'er? You go ahead. The signor 'e will not like it but maybe you don't care. Is up to you. Me, I am finished! The signor say she not 'it anyone if they stand still, but I don't know is true.'

'I'll remember that you warned me,' grinned Kate. 'But I think Meg had better stay here with you.' And she headed for the stairs.

She paused for a second outside the door, listening. Pandemonium reigned. Kate took the time to think up a suitable opening line and to marvel, briefly, at the power of the signorina's lungs; then she knocked gently and went in.

The effect was electric. Small, dark and dramatic, Gianetta del Santi paused on the backswing, clutching a vase of chased silver, and her fierce cascade of words ceased as if cut by a knife. On the far side of the room, her brother stood with folded arms amidst the shambles of his parlour and regarded their visitor with less than his usual impassivity.

Kate opened her mouth to deliver her introductory speech and found herself forestalled.

'Bloody hell,' said Luciano del Santi. 'Who let *you* in?'

'Giacomo. He says he's going mad.'

'Obviously.'

Kate raised her brows and let her gaze wander over the litter of fallen missiles on the floor between them. Then she said, 'I wanted to talk to you about Felix. I can't help having come at a bad time.'

'When else do you come? *Why* else do you come?'

'Well, be reasonable,' she grinned. 'Why else would I?'

The dark-haired tempest set the vase abruptly back on the table and faced her brother, arms akimbo. She was younger than Kate had expected and, when not scowling, probably extremely pretty. But the most noticeable thing about her was the flamboyance of her crimson silk dress and the fact that she was quite simply loaded with jewels. Pearls, dislodged by her fury, slithered snake-like from the glossy black hair, while others warred with the profusion of chains around her neck and the massive ruby brooch in the lace at her breast. An indiscriminate array of sapphire and emerald bracelets encircled both wrists and an ornate crucifix set with amethysts swung from a jewelled girdle at her waist. Kate blinked, lost in awed fascination.

'Who is she?' demanded the glittering vision, in Italian that even Kate could understand. 'What does she want?'

'Her name is Katharine Maxwell – and I imagine she wants to know why you're behaving like a candidate for the mad-house,' replied Luciano del Santi coolly in English. Then, to Kate, 'And this – as I'm sure you know – is my charming little sister, Gianetta del Santi.'

'Falcieri!' spat the girl, stamping her foot. '*Falcieri!*'

Kate searched her small vocabulary and, failing to come up with a translation, decided that it was probably a curse. Certainly, the signorina made it sound like one – and her brother's swift, razor-edged '*No!*' seemed to confirm it. He added something in infuriatingly unintelligible Italian and then, switching back to English, said, 'And unless you want to spend your life speaking only to myself, Gino or

Giacomo, I suggest you start remembering your English.'

Gianetta's reply was to sweep the silver vase violently from the table and utter a single word filled with loathing and refusal. Then she sailed across the room, brushed Kate unceremoniously aside, and went out slamming the door behind her.

Kate met Luciano del Santi's eyes and felt suddenly uncomfortable. 'I'm sorry. I oughtn't to have come. Mother's always saying it's time I learned a little diplomacy. But I didn't realise things were quite so difficult. I only hope I haven't made them worse.'

He gave the slightest of shrugs and crossed to the hearth, splinters of broken glass crunching beneath his feet. 'No. You couldn't.'

His tone was flat and held an almost imperceptible note of bitterness. Kate said slowly, 'Is she always like that?'

'Now and with me – yes.'

'Why?'

He gave a short, unmusical laugh. 'Because she doesn't want to be here. Isn't it obvious?'

'Then why did you bring her?'

'*God's teeth!*' Control finally cracking, he kicked a cushion savagely back towards the settle whence it had come; and then, in a voice still purring with temper, said, 'All right. I brought her back with me because I thought it was time she remembered who she is and stopped languishing over a boy who – however charming – is soft, weak-willed and her first cousin twice over. Satisfied? Or would you like me to turn out my pockets and let you count my teeth?'

Kate flushed. 'I'm sorry.'

'So you said. It's becoming monotonous.'

'I just thought I might be able to help.'

'Well you can't,' came the uncompromising reply. 'And neither can I imagine why you should want to.'

His voice, though still slightly abrasive, had lost the suppressed rage of a minute ago and it was this that emboldened Kate to say irritably, 'Must you be so prickly? Why *shouldn't* I want to help?'

He considered her in silence for a few moments and then

said, 'Do you really need me to tell you that? Or have you forgotten that you invited yourself into this room for no better reason than that you hoped for a little free entertainment?'

She knew an almost overwhelming impulse to say something extremely rude, and had to draw a long breath in order to repress it. Then she said carefully, 'I don't deny it – and I've already apologised. Twice. What more do you want? Blood? No – don't answer that. But though I may be vulgarly curious, what I *don't* do is gloat.'

'Don't you? Are you sure of that?'

Kate's temper rose and she said shortly, 'Don't tempt me. I suppose I'd be wasting my breath if I asked you to come to a decision about Felix?'

'Yes.' The dark eyes continued to mock her. 'I've already done so.'

'And?'

'And I'll apprise him of it later in the day when I'm in the mood to be patient.'

It could mean only one thing and an unpleasant depression settled on Kate's stomach. Swallowing, she said quietly, 'It means a lot to him, you know. You wouldn't refuse him because of me, would you?'

A slow, malicious smile wreathed the handsome face.

'Don't flatter yourself,' he said.

Felix was late for dinner and Kate's heart sank still further. She pushed her portion of beef and oyster pie around the plate and came to the conclusion that her entire morning had been a disaster. The only person to emerge with a smile on her face was Meg – who seemed to have spent a pleasant half-hour with the signor's private assassin. All in all, she herself would have done better to have stayed at home.

The door burst open upon Felix. Kate stopped rearranging her food and steeled herself to look at him. He was grinning from ear to ear.

'Mother – I'm late. Sorry. I didn't mean to be but I – well, I forgot the time. Father – it's happened! Mr Santi says I show some promise – just a grain or two, he said, but I don't mind that. It's just his way. And he says he'll take me if you give your permission – freely and without me pestering you.'

Richard's eyes held a gleam of appreciation. He said, 'Signor del Santi appears to know you rather well.'

'Yes.' Felix slid into his seat and helped himself to a hefty slice of pie. 'He says I'm an obstinate, impatient, pestilential brat and the thought of having me living in the house is sing-singularly unnerving. I think he quite likes me.'

The whole table dissolved into laughter and it was therefore several minutes before Dorothy was able to say, 'Well, my dear? Are you reconciled to having an artisan in the family – or shall we pack Felix off to Oxford with all possible speed?'

Richard sighed and laid down his knife. 'I'm not reconciled to anything yet. But I think the quickest road to a little peace and quiet is to invite the signor to dinner. But only on condition that Felix promises to let the poor fellow eat it.'

And so it was settled. After a brief conference with Kate, Dorothy despatched a formal invitation to Signor and Signorina del Santi and received a surprisingly prompt reply. The signor, it seemed, would be happy to dine with them but begged Mistress Maxwell to hold his sister excused; she was suffering – as Miss Kate would doubtless confirm – from a mild distemper of the nerves.

He arrived immaculate and saturnine in black silk. Dorothy, with only the haziest recollection of having seen him once before, found that he was not quite what she had expected but couldn't work out why. Amy stared blatantly at the slight malformation of his left shoulder until Eden kicked her under the table . . . and then successfully avoided looking at it in a manner even more irritatingly obvious. Eden himself contributed little to the conversation. Kate, as resplendent as the signor in her new and very becoming amber taffeta, chose to present a façade of maidenly gentility. Only Felix, Felicity and Richard were entirely themselves – and Dorothy thanked God for it since they saved the meal from total disaster.

When it was over, Eden pleaded an engagement with Francis and fled. Dorothy watched him go and then, hiding her thoughts, said calmly to the Italian, 'You probably don't know that Eden is shortly to be married.'

The dark eyes surveyed her enigmatically. 'Ah . . . to Mistress Celia, no doubt.'

'Yes,' she said, surprised. 'You were aware of it?'

'No. A guess, merely. I must remember to offer my felicitations to Lord Wroxton.'

Dorothy rose abruptly from her chair. 'I think we can discuss Felix's future more comfortably in the parlour – and without an audience. Richard?'

'Certainly. Don't scowl, Felix.'

'I wasn't. I just thought—'

'Then don't,' advised Richard. 'We'll summon you in our own good time. I daresay I've less need to tell you to stay within call than to remind you that I've very distinct views on people who put their ears to the door.'

It was a little over two hours later that Felix found Kate in the garden cutting roses and said smugly, 'You're going home.'

Kate stopped snipping. 'And you're not, I suppose?'

'No. You and Father and Mother and the rest of them are going home so Father can see to the farm. *I'm* going to live with Mr Santi in Cheapside.'

'Signor del Santi,' she corrected automatically. 'It's settled, then? I hope you're good at dodging pots.'

'If you mean Mistress Jenny,' said the stubbornly English Felix, 'I shan't have to. Gino says she only throws things at Mr Santi. Not that I'd care, anyway. I'm to go for a sort of trial period till my birthday – and then, if I want to stay and Mr Santi is satisfied with me, they'll let me be apprenticed properly.' He folded his arms and grinned triumphantly at her. 'Jealous?'

'Me?' Kate's brows rose. 'What on earth for?'

'Because *I* shan't have to put up with Silly Celia,' said Felix, turning to go. And, cheekily over his shoulder, 'Or maybe because you'd like to stay in London so as to encourage your admirer.'

Kate stuck out her tongue at his retreating back.

'I'd be careful, if I were you,' remarked a pleasant voice from the shadowy doorway to the house. 'The wind might change.'

She froze, resisted the temptation to swear and, composing her face, turned slowly to meet him.

'You came to say goodbye?' she inquired hopefully. 'Goodbye.'

Luciano ignored this and came out into the light, the sun striking sapphire sparks in his hair. He said, 'I'm impressed. He must be a brave man.'

'Who?' she snapped. And immediately regretted asking.

'This suitor of yours. Or doesn't he know you dip your tongue in quinine every morning?'

'No. Why should I boast? Some people dip theirs in hemlock.'

'You underestimate me,' he said, turning slightly away from her to gaze across the busy river and thus effectively depriving her of the glint of humour in his eyes. 'My gifts are entirely natural.'

Kate stared at him, wishing he'd go away. In her opinion, nothing about him was natural. But for the imperfect line of his shoulder, sharply etched in its dark silk against a cloud of white roses, he was the epitome of everything that foolish girls like Amy dreamed of. But Amy had found that one blemish repulsive. Kate didn't. For her, it gave him the sort of reality she could have done without. Distantly, she wondered if he minded . . . and then wished again that he would go. She'd come a long way in the last year, acquiring at least a veneer of the mysterious quality called poise and learning to voice the unacceptable a little less often. It worked with most people. But then, no one else turned her nerves into over-stretched lute strings and her stomach into something resembling a butter-churn. If he didn't go soon, she'd end up saying something she'd regret.

But it seemed Signor del Santi was in no hurry. He said dispassionately, 'So . . . your brother is to be married. Are you reconciled to it and ready to dance at his wedding?'

'What do you think?' she retorted. And then, abruptly, 'I suppose I ought to thank you for taking Felix.'

'Why? There's no need for such a sacrifice.' He turned

his head to look satirically at her. 'And, for all you know, I may be luring him into my evil clutches so as to corrupt, deprave and otherwise ill-treat him at my leisure.'

Kate flushed and resolutely held her tongue.

'What – no comment? How very disappointing! Any minute now you'll be virtuously telling me that you never quarrel with your father's guests and adding a prim inquiry into the state of Gianetta's health and temper.'

'Thank you for reminding me,' she said sweetly. 'How is she?'

'Busy,' he replied. 'As I was leaving, she made the mistake of becoming histrionic at the head of the stairs and broke her pearls. I imagine she's still on her hands and knees looking for them.'

With care Kate controlled the grin which threatened to disturb the studied blankness of her expression. 'How unfortunate. But perhaps you shouldn't encourage her to wear quite *all* your profits.'

Laughter flared in the dark eyes. 'Don't be diffident. If you mean ill-gotten gains, why not say so? And vulgar ostentation is the prerogative of the merchant class. You should know that. Already I'm considering how best I may impress your father with a bride-gift for your brother's wedding. Do you think he'd object to a pair of twelve-branched solid gold candlesticks set with turquoises and garnets . . . or a seven-foot salt in silver-gilt? Or no. Mistress Celia might like them.'

This time Kate had no desire to smile. 'Why,' she asked darkly, 'are you giving Eden anything at all? You hardly know him.'

'Have you forgotten that he and your father saved my life?' he mocked. 'And it's usual, is it not, when one is bidden to the wedding? Especially when – as in this case – one feels that one has played some small part in bringing it about. And then, of course, my position with regard to Felix makes me almost one of the family, wouldn't you say?' He paused, smiling on her. 'Not impressed? Never mind. You'll have plenty of time to get used to the idea before September.'

Seven

Within days of the Maxwells leaving London, the King's second long-awaited Scots war came a step closer when the Covenanting Marquis of Argyll arrested the Stewarts of Atholl and then led the Clan Campbell down on the Ogilvys, burning their castle of Airlie beneath the confused noses of the gentler garrison already installed there by the Earl of Montrose. A new violence was in the air and, although His Majesty's Governor of Newcastle did not immediately perceive it, he did begin to send weekly bulletins to Whitehall on the state of the Scots army assembling on the border. He said they could not invade; then, discovering their numbers, that they must either invade or disband; and finally, in mid-August, that they would most certainly invade, and that when they did Newcastle could not be held against them because, although he had a goodly supply of bread, cheese, muskets and cannon, he had not as yet managed to acquire any bullets.

After months of unconcerned dallying, Whitehall was thrown into a fever of activity and on 20 August His Majesty left for York with his army. My lord Wroxton went too – having sent his wife and daughter back to Far Flamstead with instructions to delay the wedding until he and Francis returned to grace it.

Celia waited until Eden's shoulder was within reach and then indulged in a fit of mild hysterics. Flattered and not a little touched, Eden swallowed his own disappointment and set out to comfort her. Richard, busy about the farm and in close correspondence with John Hampden and Lord Brooke about the chances of the Scots war forcing a recall of Parliament, plainly considered a postponed bridal of small importance beside the events which had caused it; and Dorothy's step regained its usual lightness and she started singing in the still-room again.

Unaware that on the very day the King's army had left London the Scots had crossed the Tweed, Francis Langley rode north with cheerful unconcern. The first hint that all was not entirely well came when they were greeted at York with a petition against the raising of troops from the local gentry, but the King managed to talk his way out of this and Francis was able to forget it without much difficulty. Then, on 27 August, he set off as one of the twenty-thousand-strong army to relieve my lord Conway at Newcastle – and, seeing only their impressive numbers, and the glamour of being personally led by the King, he was still able to think the army splendid. Any experienced campaigner, however, could have told a different story; indeed, that veteran of the German wars, Sir Jacob Astley, described it as a collection of 'all the arch-knaves in this kingdom'. But, in the event, its powers were not to be tested for, by the time it arrived at Northallerton, Newcastle had fallen.

The Scots, it seemed, had declined to trouble with the defences that Lord Conway had painstakingly constructed around Berwick, and advanced through the Northumbrian hills to cross the Tyne at Newburn. With very few exceptions, the English troops at Newcastle had distinguished themselves only by the speed with which they had fled from the Scots' musket-fire; and Francis, sitting snugly in a billet at Northallerton, was finally forced to admit that his confidence had suffered a severe jolt. On the following day they all rode anti-climactically back to York, leaving General Leslie to lead his Scots into abandoned Newcastle – and, thinking it all too easy, to send to Edinburgh for more men.

But, once back in York, spirits gradually rose again. My lord Strafford arrived to take command, the army was drilled until it began to shed some of its rougher edges, and a few bottles of wine soon drowned the bitter taste of the shambles at Newburn. Within a few days rumour had turned disaster into victory and Francis was able to write to Eden that the Irish forces were expected any day and that, in the meantime, 'the army is remarkably pleasant when there's no need to ruin one's appearance in nasty, sweaty battles'.

Eden smiled wryly when he read this and then put it to one side, deciding that he wasn't missing much. One did not, of course, wish to fight in such a war; but when one had been trained to fight, it was only natural to be a little sorry not to be able to do so. It was cheering, therefore, to hear that nothing much was happening.

Richard, paying a flying visit to London in mid-September, could have told him differently. With Pym, Hampden and the rest now released from the Tower again, events were once more moving towards forcing a recall of Parliament by means of a remonstrance stating all the grievances of the Short Parliament. In faraway York, the King countered this by summoning all peers to attend a Great Council; and he also arranged to rekindle Strafford's dwindling optimism by awarding him the Order of the Garter – thus successfully increasing that gentleman's widespread unpopularity and rendering him a target for everyone who disapproved of the war. No longer infected with blind faith, Strafford saw it all. 'Never,' he admitted privately to his friends, 'came a man to so lost a business.'

So, while the Great Council met in York, and the King, playing for time, listened politely to an attack on his policy whilst allowing his friend Strafford to become a scapegoat, Celia Langley entered into an uneasy truce with her mother and prepared, less extravagantly than she'd hoped, for her wedding.

The trouble was that – still smarting over her defeat in the matter of Cyrus Winter – Lady Wroxton was not disposed to be generous and, instead of sending to London for silks and seamstresses, went no further than the sign of the Ragged Staff in Banbury. Celia was furious. All the materials might be of the finest quality, but the finished gowns could not be other than provincial since they were to be sewn by Ruth Radford – who had never been more than two miles from Banbury in her life and was, in any case, as austere a Puritan as Celia ever wished to meet. But it was impossible to say anything to Lady Wroxton without releasing a fresh storm, so Celia had to content herself with pouring her troubles into the sympathetic ears of Amy Maxwell and taking out her temper on the nervous younger sister that Mistress Ruth brought with her to hem petticoats and hold the pins.

Kate stayed aloof from it all as much as was possible and then discovered that she was expected to join Amy in attending the bride. 'And that,' she said flatly to her mother, 'is hypocritical to the point of idiocy. We've never been more than civil to each other and aren't ever likely to be, so she can't exactly relish the prospect of relying on me to cherish her luck by counting up pins on her wedding-night. She'd never rest for wondering if I'd left one in just to spite her.'

'And would you?' asked Dorothy gently.

'No. I can't can I? Because it's Eden's luck too – and he'll need as much of it as he can get.'

Eden, had he been privileged to hear this statement, would have laughed. Since Celia had returned to Far Flamstead, their relationship had blossomed in a way he had never dreamed of and he was more in love than ever. She was perfect; his rose without a thorn, her petals tipped with a passion that both astonished and delighted him, and which suddenly laced the time of waiting with a new and wholly exquisite danger. He was resolved not to anticipate their marriage and did not doubt that her ardent response to his caresses was as new and unexpected to her as it was to him; but when she melted into his arms and her mouth breathed hunger and invitation into his, it was growing harder and harder to exercise restraint.

Despite the delay and her mother's parsimony, Celia was happier through those September days than she had been for a long time. Hugo started to fade a little from her mind and, now that she was away from the sophistication of Whitehall, Eden's simple taste in dress and inability to phrase clever compliments mattered less and less. He knew how to make her feel secure and how to fill her days with laughter; and, more even than this, it seemed that he could help her discover all the sweet secrets of her body which she was now impatient to experience. She began to exult in her power to arouse him – and even more in the promised ecstasy she sensed in herself. She almost believed she loved him; and it was almost true.

September became October. In York, the King issued writs for a new Parliament, asked for and was promised a loan from the City of London, and signed an expensive armistice with the Scots. The second Bishops' War was discreditably over and Lord Wroxton headed southwards for his daughter's wedding. He arrived a bare three days before the end of the month and, with the new Parliament due to open on 3 November, Celia and Eden greeted him with immense relief – having begun to wonder if, once Richard Maxwell was sitting in Westminster, they would ever be married at all.

But once the thankfulness had worn off, Celia began to realise that, in order to have the wedding before Richard's departure, the guest-list must inevitably be small, for there was not enough time to let everyone know. She came to this depressing conclusion when the two families were gathered together at Thorne Ash, ostensibly to discuss the wedding but in fact seeming to talk of nothing but the recent events in the north.

'And the terms of the truce?' Richard asked her father.

'Unfavourable,' came the heavy reply. 'Until such time as the peace is concluded, the Covenant army is to continue to occupy the six northern counties and be paid eight hundred and sixty pounds a day.'

'My God!' breathed Eden. 'Has the King uncovered a gold mine?'

'London will help,' said Lord Wroxton repressively. 'And, in the meantime, the Commissioners of both parties will transfer their discussions to Westminster so that Parliament may be consulted over further terms. Your department, Richard – and I think you'll find it a time-consuming business.'

'Yes. Well, it rather looks as though we'd all have been saved a lot of time, effort and expense if a proper peace had been arrived at last year,' said Richard dryly. 'However, it's pointless to repine. Let's just hope His Majesty has learned from his mistakes and will permit us to do better this time.'

There was a slightly uncomfortable silence before Celia took advantage of it to say tightly, 'Forgive me . . . but I thought we were going to decide about my wedding?'

Gervase relaxed and tapped her cheek with an indulgent finger. 'And so we are, my dear. So we are. Now let's see. It's Wednesday today and Richard has to be in London for the opening of Parliament next Tuesday. It doesn't give us much time, does it? But everything must be pretty well in train by now . . . so how will Saturday suit you?'

'Very well indeed, sir,' grinned Eden. And, reaching for Celia's hand, 'What do you say?'

'Oh – yes. Of course. But it's just that – that no one will come,' she said wistfully. 'And I did so want everyone to be there.'

Eden nodded understandingly and squeezed her fingers. 'Well, I daresay some of them might get here if we send out messengers immediately.'

'Of course they will,' affirmed his lordship jovially. 'You just leave it all to your new father and myself. You'll be amazed what we can achieve when we put our minds to it.'

'And failing that,' offered Kate dulcetly, 'you can always postpone the wedding. Again.'

But that, of course, as Kate confided later to her mother, was too much to hope for. And so it was that on Saturday morning she pinned a resolute smile on her face and accompanied Amy to Far Flamstead to help prepare the bride for her nuptials.

She had not expected to enjoy the occasion – and she did not. Indeed, within the hour her smile had turned distinctly brittle and she was finding it necessary to keep her jaws clamped firmly together. Celia – who was never at her best in purely feminine company – was flown with nerves and self-importance and inclined to be snappish. She carped incessantly at Ruth Radford over the gown of shell-pink silk that Kate, looking with a new and critical eye, could find no fault with at all; she had her maid running up and downstairs to bring her word of which guests had come and which had not until the poor girl was almost purple and Kate feared she might suffer an apoplexy; and then when they tried to sew on the bride-favours of rose and silver ribbon, she twisted and turned, trying to peer out of the window, complained that Kate's stitches were too tight and her needle virtually piercing the flesh – and ended by slapping little Abigail Radford's face.

It was the last straw and Kate unlocked her tongue to say bitingly, 'Well, well . . . the perfect picture of a bride on her wedding day. I'm sure Eden would have been entranced.'

Celia flushed and twisted her fingers together, looking suddenly abashed. 'I – I didn't mean it. It's just that I'm nervous . . . and the girl is clumsy.'

'She's thirteen years old and doing her best – as are we all,' returned Kate coolly. 'And it would help if you stopped worrying about who's downstairs and stood still for five minutes.'

For a moment, blue eyes met green. Then, her face hardening, Celia said, 'Very well. But for heaven's sake get on with it or we shall be late.'

And, of course, they were – but only a little, for Kate had anticipated it and done her best to speed everyone up. She herself had changed in record time into the elegant silver-green satin she'd bought in Cheapside, and managed to get Amy into her new primrose taffeta rather more quickly than anyone would have believed possible. Then, with a good deal more laughter than had been present upstairs, the bride's party made its way out into the pale autumnal sunshine and crossed the courtyard to Far Flamstead's cold, ornate chapel.

It was fuller than Kate had expected, many guests seeming to have managed to arrive on the morning itself

– but it was scarcely the major social event for which Celia had so plainly hoped. Kit Clifford was there with his sister and Sir William Davenant, and the Drydens had come from Canon's Ashby; but there was no representative from the King and most of the other local gentry such as Viscount Saye and Sele, Lord Northampton and Lord Brooke were notable by their absence; much too busy in London getting ready for Parliament, supposed Kate as she followed Celia demurely down the aisle. But then she felt all her muscles go into spasm as she caught sight of Luciano del Santi.

He was dressed in his customary black and sitting beside Felix, his gaze resting expressionlessly on Celia. Kate swallowed, managed to attract Felix's eye and grinned as she passed him. Then they were behind her and she strove to put them out of her mind, fixing her eyes on Eden's elegant tawny-velvet back in a bid to concentrate on the ceremony.

Afterwards she could never decide whether it had lasted for hours or merely minutes. Most of her memories of the occasion were blurred and insubstantial, frosted with the coldness of her feet on the marble floor and the ever-present desire to turn her head. But other moments were set immutably in her mind like flies in amber; the cloying scent of lilies and perfumed candles, the low clarity of Eden's voice repeating his vows, and the suddenly terrifying finality of it all.

'Forsaking all other . . . so long as ye both shall live . . . to have and to hold from this day forward . . . till death us do part . . . Those whom God hath joined together, let no man put asunder.'

Kate shivered. Would it be like this – would she feel like this when her turn came? For it must come, one day, she realised that now. Marriage was the inevitable lot of women – and who was she to be different from the rest? But who would be standing beside her at the altar? And did love mean that you could say those terrible words without fear? She didn't know. Eden's russet clashed subtly with Celia's pink silk. Kate hoped it wasn't an omen.

Outside the light was dazzling and the solemnity of the

last hour dissolved into a counterpoint of laughter and chattering voices as everyone made their way back to the house. Kate found herself walking beside Francis – resplendent in crimson satin with a wide lace collar and carrying the traditional bride-day gloves, embroidered and bestowed on him by Celia.

'Wondering when it will be your turn, Kate?' he asked.

She gave him a forbidding stare and said nothing. He laughed. 'I don't think you need worry. If I read the signs aright, Kit might be yours for the asking. Or, if the prospect of becoming my lady Clifford doesn't appeal to you, you can always wait on the chance of having me.' He paused, his gaze travelling appraisingly over her. 'It's not as unlikely as you might suppose, you know. You're beginning to show promise in developing that certain sort of something one doesn't see too often – though why I should find that surprising, I really can't imagine. For you never were exactly in the common way, were you?'

Kate stopped walking and met his mischievous glance with one of acidic kindness. 'You really ought to stop your tongue by-passing your brain,' she informed him. 'It'll get you into trouble one of these days.' And she walked off to join Venetia Clifford.

Inside the house hilarity was already setting in as all the young men, and one or two of the older ones, jostled to capture a knot of rose and silver ribbon from Celia's gown, while the servants were kept busy ensuring that everyone had a cup of wine. Then they all sat down to a gargantuan wedding-breakfast consisting of every delicacy known to the Gallic genius who ruled Lady Wroxton's kitchen. Kate located her mother's eye between the tail-feathers of a panoplied pheasant and detected a hint of faintly hysterical amusement before her attention was claimed once more by Francis. She could not, she discovered, see the Italian at all. An immense Chantilly cream topped with candied violets was in the way.

Finally it was over. Toasts were drunk, speeches made, and good wishes flowed through a sea of bawdy jests and hiccups. Then they all rose, some less steadily than others, and trooped into the gallery for the dancing. With rather more grace and confidence than had been his a year ago, Eden led out a now radiant Celia while Kate followed stoically behind, doing her duty with Francis. The musicians, lovingly culled from amongst Banbury's best, scraped and blew with a will and the noise level rose by several decibels.

A little later, Kate found herself partnering Mr Clifford but, after one lung-cracking attempt at conversation that ended in laughter, they gave up trying to talk and contented themselves with the more energetic pleasures of the dance – during which Kate still managed to notice the brief and apparently glacial exchange taking place between Lady Wroxton and the Italian. Later still, she escaped unseen to the cool, dark air of the walled garden, and from there – finding it inhabited by a pair of entwined but mercifully unidentifiable shapes – to the edge of the park.

The glimmer of bonfires and the strains of lusty singing drifted up from the Home Farm, where Lord Wroxton's tenants celebrated with ale and a roast ox or two. Kate leaned gratefully against a tree and reflected that, at Thorne Ash, no such division would be made and that tomorrow their own people would flood into the house to welcome the new bride home.

'It's a stupid question,' said a disembodied voice out of the darkness, 'but it *is* you, I suppose? Mistress of awkward moments and my own personal bloodhound?'

'Yes.' Kate realised that he must have been there all the time and wondered vaguely why she wasn't more surprised.

'Thank God for that,' said Luciano del Santi unexpectedly. 'I'm tired of being civil and far from feeling gallant. Fortunately, you and I are far beyond the need for either one.'

Her eyes searched for him amongst the shadows but could not find him. Tiny bubbles of laughter formed in her veins, gathered themselves together and escaped.

'Oh, God,' she said weakly. 'You'd better mind what you say. For all I know, the place may be crawling with eavesdroppers.'

'So it may.' There was the ghost of a smile in his voice and, when he spoke again, it was from much nearer at hand. 'What brings you out here? Or shouldn't I ask?'

Kate peered through the gloom and distinguished the white blur of his face. 'I didn't follow you if that's what you were thinking.'

'Another hope blighted,' he said cheerfully. And then, 'Have you spoken with Felix yet?'

'Barely. But he seems very happy.'

'That surprises you?'

'Not especially. It's what he wanted, after all. How is he getting on?'

'Rather well, as it happens,' he replied, for once without either mockery or levity. 'I have hopes of him. But of course it wouldn't do to tell him so just yet – a fact which I must remember to mention to your father before we depart for London on Monday.'

'You're all travelling together?' asked Kate.

'Yes. You have some objection?'

'No. It's just that I wondered where you'd be staying till then. Something tells me Lady Wroxton won't be offering you a bed.'

'You *do* keep your eyes open, don't you? But you're right, of course. I'm *persona non grata*, and will therefore be your parents' guest at Thorne Ash. You and I ought to be able to co-exist peaceably for a mere twenty-four hours, don't you think?'

Kate opened her mouth on a withering retort and then let it die unspoken. He was baiting her again but it didn't matter. Tomorrow, in the light, he would annoy her as much as ever; but just now, in the dark under this tree, he was the only companion she could have tolerated. Unfortunately, however, there were still duties to be performed and she said reluctantly, 'I'll have to go. I'm supposed to help make Celia ready for bed.'

'Christ. *More* ceremonial crudity?'

'I beg your pardon?'

'The traditional bedding of the bride and groom,' he said derisively. 'A time for the jests to get coarser and

141

more banal . . . and the perfect way, it seems to me, to strip the romance from anyone's wedding-night.'

Kate felt her cheeks grow warm. 'It – it's the custom.'

'It's barbaric. Take a good look at it tonight and see if your brother appreciates it. Somehow I doubt he will. And you might also care to spare a thought for how you'll feel when you're at the centre of the same circus.'

'I wish,' said Kate flatly, 'that everyone would stop assuming I'm either eager or likely to be married any minute. I'm not.'

'No?' His laughter was so soft it scarcely reached her. 'But you will be. Given time, you will be. Doubtless Giacomo would say that you haven't met the right man yet.'

'Giacomo ought to set up as a marriage-broker,' she said shortly, turning back in the direction of the path. And then, smiling, 'Who knows? He might even be able to find a bride for *you*.'

'Anything is possible.' His reply drifted after her through the trees. 'But some things are, to say the least of it, unlikely.'

The scene in the bridal chamber turned out to be very much as he had described it, decided Kate unwillingly a little later on. They brushed Celia's hair loose and arrayed her in an embroidered night-rail of the sheerest lawn and counted up all the pins from her clothes so that none might be left to bring ill-luck. Then they arranged her decoratively against the pillows as though she were a doll, and waited with much sly giggling and nudging for the groom's party to arrive. Kate kept out of the way and looked curiously at Celia. If she was shy or nervous or embarrassed, there was no sign of it, only an unmistakable glow of anticipation. 'How strange,' thought Kate. 'Perhaps she does love him after all.' Then there was a surge of noise and laughter outside the door and Eden was washed in on a tide of boisterous well-wishers.

Amongst them all he was the only one who was not flushed with wine, but he appeared perfectly composed and seemed to be taking the ribaldry in good part. Had it not

142

been for the Italian, Kate would not have questioned the fact that he was enjoying himself; now, however, she found herself searching his eyes and finding in them a hint of rigidly controlled distaste. And looking round at the rowdy gathering with their overtly blatant innuendoes and suggestive glances, she did not blame him for it.

Eventually, though, it was over. Kate was jovially bullied into sitting with Amy on Celia's side of the bed for the purpose of tossing a posy over their shoulders at the bridegroom to determine their own marriage prospects. Amy's landed squarely on Eden's chest; Kate made very sure hers didn't and managed instead to hit Mr Clifford on the nose – which turned out not to have been such a good idea after all. Then everyone wished the bridal pair goodnight and flooded back down the stairs to continue their celebrations.

As soon as they had gone, Eden got up and bolted the door. The friendly bawdiness of the last half-hour was still echoing through his mind and the formality of the great bed seemed suddenly all wrong. He turned slowly to smile at Celia and wondered how best to begin.

'Well, Mistress Maxwell . . .?'

She dimpled at him. 'Sir?'

He gestured towards the cosy hearth with its cheerful blaze. 'Will you come drink a toast with me?'

It was the right instinct. Celia slid from the bed and approached the fire; then, accepting wine from his hands, she said provocatively, 'And what toast will you make that hasn't already been drunk?'

Eden looked at her, his breath catching in his throat. The firelight danced through the embroidered shift, haloing her body in gold. He said, 'I don't know. You are so beautiful that I can't think of anything else.'

She smiled at him, perfectly satisfied.

'Then you may drink to that – and *I* to the hope that you'll always find me as beautiful as you do now.'

'You need have no fears about that.' And, touching his cup to hers, he drained it and put it aside.

Celia drank too and felt a sudden ripple of doubt. He was so good, so *sure*; why couldn't she be like that? She said urgently, 'Eden – you do love me, don't you?'

'I love you,' he said steadily. 'Can you doubt it?'

'N-no. It – it's just that I'm not as perfect as you think,' she said heroically. 'But you'll always love me, won't you? No matter what I do? I *need* you to love me.'

'Dear heart,' Eden took the cup from her hands and set it down. 'Dear heart . . . I'll love you to the edge of my life.' And, closing the space between them, took her into his arms.

For a second only, she remained taut against him and then the tension seeped out of her and her mouth opened like a flower beneath his. She felt the hardness of his body against her own and dark, sweet expectancy flowed out from the pit of her stomach into every vein and nerve. She felt the soft folds of her night-rail slither to her feet and knew the touch of hands on her skin. She closed her eyes and let the tide take her.

Eden lifted her up and carried her to the crimson-hung bed. Inextricably laced with his hunger for her was his desire to give her pleasure and he hesitated, horribly aware of his own inexperience. Then her hands were reaching out for him and everything else ceased to matter. She was the flesh and substance of his dreams and she was his.

Half the house away, in the long gallery, the revelry continued till dawn when Francis led a tunelessly inebriated consort of lutes and viols in a rendering of 'Come lasses and lads' beneath the window of the bridal chamber. By then, however, the Maxwell family – together with Luciano del Santi and his awesome servant – were half-way back to Thorne Ash, riding through the chill grey light in order to snatch a few hours' sleep before preparing to welcome the bride and groom home.

Kate's brain was blurred with fatigue. It seemed impossible to believe that Eden was even now lying with Celia – and even more impossible to imagine herself getting into bed with either Kit or Francis . . . The whole thing was too ludicrous. She really couldn't see herself sharing her bed with any man at all.

She indulged in a small, caustic smile, focused her gaze on the road ahead and experienced the most terrifying discovery of her life. Shock paralysed her lungs and froze her skin. Unsought, unwelcomed and unendurable, the truth hit her. It was not a case of any man at all, but any man save one. And the most ludicrous thing of all was that, even if she could have him, she would not. For the simple fact was that she neither liked nor understood him . . . nor even wanted to.

'Before the flame of the war broke out in the top of
the chimneys, the smoke was in every county.'

Lucy Hutchinson

The Perilous Path

November 1640 to January 1642

What Danger is the Pilgrim in?
How many are his Foes?
How many ways there are to Sin?
No living Mortal knows.

Some of the Ditch, shy are, yet can
Lie tumbling in the Myre.
Some tho they shun the Frying-pan,
Do leap into the Fire.

John Bunyan

One

Due to a sudden fit of thriftiness on the part of the King,
the new Parliament opened without the customary procession and settled down to the business of sorting out the
usual batch of incorrect electoral returns. Since this resulted
in the winnowing out of the Court party, His Majesty soon
found himself a good deal less well represented than he
had been in April and immediately compounded his disadvantage by appointing the meek lawyer, William Lenthall,
as Speaker. It was, as Richard Maxwell observed, rather
like setting a mouse to tame a tiger. For against men like
Pym and Hampden and the legal genius, Oliver St John,
Mr Lenthall stood no chance at all.

While Parliament settled in and the Scots minister,
Alexander Henderson, spoke to packed houses in St
Antholin's church, thereby putting an end to years of
sneering at the Scottish accent, Luciano del Santi received
a discreet visitor from Whitehall.

It did not surprise him. From the moment he'd returned
to discover that the King had failed to get his own candidate installed as Lord Mayor, it had been obvious that the
City would presently vote to postpone payment of their
promised loan to the Crown. All in all, His Majesty was
about to find himself up to his neck in financial embarrassment and would thus be seeking assistance. *His*
assistance.

He surveyed Secretary Windebanke clinically. The man
was a Catholic, and that, presumably, was why he had been
sent. Someone had had the bright idea that a fellow papist
might be able to make a stronger appeal. Foolish of them.

Luciano del Santi had not spoken to a priest nor paid any observance to religion since the day his mother had been buried. He'd decided then that piety and honour and sentiment were traps set for the stupid, and he had not changed his mind.

Secretary Windebanke was starting to fidget under the long silence. Finally he said, 'Perhaps I didn't make myself quite clear? His Majesty is anxious to—'

'There is no need to repeat yourself,' interposed the pleasant voice at length. 'His Majesty wishes me to advance him enough money to pay the Scots. I understand perfectly. But what you must endeavour to explain to him is that even if I could foresee the remotest prospect of regaining my investment – which, of course, I can't – my resources are not unlimited.'

'Yes – yes. We understand that. But surely it's possible for us to come to some arrangement? The City was going to begin by supplying twenty thousand. You could manage that, couldn't you?'

The dark eyes grew openly derisive. 'Perhaps. But why should I wish to? I lend money for profit, Mr Secretary. And, if you will permit me to say so, I can see no profit in lending further sums to the King. The Crown's finances have been ill managed for the last fifteen years and are now almost beyond redemption. Even by me. And I have tried, believe me. But His Majesty, as you must know, is far too inclined to follow the advice of the last person he spoke to. Certainly, had he followed mine with any kind of regularity, he would not now be in such a difficult position.' He paused and smiled coldly. 'I am very much afraid that I can't help you.'

Secretary Windebanke lost a little of his polish. 'Damn it – there must be *something* you want! A title, perhaps?'

The Italian laughed. It wasn't a particularly comforting sound. 'A title? Il Magnifico, Duke of Cheapside? Hardly.'

'Then what? A monopoly on something or other? A lucrative wardship? An official position? Men like you always have their price . . . so why don't you stop wasting time and name yours?'

There was another long silence into which Luciano del Santi finally said, 'It's possible that you are exceeding your brief, Mr Secretary. You are certainly exceeding my toleration. You may leave.'

A dark flush, partly of irritation with himself and partly pure indignation, rose to the other man's cheek. He said stiffly, 'It's possible that I've expressed myself a trifle strongly, but the case is urgent. Couldn't you just—'

'I think not.' Quite without haste, the signor rose from his seat, his long fingers resting lightly on the polished surface of the table. 'I wish the King well . . . but that's all. So make me no offers you are not empowered to fulfil – for my terms, should I have any, may not be what you expect. And now I'll bid you good-day.'

Windebanke's eyes narrowed. The fellow appeared to be hinting at something; but what? He rose, saying abruptly, 'I'll consult with His Majesty and return tomorrow. Just in case you have . . . reconsidered.'

'As you wish.' The beautiful voice did not change at all but something gleamed briefly in the black eyes. 'I cannot, of course, promise that I'll be here to receive you. There are many calls on my time these days.'

The Secretary gritted his teeth and silently damned a situation that made it necessary for him to put up with the impudence of low-bred knaves. He said, 'I see. Well, that makes the position fairly clear, doesn't it?' And snatched up his hat.

'Not at all,' came the gentle reply. 'It merely places the pieces on the board. What moves will be made have yet to be seen.'

A few minutes later Giacomo came in to find his master seated alone at the table, staring thoughtfully at his hands. Then he looked up and gave a long, slow smile.

Giacomo drew a deep breath and said in Italian, 'It begins, then?'

'Soon. It begins soon, my friend.' He paused and then in a more business-like tone said, 'The gentleman will call again tomorrow. I shall not be at home to him. You understand?'

'Yes. But why? You have waited so long.'

'Yes. So long that a few more days cannot matter. To me, that is. To them a delay can only increase the urgency of their position and make them readier to give me what I ask.' He smiled again. 'You'd better send Selim to me. If all goes well, there'll be work for him – so I think it's time I took him into my confidence.'

Giacomo sniffed. 'Him? What use is he? He understands nothing.'

'He guards my back,' came the dry response. 'As for the rest, I think you'll find that he has absolutely no difficulty in understanding vengeance. None at all.'

Selim, when he came, showed no excitement at the prospect of finally learning what his master was about. He merely gave his usual courteous inclination of the head, maintained his impassive expression and sat down to listen.

'Such restraint!' observed Luciano del Santi, with one of his rare smiles. 'You've been with me for four years and never asked a question. Haven't you been curious?'

'Curiosity,' said Selim, 'is for women. I will know what it is fitting for me to know when the time is right for you to tell me.'

'As it now is.'

'Then I am content.' The magnificent teeth gleamed. 'You saved me from the galleys, *efendim*. If you have an enemy, it will be my pleasure to kill him.'

'Thank you,' came the dry response. 'But at the moment all I require is your continued silence. Even from Aysha.'

'It is done.'

'Good. Then I'll begin at the beginning and be as brief as possible.' The Italian stared down at his clasped hands. 'When I was eleven years old, my father was arrested on a charge of treason. He was accused of hatching a Catholic plot to assassinate the King and, after months of imprisonment and torture, was discreetly tried and executed.' The dark eyes rose. 'The truth, however, is that he was quite innocent. The charges were false and the evidence all lies. I don't know if he was used as a scapegoat to cover a genuine conspiracy or whether certain of the men to whom

152

he'd lent large sums joined forces to do away with him in order to be free of their debts. All I *do* know is that my father was apparently condemned on the testimony of four men. He said so himself – albeit somewhat obliquely – only minutes before he died. And I want to know who they were.'

Selim thought about it. 'Are there names?'

'No. Not yet. But I am hoping – by putting the King under an obligation to me – to acquire them.'

'And when we have the names . . . then we find the men.'

'Yes.'

'And kill them?' Hopefully.

'Not necessarily.'

'Oh. But if we do not kill them,' said Selim reasonably, 'why are we looking for them?'

'So that I may know the truth,' came the implacable reply. 'And, knowing it, administer my own punishment. But I should make one thing clear. If there is murder to be done, it will be because other plans have failed . . . and I will do it myself.'

'It shall of course be as you wish, *efendim*. But if men have destroyed your father, do they not deserve to die?'

'Yes. But I think I am capable of devising something better.' A cold smile curled Luciano del Santi's mouth. 'I intend, you see, to ruin them. Utterly.'

Richard Maxwell's first week in Parliament passed in a blur of activity in which he and his fellows established general committees and received a multitude of petitions. Edward Hyde presented the grievances of the North and George Digby, who was currently out of favour at Court and feeling peevish, those of the West. Edmund Waller, the poet, denounced ship-money – again; and a whole clutch of prominent members hurled themselves on the system of episcopacy so vigorously that the House presently condemned every single canon recently rushed through Convocation.

Through all this, Richard was quietly aware that Pym's real goal was the removal of Laud and Strafford. Both were widely unpopular and both were close to the King and, during that first week, Laud came under strong attack in a speech which concluded that a Pope in Rome would do less hurt than a Patriarch at Lambeth. This resulted in Digby proposing that a Remonstrance be drafted against the ministers responsible for the King's civil and religious policy. The motion was carried with enthusiasm and yet another committee was formed to collect information.

On Saturday morning, Richard sat through a discussion on the cases of Prynne, Bastwicke and Burton. All three had been imprisoned for publishing violently inflammatory Puritan doctrines – and, having been privileged to read their diatribes, Richard had little sympathy with them. The bulk of the House, however, felt differently, and the debate ended with a resolution that the trio be summoned from their dungeons and brought in for inquiry. Richard abstained from the vote, stayed to hear it carried and then walked into the drizzle outside. It was time, he decided, to take a half-holiday from the affairs of the nation and call on his younger son.

He was crossing Cheapside when, through the press of carts and drays, he saw a familiar figure emerge from Luciano's door and get into a waiting carriage. Richard's eyes grew thoughtful and he drew a number of shrewd conclusions. Then he continued on his way and entered the shop. The Italian was deep in conversation with his servant and did not look very well pleased. Then, seeing Richard, his expression lightened and, switching to English, he said, 'You've come to see Felix – and I, alas, cannot produce him.'

'Buried him under the floorboards, have you?' responded Richard sympathetically. 'Very understandable.'

Laughter touched the dark gaze and was gone. 'It hasn't come to that yet. I've merely sent him out for an hour with Gino. They're both suffering from an excess of high spirits which I was beginning to find a trifle wearing. But please – come upstairs and take a glass of wine. You will have to meet my sister, of course – but no doubt you'll survive the experience.'

Gianetta del Santi was sitting at a window, staring

154

gloomily into the street. A discarded tambour-frame lay in her lap and, as usual, her person was strewn with indiscriminate jewels. She did not move until her brother introduced Richard and then, turning her head, she regarded him out of luminous dark eyes.

Smiling, Richard went forward to take her hand, saying, 'I'm happy to meet you, signorina.'

She allowed him to bow over her hand and then withdrew it, her brow creasing in a slight frown. Then she said laboriously, 'Ah. I 'ave it. You are the father of Feeleex. Is so?'

'Yes. I'm afraid it is.'

'Then I am very please to meet you,' she said more warmly. ''E is funny boy. 'E make me laugh.'

'I'm glad someone does,' remarked Luciano, moving to pour wine. 'You'll join us, Gianetta?'

'No.' She rose abruptly and allowed the embroidery-frame to fall unheeded to the floor. 'I not drink with you! But *you*, Signor Maxwell . . . I 'ope I see you again. You may visit me.'

'Thank you,' murmured Richard appreciatively.

'Is nothing.' And, executing a flawless curtsy, she sailed regally through the door.

Richard stared wordlessly at the Italian and accepted the glass he was being offered. Luciano del Santi looked astringently back and said, 'She was reared by my uncle – who has no daughters of his own and was in love with our mother. Need I say more?'

'No. An over-indulged princess, no less.' Richard sipped his wine and thought about it. 'And the . . . er . . . jewellery?'

'My uncle again. She refuses to be parted from it – even, I suspect, in bed.'

'You don't let her loose in the street like that, do you?' asked Richard, aghast. 'Someone's likely to carve her up into little pieces for the sake of those baubles.'

'I don't let her loose at all,' came the flat reply. 'I daren't. She'd be stowing away on the first boat home. But enough of that. Tell me how your business is progressing in Parliament.'

'The excitement,' replied Richard, seating himself, 'is killing. Yesterday we set up a committee to investigate the quality of the King's advisors, and today we've ordered the release of a trio of notorious Puritans. You're aware, I'm sure, that feeling is running high against Catholics?'

'When does it not?' The Italian smiled faintly. 'But it has nothing to do with me. I attend neither mass nor confession. In fact, I practise no religion at all.'

'None?' asked Richard, somewhat shocked.

'None.'

'I . . . see. You do, on the other hand, consort with known Papists. And you're still, I imagine, lending money to the King.'

'The point being that no one will stop to find out whether I'm Catholic or Presbyterian? Naturally.' There was a brief silence. Then, 'You saw Windebanke leaving this house. I suspected as much. And, having guessed what his business must be, you're wondering if I obliged him.'

'Yes. And did you?'

'In part. Enough, you might say, to pay off the Scots for another few weeks – but less than half of what was asked for.' The hard mouth twisted wryly. 'His Majesty, you see, finds himself reluctant to simply fulfil my requirements. For a man in his position, he is remarkably squeamish . . . a disadvantage he'll have to overcome, if I read the current situation correctly.'

'Oh?' said Richard. 'Enlighten me.'

'Do I need to? You must be perfectly well aware that the dogs have gathered and are already snarling. Soon they'll be at each other's throats and it will be impossible to separate them. And in the meantime, I think Mr Pym will try to remove the Earl of Strafford from his path by means of an impeachment.'

Richard thought so too. He said slowly, 'You must be uncommonly well informed.'

'So is virtually every merchant of substance in the City. It's necessary. I also know John Pym. I've dealt with him from time to time in his capacity as a shareholder of the Providence Company – which, incidentally, is floundering. It isn't hard to catch the tenor of his mind. And did he not say years ago that the Commons would never leave Strafford while his head was still upon his shoulders?'

'His very words.' Richard's face was grave. 'The question now, I suppose, is how far he meant it.'

'No. It is how many of you will support him.'

'Meaning me? It's not something I can tell you without first hearing the evidence.'

Luciano del Santi gave a short, derisive laugh. 'Strafford's doomed, then. It's said that the English love the law – and certainly they're adept at using it to their advantage.'

'That's unjust,' said Richard calmly. 'And it works both ways, you know.'

'Perhaps – if you're an Englishman. But if I were Strafford, I wouldn't care to rely on it. And I think – His Majesty permitting – I'd continue to absent myself.'

Whether on the King's command or not, the Earl returned to London the following week and on 11 November took his seat in the Upper House to accuse Viscount Saye and Sele, amongst others, of having induced the Scots to invade. He was still speaking when Mr Pym arrived at the bar to impeach him in the name of the Commons – on a charge of subverting the laws of England. He was delivered into the hands of Black Rod and his sword taken from him; his request for bail was denied and, less than a week later, he was lodged securely in the Tower.

November slid into December and Richard watched events begin to gather momentum. Ship-money was finally declared illegal; Messrs Prynne and co. received sixteen thousand pounds' compensation; and the Commons acquired the right to pry into the Privy Council. Then, while Strafford began pressing for an open trial and Laud and Finch were both also being impeached, Secretary Windebanke decided that discretion was definitely the better part of valour and fled to France before it could be his turn.

Luciano del Santi heard of Windebanke's defection without surprise and with well-concealed irritation. They would,

157

of course, send someone else, and the inevitable delay was the least of his worries. What concerned him more was whether, at the end of the day, he'd get what he wanted. And already he suspected that he would not.

Blandly and without explanations, he had asked Windebanke for a transcript of the case of *Rex versus Falcieri* or – failing that – for a list of the prosecution witnesses. For a full week the Secretary had hummed and hawed and scuttled to and fro between Whitehall and Cheapside like a mouse on a hot griddle before grudgingly promising the transcript. And that was the last the signor had seen of him.

It was perhaps fortunate that, while being forced to possess his soul in patience, there were other things to be attended to. He had done well in the last four years and was now worth substantially more than the loan he'd originally taken from his uncle; but his profits, naturally enough, had been re-lent or invested and were therefore not to hand – so the loan he had made to the Crown represented a very large portion of the capital he kept available. And, in just three months' time, he was due in Genoa with the annual interest.

He therefore spent his period of waiting working profitably at his bench at the craft that still meant more to him than anything else. He fashioned a pair of goblets for Lord Craven, an ornate salt for the Earl of Bristol, and an emerald-studded chain for Her Grace of Richmond. He put Gino to work on a set of buttons for Harry Jermyn, restrung Gianetta's pearls, and still found time to supervise Felix's first attempt at engraving on silver. Then, on a day towards the middle of the month when, despite his best efforts, his temper was beginning to shorten, Giacomo came down to tell him that one William Murray had arrived to see him.

Luciano washed his hands and, taking his time about it, thoughtfully resumed his coat. He knew about Will Murray. He was a Gentleman of the Bedchamber and supposedly deep in the King's confidence. Or as deep, reflected the signor dryly, as anyone could be with a man who vacillated as much as Charles Stuart did. Still, it was comforting to think that his business was not apparently being bandied about. Yet.

He found Mr Murray in the parlour making audacious compliments to Gianetta. For a moment Luciano remained unnoticed in the doorway and absorbed the rare sight of his sister actually smiling. Then she saw him and, her face freezing into its usual disdainful hostility, she said petulantly, 'I might 'ave known it. Always you come to spoil things when I 'ave visitor. And 'ow many times 'ave I tell you that if I *must* be in this 'ouse, I 'ave this room for my own and don't want you 'ere. You not even knock.'

Luciano's hand clenched hard on the door-latch. He had heard it all before and thought he'd mastered the art of letting it flow over him. It shouldn't hurt any more . . . yet somehow it did. A gust of temper shot through him and, completely disregarding Will Murray's presence, he said softly in Italian, 'Permit me to tell you, my dear, that your manners belong either in the nursery or the scullery, I can't decide which. But one thing I do know – and that is that if you don't swiftly learn to address me with at least the appearance of civility, I'll have you shut in a convent till you can. And now I suggest that you run along. I have business to attend to.'

For a moment she simply stared at him, white-faced with shock. In the whole of her life neither he nor anyone else had spoken to her like that and she didn't know how to begin to deal with it. Then, fury getting the upper hand, she crossed the room like a tornado to spit a brief but particularly vulgar Genoese epithet at him and fled upstairs to her bedchamber.

Will Murray stood like a stone watching her go, and it was several seconds before he remembered to close his mouth. Then he said feebly, 'I thought she was your sister?'

'She is,' came the curt reply. 'And not, I am afraid, a subject for discussion.'

'Eh? Oh – yes. Just so.' Mr Murray took the hint and struggled to remember what he'd come for. 'His Majesty asked me to give you this. I believe you've been expecting it.'

Luciano del Santi accepted the folded and sealed document and turned it over in his hands. 'Yes.'

'Good. Well, I expect you know what it is, then.'

'One lives in hope, Mr Murray . . . but it is never wise to be too hasty. Will you take a glass of wine while I examine it?'

'Why not?' said Will insouciantly. 'I'm in no hurry and someone – I forget who – told me that you keep a damned fine cellar. Well – it stands to reason that you would, doesn't it? After all, if you can't afford the best, who can?'

The Italian barely heard him. Having poured the wine and handed it to his guest, he walked away to the window; and there, above the noise and bustle of the busy street, he drew a long, slightly unsteady breath and shattered the royal seal to unfold several tightly scripted pages. The first glance told him that the thing was a copy, but he had expected that. What he had not expected, as he skimmed steadily through it, was that it should tell him precisely nothing.

He reached the end and, leaden with disappointment, turned back to the beginning in the frail hope that he'd missed something. But no. According to the document in his hand, Alessandro Falcieri had been arrested on suspicion of conspiracy and a search of his home had produced numerous incriminating letters from his fellow-plotters, none of whom could be found. He had been confronted with the evidence of his perfidy and eventually confessed to master-minding a plan to murder the King on the very day of his coronation. The court had therefore found him guilty of high treason and sentenced him to be hung, drawn and quartered.

And that was it. No names, no dates, no details. Just the bare bones of the case set down in the manner of something which had happened before man's memory. As a record of the workings of a court of law it was laughable; and to the man whose father had been at the centre of it, it was no use at all.

Luciano turned slowly to look across at Will Murray. 'Someone,' he said crisply, 'must take me for a fool. This . . . farrago . . . is not worth the paper it's written on.'

'Isn't it?' Mr Murray appeared neither surprised nor dismayed. 'Well, I can't help that. What were you expecting?'

'The truth. This, however, is not even a convincing lie.'

Will sighed, drank the last of his wine and stood up. 'Not having been privileged to read it myself, I'll have to take your word for that. But to save time, I'll tell you what I *do* know.'

'Which is?'

'That what you've got there is all there is.'

The hard mouth curled into something that ought to have been a smile but wasn't. 'Indeed? You'll have to forgive me if I say I don't believe you.'

'Well, that's up to you, isn't it? All I know is that His Majesty isn't trying to cheat you. After all, why should he? You asked to see the records of some old trial or other and he sent for them. I was in the room when he read them, if you really want to know. And his reaction wasn't that much different from yours.' Mr Murray picked up his hat and hesitated for a moment, turning it round and round between his fingers. Then, on a faint explosion of breath, he said, 'Look. The situation's fairly simple. The King doesn't remember the case himself and, if you think about it, you'll have to agree that's reasonable enough. In those days, Buckingham handled just about everything, and like as not he handled this too. Now it looks as though he may have suppressed the original trial record in favour of the one you've got there – but he's dead so we can't ask him.'

'How very convenient.'

'It's not convenient at all. It's just the way things are,' snapped Will, coming to the end of his patience. 'I'm sorry if you don't like it. But His Majesty – in case you hadn't realised it – has more important things to worry about. Good-day.'

He had been gone for several minutes before Luciano stirred himself to walk almost aimlessly to the hearth and gaze down into the fire.

'Hell,' he said bitterly, 'and damnation. Why is everything always so bloody difficult?'

Two

At Thorne Ash the weather worsened, bringing icy blasts and flurries of snow. Christmas came but Richard did not and so, although Dorothy arranged all the normal festivities, it was a tame affair which only Amy – due to having a susceptible young man in the house – enjoyed as much as usual.

The gentleman had arrived from Dublin with a letter for Dorothy from her brother, Ivo Courtenay, and been prevented from completing a cycle of such deliveries by the state of the roads. Red Irish and Catholic, Daniel O'Flaherty was possessed of a wide grin and quantities of easy charm – and Amy stalked him with a relentless vigour which he, being good-natured, was more than ready to meet half-way. Within three days of his arrival they were regularly encountering one another by chance in deserted corridors and, in just over a week, had progressed to less random assignations in the linen-closet.

Celia might have enjoyed the festival had she not started feeling queasy on the morning of Christmas Eve. She put it down to the previous day's fish and, when the process was repeated next day, ascribed it to the venison patties. By Twelfth Night she'd blamed everything from candied cherries to the October ale and was slowly coming face to face with a truth which ought to have been welcome but wasn't.

She kept it successfully to herself until Eden awoke one morning to find her retching at the wash-stand. And then his swift concerned inquiry released a pent-up storm that surprised her as much as it did him.

'No, I'm *not* all right!' she snapped, pushing back her hair to glare at him. 'And I'll get a whole lot worse before I'm better. I'm going to have a baby.'

Half out of bed, Eden took several seconds to take it in; and then an expression of mingled joy and wonder crept into his eyes. Rising, he moved towards her, holding out his hands and saying, 'Celia – sweetheart, that's wonderful!'

'Wonderful for you, no doubt. *You* don't have to go round getting fatter and uglier every day. All you have to do is accept everybody's congratulations.'

Her first words had checked him half-way across the floor. But he could not believe she meant it so he said, on a tremor of laughter, 'My heart, nothing in this world could make you look ugly. Ever.'

'This can! In a little while none of my clothes will fit—'

'Then you'll order new ones.'

'And I'll be shapeless and – and matronly. And my waist will never be the same again – never!'

A faint frown contracted Eden's brow. 'And if it isn't . . . won't it be worth it? This is our very own baby we're talking about. Yours and mine. You want children, don't you?'

Something in his tone stopped her. She drew a short, sharp breath and made a terrible discovery. The truth was that she hadn't the slightest desire to have children – now or ever; but because everyone took it for granted that all women automatically wanted to be mothers, she couldn't possibly say so. For a moment, pure rebellion seethed inside her and then, realising that she had to make some sort of answer, she said sulkily, 'Yes. I – oh yes. I suppose so. But not yet! We've scarcely been married two months and I wanted to go to London this spring. It's all spoiled now: even if we go, I'll look like a pumpkin. I'm young, Eden! I want to have some fun before I have to become dowdy and fat and be smothered with screaming brats.'

'And so you shall,' he promised. 'But not this year. It's not so great a sacrifice, surely?'

163

'Yes it is. I want to see Francis and Father – and all my friends at Court. It isn't *fair*!'

There was a long silence and finally Eden said slowly, 'I see. Aren't you even the tiniest bit pleased?'

The glance she sent him was one of faintly apprehensive defiance. 'No. I'm not. And it's no good pretending I am. Oh, I daresay I may feel differently after it's born . . . but till then the best I can do is to put up with it.'

'I'm afraid,' said Eden in a gentle tone which accorded ill with the frozen hurt in his eyes, 'that may not be enough. You may say what you choose to me. But I'd be glad if you could manage just a small show of pleasure in front of the family – mainly to preserve yourself from appearing childishly selfish.'

Celia flushed and twisted her hands together. It was the nearest he had ever come to criticising her and although she was dimly aware that she probably deserved it, his coolness was alarming. She said, 'I – I don't mean to be selfish. I just think you might try to understand a little.'

'I do understand. I can even sympathise to a degree. I'm sorry you feel all your pleasure is to be spoiled. I'm even sorrier you can't welcome our child – and I hope that, once you get used to the idea, you'll change your mind. But in the meantime I think we should delay making a grand announcement until you're more ready to accept everyone's good wishes gracefully.'

'Yes.' She looked doubtfully at him. 'Are you . . . you're not angry with me, are you?'

'No.' His smile was bleak and slightly awry. 'I'm not angry.'

'Good. And at least you're pleased about the baby.'

His brows rose. 'I'd an idea that my feelings in the matter were superfluous. But since you ask . . . yes, I'm pleased – and would be more so if you were too. The fact that you're not does rather tend to take the gloss off, you know. And now, if you'll excuse me, I'll go and dress. I've a number of things to do today.'

And for the first time ever, he walked away without either kissing her or giving her a chance to reply.

It could not be called a quarrel, but it did bring about a certain air of tension. Celia allowed it to last for three days whilst she progressed from angry resentment to nervous insecurity; and then she flung herself tearfully into Eden's arms, uttered a string of incoherent excuses and vowed she'd die if he didn't promise to go on loving her. It was, of course, a master-stroke against which he had no defence whatsoever. He smoothed her hair, told her he worshipped her, and swore he'd take her to Paris the following year. Next morning they told the family their news and Celia, finding herself the centre of everyone's attention, tried to tell herself that having a baby might not be the end of the world after all.

January became February and the weather showed no sign of improving. Letters from Richard ceased completely and the only news to arrive at Thorne Ash was that which Eden managed to glean in Banbury. It was rumoured that Lord Keeper Finch – that unpopular gentleman who Lord Falkland said had 'prostituted his own conscience and had the keeping of the King's' – had escaped impeachment by fleeing to Holland; but Archbishop Laud – less quick or less cowardly – was apparently in the Tower.

Mr Pym and the Parliament, meanwhile, were continuing to attack both His Majesty's policies and his position. They had taken charge of the royal revenues and ordered the customs officials to put no more money into the King's coffers than was needed to pay the daily expenses of his household, an innovation which Eden said was probably a good thing but which his mother found faintly shocking. They had also seemingly ordered all Papist officers to resign from the army and taken command of it away from Strafford in order to give it to the Earl of Essex.

'Essex?' said Daniel O'Flaherty. 'Sure and isn't he the one they call the Great Cuckold?'

'He is,' replied Eden defensively. 'But poor taste in women doesn't necessarily mean the fellow's a bad soldier.'

'Ah. Well . . . you'd know best, I daresay,' came the peaceful response. 'The only thing I know is that Black Tom – my lord Strafford, that is – has done a lot of good for the

Irish. And a lesser man, so Mr Ivo would tell you, will not be holding Ireland at all.' He smiled cheerfully. 'I hope your busy Parliament finds the time to remember it.'

If they did, the garbled and fragmentary news did not reflect it. Rumour said that the Princess Elizabeth – or perhaps the Princess Mary – was to marry the twelve-year-old Prince of Orange; Sir Edward Littleton had replaced Finch as Lord Keeper, and Pym's friend, Oliver St John, was the new Solicitor-General. Bishops had been – or would be or might be – abolished; and the Commons, having brought in the glaziers to make Westminster Hall less draughty, was now debating something called the Triennial Bill which meant that it must sit every three years.

All of this provoked much discussion at Thorne Ash but no change in routine. Frost hardened the roads but Danny, having developed a fortuitous ague, did not take advantage of it to ride to London with the letters he was supposed to deliver to the Earl of Tyrone's nephew. He remained, instead, to effect an unhurried recovery and resume his clandestine meetings with Amy. In his more sober moments, he sometimes wondered exactly where these were leading and what would happen if they were caught; but his nature was too sanguine for this to cause undue concern . . . and anyway it passed the time something wonderful.

Amy, with her ears full of Danny's blandishments, decided that it was a pity he was Irish – for who wanted to bury oneself amongst the peat-bogs? But while she waited for the kind of husband who could provide her with sable muffs and ruby rings, there seemed no reason why she shouldn't amuse herself in a manner as exciting as it was instructive.

It was her misfortune that she couldn't help assuming an air of mysterious smugness which Kate interpreted without any difficulty at all and which eventually, after listening to Mr Cresswell and Good-wife Flossing, brought her to say, 'Amy. If you must flirt with Mr O'Flaherty, do *try* to do it like a lady.'

Amy's jaw dropped. 'Wh-what?'

'The linen-cupboard. It's vulgar and it annoys Flossie. Also, although she's as yet only complaining of unexplained disarray, she's bound to catch you sooner or later. Or Nathan will. *He*, by the way, is on the verge of speaking to Mother about the number of lessons you've been missing. And do you *want* that young man to take you for a wanton?'

'He doesn't! He won't.'

'No? Oh well . . . perhaps things are different in Ireland.' Kate sighed. 'You're playing with fire, you know.'

'No, I'm not. I know exactly what I'm doing. I shan't let him make love to me and I shan't elope with him either.'

'I know that. He hasn't enough money, has he? But you might try remembering that he works for Uncle Ivo and that he could lose his position over this. Also, the only excuse for what you're doing is that you love him. But you don't, do you?'

'In a way I do. But I want pretty things and a house in London. I think Celia was quite mad to have Eden when she could have married Cyrus Winter and had a position at Court.'

'Quite,' said Kate sardonically. 'But if you don't want to marry Danny, you'll have to stop lurking in the linen-cupboard – or anywhere else, for that matter. Otherwise I'll tell Mother.'

'No! Don't do that!' begged Amy, alarmed. 'I won't do it again. I promise. There. Are you happy now?'

'Not particularly,' said Kate. 'But it's a start.'

Still inwardly railing against the inescapable fact of her pregnancy, Celia started to carp gently about the amount of time Eden spent overseeing the estate.

'I don't know why you have to do so much,' she said fretfully. 'That tedious Cresswell person seems to know about everything – so why can't you let him do more? He's always offering.'

'I know.' Eden frowned slightly. 'But he spends too much time in Banbury consorting with the Puritans for my liking . . . and then he comes back to spread his zeal amongst our tenants and harangue Parson Fletcher about purifying the church.'

'So?' Celia finished braiding her hair for the night and subjected her face to careful scrutiny. 'What harm can that do?'

'A lot. By and large, the older people hold by the traditional values; but a surprising number of the younger men are beginning to absorb Nathan's outlandish ideas – and I could name no less than three families who've stopped attending church in order to worship in what they call a less idolatrous fashion. I've even a suspicion that it's Nathan who leads their services.'

Yawning a little, Celia forsook her mirror and slid into bed. 'Then forbid him.'

'I've tried – but it's not that easy. He merely tells me that a man must keep his own conscience and do the Lord's work as best he can. Goodness knows I've no particular aversion to Puritans in general. But one or two of them look to me to be fanatics – and I don't want that kind of thing rearing its head here. That's why I'm restricting Nathan's activities about the estate and doing things myself. Do you understand?'

'Mm.' No longer really listening, Celia continued to investigate the contours of her abdomen. 'The baby doesn't show at all yet, does it? I believe I'll be able to ride for two or three months longer. When we get a fine day, will you take me to visit the Drydens? I'd like to pay a few calls before I start to look dreadful.'

Eden placed his hand between hers. 'Which you never will. How many times must I tell you?'

'Twice a day and thrice on Sundays.' She turned to twine satiny arms about his neck. 'Do you love me?'

'It's marginal,' replied Eden, his breath faintly ragged. 'But I believe you might say so.'

'And you'll take me to Canon's Ashby?'

'Yes.' His mouth hovered over hers. 'To the moon, if you like.'

Nathan Cresswell had always viewed the world with subconscious disapproval. This stemmed largely from being born into a family whose declining finances were in direct proportion to its increasing number of offspring. The Cresswells had once been one of Warwick's more comfortably off and well-respected families; but by the time Nathan was twenty, he had five brothers and four sisters and could recite the catalogue of his father's unlucky investments to music. He had also come to dislike his father's partiality for the bottle, his mother's addiction to bright colours and the noisy cheerfulness of his siblings. In short, he found them feckless, Godless and vulgar and was at odds with them one and all.

Then he had come to Thorne Ash and life had taken a turn for the better. Richard Maxwell, who was his second cousin once removed, had never treated him like a poor relation, and Dorothy was never less than courteous. Of course he thought them foolishly lax in their dealings with their children, but he had enjoyed his brief moments of power managing the estate in Richard's absence. Best of all, he'd made friends in the town and, for the first time in his life, known the comfort of being among men who thought as he did; men who saw the evil in the world with a clearer eye even than his and who did not scruple to say so. And through them Nathan discovered that the disapproval he had always striven to hide was not at all odd. It was right.

He learned to channel it and found that, by doing so, he earned a position of influence among his new friends. He spoke against bishops and all their works, against lewdness, idolatry and Sunday football. And he was just beginning to see the fruit of his labours when Eden Maxwell stepped in to stem his progress.

Nathan took his frustrations to his friends in Banbury and returned with renewed resolution. There was corruption in the house and it was up to him to drive it out. Eden's wife was wholly eaten up with vanity, Amy was becoming immodest as any whore, and an accursed Papist lay nightly beneath the roof. Of them all, only Kate seemed truly worth saving, for there was an austerity in her that appealed to him. He determined to do his best.

Returning one evening from the home of his friend,

Jonas Radford, Nathan found himself forced to stable his horse himself. This was not unusual, for the servants had a habit of either misconstruing his orders or eluding them altogether. But one day, decided Nathan as he set about unsaddling his mare, one day they shall attend to me and I will not be mocked.

A sound caught his ear. The soft, unmistakable sound of feminine laughter. Nathan laid down his cloth and turned his head to listen. It came again from somewhere above him and, silently, he moved towards the ladder. Cousin Richard's servants were not only impertinent – they were lascivious. He climbed quietly, hoping that one of the miscreants above was Tom Tripp. He would enjoy seeing that young oaf discomfited – or, better still, dismissed.

It was not Tom Tripp. It was even better. Nathan remained poised on the ladder, his head just above the level of the loft floor, taking in Amy's tumbled hair and the Irishman's hand at her half-unlaced bodice. They were quite unaware of his presence and he took his time, absorbing the languor of Amy's expression and the way her hands slid knowingly between the fastenings of her Papist lover's shirt. Then he pounced.

'It's my fault,' said Kate when the shouting had stopped and a sobbing Amy had been taken upstairs by Celia. 'I should have known she wouldn't keep her word. When does she ever? It's my fault and I'm sorry. I should have told you.'

Wearily, Dorothy shook her head and then regretted it. Her temples were pounding. 'You did what you thought best. If anyone is to blame, it is I. She hasn't had a thought outside her body since she was ten and we've always known we'd have to find her a husband before any harm was done. But she's not sixteen till next week. How can she have been so *stupid*?'

'Easily,' said Eden dryly. 'And how fortunate it is that Nathan should have caught her. It's just a pity he couldn't have been a bit more discreet about it.'

'I am but an instrument of the Lord,' returned Nathan.

'He directeth my footsteps and also my ears so that I may do His work and offer His counsel.'

'His – or yours?'

'Pride goeth before destruction and a haughty spirit before a fall,' observed Mr Cresswell reprovingly. 'The brand of the Lord God's displeasure is on this land and the time is coming when those who have wilfully turned their eyes from the Light shall be winnowed out.' He turned his burning gaze to Kate. 'There has been evil idolatry in this house for many months now. You must shun it as you would the plague.'

'If you're talking about Amy, I can't possibly shun her,' said Kate prosaically. 'And if you mean Mr O'Flaherty's religion, it's harmed none of us and has nothing to do with the present problem.'

'It is an abomination in the eyes of the Lord! He that toucheth pitch shall be defiled therewith.'

'Oh that's enough!' said Eden, a spark of temper lighting his eyes. 'You found Amy doing what she'd no business to be doing and have brought it to our attention. For the rest, you may go keep your own conscience and reserve your sermons for your sectarian friends. In short, from this point on, I believe we can dispense with your presence. Goodnight.'

An unpleasant gleam showed briefly in the pale eyes and was gone. 'As you wish, cousin. But I shall pray that you may comprehend the damage you do with your misguided notions of what is proper.'

The door closed softly behind him but it was several seconds before anyone spoke. Then Eden looked across to the furthest corner of the room where Danny still sat, white-faced and shaking, and said, 'It's time, I suppose, that we asked you how far this has gone. We've heard – indeed the whole house has heard – what Amy says. The unfortunate part is that, being Amy, we don't know whether we can believe her.'

Mr O'Flaherty rose and tried to assemble the remnants of his dignity. Then he said earnestly, 'You can. It's true enough I've been a great daft fool – but I've not seduced

171

your sister. And I'll swear to that on the holy cross or the grave of my mother or anything else you like.'

There was a long silence while Kate, Dorothy and Eden all eyed him thoughtfully. Finally Dorothy said, 'I think I believe you. But why did you do it? You must have known the trouble it would cause.'

Daniel bent his head and stared penitently at the floor.

'You heard him,' said Eden. 'He's a great daft fool – and he just couldn't resist the opportunity. If he'd had any sense, he'd have been off to Dan O'Neill while the going was good.'

The Irishman met his gaze slowly. 'You're right. And Mr Ivo will fillet and bread me, so he will.'

'If,' said Kate slowly, 'he's told.'

'Quite.' Dorothy caught and held the stunned blue gaze of her brother's messenger. 'But I think it would be best for all concerned if you left here. Quickly.'

February became March and, in London, Richard watched the Triennial Bill become law while the House continued to prepare for the opening of Strafford's trial on the 22nd. It compiled twenty-eight articles of impeachment – sixteen of which were aimed at the Earl's Irish policies – and then allowed the entire indictment to be printed on a broadsheet so it could be read by the public at large. Meanwhile, crushed by the responsibility of trying to deal with the rising opposition in Dublin, acting Lord-Deputy Wandesford succumbed to chill and died.

It was this, when he heard of it, that caused Richard to devote a little time pondering the Irish question and eventually, towards the end of the month, to discuss the matter over dinner with Luciano del Santi.

'I suspect,' he said at length, 'that there's going to be trouble. The Irish seem to have supported Strafford because he offered the best hope of curtailing the sale of land to English profiteers. So the burning question now, I suppose, is what line his successor will take.'

'Quite. The word in the City is that the Earl of Ormonde has been suggested – but that he'll be rejected in favour of someone less likely to provoke Lord Cork and his merry band of speculators.' The Italian's dark eyes met his friend's grey ones. 'Do you understand Irish politics?'

'Does anyone? What little I know comes from the infrequent bulletins Dolly's brother sends us. He's served under Strafford for the last couple of years – and has presumably stayed on in Ireland to try and hold things together.'

'Yes? Then I hope, for his sake, that he is well paid,' came the arid response. Then, 'We spoke some time ago of Strafford and you declined to comment. What is your opinion now?'

Richard's expression grew grave and, folding his arms, he let his chin sink on to his chest. 'I don't know. I think he may be sincere according to his lights . . . and he certainly doesn't look like Black Tom Tyrant any more.'

'No. He looks like a sick old man.'

'You've been to the trial?'

'Yesterday. I shan't go again. I've seen what I wished to see, and not even for the pleasure of hearing more of Strafford's quite masterly defence will I spend another hour on the public benches, squashed between red-faced fellows swilling ale, eating onions and relieving themselves on the floor.'

Richard nodded slowly but it was a long time before he spoke. Finally, he said, 'You admire Strafford?'

'I admire precision. I admire the ability to eschew rodomontade and stick to the facts. Yes, I think it's fair to say that I admire him. Certainly I wish him well.' He paused, smiling sardonically. 'I rather enjoyed seeing the credibility of the prosecution witnesses reduced to pulp. But it can't last, of course. I'm sure Pym has something better up his sleeve.'

'He has.' Richard stared carefully into space. 'Secretary Vane has been a mite careless with his papers.'

There was a long silence. 'Let me guess,' said the Italian with heavy irony. 'Harry Vane the younger – that well-known, fire-breathing Puritan – has been rifling through his father's drawers. Yes?'

'Yes.'

'And?'

'And, according to the notes of a Privy Council meeting held in May of last year, Strafford suggested raising "an army in Ireland you may employ here to reduce this kingdom".'

Luciano del Santi appeared supremely unimpressed. 'Which kingdom?' he asked calmly.

'Well, that is what you might call the crux of the matter. We all knew about the army Strafford was raising to fight the Scots. But what if there had also been some idea of using it here? What then?'

'Are you seriously asking me that question?'

'Yes.'

'Then either Pym's a cleverer man than I took him for – or you are a bigger fool,' came the uncompromising reply. 'Do you really suppose that if the King was planning to unleash an Irish army on the undutiful English there would be a record of it in Council? And any dozen words quoted out of context can be made to sound incriminating. You know that. But your problem is that you also know what will happen if Strafford is allowed to resume his position at the King's side. However . . . if you're going to help destroy the man, at least acknowledge why – and for God's sake don't try placating your conscience with sanctimonious clap-trap. It's not worthy of you.'

For a long time Richard stared at him without speaking. Then he said gently, 'How old are you?'

Amusement and perfect comprehension touched the sculpted face. 'Nearly twenty-five.'

'God help us, then, when you're thirty,' remarked Richard feelingly. 'All right. The truth is that Strafford needs to be removed but I don't like the way it's being done. On the other hand, because I put my country before the life of any one man, I'm unlikely to lift a finger to save him. Is that better?'

'It is, at least, honest.'

'You set great store by that, don't you?'

The dark brows rose. 'It surprises you?'

'No – not exactly. It makes me wonder why.'

174

The Italian laughed with an odd mixture of mockery and reluctance and reached out to pick up his glass. Green fire flared from the great emerald on his hand and, idly watching it, Richard wondered how much he had drunk – how much they had both drunk. He himself felt pleasantly mellow and, though the black eyes held a gleam of something he could not quite name, del Santi did not look cup-shot either. But at the back of his mind lurked the suspicion that they had somehow or other arrived at a sort of crossroads – one from which there would be no going back. He refilled his glass and waited.

'You wonder why?' came the eventual response. 'Of course you do. There's a reason for everything, isn't there? A reason for everything we do and are. And a reason why – against every sensible tenet I've ever held – I'm now obliged to take you a little way into my confidence.' He smiled wryly. 'There's a compliment in that. I always swore I'd never trust an Englishman. And, to be frank, I don't trust many people at all. Next to love, trust is probably the most dangerous condition known to man – and as such is best restricted. So I trust Giacomo who has known me since I was sixteen, and Selim to whom I owe my life; and now you . . . of whom, unfortunately, I must ask a favour.'

'I see,' said Richard neutrally. 'Regarding what?'

'My sister. In three weeks' time I leave for Genoa. I go there every year in April to acquit a financial obligation to my uncle. I can't take Gianetta with me – and I can't leave her here because Giacomo can't cope with her and Selim travels with me. So I wondered if you might possibly be good enough . . .' He stopped, plainly finding it hard to ask.

'To take her off your hands and place her in safe-keeping at Thorne Ash?' finished Richard kindly.

'Yes. It's not a small thing, I know . . . but there's no one else I can ask. And at least she's stopped throwing things.'

'I'm glad to hear it. Dolly will want a written guarantee against damages.'

'She shall have it.'

'In triplicate. Very well. How soon would you care to deliver Mistress Gianetta? Or are you hoping that I'll do it for you?'

Luciano's smile held a hint of tension.

'I hadn't thought that far ahead. First, there are other things I ought to tell you – because if I don't certain things Gianetta may say will puzzle you.'

'Ah.'

'Quite. To begin with, she wants to force me into returning her to my uncle in Genoa so that she can marry his youngest son. I've no intention of doing so – nor would my uncle wish it. Like me, he's fully conscious that – he and my father having married a pair of sisters – the degree of relationship between their children is too strong to admit marriage. Gianetta, however, can't accept that, having indulged her every whim since she was five years old, and taught her to look on me as part of the hired help, our uncle can't be brought round her thumb this time. Consequently I'm the villain of the piece – and seem destined to remain so.' He paused and sipped his wine. 'And that's why I have to tell you a long and not particularly edifying tale about the ability of English law to do a man to death on the strength of his nationality and religion.'

The room seemed suddenly airless and Richard set down his glass, aware that a turning point was upon him and that he wasn't sure he wanted it. He said, 'I think you'd better start at the beginning.'

'Yes.' A faint frown entered the Italian's eyes and he gazed down into the ruby liquid in his glass. 'After so long, it's hard to know where to start – or how to make you believe me. But in the end I suppose the most I can hope for is that you'll listen.'

'I'll listen. Where does your story start?'

'It starts here in London in the summer of 1615, when a young man left Genoa with his bride to set himself up as a goldsmith and money-lender in Foster Lane.' A crooked smile invested the hard mouth. 'His name was Alessandro Falcieri . . . and he was, of course, my father.'

176

Three

James Butler, twelfth Earl of Ormonde, was not made Lord-Deputy of Ireland. Instead the King hedged his bets by leaving the post vacant and appointing two sexagenarian cronies of Lord Cork to be Lord Justices with the task of governing in his name. Meanwhile, the trial of Strafford moved into its second week and the wider affairs of the nation waited on its outcome. His lordship continued to cast doubt on the validity of the prosecution – thus tickling public fancy for the first time in his career and forcing Pym to resort to the questionable evidence contained in the Privy Council notes. Secretary Vane was summoned but was no help, and other councillors flatly denied any treasonable implication; so that at the end of ten hours Pym left the hall with his stomach in disorder and black rage in his heart.

The King continued to attend the trial every day whilst simultaneously wooing his critics in the Upper House – to which end my lords Essex, Bristol, Mandeville and Saye all gained places on the Privy Council. And the Queen's Master of Horse, Harry Jermyn, did his bit to help by encouraging Will Davenant, John Suckling and Francis Langley to consider more tangible forms of action. With this in mind they combined under the leadership of George Goring and enjoyed a number of secret meetings where they swore oaths of silence and plotted to seize the Tower of London. For several weeks they scuttled about Whitehall, exchanging significant glances and almost bursting with cloak-and-dagger excitement until Goring gradually realised that their doings had not passed unnoticed and decided to disassociate himself from the plot. He mentioned it casually to Lord Newport – who passed it on to Lord Mandeville – who quietly informed John Pym. Goring then left Suckling, Davenant and Francis to their own devices and slipped unobtrusively back to his post as Governor of Portsmouth.

Pym filed the information away at the back of his mind and let it lie. Still intent on proving Strafford a traitor, he reluctantly produced the copy he'd made himself of Secretary Vane's notes and handed it to the lawyer John Glyn. He knew, of course, that it was far from ideal – but it was all he had.

Glyn did his best. It wasn't his fault that, as soon as he announced new evidence, Strafford instantly obtained leave to call new witnesses. Anxious to stick to the point, Glyn offered to abandon his new evidence if Strafford would do likewise with his witnesses. This was a mistake. The hall erupted into a tumult of cat-calls and the session had to be adjourned before the prosecution could be made to look any more ridiculous than it already did. Even the King was seen to be laughing.

Without lingering to speak to any of his colleagues, Richard Maxwell fought his way through the crush and into the blessedly clean air above Westminster Stairs. Then he hailed a waterman and, a short time later, was facing Luciano del Santi across a bench in the workshop.

'Tomorrow,' he said tersely. 'I've had enough and I'm taking a few days' leave of absence. I'll make an early start in the morning and, if Mistress Gianetta can be ready by then, I'll take her with me.'

The Italian's eyes remained characteristically impassive. 'She'll be ready. I'll see to it personally.'

'Good. Then we'll go an hour after it's light. In fact, it might look better if you came too – not to mention the need we have to come up with a convincing story.'

'For whom?'

'Eden and Kate, mostly. Unless you're prepared to trust them with the truth as well?'

'No.' The word was soft but implacable.

'I thought not. Of course, you may be lucky. Your sister may not say anything untoward. But I wouldn't care to rely on it.'

'Neither would I.'

'So you'll come?'

'Have I a choice?' asked Luciano with faint acidity. And then, 'You're very abrasive today. The impeachment?'

'What else?' said Richard. 'I can put up with failure. What I *don't* like is a bloody shambles.'

'So you're going home.'

'Yes. And if you've any opinions on the subject, I'd be glad if you'd keep them to yourself. Right now, there's only one matter on which we're likely to agree.'

'And that is?'

'The court-room,' said Richard. 'It stinks.'

They reached Thorne Ash just before dark on Monday evening: Gianetta, her maid and a mountain of luggage in the carriage, and her brother attended by Selim, together with Richard and his groom on horseback. It was Kate, sitting at the window, who saw them first and, rising swiftly, said, 'My goodness – it's Father!'

Only Amy was stricken silent. Everyone else exclaimed with pleased astonishment.

'Richard?' said Dorothy. 'Are you sure?'

'Yes.' Still hovering by the window, Kate's hand suddenly clenched hard on the latch. 'And he's brought Luciano del Santi with him.' She turned slowly to look at Eden. 'And Luciano del Santi's sister – and the private assassin.'

Eden grinned.

'Then we'd better lock up the maidservants. Perhaps Mother ought to—'

But Dorothy was no longer there to hear him. She was already out through the hall and running across the court-yard to throw herself into her husband's arms.

It was much later, when the travellers had been fed and a distinctly prickly Gianetta settled into the best spare bedchamber, that Richard lay with his fingers twined in his wife's hair and said, 'Out of the thousand or so things I have to tell you, only one seems important.'

She smiled at him. 'I know. And I love you too.'

'Then you'll know what I'm about to ask.'

'Yes. You want me to come to London.' She searched his eyes for the trouble that had been there earlier and found that it had lessened. 'Is it just the trial?'

'*Just* the trial? No, my darling – it's not just the trial. It's spending five months of the year away from you and everything here and being still without any prospect of release. My esteemed colleagues are preparing a bill stating that Parliament can only be dissolved by its own consent. If it gets through, the House will sit forever.'

'You could resign your seat,' she said, knowing he would not.

'In the end, I may have to.' He paused. 'Sometimes I wonder where it's all leading. The Scots army is still in the north; there's unrest in Ireland over the distribution of land, and discontent here over everything from trade to football. And what are we doing about it? We're putting all our efforts into the removal of Strafford and the increase of our own power. But what if it can't be achieved gradually and with dignity inside the House? What if, in chasing this one dream, we bring the order of generations down like a pack of cards? Will we still have been right?'

'I don't know,' said Dorothy slowly. 'I only know that you will follow your conscience – and that, if a thing is worth having, it must be worth fighting for. You can't give up now because the path is thorny – for if you and the others like you withdraw, who will there be to moderate the extremists and speak for the ordinary folk? Who will care for the man to whom acts of Parliament are nothing so long as his family is fed and his roof secure?'

Turning, Richard propped his head on his hand, the better to look at her. Then, lightly touching her cheek, he said, 'Wise Dolly. What would I do without you? And who else would put up with a husband who brings politics to bed? I'm sorry.'

'Don't be. Not for that, anyway.' A tiny laugh rippled

through her voice. 'But you might apologise for saddling me with the signor's spoiled and overly decorated sister without so much as a word. What on earth do you expect me to do with her?'

'Hand her over to Kate,' he grinned. 'You don't mind, do you?'

'Mind? Me? Now whatever makes you think I might mind? I've got a Genoese maidservant who barely speaks English and a fellow with a nasty-looking dagger running loose in the house; I've a daughter-in-law who's pregnant, a tutor-cum-steward who's turned Puritan, and I've to play hostess to a sulky Italian child and a diabolically beautiful young man whose cleverness and icy restraint I find frankly terrifying. But it could be worse, I suppose. At least we're rid of Ivo's Irishman.' She stopped and drew a long breath. 'Which brings me to the thing I've been putting off telling you about Amy.'

'Sufficient unto the day is the evil thereof,' said Richard. 'As it happens, I've something to tell you about your diabolical young man, too. But, at the moment, my mind is on other things.'

'Again?' murmured Dorothy wickedly.

'Again,' he agreed, against her mouth. 'It's amazing what a five-month separation can do – even at my age.'

By noon next day, however, with Eden's worries about Nathan Cresswell and the tale of Amy's misconduct ringing in his ears, Richard began to wonder if he might not have done better to remain in Westminster.

'You're sure,' he asked wearily of Dorothy after sending a sobbing Amy once more back to her room, 'that no real harm was done?'

'As sure as I can be – yes. That's why I sent the foolish boy packing.'

'Mm. Well, you could hardly keep him here under lock and key, could you? But the trouble is that we can't let some unsuspecting family take Amy to their bosoms if she's—'

'I know. But she isn't. Yet.'

Richard looked at the ceiling and swore quietly. 'Then we'd better find her a husband – after which, it's just a question of hoping for the best.'

'Quite. So who do we know? Someone kind and sensible who prefers looks to brains would be nice.'

Richard grinned ruefully. 'You don't want much, do you?'

'Well, she may be a troublesome baggage but she's still our daughter,' she sighed. 'Otherwise I'd ask if your alarming friend might be interested.'

'Luciano?' He gave an involuntary choke of laughter. 'God, no!'

'No. Of course, Amy is so impressed by the signorina's jewels that she'd probably be willing to overlook the fact that she finds that shoulder of his repellent . . . but then she doesn't know what *we* know, does she?'

Richard eyed her thoughtfully. He'd given her a skeletal version of the story Luciano had told him and watched her making the obvious deductions. Now, feeling that it was time to bring it into the open, he said, 'What is it that's worrying you? Felix?'

'Well, of course. You can't believe any more than I do that the signor has set himself up under a name that isn't exactly his own purely in order to earn a simple crust. Another man might do so – but not him. He's too clever for his own good. And I don't want Felix mixed up in his little games.'

'He won't be.'

'Meaning that you'll see to it that he isn't?'

'If necessary. What's the matter? Don't you trust my judgement?'

The tawny-green eyes encompassed him and seemed to refocus. She said simply, 'I'm sorry. I must be on edge. I know how rarely you're wrong about people. But in this case I just can't understand why you like him so much.'

'To be perfectly truthful, neither can I.' He smiled at her. 'But there's one thing you may be certain of. Nothing he does will ever hurt anyone in this family because he places far too high a value on his connection with us to let it. And now I suggest that we forget him. He'll not be with us for long . . . and the problem of what to do with Amy is undeniably more pressing.'

'True. But I've thought and thought – and I can't come up with any possibilities at all,' she said gloomily. 'Haven't any of your colleagues got an eligible son?'

'I can't say I've ever asked them,' he began humorously. And then stopped, an arrested expression entering his eyes. 'Wait a minute. Tall, passably good-looking, roughly twenty-five years old with a good head for business; grandfather a book-binder, father a member of the Commons with an eye to social advancement, a finger in all manner of pies and a sense of humour. How does that sound?'

'Too good to be true. What's his name?'

'The son? Geoffrey Cox. I don't know him well but he seems a pleasant young man and fairly bright. Of course, he may have too much sense to take Amy – or even have an interest elsewhere. But I'll sound his father out on the matter and, if all goes well, you can bring Amy to London with you.'

Her brows rose. 'I'm coming, then?'

'Yes. If you value my sanity.'

After an evening spent avoiding Luciano del Santi and a morning making stilted conversation with his sister, Kate sent Meg off to have someone saddle her horse and slipped away to change her dress. Luck, however, did not seem to be with her; for though Tom Tripp was in the stable-yard, he had not saddled Willow because Meg had not brought him the order.

'I'll do it now, mistress,' he said with unusual curtness. 'Won't take but a minute.'

Kate followed him, frowning slightly. 'It's all right, Tom. It's not your fault. I just wanted to get away unseen if possible. Goodness knows where Meg can have got to.'

'I could make a guess,' muttered Tom.

'Well?'

'And I'll bide my time till I'm sure, if you don't mind.' He busied himself over his task. 'No need for you to bother your head, Miss Kate. No need at all. There now. Shall I come along with you?'

'No thank you. I just want an hour on my own – and you know I'll be safe enough.' Accepting his proffered hands, she swung herself up into the saddle. 'As far as you're aware, is anyone else out riding just now?'

'Yes.' His face seemed to freeze. 'That foreign friend of the master's. Took his horse out after breakfast and hasn't come back yet that I know of.'

Kate grimaced. 'That's all I need. Still . . . he could be anywhere by now so there's no reason why I should meet him.'

'No.' He eyed her shrewdly. 'Don't you like him, then?'

'I can take him,' shrugged Kate, 'or leave him.' And rode out of the yard fervently wishing it were true.

Just exactly what was true, she didn't know. That was the trouble. Since the moment she'd seen him through the window last night she'd been terrified of experiencing another horrible aberration. Fortunately, however, she hadn't. She was still more conscious of him than she liked – but no more than that, thank God. Logic dictated that the whole business of the wedding had simply produced a passing fancy – a random attraction that was unlikely ever to be repeated. After all, despite the fact that one was supposed to be all modestly virginal one minute before being catapulted into bed with someone the next, it was stupid to believe that one stepped innocently off the rainbow on one's wedding-day. And that was how come she'd been momentarily attracted to Luciano del Santi. But she'd faced up to it now and therefore there was absolutely no possibility of it happening again. None. On the other hand, she'd just as soon that their paths crossed as little as possible for there was no point at all in tempting providence.

Afterwards, she realised she ought to have known better than to trust to luck on a day when nothing had really gone right. Life, she often thought, was either blissfully trouble-free or composed of one petty irritation on top of another. Not that the sight of Luciano del Santi riding towards her was precisely petty; in her present mood it was more like

184

incipient cataclysm. Kate jerked Willow's head round in exactly the manner she'd always deplored in Celia and set her careering across the common in the opposite direction.

He chased her – and that was something else she ought to have expected. She didn't know how well he rode and wasn't going to waste time turning round to look, but she could hear his hoofbeats drumming behind her own. If he was a good enough horseman, he'd catch her. Willow was no match for the powerful black he was riding.

Damn! thought Kate. *Why can't he see he's not wanted and mind his own business?*

Her hat abandoned the struggle and went whirling away behind her, leaving her hair to fly free of its pins and stream in the wind like a banner. Deciding she'd have to know if he was gaining on her, she swivelled her head, got a mouthful of hair and discovered that he was. Rapidly.

She tried to encourage Willow to a fresh burst of speed, but it was pointless. He came gradually up behind her and then slowly but surely drew level. Kate turned her head, spat the hair out of her mouth and glared at him. He laughed. Then he reached across to grasp her bridle.

Suddenly shaking with temper, Kate struck hard at his hand with her crop. He flinched but did not release his grip; and, in no time at all, he brought both horses to a quivering stop. There was a moment's fulminating silence while furious green eyes met faintly satiric black ones. Then Kate said unsteadily, 'Well?'

'Well what?' he asked, holding out her maltreated hat.

The mere fact of his having managed to retrieve it added fuel to the fire, but she forced herself to take it without snatching and was rewarded with a sight of the bright red weal on the back of his hand. She said blightingly, 'I can only presume that either the house is burning down or someone's dying. If not, why the—' She stopped in order to control her tongue.

'Hell?' suggested Luciano del Santi, dulcetly. 'Devil?'

'Why come chasing after me?' snapped Kate. 'It must have been obvious, even to you, that I – that I prefer my own company.'

185

'Not especially.' He smiled gently. 'I thought your horse was running away with you.'

'*Nothing* runs away with me!' she said. And then, realising he'd thought no such thing, had to use her hands to push back her hair to stop herself hitting him again. 'Oh – go away, can't you? I've had my fill of Santis this morning. Or even of Falcieris.'

'Ah.' The dark eyes surveyed her thoughtfully. 'So Gianetta told you that, did she?'

'Yes. I believe her exact words were that she, Gianetta Falcieri del Santi, was unaccustomed to waiting over an hour for water to be heated for her bath and to occupying a chamber which is of utterly miserable proportions.'

'Dear me – I'm impressed. I'd no idea her English was that good.'

Kate gritted her teeth and jammed her hat back on her head.

He laughed and said, 'Lost for words, Kate? Never did I think to see the day. Haven't you even any questions?'

'No. Your insufferable sister can call herself Queen of the May and tell us all she was taken from the Grand Turk's palace by leprechauns for all I care. The only name that interests me is my own. And, as far as I'm aware, I've never given you the right to make free with it.'

'I stand rebuked.' The slight inclination of his head was a masterpiece of irony. 'As for Gianetta . . . there are two things you should bear in mind. First, that she has a strong sense of the dramatic – and second, that she was brought up by my uncle and styles herself accordingly.'

Kate shrugged and stared balefully between Willow's ears. As usual, he was using his multiple graces to emphasise her own lack of them. She knew that. She only wished he'd stop looking at her in just that way so that her nerves might have time to settle. Instead he said, 'Why did you panic just now?'

'Panic? I never panic!'

'No? Then you give a fair imitation of it.'

Kate pulled herself together and awarded him an indulgent smile. 'I know it must be difficult for you, but try to accept that I simply didn't want your company. Neither yours nor anyone else's.' Then, deciding to attack, 'Why did you bring your sister to us? You must have other friends.'

He remained perfectly unruffled and continued to survey her with mild amusement. 'That was rather a poor shot, wasn't it? You know perfectly well that I've no friends at all – or not of the sort to whom I could safely entrust Gianetta. And, rather than allow you the pleasure of making some caustic observation on the subject, I'll do it for you,' he said, as she opened her mouth to speak. 'I'm rich and not entirely unpresentable – and therefore I am tolerated. No more and no less. But I'm also a foreigner and a usurer, and the one is no more forgivable to most of your countrymen than the other. Ah – and no; I do *not* lose any sleep over it.'

'I never supposed you did,' said Kate. And then, 'You don't like us much, do you? It makes one wonder why you're here at all.'

Something cold and dangerous awoke in the black gaze and then was gone, leaving her to wonder if she had imagined it. Certainly his tone was smooth as butter as he said, 'I'm earning a living as best I may. What else? And, as for the English, I believe I'm learning to differentiate.'

'Should I be flattered? Or no. You'd have to say that, wouldn't you? After all, Mother's chancing her best glasses on your account.' She smiled sweetly. 'And now – if you don't mind – I'd like to continue my ride. Alone.'

'As you wish.' His eyes raked her face. 'Are you sure there's nothing you'd like to ask me?'

'No,' she said. And then, formless suspicion flaring in her mind: 'Don't they say, "Ask no questions and you'll be told no lies"? I assume Father knows what he's doing.'

'Precisely what do you mean by that?'

'I don't know. But I think . . . yes. I think you're worried about something Gianetta may say.' She stopped, her eyes widening as an errant thought slipped neatly into place. 'I also think you came after me in order to deliver a prepared explanation. Not the truth, of course – just a little something to satisfy my curiosity.'

The beautifully sculpted face held not a trace of expression. If she had touched on a nerve, there was nothing to show it. He simply said, 'Having declined to hear it, you'll never know, will you? But, just out of interest . . . what makes you so sure it would have been a lie?'

'Because you wouldn't have risked your neck over unfamiliar country to make me a present of the truth,' came the prompt reply. 'You never give that away at all. It's something you play games with.'

He took his time about answering her and, when he did, it was to say reflectively, 'How well you think you know me. You should beware, however, of over-simplification.'

'You would think that, of course. I've never met anyone so determined to be inscrutable.'

'Tell me,' he invited gently, his tone at distinct variance with the devil dancing in his eyes. 'Do you have other interests – or am I the only one?'

The shock of it stopped Kate's breath and sent the blood tingling into her cheeks.

'Oh – don't misunderstand me,' he continued, an infuriating smile bracketing his mouth. 'I recognise the compliment. In a few years' time when that nettle-sharp brain of yours has matured a little, I may even be able to return it. Who knows? But in the meantime you would be safer cultivating a sense of proportion and not indulging in too many frail hopes. Marriage is a cage and love exists only in poetry. And I am not for you.'

Kate stared at him, incapable of speech but intensely capable of murder. Finally and with great care, she managed to say flatly, 'Imagination and monumental conceit must run in your family. The truth, of course, is that I wouldn't touch you with a ten-foot pole.'

'You ought,' came the mocking reply, 'to have said you wouldn't marry me if I were the last man on earth. It's equally banal but at least I might just conceivably have believed it.'

'You just want the satisfaction of telling me that I won't be asked,' spat Kate. 'Do you take me for an idiot?'

'If I did, we wouldn't be having this conversation. As it

is, I'm simply attempting to provide you with two valuable lessons.' He paused and then, when she said nothing, went on smoothly, 'The first is that other people's weaknesses are useless to you until you learn to recognise your own; and the second is that you can't read me half as well as I can read you.'

'You think not?' she asked witheringly.

'I know not. For the reality, dear Kate, is that you're fast becoming petrified by the ambivalence of your emotions – and that is why you took fright just now. You're afraid to do more than scratch the surface of your mind because you don't know what you'll find.' He gave her a slow, blinding smile. 'Hoist with your own petard, as they say. But I'm sure you'll get over it.'

He left the next day for London and the long journey to Genoa. Kate did not speak to him again before he left and, even after he had gone, it was an effort to batten down her inner violence. At any other time, she would have taken the trouble to investigate Meg Bennet's suddenly doleful behaviour; now, however, she was too busy seething to give it more than a passing thought. And when Felicity tried to tell her something that Gianetta had apparently said about her brother, Kate said baldly, 'Don't, if you love me, mention that man in my hearing. The very thought of him gives me an ague!'

On the following Sunday and with a week still to go before Easter, Richard received news which effectively crushed his hopes of celebrating the festival with his family. Pym, it seemed, had renewed his attack on Strafford with a Bill of Attainder.

'I'll have to go back,' said Richard. 'There'll be a vote.'

'What's a Bill of Attainder?' asked Kate.

'It's an act of Parliament whose purpose is to preserve the safety of the state. When the courts have failed to prove a man guilty of treason, an attainder can declare him so by law. You might call it a last resort.' He stopped and looked deep into his wife's eyes. 'I know . . . But I can't, in conscience, stay away.'

'No.' She strove to keep her voice expressionless. 'Will you go today?'

'Yes. It's barely noon so I ought to get as far as Oxford.' He rose, smiling at her. 'And you'll follow after Easter with Amy?'

'You're taking Amy to London?' asked Celia, surprised and none too pleased. 'Is she to be married?'

'One can but hope,' murmured Eden. And then, 'What are you going to do with our little Italian jewel-tree?'

'Leave her here with you,' responded Dorothy promptly. 'Since the only person she's formed some sort of a relationship with is Felicity – who won't, in any case, want to spend the summer in London – it seems the obvious answer. But what about you, Kate? Will you come?'

With her own private devil safely en route for Genoa, it was too tempting to refuse. 'Yes,' said Kate lightly. 'I believe I will.'

'I wish *I* could go,' sighed Celia. 'And really, Eden, I don't see why we shouldn't. The baby won't come till August and that's ages away yet.'

'I'm sorry,' he said, as gently as he was able. 'I can't possibly go. I'm not leaving everything to Nathan's tender mercies. And—'

'But why on earth not? He can manage – and I *want* to go!'

'I know you do . . . but you know very well why I won't leave Nathan in control. I explained it all to you.'

Her face fell. Then, brightening again, she said, 'Well, there's no reason why *I* shouldn't go, is there? It would be perfectly proper, after all.'

'You don't think,' suggested Dorothy, 'that the journey might be too much for you just now?'

'Good heavens, no! Not at all.'

'Well, I do,' said Eden, finally driven into making his stand. 'And I'm afraid I'm not prepared to let you risk both yourself and the baby by spending the best part of three days rattling about in a coach.'

Celia stood up, cheeks pink with anger and eyes flashing storm signals. 'The baby is the only thing you care about. You don't think of *me* at all!'

'Oh God,' sighed Kate under her breath. 'Here we go.'

Eden rose to face his wife, a white shade bracketing his mouth. He said quietly, 'You know that's not true. But, even if it was, this isn't the time to discuss it.'

'Why not? Why *not*?' she demanded, her voice rising shrilly. 'I'm tired of being quiet and good and not having anything I want! And I'm sick of spending my days sewing or shut up in the still-room instead of visiting my friends or doing anything the least bit entertaining. Just because *you* are content to be dull is no reason why I should be so too. And if you always meant to become a farmer and stay mewed up in the country, you should have said so before we were married!'

She stopped on a tiny gasp, suddenly aware of exactly what she was saying and of the catastrophic silence all around her. Eden had no more colour to lose and Kate looked frankly disgusted. No one else, she discovered, was looking at her at all. Fright and a grain or two of shame blotted out her temper and she did the only thing possible; she burst into tears.

Richard arrived in London on Tuesday 20 April – the day on which the official recorders were busy noting that the youthful Prince of Orange had come to claim his even more youthful bride and been given the cold-shoulder by his future mother-in-law. Richard's welcome was not much warmer, for he'd returned almost twenty-four hours too late. The Commons had already cast their votes and passed the Attainder by a majority of forty-five.

'Wouldn't have made any difference if you had been here,' observed Henry Cox with gruff cynicism. 'Walk-over for the Ayes. Not that it makes any odds. Lords won't pass it. Fellow's one of 'em, ain't he?'

Upon reflection, it seemed that Mr Cox might be right. Certainly the King did not appear at all cast down by the death-threat hanging over his friend's head. He felt he had the support of the army he'd led against the Scots and which Parliament had neglected to pay – and he'd built up a nice little party of moderates in the Lords, all of whom were committed to preserving the existing order and looking forward to substantial rewards for services rendered.

So the King ordered all his loyal officers to resume their stations; and Pym countered by demanding disbandment of the eight thousand men still awaiting orders in Ireland. On Lord Bedford's advice, the King replied by offering to retire Strafford and appoint Mr Pym Chancellor of the Exchequer . . . and Mr Pym pretended to consider the bribe whilst deciding how best to say no without *appearing* to say no. Finally he repeated his demand for the disbandment of the Irish army; and watched Bedford's plan crumble to dust on the King's refusal.

In the midst of all this, Richard found time to spend a couple of pleasant evenings in the Coxes' house on Ludgate Hill. Though unmistakably merchant-class, they were neither pretentious nor vulgar and, by his second visit, Richard was satisfied enough to broach the delicate question of a possible marriage between Geoffrey and Amy.

'I'd welcome such a match and I won't pretend otherwise,' said Henry candidly. 'But Geoffrey's five-and-twenty with a mind of his own. Now, if he were to meet your lass and the two of them were to take a fancy to each other . . . well, that'd be best all round, wouldn't you say?'

'My thoughts exactly,' smiled Richard. 'A small family occasion with nothing said and no obligation on either side. Agreed?'

'Agreed.' Mr Cox held out his hand. 'And I hope we can look forward to discussing it further.'

May came in with the usual apprentice riots – in which, Richard was relieved to discover, his son Felix had *not* taken part – and the King appealed to the Lords to reject the Attainder. Pym, mindful of the failure to impeach Buckingham fifteen years before, took the precaution of introducing the bill which made it impossible for Parliament to be dissolved against its own consent. And on 2 May, the Princess Mary married William of Orange to the accompanying rumble of yet more riots.

It was at this point that Richard wrote directing Dorothy to delay her departure for a few more days. 'We are surrounded by wild rumours,' he wrote. 'Everyone is

supposedly hatching a plot; there are Papist Plots, Gunpowder Plots, Save Strafford Plots and Army Plots. So far as
I'm aware, there is truth only in the last – and we have
promised to pay the army, so that should soon be over.
But although I long to see you, I'll be happier for knowing
you are out of London at this time.'

The Commons, meanwhile, took its own measures to
calm things down by declaring its intention to defend civil
liberties – upon which the member for Cambridge immediately interceded on behalf of John Lilburne. Having been
arrested for peddling one of Dr Bastwicke's illicit pamphlets,
this extraordinary young man had transformed himself
into a public hero by having the audacity to lecture the Court
of the Star Chamber on his own rights as a free-born
Englishman. His continued imprisonment was a scandal,
said Mr Cromwell. The House agreed and sent out an order
for his release. Then it called upon the Army Plot Committee to deliver its first report – whereupon Richard Maxwell
cursed under his breath on hearing Francis Langley named.
He need not have worried, however, for Francis was found
to have vanished – along, it appeared, with Suckling and
Davenant.

It was not till after the Lords had voted on the Attainder on the 8th that Richard encountered Viscount Wroxton;
by then, Francis's flight had paled into insignificance.

'Why did you do it?' asked Richard. 'How did you come
to let it pass?'

His lordship flushed and stared at his feet. 'Bedford's
dead – and virtually half the House absented itself,' he said.
'But it won't matter. The King won't sign it. He told us
he wouldn't. So it didn't matter how we voted. Not really.'

Hearing an echo of Henry Cox's words, Richard felt a
shiver go down his back. If Strafford went to the block for
no better reason than that everybody had passed their
responsibility on to someone else, he – Richard – would
be no less culpable than the rest.

In order to push this uncomfortable thought to the back
of his mind, he set about trying to verify the bizarre tale
told to him by Luciano del Santi. Deciding that the only

place to start was with the Inns of Court, he approached three Justices and four lawyers and drew a blank with all of them. Then, just as he was beginning to wonder if the whole thing wasn't a figment of Luciano's imagination, he finally elicited a spark from John Maynard.

'Falcieri?' he said thoughtfully. 'Falcieri. Yes. An Italian, you say? Mm. The name is vaguely familiar.'

'The trial – if there was a trial – would have taken place around the time of the coronation,' said Richard. 'February or March, 1626.'

'Mm,' said Maynard. And then, 'Ah.'

'You've remembered something?'

'Perhaps. It's simply that, at the time you mention, I was assisting a lawyer who was occasionally patronised by the late Duke of Buckingham – on matters to which I was never made privy. It seems likely that, if I have heard of this Italian gentleman at all, I did so in the chambers of Samuel Fisher.' He paused consideringly. 'Yes. Fisher rose to the bench in the autumn of '26 only to fall into disfavour on the death of Buckingham. In later years I believe he became something of a recluse . . . but he may see you. Assuming, that is, that he still lives.'

'I see,' said Richard. 'Thank you.'

'Don't mention it. He had a reputation for having the sharpest legal brain in London and an ability to make a case out of anything. If you find him, let me know. We could have done with his services during the impeachment.'

Before Richard could pursue this line of inquiry, national events gathered momentum when the Bill of Attainder was put before the King. For two days His Majesty sought legal advice and spiritual counsel until the Bishop of Lincoln pointed out that he could either save Strafford or perish with him – along with his family. Then, tears in his eyes and remarking that Strafford's position was happier than his own, Charles signed.

A bare two days later, Richard stood amidst the surging crowd and watched Strafford go to his death in the bright May sunshine. And when it was over, his mind echoed not with the Earl's simple words from the scaffold, but with an earlier speech he'd made to the Commons.

'*Opinions*,' he had said, '*may make a heretic; but that they make a traitor I have never heard till now.*'

Four

Four

Once she had got over the fright of being caught in the stable-loft with Daniel O'Flaherty, Amy was speedily able to convince herself that everything had worked out for the best. She had got what she wanted – a fact that caused her spirits to rise with every passing mile on the journey to London and made her prattle non-stop. By the time they got to the house at Old Palace Yard, Dorothy's teeth were on edge and Kate was having to grip her hands together to prevent them straying to her sister's neck.

All was forgotten, however, in the warmth of Richard's welcome, and by the following day Kate was sufficiently restored to be able to set forth in a mood of mild curiosity to dine in Ludgate Hill with a family of strangers. Since Amy had been included in the invitation, it seemed logical to suppose that Father's friend Mr Cox had an eligible son, and Kate looked forward with benign interest to seeing what he and Amy made of each other.

The evening, as it turned out, was remarkably successful. Mr Cox's wife, Alison, was characterised by a fund of cheerful common sense which instantly recommended her to Dorothy; his two daughters were lively and down-to-earth enough to appeal to Kate; and his son and heir – a tall, pleasant young man, distinguished principally by an air of quiet self-possession – appeared sufficiently appreciative of Amy's attractions to satisfy everyone.

Kate watched her sister automatically setting out to enslave and grinned to herself. So long as a man had an eye on either side of his nose, you could always rely on Amy. But the interesting bit now was whether or not she had any idea of what was in the wind . . . and, if she hadn't, whether she'd presently regret tonight's work.

The answer came later on when they were preparing for bed. After chattering about the compliments Geoffrey had supposedly paid her, Amy said coolly, 'I've an idea that Father and Mr Cox may be considering a marriage between us. What do you think?'

'It's possible,' acknowledged Kate. 'Would you like that?'

'Well, it's not exactly what I had in mind. I'd hoped for someone with a position at Court. But the Coxes are quite rich and there'd be no question of having to moulder away in the country . . . so I think I might be able to resign myself to it.'

'That's nice. And can you . . . resign yourself . . . to Geoffrey?'

'Why not? He's quite attractive, after all – though not very talkative. Not that I mind that.'

'No,' said Kate with feeling. 'You wouldn't.'

Amy shot her a suspicious glance and then continued placidly braiding her hair. 'Did you see that sapphire brooch Mistress Cox was wearing? It was even bigger than the ruby one that awful Italian girl has. I expect I'd get something like that to mark our betrothal.'

'If,' suggested Kate delicately, 'there is a betrothal.'

'There will be.' Amy rose and advanced on the candle, smiling complacently. 'If I want him, I'll have him. You'll see.'

A week went by . . . and then another.

Kate celebrated her eighteenth birthday, renewed her friendship with Venetia Clifford, and kept away from Cheapside; Felix breezed in full of technical terms and a determination to have his apprenticeship formalised as soon as possible; and Amy went shopping with the younger Miss Cox, was escorted home by brother Geoffrey, and capitalised on her opportunity by seeing to it that he stayed to dine.

Richard Maxwell, meanwhile, sat quietly in the Commons

and watched his own misgivings surface in others. A new feeling was being born: a feeling that, having taken Strafford's head, they should now cease harassing the King before they destroyed the order of generations. The truth was that, grumble and criticise as they might, the King was still the King and few members wished to show disrespect for his person or see his authority completely overthrown. Pym, on the other hand, appeared intent on doing both and, for the first time since Parliament had opened, voices began to be raised in opposition. The King, it was pointed out, was demonstrating a new spirit of reasonableness and therefore did not deserve to have his household and its expenditure put under such minute scrutiny as Mr Pym had instigated.

Pym listened and drew his usual shrewd conclusions. The King, in his opinion, was merely trying to win support whilst casting about for the best means of strengthening his arm. It was for this and no other reason that he had so far refused to dismiss the Irish troops, was quietly courting the Scots and had begun talking about raising a force to restore his nephew, the Elector Palatine, to his lands. In short, he badly wanted an army, and once he had it the days of his moderation would be numbered. Or so Pym thought. But with his own already weakened position being further undermined by an extremist Presbyterian bill to abolish bishops 'root and branch', his first concern had to be to divert attention from it as a first move towards re-establishing his control over the House.

He therefore called for a new investigation of the so-called Army Plot. Richard sighed and hoped Francis Langley would have the sense to remain in whatever patch of heather currently harboured him. He himself already had enough to do without having to negotiate the young fool out of the Tower.

At home, his eldest daughter had uncovered other problems. Her maid, Meg Bennet, was pregnant.

'Oh God,' said Kate weakly. 'You're not, are you?'

'I only wish I wasn't!' wailed Meg. 'It were only the once, Miss Kate – and I've been praying I was mistook and that

I were only late. Only it's been well over a month, now –
and I wish I was dead!'

Feeling somewhat out of her depth, Kate repressed an
inclination to remark on the futility of this wish and said,
'You'd better tell me about it. Is the baby Tom's?'

'N-no. And I can't even pretend it is,' sniffed Meg. 'I'm
not really wicked, Miss Kate. It truly were just the once
and I never thought it could happen just like that. It don't
seem fair.'

'No. I daresay it doesn't. So who was it?'

'S-Selim. You know – the foreign gentleman's servant.'

For a long moment Kate simply stared at her. 'Hell and
damnation,' she said hollowly. 'That's all I need.'

She turned the matter over in her mind until Amy was
out of the way and she was sure of being alone with her
mother. Then, bluntly and in a tone devoid of expression,
she said, 'Meg's pregnant by the assassin. What do you
think we ought to do about it?'

Dorothy stared at her for a moment. Then, 'Pregnant
by *whom*?'

'Luciano del Santi's servant. The one with the knife. I
believe his name is Selim.'

'Oh.' Dorothy sat down. 'Of course, it *would* be him. I
ought to have listened to Eden. He kept saying it was like
cats to cat-mint.' She paused, thinking about it. 'Is she sure?'

'About the baby? Yes. And there seems no choice about
who's the father. Goodness only knows what Tom Tripp
will say.'

'That's the least of our worries.' Dorothy stood up again.
'I'd better have a word with her. And then, in preference
to worrying your father just now, I suppose I'll have to call
on your assassin.'

'You can't. He's in Genoa, guarding his master's back.
And if you're hoping he may want to marry her, I suggest
you don't depend on it. With his apparently fatal fascination, this situation can hardly be new to him; and he can't
marry them all.' Kate stopped abruptly and drew a long
breath. 'Or can he?'

'I beg your pardon?'

'I'm sorry. Something just occurred to me.' She fixed her mother with an awed green stare. 'We don't know where friend Selim comes from, do we? Supposing he's a Mussulman?'

Dorothy's own eyes widened and there was a long, yawning silence. Then she said, 'Kate – I could murder you. Why should he be any such thing?'

'I don't know – but I think we ought to get Felix to find out. Unless, that is, Meg doesn't mind ending up in a harem.'

Felix, upon being asked, produced the required information in record time.

'He's a Turk,' he announced cheerfully to Kate. 'From Constantinople. *Now* will you tell me why you want to know?'

'No,' was the brief reply. And then, 'Is that all?'

'More or less. It was pretty well a waste of time asking Giacomo. I knew it would be. He never tells you much at the best of times and, if you mention Selim, he just threatens to spit. Not that he ever does, of course.' Felix appeared to find this mildly regrettable. 'Anyway, when you want to know something, it's always better to ask Gino.'

'And did you?'

'Yes. But if you're too mean to tell me why you want to know—'

'I *can't* tell you. Nor Amy, either.'

'Oh well. Please yourself.' He paused and smiled seraphically at her. 'It's a pity, though . . . because I found out something rather interesting about Mr Santi as well. And, unlike Amy, *I* haven't got a big mouth.'

For a full minute Kate struggled with temptation. Then, in as few words as possible, she told him what he wanted to know.

'God's boots!' breathed Felix, impressed. '*Meg?*'

'Yes – Meg. And if you tell a soul, I'll—'

'I won't. Word of a Maxwell.'

'All right. So tell me what Gino said.'

Felix edged closer and lowered his voice to a conspiratorial whisper. 'He said Selim spends a lot of time at the brothel with a girl called Aysha.'

'You,' said Kate calmly, 'aren't supposed to know anything about places like that.'

'Don't be stupid. I'm not a baby, you know. And it's not just any old brothel. It sort of belongs to Mr Santi.'

'*What?*' Kate swallowed hard and pulled herself together. 'What do you mean – sort of belongs to him?'

'Gino says that he owns the house but that the – the business is run by a woman named Gwynneth.' Felix grinned and casually produced his *pièce de résistance*. 'And Gwynneth, of course, is Mr Santi's mistress.'

There was a long silence. Then Kate said sourly, 'Dear me. I don't know whether to applaud his efficiency or his originality. Or both. Have you met this lady?'

'No. But if I do, I'll tell you all about her.'

'Don't bother.' She got abruptly to her feet. 'She's bound to be a voluptuous blonde. They always are. And, really, I couldn't care less what she's like. Why should I?'

Then, after first speaking with her mother, she went off to deal a death-knell to Meg's hopes of marriage, before writing to Eden so that he could do the same for Tom Tripp.

Towards the end of the month, while the King tried to live down the Army Plot by agreeing to disband the Irish, and London seethed with rumours of a Popish Plot, Geoffrey Cox gradually became aware that his father was cherishing certain expectations. He found the concept interesting. If Richard Maxwell was considering establishing his second daughter while his first remained unwed, there was probably only one reason for it . . . but it was not a reason Geoffrey felt need cause him undue concern. Amy was young enough to be moulded by her husband, and her essential frivolity meant that she was unlikely to pry into business matters. She was, moreover, better connected than any bride he had ever hoped to have – and pretty, too. All in all, he decided coolly, she would probably suit him very well; and there was an element of pleasing irony in broaching the subject with his father as though he thought the whole thing was entirely his own idea.

Henry Cox was ecstatic and lost no time in communicating the news to Richard – who, in turn, informed his wife.

'My goodness – he didn't waste much time, did he?' was her immediate response. 'But I suppose we should just be grateful. Kate says Amy is set on having him.'

'Then perhaps we'd better let her know that she's fought a successful campaign and may now lay down her arms. I just hope Geoffrey realises what he's taking on and is up to dealing with it.'

'Those,' said Dorothy flatly, 'are my thoughts exactly.'

Amy received the glad tidings with maidenly gentility and then went off to crow over Kate.

'We're to be betrothed as soon as Father and Mr Cox have agreed terms and then married in the autumn after Celia's had the baby. Geoffrey's father has even promised to build a house for us,' she announced smugly. 'I told you I'd get him. Didn't I?'

'You certainly did,' said Kate, reluctantly laying aside her lute. 'Congratulations.'

'Thank you. Don't you mind that I'll be married first?'

'Should I?'

'Well, yes. *I* would if I were you.'

'How fortunate it is, then,' came the gentle reply, 'that you're not.'

And with that, Amy had to be content. She was less than happy about Dorothy's decision to take her back to Thorne Ash at the end of July and keep her there till a couple of weeks before the wedding – but a tongue-in-cheek remark of Kate's about absence making Geoffrey's heart grow fonder slightly softened the blow. And then the excitement of her betrothal overcame all else.

The two families congregated for the event and Kate used the opportunity to study the bridegroom-to-be. He was not, as Amy had said, talkative . . . but what he did say showed sense. And though he complimented Amy and was suitably attentive to her, Kate did not think he was in the least besotted; he looked, in fact, as though he knew precisely which side his bread was buttered.

In another quarter of the room, meanwhile, her own name was about to feature in a context that would have astounded her. Having begun by lamenting the terms of the long-delayed and recently completed peace with Scotland and referred in passing to the curious, coded letter about camels and serpents that had been intercepted between His Majesty and the Earl of Montrose, Mr Cox came slowly to the point.

'And then there's this thrice-blasted Army Plot,' he said. 'Don't think there's anything in it myself and never did. But I suppose it gives Pym a good excuse to put the Papists out of office. And that brings me to what I wanted to say to you.' He stopped, drew a long breath and met Richard's eyes. 'Since their lordships agreed that all appointments to the royal households ought to have parliamentary consent, certain members of the House have been talking about supplying the King with a list of suitable names. And one of those I've heard mentioned as a possibility is Miss Kate.'

There was a long, incredulous silence. Then, 'Kate? You can't be serious! No one in the House has clapped eyes on her.'

'Lord Brooke apparently has – and Viscount Saye and Sele.'

'Oh yes. But surely neither of them would think of—' Richard broke off and tried to suspend his instinctive disbelief. 'If this is true, how come I haven't heard about it?'

'Probably because no decisions have been made. It may all come to nothing – or they may not choose Miss Kate. I don't know. I just thought you ought to be warned, that's all.'

'In case I'd as soon not have my daughter used as a spy?'

Henry looked uncomfortable. 'I don't think there's any question of that.'

'There'd better not be,' came the grim reply. 'Because

even if I'd permit it – which I won't – my Kate would quite certainly tell them to go to perdition.'

Two days later Luciano del Santi and his Turkish servant arrived back in London and went directly to the Heart and Coin. Selim, who had no use for wine, melted discreetly away with Aysha; and Gwynneth, having poured brandy for her damnably elusive love, was left staring at the length of sapphire velvet he had placed in her hands. Finally she said tightly, 'You didn't need to bring me this.'

'I know it.'

'Then why did you?'

'Perhaps,' he suggested gently, 'as a mark of my esteem and because I thought it might give you pleasure.'

She turned slowly to face him, her eyes bitter.

'Who are you trying to fool? If that were true, you know there's only one thing I want.'

'And which I, alas, cannot give you.' He sighed and set down his glass. 'We've had this conversation before, *cara*. And, just now, I'm not in the mood to repeat it.'

'Do you think I don't know that? Or that I want to quarrel with you before you've put off your coat?'

'Then don't.'

'Easy to say! Don't you realise it's been almost three months – and that I've been frantic with worry?'

'Why? Selim was with me.'

'God in heaven!' she said violently. 'Can Selim save you from shipwreck or plague? Why can't you understand that I care what becomes of you?'

'I do understand it – and wish you cared less,' he responded dispassionately. 'Gwynneth . . . I really don't need this.'

'Don't you? And what about what *I* need?' Something seemed to snap inside her and, hurling the velvet to the floor, she shouted, 'You cold-hearted bastard . . . where the *hell* have you been till now?'

'You know where I've been – and also that I've never given you the right to catechise me.' He stood up and picked up his hat. 'Forgive me, *cara*. I'm leaving.'

Her anger fell away, leaving only hurt behind it. 'Don't go. I'm sorry.'

'So am I. But you have always known the limitations of what I have to offer.'

'Yes.' She gestured helplessly with her hands. 'But what can I do? I love you.'

He looked at her for a long time out of shuttered black eyes and then said tiredly, 'To which, of course, there is no answer whatsoever. Goodnight, my dear.'

Gwynneth watched the door close softly behind him and damned herself silently for a selfish fool. Then, as desolation welled slowly up inside her, she sank down on the bright rag rug and, gathering up the beautiful material, cradled it mutely against her cheek.

Outside in the deepening twilight, Luciano del Santi experienced a feeling of unaccustomed depression. He ought to go home to Cheapside and Giacomo and the mountain of correspondence that was doubtless waiting for him . . . but he did not want to. He had lingered a full month longer than usual in Genoa, waiting to see if his uncle would recover from the apoplexy that had smitten him – and knowing all the time that, if Vittorio died, Cousin Carlo would foreclose on him before the old man was even cold. Fortunately, it hadn't happened. Vittorio had recovered enough to resume control of his affairs and Luciano had known himself safe – this time. But it had brought home the perilous nature of the path he was treading and made him realise the need to make some speedy progress with his mission. For, if he did not complete it while Vittorio lived, the chances were that he would not be able to complete it at all.

And that was why he did not want to go home yet. For days now, his mind had been going round in circles and he was tired of it. All he wanted, he suddenly realised, was an hour's simple companionship; and there was only one place he could hope to find it.

Without stopping to think further, he turned his feet towards the river and hailed a boat.

***

205

In the house at Old Palace Yard, Richard Maxwell eyed his wife and eldest daughter with rare gravity and said, 'So there you have it. Due to the dismissal of the Catholics, there are vacancies in the Queen's household and my lords Saye and Brooke want to put forward certain suitable names to fill them. Yours, Kate, is one. And I am supposed to encourage you to accept.'

'I see,' said Kate, blankly. And then, 'No I don't. Why me? Their lordships can't have laid eyes on me more than a dozen times between them. For all they know, I could be howlingly indiscreet.'

'So long as it works in the right direction, I suspect they wouldn't mind if you were,' came the dry response. 'I have been assured, however, that you will at no time be asked to eavesdrop or carry tales . . . but for which we wouldn't be having this conversation.'

'And quite right too,' said Dorothy. 'But since you *have* been assured of it, why are you still against the idea?'

'Because I don't like the hole-in-a-corner way it's come about. If Henry hadn't enabled me to force the issue by asking, I'd probably still be in the dark.'

'Well, certainly that is very bad,' Dorothy agreed. 'But I think we can acquit Lord Brooke of wishing to serve you an ill turn. And even Lord Saye is unlikely to push you against your own good judgement. So the question we ought to be addressing is whether or not Kate is to do what they want.'

'I suppose so,' he sighed. 'Well, Kate?'

'I don't know. At the moment I'm still stunned at being asked. All I can truthfully say is that it's not something that's ever particularly appealed to me . . . but that, equally, I'm not totally against the idea.'

'Oh.' Richard looked faintly nonplussed. 'I quite thought you would be.'

Kate grinned. 'Yes. A year – or even six months – ago I'd have refused to so much as consider it.'

'So what has made the difference?'

'I'm not sure. One thing is probably Venetia. Since she's already with the Queen, it wouldn't be as if I didn't know anyone. But more importantly, I think it's that I've begun to feel the need for a change of some sort. I don't want to have spent my entire life doing nothing but sit at home. So perhaps – just for a little while – this is the answer.' She stopped and looked at her mother. 'Does that make sense?'

'Yes. Perfect sense.' Dorothy rose and walked to her husband's side. 'Look at her, Richard. And try to be objective.'

Richard looked. Though no taller than she'd been at sixteen and still very slender, Kate's bones and angles had acquired delicate new curves. The face which had always seemed so pointed had gained a smoother line of cheek and jaw that rendered it almost heart-shaped; the wide cat's eyes were suddenly alluringly almond-like and the fiery mane had darkened slightly to a shade resembling beaten copper. She wasn't – and never would be – what passed in the world for a beauty; but, 'My God,' thought Richard, startled, 'she's got something that will bring most men back for a second look!'

Aloud he said weakly, 'Yes. I see what you mean.'

'I thought you would.' Dorothy smiled. 'And now look at the way her hair is falling down her back and the ink-stains on her fingers and the tear in her skirt which she hoped I wouldn't notice.'

Kate looked down with an air of vague guilt and said, 'Quite. But I'd have changed if we'd been expecting anyone.'

'An improvement I'll happily acknowledge,' replied her mother. 'But it's not enough. You've a number of unusual attributes, Kate. And I want the outside of you to reflect them.'

'In short,' said Richard, 'you want her to go to Court.'

'With your agreement, yes. I think for a time at least, she needs a wider arena than Thorne Ash and she may never get a better chance than this one. Is that so foolish?'

'No.' A smile had crept back into the grey eyes. 'I just hadn't thought of it that way. So, Kate . . . your mother wants you to become a Court butterfly. What do you say?'

'That I'm more likely to be a moth,' came the

characteristic reply. 'But I think I'd like to go. The only question is – is Whitehall ready for me?'

'As ready as it will ever be,' began Richard. And then stopped, listening to sounds clearly betokening an arrival. 'Dear me. Now who can that be, I wonder?'

A tap at the parlour door heralded a maidservant. And behind her in the shadows of the hall stood Luciano del Santi.

There was a moment of utter silence. Then, 'My point, I think. You should have changed that gown, Kate,' murmured Dorothy wickedly, before moving forward to greet their visitor.

Kate stayed where she was and waited for her stomach to settle. Then, when the signor had been shown to a chair and offered wine, she said abruptly, 'When did you get back?'

'This evening.'

'And you came straight here? How nice. What a shame your sister isn't here to appreciate it.'

'Kate!' said Richard, under his breath. And, aloud, 'Mistress Gianetta seemed happy to remain at Thorne Ash so my wife thought it best to leave her there.'

'A wise decision I'm sure.' Luciano del Santi smiled at Dorothy. 'I trust she's given no trouble?'

'None worth mentioning. Fortunately, she and Felicity have taken to each other.'

'I suppose that was to be expected. Since she came to live with me, the only other person she's deigned to like is Felix.'

'Who, incidentally,' offered Richard with some humour, 'has been daily lamenting your continued absence and is determined to foist himself on to you for a full five years.'

'Ah.' The merest hint of a smile touched the lean mouth. 'And you want to know if I'll take him.'

'Please.'

'It seems likely – subject to what I find when I go home. He shows more than average promise.'

'*When* you go home?' queried Kate. 'Haven't you been yet?'

'No. Not yet.'

'Goodness! Never say you've brought all your luggage here with you?'

'Again – no.' His voice remained perfectly courteous but there was a glint in his eyes which was not. 'It is . . . at another establishment of mine.'

The brothel, of course, thought Kate instantly. But she had more sense than to say it and, instead, went straight to the only point which interested her. 'And what about Selim? Have you brought *him* with you?'

'No. Should I have done?' He drew a sharp breath and loosed it. 'If there is a point to this inquisition, I should be glad if you'd make it.'

'Kate.' This time it was Dorothy who spoke. 'There's nothing to be gained by this.'

'There is to me. Unless Meg doesn't matter?'

'You know she matters. But—'

'Dolly.' Richard took his wife's hand. 'He's got to know at some time. Let her get it over with.'

'Excuse me,' said the Italian gently. 'But is there something I've missed?'

'You might say so.' Kate faced him witheringly. 'Your man, Selim, has seduced my maid and got her pregnant. And though it may be of small importance to you, it isn't so to me.'

'No. I don't imagine it is.' He looked back at her thoughtfully. 'You want me to apologise for him? I apologise.'

'Don't put yourself out, will you?'

'Well, what else do you expect me to do? I can't compel him to marry her – and neither, I suspect, would you like it if I did. Selim is a follower of the Crescent.'

'I know that. And of course they can't marry.'

'Then what do you want of me? Selim's dismissal? Money for the child? Blood?'

Furiously conscious that she could not, under the ears of her parents, answer as she wished, Kate remained fulminatingly silent. Taking advantage of the lull, Richard said with the suspicion of a smile in his voice, 'He has you there, Kate. You admit marriage is out of the question; you can't want Selim cast off for something that is as much Meg's fault as his, and you know we'll look after both her and the baby. So what do you want?'

'I don't know,' she returned shortly.

'Yes you do.' Luciano del Santi rose from his seat to face her. 'This is just a way of relieving your feelings, isn't it? For what you really want is a quarrel.'

There was a long, cataclysmic pause. Dorothy caught her husband's eye and then bent her head diplomatically over her hands. The Italian continued to smile provokingly at Kate and waited, without visible stress, for her to speak. Finally, in tones of the purest honey, she said, 'It's a good thing you called then, isn't it? What *would* we do without you?' And, turning on her heel, summarily left the room.

'A strategic withdrawal, no less,' remarked Richard pensively. 'I suppose you *had* to be even more bloody-minded than usual?'

'Yes,' said the Italian. 'I'm having a hellish evening.'

'In which case,' observed Dorothy, 'it was thoughtful of you to come and share it with us.'

For a second the black eyes reflected something that might have been appeal. Then he said impassively, 'I'm sorry. You're right, of course. I shouldn't have come. But, despite the unfortunate façade, I *do* regret the trouble caused by my servant and will make whatever reparation I can. And now I think it's time I removed myself.'

'Not just yet,' said Richard. 'You're not unwelcome. And there are things you should know – such as the fact that, as a Catholic, you are now forbidden to carry arms.'

'In which case, *I* shall remove myself,' announced Dorothy. And, smiling briefly at her husband, did so.

Luciano del Santi watched her go and then said slowly, 'If I have caused offence, I am sorry for it.'

'My God! Two apologies in one evening? You must be sickening for something,' grinned Richard. 'Oh – sit down and finish your wine. Dolly's not offended . . . though she's probably wondering how you've come to understand Kate so well if you can't meet without the fur flying.'

'Simple. It's *because* we can't meet without the fur flying.'

Richard raised one brow. 'Is that what you think?'

'Don't you?'

'No. I think it's because, in certain respects, the two of you are more alike than either one of you cares to admit. And I suspect that Kate's disadvantage is in knowing it.'

A strange smile touched the sculpted face. 'Not so. It is in *showing* that she knows it.'

'Meaning?'

'That I know it too. And am therefore as aware as you could possibly wish that it will be much the best for all concerned if we carry on quarrelling.'

By the end of the month and the date set for Dorothy's return to Thorne Ash, Kate had received a formal appointment to the Queen's household and was awaiting the completion of more gowns than she personally thought necessary. A slight hitch occurred when Henrietta Maria announced her intention of visiting a spa for the sake of her health and it was feared that she might be planning to raise money for an army by selling her jewels abroad; but a hint from Parliament on the undesirability of the said jewels leaving the country soon solved this problem and the Queen said she would go to Oatlands instead.

'Which,' said Richard, 'is just as well. Because if anything happens or Kate isn't happy, I want her where I can reach her – not careering all over Europe.'

With Celia's confinement due around the middle of August and Amy growing sulkier every day on account of Kate's good fortune, Dorothy was anxious to be off. She also decided to take Meg Bennet home with her and find a more experienced, London-bred girl to look after Kate. The result was that Jenny Platt joined the household and Meg wept new torrents at the thought of facing her father and Tom Tripp. Dorothy, with a hundred or so small matters still claiming her attention, began to feel frayed around the edges.

Finally, however, everything was suitably organised and she was able to spend her last evening comfortably alone with Richard.

'This is nice,' she sighed, nestling against his shoulder.

'Does Kate going to Court mean that you won't be home this summer?'

'Not necessarily. The King is due to leave for Edinburgh any day now and I can't see much happening in Westminster while he's away. Kate ought to be safe enough at Oatlands for a couple of weeks.'

Dorothy twisted her head to look up at him. 'Safe? That's an odd word to choose.'

'Possibly. I may be foolish, but I don't think the current climate is immensely stable. At the moment, Pym and the King are playing a game of cat and mouse in which they try to outdo each other in the appearance of moderation. But at the end of the day, Pym still wants the Crown brought under parliamentary control and the King still believes himself supreme by Divine Right. So the time must come when Pym will go too far or His Majesty will make a stand. And what price moderation then? But don't worry. The very worst that can happen to Kate is that her stay at Court may be a short one.'

'You're sure?'

'If I wasn't, she wouldn't be going at all.'

'No.' She relaxed again. 'And she's sensible, isn't she?'

'Very. More, perhaps, than we've ever realised.'

'What do you mean by that?'

'Merely that I suspect she may be fighting an unsuitable attraction, and one which, did she but know it, is very possibly mutual.'

'Good gracious!' Dorothy sat up. 'Who is it?'

'I don't think I'd better tell you,' he laughed. 'All your muscles will go into spasm.'

'Don't be silly. Who is it?'

'My alarming friend.' He smiled down at her. 'Well? Nothing to say?'

'Yes,' came the feeble reply. 'All my muscles have gone into spasm. Did you say *mutual*?'

'I said it could be. But, like Kate, he knows it won't do. And I doubt it's more than a passing fancy on either side.'

'I hope so. I really do hope so.' Dorothy drew a long, unsteady breath. 'Because the possibility of having that

dangerous young man and his secrets in the family is the
most unnerving thing I can think of.'

Five

According to Venetia Clifford, the palace of Whitehall was the largest in Europe; and after spending her first three days losing herself in its miles of corridor and blundering incorrectly, and sometimes embarrassingly, into some of its two thousand rooms, Kate was happy to believe her. Part of it – such as Mr Jones's exquisitely painted Banqueting Hall – were opulent; other parts – such as the rooms occupied by the ladies-in-waiting – were decidedly shabby. But no matter where you were, Kate soon discovered, personal elegance was the order of the day. If your collar was askew or your hair mildly adrift, someone was sure to remark on it; and if your deportment was less than perfect or you missed your step in the dance, there was always at least one sharp-eyed young lady to mimic you later on. Also, as if this were not enough, Kate could not help but find it ironic that she should have conceived a strong liking for Venetia – who was not only permanently and effortlessly immaculate but also, with her silver-gilt hair and eyes of shifting amethyst, staggeringly beautiful. Some people, Kate was beginning to realise, had a whole arsenal of unfair advantages.

Her duties, however, seemed vague almost to the point of non-existence and consisted mainly of a lot of standing around. As for the diminutive Queen with her snapping black eyes and slightly prominent teeth – Kate made her curtsy under the aegis of my lady Carlisle, was given an uninterested hand to kiss and thereafter largely ignored. Ignored, that was, by Her Majesty. Lucy Carlisle, on the other hand, showed an inexplicable amount of interest in

214

her and asked rather more questions than Kate, who was trying to make a cautious beginning, thought needful.

'Avoid her as much as you can,' was Venetia's advice when she realised what was happening. 'She thrives on intrigue and – for all she's one of the Queen's intimates – she isn't to be trusted. In fact, to be absolutely frank with you, she's rumoured to be Pym's mistress.'

'Is she?' Kate's eyes widened thoughtfully. No wonder she herself hadn't been asked to search out juicy titbits of information. 'Does Her Majesty know?'

'I doubt it. After all, who's likely to tell her? And it may not be true. This place is a hive of gossip.'

'So I've noticed. It's also, unless I'm mistaken, more than a little on edge.'

'Yes. But what did you expect? Strafford lost his head, all the Papists have been politely shown the door, bishops are still being impeached by the dozen and half the Court is under suspicion of plotting. Nobody knows where they are any more.'

'Speaking of which,' said Kate smoothly, 'I've been meaning to ask you. Where's Francis?'

'In France with Suckling and the rest of them – where, if he's wise, he'll stay,' came the caustic reply. 'Hasn't he written to Celia?'

'Not to my knowledge. But nobody's going to hurt Francis, surely? He's all talk. And so, I should imagine, is Sir John.'

'You know that and *I* know that. But even if Pym knows it too, I doubt it will suit him to admit it. And it's an ill wind, I suppose. Poor Suckling's so deep in debt that he needed to leave the country for a while anyway. It's just a pity it had to come about over such a silly plan. I mean – what good would come of seizing the Tower? Kit says they must all have been suffering from necrosis of the brain.' Venetia paused and awarded her friend a slanting smile. 'And talking of Kit, I've had a letter from him.'

'Oh?' said Kate warily.

'Yes. He says that there's no moving Harry so—'

'Harry?'

'Our brother – Kit's twin. I've told you about him, haven't I?'

'You mentioned that you had a brother but not that he and Kit were twins. Are they alike?'

'Only,' responded Venetia, 'in appearance. Harry is the serious one of the family – which is why he's insisting on staying at Ford Edge instead of coming with Kit to join us at Oatlands.'

'Ah. I see.'

'Is that all you've got to say?'

'Yes. What else would you *like* me to say?'

'You know perfectly well.' The violet eyes assumed an expression of mock gloom. 'As a friend and confidante, you can be a terrible let-down.'

'I know,' agreed Kate sympathetically. 'No fun at all. But it has to be said that you don't set much of an example.'

'What do you mean by that?'

'Well – you don't discuss *your* preferences, do you? And, from what I've been privileged to see so far, you've got half the gentlemen at Court languishing after you.'

'Oh – that doesn't mean anything.' Venetia paused and then, smiling a little, said, 'All right. The truth is that I'm as good as betrothed.'

'Are you?' Kate looked faintly taken aback. 'To whom?'

'A man I've known all my life. His father's lands march with ours and he's Kit's best friend,' came the calm reply. 'His name, if it interests you, is Ellis Brandon.'

Four days later and with a good deal of fuss but surprisingly few mishaps, the Queen's household transferred itself lock, stock and barrel to the Palace of Oatlands where it resembled the proverbial quart fitting into a pint pot. Kate and Venetia found themselves sharing a dormitory with six other ladies – which, in Kate's opinion, was at least three too many – and their respective maids immediately embarked on a battle for closet-space as they tried to unpack. From this, Kate was amused to discover that her own Jenny Platt emerged in victorious possession of a large oak chest; this, however, did not prevent her mislaying both brushes and hairpins on the first evening and leaving Kate with a choice between running or being late for supper.

She chose the former – partly because it wasn't always easy to take one's place unobtrusively, but mainly because she was hungry. And that was how she came to round a corner and ram her nose into someone's silk-clad shoulder-blades.

Kate gasped and ricocheted backwards but the man in blue was quicker and, wheeling round, he gripped her elbows in what felt like a steel trap. Kate gasped again and found herself staring up into the lightest, most piercing eyes she had ever seen.

'Oh lord!' she said weakly. 'I *do* beg your pardon.'

The bruising grip relaxed a trifle but did not leave her. She had time to notice that his hair was silver too – though the face it framed belonged to a much younger man. And then, when he still did not speak, she said politely, 'Would you mind releasing me? I'm already dreadfully late.'

'Are you?' His teeth gleamed in a predatory smile. 'Then I won't detain you. But first, my dear, a forfeit.'

And, pulling her against him, he claimed her mouth in a casually expert kiss. Then, while Kate remained dumbstruck before him, he made her the merest of bows and sauntered off towards the staircase.

Kate took a deep breath and continued thoughtfully on her way. He probably kissed anyone who came to hand. She, on the other hand, had never been kissed at all. Or not like that. Mother had been right. Court life *was* an education.

The gentleman did not appear at supper and she decided to keep the incident to herself. Then, two days later, she saw him again – this time conversing with Lady Carlisle in the garden.

'Who's that?' she asked swiftly of Venetia. 'Over there in blue with my lady.'

Mistress Clifford's brows rose provokingly. 'You mean you don't know?'

'I wouldn't ask if I did. Who *is* he?'

'That, dear Kate, is probably the richest and certainly the most dangerous libertine you're ever likely to meet. In short, it is Cyrus Winter. Why do you want to know?'

'Because he kissed me the other night,' responded Kate absently. 'Winter. Now where have I heard that name before?'

'Kissed you?' echoed Venetia. And then, 'Yes. He would. But, if you're wise, you'll forget it. Forget it and stay out of his way. *His* reputation doesn't bear thinking about – and he'd destroy yours without a second thought.'

'Winter!' exclaimed Kate. 'My God! *Not* the one Celia wouldn't marry?'

This time Venetia looked frankly stunned. She opened her mouth, closed it again and finally said faintly, 'Celia? He actually offered to marry Celia? And she wouldn't have him? I don't believe it!'

'Which?'

'Either – both. He – they say he's had hundreds of mistresses but vows to die a bachelor. While as for Celia . . . well, with all due respect to your brother, I'd have thought Cyrus Winter would have filled her requirements to the letter.'

'Yes,' said Kate meditatively. 'Now that I've seen him, so would I. Odd, isn't it?'

A week later the King left for the opening of the Scottish Parliament and Kate recognised for the first time that a deep and abiding affection lay between him and the Queen – a revelation which subtly changed her view of both of them. And then her attention was claimed by the arrival of Christopher Clifford – along with his lady mother.

As things turned out, the manner of their meeting was less than fortuitous. It was a beautiful day, the sky dazzlingly blue over a shimmering heat haze; and Kate, rebelling against the usual dawdling progress around the gardens, volunteered to exercise the Queen's spaniel in the park beyond. Permission was granted and, equally glad to be free, Jemmy scampered away across the grass with a series of excited little yaps. Kate grinned and set off after him, enjoying both the rustle of her new primrose taffeta and the moment of all-too-rare solitude.

Their meandering progress took them in due course to the river. And that was when it happened. One minute Kate was watching the spaniel trailing his ears in the water and the next he was plunging in the wake of some small, unwary river-creature.

'Drat!' said Kate cheerfully. 'Come back, you silly animal! Don't you realise that if you get dirty, I'll have to bath you?'

Jemmy, however, was having too much fun to attend to logic – or even to care that his quarry had vanished. The water was not deep and half splashing, half swimming, he made it to the far bank where a tree hung low enough to dip its branches. And then, just as he was considering doing Kate the favour of returning to her, his collar became inexplicably caught fast on a twig.

Not immediately recognising the problem, Jemmy continued swimming. The branch swayed but did not give him up. Unable to understand his lack of progress, Jemmy stopped paddling and was towed gently back to where he'd started. Eyes widening with consternation, he tried again; and then, managing to turn an appealing brown gaze on Kate, he uttered a forlorn bark.

She found it quite difficult to stop laughing. Then, descending to the water's edge, she said severely, 'I suppose you're expecting me to come and rescue you? Well, it's all very well for you – but this gown won't wash. And how we're to get back without anyone seeing us, I just don't know.'

Talking all the time to reassure the animal, she took off her shoes and attempted to loop her taffeta skirt over one arm. Then, sighing, she stepped into the water and sank up to her ankles in cool, soft mud.

By the time she had reached the place where the Queen's pet hung helpless, her petticoats were soaked to the knee but her gown was still relatively unscathed. It might have stayed that way, too – had not Jemmy, upon being freed, chosen to hurl himself upon her in gratitude and knock her off balance. Kate sat down up to her arm-pits in water and found herself in receipt of a soggy bundle of wriggling fur whose sole aim appeared to be to lick her face.

'You,' she told him flatly, 'are a four-legged disaster. And this is absolutely the last time I volunteer for anything. Come on – let's go.'

They gained the other bank without further mishap and Kate, disarrayed, muddy, and weighted down by several ells of sodden petticoat, stepped squelchingly back into her shoes. Then she clambered slowly up the bank . . . and found herself impaled without warning on some two dozen startled pairs of eyes.

The Queen, it appeared, had also taken a fancy to stroll by the river. And amongst the inevitable entourage was Venetia, Venetia's brother Kit – and a fair, faded beauty who could only be their mother. Kate experienced a sensation of distant hilarity. Kit's face was positively alight with laughter; his mother's definitely wasn't.

'*Mon Dieu!*' said the Queen blankly. And then stopped as, at the sound of her voice, Jemmy came catapulting, mud and all, against her silk embroidered skirts.

A collective gasp filtered through the entourage and at least three ladies-in-waiting uttered exclamations of consternation. The only movement, however, was an outward one away from the dirty, excited paws. Then, as Kate stepped resignedly forward, Lady Carlisle said sharply, 'Mistress Maxwell – pray remove the dog and see to it that he is thoroughly washed. Then, when you have made yourself presentable again, I will receive your explanation.'

Kate's brows rose and an acidic glint entered the green eyes. 'In most particulars, that was just what I had in mind.'

'Wait!' said the Queen. 'It is perfectly clear that my Jemmy has been in the river and that you have brought him out again. Is it not so?'

'Yes, Madam,' agreed Kate with a small curtsy. 'His collar was caught on the branch of a tree – and though he was in no danger, I couldn't just leave him to go off and find a servant.'

'And so you sacrifice that pretty gown.' Henrietta Maria

nodded decisively and then smiled. 'I shall see that it is replaced with one better. But first you must go and change before you take cold.'

'Your Majesty is more than kind.' Kate curtsied again. 'Shall I take Jemmy with me?'

'What need? It is time, I think, for another to perform some small service.' The bright, black eyes scanned the circle of courtiers with faint malice. 'Now whom, I wonder, should I choose?'

'If it please you, Madam, let it be me.' Still smiling, Kit Clifford stepped forward and bowed. 'And, with your permission, I can also escort Mistress Kate back to the palace.'

Henrietta Maria laughed and shook an admonitory finger. 'You are a rogue, Monsieur Clifford – and it will serve you well if the lady will have none of you. But go – go! Before *mademoiselle* catches cold.'

'At once, Madam!' He swept a second, more extravagant bow, scooping Jemmy up in the same movement and then, turning, offered his arm to Kate.

She grinned and accepted it but said nothing until they were out of earshot of the royal party. Then, judiciously, 'In my present condition, I think you might have been wiser not to have acknowledged me. Your mother – if it *was* your mother? – didn't look impressed.'

'It was – and she wasn't,' he replied cheerfully. 'But I daresay she'll get over it. And the only difficulty I'm experiencing right now is how, without appearing insane, to compliment you on your appearance.'

'You can't. No one could. Are you *really* going to bath that dog?'

'Not,' said Kit, inspecting Jemmy with unruffled calm, 'if I can find someone else to do it for me. After all, I've already cheerfully ruined my coat for the privilege of five minutes of your company; and if that hasn't impressed you, I don't know what will.'

'Well, be reasonable,' said Kate. 'How would you?'

He laughed and tucked Jemmy unceremoniously under one arm while he opened the gate to the garden and allowed her to pass through. Then he said lightly, 'Do you realise that it's nearly a year since we last met?'

'Is it really? Good heavens!'

'Yes – and *doesn't* time fly!' he retorted. 'Why are you walking so quickly all of a sudden?'

'I should have thought that was obvious,' Kate replied. 'Look at me!'

'I have – and will happily go on doing so as long as you'll let me. Kate – will you wait a minute!' He caught her hand and brought her to a halt. 'What I'm trying to tell you is that I've thought about you. Often.'

'Oh. Have you?' said Kate, slightly flummoxed. 'That's nice.'

'Isn't it? I suppose you wouldn't like to say whether or not you've also thought of me?'

For a moment she stared at him with a careful lack of expression and then said baldly, 'No, I wouldn't. In fact, if you *must* know, I'd as soon we didn't have this conversation at all.'

'Ah. Too soon?'

'Much.'

'Fair enough.' Kit released her hand and smiled at her with unimpaired cheerfulness. 'How are you enjoying life in the hen-coop?'

'It has its moments,' she replied, her voice quivering on the brink of laughter. And then, walking on again, 'I'm here to be turned into a silk purse but, fortunately for Jemmy, the transformation is still incomplete.'

'Fortunately for you, too. Or hasn't it occurred to you that you've just earned Her Majesty's regard?'

'Well, of course. How else do you think I was going to get myself noticed? Not that I expect it to last. Someone is bound to point out that my presence here is more or less solely due to the Parliament.'

'Is it?' he asked, startled.

'Yes. Didn't you know? I'm Lord Saye's idea of a "tactful suggestion".' She eyed him obliquely. 'But there's no accounting for taste, is there? And my only regret is that he can't see me now.'

222

Later, whilst bathing and changing her dress, Kate devoted some careful thought to Mr Christopher Clifford. In the months since she had last seen him, his image had become somewhat indistinct, but she knew now that he was the same as ever. Bright, golden, fun-loving; and, in many senses, a less egotistical version of Francis – whose absence she occasionally caught herself regretting. So, although the mere sight of him had not caused her heart to turn over, nor her bones to melt, she was genuinely pleased to see him; and it was, of course, naturally difficult not to respond favourably to someone who had the good taste to admire one quite so steadfastly. Surprisingly difficult, in fact – for Kate had never considered herself prone to the same silly desire to attract male attention that seemed to afflict girls like Celia and Amy. But there it was. Kit admired her and she liked it. The only problem was in deciding whether or not she wanted something to come of it.

It was at this point that the face of a dark, Renaissance angel swam uninvited into her mind. Kate frowned balefully and banished it. Luciano del Santi was not for her. He'd told her so himself and she entirely agreed with him. After all, just because someone had the power to make your blood run faster didn't mean that you necessarily had to like them. And even if you *did* like them . . . well, as Mother said, the things you liked weren't always good for you – and, if proof of that were needed, one only had to look at Eden. Unfortunately, however, the fact that one could recognise and dismiss a man who was unsuitable did not mean that one would automatically welcome an offer from another who wasn't. All of which, decided Kate, was logical, sensible, and unaccountably depressing.

The result of these deliberations was that she embarked on an immediate regime of enjoying Kit Clifford's company whilst making it subtly impossible for him to utter any declarations she wasn't ready to hear. If he invited her to walk with him in the gardens, she made sure others always went too; and when as sometimes happened they were unavoidably alone, she either used her wit to make him laugh or opened some topic of conversation which she knew would make him temporarily forget his desire to flirt with her.

They discussed with perfect agreement the recently passed ordinance which defined how the Sabbath should henceforth be kept and strictly forbade all the usual games; they wrangled about the Parliament's intention to draft a Remonstrance listing every so-called error of the King's reign, and laughed over George Digby's discomfiture at having his idea taken up just when he had got himself back into royal favour. And while Venetia, cynically misconstruing Kate's motives, silently applauded her tactics, Lady Ellen Clifford came to the reluctant conclusion that the girl with whom her favourite child was so obviously in love might possibly be a lady after all.

The third week in September brought Kate a letter from Felicity which contained a whole budget of news. Celia, it appeared, had been safely delivered of a son and was enjoying basking in everyone's attention. Eden was as proud as a peacock; and the baby – whom Felicity described as a perfect little cherub – was to be named Jude. As for the rest, Father had been at home throughout August but would return to London soon; Meg Bennet – who was beginning to swell like a pumpkin – and Tom Tripp weren't speaking to each other; Amy was full of airs at being a betrothed lady and talked of nothing but bride-clothes; and Mr Santi had visited them briefly to reclaim his sister.

'Speaking of which,' wrote Felicity, 'I've found out a lot of things which are too interesting not to tell you even if you do hate Mr Santi. For example, did you know that he and Jenny were born in London and that their father was executed on account of being a Catholic? Imagine it! Then, after he died, Jenny and Mr Santi and their mother had no money and nowhere to live so they set off back to the rest of their family in Genoa – only their mother fell ill and died before they got there. Isn't that awful? Jenny was only five years old and, although Mr Santi couldn't have been more than twelve himself, he had to look after them both and earn money by sweeping floors and the like so they could eat. Then, when they got to Genoa, their uncle took Jenny to live with him and gave her all those jewels – but he just put Mr Santi to work as an apprentice! And that, of course, is why Jenny treats her brother like a servant – even though, if it hadn't been for him, she'd have died on the journey. Quite honestly, Kate, it makes my blood boil! So I gave Jenny a piece of my mind and we had a terrible quarrel – which I'm sorry about of course, but I still think I was right. Don't you?'

What Kate thought was that she'd very much like the chance to cross-examine Signorina Gianetta, but that she almost certainly wasn't going to get it. But if what Felicity had written was true, it cast a new and interesting light on Luciano del Santi which, under the circumstances, was something she could well do without. The only sensible course, therefore, was to put the matter firmly from her mind and concentrate on convincing Venetia that she was *not* playing games with Kit now in order to trap him all the more securely later.

September became October and the Court grew progressively more uneasy. News from outside spoke of widespread unrest; of unemployed soldiers turned robber, rioters pulling down fences and bands of poachers in Windsor Great Park. In Puritan districts, statues were removed from churches and whitewash started to cover paintings of the archangels. And from Scotland came word that one Colonel Hurry had revealed a plot to solve the King's worst difficulties in that land by kidnapping the Covenanting Earl of Argyll. The calamitous implications of this last caused the Queen to lose a little of her determined sparkle; but she kept her head high and continued her programme of canvassing support through a stream of discreet visitors.

Discussing these things with Kate and his sister, Kit had admitted that things looked pretty black but voiced the opinion that it couldn't get much worse. The passage of a few weeks proved him wrong. He, like everyone else, had forgotten about Ireland – where the rise of Puritanism in the English Parliament threatened the lives, land and freedom of the Catholic Irish. And then the O'Neills rose in force to remind them – taking Carrickmacross and

Newry and lighting a torch of desperate and dangerous rebellion.

'You know what this means, don't you?' said Venetia flatly to Kate and her brother. 'The King will ask for an army to put down the rising and Parliament will say no as usual because they're determined not to trust him. And then Pym will think it all over and start convincing everyone that it's not a rising at all but just some action on behalf of the King's friends.' She paused to draw a long, unsteady breath and the amethyst eyes blazed oddly. 'The world is running mad. We've had two wars with Scotland, the quarrel between His Majesty and the Parliament is growing bigger every day and breeding civil unrest throughout the land – and now Ireland is in flames. Can't you see where all this could be leading us? Or am I mad as well?'

Kate surveyed her friend in silence and felt a chill slide slowly down her back. Venetia was right, and the unspeakable thing she had refused to name was actually possible. For months now – even years, perhaps – the old comfortable life had been gradually changing. Old laws had been overset and new ones made; the traditions of the church had been turned upside down and private religious practices were coming under suddenly strict scrutiny; and, most serious of all, the King's position – which had always been at the very core of all their lives – had been so undermined that he stood on a knife-edge. No one, as Venetia had said, knew where they were any more. No one. And unless they were all very careful, the next step could take them over the brink.

'What are you saying?' asked Kit slowly. 'That the present difficulties could lead to rebellion here?'

The girls stared at him without speaking.

'But that's preposterous! This is England, not Germany – we like our peace too much. What you're suggesting would amount to civil war: that could never happen here.'

'No?' said Venetia.

'No,' echoed Kate flatly. 'For if we and people like us don't believe and go on believing that it's impossible, it

226

may become possible. And I'm not sure that any of us could bear it.'

By mutual consent, they did not refer to the matter again, and three days later Kit at least was cheered by news of a different kind.

'Rupert's been released!' he announced, catching Kate around the waist and whirling her down the otherwise empty antechamber in a wild fandango. 'Hurrah for the King's ambassador!'

Kate waited patiently for his excitement to abate and then said calmly, 'And who, precisely, is Rupert?'

'Rupert of the Rhine – the Elector Palatine's younger brother. He's been the Emperor of Austria's prisoner for the last two years. You *must* have heard of him! He's the King's nephew.'

'Oh,' said Kate. 'Yes. Now you come to mention it, I believe I have. Isn't he a professional soldier?'

'The best, my dear!' grinned Kit. 'And, since the terms of his release apparently forbid him taking up arms against the Emperor again, the burning question has to be, who *will* he choose to fight for?'

Kate's breath leaked away. 'Uncle Charles?' she suggested weakly.

'Uncle Charles,' agreed Kit. And then, 'But only if necessary. And he's a splendid fellow, Kate. Just the mere fact of his being here will cheer the King up no end – and ought to make Pym think twice before provoking matters any further.'

'Or make Pym doubt the King's intentions even more than he does already?'

'Oh. Yes. Well, there is that I suppose. But let's look on the bright side for once. It will probably be months before the Prince gets here – and meanwhile, from what I hear, Pym's got other things to worry about. They say that the disbanded troops are daubing threatening slogans over every tavern in the City and that Parliament's being guarded by trained bands for fear of violence.'

'If that's supposed to comfort me,' snapped Kate, who

had heard exactly the same gossip, 'I can only say that it's wide of the mark. Have you forgotten that my father sits in the Commons?'

'Oh hell. I'm sorry.' Kit took her hand and pulled her down beside him on a window-seat. 'No one will touch your father, Kate. It's Pym they're after – and even that probably won't last. Or Venetia says not. And, much though I hate to admit it, she generally has a sounder grasp of these things than I do.'

Kate relaxed a little and summoned a smile. 'Don't worry. I won't tell anyone.'

Somewhat to her surprise, he continued to frown down at her fingers, still clasped in his own. Then he said abruptly, 'I want to marry you, Kate. How much longer must I wait before asking?'

The suddenness of his declaration scrambled Kate's wits and, unable to bear her silence, Kit released her hand in order to grasp her shoulders and pull her round to face him.

'Listen. It's obvious that if – if you felt as I do, you wouldn't be hesitating. But what I have to know is whether there's any hope. If there is, I'll wait as long as you like. If not . . . well, it would be kinder to tell me now, that's all. I don't think that's too much to ask, is it?'

'No,' said Kate truthfully. 'Not at all.'

'Well, then?'

'I – I don't know. I like you very much indeed. And if there is anyone I could consider marrying at this time, it would be you. But that isn't an answer.' She paused to look him straight in the eye. 'I think what I'm trying to say is that with the world as it is we have to be doubly sure. And I'm not.'

'I see.' His mouth twisted wryly. 'Well, that's plain speaking with a vengeance. But I can't pretend I didn't ask for it.'

'N-no. But you do understand what I'm saying?'

'Yes. And you're right, damn it. We *do* have to be sure.' He lifted one hand and lightly traced the line of her cheek. 'My misfortune, however, is that I already am.'

Six

In the end, Richard Maxwell was sufficiently satisfied about his eldest daughter's security to remain at Thorne Ash until just before Parliament reassembled on 20 October. And then, since the family was not due to join him until the end of the month, he divided his time between listening to Pym's continued attack on the King's authority (now being channelled into the Remonstrance) and making a concerted attempt to find the one who might just possibly be able to tell him the truth about Alessandro Falcieri.

He was still not entirely sure why this mattered, or whether, if Justice Fisher should prove helpful, he would pass the information on to Luciano. But, having begun, he found the task absorbing enough to justify the effort required; and it made a pleasant diversion from Pym's depressingly long catalogue of the King's mistakes – or Ned Hyde's incessant bickering with Oliver Cromwell over control of the armed forces. The first, so far as Richard could see, was only going to aggravate matters and kill any spirit of compromise; and the second ought to be set aside in favour of some discussion on the rapidly escalating rebellion in Ireland.

It took him over two weeks to trace Samuel Fisher to the decaying grandeur of a mansion in Lambeth, and a further week to persuade the old man, by letter, to receive him. By then Dorothy, Amy, Felicity and Celia, but not – Richard was unsurprised to discover – the baby, had all arrived to join him and the house had become a hive of preparation. Eden, it appeared, had elected to follow later in order to keep Nathan Cresswell under his eye for as long as possible, and Richard, beset by pre-nuptial chaos, was rather inclined to regard this as a shrewd move.

The crumbling exterior of the house in Lambeth accorded perfectly with the moth-eaten hangings and the faint odour of cabbage inside it. Richard followed a pock-marked maid upstairs, hoping the rotting wood would bear his weight, and entered a room with a roaring fire where the smell of cabbage was all but lost in things even less pleasant. And there before him, his body spilling out of a great carved chair, sat the bloated remains of the man who had once been the sharpest lawyer in London.

Thinning grey hair hung in matted wisps around a vast, pendulous face and the numerous chins rested on a filthy, food-encrusted coat. The swollen hands ended in long, blackened claws; a mountainous stomach sagged over heavy thighs; and, propped on a stool, one foot was unskilfully wrapped in foul, reeking bandages.

Half choking in the stench and already recoiling from the heat of the fire, Richard said abruptly, 'It's not my place to interfere – but is there no one who can look after you better than this, sir?'

A peculiar wheezing sound that might have been laughter emanated from the carved chair. Then, in a voice that – though breathless – was surprisingly strong, Justice Fisher said, 'No, my fine gentleman, there isn't. Neither do I want a pack of idle servants poking round my house, eating their heads off at my expense. And you're right. It's not your business. So if I'm not a pretty enough sight for you, you can take yourself off. Nobody asked you to come.'

'True,' agreed Richard. 'But I came to ask you a question – and it would be stupid of me to leave without doing so, wouldn't it?'

'Ask it then.'

'I'm interested in a case that would have come to court early in '26, in which the defendant was condemned for participating in a Papist plot to assassinate the King. His name was Alessandro Falcieri.'

Between the puffy folds of flesh, Mr Fisher's eyes seemed suddenly to focus and there was a long, echoing silence.

230

Then he said softly, 'And what can the fate of a dead traitor possibly be to you, Mr Maxwell?'

'Very little,' responded Richard with cool caution. 'I merely seek confirmation of a story I've been told.'

'By whom?'

'A friend. Does it matter? All I'm asking is whether, to the best of your knowledge, such a trial ever took place.'

'All? *All?*' Again that creaking laugh. 'I may be unsound of body but I'm not senile. Which one of them sent you here?'

'I beg your pardon?'

'Deaf, are you? I asked who sent you.'

'No one sent me.' Richard's stomach was beginning to rebel and he could feel himself sweating, but he guarded his patience. 'You said "which one of them". Which one of who?'

'Never you mind!' The old man relapsed into silence again and then said, 'I've been out of the world long enough for it to have forgotten me – yet someone has given you my name. Either tell me who it was or get out.'

The first glimmerings of suspicion stirred in Richard's mind and he decided to put his theory to the test. 'Who do you think it was? One of your four witnesses?'

The heavy jowls quivered. 'And who might they be?'

'You tell me,' invited Richard. 'You might as well – for I think you've already answered my original question. Alessandro Falcieri was indeed tried for treason . . . and you handled the prosecution.'

'*Who sent you?*' Mr Fisher hissed. 'Who?'

'Confirm what I've said and I'll tell you.'

'Be damned to you, then! You'll get nothing from me!'

'Then I may as well leave.'

A tide of apoplectic colour filled the gross countenance as Justice Fisher struggled with himself. 'Go, then – and good riddance. Don't think you'll trick me into telling you who they are. You don't know anything. If you did, you wouldn't be here.'

'True. I begin to suspect, however, that you sent a man to his death on evidence which you knew at the time to be false,' remarked Richard gently. 'And that is all I came to find out.'

This time the silence was of epic proportions and Richard had almost given up hope of an answer when the old man said slowly, 'Falcieri had children.'

It was unexpected but Richard merely raised his brows and said nothing.

'Children,' muttered the Justice. 'A son, perhaps? Yes. That's it. It has to be. When a man's been dead for fifteen years, who else remembers or cares but his son?' He paused and gave a flabby, unpleasant smile. 'He ought to have come himself.'

'You really do jump to conclusions, don't you?'

'I'm a lawyer – or was. It's what we do. But I'm right in this. I can smell it. You've come from Falcieri's son.'

'I've come of my own volition and know no one bearing that name,' responded Richard with perfect truth. 'But if you're willing to tell what you know to the man's son – supposing, of course, that he had one – why not to me?'

'Because I don't waste my time on lackeys,' wheezed Mr Fisher. 'But I'll say this. You can tell your Italian master that if he wants to know more than he does, he'd better come himself. And then we'll see whether I feel like helping him . . . and if I do, whether he can meet my price.'

With Amy's wedding fixed for 26 November, it was fortunate that the King's return from Scotland brought the Queen's household back to Whitehall in time for Kate to request immediate leave of absence and arrive home at the eleventh hour. She walked in just before supper to a barrage of questions and half-teasing, half-congratulatory remarks on her appearance from everyone except Celia and Amy . . . and then spent an enjoyable evening listening to Eden's glowing descriptions of his son and Felix's enthusiasm for his work, in between talking politics with her father and delivering her own witty exposé on life at Court.

It was therefore not until much later that she was finally alone with her mother and able to say simply, 'You sent me away to be polished. Will I do?'

'Very well indeed,' smiled Dorothy. 'Have you enjoyed it?'

'Yes. Much more, in fact, than I'd expected. The only worrying part has been discovering that this quarrel between Parliament and the King has left all the things we take for granted hanging by a thread. But you live with that thought every day through Father – so we won't speak of it now. And instead I'll tell you that I've been kissed by the man Celia wouldn't marry, that the gown I intend to wear tomorrow was a gift from the Queen herself and – and that Kit Clifford wants to marry me.'

For a moment Dorothy simply looked at her. Then she said calmly, 'I see that the changes are only skin deep. Do you love him?'

'I don't know. I'm comfortable with him and I enjoy his company and I realise that I could do much, much worse. But I'm all too aware that his family is no less involved with the Court than Celia's and I don't want to make the same mistake as Eden.'

'I see.' Dorothy thought for a moment. 'But Eden's problems are caused less by Celia's background than by her nature – and, from what I've seen of him, your Kit is a very different kettle of fish. On the other hand, things have worsened in the last year and people *are* beginning to take sides – so there's little doubt that a difference of allegiances could become a serious obstacle.' She paused. 'I suppose the only advice I can give you is to weigh these things in the balance. If you find that you love him, you'll regret allowing this present quarrel to come between you, and if not, there's no question to be answered. Mere liking does not make a marriage.'

Kate nodded. 'That's more or less what I've told him.'

'And he's willing to wait?'

'Yes.'

'Then I suggest that you stop worrying and allow matters to take their course,' said Dorothy. 'And now . . . *what* was it you said about Celia's rejected suitor?'

On the following morning, and despite the pandemonium

caused by preparing Amy for her wedding, Kate became aware of a certain hostility radiating towards her from Celia. She said nothing until Amy was satisfactorily arrayed in forget-me-not silk and then, snatching a moment's privacy with Felicity, said, 'I know Celia and I have never really got on – but have I done something new to upset her?'

'Well, of course,' came the faintly surprised reply. 'You've spent four months at Court and come back more stylish than she is herself – and she hates it. So does Amy, come to that.' And then, 'Do you like my locket? Jenny gave it to me.'

'I was under the impression,' remarked Kate, examining the pretty thing, 'that you and Gianetta had fallen out.'

'We did. But then we made it up again. And Mr Santi says she's been a bit more polite since he took her home again, so she obviously took some notice of what I said.'

'You've seen him?'

'Yes. He came to dinner last week.' Felicity grinned and gave one last tweak to her primrose taffeta. 'You'll be able to see him yourself shortly. He's bringing Jenny to the wedding.'

And that, thought Kate sourly, was no more than she should have expected.

Precisely what Luciano del Santi should have expected was something he found himself unable to decide. He'd been prepared for changes. What he found he *hadn't* been prepared for was something that – for no good reason he could see – amounted to a complete transformation. Throughout the ceremony and the round of kissing and congratulations that followed it, his eyes brooded on the elegant creature in the daring bronze and amber gown; and by the time they sat down to the wedding-breakfast, he was still no nearer finding an answer.

Her hair was intricately dressed . . . but that was not it; nor was it the fact that someone had apparently taught her the art of darkening her brows and lashes. And presumably the lines of cheek and jaw, neck and shoulder, had always possessed that delicate, cameo-like purity. So what was left? That graceful, swaying walk? Yes, perhaps. And something else that – since it could not be learned – must have been there all along, though he'd never previously noticed it; the dangerous, indefinable quality that – for want of a better word – one had to call allure.

The procession of dishes came to an end and the boards were drawn to make room for the dancing. Amy frolicked down the room with her Geoffrey and Dorothy did her duty by Mr Cox Senior – now entering the first stages of inebriety. Kate, the signor observed sardonically, had steered Felicity and Gianetta into the furthest corner for a purpose one did not need to be a genius to work out; and that, considering how carefully she was avoiding *him*, was not without a certain ironic humour.

'You're supposed to kiss the bride, shake the groom by the hand and tell everyone what a handsome couple they make,' said a pleasant voice beside him. 'And if you were a *really* good fellow, you'd follow it up by dancing with one of the Cox girls.'

The dark gaze moved to encompass the groom's good-natured but undeniably homely sisters and returned blandly to Richard's face. 'I'm afraid you'll have to hold me excused. I rarely dance.'

'Rather look at Kate, would you? Well, I can't say I blame you. But you'd better be careful. She says your eyes are like knives and it's high time someone told you it's rude to stare.'

'Time was when she'd have done so herself. Or has Court life made her too much of a lady to say what she thinks?'

Richard laughed. 'I doubt it. She's probably on her best behaviour for the day – or living up to that dress. Either way, Dolly assures me that the changes are purely superficial.'

'Should I be comforted?' asked the Italian dryly. And then, 'Do you intend to let her go back to Whitehall?'

'I haven't decided. It mostly depends on what response the King makes to the Remonstrance. You know that it's been passed?'

'By a mere eleven votes and with a lot of unseemly jostling. Yes. What I don't know, however, is what Pym expects to gain by raking over old grievances other than alienating the Lords and the Moderates.'

'That's what Falkland said. Pym, on the other hand, argues what he calls the "necessity of the times".'

'Meaning that now the Providence Company is bankrupt, he and the other shareholders can't be arrested for debt while Parliament sits?'

'Meaning,' corrected Richard with irony, 'that the Moderates are fast gaining control of the House and Pym daren't let the King raise an army to send to Ireland because the Irish are claiming royal authority for their rebellion. So his answer is to blast the King's reputation to perdition with every discreditable item he can find. And the unfortunate part of *that* is that, amidst all the dross, the King has actually given him the grounds on which to do it.'

'Daniel O'Neill's plot to overawe Parliament by marching on London last summer? Yes. I've heard that one.' Luciano del Santi paused and then said thoughtfully. 'O'Neill's a name we're hearing a lot of recently. They say, for example, that Phelim O'Neill is poised to take Drogheda. Is your brother-in-law still in Dublin?'

'To the best of my knowledge, yes. We keep hoping one of the fugitives will bring us a letter, but there's been nothing so far. Fortunately, Ivo's thick as thieves with Dan O'Neill and Ormonde and the rest of them – so he ought to be safe enough. Or so I've been telling Dolly.' Richard stopped and smiled ruefully. 'But enough of that. How are your affairs progressing?'

'They're not,' came the flat reply. 'Since seeing the trial record – which, as I told you, was less than useless – I've opened up other lines of inquiry, put pressure on any number of financially embarrassed gentlemen and achieved precisely nothing. In short, I seem to be banging my head against a brick wall.'

Richard considered him for a moment and then said, 'In plain terms, what would you do with the information if you had it?'

236

'You mean – would I commit murder and mayhem?' The ghost of a smile touched the sculpted face. 'No. But what I *would* do isn't likely to be much less destructive.'

'I see.' Richard drew a long breath and finally made up his mind. 'Then you'd better go and see a man called Samuel Fisher in Lambeth. It seems to me – though I couldn't get him to admit it – that he probably presented the case for the prosecution.'

Silence stretched out on invisible threads and shock drained the blood from Luciano del Santi's skin. At last, in a voice that was oddly remote, he said, 'You've found someone who knows something? How? And why? Why would you put yourself to so much trouble?'

'Well, as to that, it wasn't so arduous,' replied Richard. And related his conversation with John Maynard. 'For the rest . . . I suppose you might say I was curious.'

'Ah.' The colour began to seep slowly back into the Italian's face. He said, 'Of course. You wanted to find out whether or not I'd told you a pack of lies. How foolish of me not to have anticipated it.'

'It'll be foolish of you to start letting your damned temper get the upper hand,' retorted Richard crisply. 'If you really want to know, I never doubted you'd done anything but tell me the truth as you saw it at the time. But you were only a child then, for God's sake! What did you expect me to think? What would anybody think? And whether or not you're happy with my motives, the result may well be a trail worth following. So don't sharpen your tongue on me, Luciano. I won't put up with it.'

For a long moment the black eyes stared imperviously back at him until, on a tremor that might have been laughter, Luciano said, 'Oh God. You're right, of course. But have you the remotest idea what you've done? I spend three years preparing the ground and a further two stumbling into dead-ends . . . and then you come along and blithely announce that you've found the prosecuting counsel.'

'No justice in the world, is there?' grinned Richard, tacitly accepting the equally tacit apology. 'And correction; I *may* have found him. The signs certainly point to it:

mainly the fact that – if you go to see him – he'll know who you are. But perhaps I'd better start at the beginning?'

Luciano listened attentively to Richard's account of his meeting with Samuel Fisher and at the end said reflectively, 'You're right. He obviously knows something. What's he like?'

'Old – but not, he'll doubtless inform you, senile. He's got gout and dropsy and doesn't look as though he's got fourpence for a groat – which is why, if he tells you anything at all, he'll make you pay through the nose for it. And that brings me to the most useful piece of advice I can offer.'

'Yes?'

'Drench yourself in chypre and take a pomander with you. The stench in that house is enough to make a dog vomit.'

Having successfully avoided him all day, it was just sheer bad luck that Kate should run into Luciano del Santi in the hall where he was awaiting Gianetta prior to leaving.

'Going already?' she inquired cordially. 'What a shame. You'll miss all the bawdiest jokes.'

'Since I've already given you my views on that subject,' he sighed, 'I can only call that remark fatuous.'

Kate smiled brilliantly and proceeded to turn her mistake to good account. 'Which it would be – if, of course, I could possibly be expected to remember every word you utter.'

'Ah – now that's better. I could almost believe that.'

'Try.'

'As you see, I still live.' He smiled back at her with deadly charm. 'Tell me, did Gianetta manage to produce enough sordid details for you – or are you still in the market for more? Because, if so, I suggest that next time you apply to me. You'll find that my recall is by far the clearer. In fact, dear Kate, I think I can safely promise to give you more than you bargain for.'

A colourful and seemingly rapturous reception having been organised for him by the newly elected, royalist Lord

Mayor of London, King Charles felt best able to demonstrate his disdain for the Remonstrance by politely ignoring it. He therefore made no official visit to Parliament and presently retired to Hampton Court pleading a sore throat. Kate, alerted to this move by a frantic note from Venetia, sought and finally obtained Richard's reluctant permission to return to her post. Celia, who had been counting on passing a few pleasant evenings at Whitehall before being dragged back to Thorne Ash, threw a tantrum of monumental proportions and was only pacified by Eden's weary promise to take her to Hampton instead.

'She doesn't change much, does she,' said Kate trenchantly to Eden in the midst of her final preparations to depart. 'In fact, I'm tempted to say that she's getting worse.'

'Then don't,' he retorted. 'Just try to remember that Celia is my wife – and, unless you learn to like her, you and I can't ever be close again. Is that what you want?'

'No. And though you won't believe it, I've really tried to find something in her worthy of respect. Only I can't – so the best I can do is to be civil to her. Which is more than she appears to be doing for you; and that's what I can't tolerate.'

'There's no question of your tolerating it. It isn't your business.'

'Isn't it?'

'No,' he said, sticking doggedly to his point. 'She'd be your friend if you'd let her.'

'You mean,' returned Kate acidly, 'that she'd be happy to have me worship at the shrine. She doesn't have friends – she has votaries.'

'Jealous, Kate?'

'You know I'm not. I'm just wondering how she's going to get on now that her chief hand-maiden is married and gone. After all, there's no denying that Amy was an absolute god-send in certain respects.'

'Christ!' Eden was suddenly angry. 'You're so awash with blind prejudice you can't even make a few allowances. Celia's just had a baby, damn it!'

'Don't tell me. It's Celia herself you need to remind. I don't think I've heard her mention Jude above once – and she doesn't seem exactly panting to get back to him, does she?'

It was only then, looking into his eyes, that she finally realised that he knew all of this but could not bear the pain of acknowledging it. Feeling suddenly rather sick, Kate sought desperately for some means of undoing the damage . . . but too late. With a muttered curse, Eden pivoted on his heel and slammed out of the house.

Within twenty-four hours of resuming her duties at Hampton Court, Kate was informed that they were all returning to Whitehall. London, it appeared, was suffering a recession caused by the growing maritime trade of the Dutch – added to which the cost of paying off the victorious Scots had been enormous and investments were currently being lost hand over fist in Ireland. Or so said a deputation of aldermen who came to beg the King to bring his Court and its purses back to the City for the festive Yuletide season. And His Majesty, knighting the worthy petitioners one and all, was magnanimous enough to agree; thus leaving his courtiers no alternative but to have their boxes repacked and causing Kate to reflect that at least Celia ought to be pleased.

The move was accomplished with what Kate was fast coming to recognise as the usual chaos. Items were forgotten until the last moment or mislaid altogether; tempers grew frayed and Lucy Carlisle quarrelled with the Duchess of Richmond about the privilege of guarding Her Majesty's chest of correspondence. Kate kept her tongue very firmly between her teeth and attended to the duties assigned to her with ruthless efficiency.

Once back at Whitehall, she soon became aware that the strain of the early autumn had been replaced by a sort of half-confident, half-nervous excitement. The confidence was inspired by the fact that the King's party in the House now apparently rivalled Pym's in size, and also by the exuberant buoyancy evinced by Lord Digby; the nervousness came from speculation about what reply His Majesty would eventually make to the Remonstrance, coupled with fear that the Parliament's attempts to take control of the militia away from the King would precipitate a crisis.

Considering the angry murmurings outside the palace about the shocking price of coal and the King's appointment of several new bishops, Kate thought His Majesty showed quite remarkable sangfroid. Her own opinion was that, given the weekly bulletins on the activities of Parliament now being printed, and the number of apprentice lads at a loose end due to flagging trade, violence was likely to flare up at any minute. And if the pugnacious young fellows now guarding Westminster under the haughty Earl of Dorset – in place of the London Trained Bands under peaceful, pipe-smoking Essex – chose to retaliate, it would not take Parliament's expected Militia Bill to force that crisis.

In the midst of all this, Eden brought Celia to Court but somehow managed to deny Kate any opportunity to either explain or apologise; and, escorted by Kit, Venetia and her mother left Whitehall to spend Christmas at home in Yorkshire. The result was that, for the first time in her life, Kate knew what it was to feel isolated . . . and so, when Cyrus Winter took to seeking her company, she found herself less inclined than usual to discourage him. For one thing, it seemed to annoy Eden and there was therefore every possibility that he would eventually break his self-imposed silence to tell her so; and, in the meantime, Mr Winter was a well-informed and amusing companion from whom she swiftly learned a few long overdue lessons in the art of flirtation. It wasn't the most absorbing skill she had ever tried to acquire, but it was better than nothing. And life, if not perfect, at least remained reasonably tranquil until, on the evening that the Militia Bill passed its first reading, Luciano del Santi walked in and caused chaos without even trying.

Kate saw him immediately and felt the usual involuntary tightening of her nerves. Clad in his customary superbly cut black, he looked like a raven amongst peacocks, she thought irritably. Worse still, he was without doubt the most attractive man in the room, his dark austerity far outstripping even the much-admired angelic fairness of George Digby. And that wasn't just annoying: it was totally and utterly unfair.

'Damn,' said Kate weakly under her breath. 'Damn!'

'I beg your pardon?' Sitting forgotten at her side, Cyrus Winter regarded her with mock-alarm. 'Have I said something I shouldn't?'

With an effort, Kate brought her gaze back to his face and managed a cursory smile. 'At least a dozen, I should think. But I'll forgive you if you'll be good enough to excuse me for a while. I – the heat is beginning to overpower me.'

Since the vast chamber was no more than passably warm, his brows rose a trifle; but he was not the man to lose such a promising opportunity so he said smoothly, 'Why of course, my dear. But you can't surely suppose me so ungallant as to let you go alone. Come – let me escort you.'

Not particularly caring whether he came or not so long as she was able to avoid Luciano del Santi, Kate did not bother to argue. She merely rose, placed her hand on his arm and allowed him to lead her out into the gallery and from there to a small, little-used antechamber. Then, suddenly realising that conversation would be required of her, she said abruptly, 'Tell me something. Why do I continue to interest you? For you must by now have worked out that I've no intention of being seduced by you – or anyone else, come to that.'

The silver head was thrown back in what sounded like genuinely amused laughter and he said, 'You do favour the blunt style, don't you?'

'Only when I see a need for it. Well?'

'Perhaps I simply enjoy a challenge. I don't get many.'

Kate's expression grew faintly sardonic but she said merely, 'I see. And is that what Celia was?'

'Ah.' He eyed her consideringly. 'So you know about that, do you?'

'A little. I've also noticed that your interest in me coincided with Celia's reappearance at Court.'

242

'And you are wondering if I'm only flirting with you in order to annoy her.'

'Partly. I'm also wondering if you're toying with the notion of upsetting my brother through me.'

'Dear me!' he drawled plaintively. 'You must think me utterly Machiavellian.'

'Not necessarily. As yet I haven't decided *what* I think of you. It's just that I like to consider all the possibilities. But you haven't answered my question.'

'Which one? It's my impression that you've asked at least four,' he replied easily. And then, closing the space between them, 'In fact, my dear, I'm beginning to feel that you talk altogether too much.'

Unperturbed but aware that, if the situation should get out of hand, she had only herself to blame, Kate turned easily away from him. 'I don't know what else you had in mind. But I ought, without prejudice, to inform you that I bite.'

'Do you?' His teeth gleamed and one arm caught her effortlessly about the waist. 'So do I.'

Kate looked him straight in the eye with what was meant to be withering kindness – and suffered her first moment of doubt. His expression suddenly owed nothing to the idle, womanising gallant she had thought him; the charm had gone, the smile was empty of everything except purpose . . . and there was a hint of something more. Something she could not quite put a name to but most assuredly did not trust. She said calmly, 'I have excellent lungs. Take your hands off me or I'll use them. And what price your beautiful reputation as a seducer then?'

'One swallow neither makes a summer nor banishes a Winter,' he quipped. 'So don't threaten me, sweeting. For what I want, I invariably have.'

The green eyes filled with acidic interest. 'Celia being the exception that proves the rule, presumably?'

This time the smile vanished completely. 'Leave Celia out of this. Are you obsessed with her?'

'No. Are you?' she retorted. And then, 'Oh do stop posturing and let me go. This is becoming tedious.'

'Tedious?' His hold on her shifted and tightened. '*Tedious?* Then by all means let us progress.'

His intention was perfectly plain and, seeing it, Kate stamped on his foot, took a swipe at him with her free hand and opened her mouth to scream. Then, from the doorway, a melodious voice said blandly, 'I know you like to live dangerously, Kate . . . but isn't this carrying things a little too far?'

Kate's breath drained away and, on the same instant, she found herself free. She stared at Luciano del Santi and said faintly, 'All you need is a puff of smoke. How *do* you do it?'

'With mirrors,' came the laconic reply. 'But I believe we are delaying Mr Winter.'

For a brief, inimical moment, silver eyes met black. Then Cyrus Winter said softly, 'Well, well. The gutter-bred hunchback. Are you still bedding Mary Langley?'

Kate made a tiny strangled sound and clenched one hand hard over the other.

'No,' said the Italian with mild surprise. 'I thought you were.'

The pause this time was longer and more dangerous but at length Cyrus Winter strolled unhurriedly towards the door, saying, 'Take a word of advice. Don't cross my path again if you can help it. I don't bandy words with back-alley scum; I tread on it.' And brushing the signor contemptuously from his path, he was gone.

Kate sat weakly on the edge of a chair. 'Was that just witty repartee? Or have both you and he really—'

'Slept with Lady Wroxton? Yes.' He hesitated, resisted a strong impulse to swear and then added irascibly, 'Why else do you think Celia's father wouldn't have friend Cyrus as a son-in-law?'

'Oh.' Kate swallowed and thought about it. 'Does Celia know?'

'I doubt it.'

'And – and Eden?'

'I don't know. Why don't you ask him?'

'Because I'm not that stupid.' She frowned absently

down at her hands. 'It's all particularly nasty, isn't it?'

'Yes.' He stared at her, wishing he didn't know what she was thinking. Then, on a breath of pure irritation, he said, 'Once, Kate. I slept with the bloody woman once – and regretted it immediately. As for the rest . . . I'm sorry you've learned something you were never meant to know. But at least now perhaps you'll have the sense to keep away from Cyrus Winter.'

'I think,' remarked Kate, distantly, 'that you can be fairly sure of that. Is it why you followed me in here?'

'What do you think?'

'Then I suppose I ought to thank you.' She rose and awarded him a brittle smile. 'Thank you.'

'Don't mention it. And now you'd better go before the gossips get busy . . . while I try and interest His Majesty in the no doubt trivial fact that Anthony Van Dyck is dying.'

'Van Dyck? The court painter?' Kate's eyes widened. 'I didn't know that he was a friend of yours.'

'No. But then there's still quite a lot about me that you don't know,' he responded sardonically. 'However, by the time Gianetta has spent a few more months at Thorne Ash with Felicity, I daresay you'll be much better informed.' He paused and then said, 'Has that come as a surprise? I thought Eden would have told you.'

'Well, he didn't. How did that come about? You can't be off to Genoa again already.'

'I'm not. But Felicity asked for Gianetta's company and, since she's such a good influence, I was glad to agree. I'm hoping that this time she can talk Gianetta into occasionally discarding the odd ring or two.'

'I'm sure she'll do her best.' She looked back at him and felt the mood between them shift. 'I'm truly sorry about Sir Anthony. I can't understand why no one seems to know of it.'

'It's a sign of the times, Kate.' A cynical smile touched his mouth. 'And Blackfriars is a long way off.'

A few minutes later Kate stalked purposefully up to her

brother and said baldly, 'I'm sorry. I had no business to say what I did and I'm sorry.'

He did not look at her. 'Mother has asked me to tell you that we're leaving next week. Not Father, of course – but the rest of us. She seemed to think you might want to honour us with a visit.'

'Yes. I do.' She sighed and shook his arm. 'Will you *listen* to me?'

'Why should I?'

'Because I'm trying very hard to grovel.'

For a moment or two he said nothing and then the hazel eyes encompassed her with faintly bitter appraisal. 'Do you mean it?'

'Yes.' She drew a long breath. 'I – it's possible that I completely misunderstood, that's all.'

'You did. You misunderstand a lot of things, Kate. But one day you'll lay eyes on the only man you'll ever want; and then perhaps you'll know how it is with me.'

Quite without warning, Kate's nerves snarled themselves into a painful tangle and left her shivering on the edge of the vortex. For an instant every function of her body was suspended and she was incapable even of thought. The timing was all wrong and the knowledge was worse . . . but for once she was powerless to stop it. Quite slowly, she drew the shutters of her mind and focused her eyes once more on Eden's face. Then, with curious detachment, she said: 'I rather think I've already seen him. And it makes no difference. None at all.'

His brows rose. 'If you mean the elegant and eligible Mr Clifford, I can well believe it. And who else is there?'

'No one that I can possibly marry.'

He continued to stare at her, searching for an answer; and then, suddenly finding it, 'Oh God. No. You couldn't be so stupid.'

'No,' came the arid reply. 'I couldn't. And that, of course, is the whole point.'

Seven

In the days that followed, Kate did her best not to think about Luciano del Santi. There was, after all, no point. He was an Italian-Catholic money-lender whose father had gone to the gallows . . . on top of which he owned a brothel, kept a mistress and had slept with Eden's mother-in-law. And those were just the things she'd found out about. So even if he had wanted her, which he plainly didn't, there was no possibility of a relationship between them – nor could there ever be. And that was that.

Thanking God she was too sensible to let the matter distress her, she paid a fleeting visit to her family on the eve of their departure for Thorne Ash and successfully astounded her parents by calmly announcing that, if Kit Clifford should seek her hand in marriage, and they had no objections, she would like to accept him.

'What?' asked Richard blankly. And then, to Dorothy, 'Did you know about this?'

'Yes. I didn't tell you because it was all "Shall I or shan't I?",' she replied. 'So what's changed, Kate?'

'Nothing – except that I've thought it all out and decided that it's what I want,' said Kate obscurely. 'Would you dislike it?'

Richard looked at his wife. 'You know him better than I do. *Would* we dislike it?'

'No. It's exactly the kind of match we'd always hoped for. The only thing that bothers me is Kate's motive.'

'Well, it needn't,' said Kate firmly. And thought, 'What else can I say? I can hardly tell them that I need to keep away from Luciano del Santi and that, under the

247

circumstances, marriage to Kit is the best I can hope for.' She drew a long breath and said, 'I – I've missed him a great deal while he's been in the country . . . and it's helped me clear my mind. So you see, there's no need to worry. None at all.'

And with that they had, for the time being, to be satisfied.

Leaving Amy secure in the bosom of her new family and taking Gianetta in her stead, Dorothy, Eden, Felicity and a reluctant Celia duly set off next day through the mud and drizzle to spend Christmas at home. Richard, meanwhile, continued to watch national events gathering momentum, voted more and more often with the Moderates, and was grimly prepared to remove his daughter from Whitehall the moment the need should arise.

That moment, it seemed to Kate, could not now be long delayed. The Grand Remonstrance had been printed for any Tom, Dick or Harry to read and, by Christmas Eve, the King had not only been accused of breaching parliamentary privilege by openly refusing to pass the Militia Bill as it now stood, but was also rumoured to be toying with the notion of soothing the Catholic Irish with a promise of full religious liberty. And, as if that were not enough, he had also upset just about everyone, including his friends, by making bold, hot-headed Tom Lunsford lieutenant of the Tower of London.

The result was that throughout the course of a very uneasy Christmas Day, holidaying apprentices were able to add cries of 'Down with Butcher Lunsford' to their usual chorus of 'No bishops'. And by the following afternoon, the Lord Mayor was so frightened of losing control of the City that he finally persuaded the King to replace Colonel Lunsford with the equally loyal but distinctly more popular Sir John Byron. It was just unfortunate that, having leapt into the public eye, the Colonel decided to keep himself there by regularly beating up rioting apprentices outside Westminster Hall; all of which – along with implications that the Queen was hand in glove with the Irish – rather took the gloss off His Majesty's long-awaited and beautifully reasoned response to the Remonstrance.

And suddenly everything began to crystallise. The King instructed the City's Trained Bands to stand ready against 'the mean and unruly people' who were blocking Westminster Stairs to prevent the bishops taking their seats in Parliament, and the Commons asked for those same Trained Bands to guard them against the violence of the 'malignant party', whilst simultaneously impeaching a dozen bishops for protesting at their exclusion from the Lords. The Queen unwittingly coined a nickname for every disloyal knave from Pym downwards – calling them all Roundheads, after the crop-haired apprentice lads; and the apprentices retaliated by labelling the King's friends Cavaliers – which was the worst thing they could think of since it derived from the national enemy, Spain.

The old year passed away in an increasing dither of uncertainty and, on the first day of 1642, the Commons removed itself to the Guildhall 'for reasons of safety' and discussed new evidence of Henrietta Maria's involvement with the Irish. By evening, Whitehall echoed with whispers that Pym was planning to impeach the Queen, and Kate lived in hourly expectation of seeing her father come to take her home; instead of which the following afternoon found her face to face with Venetia Clifford.

'I don't believe it!' she said weakly, trying not to let her eyes slide past Venetia to Kit and the unknown man who was with him. 'You said you wouldn't be back till after Twelfth Night – and the roads are appalling. How on earth did you get here?'

'With difficulty,' responded Venetia crisply. 'But I thank God we did. I've been with Her Majesty too long to desert her now. And Ellis has been in the Low Countries and seen Prince Rupert, so naturally he wanted to – oh! This *is* Ellis, by the way.'

Kate grinned at the satin-clad exquisite, complete with chestnut love-locks and a moustache, and saw that he was not in the least put out by this careless introduction.

'Mistress Kate, I presume?' inquired Ellis Brandon,

performing a graceful bow. 'I'm delighted to meet you at last – having had your praises sung to me, *a capella* and *basso ostinato* as it were, throughout Yule. And no – ' as Kate looked at Venetia – 'not by my beautiful betrothed – whose mind is almost wholly concerned with political matters these days. So I will leave you to guess who you must blame and confess instead that we share a common embarrassment. *The* Commons in fact – for I understand that your father sits in it, just as mine is its greatest admirer and advocate.'

Amusement faded and Kate raised her brows. Seeing it, Kit said quickly, 'Not everyone disagrees with their father on principle as you do, Ellis. And now let's get out of this crush to somewhere a bit more private so Kate can tell us what's been going on.'

'Yes, let's,' nodded Venetia. 'Come on. I know a little room.'

So did Kate but she forbore to mention it. And instead, when they were all seated, embarked on a concise resumé of the past three weeks. Mention of Colonel Lunsford caused Mr Brandon's eye to brighten and he said, 'Sounds as if old Tom's been having fun. He's a real Roaring Boy!'

'He certainly is,' returned Kate dryly. 'It's just a pity, as my brother would say, that he seems to think with his stomach.'

'Quite,' said Venetia. 'But tell us about the Queen. What exactly is it they're saying?'

'That Pym is preparing to impeach her. He's supposedly received evidence from a kinsman of his in Ireland that she authorised the rebellion there in defence of the Roman Catholic Church. Whether or not it's true—'

'Of course it's not!' snapped Venetia hotly. 'Oh, I know she favours the Papists . . . but how can anyone think she's stupid enough to stir up the Irish?'

'Because the Irish themselves have been claiming royal support,' Kate replied. 'And it's taken the King until today to deny it. If he'd done it right away, the Queen might now be in less danger and the Londoners wouldn't be getting hysterical at the thought of Papist forces subduing Ireland and England both.'

'*Is* that what they think?' asked Kit slowly.

'Well, of course. You know what people are like. And right now, with rumours spreading like wildfire and violence erupting on every other street corner, it probably doesn't seem all that far-fetched to them.'

For a moment there was silence and then, her voice oddly strained, Venetia said, 'The King will never allow Her Majesty to be impeached. He can't.'

'No,' agreed Kate. 'He can't. And if the gossips are to be believed, he's spent today trying to bribe Pym by offering him the Exchequer again – only Pym, of course, refused. So they say the post's gone to Culpeper instead and that Lord Falkland's been made Secretary of State. But what will happen next, I'm afraid, is anybody's guess.'

'If you ask me,' remarked Ellis languidly, 'it's high time His Majesty ceased pandering to these impudent dogs and took his stand.'

'I imagine he very probably will,' retorted Kate. 'But the question that's obsessing the rest of us is – how?'

A little later, when Venetia had gone to report her return to Lady Carlisle and Mr Brandon was making his bow to the King, Kit looked at Kate and said, 'You think we've reached the point of no return, don't you?'

'What other conclusion is there? The King can't give way on this one and Pym knows it. So the only loophole will be in how he chooses to act – and he hasn't too many options.'

'Short of having Pym assassinated, I can't think of *any*,' replied Kit. 'However. That's not what I wanted to say to you.'

Something shifted behind Kate's elegant green bodice and she kept her eyes discreetly on her hands. 'No?'

'No. Quite simply, it's this. If matters reach a crisis, I imagine your father will have you out of here with all possible speed. And that being so, you and I no longer have any time to waste.' He paused, his colour slightly heightened. 'The circumstances are a little awkward but I've taken what steps I can to do things properly. I've obtained my father's leave to address you and have in my pocket a letter from him to your father. What I need to know is whether or not I've your consent to – to deliver it.' He stopped again and grasped her hands. 'Oh God. I'm doing it all wrong, aren't I? Kate . . . I love you. Will you please marry me?'

There seemed to be a fog inside her head and she felt rather cold; but for the sake of safety and good sense and peace of mind, she knew what she had to do. The only difficulty, it appeared, was in getting the words out. So she swallowed, drew a long steadying breath and then said remotely, 'Yes, Kit. I will.'

By mutual consent they elected to keep their understanding strictly to themselves until Kit was able to speak with Richard; and Kate – on seeing Kit's transparent happiness – silently salved her conscience by vowing that he should never, ever know to what he owed it. Meanwhile, for better or worse, there were more important things to think of.

On Monday 3 January, the King followed Lord Digby's advice and had his six main opponents accused of high treason before the House of Lords. Pym's name headed the list – followed by Hampden, who'd fought so hard against ship-money, Strode and Haselrig for their part in the Militia Bill, Denzil Holles for just about everything else and, last but not least, the principal architect of opposition in the Upper House, Lord Mandeville. The plan had been for Digby to propose their immediate arrest but, unreliable to the last, he somehow failed to do so – with the result that both Houses joined in hasty consultation and announced that the said accusation constituted a breach of parliamentary privilege.

Before evening, His Majesty had retaliated by making the articles of treason public – and presumably found a certain satisfaction in so doing since it had, after all, been done to his friend Strafford. He also forbade the Lord Mayor to send any Trained Bands to guard the Commons and called all the gentlemen volunteers at the Inns of Court to stand ready to defend both King and Kingdom.

All that night and into the next day the tension at Whitehall was so strong as to be almost tangible. The Queen stayed closeted in her rooms with only the Duchess of Richmond, Lucy Carlisle and a handful of other trusted confidantes, while in the palace at large, the same questions were to be read in everyone's eyes. 'Will His Majesty manage to lay Pym by the heels – or will the House thwart him? And, in either case, what will happen then?'

Kate spent the morning gleaning what news she could in between letting Kit hold her hand. Then, tense to the point of screaming, she went off to prowl restlessly about the antechamber outside the Queen's door . . . which was how, at a little after two, she came to see my lady Carlisle emerge hurriedly from the royal presence.

'What are you doing here?' demanded her ladyship sharply.

'Nothing,' said Kate with perfect truth. 'I just thought I'd stay within call in case I'm wanted.'

'Well, you're not. Her Majesty has the Duchess with her and doesn't require you,' came the tart reply. And then, 'Ah. Is that your cloak?'

'Yes.' Faintly surprised, Kate glanced to where it lay across a chair. 'I went out for a breath of air and couldn't be bothered taking it all the way—'

'I daresay you've no objection to my borrowing it?' Even as she spoke, Lady Carlisle had crossed the room and picked the garment up. 'I, too, need a little fresh air – and I'll see that it's returned to you presently. In the meantime, I suggest that you go and seek occupation elsewhere.' And with that, she was gone.

Kate stared thoughtfully after her and toyed with the notion of following. However, before she could reach any conclusion on the possible usefulness of this course of action, Venetia flew into the room saying, 'Kate – have you seen Ellis at all?'

'Not since this morning. Should I have done?'

'No. It's just that he and Roxburgh and quite a few others I could name are nowhere to be found. And I've got a feeling that it's because something is happening.'

Kate eyed her forebodingly.

'Something, perhaps, that might account for Lucy Carlisle rushing out of here in my cloak? Yes. What a pity I didn't follow her, after all. It would be nice to know what's going on, wouldn't it?'

After an uneasy morning in the Commons, Richard Maxwell would also have given a good deal to know what was going on – for it did not need a genius to work out that something was. For one thing, after the fears and alarums of the previous week, the House had that morning unaccountably chosen to quit the Guildhall and return to Westminster; and for another, it seemed damned odd that Pym, Hampden, Haselrig, Strode and Holles should all be present and correct upon their benches when they'd only yesterday been accused of high treason. It very much looked as though His Majesty – if he wished to lay hands on the five – was being invited to breach parliamentary privilege by doing so with force in the House. And if that were so, it was as nicely baited a trap as Richard had ever seen. All that remained was to see if the King would step into it.

They spent the morning trying to countermand the orders His Majesty had given overnight, and then paused to fortify themselves with the noon-day meal, after which Richard resumed his seat with the rest and prayed that the afternoon might be uneventful. It was, he realised later, too much to hope for. At around three o'clock word came that the King was coming in person to Westminster, along with all his guard, his pensioners and two or three hundred soldiers and gentlemen.

It was all Pym had been waiting for and, rising, he immediately asked the Speaker's permission for himself and his friends to depart. It was granted and within minutes they were gone – dragging a plainly reluctant Strode out of the Hall by his cloak. Then, almost before the House had resettled itself, the King was at the door.

Richard watched him come in, that small slight man on whom the grievances of years had now fallen, and thought, 'He ought not to have come himself. They'll never forgive him.'

The doors were open and through them, as he rose with the rest and removed his hat, Richard could see soldiers playfully levelling their pistols. The Earl of Roxburgh and a maliciously smiling individual whom Richard did not recognise leaned against either side of the door, and the Elector Palatine followed his uncle the King down towards the Speaker's chair.

Punctilious to the last, Charles had also uncovered his head and, reaching William Lenthall, said gravely, 'Mr Speaker . . . I must for a time make bold with your chair.'

Lenthall made way for him but the King did not sit, merely standing upon the steps surveying the House before finally saying, 'I would not for anything break your privilege, gentlemen. But I fear that treason *has* no privilege and I am come for those five members whom you know of. Is Mr Pym here?'

Silence.

'I ask you again. Is Mr Pym here? Also, Mr Holles and the rest?' He waited but still received no answer. Then, sharply, 'Speaker Lenthall – are the five I seek present within the House?'

Driven into an impossible corner, William Lenthall did the only thing he could think of. He knelt before the King and said loudly, 'I pray you to excuse me, sir. I am the servant of the House and have neither eyes to see nor tongue to say anything but what I am commanded.'

For a long moment he was subjected to bitter scrutiny. Then, 'No matter,' said the King with irony. 'I think my eyes are as good as another's – and I see that my birds are flown. I expect, however, that the House will send them to me. And if you do not, I shall be forced to seek them out myself that they may stand their trial for a most foul treason.'

And so saying, he descended the steps and trod briskly out of the chamber, his footsteps ringing loud in the continuing deathly hush.

News of the King's failed coup broke quickly at Whitehall, turning nervous excitement into appalled grimness. Kate, knowing that her departure from Court must now be imminent, told her maid to start packing and went to wait in the Stone Gallery with Kit. When – as she had expected – Richard arrived, she said baldly, 'How bad is it?'

'Bad enough,' he replied, briefly kissing her. 'Shops are shut and the streets are full of people. Some fellow's even handing out leaflets saying "To your tents, O Israel!". So if the King lets any of his young hot-heads try to drag Pym out of the City, I wouldn't wager a groat on there not being a mass riot.'

Kate had already guessed as much so she merely said, 'And you want me to come home. Yes. I'll go and see if Jenny has finished packing. But, in the meantime, Kit would like a word with you.' And she was gone.

Richard looked resignedly at Mr Clifford and thought, 'Blast. I really could do without this right now.'

And, seeing it, Kit said ruefully, 'This isn't a good moment, is it? So perhaps it would be best if I simply gave you this letter from my father and asked if I may call on you at home.'

'Much the best,' agreed Richard, accepting the missive. 'With the roads as they are, it will be a while before I can get Kate back to Thorne Ash. I assume this *is* to do with Kate?'

'Yes,' said Kit, colouring a little.

'Ah. Well, don't be too despondent. I've no objections to you that I'm aware of – and my wife approves of you. So if your father's happy with the match and Kate herself wants it, the only problem you have is the same one facing us all.'

Something altered subtly in Kit's face.

'Rebellion?' he asked gravely.

'No,' came the flat, terrible reply. 'Civil war.'

During the week that followed, Richard's reluctant prophecy

seemed to come ever closer. The King entered the City with promises of a free Parliament and security of religion only to be greeted with cries of 'Privilege!' In defiance of the Lord Mayor, petitions were drafted against papists and Sir John Byron's command of the Tower – while apprentices built barricades against the King's marauding Cavaliers. Sailors and river-boatmen flocked into the City, swearing to 'live and die for Parliament' and the London Trained Bands (finally placed in the experienced hands of Philip Skippon) took to drilling in the streets.

It was at this point that the King, realising the full extent of his failure to subdue his opponents, left Whitehall under cover of darkness and took his wife and three eldest children to the greater safety of cheerless, unprepared Hampton Court.

That was on Monday 10 January. On Tuesday the 11th, Luciano del Santi at long last met the old man who – for almost two months – had been refusing to see him: Justice Samuel Fisher.

Just as Richard had done before him, he followed the slatternly maid up the rotting staircase. The only difference, though he did not know it, was that this time the odour was of fish. And then he was in the hot, foul atmosphere of Mr Fisher's room.

For a moment neither of them spoke, and Luciano was happy to have it so while he mastered his sudden nausea. Then the old man said slowly, 'So. The traitor's brat, I presume?'

'My name,' came the carefully controlled reply, 'is Luciano del Santi. But you may call me whatever you like. I'm only here because I understand you've some information to sell.'

'Not so fast, my buck – not so fast. I don't know yet that I choose to do business with you. First you can come over here into the light so I can get a proper look at you.'

Luciano took his time about obeying this command but at length he advanced without haste towards the window. Although he was a little pale, his face was entirely without expression and his hands appeared perfectly relaxed.

Justice Fisher examined his visitor from head to foot, taking in the elegantly cut black coat and the beautiful lace collar lying beneath long, crisply curling dark hair. Then, erupting into wheezing laughter, he said spitefully, 'My God – it's an Italian crookback! Fortune certainly didn't smile on you, did it? Gallows-meat for a father and deformed to boot! Born that way, were you?'

'Due, I'm told, to inexpert midwifery – yes,' responded Luciano coolly. And then, 'You won't annoy me, you know. So unless my physical imperfections have an especial fascination for you, I suggest we progress to the matter that brought me here.'

'Which is?'

'The case of Alessandro Falcieri.'

'Your father, you mean.'

'That is your assumption, Mr Fisher. Cling to it if you will – but try to remember that I do not confirm it.'

With an irritable grimace, the Justice shifted his position in the great, carved chair. 'Cautious, aren't you?'

'What did you expect? Impassioned confidences and entreaties? If so, prepare yourself for a disappointment. All I have to offer is a simple business transaction which can be accomplished in a few minutes and leave you substantially better off. Well?'

There was another long silence. Then, 'What is it you want to know?'

'First of all,' said Luciano remotely, 'whether or not you had any dealings with Alessandro Falcieri's trial.'

'And if I did?'

'The names of the chief prosecution witnesses.'

'Why?'

'That, Mr Fisher, is my affair. Yours is whether or not you intend to answer my questions.'

'Wrong, my fine popinjay. It's to find out if you've the resources to make it worth my while.'

'You mean you haven't already made inquiries about my financial status?' asked Luciano dryly. 'You surprise me. However, you may take it that I'm well able to pay you.'

'Good.' A malevolent smile revealed a mouthful of rotting teeth. 'Then I'll take a thousand pounds.'

The narrow brows rose a fraction but the mellow tones remained unchanged. 'I said I would pay you, Mr Fisher. I did not say I was willing to be fleeced. Five hundred.'

'What's the matter? Don't the poor bastards you feed off bleed freely enough? Or have you forgotten that I'm the only one who can help you?'

'Not at all. At present, however, I'm still awaiting proof of it.' Impatience stirred and, repressing it, Luciano continued implacably, 'I ask you again. Did you play any part in the trial?'

Samuel Fisher spread his swollen fingers on the arm of his chair and smilingly made his visitor wait for an answer. Then he said softly, 'Yes. I was – as your clever friend was so quick to work out – the counsel for the prosecution. And that is all you'll get without showing me the colour of your money.'

Something turned in Luciano's stomach. It was what he had come to hear and he ought to have been prepared for it, but somehow he wasn't. Drawing a long, steadying breath, he pulled a heavy purse from his pocket and dropped it on the table, saying, 'You'll find it the same as anyone else's. Now tell me why the trial record was suppressed – and by whom.'

'So you know that, do you?'

'Obviously. Well?'

Grunting a little, the old man reached out for the purse and weighed it thoughtfully in his hand. He said, 'I wonder what it cost you to find that out? Enough, I'll wager, to double the disappointment. Yes. I imagine you'd give a good deal to see the original of that particular document, wouldn't you? Much more, shall we say, than this paltry five hundred.'

The dark gaze sharpened. '*You* have it?'

'What's the matter? Hadn't the possibility occurred to you? You can't be as bright as you look.'

'Perhaps not. But I'm by no means stupid enough to

put my trust in veiled allusions.' An ominous silkiness invested the courteous voice. 'Do you have it or not?'

'What's it worth?'

Without a word, Luciano pulled off the great, square-cut emerald that adorned his left hand and held it up to the light where it gleamed with fitful green fire.

A change came across the puffy, glistening face and Samuel Fisher said hoarsely, 'Let me see it.'

'Ah. You like emeralds? But of course you do. Who doesn't? And this one – unusually for so large a stone – is quite flawless. I myself have never seen another like it.' He paused and smiled invitingly. 'Your move, I think.'

The Justice's answer was to withdraw several folded sheets of paper from the breast of his filthy coat and clutch them mistrustfully to his chest. 'Give me the ring.'

'All in good time. First I'd like to point out that we are alone here and that it would be a mistake to try and cheat me.'

'Slit my throat, would you?'

'No. But there are, fortunately, other options.' The stench in the room was fast becoming unbearable and Luciano wondered briefly how much longer he could control his stomach. 'If you took the trouble to steal that document, you must have had a use for it. In which case, how come it's still in your possession?'

'That's my business. But it's genuine enough, if that's what worries you.' Clumsily, the fat hands unfolded enough of the papers for Luciano to catch a glimpse of faded script. 'And it's complete. Now put the ring on the table.'

Slowly but without hesitation, Luciano did so – and had to catch the papers mid-air as the old man threw them at him in order to dive on the emerald. He scanned the sheets rapidly before refolding them with hands that were no longer entirely steady. Then, realising that he had to get out or risk being sick on the spot, he said evenly, 'Our meeting may not have been a pleasure, Mr Fisher, but at least it seems to have been to our mutual advantage and, with luck, need never be repeated. Enjoy your emerald.' And, pursued by the eerie echo of Samuel Fisher's laughter, he was gone.

Luciano had travelled to Lambeth by boat from Puddle Wharf but he knew he couldn't return the same way. The tide was against him. So after he'd got rid of his breakfast in the Justice's overgrown garden, he walked down to the Stangate Stairs to look for a lighterman who would row him across to Westminster. He felt cold and curiously detached from everything except the folded papers in his pocket. Later, he knew he would be glad that he hadn't had to discuss his father with that rank and vicious old man; but for the time being it was beyond him. He only wanted to go home.

The river was remarkably busy. Indeed, a noisy and oddly assorted flotilla of gaily bedecked craft appeared to be sailing towards them from the City and eventually Luciano pierced his chilly cocoon to ask what was happening.

'Don't you know?' was the boatman's surprised response. 'It's John Pym and Mr Hampden and the rest. Now the King's run off, they're coming back to Westminster so we can have a proper Parliament at last.'

'Then let us hope that it lives up to your expectations,' said Luciano indifferently. And relapsed once more into silence.

He left the boat at Westminster Stairs and set off on foot along King Street towards Charing Cross. It was a mistake. The way was virtually jammed with cheering crowds, through which marched the London Trained Bands with colours flying and drums beating as though in celebration of a huge victory. And outside the deserted palace of Whitehall was a chant of 'Where is the King and his Cavaliers?'

Although he was well aware of the ominous significance of it all, Luciano merely continued to elbow his way through the jostling throng and head for Cheapside. The perilous path this nation was treading could wait; today was for his own affairs.

It was much later, in the solitude of his parlour, that he was finally able to examine his prize and find it everything he had hoped and feared it would be. The precise nature of the evidence was set down in meticulous detail and, with it, the names of the men who had given it. Luciano read and reread the pages . . . and then sat simply staring at them while he waited for the reality of it to strike him.

Four names. Giles Langley, Ahiram Webb, Thomas Ferrars and Robert Brandon. Four faceless names.

All he had to do now was find the men they belonged to.

'The God of peace in his good time send us peace – and in the meantime fit us to receive it. We are both upon the stage and must act those parts that are assigned to us in this tragedy. Let us do it in a way of honour and without personal animosities.'

Sir William Waller to Sir Ralph Hopton

Debatable Land

June 1642 to November 1643

Now that the world is all in amaze
Drums and Trumpets rending heavens,
Wounds a-bleeding, Mortals dying,
Widows and Orphans piteously crying;
Armies marching, Towns in a blaze,
Kingdoms and States at sixes and sevens;
What should an honest Fellow do,
Whose courage and fortunes run equally low?
Let him nothing do, he could wish undone;
And keep himself safe from the noise of a Gun.

Thomas Flatman

One

'I wonder,' remarked Felicity, without raising her eyes from her embroidery, 'if anything is ever going to actually happen?'

Everyone knew what she meant, of course, but for a moment it seemed that no one could be bothered to reply. Unmindful of her expensive silks and trailing the inevitable pearls, Gianetta Falcieri del Santi sat on the grass and continued amusing Meg Bennet's baby daughter, Eve, with a string of amber beads; Kate put the finishing touches to a sketch of her sleeping nephew whilst considering the peculiar but not unlikely possibility that both babies – when they began to talk – might do so with Italian accents; and the bees droned on undisturbed amongst the roses until the peace was shattered by a violent discord as Celia's hand swept angrily across the strings of her guitar.

'Going to happen? It's already happening – and has been for five months! Or do you suppose the Queen's gone to the Low Countries on holiday and the King's in York for his own amusement?'

'No. As I understand it, she's gone to pawn her jewels and he's raising an army. Just the same,' said Felicity with a mischievous, glancing smile, 'as the Parliament's supposedly doing. But what I meant was – is it ever going to amount to more than a few heated words in the marketplace?'

'No.' Gianetta put down the beads in order to move little Eve more securely into the shade. 'Englishmen do not fight – they talk. Always talk, talk, talk. Is very boring.'

'That's all you know!' grinned Felicity. 'And Eden

265

doesn't just talk. He's recruited twenty men already and—'

'Felicity.' Kate stopped drawing and looked up. 'It's a beautiful day. Stop ill-wishing us all for the sake of a little excitement.'

'I wasn't. It's only that I can't help wondering if Eden's ever likely to wear this.' She held up the tawny silk sash, lovingly worked with silver thread. 'You must admit that it will be a pity if he doesn't.'

'A pity? Is that what you think?' Celia surged to her feet in a flurry of cherry taffeta. 'My God – can't any of you get it into your heads that taking up arms against the King is treason?'

'If,' said Kate, 'it should come to that. And we must all go on hoping it won't. But if it does . . . has Eden said that's what he'll do?'

'No. He hasn't *said* anything. But if he isn't planning to throw in his lot with the Parliament – *where is he now?*'

'I've no idea. You tell me.'

'Consorting with Lord Saye and Sele at Broughton – or counting guns with one or other of the old man's sons in Banbury,' came the hot retort. 'And you can stop pretending you don't know what he's up to. You do. All of you. But there's a conspiracy to keep me in the dark.'

'And if there is, can you wonder at it?' sighed Kate. 'We know how you feel. Goodness only knows you make it plain enough. But none of us wants the house to become a battle-ground.'

'And *I* don't want to find myself branded a rebel! My father's with the King and my mother's gone with the Queen. And—'

'And our father sits in the Commons,' interposed Kate, her patience beginning to wear thin. 'How many times do I have to say it? Can't you realise that it's difficult for us all?'

'She realise nothing.' Gianetta raised a critical dark gaze to encompass Celia and stated the point of view dearest to her heart. 'She is also very bad mother.'

'How *dare* you?' Celia spun round to meet the

unexpected attack. 'Just because I don't choose to spend my days cooing over a cradle like some Italian peasant—'

'I,' said Gianetta flatly, 'am no peasant. Is just that I like babies.'

'Well you're certainly marvellous with these two,' offered Felicity pacifically. 'Mother says she's never seen such a well-run nursery.'

'I enjoy,' shrugged the other girl. 'And Meg is very good nurse-maid. But she love *her* little girl.'

'Her little bastard, you mean.' It was a sore point with Celia that Dorothy had not only insisted on Meg's baby being brought up at Thorne Ash but also installed Meg herself as nurse to both infants. 'It's absolutely disgraceful that my son has to share his nursery with that slut's by-blow.'

'Oh don't start that again!' Kate got up, brushing bits of grass from her skirt. 'Meg's not a slut. And as for Eve sharing the nursery – I don't see how it can matter to you. You never set foot in the place if you can help it – and I honestly doubt if Jude knows you're his mother.'

'You wicked creature!' gasped Celia. 'It's not true!'

'No?' Kate's attention had wandered. 'Well, I wouldn't lose your temper over it just now. We have visitors.'

Celia checked herself and, along with the others, followed the direction of Kate's gaze. Then, on an incredulous breath, 'My God . . . *Francis*!'

'Francis,' agreed Kate, her tone still oddly remote, 'and Kit. Ah well, I suppose I'd better go and greet him.'

Celia was already skimming across the grass towards her brother. Watching Kate set off sedately in her wake, Gianetta said meditatively, 'This Kit is the man she marry, yes? Which is he?'

'The fair-haired one,' replied Felicity obligingly. 'The other one is Celia's brother.'

'Is so?' A pause; and then, 'He is very elegant.'

'Francis? Isn't he just!' Felicity looked her friend full in the eye and grinned. 'And – so far as we know – unmarried.'

Tilting her head in almost imperceptible acknowledgement, Gianetta elected to change the subject. 'But why is it not Kate who runs?'

'That's a very good question – but one which I doubt she'll answer.'

Just at that moment, meeting Mr Clifford's eyes and letting him kiss her hands, Kate would have been hard-pressed to explain her feelings to anyone. *His*, it was perfectly obvious, were the same as they had been in January; but that was less a relief than a responsibility. And though she was pleased to see him, she was just as pleased to see Francis . . . which, though faintly depressing, wasn't particularly surprising, for Francis didn't come imbued with the same complications.

'My dear, my dear!' murmured Kit, still holding fast to her hands. 'At last. Had you quite given me up?'

'I never give anything up,' returned Kate lightly. 'And your letters suggest you've been trying to girdle the earth since we last met.'

'Something very like it. Windsor, Dover, Holland with the Queen; then to France bearing letters and back to York with yet more. Which reminds me – I've one for you from Venetia. And somewhere along the way I ran into our prodigal friend here.'

'So I see.' Kate withdrew her hands whilst watching Francis similarly and carefully disentangling himself from Celia and then said, 'French tailoring, Francis? It looks expensive.'

'Exorbitant!' he agreed, descending on her with an all-too-familiar glint in his eye. 'Kate, my beloved – I'm stunned! Someone should have warned me such a metamorphosis was taking place and I'd have returned forthwith.'

'Even at the risk of spending a few months in the Tower?'

He snapped his fingers. 'A mere bagatelle compared to losing you to such an unspectacular and undeserving fellow. However. I understand there is as yet no formal contract between you, so I don't despair. And – as a friend of such long-standing – I really don't think Kit can object if I salute you as such.' Upon which he placed his hands on her waist and lightly kissed both cheeks. 'There! Aren't you sorry you didn't wait?'

'Mountebank!' said Kit, laughing.

And, 'I'm glad to see,' remarked Kate dulcetly, 'that you've lost none of your customary elan.'

'My dear – only give me time and I'll prove to you that I've lost absolutely nothing! But seriously now . . . it seems that I've to wish you joy. When is the great day to be? I insist on being the first to know.'

Kate silently damned him and responded with her best smile. 'And so you shall be – when it's been decided. But in the meantime, why not come and see if you can dazzle Gianetta? Or, alternatively, if *she* can dazzle *you*.'

His brows rose. 'Meaning?'

'Meaning,' cut in Celia shrewishly, 'that the low-bred creature is simply laden with the most vulgar display of jewels you've ever seen.'

'Dear me!' Francis evinced signs of mild interest. 'Do I detect a hint of dislike? How intriguing. By all means let us go immediately.'

Still sitting on the grass, Gianetta acknowledged the introduction of Messrs Langley and Clifford with nothing more than a smile and a gracious inclination of her dark head. But the quality of the smile – languidly tantalising and full of subtle promise – was apparently enough to make Francis decide to sacrifice his crimson silk; or it might, thought Kate cynically, have been the pearls and rubies. One never knew with Francis. At any rate, he tossed a bantering greeting to Felicity and then dropped artistically on one knee beside Gianetta in order to kiss her dimpled wrist.

'Signorina Gianetta, how fortuitous. I believe I can give you news of your brother.'

Kate's heart lurched. Gianetta, on the other hand, merely raised uninterested brows and said, 'Oh? He is back from Genoa?'

'Very much so. He is in York.'

'Really?' Two syllables of complete indifference.

This time even Francis looked faintly nonplussed. Then Felicity said helpfully, 'York? What on earth's he doing there?'

'Principally, asking my father a stream of – dare I say impertinent? – questions about his late lamented cousin.'

'Cousin Giles?' Celia stared at him. 'But he's been dead for years!'

'Precisely. So one naturally wonders what the signor's reasons might be.'

Gianetta shrugged. 'Business. With Luciano, is *always* business. Me – I know nothing and do not care.'

'Ah.' Francis flicked an imaginary speck of dust from his cuff and then looked up. 'Kate?'

'Don't be silly,' she said. 'How would *I* know?'

'Just a thought. I'm told that your esteemed parent has become the signor's very good friend.'

'Then you'd better ask Father himself, hadn't you? He'll be home in August.'

'August? But that, dear Kate, is still some six weeks away, and who knows where I may be by then? So little time and so much to do, you know. Ah well. This sudden interest in our deceased relative will just have to remain one of life's little mysteries.' He paused and then, waving a graceful hand at the two sleeping infants, said, 'I thought you'd only the one, Celia. Never say I'm an uncle twice over already?'

'How could you be with Jude not a year old yet?' she snapped. 'That one is Kate's tire-woman's bastard. *This* is my son.' And, scooping Jude up, she held him out for inspection.

Rudely awakened, he opened his eyes and began to cry. Kit chuckled, Gianetta made a sound of pure exasperation, and Francis eyed the screaming bundle dubiously.

'Very nice. And his lungs are excellent,' he said. 'No, no – I've no ambition to hold him. Babies are not my forte.'

'Give him to me,' said Gianetta, holding out her arms.

Celia looked at her, plainly torn between wanting to prove her maternal ability and a desire to be free of the noisy, wriggling baby. Then her normal instincts won and she dumped Jude unceremoniously in Gianetta's lap – where he instantly stopped crying and settled back with a beatific smile.

Still laughing a little, Kit strolled over to look down at

270

him, saying, 'A lusty little chap, isn't he? You and Eden must be very proud of him, Celia.'

'Yes,' came the careless reply. 'We are.'

'He certainly looks to have inherited Eden's colouring,' observed Francis idly. And then, 'Speaking of which . . . where *is* Eden?'

Kate and Celia's eyes met and locked.

'Out,' said Kate. 'I think there was some question of missing livestock.'

'Why bother to lie?' Celia's gaze swept back to her brother. 'You might as well know that Eden is thick as thieves with Old Subtlety and his sons these days – and at this very moment is probably helping one of them grease a cannon or some such thing.'

'Does one grease a cannon?' asked Francis, not noticeably perturbed. 'No matter. I'm sure Eden knows. And, as for the rest . . . it is, of course, entirely regrettable – but not, I would have thought, especially surprising. And, to be truthful, my dear, it's one of the reasons I came.'

'To talk him out of it?' asked Celia eagerly.

'Let us rather say – to discuss the matter.'

Frowning a little, Kate said, 'That sounds remarkably philosophical.'

'No, no – merely civilised. One's opinions may differ from those of one's friends – one may even eventually find oneself fighting on the opposing side. But there's no need to allow the thing to become *personal*, is there?'

'I imagine it becomes *damned* personal when you're facing each other over a couple of loaded pistols,' observed Kit with unusual dryness.

For a moment, brief, airless silence gripped the garden. Then Kate said remotely, 'You're talking as though war is inevitable.'

'Quite,' said Francis. 'It's been so ever since the Parliament decided to wrest control of the armed forces from the King by means of this so-called Militia Ordinance. His Majesty can never – and *will* never – agree to it.'

'So he'll fight?' asked Felicity.

'What else can he do?' It was Kit who answered her.

'He's been turned away from the gates of Hull; his friends are being persecuted and all his appointments revoked; and the Commons has declared him "seduced by evil councillors" and usurped his authority. He's the Lord's Anointed . . . but he's been treated as no king ever was before him.'

'Condemned, you might say, on less evidence than would hang a fellow for stealing a horse,' finished Francis quietly. 'So the only question now, I fear, is who will strike the first real blow.'

Later, when the others had gone into the house to partake of refreshments with Dorothy, Kate looked at Kit and said slowly, 'We have a problem, haven't we?'

'Yes. But not, I hope, one that is either permanent or without a solution.' He drew a long breath and then loosed it. 'Kate – it rather looks as though whatever's going to happen will happen quite soon. The King has issued his Commissions of Array – his call to arms, in effect – and the Parliament is currently appealing for loans to pay an army. But England has been peaceful for so long that I suspect neither side really knows what it's doing – and both are reluctant.'

'So?' asked Kate. Her face was slightly averted and her fingers toyed aimlessly with the roses.

'So it could all be over very quickly. With the first big battle, in fact. And, if it is, life ought to return to some semblance of normality.'

'I see.' Care kept her tone free of any traces of relief. 'And that being so, the best thing we can do is wait?'

'Either that – or marry immediately and hang the consequences,' he replied. 'But I don't somehow think you're ready to do that. Nor, I imagine, would your family permit it.'

'No. Probably not. Any more than I could leave Thorne Ash just now.' She turned and looked at him, her eyes perfectly stark. 'With Father at Westminster and Eden – well, who knows where Eden may go? – I'll be needed here.'

'By your mother? But surely she has Celia?'

Kate gave a brief, sardonic laugh. 'Unless Celia changes

overnight, she'll be more of a hindrance than a help. And even if her sympathies ran with ours – which you must surely have noticed they don't – I can't see her caring for the tenants or helping with the harvest. Or even, should the need arise, defending this house.'

Kit regarded her thoughtfully. 'But you would?'

'Yes.' Her hands moved in a gesture half-helpless, half-defiant. 'I don't approach this quarrel the way you do – or Francis or even Eden. You might say, I suppose, that I'm politically indifferent – though I don't think that's true. I can understand what the Parliament is trying to achieve and sympathise with the view taken by the King. But at the end of the day, only two things really matter to me. One is loyalty to my father – for no better reason than that's who he is and I respect him; and the other is Thorne Ash, our lives here and everything we've always held dear.' She paused and awarded him a small crooked smile. 'And because of that, I'll hold this place against the King and John Pym both if I have to.'

It was a long time before Kit answered her. And when he did, it was to say, in a tone of wry understanding, 'I see. Then it seems that the matter is decided, doesn't it?'

By the time they rejoined the party, Francis had failed to ascertain Dorothy's feelings on the matter of her daughter's betrothal but succeeded rather better – once the babies had been taken back to Meg in the nursery – at beguiling Gianetta into mild flirtation. He had also, with reluctance, decided that it behoved him to have a quiet word with his sister and, deftly removing her to the winter parlour on the score of having messages to deliver from their mother, said meditatively, 'I suppose you realise how shrewish you're beginning to sound?'

Celia's jaw dropped and she simply stared at him.

'Take, for example, that remark you made just now about Eden,' he continued smoothly. 'He is – as you very well know – neither a fool nor a traitor. And calling him so before his mother and sisters is both ill judged and futile.'

'I can't believe I'm hearing this,' she said jerkily. 'If you, of all people, can't understand how I feel – then you've changed beyond all recognition!'

Francis appeared to contemplate his fingernails. 'I've been away a long time and made a number of discoveries, Celia . . . not least among them the realisation that we'll all need to preserve a sense of proportion if England is not to go the way of the German states.'

Neither understanding nor caring what he meant, she said hotly, 'It's all very well for you to say that. *You're* not shut up in this dreary place – cut off from all your friends and everything that matters.'

'That is a very peculiar remark. Doesn't Eden matter? He is, after all, both your husband and the father of your child. And if it's merely a question of his not giving you the life you want, I can only point out that you have no one but yourself to blame for that. You had the option, my dear. If you wanted to be an ornament to the Court, you should have married Cyrus Winter. But you chose Eden instead. And, having done so, you now owe him a small degree of loyalty.'

'And what does he owe me – or don't my feelings matter?' she demanded, angrily shredding her handkerchief. 'My God! At this rate, I wouldn't be surprised to hear you tell me that Eden's quite right and you're going to fight against the King yourself!'

There was a pause. Then Francis drawled blightingly, 'Try not to be any more stupid than you can help, Celia. And take a piece of good advice. Strive for a little moderation and stop quarrelling with everyone – for, if you don't, life over the next few months could be more than just dreary.'

'Then I'll join Father in York!'

'Or our mother in France?' he mocked, knowing perfectly well that Lady Wroxton had not willingly seen Celia since her marriage. 'I think not. Whether you like it or not, you are now a Maxwell – and neither our parents nor myself will welcome any attempt on your part to change that. So if you're harbouring some insane notion of leaving Eden

274

because you disagree with his politics, I can only suggest you banish it forthwith. Do I make myself quite clear?'

Celia's mouth quivered. 'How can you be so cruel? You're my brother. You're supposed to care about me!'

'Exactly. Which is why I'm attempting to bring you to your senses and stop you contemplating ruin.'

'No you're not! You're just pushing me out of the way the same as everyone else. I *hate* you!' And, storming past him, she wrenched open the door to come face to face with Eden.

For a moment she regarded him in bitter silence. Then she said savagely, 'Well? Did you manage to hear all that? But no matter. I'm sure Francis will be delighted to repeat it all for you – so I'll leave you to be cosy together. It would be a terrible shame if I were to get in the way, wouldn't it?' And, brushing him violently aside, she was gone.

His face rather pale, Eden watched her go before turning slowly back to Francis. 'What was all that about?'

'I've been trying,' came the slightly tense reply, 'to shake a little sense into her. But without, as you saw, any pronounced degree of success.'

'Ah.' Closing the door behind him, Eden advanced into the room. 'Perhaps you'd better be more specific.'

'Had I?' Francis raised sardonic brows. 'Very well. I told her it's time she started cleaving unto her husband.'

'I see. Am I supposed to thank you?'

'What do *you* think?' A pause; and then, 'Does she often speak to you like that?'

'Sorry, Francis.' Eden's reply was swift, pleasant and final. 'I don't discuss my wife – even with you.'

'No. You wouldn't, of course. But you can't stop me telling you that you're a bloody fool.'

'Quite.' Eden grinned suddenly. 'And you're an over-dressed mammet. Where the *hell* have you been all this time?'

The tension evaporated into laughter so that at last their hands met and gripped.

'In Paris,' said Francis, finally. And, with a brief return to his usual languor, 'Amusing enough for a time, beloved, but I believe I'm glad to be back. Poor Suckling's drinking

275

himself to death over there, you know.'

'And what did you do?'

'Need you ask? I wrote a little poetry and paid court to all the prettiest girls. Speaking of which – I find the signorina entirely delicious. What a pity her brother's a usurer! However. One can't have everything, I suppose.' Francis smiled and dropped his pose. 'I haven't congratulated you on my nephew.'

'How like you to put it that way,' retorted Eden. 'If you hadn't got yourself mixed up in all that cloak-and-dagger stuff, you could have stood sponsor to him.'

'Yes, well, we all have Goring to thank for that; and now, to add insult to injury, I hear he's holding Portsmouth on behalf of the Parliament.' There was silence for a moment as suddenly austere sapphire eyes met watchful hazel ones. 'But that's not what I came to tell you.'

'No?'

'No. Not to put too fine a point on it, I've come from York with the King's Commission of Array. And I intend to read it.'

'In Banbury market-place?' asked Eden with apparent lightness. 'If so, I'd advise you not to wear that coat. The flying vegetables are likely to spoil it.'

'Possibly. The question is – is that all?'

'You mean will I try and stop you? No. I won't need to. John Fiennes will do it.'

'Ah. The ubiquitous Lord Saye's son. Yes. Celia mentioned something about that.' Francis stared thoughtfully at his hands. 'I imagine you're aware that his lordship's been arresting the King's friends hereabouts for merely organising petitions?'

'Yes.' Eden saw no need to mention that he'd had a monumental row with Lord Saye on this subject. 'I don't want to quarrel with you, Francis – particularly not today. We may not . . . oh hell! It may be a long time before we're able to meet again as friends.'

'I know it. So what are you suggesting? That we simply agree to differ?'

'There's no point in anything else. We both know the

other's views – and neither of us can change tack just for friendship's sake. You believe it's the King's right to command Parliament; I don't. You'll fight to preserve His Majesty's prerogative; I won't. And we could argue till kingdom come without it making a blind bit of difference.'

'You want His Majesty turned into a puppet?'

'No. I want Parliament turned into something more than a mere cipher,' came the swift reply. And then, 'A balance has to be struck. The King stands for stability and tradition – and no one wants to see him safely back on his throne more than I do. But Parliament represents the people and must be allowed to act in their interests without fear of being dissolved on a royal whim.'

'"'Tis to preserve His Majesty that we against him fight"?' quipped Francis. 'No. Don't answer that. Tell me something else instead. You say you can't support the King . . . but must you necessarily take the field against him?'

'How long do you think I'll have a choice?' returned Eden dryly. 'If you perch on the fence, it's everyone's business to knock you off. Like Father, I wish it need not have come to this. But it has – so I've no choice but to follow my conscience as you do yours and hope for a quick end. And now . . . will you please sit down and let me send for a bottle of wine?'

There was a pause. And then, 'Make it two,' said Francis, dropping gracefully into a chair. 'Quite frankly, I thought you were never going to ask.'

Eden and Francis got gloriously drunk together – which further infuriated Celia because she couldn't understand why they should do such a thing. And two days later, Francis proclaimed the King's Commission amidst a good deal of booing, cat-calling and unseemly jostling, but without coming to any real hurt. John Fiennes arrived from Broughton towards the end of the proceedings for the purpose of informing him that the said Commission was unlawful, but this was accomplished with a brisk, business-like efficiency and no incivility from either side.

277

And, true to his word, Eden stayed well away so that he and Francis might avoid direct confrontation for as long as possible.

By the end of the month a letter from Richard told his family that the King had rejected the nineteen proposals for government sent to him by both Houses on the grounds that they had been drafted by 'raisers of sedition'; but since these had included parliamentary control of all major military and civil appointments along with that of all fortresses, together with prosecution of the laws against Papists, no one could be surprised that they'd met with a refusal. Slightly less easy to follow was the fact that His Majesty had flatly denied any intention of making war on his Parliament immediately before issuing his call to arms. 'And having the latter read in London,' concluded Richard, 'has not only cost the Lord Mayor his office but also placed him in the Tower. But with five hundred parliamentary cavalry drilling every day in Tothill Fields, he must have expected that. And one can't but appreciate his difficulty. With so many declarations emanating from both the King and Westminster, there's not an officer in the land who isn't now a traitor to one side or the other.'

'Upon which intriguing thought,' sighed Dorothy to Kate, 'I suppose you and I just carry on filling the larder and praying there'll still be some men here at harvest time.'

'Quite. And goodness knows there's little enough getting done around the estate even now,' said Kate. 'The ones with horses seem to spend half their time practising cavalry manoeuvres with Eden, and the ones without are now marching up and down in front of Tom Tripp, clutching pitchforks. Adam Smith hasn't time to repair the winding-jack because he's too busy renovating all those old swords and rusty halberds Eden's been collecting from just about everywhere. And Meg's father nearly blew his head off last night trying to repair an antiquated blunderbuss that probably hasn't been fired in twenty years. What is it,' she finished irritably, 'that turns grown men into little boys playing at soldiers?'

'I've no idea. But I wish it would affect Nathan. He tells

278

me that God has given him the duty of caring for us all during the Conflict's Rage,' said Dorothy gloomily. 'I must say, I wish he wouldn't. His abhorrence of Gianetta's rosary and Meg's lapse from grace are beginning to get on my nerves.'

'Nathan,' observed Kate, 'needs setting right on a few things. He appears to feel that we poor females ought to allow him to organise matters as he sees fit. Added to which, he had the effrontery this morning to congratulate me on putting an end to my foolish involvement with one he can only call a Licentious Cavalier.'

'Kit?' asked Dorothy calmly.

'Kit,' agreed Kate. 'So I told him that he seemed to be labouring under a misapprehension – which wasn't all that surprising since the matter was absolutely none of his business.'

Dorothy regarded her daughter thoughtfully. 'I suppose you realise that allowing your betrothal to stand but remain unofficial leaves you in a somewhat debatable position?'

'Of course. But with Father in Westminster and Kit returning post-haste to York, we couldn't really have done anything else, could we?' came the glib reply. And then, with creditable negligence, 'Which reminds me. I suggested that if Kit should happen to meet Signor del Santi, he might take the opportunity to remind him of his sister's existence. After all, it would be nice to know whether or not Gianetta will be with us for the duration, wouldn't it?'

During the third week in July, news came of a skirmish in the muddy streets of Manchester in which one of my lord Wharton's parliamentarian recruits had been personally despatched on behalf of the King by Lord Strange.

'And that,' announced Celia gleefully, 'is an omen.'

'It's also the first gravestone,' returned Eden caustically. 'And if you can find anything cheering in that, I'd be glad to have you share it with me.'

An hour later he was in the courtyard wrestling moodily with the corroded firing mechanism of Thorne Ash's ancient saker, when a voice he had no expectation of hearing said jovially, 'I might have known. Anything involving moving parts and a tub of grease. But I half thought you'd have built your own catapult by now.'

'Ralph.' Straightening his back, Eden stared incredulously at his friend. 'My God . . . *Ralph*!'

'The very same.' Mr Cochrane grinned magnificently down on him and extended one large calloused hand. 'How are you, my midget?'

'Astounded,' said Eden, gripping the hand in his own. 'And less of the insults. Can I help it if you've grown?'

'Or I if you've shrunk? I take it I've surprised you.'

'Don't you always? And what have you done with your horse?'

'I met that fellow of yours – Tripp, is it? He said you were out here and offered to stable my nag so I could check your reflexes. Not very good are they? But,' waving a dismissive hand, 'we'll let that pass. I don't suppose it's your fault you've grown slack. And I'd sooner catch up on your news.'

'Would you?' laughed Eden. 'Well, let's see. I'm married to Francis's sister, Celia, and we have a son. Father's in the Commons helping to set up the Committee for Defence; Amy's married and living in the City; Felix is apprenticed to a goldsmith whose sister you'll find in the house; and Kate . . . Kate spent six months at Court and came back more or less betrothed.' He stopped and drew a long breath. 'How's that?'

'It'll do for a start. Though to tell you the truth, I'm still reeling from the notion of you as a father,' retorted Ralph. 'But tell me: what exactly are you trying to do to that cannon?'

'Give it a new lease of life. I doubt, quite frankly, that it's ever been fired in earnest, but you don't know what you'll need these days, do you? The problem is that I can't release the damned pin.'

'Stand aside, my boy. This job requires the brute force of a professional.' Already half out of his coat, Ralph cast it aside and bent over the saker. 'I assume that – though you're readying this piece for action – you don't intend to stay and man it personally?'

'No. John Fiennes seems eager to have me help garrison Banbury Castle, but if I'm going to fight, I'd sooner do it in the field.'

'What do you mean – *if*?' demanded Ralph, heaving forcefully at the recalcitrant pin. 'You're a trained man, for God's sake! I'd have thought you'd already be raising levies.'

'I am. And eventually I'll take them to join a larger force – Essex probably. But I can't just go charging blithely off into the blue, Ralph. I've other responsibilities.'

'You mean your son?'

'He's part of it. Also the estate and the family and so on.' Eden hesitated before saying lightly, 'And there's Celia.'

The pause was not lost on Ralph and he shot a hard, searching glance at his friend's face. Then, addressing himself once more to the saker, 'Ah yes. Celia. Thinks like Francis, does she?'

'More or less. So living here is difficult for her.'

'Difficult for all of you, I should think. Hallelujah! I believe this thing's moving at last. Well . . . you'll do what you must, I suppose. Pity though. I'd hoped we might go together.'

'Go where?'

'To war, you idiot!' He gave one last tremendous tug and sat back with a bump as the pin came free. 'There you are – all yours to play with to your heart's content. The mercenaries are homing in from all over Europe for the fray. The fellow I fought under in Germany is one of 'em – another nasty, common soldier like myself. Matter of fact, I'm meeting him in London next week and we're off to join someone named Waller.'

'Sir William Waller? The member for Andover?'

'That's him. Gabriel says he's good – and, more to the point, experienced. A quality which is going to be in short supply.' Rising, Ralph dusted himself off and reached for his coat. 'Speaking of which, they say Prince Rupert's coming in for the King.'

'I know.' It was a source of regret to Eden that fate had

decreed he would never fight beside this legendary young man. 'Rumour has it that he's busy collecting arms and experts in Holland.'

'Quite. So it's going to be interesting, isn't it? Because if a tithe of what's said of him is true, we're going to need all the help we can get.' Ralph stopped and grinned. 'And now – before I start boring the arse off you with war stories – perhaps I'd better go and make my bow to your lady mother. Do you think she'll give me a billet for a few days?'

'I'm sure she'll be delighted,' replied Eden. And then, his eyes gleaming, 'Provided, of course, that you refrain from being nasty and common.'

With the inevitable exception of Celia, the entire household was pleased to welcome Ralph, and the faint air of tension which had begun to invade Thorne Ash fled before his bluff good cheer and wholly uncomplicated nature. He told a stream of hilarious and frequently suspect tales of his antics abroad to Dorothy and the girls, whilst reserving for Eden alone the grim realities and military details. He declared himself both alarmed and stunned by Kate's metamorphosis, teased Gianetta unmercifully about her jewels but restored himself to grace with his readiness to play with Jude, and allowed Celia to snipe at him almost continuously without ever being provoked into anything more than a discreetly contemptuous glance.

In the end, however, it was to fifteen-year-old Felicity that he found himself saying grimly, 'That girl is the most beautiful shrew it's ever been my misfortune to meet. How on earth do you all put up with her?'

'With difficulty,' came the candid reply. 'But it's for Eden, you see.'

'No. I don't see. It seems to me high time someone stopped her in her tracks with a few home truths.'

'I daresay. But the trouble is, it *doesn't* stop her. It only makes her worse. Do you think Kate hasn't already tried? And Francis too, I suspect – before he and Eden got rolling drunk together. She couldn't understand that at all, of course.' Felicity bit off her thread and shook out the shirt she'd been mending. 'There you are. Good as new.'

'Thank you. And you *did* understand it, I suppose?'

'Oh yes.' She caught the grin in his eye and responded to it. 'They've been friends for years and one can't expect that to vanish overnight just because they're on opposite sides. So, in a sense, it was a sort of goodbye before Francis went back to the King. Eden's very conscious, you see, of this being what he calls "a war without an enemy".'

'Eden,' said Ralph flatly, 'is permitting Celia to influence his views. And it's making him tepid.'

Felicity's brows rose. 'If you think that,' she said, 'you can't know Eden nearly as well as you think. The truth is that he's itching to go because it's what he's good at. You've seen him with that troop of his. Would he be going to all that trouble if he planned to stay out of it? Of course he wouldn't! And when the time's right, he'll go. It's true that he loves Celia very much. But have you ever known anyone make him do anything he didn't want to do or didn't believe to be right?' She paused and finished a trifle breathlessly, 'Really, Ralph – I'm surprised at you.'

For a long moment, he simply looked at her while something entirely unexpected stirred inside his chest. Then, putting it sensibly to one side, he said humorously, 'I take it I'm having my knuckles rapped?'

'Yes. And you deserved it, too.'

'Did I? Yes – I probably did. No tact, you see.'

Felicity got up and fixed him with a stern, grey gaze. 'What's tact got to do with it? The general idea was that you should *understand*.'

Proof – if proof were needed that what Felicity had said of her brother was true – arrived on the following morning. Ralph was helping put a score of motley individuals-turned-well-drilled-cavalry-unit through their paces when a messenger galloped up in a cloud of dust. And two minutes later, Eden was saying cheerfully, 'Time to put our skills to the test, boys. It appears Lord Brooke requires some assistance on the Warwick Road. A matter, I believe, of preserving some artillery from the marauding hands of my lord Northampton. How fortunate we're mounted and ready. So fall in, gentlemen – and try to remember what you've been taught. Coming, Ralph?'

'What do you think?' responded Ralph, turning his horse's head. 'Anything to pass a dull Saturday. Where are these guns supposed to be going?'

'Warwick. They were delivered to Banbury and have been awaiting collection.'

'And the odds?'

'Not, I gather, in Lord Brooke's favour – which is why he's very wisely summoned help,' came the crisp reply. 'Are you going to talk all day – or do you think we might get on?'

Ralph opened his mouth on a pithy retort and then thought better of it. Setting spurs to his horse, he drew abreast of Eden once more and said casually, 'Are we expecting a fight?'

Eden awarded him an amused, sideways glance. 'Why don't you say what you mean?'

'All right – I will. Are you *prepared* to fight?'

'Yes, but only if necessary. Our sole objective is to prevent those pieces of ordnance from changing hands. So we only break heads if we have to. Clear?'

'Christ!' said Ralph with mingled laughter and irritation. 'Who do you think you're talking to? Some damned tyro?'

'Not at all. But my respect for your superior experience is tempered by my awareness of your besetting sin.'

'Which is what?'

'Thinking with your stomach,' grinned Eden. 'And don't tell me you've grown out of it. If you had, you wouldn't need to ask if I'm prepared to fight, would you?'

Two

With the disputed cannon successfully rescued and returned to Banbury for safe-keeping, Ralph packed his bags and departed for his rendezvous with a man called Gabriel in London. Eden saw him off with faint but well-concealed envy, Celia with a waspish expression of relief, and Felicity with untouched equanimity.

Four days later, Richard arrived.

He waited until the natural excitement of welcome was over and he found himself alone with his wife and two eldest children; then he said flatly, 'I think we must finally abandon all hope of a peaceful settlement. Some of the other members and myself have been doing our best but neither Pym nor the King is prepared to give an inch.'

Seconds ticked by in silence. And then, with suppressed violence, Dorothy said, 'God help us all then.'

'Amen to that.'

She took his hand in hers. 'What will you do?'

'Continue to occupy my seat in the hope that there may be some way of minimising the damage. So you needn't worry yet. Just tell me how matters stand here. Are we ready?'

'As well as we can be. We're stocked up with salt and flour and everything else that will keep. Kate's been preserving fruit and devising ways of storing the vegetables; Felicity's got the dairy under full production with hard cheese – which tastes rather like soap but stores better than the soft kind; and I've been making vast quantities of various salves and cordials which I hope not to use. As to the rest . . . we're almost ready to start harvesting, aren't we, Eden?'

'Within the week,' he nodded. 'In the meantime, Jacob's repairing roofs and fences where necessary and I've had Adam fit a new locking-bar to the front gate. The saker in the courtyard is now operational but we've precious few balls to put in it; there are four muskets and two pistols in the hall chest; and I've laid in a barrel of powder along with as much shot as I could get hold of.' He paused and smiled wryly. 'All of which sounds very fine till you add the fact that this house could be taken by a dozen men inside two hours.'

'Quite,' said Richard grimly. 'What men are you leaving?'

'Jacob, of course – and old Silas and the Woodley brothers. And there's Nathan.'

'Nathan,' asserted Kate, 'is likely to be as much use in a crisis as a stale custard. He can't even load a pistol, much less fire one. So if anyone attacks us, the best we can hope for is that he'll talk them to death.'

'That's a fairly accurate assessment,' Eden acknowledged ruefully. 'Unfortunately, he's all we've got.'

'He isn't, you know.' Kate eyed him squarely. 'There's me. All you have to do is tell me what to expect and teach me a basic plan of defence. I can shoot – quite well, as it happens. And I couldn't do worse than Nathan. No one could.'

'That,' said her father, 'is probably true.'

'Thank you.' She looked at Eden. 'Well?'

He thought about it for a moment and then shrugged. 'Why not? We'll start tomorrow. But you'd better get used to taking orders or I'll return you to the ranks and train Nathan instead.'

As luck would have it, the middle of August brought wet and blustery weather that turned the harvesting into a hurried and dismal affair. The King, they heard later, had also suffered from it, having raised his standard at Nottingham only to have it topple ignominiously into the mud.

Of the other news, all was fragmentary and none good. The Earl of Northampton, Eden was incensed to hear, had somehow managed to seize the cannon John Fiennes was supposed to have been holding; Prince Rupert had arrived and extorted five hundred pounds for the King from the people of Leicester; the Cavaliers kept Sir William Brereton out of Nantwich while, in Portsmouth, George Goring suddenly declared for the King; and the Irish rebellion grew daily more complex and showed no sign of abating.

Kate, meanwhile, took lessons from Eden in defence and siege-craft but still found the time to go riding with her father in order to ask him a simple question in private.

'Francis,' she said, 'was asking about Gianetta's brother. He wanted to know why the signor was so interested in his second cousin Giles.'

'Giles Langley?' Richard's brows rose a little. 'He's dead.'

'I know. Since Celia was about six. So why should Signor del Santi want to know about him?'

'I haven't the remotest idea,' replied Richard untruthfully. 'And neither, I have to say, do I much care. What I *would* like to discuss while we've a moment alone is this betrothal of yours.'

'Oh.' Kate bent down to adjust the folds of her skirt and kept her voice carefully blank. 'Why?'

'I think you know very well. I like Kit Clifford, but the times are against him. And I'd be a very poor father indeed if I didn't object to seeing you placed between two stools.'

'That was my decision – not Kit's. And I still don't see what else I could have done.'

'Don't you? Surely the truth is that – if you loved the man – the threat of war would make you marry him like a shot. But you don't love him. And I can't say I'm surprised because – pleasant and eligible as he is – he's not the man for you. To put it bluntly, he's not up to your weight. So I can't understand why you ever agreed to marry him in the first place, let alone why you haven't terminated this silly half-and-half arrangement.' He smiled at her. 'Well? I'm listening.'

Oh hell, thought Kate. And said, 'It's not as simple as that . . . but I promise I'll think about it.'

'Do,' said Richard cordially. 'It would be nice to see you recover your common sense.'

The green eyes rose to meet his with an expression of bitter irony. 'Personally I think I'm displaying commendable good sense already. And so would you if you considered how much more unsuitable my choice might have been.'

'Possibly. But then, of course, you might find my views on a suitable match something of a revelation,' he retorted with an involuntary choke of laughter. 'If, that is, I could be persuaded to tell you what they are.'

'Then why don't you?'

'Because there's no point while you're tied to Mr Clifford. I will say one thing, though. Don't grasp at straws and don't settle for half a loaf. You're worth more than that, Kate. And, to be frank, I thought you already knew it.'

Richard returned to Westminster on the day his colleagues decided to shut down London's playhouses: an act which annoyed him so much that he left the House early and went to Cheapside.

Giacomo admitted him with a pleasure that bordered on rapture and informed him that the signor would be most 'appy.

Richard stopped mid-stride. 'He's back?'

'*Si*. Three weeks – maybe four. There is much work now.'

'Is there? The last time I was here, Felix led me to believe that work was more or less non-existent.'

'That was then,' Giacomo shrugged. 'Now is different. Every day people come. You go in the work-room and you see.'

'I will. No – don't trouble yourself. I know the way.'

The door to the work-room stood wide and, inside it, Luciano del Santi was sitting at his bench in minute examination of something he held in his hand while Felix and Gino appeared to be pouring molten gold into a mould. Very sensibly, Richard stayed where he was until they had finished and then, walking forward, said gently, 'Hell's kitchen, I see. Are you too busy for visitors?'

'Father!' Beneath the dirt and sweat, Felix grinned broadly. 'I thought you were still at home.'

'Until yesterday, I was – and might as well have stayed there if today's trivia is to continue . . . No, Felix. I believe I can wait to embrace you until you've washed. I'm quite fond of this coat.'

'And have been for some years?' The Italian laid down the exquisite, antique cameo he had been inspecting and advanced with his usual lurking smile. 'You are, as ever, thrice welcome. But do I detect a note of discontentment?'

'Why bother to be tactful?' returned Richard, grasping the outstretched hand. 'The truth is that I'm in a bloody bad mood because I've torn myself away from Thorne Ash, when I'd much sooner have stayed, only to find the House wasting time on the nation's morals instead of its safety.' He paused and looked around. 'Giacomo says business is booming. Is it?'

Felix snorted and muttered something unintelligible.

'Giacomo,' explained the signor, 'is not a goldsmith. This basically means that as long as customers bring us commissions, he's happy. Felix, on the other hand, regards most of what we are doing at present as sacrilege: a point of view with which I occasionally find myself in sympathy. In short, we are melting things down.'

'Ah. Yes . . . I suppose you would be. In times of uncertainty people prefer ready coin.'

'They also like their assets to be easily portable. Salts and candlesticks, for example, are becoming ingots. As for the family jewels we've been buying, most of those go for the melt as well because there is no market for such pieces in wartime and the majority of them are clumsily made. One has one's reputation to consider, after all.'

'Not to mention making the odd crust on the transaction?'

'Quite. How else,' asked Luciano sardonically, 'do you think we poor artisans are able to meet the forced loans demanded of us by your friends?'

'Ouch!' Richard winced. 'Enough said. But rid your mind

of any notion that you're the only sufferer. The taxes on Thorne Ash have risen to the point of iniquity.'

'And this is only the beginning.' Luciano paused to look across at Felix. 'If you've finished what you were doing and would care to make yourself presentable, you may join your father and me upstairs.' And then, to Richard, 'You'll stay to dine?'

'With pleasure.'

'Good. And then later perhaps we can talk.'

The hint was unnecessary. Throughout the meal Richard automatically confined himself to family matters, giving his son all the news from Thorne Ash. And it was thus that he discovered that Felix had been seeing a good deal of Amy . . . and, more importantly, Amy's husband.

'He's a good fellow – though how he puts up with Amy I don't know. She seems to get sillier every day,' said Felix. 'Geoffrey's all right, though. He's been showing me how his new presses work.'

'I thought,' remarked Richard, 'that he was continuing in the book-binding business?'

'He is. But he says the future lies in the printed word.'

'Thinking of changing trades, Felix?' asked the Italian.

'Not at all. But I wouldn't mind having a go on one of those machines. In my time off, naturally.'

'Naturally,' agreed Richard mildly. 'And what, precisely, is Geoffrey printing?'

'Oh – this and that.' Felix became suddenly vague. Then, 'Felicity wrote that Kate's Mr Clifford is with the King. I suppose that means she won't be able to marry him, doesn't it? After all, it's bad enough having Celia in the family.'

Richard's answer was to bend a satiric gaze upon his son and make a mental note to visit Geoffrey Cox quite soon. But later, when Felix left him alone with his host, he said reflectively, 'He's right, of course. Celia is becoming a problem – for which I blame myself. I should have played the magisterial father for once.'

'Perhaps.' Luciano refilled his glass and pushed the bottle across the board. 'You could hardly have foreseen the current situation, however. And I don't imagine Eden has voiced any regrets.'

'No – but then, he wouldn't.' Richard stared gloomily into his glass. 'You know, Dolly and I used to congratulate ourselves on having reared sensible children. *Now* look at them. Eden's married a selfish brat; Amy had to be hustled to the altar before she could ruin herself; Felix is apparently up to something nefarious with son-in-law Geoffrey; and God alone knows what Kate thinks she's doing. All we need is for Felicity to run off with a groom or decide to take the veil and we'll have a full set.'

'My God. You really are depressed, aren't you?'

'Wouldn't you be?' Richard emptied his glass and then sighed. 'The world's going mad. And as if that weren't enough, my eldest daughter's half-tied to a man who – were she to marry him – would let her lead him by the nose.'

'Then stop her.' The tone was negligent but the dark eyes were watchful. 'On the other hand, if what you want is a man with strength and wit enough to hold her, you may wait a long time.'

'And that would be a pity. Especially when I know a man who is eminently suitable in every respect save one.'

'Only one? You've found a paragon.'

'Far from it.' An odd smile invested Richard's mouth. 'Do I really have to spell it out?'

The dark gaze grew suddenly opaque. 'Why should you? It's no business of mine.'

'Isn't it? My mistake, then. I thought it was.'

'Forget it, Richard.' Luciano came abruptly to his feet. 'I recognise the compliment – and am honoured by it. But marriage is something I neither want nor have time for; which is just as well, since I'd make a disastrous husband. And now, if you don't mind, we'll change the subject.'

'As you wish.' With perfect equanimity, Richard refilled his glass and leaned back. 'Tell me about Genoa.'

'You want the minutiae? I paid my dues and found my uncle in mercifully robust health. Then I listened to all my cousin Carlo's usual reminders of what will happen when that health fails – or, better still, I can't repay on time.'

'I don't follow. What *will* happen?'

'Didn't I tell you?' Luciano shrugged and sat down again. 'It's very simple. My uncle lent me a spectacularly large sum of money for a period of ten years. The term expires in April of 1646. But if Vittorio dies before then and my bond falls into the hands of my beloved cousin, he'll foreclose on me.' A wry smile touched the sculpted face. 'You will therefore appreciate that for the next three-and-a-half years I remain within a hair's breadth of ruin. If I'm astute and – more important – lucky, I may avoid it. Otherwise . . . not.'

'You don't need luck,' said Richard, aghast. 'You need a bloody miracle! And all so you can play Nemesis to four men who may not even be alive any more? It can't be worth it!'

'That depends on your point of view. In other respects, however, you're quite right. They *may* all be dead. I already know that one of them is.'

'Giles Langley? Yes. I could have told you that.'

There was silence for a moment. Then, his tone suspiciously mellow, the Italian said, 'I am aware of it. I believe, however, I had some idea of not involving you further on account of your connection with the family. It seems I wasted my time. But what really interests me is how you know.'

'Kate told me.'

'*Kate?*'

'Yes. It's not so surprising really. You spoke to Francis; Francis spoke to Kate; and Kate was curious enough to mention it to me. I, of course, simply put two and two together.'

'I see.'

'Well, you must have expected something of the sort,' argued Richard reasonably. 'And as for keeping me out of it – it's a bit late for that, surely? So you might as well tell me what, if anything, you found out about the late Mr Langley . . . and also the names of the others on the list. Who knows? I may be able to help you.'

'Are you sure you want to? As I understood it, you consider the whole business futile to the point of lunacy.'

'The word,' said Richard, 'is suicidal. But since no amount of talking will stop you, the sooner you get it over with the better it will be.'

A glint of humour appeared. 'So I can rescue Kate from her betrothal?'

'No. So you can keep the shirt on your back. Well?'

Sighing faintly, Luciano laid his fingers on the edge of the polished board and, gazing down at them, said, 'Giles Langley died ten years ago when he fell downstairs and broke his neck. It would be helpful to know whether or not this was an accident, but I doubt we ever shall. As for the rest – the only other thing I know is that he invested somewhat catastrophically in the Cadiz expedition.'

'That fiasco? Well, I suppose it would account for him borrowing from your father – if he in fact did so. Anything else?'

'No. The difficulty lies in knowing what questions to ask. So rather than waste any more time on what will probably prove a dead end, I've got Selim scouring London for some trace of one Thomas Ferrars. Ever heard of him?'

'No. I can't say I have.'

'Pity. What about Ahiram Webb or Robert Brandon?'

The grey eyes narrowed a little and Richard took his time about answering. Then he said slowly, 'Webb . . . no. But the name Brandon rings a distant bell.' He paused again and then shook his head. 'No. I can't place it. I can, however, make a few inquiries for you.'

'Thank you. I am, as ever, in your debt.'

'Mm.' Richard surveyed him aridly. 'You still haven't told me what you intend to do if and when you catch up with these people.'

'No.' The hard mouth curled in a brilliant, impersonal smile. 'I haven't, have I?'

A week later and acting on the only scrap of information that Selim had managed to glean, Luciano del Santi left Felix with enough work to keep him gainfully employed till All Saints, and Giacomo with instructions to keep a close eye on him – and then departed quietly for Buckingham.

293

He had mistimed his journey, he soon realised, by at least a day.

The trouble was that the Great Cuckold, sometimes known as the Earl of Essex and currently Parliament's commander-in-chief, had chosen the same day to lead his motley troops out of London for the purpose of joining with the Midland forces at Northampton. And the result was that the road was jammed tight, not only with a slow-moving column of men and horses, but also with baggage-waggons, heavy artillery and Lord Essex's private coach, to the rear of which was strapped a rather splendid coffin.

This, at first sight, was undeniably amusing and, beneath its magnificent moustaches, even Selim's mouth was seen to twitch. But by the time they had been condemned to idling along behind the lumbering cavalcade for the best part of a day on a road bounded by high hedges, Luciano had lost all desire to laugh and most of his patience. Fortunately, however, the parting of the ways came in the nick of time to avert an explosion. The army headed north by way of Stony Stratford and the signor, with relief, set his face towards Aylesbury.

They arrived in Buckingham only a day later than expected and racked up at the Bush Tavern. Selim found a serving-girl to dally with and Luciano spent the majority of the night trying to keep a curb on his hopes.

This, as it turned out, proved to have been a useful exercise; for when they finally arrived at the modest manor on the outskirts of the town to which Selim had received vague direction, it was to be met with the frigidly delivered intelligence that the Thomas Ferrars they sought, being but a distant cousin, was at no time to be found there. And then, with barely concealed distaste, the information that if Tom owed them money they were unlikely to get it, but could best find out by pursuing him to his own house near Worcester.

Having subsequently been summarily shown the door, Luciano saw nothing to be gained by lingering. He therefore turned calmly on to the Brackley road and resigned himself to another tedious ride.

Selim followed silently, his hawk-like countenance swathed in gloom. Finally he said heavily, 'A thousand pardons, *efendim*. I have failed you.'

Pulled from his abstraction, the Italian looked back at him with faint surprise. 'Failed me? How? It's entirely due to you that we now know where to look. It would be stupid to expect everything to fall neatly into place for us, you know. And I'm well satisfied with what you've done.'

'Then what are you thinking?'

'That the road to Worcester leads through Banbury and Stratford – and is likely to be alive with troops from either side.'

'Oh.' Selim considered this in his own way for a mile or so and then said cautiously, 'Since our way lies close, will you visit your lady sister?'

'With your misdemeanour still so fresh in everyone's mind? Hardly. Unless,' finished Luciano del Santi smoothly, 'you are eager to see your daughter?'

Selim sniffed disdainfully and relapsed into silence.

They entered Brackley in the early part of the afternoon and immediately found Luciano's forebodings justified. A dozen or more horses were tied up outside the inn and an unlikely collection of would-be soldiers lounged against walls or strolled aimlessly about the street.

'Damn,' said Luciano softly. And then, looking more closely, 'And thrice damn. Now . . . do we possess our stomachs in patience and slip quietly through?'

'*Efendim?*'

'Or . . . no,' sighed the signor. 'Too late.'

'*You!*' spat Tom Tripp, erupting at Selim's side. 'Been sneaking after Meg again, have you, you bloody heathen bastard?'

Selim stared down his magnificent nose. 'I,' he announced, 'do not sneak. And if you cannot hold your woman – is this my fault?'

White with temper, Tom grabbed the Turk's bridle. 'Get down.'

Selim smiled and fingered his knife. 'You wish to fight?'

'I wish to ram your teeth down your throat,' snapped

Mr Tripp. 'Get down, you fornicating bugger.'

'Tom.' His voice crisp and cool, Eden stood framed in the tavern doorway. 'I have every sympathy, believe me – but I can't have you brawling in front of the men. If you must settle this, get yourselves off behind the inn and do it in private.'

'Suits me,' said Tom grimly. And to Selim, 'Coming? Or are you too scared?'

'Scared? Of the braying son of an ass? Ha!' scoffed Selim, already preparing to dismount. Then, belatedly, 'I may go, *efendim*?'

'I suppose you'd better,' sighed Luciano del Santi. 'There is, however, just one small stipulation. Your knife stays with me.'

'But, *efendim* . . .'

'With me, Selim – or you'll just have to let Mr Maxwell's groom think what he will of you.'

For the first time, Eden allowed his gaze to encompass the man who'd bedded Celia's mother and spoken of Celia herself as if she were an inanimate object with no feelings worth considering. Then, putting aside his instinctive dislike, he said, 'Quite right. And I'll take Tom's sword.' He looked back at the two protagonists. 'Well? It's fists or nothing. Take it or leave it.'

'We'll take it,' said Tom, pulling off his sword and watching his foe reluctantly handing over his ornate knife. 'Let's go.'

When Selim had departed in Tom's wake, Luciano came lightly down from the saddle and approached Eden. 'It seems that you and I are left to be sociable. Will you share a bottle of wine with me?'

'I'll take ale, if it's all the same to you,' replied Eden tersely. 'We've a four-hour march to do this afternoon.'

'Ah. Don't tell me. You're off to join Lord Essex in Northampton.'

'Yes. So the sooner Tom and your fellow finish pulverising each other, the better.'

It was not until they were sitting inside and the Italian had ordered food that Eden asked the obvious question.

'*Have* you been to Thorne Ash?'

'No. And neither am I going there.'

'Oh.' It wasn't, Eden decided, worth asking the fellow where he *was* going; nor did he really care. So, in an effort to maintain conversation he said, 'How's Felix?'

'Taller, I think, than when you last saw him – but otherwise much the same. His latest craze – fostered by your brother-in-law, Mr Cox – is for printing. But I suppose that's better than rushing off to join somebody's little army.'

Eden surveyed him without favour. 'Is that what you think I'm doing?'

'Does it matter?'

'No. But before you start sneering, you might try remembering that we're only doing this because we care about our country. Nobody wants this war, but—'

'Don't they? You surprise me,' interposed the Italian sardonically. 'If that were so, surely everyone would be staying by their own hearth? But no doubt the finer points are lost on a mere foreigner.'

'No doubt,' snapped Eden, annoyed that he couldn't think of a good answer. 'But I'm sure that won't stop you from making a healthy profit.'

'We can but hope,' came the silky reply. 'And now, before we end up finishing this in the back yard with Selim and your groom, I suppose I'd better ask how Gianetta is.'

'Vastly improved in temper.'

'Due to reduced contact with me. Quite.' Impassive black eyes met and held irritable hazel ones. 'Is that all?'

'No. She's also having a cataleptic effect on pretty well every man under sixty.'

'I see. Anyone in particular?'

'Not that I know of; though I do recall Francis being quite stunned.'

'Francis Langley? Yes. I suppose he would be. The instant lure of the obvious. *Oh Christ!*'

It was a second or two before Eden realised that this exclamation was a comment, not on his friend's disposition, but on something else entirely. Then, following the signor's gaze, he too muttered helplessly, 'God's teeth!'

It wasn't just the myriad cuts and bruises that adorned Tom and Selim or even their torn and muddied clothing. It was mainly what they'd managed to do to each other's faces. Tom had a split lip whose swelling was bidding fair to take over his face; and Selim's right eye was completely shut and already darkening to several exquisite shades of purple.

'Well, I hope honour is satisfied,' said Luciano, at length. 'Because you and I now have the pleasure of continuing our respective journeys with two apparently desperate ruffians. The only good thing to be said for it is that at least they're still standing.'

Three

It took a further three days to reach Worcester, by which time Selim's eye – though it had begun to open again – was becoming a veritable kaleidoscope of colours. The landlord of the Cardinal's Hat looked first at the eye and then at the knife and suffered severe misgivings which were only allayed by Luciano ordering every available comfort . . . and paying for them in advance.

The town, they soon discovered, was alive with nervous excitement and rumour. It was also full of Royalist soldiers – namely the Earl of Worcester's regiment of dragoons under the command of Sir John Byron. These, it appeared, had but that day arrived from Oxford with quantities of gold and silver plate which they were transporting to the King at Shrewsbury. But the town was by no means wholeheartedly sympathetic towards His Majesty and had only let Byron in because the rotting gates and crumbling walls would not suffice to keep him out.

'And that,' said Luciano grimly to Selim, 'is not all. For since it seems that just about everyone between London and Shrewsbury knows exactly what Sir John is carrying, I wouldn't wager a groat against a parliamentary force coming to take it from him. Which basically means that the sooner we get out of this place, the better.'

So it was that the following morning saw them riding south out of town through the village of Powick, towards a place called Callow End and the house of Thomas Ferrars.

It was an eye-catching structure: partly on account of its relative newness, but mostly because it was vastly too ornate for its size. Someone, decided Luciano, had grand designs but insufficient money and no taste.

He was admitted by a harassed-looking manservant and then shown into a grossly over-furnished parlour where a woman's voice immediately said coldly, 'Make haste to state your business. I don't waste time on tradesmen.'

Luciano surveyed her clinically. She was tall and had once probably been a great beauty; but the golden hair was fading and the lines on her face were those of discontent. Her gown, however, was of the best quality velvet, trimmed with silver lace, and the pearls encircling her throat were amongst the finest he had ever seen.

Without smiling, he accorded her a slight bow and said, 'Your pardon, madam – but I had hoped to see Mr Thomas Ferrars.'

'I know that. I am Alice Ferrars. And you can discuss your business with me as well as with my husband.'

'I think not. But if your husband is otherwise engaged just now, I have no objection to waiting.'

'Your wishes don't interest me, Mr . . . What did you say your name was?'

'Sandy. Lucius Sandy,' came the mendacious reply.

'Well, Mr Sandy, it would be a waste of time waiting. My husband is from home.'

'Ah.' Frustration stirred but he controlled it. 'And may I ask when you expect him back?'

'No. You may not. Either tell me what you came for or go.'

'I am sorry to disoblige you,' said Luciano, his voice growing noticeably mellow, 'but I can only repeat that my business is with your husband. And I would be even sorrier to inconvenience you by calling twice a day until he returns.'

The frost in Alice Ferrars' blue eyes turned to ice. She said slowly, 'Are you having the impertinence to threaten me? If so, allow me to tell you that I don't take that tone from anyone alive – let alone some jumped-up shop-keeper!'

Luciano allowed her words to linger uncomfortably on

the air for a moment. Then, invitingly, 'Is that what you think I am?'

'What else? And instead of trying to dun my husband in his own house, you should count yourself fortunate in having received his custom at all. Now get out.'

The realisation that he had conceived, in a very short time, a profound dislike for Mistress Ferrars made Luciano decide on one last throw. It was a gamble, of course; but not, he calculated cynically, a very big one.

'I am afraid,' he said, with just the right note of reluctance, 'that you place me in a very difficult position. You see, it isn't a question of money . . . but of certain designs.'

'What designs?'

'Forgive me. I've said too much already. Mr Ferrars was most insistent about surprising you.'

'Ah.' Her expression relaxed and something approaching a smile touched her mouth. 'I see. A surprise, you say? Well, that is quite a different matter.' She disposed herself in a particularly ornate chair. 'Tell me, precisely what business are you in?'

'I . . . am a goldsmith.'

'A goldsmith? How nice.' Suddenly she was almost purring. 'Well, let us see. I wouldn't for the world spoil my husband's little surprise . . . but equally it seems a pity not to take this opportunity to improve upon it. The truth, of course, is that his taste is sometimes quite execrable.' She leaned back, eyes narrowed but smiling. 'So why don't you sit down, Mr Sandy – and tell me all about it?'

Thirty minutes later, and having sketched an idea for what (if he ever actually made it) would be the most vulgar and extortionately expensive necklace of his career, Luciano del Santi was riding cheerfully back to Worcester with Selim.

'The master of the house – and I use the term in its loosest sense – is away,' he announced presently. 'His lady has taken a fancy to live in Oxford for a while and has duly despatched him to hire a suitable residence for her.'

'So now,' sighed Selim, 'we go to Oxford?'

'No. I don't want to run the risk of missing him again.

She says she told him to be back here no later than next Friday – and, from what I've been privileged to see of her, I doubt he'll disobey. So you take steps to keep the house under some sort of observation . . . and we wait.'

'For nearly a week?'

'For as long as necessary,' replied the signor calmly. 'I agree that it's unfortunate – but needs must when the devil drives. My biggest problem is how to pass six days in Worcester without coming to the attention of Sir John Byron and being forced to contribute to the King's coffers. But, if we're lucky, he'll take himself off to Shrewsbury.'

'And if we're not,' said Selim gloomily, 'he'll bring the Roundheads down on us.'

'Quite.' Luciano smiled wryly. 'A situation fraught with possibilities. But I'm sure that, should the need arise, we'll think of something.'

Although the rumours grew ever wilder and Sir John Byron showed no sign of departing, the days passed uneventfully enough until, in the grey light of Thursday's dawn, someone stuck an axe in the Sidbury Gate and then fired a musket through the hole. This roused a lone Royalist sentry to the discovery that roughly a thousand parliamentarian Horse commanded by Nathaniel Fiennes stood outside it – which was rather surprising since the gate had no fastenings and would have yielded to a simple push. However, no one outside seemed to suspect this, so the sentry gamely refused to surrender the town and then made haste to call out his slumbering comrades.

The noise and confusion as the garrison piled out of bed to meet the unexpected attack woke and alarmed half the town. Fortunately, it also alarmed the would-be attackers who, for reasons best known to themselves, beat a hasty retreat and were out of sight before Byron's men had got the gate open.

Luciano heard the tale over breakfast but was not tempted to laugh. Instead, when the landlord left him alone with Selim, he said brusquely, 'Pack.'

'Pack? But why, *efendim*? They have gone.'

'I doubt it. Fiennes was with Essex – which means that the main army can't be far away. The plan now is probably to trap Byron here until it arrives; and with Ferrars due home tomorrow, the very last thing I need is to find myself shut in a beleaguered town.' He paused, frowning thoughtfully. 'There is also the possibility that Byron is expecting rein-forcements. I can't think of anything else that would have caused him to linger here. And if he is, we could end up playing grandmother's footsteps with both sides if we don't want to have to follow Ferrars all the way back to Oxford.'

Selim awarded this due consideration. Then, 'I think,' he said simply, 'it will be best if we go quickly.'

'Brilliant,' sighed the Italian. 'Why didn't I think of that?'

Getting out of Worcester was nowhere near as difficult as it ought to have been and, on the assumption that the Roundheads had gone north to blockade the Shrewsbury road, Luciano set off across the Severn through Bridge Gate and turned south towards Powick. It was not his fault he'd miscalculated. But by the time he realised his error, they had ridden more or less straight into the arms of Nathaniel Fiennes.

It was not Nathaniel but his brother John, however, who recognised the importance of their catch and said, 'Well, this *is* a surprise. You're a long way from home, aren't you?'

'Business,' shrugged Luciano, 'demands mobility.'

'You're likely to run into difficulties, then. Or haven't you noticed there's a war on?'

'Dear me. Is there really? But that's no concern of mine.'

'No?' John Fiennes folded sarcastic arms. 'Then what have you been up to in Worcester with Byron? Helping melt down his spoils – or just adding to them?'

'Neither.'

'What's all this about?' demanded Nathaniel irritably of his brother. 'Do you know this man?'

'Don't you?' John's tone was laced with bountiful satis-faction. 'You should. He's a money-lender – and reputedly one of the richest men in the three kingdoms. So we can't just leave him wandering around loose. He might fall into

303

the wrong hands. And a lot of people would consider that worse than losing Byron.'

After almost twenty-four hours of polite captivity that had included a very uncomfortable night, Luciano was beginning to lose his temper. It was Friday and he'd expected to be at Callow End by now, confronting Thomas Ferrars – not sitting in a field at Powick under constant guard while the citizens of Worcester came in their droves to gape at the novel military peep-show.

'This,' he said savagely, 'is bloody ridiculous.'

Selim looked at him. 'I still have my knife,' he said hopefully.

'Don't be a fool. How many of them do you think you can kill? And our horses are back there with the rest. We can't do a thing until they decide to move – and, on present showing, that could take till Doomsday.'

There being no real answer to this, they sat in silence for a further hour until the air of rising excitement around them culminated in a mêlée of activity. The troop, it appeared, was finally planning to depart . . . and at length a youthful lieutenant arrived, leading their horses.

'Mount up,' he said cheerfully. 'We're going.'

Luciano rose slowly. 'Going where?'

The fellow hesitated and then shrugged. 'Worcester. Byron's on the move and we're off to stop him. But don't worry. Captain Fiennes says you're to be protected at all times.'

'I bet he did,' came the acidic reply. And then, 'Well, Selim? You heard the man. Let's go.'

The men fell in on a large meadow just below the village and then indulged themselves with a heartening psalm.

> 'God is our refuge and strength, a very present
>   help in trouble.
> Therefore will not we fear, though the earth be
>   removed . . .'

Luciano looked on beneath faintly amused brows. 'A

goodly clutch of Puritans, no doubt. But I wonder if they fight as well as they sing?'

Selim sniffed. 'Singing is for women.'

'You're missing the point. Why would Byron choose to leave today of all days, knowing as he does what's out here waiting for him?'

Selim cast his mind back and then, finding the answer, opened his mouth to deliver it.

'Exactly,' said Luciano softly. 'But if dear Nathaniel hasn't worked it out for himself, I don't think we'll help him. Just keep your eyes and ears open and be ready for any confusion. I imagine we can rely on these gentlemen not shooting the golden goose.' He paused and met his henchman's eye with a sudden smile. 'But, in case those are famous last words, you'd better get ready to duck as well.'

The cavalcade made its ponderous way along the lane towards the bridge that would take it across the River Teme. Luciano knew that bridge moderately well. It was old, brick-built and no more than twelve feet wide – which meant that the troops would have to break formation to cross it. And on the far side of the river lay an equally narrow lane bounded by high hedges which wound up into a large field from where one could see Worcester. So if a surprise lay in store, this was presumably the place to look for it.

Rather less alert than his Italian captive, Nathaniel Fiennes led the column over the bridge and down the lane into Wickfield, aware but undismayed that, behind him, his force was being squeezed into a long, thin ribbon. And then he stopped dead, staring at a sight too incredible to be believed.

On the other side of the field four or five hundred Royalist cavalrymen were taking their ease on the grass. Some had disarmed and lay dozing in the sun, some were still eating their noon-day meal and others were grouped about their officers in the shade of a thorn tree. All appeared totally oblivious to the presence of the enemy.

Nathaniel stared and stared again, still unable to take it in while, at his back, the entire troop came to a shuddering stop as each man's horse cannoned unwarily into that of the man in front. And then everything changed as a tall Royalist officer surged to his feet and alerted all the others by throwing himself astride the nearest horse.

'Boot and saddle!' he yelled. '*Charge!*'

The spell broke.

'God rot it!' swore Nathaniel. '*Rupert!*'

And then all hell broke loose.

Somewhere towards the back of the column, Luciano and Selim were barely over the bridge.

'Christ!' muttered Luciano, as they ground to a halt. 'Already?'

He dropped one hand on Selim's bridle and strained his ears. Then, as the first shock waves rippled through the ranks, '*Now!*' he said. And, dragging the Turk from the saddle as he dropped neatly from his own, took a sort of flying dive at the hedge.

It parted unwillingly to let them through but took its toll on skin and clothing. Without pausing either to assess the damage or heed the pandemonium breaking out on the other side of the hedge, the Italian said briefly, 'Across the river – before our psalm-singing friends start dropping on our heads.'

Shouts and screams of escalating panic and confusion rose from the lane as those in front turned and rode down those behind in an attempt to retreat; while further away pistol shots and the clash of swords bore witness to the fact that at least some of Nathaniel's men were staying to fight.

'What now?' asked Selim as, soaked and muddy to the armpits, they gained the opposite bank. 'We run?'

'No. We hide. That clump of willows ought to do,' replied Luciano, already squelching towards it in boots full of water. 'We need horses. Preferably our own – though I suppose that's too much to hope for. Either way, we stay out of sight until the gentlemen over there complete their business with each other. And then we try to keep our rendezvous at Callow End.'

Selim resisted the impulse to say, 'Like this?' but could not forgo a gloomy, '*Inshallah.*'

'Quite. But just now I'd prefer a less fatalistic approach. So let's try "God helps those who help themselves", shall we?'

The skirmish taking place on the opposite bank turned out to be brief but remarkably unpleasant. Long before the Royalists appeared, the lane was a seething mass of confusion as Fiennes' men rode over each other in their efforts to escape that damnably restricted space. They swarmed back on to the bridge where John Fiennes tried to turn and rally them – only to find himself driven aside by the terrified stampede. And then the Royalists were upon them from behind: cutting men down, forcing them into the river to drown, and trampling others beneath their horses as they swept on in relentless pursuit.

The whole thing probably lasted less than twenty minutes, thought Luciano grimly; but it was as comprehensive a rout as anything he could have imagined.

'Tenant-farmers versus gentlemen,' he murmured. 'What chance have they got?'

'*Efendim?*'

'Nothing.' Luciano began pulling off his boots to empty them. There was no use in letting the scene he'd just witnessed touch him. It was nothing to do with him; he'd decided that long ago and it would be stupid to let it change. 'Let's get out of here. It would doubtless be safer to wait till the Royalists give up the chase and head back for Worcester . . . but if we do that they'll round up all the loose horses and we'll be left to walk. And I, personally, would rather risk it.'

Selim – who disliked being wet – agreed with him. He said persuasively, 'And then we find an inn?'

'Perhaps. But let's take one thing at a time, shall we?'

He had not bargained for the nightmare on the bridge. Dead, dying or wounded, men and beasts lay tangled in grisly carnage: the very air was filled with sounds of pain and terror. Never having been near a battlefield before, Luciano felt his stomach tighten. He did not think his life had been particularly cushioned: poverty, fear, gruelling work and the disease and desperation of the back-streets,

307

he knew all these things. But nothing had prepared him for what lay on Powick Bridge; and for the first time he found himself wondering how many people in sleepy, self-satisfied England were prepared for it either.

'Oh Christ,' he said, sickened. 'What a bloody mess.'

'Yes. But we can do nothing, *efendim*. There are too many. And soon the King's men will return – so we must cross the bridge.'

At the back of his mind, Luciano could see the sense in this; and so, although it was the very last thing he wanted to do, he pulled himself together and began picking his way through the human wreckage at his feet. The necessity of looking where he was going brought nausea several steps closer, and the sight of a man whose skull had been virtually split all but undid him. Then a hand grabbed his ankle.

'Thank God,' said a weak voice. 'Help me. I'm stuck.'

Luciano looked down into the paper-white face of a boy who couldn't have been much older than Felix. A long scratch adorned one cheek and he wore a blue sash over his buff-coat, proclaiming allegiance to someone or other. As for his legs, they lay hidden beneath a dead horse.

'For God's sake!' said the boy. 'It hurts like hell.'

'I daresay.' The signor became suddenly brisk. 'If we were able to move the horse a little, do you think you could drag yourself clear?'

'I'll do my best.'

Moving a dead weight is never easy, and the horse was a powerfully built cavalry charger, but eventually Luciano's scientific approach succeeded in putting Selim's brawn to its best use and the thing was done.

'Well done,' said Luciano. 'Now Selim will carry you out of this charnel-house and we'll see if we can get your boot off.'

The Turk did as he was bidden and then, setting his burden down on the far side of the bridge, said despairingly, 'Please, *efendim* – we've done what we can and must go.'

'Why is he in such a hurry?' asked the boy, wincing as

Luciano explored his ankle through the leather. 'You're not Roundheads, are you?'

'Perish the thought.' The Italian smiled briefly. 'Your foot's already very swollen. We'll have to cut your boot.'

'Hell. Just my luck. My only pair, too.'

'Quite. Selim – your knife, if you please.'

It was produced, albeit somewhat reluctantly. Then Selim said sharply, '*Geliyorlar! Efendim* – they come!'

Luciano looked up from his task and then, with a sigh, calmly continued with it. 'Then we'll just have to rely on this gentleman's good offices, won't we? Tell me, who's in command of this little expedition?'

'His Highness,' came the reverent reply. 'Prince Rupert.'

'*Efendim!*' Selim adopted a belligerently purposeful stance between his master and the approaching Royalists. 'Give me back my knife and go. I will delay them.'

'Selim.' The Italian sat back on his heels and looked up with a glimmer of patient amusement. 'Don't think I don't appreciate the offer. I do. But you've got to stop taking on whole armies. Just try to remember that I've no ambition to see you commit suicide in my service, and that, for the time being at least, no one is going to shoot us deliberately. Do I make myself clear? And now I suggest you turn round. The gentleman behind you looks as though he has a number of questions to ask.'

'Not me. I'm the least curious of mortals,' said the officer as Selim spun round. And then, grey eyes twinkling a little as they rested on the boy, 'Well, Jack? We thought we'd lost you.'

'Lord, no. But it was close, Captain Legge, sir. Jupiter fell on me and I'd be there still but for – for . . .' He looked inquiringly up at Luciano. 'I'm sorry. I never asked your name.'

'A matter of no importance compared to the removal of this boot,' said Luciano suavely. He rose. 'A task which I think I should now hand over to your friends.'

'His friends will probably just remove the whole leg,' remarked the captain humorously. 'But in the meantime, I daresay Jack would like to know who to thank.'

'For what? It was nothing.'

The grey eyes grew thoughtful.

'You're very shy,' he began. And then stopped as two exceedingly tall young men came striding across the bridge towards them.

One of these was fair-haired with a handkerchief picturesquely tied about his brow; the other was dark with a scarlet cavalry cloak dropping even more picturesquely from his shoulders. And between them was a very distinct resemblance.

'Sir?' Captain Legge saluted and then, with a grin, said, 'For a first charge, that wasn't at all bad. Your Highness must be moderately pleased.'

'Not particularly,' replied the dark young man tersely. 'We were caught napping and would have been trounced if they'd had an officer worth his salt. As it is, we were lucky.'

'Perhaps, sir. But you were quick to redeem the situation.'

'Quick to redeem my own mistake, you mean. But it won't happen again. Do you know – nearly all of our fellows are injured? Wilmot, Dyve . . . even Maurice here.' He looked as if, but for the handkerchief, he had half a mind to cuff his brother about the ear. 'Oh – go and get yourself seen to, Maurice. You're bleeding like a stuck pig. And find someone to attend to Cornet Alsopp while you're at it.'

The boy at his feet coloured, overcome by the honour of having his name remembered. Meanwhile, the dark eyes had swept on to encompass Luciano and Selim.

'Where did these two spring from?'

'I don't know, sir,' answered Will Legge. 'I've yet to discover their names.'

'Well?' demanded the Prince of Luciano.

The Italian sighed. There was little point in offering a false name only to be exposed by someone who knew him. He therefore said calmly, 'My name is Luciano del Santi. I have business with a gentleman living not far from here and was detained on my way there yesterday by Captain Fiennes. When—'

'Fiennes?' His Highness interrupted. 'Was he commanding?'

'I believe so.'

'Then he deserves to be court-martialled. Go on. Why would he take you prisoner?'

'So that I might be persuaded to finance his cause.'

'Hah! You hear that, Will? And they call *us* thieves and robbers. So. He lifted you, did he? And I suppose you got away when he ran into us.' Rupert grinned. 'Wise of you. And no doubt you can afford a new coat.'

A faint answering gleam lit Luciano's eyes. 'God gives and God takes away, as they say. But if our horses could be found, I believe we should be glad of it.'

'Your Highness – I really m-must congratulate you!' said a softly drawling voice from behind. 'Brilliant. Quite b-brilliant!'

'I'm glad you think so.' Turning slowly, Rupert fixed the newcomer with a heavy-lidded stare. 'For myself, I can only say that you're easily pleased.'

Lord Digby raised his brows over angelic blue eyes and opened his mouth to reply. Then he saw Luciano.

'Dear me! Crookback Luke, by G-God! What are *you* doing here?'

'Getting very tired of being asked that question,' retorted the signor coolly. 'But if it's any comfort, I'm just as surprised to see you. I wouldn't have thought this was quite your milieu either.'

Captain Legge hid a grin. Prince Rupert didn't.

'Possibly not. But one serves as best one can,' came the frigid, unstammering reply. And then, with an acid-edged smile, 'Your Highness has obviously been doubly fortunate. I'm sure His Majesty will be delighted to see his favourite money-lender again.'

Rupert looked at Luciano and then, with mild irritation, at his lordship. He said abruptly, 'If you've nothing else to do, I suggest you go and see if there are any officers among the prisoners we've taken. Will – you can help him.'

'By all means, sir.' Captain Legge took Digby's arm and led him amicably but firmly away.

The Prince continued to stare at the Italian. Finally he said broodingly, 'Is it true?'

'Lord Digby is prone to . . . exaggeration.'

'I know that. But is he *right*?'

Luciano drew a long breath and then loosed it. 'More or less. I am a usurer . . . and I am known to the King.'

'And where do you live?'

'In London.'

'Ah.' Rupert thought about it. 'Well, I'd be failing in my duty if I let you go back there. Wars cost money and the longest purse tends to win. You'll have to come with us. Nothing else for it.'

'Isn't there?' Luciano's voice was suddenly crackling with temper. 'I've already poured thousands into His Majesty's bottomless pit. Am I now supposed to finance this – this latest débâcle? Hell's teeth! I'm not even English!' He checked himself and strove for a more moderate tone. 'Your Highness – I've spent more than two weeks chasing a man who is now probably no more than three miles away and I need to see him today. It really is of vital importance.'

'So is getting Byron safely to Shrewsbury – and if I delay now, I risk running into Essex,' came the blunt reply. 'The best I can do is to see that you're not kept kicking your heels any longer than is necessary – and then issue you with a pass. Sorry.'

'You can't possibly be as sorry as I am,' remarked the signor bitterly. 'From where I stand, it's beginning to look as if the only thing at stake in this war is possession of my person.'

Four

By the third week of October, bereft of both Richard and Eden and enlivened only by Celia's sporadic bursts of petulance, life at Thorne Ash was once more verging on tedium. The shelves were laden with everything from bandages to quince jelly; Kate had buried as much of Gianetta's hoard as the girl was prepared to part with, along with the best of the family silver, in a hole behind the hencoop; and everyone could recite to music their duties in the event of an attack. In short, they were as ready as they would ever be, and all they lacked, according to Felicity, was the opportunity to prove it.

'Which is only true up to a point,' observed Kate to her mother. 'I didn't really believe Eden at first – but he was perfectly right. We haven't a hope of holding the house against anyone who really wants to take it. And if Celia's not watched, I suspect that the first sign of the King's troops at our gates will have her out there welcoming them with cherry cordial. But I suppose we can hope that our very vulnerability may protect us. After all, if a place can't be held, why bother to take it? Or is that too logical?'

'Probably,' replied Dorothy. 'If common sense prevailed, the country wouldn't be in this mess. And that being so, I don't think we can rely on—' She stopped as the door opened to admit Mr Cresswell; and then, with courtesy but no pleasure, said, 'Well, Nathan, you're back early from Banbury today. Is there news?'

The tutor regarded her sombrely. He had recently had his pale hair cropped in the style responsible for the much-hated nickname that now clung to the Parliament's entire army – and it did not suit him.

'News, madam? Yes, I fear there is.' He paused weightily. 'The King is at Southam. They say he is marching on London with a dozen thousand men.'

'Southam? Dear God!' Dorothy exchanged a brief, startled glance with her daughter. 'And my lord Essex?'

'His lordship is vastly superior in numbers and has the goodwill of Almighty God. There can be no doubt that he will prevail. His exact whereabouts, however, are not yet known.'

'In which case I don't see how you can be so sure of his numerical superiority,' remarked Kate. 'And the last thing we heard was that his cavalry had just failed to prevail in that place near Worcester. But, since it looks as though the Cavaliers are about to march more or less past the door, I suppose we'd better hope you're right.'

'You must not doubt so much, Kate,' chided Mr Cresswell with a small indulgent smile. 'God is our strength.'

'I daresay His Majesty is saying the same,' she returned dryly. 'I think we'd better send someone to keep an eye on the main road. If they're making for London, they should simply pass us by; if not, we could do with some warning. And it would be nice to know when they've gone. But in the meantime, Nathan, you might be wise to stay away from Banbury. If the King's men catch you looking like that, I shudder to think what the consequences might be.'

So, privately, did he – but he merely looked disapproving and informed Dorothy that there was another matter to discuss.

She smothered a sigh. 'Yes?'

'As I have long expected, the Godly are aflame with the spirit of purity. In Rochester, seafaring men have cleared the cathedral of its graven images and in Canterbury, soldiers have destroyed a Papist representation of the Crucifixion. In short, the Lord's houses are at last being swept clean.'

'Ah.' Laying aside her needlework, Dorothy fixed him with a steady green gaze. 'Come to the point, Nathan.'

A spasm of irritation crossed his face. 'It is one I have tried to make before. The chapel here is filled with statues and ornaments and other unsuitable decoration. It should be cleansed without delay – for the time is coming when, if *you* do not do it, others will.'

Kate kept her mouth tightly shut and waited for her mother to speak. Finally, in a deceptively calm tone, Dorothy asked, 'Is that some sort of threat?'

'No. But it is a warning you should heed.'

'Should I?' She rose and faced him coolly across the width of her parlour. 'As you say – we have had this conversation before and my answer has not changed. But in case I failed to make myself sufficiently clear, I will say it once more. There is nothing remotely Papist about the services we hold here; and, as for the furnishings of the chapel, they have been placed there over successive generations by my husband's forebears. Consequently, I will have nothing moved, touched or altered in any way. And if you can't accept that, I can only suggest that you consider returning to your own family.'

A tide of rare colour washed over the pallid cheeks and Kate, silently rejoicing, perceived that for once in his life Mr Cresswell seemed lost for words.

'Well?' asked Dorothy crisply.

Something flickered in the colourless eyes and then was gone. 'How can you ask? You know I could never reconcile it with my conscience if I were to abandon you in your hour of need. It saddens me that I am unequal to the task of opening your eyes to the Light . . . but I will pray that you find understanding. Nothing, however, can render me so base as to desert you now.'

'How comforting,' said Dorothy, resolutely avoiding Kate's eye. 'And now perhaps you'd be good enough to go and consult with Jacob about the pigs. I understand there's some difficulty over where best to keep them if they're to stand any chance of escaping the notice of passing troopers and yet not be so close to the house that we can smell them.' She smiled. 'Life is full of small complications, isn't it? But I'm sure you can sort it out.'

Swathed in a cloak, Kate spent the latter part of the afternoon sitting behind the coping on the flat roof of the gallery – partly because it presented a good view of the country towards the road between Banbury and Southam, and partly because it was as good a place as any to be alone. Access to it was from one of the attic windows and posed no particular problem. Kate might have retained the façade of Whitehall elegance (now suitably adapted to rural practicality) but she also remembered how to climb out of a window and perch crow-like in the one place that offered reasonable comfort.

After mentally dropping Nathan down the nearest well, she moved on to ponder the news from outside. Although Thorne Ash was as yet in no real danger, Southam was just a little too close for comfort and twelve thousand men sounded an awful lot. And where, she wondered, was Essex? For if Nathan knew where the King's army was, it was reasonable to assume that Parliament's Commander-in-Chief must know it too and be taking steps to get between His Majesty and London.

It still didn't seem possible that this thing was actually happening; that somewhere out there, two armies of Englishmen were marching against each other. And the worst of it was that no one seemed to know what to expect. Would houses like theirs be left alone – or become part of the struggle whether they liked it or not? Would the twin armies really fight that 'first big battle' that everyone talked about, or would they continue to manoeuvre around each other because neither wanted the responsibility of striking the first blow? And was there no one, even now, who would find a way of stemming the tide before it was too late? Kate didn't know, and she suspected that no one else did either. It was like standing blindfold on top of a cliff, unable to move in any direction because just one step could take you over the edge.

And as if all this were not enough, thought Kate, pulling her cloak more closely about her against the chill north wind, there was her own position to consider. She didn't know if she herself had changed during the last few months or whether it was simply a matter of circumstances altering cases. But it did now seem that she had been somewhat hasty – if not downright stupid – to let her feelings for Luciano del Santi panic her into betrothal with Kit. Indeed, she was no longer certain those feelings still existed; and if they did . . . well, surely she was mature enough to cope with what could never amount to more than the odd, random meeting?

Sometimes she even wondered if she had ever seriously intended to marry Kit at all or had merely been using him as some sort of shield. A lowering thought when she had always made such a parade of her honesty and common sense. But what really mattered was the harm she was doing: first and foremost to Kit, who did not deserve to be cheated; and also to her parents, who had more important things to think about these days.

Kate sighed and stirred restlessly. It wasn't that she didn't like Kit. She did. She liked him very much, in fact, but she was very definitely not in love with him and nor did she truthfully think she ever would be. All of which – when added to the present complications – meant that the only sane course was to do what the King and John Pym ought to be doing: put an end to the situation before it got any worse. The only question left, therefore, was how best to do it. A letter was probably the quickest and easiest way out but seemed rather cowardly; and anything else meant waiting.

'Damn,' she thought crossly. 'I don't know what to do for the best – and it's all my own stupid fault.'

There was no use in brooding, however . . . and in any case it was beginning to rain. Kate sighed again and came cautiously to her feet. It wouldn't do to slip and break her neck either. Gathering up her skirts, she placed one hand on the window-ledge and then stopped, staring intently down at the lane.

Two horsemen appeared to be heading for Thorne Ash.

Kate strained her eyes but to no avail. Kit? she wondered. No. Possible . . . but surely too much of a coincidence.

Eden? Oh God, hopefully not – for that would mean Essex's army was also close by. Who, then? *Who?*

The truth dawned slowly and took time to sink in. Then, 'I should have known,' she breathed. 'As ever, dead on cue. Ah well . . . at least I'll find out how mature I really am. And, with any luck, Meg will spit in the assassin's eye.'

Once safely back in the house and already aware that she was in no hurry to go downstairs, she stalked purposefully off to the nursery. Then, without looking at Meg, she informed Gianetta that her brother was on his way to the door.

'Oh?' The dark brows rose suspiciously. 'What for?'

'To see you, probably,' shrugged Kate. 'Go and warn Mother, will you? I'll be down when I've tidied my hair.'

Gianetta thought about it for a moment and then, with a glance at Meg, said flatly, 'The fool. He has brought Selim with him, hasn't he?'

Kate sighed and met her maid's widened gaze. 'Yes.'

'*Men!*' said Gianetta disgustedly. And swept out of the room.

Meg's hands closed hard over the rim of her daughter's cradle. 'I . . . Miss Kate, I don't want to see him.'

'I don't blame you. And there's no reason why you should. They'll probably only stay one night anyway.'

'But what if he wants to see Eve?'

'I'll tell him he can't,' replied Kate. 'In fact, I'll quite *enjoy* telling him. Don't worry. He won't come near either of you. And I doubt, after this visit, that he'll be in too much of a hurry to come back.'

By the time she had completely re-dressed her hair and decided that changing her gown would leave her open to misinterpretation, an hour had passed and she was unable, reasonably, to delay further. With the exception of Selim, of whom there was no sign, she found everyone gathered uneasily in the parlour. Dorothy looked mildly fraught, Gianetta stubborn, and Celia frankly bored. Only Felicity appeared pleased to see their visitor; but then Felicity would probably smile just as sunnily at the devil himself.

'Down so soon, Kate?' The signor rose to greet her with a provoking smile. 'You shouldn't have hurried.'

She allowed herself to look at him. There was a suspicion of fatigue in the fine-boned face and the inevitable, exquisite black coat showed unaccustomed signs of wear . . . but otherwise he was just the same.

She smiled back with killing sweetness. 'How could I help it? I'd have been sorry to miss you altogether. And I don't suppose you'll be staying long.'

'Now why should you suppose that? Wishful thinking?'

'Not in the least.' She avoided the necessity of offering her hand by moving to a stool and sinking gracefully down upon it. 'I merely assumed that you wouldn't otherwise have had the audacity to bring Selim with you.'

Luciano del Santi looked down on her with unbroken composure. 'You're too late. I've already been taken to task on that score by Gianetta and arranged matters to the satisfaction of your lady mother. It's a shame you missed it, but the subject is now closed and you're left with nothing to do but greet me politely and say how delighted you are to see me again after all this time.'

'Consider it done,' said Kate shortly. 'And tell us, instead, to what we owe the honour. Or have I missed *that* as well?'

'No.' It was Gianetta who spoke. 'And if he has come to take me away, I tell him now I will not go.'

Five pairs of eyes rested on the Italian while he took his time about answering. Then he said pleasantly, 'Your English has improved beyond recognition, Gianetta. What a pity the same can't be said of your manners.'

'I don't care. I don't want to live with – to live in London.'

'Tact at last,' he marvelled. 'It might be more to the point, however, to consider whether you've outstayed your welcome. Mistress Maxwell has been kindness itself, but she can't have bargained on your visit being quite so prolonged.'

Dorothy immediately found herself impaled on a mutely appealing stare. And, because she had become quite fond of her charge, she said lightly, 'My goodness, Signor del Santi – you can't take her away now! Who's going to supervise the nursery and dazzle any visiting soldiers into forgetting to ransack the house?'

Faint amusement bracketed the Italian's mouth. 'I take it that means you're happy to keep her – and not merely being civil?'

'Civility – in *this* family? God forbid!' Dorothy's glance strayed briefly to Kate. 'But no. She's welcome to stay.'

'Aunt Dolly!' Gianetta flew to kiss her. '*Grazie!*'

'*Aunt?*' queried Luciano.

'Why not?' Felicity's smile brimmed with mischief. 'What does Felix call you?'

'Sir,' came the arid response. 'And, speaking of Felix . . . I daresay you'd like to have him with you for Christmas?'

'We would,' agreed Dorothy cautiously. 'But with the countryside in turmoil, I don't really see . . .'

'How he's to get here safely?' finished the signor. 'Don't worry. I won't send him if the signs are against it – and I'll see that he's well escorted. But not – ' to Kate – 'by Selim.'

'Obviously.' Her brows rose. 'You can't unless you cut the cord, can you? And you're plainly not thinking of bringing Felix here yourself.'

'Is that an invitation? If so, don't think I'm not tempted. Unfortunately however, having already been politely detained by both sides, I can't help but feel that Felix will arrive quicker without me.'

'Goodness!' said Kate amicably. 'I'd no idea you were so popular. But it seems they soon let you go again.' She paused, catching a glimpse of something unexpected in his eyes. 'Or did they?'

'Not particularly. I escaped the singularly inept clutches of Nathaniel Fiennes only to fall into the rather more efficient hands of the King's nephew – with the result that I've wasted the last month getting from Worcester to here via Shrewsbury.'

Celia sat up, displaying faint signs of animation. 'The King's nephew? Prince Rupert? Heavens! Is he really as romantic as they say?'

'Romantic?' A sardonic smile curled the Italian's mouth. 'I doubt I'm qualified to judge. The words that spring to my mind are self-willed, single-minded and blunt. Rather,' he finished blandly, 'like Kate.'

There was a ripple of laughter.

Bastard, thought Kate appreciatively. And then, in an effort to disguise the fact that, for the first time in months, bubbles of exhilaration were bursting in her veins, said calmly, 'I'm flattered. And I suppose you travelled in this exalted company as far as Southam?'

'Further than that. When I took my leave of him earlier today, the King was at Fenny Compton with the intention of spending the night at Edgecote.'

There was a sudden silence. Then Dorothy said remotely, 'If that's the case, they're all around us. Wonderful. And where is Lord Essex?'

'Supposedly marching east from Worcester to prevent the King's progress south,' came the brisk reply. 'But whether or not he'll do it is anybody's guess – so at the moment I think all you have to worry about is escaping the attention of the Royalists.'

'Oh,' said Kate feebly. 'Is *that* all?'

'Yes. But look on the bright side. You're well away from the main road here – and I rather gathered that their immediate objective is to take Banbury Castle. Consequently, they're unlikely to come here either by accident or design. And just in case they do, I've despatched Selim to the tavern in the village so that we may have some warning.' He smiled mockingly. 'What's the matter, Kate? Surprised I should think of it, or unable to accept that I'm not quite as crass as you'd like to think?'

'Both.' She drew a long breath. 'If you've been with the King, I imagine you've probably also seen Celia's brother and – and Kit Clifford.'

'Yes – and both are well. But I'm afraid I bear no messages because it seemed wiser not to mention that I was coming here. Ah. And that reminds me.' Sliding one hand into his pocket, he pulled out a rather crumpled letter. 'Gianetta. This is for you.'

Surprise marking her brow, she rose to take it from him; and then, staring at it, said slowly, 'This is from Mario. If you brought it yourself from Genoa, why didn't you give it to me before?'

He shrugged. 'I believe I was too busy.'

'You could have sent it.'

'It slipped my mind. Aren't you going to read it?'

'Yes – but alone.' And, without another word, she went swiftly from the room.

Felicity frowned at the signor. 'You know what it says, don't you?'

'More or less. But I don't think I'll compound my offence by telling you.'

'Meaning,' said Kate, 'that the news will not be welcome.'

'Exactly. But the storm it raises shouldn't last long.' Again that cool, impersonal smile. 'Displays of temperament require the right audience, you see. And I am leaving for Oxford first thing in the morning.'

For two equally good reasons, Kate retired that night only to find that sleep was entirely beyond her. And after two hours of tossing and turning and trying to think neither of Luciano del Santi's presence in the house nor the Royalist army's all around it, she finally admitted defeat and got up. A hot posset was probably the answer; and, even if it wasn't, at least the task of making it would give her something else to think about.

She lit a candle, pulled on her chamber-robe and rammed her feet into a pair of slippers. Then, taking care to make as little noise as possible, she went down to the kitchen to set some cream to warm and savagely beat up some eggs.

This made her wrist ache but unfortunately didn't touch her mind.

'All right,' thought Kate, irritably setting down the basin and reaching for the cinnamon. 'Address the problem. The Cavaliers may be close by but, if they haven't come here yet, the chances are that they won't. And tomorrow they ought to be too busy trying to take the castle or march on London to bother about small country manors like this one. As for Luciano . . . in a few hours he'll be gone too. It's unfortunate that he manages to make me feel so alive and attracts me in a way Kit doesn't . . . unfair, even. But it's hardly the end of the world and I can cope with it.' She poured a generous measure of sack into the spicy eggs. 'So that's that. No problem at all.'

The cream was just coming to the boil. Kate lifted it from the heat and, holding it high in the air, let it cascade smoothly down on the eggs and sack.

'"Eye of newt and toe of frog", I presume,' said a thread-like voice from the door. 'You must have known I was coming.'

Kate jumped and a splash of hot cream landed on her hand.

'"By the pricking of my thumbs"?' she retorted, slamming the pan down and wheeling to face him. 'Haven't you *any* sense? I might have been scalded. And why aren't you in bed, instead of creeping round like a blasted burglar?'

'My apologies. It's not through choice, I assure you,' he replied, advancing a little into the light. And then, before she had time to do more than think how odd he looked, said desperately, 'Oh hell. Sorry, Kate.' And threw up neatly into the nearest available receptacle.

Shock paralysed her for at least thirty seconds. Then, having waited for the paroxysm to pass, she moved slowly towards him saying, 'Well, well . . . another illusion shattered.'

He remained where he was, leaning heavily on the dresser and trying to steady his breathing. 'I knew I could count on your sympathy.'

'Quite. How long have you been like this?'

'Not long.' A faint shudder passed over him. 'An hour, perhaps. Could I trouble you for some water?'

'Milk might be better.'

'Only if you like watching me vomit,' he snapped, looking up at her. And then, 'Kate. Enjoy yourself by all means, but just for once do as I ask.'

'When does anyone ever do anything else?' she asked furiously. 'Oh – sit down, for God's sake. And take the damned bowl with you.'

When she came back with the water, she found that he had done as she asked but was still looking decidedly green. She handed him the cup without a word and stalked back to the stove as if she didn't care a jot. Which of course, she told herself firmly, she didn't. From behind her came the unmistakable sounds of further unpleasantness. Kate stared fixedly into the posset and discovered that, like her insides, it appeared to have curdled.

Presently, his voice low and controlled, he said, 'I don't suppose you'd consider going back to bed?'

'*And leave you like this?*' she thought. But of course she couldn't say it. So she turned a brittle smile on him and said, 'And miss all the fun? Don't be stupid. But it does rather look as though I ought to fetch Mother.'

'No.' For some obscure reason, Luciano suddenly realised that – if he couldn't be left decently alone – Kate's was the only company he could tolerate. 'Don't worry. I haven't brought some unspeakable disease with me. I think I know what this is . . . and it shouldn't last much longer.'

'So now you're a doctor as well!' She marched to the table and sat down facing him. 'Is there no end to your accomplishments?'

The dark eyes were a little dull but he achieved a semblance of his customary acid-edged smile. 'Don't tempt me. It doesn't take much, however, to spot the effects of an emetic.'

Temporarily silenced, Kate stared at him. Then she said uncertainly, 'If that's a joke, it's a poor one.'

'As you wish.' The smile lingered. 'So . . . what shall we talk about now? *Your* reasons for being up at this hour?'

He was obviously feeling better. Planting her elbows on the table and resting her chin on her hands, Kate said severely, 'All right. I'm listening. Who and how?'

'I'm inclined to suspect the mulled ale, so conveniently placed at my bedside. As for who . . . I can only suppose that Gianetta is taking her revenge.'

'*Gianetta?* But she's your sister!'

'Only by blood,' he excused dryly. 'And, on top of parting her from her beloved cousin Mario, I'm also guilty

324

of withholding his letter announcing his intention to wed elsewhere until the deed was done.' He paused, reflectively. 'I ought to have expected it really. Her admirable restraint throughout supper didn't quite match the look in her eye.'

'But it's ridiculous!' said Kate crossly. 'If you ask me, she no longer cares a fig for this cousin. And it's certainly no reason to – to half poison you!'

His brows rose. 'This unlooked-for support is very touching, Kate, but don't get carried away. It was only an emetic, you know, and a relatively mild one at that. I'm surprised you're not laughing.'

'Give me time,' she retorted, annoyingly aware of her error. 'Right now I don't find anything particularly funny in having to clear up the results of Gianetta's little prank.'

'Understandable . . . but unnecessary.' The pause held a subtle element of disbelief. But before she could speak again, he came slowly to his feet saying, 'I'll do it myself. I'm quite capable.'

'I daresay you are. Unfortunately, however, you're a guest. And Mother would never forgive me.'

'She won't know anything about it.'

'I beg your pardon?'

'You heard me.' He held her gaze with pleasant implacability. 'Quite simply, dear Kate, if this becomes public I'll be forced to box Gianetta's ears. Metaphorically speaking, of course. And that isn't going to solve anything.'

'It might stop her doing it again.'

'There's no need for that. She may be Italian, but she's not a Borgia. And if I can forget it, why shouldn't you?'

'I'll think about it,' said Kate curtly. Rising, she took the foul bowl from beside him and bore it wordlessly away to the scullery.

When she came back, he was once more sitting motionless at the table, staring thoughtfully at his hands. Kate replaced the bowl on the dresser and then, turning, said abruptly, 'You say Gianetta is Italian. Aren't you?'

He looked up at her and gave an almost imperceptible shrug. 'Not really. Not any more. I believe the expression is "Neither fish nor fowl".'

She knew she ought to leave, that there was no further excuse to stay; but she could not resist the temptation to sit down again, saying slowly, 'That sounds rather uncomfortable.'

'Only if one allows it to be.' He paused and, for the first time since he had entered the kitchen, took in the russet-coloured robe that had seen better days and the waist-long hair, once loosely confined at the nape but now wildly straying. Most women – even Gwynneth, with whom he still slept from time to time – would resent being caught at such a disadvantage. Kate did not appear to have given it so much as a passing thought. He found he rather admired that. And so, although he had not planned to interfere, he chose to say mildly, 'But I imagine you'd know all about that.'

Wariness flickered in the jewel-green eyes. '*I* would? Why?'

'The peculiar nature of your betrothal.'

'Oh God – not you too!' she snapped. And then, 'You've been talking to Father.'

'*Vice versa*. He's concerned about you, Kate.'

'Do you think I don't know that?'

'No. I've even a suspicion that it occasionally keeps you awake at night. So what are you going to do about it?'

She stood up again and faced him over the table, shaking with an emotion that she told herself was anger. 'That's no affair of yours. And even if it were, you are the very last person I'd discuss it with. I don't even know why you're asking me. You must, as someone once said, have other fish to fry.'

He gave the ghost of a laugh. 'One or two.'

'Quite. So if you'll refrain from prying into my affairs, I won't ask why you're hot-footing it round the country inquiring about dead men.' She smiled disquietingly. 'I'll even promise not to ask Father.'

Luciano remained completely unperturbed. 'It wouldn't do you much good if you did. Are you going? If so, good-night – and goodbye.'

Kate promptly sat down yet again and broke all her rules. 'The country is heaving with troops and you've just been as sick as a dog. You can't still mean to go to Oxford!'

'Why not? In fact, since it hardly seems worth going to bed now, I can start even earlier than I'd planned.'

'Fine.' She folded her hands carefully together and laid them on the table. 'And I'll make such a noise about tonight that neither you nor anyone else will ever forget it.'

She had anticipated the silence but not the look in his eyes; and when he didn't reply, she was finally driven to say, 'Well? Will you do yourself the favour of getting some sleep?'

'I don't respond to threats,' he informed her silkily. 'And neither do I need you to decide what I should or should not do.'

'You need someone – and unfortunately I'm all you've got.' She drew a ragged breath. 'I'm only trying to make you see sense.'

'Are you? Somehow I don't think so.' The force with which he rose sent his stool screeching over the flagstones. 'How many times must I say it? I am not available. And this kind of thing can't go on.'

Later, she would realise how easily she could – and should – have dissembled. Instead, she opened her mouth on the first thought that came into her head. 'I know. Why else do you think I said I'd marry Kit Clifford?'

Catastrophe yawned all around them. Kate shut her eyes. Then, 'Oh Christ,' said Luciano wearily. 'Not clever, Kate. Not clever at all. If you wanted to call me a bastard, all you had to do was say it . . . remembering, of course, that it takes one to know one.'

And walked quietly away, leaving her alone.

There was no possibility of sleep after that, and neither did the dawn bring counsel. Kate rose early with shadows under her eyes, a lead weight in her chest and just one question beating sickeningly in her brain. '*What have I done?*'

Once downstairs, however, she was given little time to brood. First there was Goodwife Flossing demanding to know who had been wasting precious spices on undrunk possets . . . and then, almost before Kate had finished apologising, Dorothy appeared in the hall.

'I see,' she said wryly, 'that you didn't sleep either. Do you think it would be asking for trouble if we sent Nathan to find out what's happening?'

'There's no point. Selim is supposed to be keeping his ear to the ground in the village and I've had one or other of the Woodley brothers watching the Southam road since yesterday. So if there was anything to know, presumably we'd know it.'

'In other words, no news—' She broke off in response to an urgent hammering on the door.

'Is good news,' finished Kate, moving swiftly to release bar and bolt. 'Or should that be *was?*'

It was Selim – a fact which immediately told her that the signor must still be in the house. But in the face of the Turk's obvious agitation, this was plainly not the moment to think of it; so without stepping aside for him to enter, she said flatly, 'What's happened?'

'The Roundheads have come and the King's men are marching to meet them,' came the equally bald reply. 'I think they will fight.'

An unpleasant plummeting sensation took place behind Kate's ribs and she turned to stare mutely at her mother.

'He'd better come in,' said Dorothy, in a voice that was not quite her own. And, when he had done so, 'Now. Tell us everything you know.'

'As soon as the light came,' explained Selim, 'I rode to the next village – the one named Cropredy – to see if there were soldiers. I found many. They were getting ready to leave and so I talk to them and ask where they are going. They say that they march to meet Prince Rupert's men because the Roundheads have come in the night to Kineton.'

'I see.' Dorothy drew a long breath. 'And where exactly are the King and his nephew planning to meet?'

'By the Vale of the Red Horse . . . in a place which is called Edgehill.'

'Edgehill.' Kate's eyes locked once more with her mother's. 'And Lord Essex is at Kineton. This is it, isn't it? And we're going to be able to hear the guns from here.'

There was silence. Then Dorothy said, 'Eden must be there. And Tom Tripp and all our people.'

'I know.' Kate looked sick.

Selim glanced uncomfortably from one to the other of them. Then he said diffidently, 'Is it possible I can speak with my master?'

'He – he's still asleep.' Kate tried to pull herself together. 'And with two armies on the move, I wouldn't have thought today an especially good time to leave for Oxford.'

'No. This is what I have come to say.'

'In which case, it hardly seems necessary to wake him, does it? And in the meantime I'd be grateful if you rode up the lane to the road and brought back the man you'll find there – if only he hasn't perished in this frost. Then, when you come back, there will be breakfast for you both in the kitchen.'

Mention of breakfast made the moustaches quiver. 'A thousand thanks, *hanim-efendi*. I will go at once.'

'There is,' said Kate austerely, 'just one more thing. Stay away from Meg and keep your hands to yourself in general. Otherwise I'll feed you to the pigs myself.'

When he had gone, Dorothy looked thoughtfully at her daughter and said, 'Why are we trying to stop the signor leaving?'

'We're not.' Kate kept her expression perfectly blank. 'But a small delay can't matter. And who's to say that we may not find a use for him before the day's out?'

Afterwards, Kate always thought of that day as the one on which, for Thorne Ash, the war began in earnest. It was Sunday, but no one went to church. Instead, Dorothy gathered her household for the usual morning prayers and then, as calmly and simply as she could, told them the news.

The little scullery-maid burst into frightened tears, Celia dropped her prayer-book and Gianetta crossed herself. It was the last of these, Kate suspected – along with a natural reluctance to miss a good opportunity – that inspired Mr

Cresswell to fall instantly on his knees and exhort them all to join him in praying for Lord Essex's triumph. Dorothy, however, nipped this overture firmly in the bud by saying coolly, 'Most commendable, Nathan. But it seems to me that this is less a moment to ask for victory than for the preservation of those we love . . . and that is something we can each do best in our own way.'

It was not until everyone was dispersing to attend to their various duties and concerns that Kate saw Luciano standing quietly in the doorway, listening. He looked a little drawn but otherwise fully restored; and, her heart sinking still further, she thought dismally, 'Oh God. Please let him not have believed me. He's good at that, after all. And if he *did* and is going to say something dreadful, please let him not do it now for them all to hear. Today's likely to be quite bad enough without having to fend off personal humiliation as well.'

Perhaps Luciano was himself aware of this . . . or perhaps he had other reasons altogether. At any rate, he did not so much as glance in her direction but confined himself to exchanging a few words with Dorothy about the news his henchman had brought, before drawing his sister to one side for a rather longer and less audible conversation, from which she emerged faintly pink and more than usually subdued. Then he summoned Selim from the kitchen and took him off in the direction of the stables.

The morning dragged by on leaden feet. Kate spent most of it greasing the mechanisms of the small collection of firearms left by Eden, in between lurking at any window that afforded a view of the lane. By the time the family assembled for the noon-day meal, they were still no wiser than they had been five hours earlier and Kate was forced to take the risk of asking her mother what had become of their guest.

'I don't know. He said he was going to see what's going on. Presumably he'll come back when he has something to tell us.'

'Well, I wish he'd hurry up,' said Felicity. 'All this waiting and not knowing is hard on the nerves. I don't know why, but all I can think about is Eden, wearing his new silk sash.'

'You would,' remarked Celia pettishly. 'It seems to me that stupid sash is the only thing you care about.'

'Does it?' Fatigue and strain were taking their toll on Kate's temper and she came abruptly to her feet. 'And what, may we ask, do *you* care about?'

The afternoon passed no quicker than the morning. Wrapped in a thick cloak against the biting wind, Kate took her ill humour outside to the top of the gatehouse and paced up and down its brief length until her head started to spin. And then she heard it: a deep, distant thud, repeated over and over.

She froze, her fingers tightening painfully on the stone. Nothing to see, of course . . . nothing even to hear but for that irregular, menacing boom. But imagination was a terrible thing; and worse still was the knowledge that they were all over the cliff with a vengeance now, and that, whatever happened today at Edgehill, nothing would ever be the same again.

A pall of silence grew in the house as the light began to fail. Candles were lit, curtains reluctantly drawn and they all assembled once more for a meal which nobody really wanted. And then, just as they were about to rise from the table, came the long-awaited sound of hooves on the cobbles.

'Thank goodness!' said Felicity in heartfelt tones. 'That will be Mr Santi. Now at last we'll know what's happening.'

Kate did not speak. Without stopping to think, she was out of her seat and into the hall to throw open the door.

He looked cold . . . but that was natural. What she hadn't expected was to see something in his face that effectively prevented all the obvious questions and caused her to say merely, 'Give me your cloak and come in to the fire. Where's Selim?'

'Stabling the horses – after which I've told him to go to the kitchen.' His voice was remote and his manner uncharacteristically passive. Looking down at his boots, he said, 'I'm rather dirty, I'm afraid.'

331

'It doesn't matter,' she began. And then, understanding dawned. 'But go and change if you wish. I'll have some brandy sent up to you.'

His smile was faintly twisted. 'That is the best offer I've had all day – but I'd better not take it. You will want the news; and if I go to my room with a bottle, I may not come out again.'

'Then you'd better come and get it over with,' said Kate. And led him in to face the others.

Felicity and Gianetta had been swiftly clearing the board of half-empty plates while Dorothy set a fresh place for the signor and put the chicken cullis within easy reach. When he entered the room, all three looked expectantly from their tasks and Dorothy immediately saw the same thing that had struck Kate. It brought her the nearest she had ever come to liking him.

'Come and sit down,' she said. 'There is food if you want it.'

'Thank you.' He eyed the chicken without enthusiasm. 'Perhaps later? And in the meantime, while I tell you what's been happening, there was some mention of brandy . . .?'

'Here it is.' Kate poured a generous measure and set the squat green bottle down at his elbow. 'Take your time. We've waited all day – so a few more minutes won't kill us.'

Luciano downed half the glass in one swallow and waited while the warmth of it began to invade his veins. Then he said slowly, 'I imagine you already know that there was a battle. It finally began at around two this afternoon on the ground between Kineton and Radway – and Selim and I watched as best we could from Avon Dassett. Lord Essex fired the opening shot . . . and then the Royalist Horse made a charge that scattered half of his lordship's cavalry and a part of his Foot as well. The chase seemed to go on for miles.' He paused and took another drink. 'After that everything got rather confusing – or so it appeared to me. But then, I'm no expert. Suffice it to say that other parliamentary regiments arrived on the scene and the King looked to be in some difficulty until part of his cavalry came back to the field to help him. And then it got dark.'

There was a long silence when he stopped speaking but eventually Kate said baldly, 'Who won?'

'I don't know. It didn't look to me as if anyone did . . . but then I don't know how these things are measured. So far as I could tell, no ground was either gained or lost today, and when I left, it looked as though both armies were preparing to spend the night more or less where they were.'

'But it's so cold!' exclaimed Felicity, shocked.

'Yes.' He stared grimly into his glass for a moment before draining it.

Kate reached out and refilled it, leaving her mother to say flatly, 'I'm sure you would rather spare us the details, just as we ourselves would prefer to be spared. But one thing we must know. How great were the – the casualties?'

He met her gaze sombrely. 'Heavy on both sides, I believe. The field was littered . . . though how many were dead, it's impossible to say.'

'I see.' Dorothy swallowed but managed to keep her voice level. 'I don't suppose you saw anything of Eden?'

'No. I'm sorry. We were some distance away and as yet the various colours mean nothing to me. I could perhaps have gone down when it was over and tried asking, but the confusion was such that I doubt it would have proved helpful.' He stopped and then, on a sudden explosion of breath, said, '*Hell!* That's a lie, of course. I didn't go down because I didn't think my stomach would stand it. And I ought to tell you that, if I'm not to disgrace myself still further, someone had better remove that damned chicken.'

Five

Having taken the bottle to bed with him and finished it, Luciano awoke next morning with knives grinding inside his head. He decided, quite sensibly, to stay where he was, and ten minutes later a gentle tap at the door was followed by Gianetta's head.

'Luciano? May I come in?'

'Can I stop you?' She had spoken in Italian and, closing his eyes again, he answered her in the same. 'I hope you haven't brought me anything to eat or drink, because a refusal, as they say, often offends.'

She put the laden tray carefully down on the clothes chest. 'That's why I came. I want to apologise.'

'Did you? Why?'

'You know why. Because that emetic was a stupid, child-ish trick and if I'd thought for even a minute, I wouldn't have done it. Only I didn't think. I just lost my temper because you didn't trust me enough to give me Mario's letter. And now I'm sorry.'

He opened his eyes and, not without difficulty, forced them to focus on her. 'Have you been talking to Kate, by any chance?' Then, when she looked completely blank, 'Obvi-ously not. So why are you honouring me with an apology?'

Gianetta sighed and sat down on the edge of the bed. 'It was partly what you said yesterday about trying to do your best for me. I suppose that's always been true . . . only it was easier for me not to believe it.' She hesitated, toying restlessly with her rosary. 'I can't really remember that time after Father died and you and Mother and I left for Genoa.'

'That,' he remarked rather grimly, 'is just as well.'

'Is it? I used to think so. Indeed, I don't think I really *wanted* to remember it. Only, perhaps if I had, I wouldn't have taken so long to remember that you are my brother.'

Very, very cautiously, Luciano sat up. He said, 'It wasn't your fault that you forgot. Vittorio and I did that between us. If you remember it now, that's enough.'

'Perhaps.' She raised doubtful eyes to his face. 'But in every sense that counts, we're almost strangers. And last night, watching Kate and Felicity, I realised that it shouldn't be so – particularly now, with life so uncertain.'

'You're worried about mild regret becoming life-long guilt? Don't. I have no intention of dying.'

'I'm glad to hear it.' She smiled a little. 'But don't misunderstand. I'd like to know you better and hope that, in time, we can be friends. But I still don't want to live with you in London; and—'

'That's fortunate, because I wasn't about to ask you.' He met her gaze wryly. '*Mea culpa*. Perhaps in future I should correct your misconceptions. But if it interests you, I'm well aware that you're better off here – mainly because life in London is likely to become rather uncomfortable. And I shan't be there much myself.'

She considered this and then said unexpectedly, 'You're up to something, aren't you?'

'Yes. And one day I'll tell you about it. But not yet.' His tone was pleasant but final. 'I believe you had a second point to make?'

'Yes. I want you to try *talking* to me before you interfere in my life. I've grown up, Luciano – and you may find I'm less stupid than you think.'

The knives were still grinding and it was an effort to smile but he did it. 'You're asking me to be less high-handed . . . and I'll promise to try. But on one condition.'

'Which is?'

He sighed and lay down again.

'Did anyone ever teach you to make a tisane? My skull is splitting.'

***

Never having been in the habit of confiding in Kate, Gianetta saw no reason to begin now – but eventually passed on an edited account of their conversation to Felicity. Consequently, by the time Kate was told of the budding rapprochement, she had spent several hours viewing the new, inexplicable cordiality with suspicion and wondering precisely what had caused the signor to delay his departure for yet another day.

She was also, now the initial crisis of Edgehill seemed to be over, able to think once more of that criminally stupid admission she had made about her betrothal – and the disaster that could befall her as a result. But although she knew that no amount of brooding would cure it and the most sensible course was to reopen the subject with Luciano – so that, with the aid of a little cunning, she might nurture disbelief – she could not find the courage to do it. He had never, in the entire course of their acquaintance, reacted as he was supposed to – and he had no tact whatsoever; so rather than give him the chance to cut the ground from beneath her feet, it was probably better to leave well alone and simply avoid him altogether. If, of course, he chose to let her.

Miraculously, it seemed that he did – which, irritatingly enough, was less of a relief than it should have been. And during the hours that followed, in which they barely exchanged two words with each other – and then always in the company of others – a second question began to grow in Kate's mind. Twice now he had accused her of regarding him with more than mere liking . . . and he was right. *But how did he know?* She did not think she was especially transparent, and in the last year she had used every art of concealment at her command. No one else, moreover, appeared to have noticed anything. So how *did* he know? Sorcery? Inspired guess-work? Or could it possibly be that he was rather more interested in the state of her emotions than he cared to admit? The sudden closing of her throat told her that this concept was too dangerous to be pursued . . . except just possibly as a last line of defence.

On the following morning, the Royalists came.

Meg Bennet's father, Jacob, was the first to see them when, having set out to call at one of the outlying farms, he espied a cavalcade of horsemen wending its way up the hill towards him from Cropredy. Then, since he too was unfamiliar with the banners and devices that were the only means of distinguishing friend from foe, he had to tarry for several agonising minutes before a ragged burst of song gave him the clue he had been seeking.

'The cuckoo then on every tree mocks married men
For thus sings he – Cuckoo! Cuckoo!'

It seemed an unlikely choice for men serving under one who had for years been popularly known as the Great Cuckold; and that left only one alternative. Jacob set spurs to his horse and rode *ventre à terre* back to Thorne Ash.

'Oh God,' said Dorothy weakly, when she had heard him out. And then, to Kate, 'What do you think? Have we any chance at all of defying twenty or thirty men?'

'I don't know.' Kate was already half-way to the door. 'We'll soon find out though, won't we? Sound the alarm, make sure everyone does what they're supposed to – and keep an eye on Celia. I'm going outside.'

By the time the Cavaliers came into view, the gate was securely barred, the ancient saker loaded with ball and shot and Kate herself was on the wall, armed with a musket. She was just trying to see whether or not the Royalists had brought any pieces of ordnance with them when Luciano del Santi materialised at her side and said crisply, 'What the hell do you think you're doing?'

'What does it look like?' she responded without turning.

'Lunacy. Half a regiment couldn't hold this house – let alone a handful of women. It just isn't built for it.'

'I thought you said you were no expert?'

'I'm not – but I do know a lost cause when I see it. And this is no time for heroic gestures.'

'Isn't it?' She turned suddenly and eyed him fiercely. 'What did you expect? This is our home; and I'm not about to give it up to strangers without a fight. So if you don't want to help, you'd better go and make yourself comfortable in one of the cellars because I haven't got time to argue with you now.'

Luciano looked back at her for a long, reflective moment. Then he said resignedly, 'I must be suffering from necrosis of the brain. All right. What do you want me to do?'

He had the satisfaction of surprising her. She said, 'If you mean it – and can shoot – there's a pistol over there. But we can't afford to waste shot.'

She half expected a tart response, but he merely picked up the weapon with the ease of one who knew exactly what he was doing and said mildly, 'Are we really planning to fire at them?'

'If we have to – yes,' came the grim reply. 'My goodness, look at them! They've certainly come dressed to kill, haven't they? And they've brought a cannon . . . though it doesn't look any bigger than ours.'

Luciano said nothing. Someone appeared to have gone to the unusual expense of providing two dozen men with matching grey coats, blue silk sashes and plumed hats, and the results were impressive. On the other hand, looks weren't everything and a troop in such pristine condition was unlikely to have fought at Edgehill.

'With any luck, they'll want to keep their coats clean,' he said. And then, 'Ah. They're starting to deploy.'

'Yes. But they can't do anything until they send us a summons to surrender – or so Eden said.'

'And God forbid that anyone should fail to play by the rules!' observed the Italian sardonically. 'But no. Here it comes.'

A solitary grey-coated rider had detached himself from his comrades and was approaching the gates. Then, reaching them, he produced a bugle from his saddle-bow and blew an inexpert fanfare.

Kate peered indulgently down on his head. 'I'd take a few more lessons if I were you. However. What do you want?'

For a moment he looked completely at a loss. Then he said importantly, 'Captain Winter presents his compliments and asks that, in the interests of property and for the preservation of life, you open your gates to His Majesty's troops. In such a case, the captain is prepared to guarantee the safety of all within your walls, for it is not our desire to make war on women.'

'That's nice.' Kate temporarily withheld the obvious question. 'We don't want to make war on you either. So if your captain will withdraw his men, *I'll* guarantee *their* safety. How's that?'

The young man was baffled again. This wasn't how the exchange was supposed to go and it made it difficult to know what to say next. He cleared his throat and tried again. 'You don't quite understand, madam. We don't want to inconvenience you but – but we can't permit you to hold this house in defiance of our sovereign lord the King.'

'Which is just a grandiose way of saying that I'm supposed to let you and your friends tread mud all over the house and make off with the chickens.' She was aware that, beside her, Luciano del Santi was sinking down upon his haunches, laughing immoderately. 'Well, I won't. So you'd better tell Captain . . . what did you say his name was?'

'Winter, madam. Captain Cyrus Winter.'

'Ah.' Kate shot a brief, quelling glance at Luciano. 'Then you may present Kate Maxwell's compliments to the captain and tell him we've no intention of opening our gates to him or anyone else coming here with a similar demand. And if it becomes necessary, we are prepared to meet force with force.'

The envoy looked understandably downcast. 'Is that your last word?'

'Not quite.' She smiled maliciously. 'You may like to remember that – whatever customs prevail in the army – it's usual elsewhere for a gentleman to remove his hat when addressing a lady. And now, goodbye.' Upon which note, she sank slowly down beside the signor.

He had stopped laughing but the signs of it were still in his eyes. For a moment Kate surveyed him in silence; and then she said severely, 'It's not funny. That's Cyrus Winter out there . . . the one Celia wouldn't marry and I wouldn't go to bed with. The very last man we want in the house and the one least likely just to go away. In fact, all he needs for the perfect day is to discover that you're here too.'

'I know.' He gave his rare, devastating smile. 'So we'd better have a damned good try at keeping him out, hadn't we? What words of wisdom did Eden leave you with?'

'He said they'd probably just use a cannon to blow out the gates – and that our best course would be to use our saker to stop them planting it. The only trouble with *that* is that we've only got about a dozen balls and no one with enough experience to get the range right without wasting most of them.'

Luciano considered the matter. Then, 'Mathematics,' he remarked cheerfully, 'are my forte. I'll see what I can do. But is this all the help we've got? Where's that long-faced tutor of yours?'

'In the house,' said Kate. 'He'd only get in the way. But there's Adam ready to fire the saker and his brother Jack down there in the yard. Felicity should be here soon and, though she can't shoot, she can load. As for Goodwife Flossing and the maids, their job is to fetch and carry for the rest of us . . . and Mother and Jacob are at that window with muskets, ready to join in if needs be. Ah . . . and here comes Selim.'

'Amateurs' day with a vengeance, then.' He eyed her thoughtfully. 'One more question. Are you willing to open fire before they do?'

She grimaced. 'I'd rather not – but we'll have to.'

'Good. Then let's get to work.' He stood up and looked out across the wall. 'They're still awaiting orders, but that can't last long so we'd better make the most of it. If you keep them under observation, I'll go and see what I can learn about artillery.' He turned. 'Felicity's on her way. And Celia.'

'Damn!' said Kate irritably. 'The only thing I ask Nathan to do and he can't even manage *that*!' And, since the very last thing she wanted was to allow Celia up on the wall, she stamped down the stairs to meet her. Then, having sent Felicity to watch the enemy, she said bluntly, 'You'd have done better to stay inside, Celia. This is only going to distress you.'

'As if you cared for that! You just want to stop me finding out what's happening – but I've a right to know!'

Kate sighed. 'All right. I've just refused to surrender the house to a troop of Royalist Horse. Happy now?'

'*Happy?*' The sapphire eyes widened incredulously. 'You must be out of your mind! I know you always *said* you wouldn't let anyone in without a fight – but I never thought you'd be stupid enough to actually do it.'

'Well, now you do. So if that's all—'

'No, it isn't!' snapped Celia. 'For God's sake – have one of the men open the gates before it's too late. Don't you realise that we could all be killed?'

'That's extremely unlikely.' Kate could feel her patience beginning to run out. 'I'm not letting them in, Celia – so you might as well go back in the house.'

'Oh no – you're not going to brand *me* a rebel! If you won't open the gates, I'll do it myself! Francis could be out there – or my father—'

'Or Cyrus Winter,' said Kate, with sudden deadly savagery. 'Oh yes – I'm quite serious. And if you go one step nearer to the gates than you are now, I'll have you forcibly removed and locked in the linen-closet. In fact, if you don't get out of my way, I'm tempted to do it anyway.'

'Kate?' Felicity's voice drifted anxiously down. 'I think they're going to move their gun.'

'Tell the signor.' Kate continued to fix Celia with an implacable gaze. 'Well? Will you go on your own or do you want an escort?'

For a moment Celia stood her ground, shaking with outrage. Then, 'Damn you!' she said furiously. 'I'll never forgive you for this – *never*!' And, spinning violently on her heel, swept back inside the house.

After that, everything happened very quickly. Having already drawn certain conclusions of his own about the probable course of events, Luciano had lined up the saker accordingly and, when Kate reached his side, he therefore said calmly, 'Just there, I think – that patch of slightly higher ground some yards to their left. Are you sure you want to go through with this?'

She stared at the slow-match in Adam Woodley's fingers and swallowed hard. 'Now?'

'If you'd prefer not to start by killing somebody – yes. We've a chance of ruining the ground and making them think again. Well?'

Her eyes rose to meet his and, for the first time, he saw that she was only too aware of the enormity of it all. Then she said tonelessly, 'All right. Do it.'

His expression did not vary by so much as a hair's breadth and, if he hesitated, it was only for a split-second. 'Stand back, then,' he said curtly. 'Mr Woodley?'

Adam nodded and, without troubling to hide his satisfaction, applied match to powder.

The time Eden had spent renovating the saker had not been wasted. It fired faultlessly and, half-deafened, Kate watched the ball explode the earth a mere eight feet or so in front of the point Luciano had indicated . . . while startled and choking but otherwise unhurt, the Cavaliers hurled themselves aside.

'A bit short,' remarked the signor critically, 'but not bad. I think we'll give them time to wonder what we're doing and then try again. Who knows? If we can hold them off till dark, they may give up and go home.'

Thus began the pattern of the next two hours. Every time the would-be besiegers tried to plant their cannon, Thorne Ash answered with a shot that caused confusion but little actual hurt. It began to seem like a harmless but surprisingly successful game and Kate's spirits lifted accordingly until, during a brief lull, Luciano said dampeningly, 'Don't get too optimistic. The only reason this is working is that they're about as experienced as we are. And quite soon they're going to chance relying on the fact that we're obviously not trying to kill them – at which point we'll be forced to stop playing and do some damage.' He paused and looked up at the sky. 'It can't be much after three, which gives them a good couple of hours of daylight yet. And we've only got five cannon-balls left.'

'Call it four.' Kate pushed back her hair with one powder-blackened hand and left a smear across her brow. 'They're trying again.'

'Damn! Adam?'

'Ready,' said Mr Woodley. And nonchalantly performed his function.

But this time the accustomed roar was followed by a sharp, ominous, cracking sound and Adam leapt back clutching one hand to his chest and swearing.

'What happened?' Kate was at his side in an instant. 'Adam – stop jumping about and show me your hand.' Then, as he did so and she saw the shard of metal embedded in his palm, 'Oh God. How on earth . . .? No. It doesn't matter. Just go into the house and let Mother see to you. Felicity – make sure he gets there, will you?'

Rather pale herself, Felicity merely nodded and helped Mr Woodley down the stairs to the courtyard. Kate turned back to find Luciano and Selim on their knees grimly inspecting a great crack in the barrel of the saker.

'Now we *are* in trouble,' said Luciano, looking up. 'I personally think it may be time to make sure we've got a white flag. But I'm open to suggestions.'

'We still have the muskets and pistols.'

'Which are no use at this distance. Next?' And then, when she said nothing, he rose to face her. 'They're going to plant that gun, Kate. We can't stop them. And then they're going to blow a hole through your gates. Again, we can't stop them. So it's only a matter of time before they get in – and the longer we hold out, the more excuse they have for pillaging the house and being generally unpleasant.'

'I know.' Depression was filling every vein but she refused to let it show. 'I know. But they don't know our saker has split and you said yourself that they aren't very experienced.'

'True. But barring divine intervention, I don't see how they can fail.' He held her gaze in silence for a moment. Then, sighing, 'All right. It goes against my better judgement, but we'll give it another half-hour or so and see what happens. Or *I* will. *You* will go into the house. It's not safe up here any more. And since there's nothing to do but watch, the fewer people there are out here, the better. Selim and I can manage. Now go.'

Kate stood her ground. 'I agree with everything you've said,' she replied amicably. 'But you've overlooked just one small thing. I live here and I'm the one who won't give up. So I've no intention of hiding meekly inside while you do the dirty work. Sorry.'

Luciano stared back at her, pure exasperation in every line of his face. 'You,' he announced bitingly, 'are a bloody liability.'

'No I'm not. I'm the one with the white flag,' she grinned, hitching up her skirt to reveal an inch or two of petticoat. 'You see? No detail too small, no sacrifice too great. So you could be glad of me yet.'

'I doubt it. I feel more inclined to wring your neck.'

She tutted reprovingly. 'You can't do that. Father wouldn't like it. And—'

'*Efendim!*' shouted Selim urgently. 'Get down!'

Luciano did not waste time seeing the cause of Selim's alarm for himself. He simply grabbed hold of Kate and, in the same movement, threw them both to the ground. Seconds later there was a roar, a massive vibrating thud, and fragments of earth and stone were dropping on them like rain.

Kate lay mouse-still and looked into the black eyes only inches from her own. Then, before she could open her mouth, the Italian said dryly, 'Don't. This is not a good moment for saying something clever.'

'I know. I was only going to save you the trouble of saying that you told me so,' she replied somewhat breathlessly. 'How close was that?'

He got up and looked. 'Close enough. Slightly short and a few feet off course – but nothing that can't be mended. *Stay where you are!*' And dropped down beside her again as the second shot arrived.

This time the vibration was greater and splinters of

masonry joined the falling earth. Luciano swore under his breath and sat up.

'That's it,' he said. 'Enough is enough. Are you going to give me a petticoat or do I have to take it?'

'You wouldn't,' said Kate, struggling to her feet. And then, recognising the look in his eyes, 'All right – all right! But at least have the decency to turn away while I untie it.'

'Hell's teeth!' he breathed. 'If you want to save the gates, there's no time for niceties.' And, pushing her skirt out of the way, he grasped her petticoats in both hands and gave a sharp jerk.

There was a tearing sound as the tapes gave way and Kate had to hold on to the wall in order to keep her balance. Then, as eight ells of cambric slithered to her feet, she stepped out of them, saying furiously, 'Now look what you've done! Surely one would have been enough?'

But the Italian wasn't listening. He gathered up the whole bundle, gave it a brief shake and then stood up to wave it over the wall. One by one, three of the garments fluttered down to lie on the ground outside. A ragged cheer arose from the ranks of the besiegers.

Luciano looked from the petticoat in his hand, to the ones on the ground, to Kate. 'My God. How many of the things were you wearing? Not that it matters. They seem to have had the desired effect.'

'I daresay. Cyrus Winter is probably laughing his boots off,' snapped Kate, snatching what was left of her under-wear from his hand. 'Well? What are you waiting for? You might as well go and let them in.'

'In a minute.' His attention was still fixed on something outside. 'Somebody's got visitors.'

Kate looked – and promptly forgot all about her ruined petticoats. Three horsemen were riding very fast up the lane towards the Cavaliers.

'Reinforcements?' she murmured. 'How very odd.'

It became progressively stranger. The newcomers rode straight into the middle of Captain Winter's little force and, without troubling to dismount, promptly embarked on something that looked suspiciously like an argument. Then, after a good deal of arm-waving and pointing, the impossible happened.

'I don't believe it,' said Kate weakly. 'They're going.'

'So they are.' Luciano watched their erstwhile attackers mounting their horses and hauling their cannon sulkily back to the lane. 'I wonder why? Ah. It looks as though we're about to find out, doesn't it? Do we shower them in rose-petals and kiss their feet – or will a simple thank-you be sufficient?'

Kate was still staring at the approaching riders. 'Please yourself,' she said in hollow accents. 'It's Kit.'

Very, very slowly, he turned to face her. 'Dear me,' he said blandly. '*What* an interesting day we're having.'

Horribly aware that time was running out, she met his eyes and took a deep breath. Then she said rapidly, 'Look. Don't start pretending to believe what I said the other night about my betrothal because it won't work. We both know you're not that credulous. I'll admit that it was fairly stupid – just as you, if you've a grain of honesty, will admit that you asked for it. But none of that constitutes a good excuse for . . . for making mischief.'

'Doesn't it?' He smiled disquietingly. 'I should think that would depend on your point of view. Are you still determined to marry him?'

'That's none of your business.'

'Not true. You made it my business when you named me as your motive.'

'But you know perfectly well I didn't mean it!'

'No. In fact, I don't – although I'll agree it's possible.' His eyes mocked her. 'But even *that* has its suspicious side.'

Kate felt herself go pink and was damningly aware that she was doing more harm than good. She said crossly, 'Oh – it's a waste of time talking to you. Believe whatever you like. I'm going to let Kit in.' And, snatching up her now overlong skirts in both hands, she stamped away down the stairs to the gate.

Luciano watched her go. Hands, face and gown were all liberally smeared with dirt, her hair was escaping in all directions like a nest of vipers . . . and the once buoyant skirts trailed forlornly along the ground behind her. Mr Clifford, he told himself carelessly, was in for a surprise. It would be interesting to see how he took it; or then again, perhaps it wouldn't.

'Hell,' he said rather desperately to the empty air, 'and damnation.' And then, catching Selim's eye resting curiously upon him, 'Come on. After all the trouble we've been to, it would be a shame to miss the grand finale. And then, God willing, we can get back to the straightforward business of chasing perjurers.'

For a whole battery of reasons, Kit had no difficulty at all in taking Kate's appearance in his stride. His two companions, on the other hand, had no such defences. Lieutenant Verney greeted the vision with flying brows and a grin; Lieutenant Harry Clifford looked first horrified and then frankly confused. But Kit, with Kate's hands in his and his eyes on hers, was aware of neither of them. He merely said, 'Kate, my dear . . . Are you all right?'

'Perfectly.' A faint frown marked her brows. 'I don't understand what you're doing here. Or how – and why – you were able to send Cyrus Winter away.'

'It wasn't very difficult. He arrived too late to fight at Edgehill and must have decided to blood his fellows this way . . . or perhaps he wanted to make an impression, I don't know. But he was acting without orders – and that's something Prince Rupert won't tolerate. He's said over and over again that officers rushing off on their own initiative only leads to disorder. So when Harry got wind of what Winter was doing, all I had to do was to get His Highness's authority to stop it. Simple. And as good a way as any for you to meet my twin.'

Kate smiled somewhat absently into blue-grey eyes that were so like Kit's and yet so unlike. 'It certainly is – and we're all in your debt. As you no doubt saw, we were just on the point of surrendering.'

'And very charmingly too.' Lieutenant Verney stepped

forward with a mischievous smile and held out her maltreated petticoats. 'Yours, I think.'

Long past being embarrassed, Kate accepted them with complete composure and a simple, 'Thank you', before forcing herself into a greater degree of attention. 'But haven't we met before?'

'We have indeed – and I'm honoured that you remember it,' he began cheerfully. And then stopped, apparently transfixed by something beyond her shoulder.

Kate turned. Dorothy and the girls were crossing the yard towards them; all, that was, except for Celia, who had stopped dead as if she too had walked into a wall.

The pieces fell into place. Kate's gaze swivelled back to the lieutenant and she said expressionlessly, 'Of course. Sir Hugo Verney. I remember you very well indeed – as, I'm sure, does my sister-in-law.' She paused; and then, with a bright smile, 'Dear me. I wonder how many *more* surprises today has in store for us?'

Once the inevitable greetings and introductions were out of the way, Dorothy ushered them all inside to partake of honey-cakes and wine and Kate, uncomfortably aware of Luciano del Santi's sardonic eye, took herself off to wash and change. It wasn't, she told herself irritably, that she much cared how she looked, but she didn't particularly want to watch Celia and Hugo Verney alternately meeting and avoiding each other's eyes; and her chances of saying the things she wanted to say to Kit looked fairly remote if Luciano was going to dog her every step. And then, of course, she needed time to let her nerves settle after the maelstrom produced by those last minutes up on the gatehouse.

Downstairs in the parlour, Hugo finally managed to sit beside Celia. He had been prepared for the sight of her but not what it did to him and he was still in shock. He tried to hide it, however, and said merely, 'It's a great pleasure to see you again, Celia – and looking, if I may say so, more beautiful than ever. Eden is a fortunate fellow.'

348

'Eden,' said Celia bitterly, 'is fighting for the Parliament.'

Faintly taken aback, Hugo looked around them to see who else was listening.

'You needn't worry.' Celia's smile was brittle. 'They all know how I feel – and couldn't care less. But let's not talk of that. Tell me . . . how is your wife?'

'To the best of my knowledge, very well.' A knife was twisting in his chest. It was bad enough that *he* still cared; but if it should turn out that she, too . . . or no. Best not to think of that. He said quietly, 'If you don't agree with the politics of this house, living here must be very hard for you. I'm sorry.'

'Yes. You should be.' For the first time, the blue eyes looked full into his. 'Why did you come? *Why?* It's the very worst thing you could have done.' And, rising, she walked quickly away to the window.

He was still staring at her unyielding back when Kate came in. And, because his mind was in turmoil, he was the only one not to be struck by the transformation she had wrought. But Harry broke off his earnest conversation with Gianetta in order to stare, Luciano del Santi conducted a leisurely head-to-toe appraisal, and Kit surged to his feet, saying blithely, 'If that's the silk we chose at the Exchange, it suits you even better than I'd expected. And how quick you've been! I was afraid I'd have to leave again without seeing you. We have to be back by six – or at least, *I* do. That's the trouble with being a glorified errand-boy. Your time's rarely your own.'

'Then we shouldn't waste it.' Standing demurely in her jade silk and resolutely ignoring the signor, Kate directed a bland look at her mother. 'Will you excuse us for a few minutes? I've a letter to give Kit for Venetia – and several messages I want to add to it.'

'Of course.' Dorothy recognised the look but not what lay behind it. 'Why not take Kit to the book-room? I believe Flossie had the fire lit.'

'Thank you,' said Kate. 'I will.' And, without more ado, led her betrothed unceremoniously away.

As soon as they were alone, Kit slid an arm about her

waist and said conspiratorially, 'This is a privilege I'd not dared hope for. Have you really a letter for Venetia?'

'Yes. But that's not what I want to talk to you about.'

'Better and better.'

'On the contrary.' Kate eluded his arm to close the book-room door behind them and then faced him grimly. 'It's damnable.'

Quite slowly, the pleasure in his face turned to wariness. He said, 'Something is wrong. What?'

She drew a long breath and gripped her hands together. 'I don't want to hurt you, but it's become increasingly plain to me that the situation between us can't go on. And to put it bluntly, I'd like you to release me from my promise.'

During the long silence that followed, her words hung unpleasantly on the air. Then he said abruptly, 'Has someone been brow-beating you?'

'No – of course not! Though it *is* true that neither of my parents is particularly happy for me to remain neither formally contracted nor free. But—'

'I don't blame them. But that's easily mended, isn't it?' His smile was tense. 'I'll have my father contact yours and we can be contracted before Christmas.'

'No,' said Kate, annoyed with herself for stepping so neatly into a pit of her own making. 'Kit, no. With things as they are, it would be a mistake.'

'Ah.' He rested his hands on the back of a chair and looked down at them thoughtfully. 'The war.'

'Well, of course the war! We can't ignore it, can we? And I, for one, can see all too clearly what it's doing to Celia and Eden to want to put you and me in the same position. Oh, I know it's Celia's nature to be discontented – but since she found herself trapped on what she plainly considers to be the wrong side, she's been a hundred times worse. And it's tearing Eden in two. Do *you* want that?'

'It wouldn't *be* like that for us.'

'How do you know?' She paused to collect her thoughts, still determined to try and accomplish this without having to hurt him any more than necessary. 'I won't marry you while the war places us on opposite sides, Kit, and that is quite final. Neither do I see any point in continuing as we are. So I'll ask you again: will you release me from my promise?'

'I don't seem to have much choice, do I?' Sighing, he let his hands fall to his sides and looked bleakly across at her. 'What you're really saying is that you don't love me enough to take the risk . . . and I suppose that, deep down, I've always known it. I, on the other hand, have no such qualms, so you'll have to forgive me if I can't quite give up. I love you, Kate. Therefore, although I'll do what you want now, I'll be back when the war's over to ask you again. You have my word on it.'

It was the very last thing she wanted but, because her throat already ached for him, she could not say so. And then, as she sought for some gentle way round it, the door swung open.

For an instant, a gust of pure temper took Kate's breath away and, when it came back, her first impulse was to scream with vexation.

'God in heaven!' she snapped. 'Don't you ever knock?'

'I beg your pardon.' Luciano's tone was smooth as butter and there was nothing to indicate that he was drawing certain shrewd conclusions from the look on her face and Kit's. 'In fact I'd forgotten that you were here and only came to collect a book your father was kind enough to say I might borrow.'

'You're leaving?' asked Kate, sharply. And then, to cover herself, 'What book?'

'Machiavelli's *Prince*. Richard tells me it's recently been translated and I've yet to read it in English.'

It sounded reasonable enough. Kate didn't believe a word of it. Before she could say so, however, Kit said quietly, 'I, too, should be leaving. So while you find the signor his book, I'll just go and see if Harry and Hugo are ready. Excuse me.'

Kate watched him walk across the hall towards the parlour and then looked back at Luciano. She said flatly, 'Someone will murder you one day.'

'Very probably.' He began scanning the book-shelves.

'But I don't somehow think it will be you.'

'If you're going to start all that again, it almost certainly *will* be me!' She stormed over to the window-seat and snatched up a leather-bound volume. 'Is this what you're looking for?'

'Yes – and no.' He took it from her and placed it on the desk. Then, closing in to lay his hands on either side of her face, 'Is this what *you're* looking for?'

Paralysed by shock, Kate stared unwinkingly back at him. And when no more clues appeared to be forthcoming, she said unevenly, 'What are you doing?'

He said nothing, but his smile melted her bones and his eyes suspended her in liquid darkness. Entirely without haste, one hand moved down over shoulder and arm to her waist and drew her even closer, while the fingertips of the other explored her cheek and jaw with tantalising lightness. She knew she ought to move or say something to break the spell. Instead she let the unfamiliar tide continue to flow tingling along her veins and ceased caring what motive – if any – possessed him. All that mattered was the warmth of his body against hers and her own growing need to hold him.

Yielding to it, she slid her arms up around his neck and buried her fingers in the long, crisply curling hair. He smiled again and, as if it was the signal he had been waiting for, finally bent his head to hers.

Slowly, willingly, Kate's mouth parted under his, and the world promptly exploded, taking her with it. The floor dissolved beneath her feet, fire licked her skin, and suddenly she was drowning in fathom upon fathom of unimaginable sweetness. All the sensible denials and sterling resolves of the last two years fell away in as many seconds, leaving only one shining truth behind. She loved him.

The kiss stretched out into infinity . . . and ended too soon. Then, still holding her close, Luciano looked first into the dilated green eyes before turning, almost reluctantly, towards the doorway; and, presently, feeling his unnatural stillness, Kate stirred herself sufficiently to follow his gaze.

Kit Clifford stood there, his face white with shock. Luciano's hands fell from Kate and he took a small step away from her . . . while heavy, airless and unpleasant, the seconds ticked by in silence. Then finally, in a tone of splintering glass, Kit spoke.

'I see now why you were so anxious to be free, Kate. It's a pity you couldn't bring yourself to tell me . . . but, in the circumstances, I suppose I shouldn't find it all that surprising.' And with one last, bitter glance, he was gone.

The silence lingered. Kate discovered that she was shivering. Or shaking. She wasn't sure which. She looked at Luciano. He too looked a trifle pale but otherwise quite composed; more than that . . . he looked satisfied. *Satisfied?* Her eyes widened in sudden, soul-searing suspicion.

'Sorry, Kate.' He smiled crookedly and permitted himself a slight shrug. 'Dirty tactics – but effective. And someone had to do it.'

Six

Although it was completely uneventful, the ride from
Thorne Ash to Oxford was far from pleasant, and when
Selim's third attempt at conversation brought forth a third
sarcastic response, he relapsed very sensibly into silence.
The *amir* was clearly ripe for the vengeance that lay ahead
... which, although it was entirely proper, probably meant
that he was best left alone.

So Luciano rode on with a face like thunder for the simple
reason that he was utterly and mind-blowingly furious
with himself. He had walked in on Kate and Christopher
Clifford for the sake of Richard – to whom he already
owed so much and who, outside Giacomo and Selim, was
the only friend he'd ever had – and because Kate's catastrophic revelation made it impossible to do anything else.
So far, so good. But he wished to God he could change
the means he had used thereafter; for with the consequences of them clamouring in his head, he could see now
how monumentally stupid he had been.

They passed the night at Deddington. Luciano sent
Selim away and shut himself in his room with a bottle of
brandy which, in the end, he did not touch because becoming drink-sodden twice in one week suddenly looked like
a habit. So instead he sat and stared moodily into the fire
and contemplated the results of his idiocy.

He had kissed Kate because it was the quickest and surest
way to put an end to what she appeared unable to end
herself. And it had worked. But what he hadn't bargained
for was the burden of unwanted knowledge it brought
with it about the precise nature of Kate's feelings for him.

354

It had been one thing to guess at some transient infatuation which, if it did not wither of its own accord, could gradually be eroded by the occasional blighting taunt; it was quite another to know, beyond all doubt, that she loved him: for, if the first was unacceptable, the second was nothing short of disaster. But so it was. Her response to his mouth had not been that of a child but that of a woman with the moon in her hands. And he had brought them both face to face with a truth that would have been better left hidden. He wasn't sure how to handle it, any more than he seemed able to forget the look in Kate's eyes when she'd realised what he had done.

Well, he'd acted without due consideration and was being made to pay for it, in more ways than one. He would have to live with the responsibility for Kate's hurt, stay away from Thorne Ash and be prepared for Richard to knock his teeth down his throat. It shouldn't be too difficult: he was used to isolation and had managed well enough without the Maxwells before. So why, beneath the core of anger, was he conscious only of emptiness and a terrible feeling of loss?

He became aware that his hand was reaching out for the bottle. 'Oh Christ!' he said raggedly. 'Not that way. I might as well cut my throat.' And, without thought, hurled it violently against the wall.

It didn't, unfortunately, help very much.

The following morning found him grimly composed but still disinclined to talk and, having seen the mess made by the brandy bottle, Selim recognised the wisdom of keeping his own mouth very firmly shut. Their journey was therefore completed more or less in silence and the Turk was heartily glad when it was over.

Having been in the parliamentary hands of Lord Saye and Sele until just before Edgehill, Oxford was understandably nervous and had taken to keeping its gates closed twenty-four hours a day. Luciano unlocked his tongue long enough to get them inside and then led the way uncommunicatively to the Mitre Inn where he engaged two rooms and ordered food before leaving Selim to his own devices again. Having glimpsed a particularly trim serving-maid, Selim accepted this philosophically and hoped that the morrow would bring forth improvement.

It did – but not much. He was summoned to his master's quarters at a little after eight and subjected to a barrage of crisp orders, the point of which largely escaped him.

'You will begin,' said Luciano, 'by uncovering the where-abouts of Thomas Ferrars. His wife referred to the New College district so it shouldn't be too difficult. And then the real work starts.'

'*Efendim?*' A hopeful gleam lit Selim's eye and he fingered his knife.

'No – not that. I want to know everything about them; their friends, their habits, their comings and goings. I want to know which shops they use – where they buy literally everything from candles to capons. Again – given your way with maidservants – it shouldn't be a problem. Well?'

'It is as you wish,' said Selim weakly. 'But why? Why cannot we just find him and visit him as before?'

'Because you can't play the same game twice and expect it to succeed,' came the cold reply. 'Also, this time I don't intend to take any chances. *This* time I want friend Ferrars in the palm of my hand. So if you've no further questions, perhaps we could get on? Surprising as it may seem, you're not the only one with work to do.'

Luciano began by paying a series of apparently idle calls on various town goldsmiths, during which he learned that, while the universities wholeheartedly supported the King, the town did not, and was enthusiastic only about staying out of the quarrel. True, chains and posts had been hurriedly erected in the last few weeks, but against whom seemed open to debate. And though the students had 'galled their hands with mattocks and shovels' digging defences on the north side, everyone else had remained perfectly philo-sophical when Lord Saye immediately destroyed them again. It lent a new dimension to the old town-and-gown feud and was not helped by uncertainty over the late battle. Since Lord Essex had left the London road clear by moving towards Warwick, it seemed likely that His Majesty had indeed won; but rumour had it that, in Westminster, bells and bonfires had been celebrating a victory for the Parliament. So, all in all, no one really knew what to believe.

The goldsmiths also waxed loud and long in their complaint about the arrival in Oxford of some of the most powerful Lombard usurers from the capital. Luciano sympathised and collected names and locations; then, well satisfied, he set off on a tour of his compatriots' establishments.

Since, apart from occasional Guild meetings at the Goldsmiths' Hall, he had generally had very little to do with them, he was not exactly welcomed with open arms; but respect for his skill with the gold meant that nobody actually turned him away and, when he was able to allay certain very natural fears, he was even offered wine.

The fourth glass was taken with Giuseppe Morello, an elegant grey-haired gentleman of roughly his uncle's age who appeared almost pleased to see him. Luciano kept his surprise to himself, asked no questions and answered those put to him with polite suavity. Yes, he was but lately arrived in Oxford; no, he did not intend to remove his sign from Cheapside; and yes, he was pursuing a matter of business which – though really quite insignificant in itself – demanded his personal attention.

Signor Morello relaxed still further and broached his second glass. 'I wonder,' he said tentatively, 'if you might feel inclined, then, to do me a small favour?'

Luciano professed himself happy to serve the signor in any way that lay in his power and inquired the nature of the favour.

'It is this. I have been approached to assist in the setting up of the King's own coinage here in Oxford. It is hoped that the Master of the Mint will succeed in leaving London with the authentic dies – but if he doesn't, new ones will have to be made.'

'And that, no doubt, is where you come in?'

'It is where I have been asked to come in,' replied the signor wryly. 'Unfortunately, I have lost my best apprentice and my own hands and eyes are not what they were. As for the others I might ask, they are mostly intent on staying neutral.'

'Unlike yourself, it seems.' Luciano's gaze remained fixed on the ruby brightness in his glass.

'What can one do? It is a matter of self-preservation. We are foreigners and Catholics – and if this Parliament has its way, we will all be ruined and cast out. Our only chance lies with the King . . . so it seems common sense to help him.' He hesitated and then added delicately, 'It was my impression that you had long held this view yourself?'

'Meaning that I'm known to have thrown good money after bad into the quicksands of Whitehall?' The hard mouth curled astringently. 'But I didn't do that for love, you know – and would sooner not go on doing it. However, I suppose that I, too, would prefer the throne to be occupied by King Charles rather than King Pym . . . so I'll do what I can to aid you.'

'You will?' The older man beamed. 'That is uncommonly good of you! And if there is anything I may offer you in return, I hope you won't hesitate to mention it.'

'Recompense? Perish the thought.' Still twirling the stem of his glass between long, slender fingers, Luciano looked blandly into the other man's face. 'On the other hand – now that you mention it – there *is* a small matter that you might perhaps be able to help me with.'

'Of course!' Signor Morello reached out and refilled both of their glasses. 'And this is?'

'A simple business transaction. There is a gentleman currently residing in Oxford who I have reason to believe is indebted to one or other of our colleagues. I would find it useful to acquire any bond he may have incurred . . . and even more useful to do so without becoming prominent in the affair.' He paused. 'It is a question of honour, you understand.'

'Perfectly,' nodded the signor; and thought, *Caught some fellow trifling with his sister and plans to teach him a lesson, no doubt. Good luck to him.* Then, aloud, 'You may rely on my absolute discretion. But I will need the gentleman's name.'

'By all means.' Eyes and voice were smooth as silk. 'His name is Thomas Ferrars.'

Selim eventually ran the Ferrars' household to earth in Holywell Street and then set about the not entirely unrewarding task of ingratiating himself with Bess, the maidservant. This was the easy part. More difficult was the process of getting the information he wanted without arousing the girl's suspicions; but by the time he'd given her a spangled scarf, a silver posy-ring and a vial of ambergris, his path became much smoother; and after he'd seduced her by the riverside his problems were non-existent.

The town, meanwhile, was thrown into chaos when the King arrived with both nephews and his army. The university professed itself 'gilded by the beams' of His Majesty's royal presence; but the town fretted over the alarming profusion of buff-coats and the artillery compound in Magdalen Grove. Luciano stayed quietly out of sight and wondered if the talk of Banbury Castle having surrendered to the King almost without a shot was any more accurate than the much-vaunted Royalist victory at Edgehill. And then, as quickly as they had come, they were gone again in the direction of Reading and – presumably – London. The town heaved a sigh of relief; the university applauded His Majesty's decision to make Oxford his headquarters; and Luciano bought Thomas Ferrars' bond from Signor Morello for the sum of two thousand seven hundred and twenty pounds.

Well-satisfied with his progress, he allowed the first days of November to slip by while he waited for Selim to complete his mission and spent his own time working on the currency dies with Giuseppe Morello. Since misuse of these could leave him open to the capital charge of counterfeiting, he had no intention of quitting Oxford without first seeing them bestowed in the correct quarter; and in the meantime a sudden influx of news provided daily stimulation.

The Earl of Essex, for example, had reputedly arrived

in London to a victor's welcome and a five-thousand-pound incentive at around the same time the King was receiving commissioners from the Parliament for the purpose of discussing peace. But if the latter was true, it did not appear to have done much good – for the next thing Oxford heard was news of twin skirmishes at Brentford and Turnham Green which effectively prevented His Majesty from entering his capital. The result of this was that the House of Commons became less eager for a Peace Treaty which Luciano seriously doubted they had ever really wanted in the first place, and the King fell back to Reading where the heir to the throne contracted measles.

By the latter half of the month, Selim was able to furnish his master with a remarkably extensive list of shop-keepers patronised by Thomas and Alice Ferrars. Luciano examined it at length and then, looking up at his henchman, said expressionlessly, 'You've done well. I think we are in a position to begin at last.'

Selim evinced signs of cautious pleasure. '*Now* you will seek the man out, *efendim*?'

'No. I shall cause *him* to seek me.' He smiled slowly. 'So much more poetic, don't you think? Or no. You would probably prefer me simply to bob him on the noll and have done with it. But cheer up. The end will be worth the means, I assure you. And, in the meanwhile, you may take a holiday.'

While Charles Stuart was swallowing his disappointment over his uncle of Denmark's reluctance to help him, and simultaneously rejecting the Parliament's suggestion that he should return to Westminster and abandon his supporters to parliamentary justice, signs of incipient crisis became evident in Holywell Street. And by the time the King had returned to make Christ Church both his own residence and the centre of his Court, the first fissures had already appeared in Alice Ferrars' perennially uncertain temper.

Her husband wilted, as always, under her tongue, and vowed to put matters right. He only wished he knew how he was going to do it. The trouble was that money slipped through Alice's fingers like water and always had. From the moment he'd first fallen victim to that cool, blonde beauty, he'd never been out of debt; and just now – in addition to the increasing number of tradesmen that were suddenly and inexplicably demanding settlement in full before supplying further goods – he owed seven thousand to a Jew in Worcester and another two to the Lombard, Bernardo Ricci. It was enough to make a braver man blow his brains out. But Thomas lacked that kind of resolution and was, in any case, less distraught about the size of his debts than about his inability to provide Alice with all the luxuries she demanded. For this was his life-long, driving compulsion: a deep-rooted fixation that, whatever she wanted, he had somehow to find a means of producing. It would be his undoing one day; he knew that. But still he could not help himself, and at least it lured Alice to be kind.

Unfortunately, however – unless he could sweet-talk the vintner, the silk-merchant and the fish-seller (to name but three) – the kindness was destined to disappear for good. And if *that* happened, Thomas knew that he might just as well put a pistol to his head.

He visited all the tradesmen in turn; threatening, cajoling and finally pleading – but all to no avail. And then, in desperation, he sought out Bernardo Ricci and attempted to extend his bond by an extra thousand.

Signor Ricci listened courteously and with attention. Then, without knowing it, he delivered what to Mr Ferrars felt like a death knell.

'But, my dear sir,' he said gently, 'I no longer hold your bond. Surely you knew? It was purchased from me some weeks ago by one Giuseppe Morello. And I have to say that – from what you describe of your affairs – it seems I was wise to sell.' He smiled a little. From the look on Ferrars' face, it appeared that Giuseppe might catch cold over this one – and he, Bernardo, was not averse to letting him. A quiet word in the other usurers' ears, he reflected, might be no bad thing. The smile grew and he said, 'I sympathise, Mr Ferrars. I do indeed. But the only advice I can give is to suggest that you place your difficulties before Signor Morello. You will find his house opposite the Corn Exchange. And now I'm afraid I must bid you good-day.'

Afflicted by a palsy-like tremor, Thomas made it out into the street and turned his feet in the direction of the Corn Exchange. Buff-coats and scarlet cloaks mingled with gay, exquisitely gowned Court ladies. He pushed his way through them, conscious of nothing save the fact that – now His Majesty resided in Oxford – nothing would persuade Alice to leave it. She wanted to be part of that bright, elegant company and would have preferred it if he'd donned a buff-coat and gone to war with the rest. But he couldn't do that, not even for Alice. And therefore it behoved him to please her in other ways.

Signor Morello was not at home. Thomas left his name, returned home to a taste of his wife's temper, and went back again the next day. This time the signor received him – and within ten minutes, he wished he hadn't.

'I cannot extend your bond, Mr Ferrars, for the simple reason that it is no longer in my possession. Indeed, having purchased it on behalf of another, it was barely in my hands for a day.'

Thomas began to feel that he was in the grip of a night-mare. He said unevenly, 'So – so who owns it now?'

'I am afraid that I'm not at liberty to tell you,' came the unhelpful reply.

'But you've got to tell me! I'm desperate, can't you understand? I need money *now* – and if I don't know who holds my bond, how am I to enlarge it?'

'It doesn't look as though you can.'

'But the d-damned butcher won't supply us with meat!' cried Mr Ferrars with unwary candour. 'God rot it – I've got to do something!' And then, violently, 'Will *you* lend me money?'

'No. I won't.'

'But why *not*?'

'Because, from what you say, you are not a good risk. For example – what collateral can you offer me? House? Lands?'

Mr Ferrars' gaze dropped. 'Mortgaged,' he muttered. And then, with one last flicker of hope, 'But my wife's jewels are worth a fortune.'

'Then I suggest you sell them, sir. I am not a pawnbroker. Alternatively, you might try one who is – or go to the other money-lenders in the town. Someone may be prepared to accommodate you. I, unfortunately, am not.'

'But—'

'You have my last word, Mr Ferrars, and there is nothing left to be said.' Signor Morello opened the door and bowed slightly. 'I'm sorry your visit was wasted. Good-day, sir.'

White to the lips, Thomas went. The signor shut the door gently behind him . . . and seconds later, Luciano del Santi walked in from the other room where he had been listening.

'That,' he remarked, 'was quite masterly. I'm in your debt.'

'It was nothing.' Signor Morello looked curiously at him. 'What will you do now? Call him to see you and then foreclose?'

'Eventually perhaps.' Luciano contemplated the diamond that had replaced the lost emerald on his finger and then looked up. 'But it would be a pity to end Mr Ferrars' lesson too soon. And I really don't think I can resist the temptation to let him sweat a little longer.'

He was smiling. But Signor Morello, meeting that smile, felt a chill make its way down his back.

Towards the end of the month, the Master of the Mint reached Oxford with his own original dies and a goodly part of the bullion from the Tower. He took cheerful possession of Luciano's handiwork and complimented him on its quality before destroying it; then he sought out the medallists Rawlins and Briot and got down to the serious business of making money at New Inn Hall.

His Majesty also returned to turn the town and its environs upside down with war preparations – which might have annoyed the worthy citizens a good deal more than it did but for the money they were suddenly able to make on food and clothes and beds. So few people complained about plundered cattle inhabiting the Christ Church quadrangle or New College being stuffed with explosive devices or even the incessant hammering accompanying the construction of drawbridges in the School of Rhetoric; and the Wolvercot sword factory was actually a welcome new source of employment, along with the Osney gunpowder mill. In short, the town – though chaotic – was thriving; and in no time at all this, coupled with the news that the Londoners were paying forced loans to the Parliament, had the townsfolk happily building earthworks alongside the students.

Relieved of his responsibility towards Giuseppe Morello, Luciano let another week go by before inviting Thomas Ferrars to call on him at the Mitre. Then he told Selim to keep out of sight, put on his best sable satin and sat down with his back to the light to await his guest.

The knock on his door was a little early, causing Luciano to smile. And then, for the first time, Thomas Ferrars was before him, hovering uncertainly on the threshold while he peered into the shadows. Luciano remained motionless in the great carved chair and conducted his own leisurely appraisal. Of moderate height and angular build, the fellow had slightly receding dun-coloured hair and the glassy, myopic gaze of a rabbit. His clothes were good but by no means extravagant, and he looked eviscerated with sleeplessness and worry. Not, thought Luciano, the villain of one's imagination – but appearances, as everyone knew, were often misleading.

He said dispassionately, 'You may shut the door, Mr Ferrars. I rarely bite.'

Thomas started and did as he was bidden so fast that a gust of smoke billowed from the fireplace. He coughed and took a couple of hesitant steps towards the disembodied voice in the chair. 'Mr – Mr Santi?'

'None other.' A pause; and then, 'I have no objection to you being seated.'

Mr Ferrars sank unhappily down on the only other chair, which was placed at some distance from his host and bathed in pale, merciless sunlight. Then, twisting his hat nervously between his hands, he said, 'Are you the – is it you who—'

'Holds your bond?' inquired Luciano helpfully. 'Yes. It is. You wish to discuss the matter?'

'No. I just want to increase it,' came the bald reply. 'Now.'

'I see. By how much?'

'Fif-fifteen hundred.'

'As much as that?' The bland voice was mildly astonished. 'And can you afford it?'

'Yes – yes. You needn't worry about that.'

'But I do worry, Mr Ferrars. If I didn't, I could soon find myself in a position not dissimilar to your own. But let us consider the figures.' Luciano reached out to the table at his side and picked up the topmost paper from the neat pile lying there. 'As matters stand, you owe me two thousand eight hundred and forty pounds – and—'

'But I only borrowed two thousand!' said Thomas, aghast.

'Quite. There is, however, the small matter of the interest – and, as you are doubtless aware, quarter-day is fast approaching. I'm sure you see my difficulty, Mr Ferrars. If you are in urgent need of fifteen hundred pounds now, it seems unlikely that you will be able to produce the necessary nine hundred or so in a couple of weeks' time. And if I advance the extra funds you require and the interest is not forthcoming, you will then be in my debt to the tune of almost four-and-a-half thousand.' Luciano smiled and spread his hands. 'Without some rather more . . . tangible security, I really don't think I can help you.'

There was an odd sort of buzzing in Thomas's head. He said chokingly, 'You don't understand – I've got to do something! None of the damned tradesmen will supply us with as much as a candle – and my wife . . . my wife . . .'

'Yes?'

'She's w-worn down with anxiety.'

Something about the quality of the silence told Mr Ferrars that the euphemism had failed to convince and he racked his tired brain for a way of putting it right. Then the beautiful, disturbing voice said invitingly, 'You appear to be in a great deal of trouble. Perhaps it might help if you were to tell me how it has come about?'

There was a moment's hesitation. Then, at his wits' end and past caring, Thomas told him.

Luciano listened without surprise to the catalogue of Alice Ferrars' extravagance and with faint contempt to that of her husband's foolish indulgence. And finally, when it was done, he said with apparent carelessness, 'You must love her very much. How long have you been married?'

'Since the summer of '26,' said Thomas wretchedly. 'And even then I had to—' He stopped abruptly and drew a long breath. 'None of this matters. Will you advance me some more money or not?'

'All things – however unlikely – are possible. I will consider it.'

'But—'

'I said I will consider it, Mr Ferrars – and with that you will have to be satisfied. You may call on me again . . . shall we say the day after tomorrow? And, in the meantime, I suggest you decide what collateral you can offer me and whether, should I choose to impose any other conditions, you will be prepared to meet them.'

'Will you take my wife's jewels?' he asked jerkily. Alice had so far refused to part with so much as a pin, but if he could tell her the stuff was merely being held in trust, she might . . . And if the worst came to the worst, he would have to steal them. He couldn't take much more of this.

'Perhaps.'

'Then I'll bring them.' He rose, still crumpling his hat. 'As for the rest – I'll do anything. Anything. Only you'll have to advance me some money now. I can't last two days. There's scarcely a crumb in the house.'

There was a long, poisonous silence and then Luciano tossed a small purse to him. 'Five pounds, Mr Ferrars. Tell your wife that several families could eat well for a week on that.'

The purse dropped with a clink at his feet and Thomas bent stiffly to pick it up. He'd never had much in the way of pride, but just now he felt like a whore. Worse still, he was cold with fright and wishing he need never see this man again.

He said dully, 'You don't have to humiliate me. I've no choice but to dance to your tune, have I?'

'Unless you resign yourself to a debtor's prison – no,' began Luciano pleasantly. And then stopped in response to an imperious tattoo on the door.

For a moment, he hesitated. He neither expected nor wanted visitors – and he hoped to God it wasn't Selim. Then, when the summons was repeated, he irritably bade the intruder enter.

It was, ludicrously, the last person he'd have thought of.

'Well, well,' drawled Francis Langley. 'It really *is* you. I was utterly convinced when Goring said he'd seen your servant leaving here that he must be mistaken. I even wagered a bottle of canary on it. Ah well, one mustn't repine.' He paused, as if becoming aware for the first time of a third presence. 'But I interrupt, it seems. A thousand apologies!'

'One will suffice.' The smooth tones had suddenly acquired an edge like a razor. 'But as it happens, this gentleman is just leaving.'

'Dear me! Not, I hope, on my account?'

'N-no. Not at all.' Thomas rammed the purse in his pocket and headed gratefully for the door. Then, turning, 'Till Wednesday then, Mr Santi. G-good day.' And, slithering past Francis, vanished.

For a moment, the sapphire eyes followed him thoughtfully. 'Now where have I seen him before?' mused Francis. 'And quite recently, too.'

'Does it matter?' Rising wraith-like from his chair, Luciano crossed to the hearth. 'Or do you want a list of *all* my debtors?'

'Ah – of course!' Francis closed the door and sauntered into the room. 'I saw him yesterday with Cyrus Winter – presumably on the same errand that brought him to you and, judging by the look on his face, with as little success.

What it must be to have money! You, for example, seem to fall somewhere between the Chancellor of the Exchequer and God. Does it please you, I wonder? Or would you prefer the rags of respectability?'

'Do you have a point to make?' The Renaissance face was bereft of expression. 'Or did you merely call to indulge in a little moral philosophy?'

'You don't find it amusing?' Francis dropped his hat and gloves on the dresser. 'Then I'll have to do better. Here's a riddle. Does debt lead to drink – or drink to debt? And do you care that poor Suckling lies dead in France as a result of both?'

This was news to Luciano but he said merely, 'You're saying it's my fault?'

'Isn't it?' There was a brief pause; and then, dropping the theatrical manner, Francis said, 'But that wasn't what I came to say. I want to know what the devil you mean by meddling with Kate Maxwell?'

'Ah.' Understanding dawned. 'You've been talking to Mr Clifford. How is he?'

'Distraught – but that's no concern of mine. Kit can look after himself.'

'And Kate can't?' The dark gaze was politely incredulous. 'Either you don't know her very well or, with Mr Clifford so neatly disposed of, you're hoping to step in yourself. If you still want to amuse me, you could try telling me which.'

Francis curbed a distressingly crude impulse to hit him and said contemptuously, 'I've a better idea. Why don't you try accepting that – though Richard Maxwell may be happy to associate with a gutter-bred leech – he's not so lax that he'd ever give his daughter to one. Unless, that is, the bastard had seduced her.'

Luciano's flicker of ironic amusement died still-born. In a voice that could have cut bread, he said, 'I think you have said enough, Mr Langley. More than enough, in fact. I am willing to overlook your unflattering views on myself; but if your long association with Kate doesn't thunder the impossibility of her becoming any man's light o'love, I can only suggest that you've been spending too much time with rakehells like George Goring. And now I think you had better leave.'

Francis coloured faintly but stood his ground. 'Very well. I take the point. But I've known Kate since she was six. And with Richard in London and Eden God knows where, I still feel entitled to ask why you—'

'*Christ!*' Luciano was within a hair's breadth of losing his temper. 'Isn't it obvious? I was cutting the bloody cord! But perhaps you *wanted* her put on the same knife-edge as your sister?'

'Oh.' Completely taken aback, Francis thought about it for a moment or two. 'Yes. I see what you mean.'

'Bring on the drums and cymbals.'

'A grain or two of fairness, if you please! How could I be expected to guess that? You're not exactly well known for your altruism, are you?'

'No. And, having been cast as Beelzebub, it's unfair of me to step out of character, isn't it? But if you're going back to hold Clifford's hand and bathe him in solicitous comfort, I may as well have saved myself the trouble. Well?'

'I,' remarked Francis, recovering his sangfroid, 'am discretion itself. If required, I will even swear an oath of silence . . . or, better still, drink to exquisite secrecy.' He smiled artlessly. 'Having cleared the weeds, let us discover the lily. Did I mention that I had met your sister?'

While Luciano was entertaining first his unsuspecting quarry and then Francis Langley, a party of dragoons under the twin leadership of Harry Wilmot and Lord Digby were rampaging their way through Marlborough – partly for the sake of the cloth, cheese and hard cash they brought back, but mainly for the greater glory of Wilmot and Digby. They returned, in due course, full of bravado and beer to cock a metaphoric snook at Prince Rupert, whose growing reputation and influence was already beginning to chafe them; and then, well satisfied, they rounded off the affair in style by keeping half the town awake all night with a wildly successful supper-party at the Angel.

On Wednesday morning, Luciano prepared precisely as before for what he expected to be his final meeting with Thomas Ferrars. Having equipped himself with every advantage he could think of, it did not seem that anything could go wrong this time . . . nor, with the clock ticking steadily away in Genoa, must it be allowed to do so. This time he had to get it right.

Thomas arrived, shaking, on the stroke of eleven, and sat on the same strategically placed chair he had occupied before. Then, addressing the shadowy figure of the man who was either his torturer or his life-line, he said abruptly, 'I – I've brought them. Alice's jewels.'

'Place them on the table before you. I'll look at them presently. I trust your wife saw the wisdom of surrendering them?'

'No.' Thomas tugged at his neck-cloth, recalling the horrible scene when Alice had caught him emptying her coffer and the unbelievably cruel things she had said. 'No. I don't want to talk about it.'

'Then let us get straight down to business.' Luciano surveyed his prey clinically and took his time about continuing. Then he said coolly, 'As matters stand, you are completely insolvent, Mr Ferrars. The shopkeepers of the town will supply you with no further goods until your various bills are paid – but you can't do this without increasing the already substantial amount you owe me. None of the other money-lenders will touch you with an eighteen-foot pike . . . and even wealthy friends such as Cyrus Winter are loth to help you.' He paused and then, in response to the other man's expression, said, 'How do I know? Suffice it to say that the extent of my knowledge might surprise you. However . . . to resume. You've brought me security in the form of jewellery to support both your existing bond and the additional sum you have asked for – and presently we shall see if it is equal to the task. But first we have to consider the fact that, in a little over a week, I shall require you to pay me the last quarter's interest. And we both know you're going to be unable to do it.'

Ferrars' skin felt clammy and he could see the bottom

of the pit rushing up to meet him. In a voice which seemed to come from a long way off, he said, 'You're refusing me?'

'At the moment I am merely establishing the precariousness of your position,' came the maddeningly calm reply. 'It seems to have escaped your notice that this is not simply a question of whether I will or will not help you out of your present predicament. It is whether or not I will ruin you.'

'Oh God.' Ferrars drove his face into his hands. 'Oh God. What can I do?'

'You can cast your mind back to the year of your marriage,' said Luciano with severely controlled impassivity. 'And you can tell me everything you know about the trial of Alessandro Falcieri.'

The lank brown head came up revealing a face contorted with shock. '*Wh-what?*'

'You heard me. The case of *Rex versus Falcieri*, in which you and three others gave evidence for the prosecution.' There was a long, terrible silence. 'The case in which you perjured yourself for the purpose of sending an innocent man to the gallows. I'm sure you remember it. And please don't try convincing me that you don't know what I'm talking about or that you didn't lie under oath. I've spoken to Samuel Fisher.' Luciano took a folded document from the table and held it lightly between his fingers. 'I also have the trial record.'

Ferrars seemed to shrink in his chair. He said, 'Then you know it all. Th-there's nothing I can tell you.'

'On the contrary. You can tell me how it was done . . . and why.' An undercurrent of nameless danger flowed through the beautiful voice. 'You ought to be grateful, Mr Ferrars. I am giving you the chance to unburden your soul and engage my sympathy. Or would you rather I had simply sent a hired bravo to knife you in the back one dark night? Surely not. And you must have realised that – after so long and with what I already know – nothing you can say is likely to make matters any worse for you than they are at this minute.'

Slowly, very slowly, comprehension filtered into the numb disorder of Thomas Ferrars' brain.

'You – you bought my bond because of this? And the shops . . . it was you who – who made them stop my credit. It was you. All the time, it was you . . . because of *this*!' He stopped, trying to suck some air back into his lungs. And then, with a kind of compulsive horror, '*Who are you?*'

'I think you know.' For the first time, Luciano came out of the shadows into the light and gave Ferrars time to look at him. 'I am Alessandro Falcieri's son.'

Ferrars stared at him, incapable of speech, movement, or even coherent thought. He looked at the well-cut black clothes, the long, fine-boned hands and the crooked left shoulder; and then, with petrified reluctance, into the sculpted face with its hard mouth and cold, purposeful eyes. His heart gave a single, heavy thud and seemed to plummet into his stomach. He found that he was sweating.

'And now,' continued Luciano inexorably, 'we will proceed. You robbed me of my father, my home, my childhood – and caused the death of my mother. And I have brought you to this point so that you may attempt to justify yourself. What, for example, did Alessandro Falcieri do that made you hate him so much?'

'N-nothing.' The word arrived on a choking gasp. 'I never hated him. It . . . it wasn't like that.'

'No? Then how *was* it?'

'It wasn't my idea – you've got to believe that! I was in d-debt to your father and I couldn't pay because I'd have lost Alice even before the b-betrothal contracts were signed. But I never meant to harm anybody! I – I just did as I was told.'

'By whom?'

Ferrars' eyes slid away and his knuckles glowed white on the arms of his chair. 'Giles Langley.'

Luciano took his time about replying. Then, silkily, 'How very convenient. He's dead.'

'I can't help that. He'd lost a fortune on the Cadiz expedition and if Falcieri had foreclosed on him, he'd have found himself in Newgate. So he – he – oh God. It was his idea, I tell you!'

There was another eviscerating silence.

'Mr Ferrars . . . I don't believe you. *Look at me.*' Luciano waited till he'd collected the frightened gaze and then said crisply, 'Rid yourself of the notion that there is any easy way out. There isn't. I want the truth. Now start again.'

'All right – *all right!*' His nerves at breaking point, the only thing Thomas Ferrars wanted was to be allowed to leave. 'I – I had a letter. It w-wasn't signed so it may have come from Langley or – or one of the others. Or perhaps they all had one too. I don't know. And that's the truth. I d-don't know. We never – we never spoke of it. And when it was over, we w-went our separate ways. I don't even know wh-where they are any more – and I'll swear that on anything you l-like!'

This, decided Luciano clinically, had both a certain logic and, at last, a ring of truth. He said, 'And the letter?'

'The l-letter told me what to do. I was to tell Buckingham that I'd overheard Falcieri and some others conspiring to shoot the King on his way to the coronation. I was to s-supply certain dates and places and say . . .' He stopped, the sheer hopelessness of it overcoming him. 'But you've got the record. You know what I said.'

'Yes.' Luciano turned unhurriedly to the requisite page and read aloud from it. '"I heard the accused say that a clear shot might be taken from the upper window of one of the buildings facing the Abbey and that he had found an expert marksman who was willing to undertake the commission in return for two thousand in gold."' He stopped and looked up. 'Since this conversation is supposed to have taken place with a Florentine, it's odd that it appears to have been held in English. Or perhaps you understand Italian? No? I thought not.' He threw the document back on to the table. 'And Buckingham believed this farrago?'

'Yes – no. I don't know. I don't suppose he could take the risk,' came the weary, miserable reply. 'You wouldn't . . . I don't suppose you'd remember how it was at that time. Rumours of Papist plots were everywhere and people were denouncing each other at the t-top of their voices. Catholic lords were fined and disarmed and had their houses searched. So, with conspiracies in every corner, what was one m-more?'

'Fabricated, malicious and one too many,' responded Luciano damningly. 'So . . . you were told what to do and you did it. But not, I suspect, purely to escape your debt.'

The hunted look came back with a vengeance. 'Why n-not? What other reason could I have?'

'That is what I'm trying to discover.' The dark eyes surveyed him with chill implacability. 'I am finding it quite difficult to believe in this tale of anonymous letters. Convince me.'

'H-how?'

'By telling me what else it said. I am not entirely stupid, Mr Ferrars. The letter – if it existed at all – suggested a way to solve your financial problems and save your betrothal. I can see how that would have appealed to you. But you'd have been foolhardy in the extreme if you'd involved your-self in such a matter for that alone – for, if the plot had failed, you'd have found yourself in very deep water indeed.' Luciano smiled disquietingly. 'It therefore follows that either the letter contained some further inducement, or you are lying. Which?'

'It wasn't my fault!' cried Ferrars wildly. 'I tell you I had to do it! I didn't have any choice.'

'Why not?'

'Because the letter threatened to tell the world that I – that I'd got a girl killed because I was too c-cowardly to defend myself!'

'And had you?'

'Yes – damn you, *yes*! It was years ago in Gloucester. We were in a tavern and there was a quarrel and before I knew what was happening, this fellow was challenging me to fight him. And then he was coming at me . . . I'll swear he meant to kill me . . . and I was afraid. So I grabbed a serving-girl and pulled her in front of me – and somehow she ended up on the other man's blade. It – it was an acci-dent. I never *meant* it to happen! It was just – just . . .' Control had gone and suddenly the man was sobbing. 'You don't know what it's like – always being afraid! But I can't help it. *I can't help it!*'

For a long, timeless moment, Luciano remained quite

still. And then, very slowly, he expelled a breath he hadn't even known he was holding. He said distantly, 'And if this had become known, you would have lost your bride-to-be?'

'Yes. Alice knows I'm n-not brave – but not . . . not—'

'Precisely what degree of coward you are?' finished Luciano helpfully. 'So, to prevent her finding out, you did as you were told and helped destroy my father. Quite frankly, despicable as it is, I'm surprised you had the guts even for that – and please don't tell me yet again that you had no choice. There is always a choice and you yourself made it.'

Feeling as though his bones had been laid bare, Thomas Ferrars huddled deeper into his chair and said desperately, 'What – what are you going to do?'

'Ah. The two-thousand-eight-hundred-and-forty-pound question. What am I going to do?' Almost idly, Luciano up-ended the bag Mr Ferrars had left on the table and watched as a tangle of pearls, sapphires and rubies came winking into the light. Then, gazing maliciously down into the other man's eyes, 'I'm going to keep these in return for the money you already owe me. I'm not, obviously, going to advance you so much as a groat, and I'm going to continue to ensure that no one in Oxford will supply you with even a pin. Then, Mr Ferrars, I'm going to do the worst thing I can think of. I'm going to send you home to your wife – and wish you joy of one another.' Again that slow, brittle smile. 'If you're wise, you'll stay out of my sight. And if you attempt to warn your colleagues in legalised murder of my interest in the matter, I'll take pleasure in personally informing dear Alice of your inglorious past. I trust that takes care of everything?' He strolled to the door and opened it. 'Goodbye, Mr Ferrars. You may now go to the devil your own way.'

He was never to know precisely what happened that night in the house on Holywell Street – and neither, to be truthful, did he care; but within forty-eight hours the aftermath was revealed to him as it went reverberating pleasurably through the taverns, shops and boudoirs of Oxford. For it appeared that Alice Ferrars had eluded her husband's creditors and fled starvation and disgrace by slipping quietly away with a rich Bedfordshire cloth-merchant; and Thomas, in response to the final irony, had put a pistol to his head after all.

Seven

Having been summoned to dine with Luciano in Cheapside, Richard Maxwell cradled a goblet of wine between his hands and listened, without comment, to the tale of Thomas Ferrars. Then, when it was over, he said somewhat coolly, 'So . . . one dead, two to go. Are you pleased with yourself?'

'I'll admit to a certain satisfaction. Why not?' shrugged Luciano. 'After all, it wasn't my fault that he killed himself. The credit for that belongs to his wife.'

'Comforting for you. And Ahiram Webb?'

'May not *have* a wife,' came the flippant reply. Then, 'Richard, it's Christmas Eve and I'd as soon not quarrel with you. I did what needed to be done and I've no intention of rending myself with self-recrimination now. As for Webb and Brandon, it seems likely that one of them planned the whole charade and blackmailed the others – so I'm obviously not about to leave them unscathed. And if you really want to pick a fight, I can offer you a better reason.'

'Ah.' Richard set down his goblet and folded his arms. 'I wondered if we'd come to that. It's Kate, of course.'

'She's written to you?'

'No – but Dolly has. From which I know that Kate's betrothal is at an end and that, from the look on her face whenever your name is mentioned, there's a suspicion that you may have had a hand in the matter. Did you?'

'Yes. Clumsily, as it turned out. I may even have done more harm than good. But Kate can tell you that better than I.'

'And – even though you know I'm relieved to have her freed from Clifford – you'd rather she did so?'

'Yes.' The lean face held more than a hint of tension.

'I see. Then I'd better withhold my gratitude, hadn't I?'

'Or banish it altogether.' Luciano left his seat and moved restlessly away in search of more wine. 'Can we talk about something else?'

'By all means,' replied Richard equably. 'How about the degree of trouble Dolly tells me you put yourself to in October to save Thorne Ash from capture?' And then, when no answer was forthcoming, 'All right. Try unlocking your jaw to tell me whether or not Giacomo has come back yet.'

'He has. He arrived late this afternoon, having deposited Felix safely at home.' Luciano returned to the table to fill two glasses and then sat down again. 'There's no chance of your going there yourself, I suppose?'

'Aside from the fact that being here occasionally gives me the chance to see Eden when the army is nearby – I only wish there was! But with the House already seriously depleted and unrest all around us, I've no choice but stay. I suppose you've heard about the recent unpleasantness at the Guildhall?'

'Trained Bands dispersing petitioning merchants? Yes. But you can hardly find it surprising. Food prices are rising, the blockade of Newcastle is making coal scarce and, due to the absence of the Court and the controls on traffic in and out of the City, trade has come to a virtual standstill. So when you add an obligatory fast-day each month, a rapidly growing black-list of so-called Malignants and His Majesty's exquisitely timed and wonderfully ironic denunciation of Parliament's illegal taxes and arbitrary arrests, you can't wonder at the all-pervading atmosphere of dreariness and suspicion.' Luciano paused and smiled a little. 'The only thing likely to put fresh heart into the waverers is a victory – and not just a minor one such as this fellow Waller taking Winchester. You need something to rival the lustre of Prince Rupert.'

'Peace,' responded Richard flatly, 'would be better. Denzil Holles and a few of the rest of us have been press-

378

ing for more negotiations but I don't know if anything will come of it. To tell you the truth, what with the Peace Party, the War Party and the Let's Copy the Scots Covenanters Party, there's more division inside the House these days than there is outside it.'

'And Pym?'

'Pym's so bloody subtle I sometimes wonder if his right hand knows what his left is doing. But he's still the only man with any kind of substantial following – and therefore the only one with enough influence to unify the factions.' Richard rolled a walnut idly between his fingers. 'For what it's worth, I think he's steering a middle course in order to pacify the nervous. But I doubt very much that he wants a peace treaty just yet.'

'In which,' said Luciano sardonically, 'he is almost certainly not alone. For I doubt very much if the King wants one either.'

Despite both the unaccustomed pleasure of having Felix home and Dorothy's attempts to generate a little Yuletide spirit, Kate spent the festive season carrying hods in Egypt and trying desperately not to allow it to show. For though her feelings towards Luciano del Santi were now so complex as to defy definition, there was one point on which she was very clear indeed. His interference in the matter of her betrothal had arisen directly from what she herself had said to him; but in his usual malicious fashion, he had chosen to do it in a way which not only demonstrated his own complete indifference to her but also lured her to make a complete fool of herself. And she did not think she would ever forgive him.

Burning embarrassment gave way to silent brooding and then to frenetic, purposeful activity. And meanwhile, 1642 became 1643 and Giacomo reappeared to escort Felix back to London, while Gianetta seized the opportunity to embark on what was to become a regular correspondence with her brother. It soon became apparent that she was not the only one taking up her pen for, in no time at all, the entire country was knee-deep in propaganda. It began with the advent of the Royalist news-sheet *Mercurius Aulicus* – which in its turn begat an unofficial parliamentary reply entitled *Mercurius Britanicus* and caused Kate to observe sourly that someone couldn't spell. And then every week saw fresh ballads and pamphlets rolling hot from the presses and selling in their hundreds for a penny or less, with the result that everyone, whatever their allegiance, was able to enjoy the Parliament's efforts to substitute Soundhead for Roundhead – or, failing that, drag the Cavaliers down with them under names like Rattlepate or Shagamuffin.

But the news-sheets were informative as well as entertaining. The Maxwells read about the peace deputations scuttling fruitlessly between Westminster and Oxford, about His Majesty giving John Pym renewed support from the City by accusing its Lord Mayor of treason, and about an unqualified Royalist victory at a place called Braddock Down. They learned that Rupert had braved the late January snow to take Cirencester; that Richard's friend Lord Brooke had been shot in the head by a sniper at Lichfield just before his old adversary Lord Northampton had his skull staved in by a halberd at Hopton Heath; that Ralph Cochrane's commanding officer had been made major-general of Gloucestershire. And by the end of March, they discovered that the Queen had narrowly escaped both shipwreck and her enemies' guns to land safely at Bridlington Bay – along, presumably, with Celia's mother and Venetia Clifford.

To those at Thorne Ash, most of these things had a curious unreality; for though Sir William Compton now held Banbury Castle for the King, his tenancy had so far made little difference outside the town. And then, on an afternoon at the beginning of April, the war swung dizzily back into focus again.

Spring had come early, causing Dorothy to turn the house upside down by setting every pair of hands to the task of cleaning. Kate, consequently, was perched on a settle taking down curtains while Felicity, who should have been helping, regaled her with random snippets from the latest edition of *Aulicus*.

'Oh – and listen to this,' she grinned. '"Sir Jacob Astley, lately slain at Gloucester, desires to know was he slain with a musket or a cannon bullet."' And, looking up, 'It's a great pity that the Cavalier stuff is always so much more wittily written than ours, isn't it? After all, there must be *somebody* on our side with a neat turn of phrase.'

'No doubt,' said Kate dryly. 'But perhaps they have better things to do. I don't suppose you could put that thing down and give me a hand, could you?'

'In a minute. I just want to finish this. It says the writer understands that Mr Pym is trying to legalise the robbery of the King's friends by setting up Seques . . . Sequestration Committees.' Felicity's brow wrinkled over the unfamiliar word. 'What does that mean, do you suppose?'

'I haven't the faintest idea. Neither – just at this moment – do I care,' snapped Kate, her arms full of heavy damask. 'For God's sake come and hold this stuff.'

Felicity rose obligingly and received the curtain but said, 'You know, you've been in a foul mood ever since you told Kit you wouldn't marry him. And if it's going to carry on, all I can say is that it would be better for the rest of us if you wrote and told him you've changed your mind again.'

Kate affixed her with a blighting stare. 'But I haven't.'

'No?'

'No.'

'Then why,' asked Felicity, 'are you as cross as two sticks?'

'I'm not. And if I were, it's none of your business.'

'It is when you bite my head off every time I open my mouth,' came the rancourless objection. And then, 'But if you're really not pining for Kit, then I suppose it must be Mr Santi.'

For a brief instant, Kate remained perfectly motionless and then, eyes blazing with temper, she stepped carefully down from the chair. 'What an utterly witless remark. If you can't stop your mouth by-passing your brain, perhaps the answer is to open it a little less frequently.'

She regretted this remark as soon as it was made and the look in her sister's eyes made her feel even smaller. But before she could put matters right by apologising, the door had burst open and one of the maids was babbling that Sir William Compton had called with another gentleman and there were troopers in the yard.

'Troopers? How many?' asked Kate sharply.

'F-four, I think. What shall we do, Miss Kate?'

'Show Sir William in and stop worrying. Six men don't make an invasion party.' Kate drew a long breath and took a second to think. 'But get Adam or somebody to watch them just the same. And then go and find Mother.'

White-faced but a little calmer, the girl nodded and left them.

'Will Compton?' said Felicity. '*In person?* Why?'

'That,' replied Kate grimly, 'is what I'm wondering. But I doubt very much if it's a social call.'

Since the Maxwells had never aspired to the lofty orbit of the Earl of Northampton, neither Kate nor Felicity had ever met his late lordship's third son. It therefore came as something of a surprise that he was rather younger than Kate herself and darkly good-looking. But all this was quickly overshadowed by the even greater surprise entering the room in his wake – for the gentleman he had brought with him was Sir Hugo Verney.

Kate's brows rose but she adhered to strict formality and offered her hand first to the lieutenant-governor.

'Sir William? I am Kate Maxwell. My mother will be with us shortly – but, in the meantime, perhaps you would care to take some wine?'

'Thank you – but no.' Sir William accepted her hand and bowed over it with practised grace. Then, looking her straight in the eye, he said, 'I'm not here on a very pleasant errand, I'm afraid. But first I believe that Lieutenant Verney would like a word with you.'

'With *me*?' The green gaze encompassed Sir Hugo with nicely judged incredulity. 'Really?'

Hugo looked back at her with mingled discomfort and unusual gravity. He said, 'Yes. If – if you would accord me a few moments in private, I believe I have some news for you.'

Something moved unpleasantly behind Kate's russet taffeta bodice. Swallowing, she said tonelessly, 'Then – since I assume that Sir William knows what you want to tell me and there is nothing you can say to me that my sister should not hear – I suggest you get on with it.'

He exchanged a helpless glance with his senior officer and then, shrugging slightly, said, 'As you wish. I am aware that you . . . severed your connection with Kit Clifford some months ago . . . but I thought you might wish to know that he . . . he fell at Lichfield last month.'

For a long, airless moment, no one either moved or spoke. Then Kate said oddly, 'Kit's *dead*?'

'Yes. I'm sorry.' Hugo looked appealingly at Felicity.

'Kate?' Felicity laid an unsteady hand on her arm. 'Are you all right? Come and sit down.'

'No – no. I'm fine.' The blood drained slowly from her skin, leaving her eyes unnaturally brilliant; all she could see was Kit's face when he had found her in Luciano's arms. Nausea stirred and grew. Kate held her head very high and said courteously, 'It was very good of you to come and tell me. I appreciate it. And now, if you will excuse me for a few moments . . .?'

Only will-power got her out of the room with dignity. Once on the other side of the door, instinct sent her flying to the close-stool where she spent several nasty minutes retching helplessly and without relief. Then, still feeling as though she'd been kicked in the stomach, she slipped out through a side-door into the garden.

Shivering slightly, she leaned against the sun-warmed wall and tried to come to terms with the unbelievable fact that all Kit's youth and vitality had been snuffed out. It was hard. And harder still was the knowledge that she would never now be able to mend the destructiveness of their parting. It was too late.

'Kate . . . my dear, is something wrong?' Inappropriate

and unctuous as ever, Nathan had materialised at her elbow. 'You're crying.'

'Go away,' she said baldly.

'And leave you so upset? How can I? Come, dearest cousin . . . surely we're good enough friends after all this time for you to be able to share your grief with me?'

Kate turned her head and stared at him. He'd shown an increasing tendency towards affectionate familiarity of late and she loathed it. She said coldly, 'Wrong on all three counts, Nathan – and I'd be glad if you would keep your endearments for someone who appreciates them. I don't. Now leave me alone.'

The pale eyes bathed her in righteous concern and half-veiled calculation. 'I only want to help you, Kate. Goodwife Flossing tells me that Sir William Compton has called. If the God-cursed Malignant has done something to distress you . . .' He paused and then, laying a hand on her arm, said with mounting horror, 'Or has he brought bad news of Eden? No – no. I cannot believe that the Lord can have so ignored my prayers.'

'When you pray, God listens?' demanded Kate mockingly, recoiling like a whip from his touch. 'If you won't go, then I must.' And she was off across the garden before he could stop her.

By the time she returned with renewed control to the parlour, Sir William was apparently on the point of leaving and her mother's face wore a look that Kate did not recognise.

'Kate – thank heavens!' Felicity arose, pink with indignation. 'You won't believe what this – this *gentleman* has had the effrontery to say!'

'Not now, dear.' Dorothy gently silenced her youngest daughter and looked searchingly at her eldest. 'What can I say, Kate? I'm so sorry.'

'Yes,' came the stony reply. 'So am I.' And then, looking across to the window where Hugo Verney stood with Celia – who was as pink as Felicity but for presumably different reasons, 'Kit's mother and sister were with the Queen. Will they have been told?'

'I believe so.' He took a step towards her and then

stopped. 'If – if you want the details, I have told your mother what little I know.'

'Then there's nothing more to be said.'

There was a short, uncomfortable pause and then Will Compton said quietly, 'Mistress Maxwell – my apologies once again for the unfortunateness of my demands. I hope you will believe that only the necessities of war could have occasioned it. I'll send a couple of my fellows over again in a few days' time . . . perhaps your acquaintance with Lieutenant Verney will make him more acceptable to you than most? And in the meantime, we'll relieve you of our presence.' He picked up his hat and swept her a deep bow. 'I have the honour to bid you good-day, mistress.'

After the two men had left, Dorothy and the girls looked at each other in silence for a long time. Then Kate said abruptly, 'Demands? What demands?'

'It will keep,' replied her mother calmly. 'You look as if you'd be better lying on your bed.'

'No. I'm perfectly all right. Tell me what they said.'

Dorothy sighed and sat down again. 'Very well. Sir William has the King's authority to . . . divert our rents into his own purse. And he intends to do it.'

A hint of colour returned to Kate's face. 'But that's simple robbery!'

'No more than your precious Mr Pym's orders for committees to seize Far Flamstead and the like,' remarked Celia sweetly. She floated smilingly past Kate to the door and then looked back to say tauntingly, 'As far as I can see, this is just His Majesty giving you your own again. And about time too.' Then she was gone.

Ignoring the interruption, Kate moved slowly towards her mother. 'We can refuse to comply.'

'Oh yes. And give him the excuse to denude all our tenants of their livestock.'

'He'll do that anyway.'

'He says not. Or not if it can be avoided.'

'That,' said Kate pungently, 'is uncommonly civil of him. So what do you suggest? That we meekly hand over every penny we've got?'

'No.' Dorothy smiled wryly. 'I suggest we get to work

preparing a full set of fraudulent farm accounts that reduce our revenue from rents by half – preferably without Celia being any the wiser.'

'Goodness, yes!' exclaimed Felicity. 'She'd tell Sir Hugo before you could say wink. But if she doesn't know he'll probably be too busy making eyes at her to notice that anything's wrong.'

'Quite,' said Kate. 'But the question is – do we want to let him flirt with Eden's wife?'

'No.' A shadow crossed Dorothy's face. 'I can't say that we do. But, short of chaining Celia to the bedpost, it's going to be rather difficult to stop him. And, provided they're not left alone together, I don't really see that any harm can come of it.' She hesitated and then said, 'Kate, my dear, you can't feel like coping with any of this yet – or indeed even simply talking. Why don't you go to your room and let me have Jenny make you up a posset?'

Ice was spreading into Kate's every vein and it was becoming increasingly difficult to ignore the leaden weight in her chest, so she nodded and said wearily, 'Yes. I think I will. Only I ought to write to Venetia.'

'Tomorrow. Do it tomorrow.'

'Yes. I suppose that would be better. Perhaps by then I – I'll know what to say to her.'

She was half-way to her room when a lone positive thought forced its way through the mists into her brain – and, turning aside, she went instead to the nursery. Gianetta was there, playing peacefully with Jude and Eve, but she looked up when Kate entered and said quickly, 'Something is wrong?'

'Yes. You could put it that way.' Kate fought to control her breathing. 'And I've a message for your brother next time you write to him.'

Surprise marked Gianetta's brows. 'Yes?'

'You can tell him that Kit Clifford is dead. I'm sure he'll want to know. And if he doesn't,' said Kate unevenly, 'if he doesn't . . . it's high time someone gave his conscience a thorough scouring.'

April dragged by on leaden feet. In the outside world,

Prince Rupert battered his way into Birmingham and moved on to retake Lichfield, while Lord Essex settled down to besiege Reading and the Parliament finally recalled its last batch of Peace Commissioners from Oxford. Reading fell and gave Essex the opportunity to inform his masters in the House that he could undertake no further action until his troops were paid; London was full of beggars, Irish refugees and wounded soldiers and still being forced to pay for the war on no better security than 'the public faith'; and the King, with an eye to his long-term prospects, wrote to the Earl of Ormonde in Dublin and told him to obtain a truce with the rebel Irish so that he could recruit and despatch to England as many troops of either nationality as could be raised.

At Thorne Ash, meanwhile, Hugo Verney arrived to examine the accounts in a manner as cursory as it was embarrassed and then took reluctant possession of the quarter's rents. He made no attempt to get Celia alone and indeed, as far as anyone was aware, barely spoke to her; but when he had gone, Celia's mood was noticeably mellower and Felicity insisted that she had actually heard her singing.

'I daresay you did,' was Kate's caustic reply. 'She's so pleased to see us contributing towards the King's war, she hasn't the sense to work out that it's her son's inheritance His Majesty is playing ducks and drakes with.'

Brief letters arrived from Amy, who was finding wartime London a big disappointment and thinking it might be more entertaining to spend the summer in the bosom of her family, and from Richard, who was apparently enmeshed in the intricacies of the various County Committees and missing both his wife and the civilised company of Luciano del Santi who had departed once more for Genoa. Kate wondered precisely what fun Amy thought they were having out here in Oxfordshire; said it would be a good thing for all their sakes if Father could take a holiday; and kept her mouth firmly closed on the subject of the man whom she personally considered about as civilised as a sewer-rat.

It was, however, all very well to indulge in this kind of heartening anger when he was several hundred miles away, Kate acknowledged irritably to herself later. The problem came when he was standing in front of her . . . and, unfortunately, it was always the same problem. She sat back on her heels and stared unseeingly at the rose bush she was transplanting. Just now she hated him for causing her to send Kit away, hurt and angry, to his death . . . but that wouldn't last. The lasting truth, as she had once obliquely admitted to Eden, was that Luciano del Santi was the only man she would ever want; and it seemed that nothing he did could change it.

'In which case,' she muttered, furiously hammering down the earth, 'I may as well resign myself to lifelong spinsterhood.'

'Kate? *Kate!*' Felicity's voice drifted excitedly down from the gate-house. 'Somebody's coming.'

'Troopers?' Kate scrambled to her feet and started up the steps, brushing soil from her hands as she went. 'Or friends?'

'I don't know. Oh, heavens! No – it can't be!'

'Can't be *who*?' snapped Kate, emerging at her side. And then, in tones of complete disbelief, 'No. I'm seeing things.'

'That makes two of us then,' grinned Felicity, gathering up her skirts. 'Either that – or it's Uncle Ivo.'

Kate stayed where she was while Felicity ran on ahead. It wasn't just Uncle Ivo. It was also another man she'd never seen before, a couple of servants, and a familiar marigold head. Whether by accident or design, Ivo Courtenay appeared to have brought Danny O'Flaherty with him. For the first time in several weeks, Kate smiled and, as she made her way back down the steps, reflected that it was just as well Amy had not come home to roost just yet.

Richard Maxwell always maintained that Dorothy's brother had a unique talent for mayhem that would hang him one day, and it was certainly true that Ivo was anything but dull. Tall and loose-limbed, his hair the colour of beech-leaves, he led his little cavalcade into the courtyard

388

and dropped carelessly from the saddle to give his sister a quick, hard hug.

'Well, Dolly, surprised to see me?'

'Not at all. We were beginning to wonder what was keeping you,' she retorted. And then, 'You look tired.'

'And you look younger than ever. I don't know how you do it with that lunatic brood of yours running wild in the house.' He winked at Felicity, making her giggle.

'Well, you know how it is,' shrugged Dorothy. 'We keep leaving them out in the woods but the fairies don't take them. Not that they *can* take Eden or Felix or Amy because they aren't here. Kate, on the other hand, is just behind you.'

He swung round and stopped dead, saying, 'Little Kate? It can't be! I haven't been away that long, surely?' Then, turning to his unknown companion, he said, 'Will you look at this, Liam? A houseful of beautiful women, no less! Where are your complaints now, I wonder?' And, without giving him time to reply, 'But come down from your horse, man, and be introduced. Dolly – this is Liam Aherne of Kildare and, if you're especially nice to him, he may overlook the fact that I'm only a Protestant Englishman and allow me to marry his sister.'

Tall, dark and possessed of stormy grey eyes and a mouth like a steel trap, Liam Aherne bowed to Dorothy and calmly remarked that pigs might fly.

'He'll come round to the idea,' said Ivo, airily. 'And in the meantime I daresay you remember Danny-boy, here. I sent him to you a while back with some letters.'

'Yes.' Dorothy surveyed the understandably anxious young man with faint amusement. 'How could we forget him? But why are we standing here? I presume you've time to come in and take a glass of wine?'

'At last! And there I was thinking it was a damned dry house you were keeping and wondering if you'd all turned Puritan while I'd been away.'

'Goodness, no,' responded Kate, mildly indignant. 'Why, a bottle of raspberry cordial doesn't last the month in this house.' And then, grasping Felicity's wrist while the others went inside, hissed urgently, 'Where's Celia?'

'Out riding again, I suppose. Why?'

'Because if Uncle Ivo and that dangerous-looking friend of his don't know what Daniel got up to with Amy, it might be better to leave it that way.' And then, 'What am I saying? If Celia wants to tell them, there's nothing we can do to stop her. Oh, let's go in and enjoy Uncle Ivo while we've got him.'

In the parlour, Ivo was fortifying himself with Richard's best burgundy in between a stream of airy witticisms. The sight of Danny O'Flaherty lurking miserably in a corner immediately roused Felicity's ready sympathy and sent her over to join him. Kate, on the other hand, sat down by her mother and took a long critical look at the grimly silent Mr Aherne.

He was younger than Ivo, probably not much past thirty, and he looked as though he'd be more at home in the saddle brandishing a sword than sitting in Mother's best chair, sipping wine. If he'd trouble to smile, thought Kate, he'd probably turn out to be quite spectacular. But he didn't look as if that was something he did often . . . and a more unlikely friend for Uncle Ivo she couldn't imagine.

Then, as Ivo paused for breath, the Irishman said suddenly to Dorothy, 'I'm told your husband sits in the Parliament?'

Her brows rose a little. 'Yes. He does.'

'Ah. And was he sitting there, by any chance, on the day they decided to murder Black Tom Strafford?'

'If you mean, was he there at the time of the trial – yes, he was,' replied Dorothy calmly. 'But if you're asking whether he voted for the impeachment, the answer is that he didn't. Does that mean that you may now drink your wine with a clear conscience?'

Liam Aherne crossed one long leg over the other and looked austerely back at her. 'Well, now, it might at that. But at this stage, I wouldn't like to be sure of it.'

There was a brief, tricky silence. Then Ivo sighed and in a tone of surprising crispness, said, 'All right. Having dispensed with the pleasantries, I suppose it's time for the nasty truth. You can't fail to know something of what's happening in Ireland. The removal of Strafford paved the way for it and, to my mind, his death lit the fuse. But the rebellion is not against the King. It's against the Puritanism coming out of Westminster and the more recent Protestant settlers and the rank mishandling of both the Catholics and the Anglo-Irish by Justice Parsons.' He paused and then, spreading his hands, said, 'Dolly, I don't want to let this become personal. But Ireland's my home now and I don't like what's happening to it.'

'So why are you here?' she asked.

'To see the King and hopefully persuade him of a few realities, if nothing else.'

'Have you heard of the Irish Catholic Confederacy at all?' asked Liam Aherne softly. 'It's been set up these several months in Kilkenny and on its seal are the words "Irishmen united for God, King and Country". It would be a nice thing, so it would, if His Majesty were to recognise it.'

'He can't,' said Kate bluntly. 'After all the tales of rebel atrocities we've heard, it would cost him support here that he can't afford to lose.'

Ivo and Liam exchanged enigmatic glances.

'Well, we'll see,' said Ivo, at length. 'But Ireland needs a truce and needs it badly if we're not to go on living in futile, bloody stalemate.'

'Is it really as bad as we've heard?' asked Felicity.

'That would depend, would it not, on what you've been told?' responded Liam. 'But it's bad enough. The land's been devastated and filled with the starving and homeless, while here in England soft-skinned gentlemen take their ease from the profits they've made off the backs of the Irish.'

'You don't like us much, do you?' said Dorothy. 'And I'll admit that you probably have cause. But it does rather make me hope that Ivo isn't serious about marrying your sister.'

For the first time since he'd arrived, the hard mouth softened a little and he said, 'Oh he's serious about it – and so, God strengthen her wits, is she. But for my part it's not just the matter of him being Protestant English.'

'No?'

'No,' grinned Ivo. 'Accustomed as he is to being accounted the biggest madman in Kildare, he's not sure he wouldn't rather have Gibbaloney the Devil for competition than myself. True?'

'True enough,' agreed Liam. And smiled.

Felicity's jaw dropped and Kate suddenly found the affinity she'd been looking for. Then the door opened and Gianetta walked in.

She was wearing dark blue satin and with it every jewel not buried behind the hen-coop: most prominent of all, as usual, was the amethyst crucifix. Ivo and Liam rose as one while Dorothy made the introductions, and across the room, night-dark Italian eyes met misty-grey Irish ones and locked. Gianetta stopped dead three steps into the room and Liam Aherne did not even appear to be breathing. Kate looked from one to the other and then, with a shrug, at her uncle, whose face was alight with unholy glee.

The moment stretched out to infinity before Liam, with an effort that could be felt, drew a long, uneven breath and crossed the room to the girl. He said, '"Fairer she is than the wings of the morning." I'm sorry, alannah. I didn't hear your name.'

'It is Gianetta,' she said wonderingly. 'And – and you?'

'I am the Aherne.' He took her hand and raised it to his lips. 'Liam, if it pleases you.'

'Liam,' repeated Gianetta softly. And again, with a smile, 'Liam.'

They stayed two days – which was twenty-four hours more than had been planned before Mr Aherne had laid eyes on Signorina Falcieri del Santi – and left before Celia's mood of strangely tranquil detachment broke sufficiently for her to reveal Daniel's previous misdeeds.

Gianetta stood on the roof of the gatehouse and watched until they were out of sight. Felicity eyed her curiously for a moment and then said, 'I don't mean to be a killjoy, but do you think you'll ever see him again?'

'But of course.' Gianetta gave a smile of complete serenity. 'How can I not? I am going to marry him.'

April became May and Celia's remoteness survived even
the news that John Pym had finally succeeded in getting
Parliament to impeach the Queen. And then, discreet in
the deepening twilight on an evening towards the end of
the month, Eden came home.

He was leaner than when he had left; leaner, harder and
more tanned. And he'd also acquired a new air of command
which Kate realised they ought to have expected but
somehow had not.

'How long can you stay?' asked Dorothy when the first
shock and excitement of welcome was over.

'Three or four days, provided I don't advertise my presence,' he grinned. 'The truth is that I've had enough of
Lord Essex and have decided to leave him.'

'*Leave him?*' echoed Celia. And then, suspiciously,
'Why?'

'Because there are other generals better worth following. It was bad enough that Essex left the London road
open to the King after Edgehill and then dallied about getting
there himself. But since we took Reading he's done nothing
but complain about the lack of money, with the result that
half the army is either indulging in petty squabbles or
deserting through sheer boredom,' said Eden flatly. 'So
I've been in touch with Ralph and he's paved the way for
me to transfer to Waller.'

'Sir William Waller?' asked Kate. 'The one who's been
made major-general of Gloucestershire?'

'And Worcestershire, Wiltshire, Shropshire and Somerset,' he nodded. 'Last autumn, he took Portsmouth,
Winchester, Arundel and Chichester – which means he's
achieving more than most of our other commanders – and
I'm told he's a gentleman who inspires loyalty. He's inspired
it in Ralph, anyway – along with this fellow Gabriel he told
us about, who it seems is a major.'

'And what are you?' demanded Felicity. 'Still a lieutenant?'

'For the moment. But I've reason to believe that my removal to Waller will result in a captaincy.' He paused, still fondling his wife's unresponsive hand. 'And now, if no one minds, I'd like to see my son.'

'He'll be asleep,' objected Celia. 'Leave it till tomorrow.'

'Oh no. I've already waited the best part of nine months and that's more than enough.' He rose, drawing her up with him. 'Come on. I promise I won't wake him. And then I think you and I are due for a little time to ourselves while you tell me all the news.' He turned a cheerfully audacious gaze on his mother and sisters. 'I don't mean to be rude and will talk all you like tomorrow. But tonight is for my wife.'

When they had gone, Felicity looked at her mother and said, 'Well, what a let-down! He didn't even ask about our bit of excitement with Cyrus Winter!'

'You heard him,' replied Dorothy. 'Tomorrow.'

'Quite.' Kate achieved an acidulous smile. 'And meanwhile, if it helps, you can cherish the thought that Celia's no more thrilled with the situation than you are.'

Upstairs in the nursery, Eden smiled a silent greeting at Meg Bennet and then bent an avid eye upon his sleeping son. At two-and-a-half, Jude was already bidding fair to become the image of his father and, when awake, was a placid, laughing child who never showed a hint of his mother's temperament. Eden touched one chubby fist and whispered wonderingly, 'I can't believe how much he's grown.'

Celia shrugged and said nothing.

'You needn't worry about waking him,' volunteered Meg quietly from the corner where she sat sewing. 'Nothing disturbs him once he's properly asleep.'

Eden bent and kissed Jude's brow. Then, looking across at the maid, said, 'Or yours either?'

'No,' she smiled. 'They're both perfect babies.'

'Well, of course!' He hesitated and then said, 'I brought Tom with me. If the two of you are still not speaking to each other, I thought you might want to know so that you can avoid him.'

Meg's colour rose. 'That's up to Tom. I-I'd be happy to – to—'

'To be friends with him if he'd be friends with you?' offered Eden helpfully. 'I'll tell him – though I can't promise it will help.'

'If you want to have a long cosy chat with all the servants,' said Celia suddenly, 'I'm going back to the parlour.'

'No, don't do that.' He slid an arm round her waist. 'Let's go and sit by our own hearth and you can pour me wine as you used to.'

'As you wish.' It was the last thing she wanted but it wouldn't do to say so; and, realising that she had also better put a smile on her face, she summoned all she could of the old, practised charm and said, 'Come, then. But if you don't take off that horrid buff-coat, I swear I'll have no more to do with you.'

'And that would be a pity,' he murmured. Then, wickedly, '*Just* the buff-coat?'

She sent for wine and then, when it came, was assiduous in keeping his glass filled while she gave him her own version of everything from Cyrus Winter's attempt on the house to Gianetta's fancy for a bog-trotting Irishman . . . and all the time she was thinking, evaluating, planning. She could not decide whether, under the circumstances, she wanted to keep him at arm's length or not. But one thing was plain enough; she could not risk going to Far Flamstead tomorrow.

'Celia?' Eden's voice cut across her thoughts. 'You look a million miles away.'

'Do I? I was just wondering if joining Waller means you'll be home more often.'

'I doubt it,' came the rueful reply. 'With such a large area in his charge, I imagine Sir William has to keep on the move. At the moment, for example, he's busy securing the lower Severn valley.'

'Oh.' Celia examined the particularly fine ruby on her finger. 'So we may not see you for some time, then?'

'No – though I'll naturally do my best to get here as often as I can.' He paused and then said, 'You know, you've told me about everyone else but said virtually nothing of your-self.'

'There's not much to tell. Aside from your uncle and his friend – and Gianetta's ghastly brother, of course – we've had no visitors to speak of. And the only place I ever go is Far Flamstead. With Father and Mother and Francis all away, it's up to me to keep an eye on the place, so I try and get over there a couple of times each week.' She shrugged. 'It's just to look in on some of the tenants and see that the house is being properly maintained. And at least it gives me something to do.'

'You could always pass the odd half-hour writing to me,' remarked Eden lightly. 'In fact, I rather wish you would.'

'Well, I'll try if you like. But you know perfectly well I'm not much good with a pen. And if I don't know where you are, how am I to know where to send my letters?' she finished brightly.

Eden dropped on one knee beside her and captured both her hands in his. 'Do you miss me?' he asked.

'Of course. You know I do.' Her colour deepened frac-tionally and she tried to distract him with her most blinding smile. 'And what about you? I'll wager you've flirted with a score of girls while you've been away.'

'Neither a score nor a dozen – nor even one,' he replied, drawing her down out of her chair and into his arms. 'As you're very well aware, I've no interest in second-best. And since the most beautiful woman in the world happens to be my wife, all I've done since I left is dream of this moment.'

His fingers, defter than they used to be – or perhaps simply more impatient – had removed the pins from her hair and were already at the laces of her gown. She said feebly, 'You – you're very importunate.'

'Yes, my heart.' And with a tremor of laughter, 'Aren't you?'

Celia closed her eyes and kept her mind carefully blank.

On the following morning, Eden talked privately with his mother for a long time and then went in search of Kate to say bluntly, 'I'm sorry about Clifford. He was a good fellow – for a Cavalier.'

'Yes.'

He looked at her obliquely for a moment and then said, 'Is there anyone else?'

'Is it any of your business?'

'Meaning that it isn't. All right. Have it your own way. But you can't still be hankering after that bloody Italian, surely?'

Kate eyed him with acute disfavour. 'Another brilliant conversation-stopper. Did you want to talk to me or not?'

Eden sighed and gave it up. 'Yes. Firstly, congratulations on keeping Cyrus Winter out and commiserations on the fate of the saker. And secondly, how come Will Compton was able to ride, unchallenged, right up to the front door?'

'Mainly because we were all otherwise engaged. But it wouldn't have made any difference. We might have kept him out of the house but we can't seal up all of the farms – as you very well know.' She hesitated for a moment and then said, 'Has anyone mentioned that Hugo Verney is presently attached to the garrison and was sent to collect the quarter's rents?'

'Yes. Celia told me. Did you think she wouldn't?' He regarded her forbiddingly over folded arms. 'No – don't answer that. I'd hoped you'd have learned a little tolerance by now.'

'Oh, I have,' responded Kate sweetly. 'I have. The only trouble is that, like most things, it's supposed to work both ways.

While Eden was slipping quietly away from Thorne Ash to join Sir William Waller somewhere in Shropshire, Sir William's cousin Edmund found fame in the news-sheets by being arrested for plotting to seize London for the King. This, not unnaturally, sent Mr Pym's nerves into spasm and caused him to impose a new Oath of Loyalty on all Members of Parliament and men of authority everywhere. And, with this furore barely over, worse was to come. On

17 June, Prince Rupert led one of his lightning raids on the village of Chinnor and followed it up with an equally successful engagement in Chalgrove cornfield where John Hampden was severely wounded in the shoulder. Six days later he was dead.

It was a great blow to the Parliament. Hampden was not only the man who'd once rocked the nation by taking his ship-money case to court; he was also the most popular, persuasive and shrewd member of the Commons. And with the Royalist fortunes so firmly in the ascendancy, his loss was something Westminster could ill afford.

Time was when Celia would have crowed with delight but, by the end of June, she had other things on her mind. There was no doubt that she was pregnant again – and the condition was no more welcome to her than it had been before. The only difference was that, this time, her dismay was better founded.

Eight

On the late afternoon of Monday 24 July, Luciano del Santi sat with his servant at Clifton and stared moodily across at Bristol. It had taken the best part of six painstaking months to trace Ahiram Webb, in the midst of which he'd had to make the annual and increasingly difficult journey to Genoa – and then, on discovering that Bristol's governor was none other than Nathaniel Fiennes, to spend yet more time and money acquiring a safe conduct from the Parliament. Not – with Lord Essex threatening to resign if his troops weren't paid – that this had presented any particular problem. And with a pass signed by John Pym in one pocket and a second signed by the King's nephew in the other, life should become demonstrably simpler.

As always, however, the complications were never where one looked for them. A mere ten days ago, Sir William Waller had been soundly thrashed at a battle the Cavaliers were already calling Runaway Down, and had retreated to lick his wounds at Gloucester, thus giving the Royalists a perfect opportunity to subdue the West. And, naturally enough, they had started with the second city and port of the kingdom.

Bristol. Moated on two sides by the Avon and the Frome, and protected on the west by a new earthwork, starred by five ditched and pallisaded forts within which the old medieval walls, studded with squat towers, enclosed both the city and part of the sprawling suburb of Redcliffe. Bristol, with its twenty fair churches, high gabled houses and underground sewerage system; its quays, roperies, soap manufactories and dockside stews. And brooding over all of these, its massive eighteen-acre castle, perched on a slope of solid rock and crowned with towers and galleries. Bristol, which Colonel Fiennes had to hold with less than two thousand men and ninety-eight cannon against a force of roughly fifteen thousand under the personal, ironic direction of Prince Rupert.

After twenty-four frustrating hours of waiting, during the course of which his night's sleep had been ruined by a pair of twelve-pounders bombarding Brandon Hill Fort and his morning depressed by Colonel Fiennes' polite refusal to surrender, Luciano knew all about Bristol. He'd also collected the sardonic Palatine gaze long enough to be informed that he might stay if he liked but had better keep out of the way and expect no favours.

'It's nothing personal,' murmured Francis Langley who, having finally succeeded in getting himself transferred to Rupert, was finding fighting less tedious than he'd previously thought it. 'His temper's balanced on a knife-point and we're all madly busy not invoking it. There are subterranean rumblings of a woman but no one cares to say too much in case they go the way of Dan O'Neill.' He leaned closer and achieved an artistic shudder. 'Stripped of his command for an ill-timed pleasantry. Only think of it! It might have been me.'

'It may still be you,' returned Luciano dryly. 'Only think of it.'

Francis smiled faintly and then, with a complete change of manner, said, 'You've heard about Kit Clifford?'

'Yes.' Expressionlessly.

'And regret nothing. How nice for you. But a word to the wise, my dear. Stay away from Sister Venetia or you may find yourself being taught repentance.'

Luciano had only the haziest recollections of Venetia Clifford. He said slowly, 'Isn't she still in the North with the Queen?'

'No. She's in Oxford with the Queen. Didn't you know? The She-Generalissima met His Majesty at Edgehill two weeks ago. With the result,' finished Francis, preparing to get back to his duties, 'that we're all packed in like herrings in a barrel.'

'Wait.' Luciano detained him. 'I believe Dorothy Maxwell's brother is in Oxford, along with an Irishman named Liam Aherne. Have you met him?'

'Aherne? Barely. He was a disappointment. I was expecting saffron and leggings. And an axe.'

'You would. And his politics?'

'Who can fathom the Irish? But,' said Francis, sighing, 'I gather he's walking a fine line between Ormonde and the rebels and looking for support for the idea of a truce.'

'I see. And will he get it?'

'That will depend on how badly the King wants some Irish levies. What is it to you?'

'As yet, very little.' Luciano smiled with affable finality. 'But I find it always pays to be well informed.'

After a day rent with volleys of musket, cannon and loose shot from both sides, darkness finally brought some respite, and Luciano lay down once more in a corner of Bernard de Gomme's tent in the feeble hope of repairing last night's omissions. Comfort, after all, was only a matter of custom, and he'd spent a good many nights in worse places than this. On that first terrible journey to Genoa with his small sister and rapidly ailing mother, for example. They'd slept in stables and byres, caves and ditches – anywhere that offered some sort of shelter. And all the while his beautiful, bewildered mother had been disintegrating into a ragged, prematurely aged consumptive, drowning in her own blood.

Luciano sat up abruptly and tried to block out the memory. 'Don't think of it,' ran the pattern. 'Or not now. Think of it, if you must, when you're face to face with Ahiram Webb.' Which was undeniably sensible but, as usual, no cure.

He finally fell into an uneasy doze, only to be rudely awakened around midnight by what he later learned was a salvo designed to unnerve the defenders of Prior's Hill. It probably worked. Certainly, coming out of the silence as it did, it was enough to wake Bernard de Gomme, who immediately dragged his guest outside to admire the ensuing hour-long display of fireworks.

'Do you not think,' asked de Gomme fondly, 'that it is not a beautiful piece of danger to see so many fires incessantly in the dark?'

'I'm sure it's marvellous,' came the arid reply. 'But is it achieving anything?'

By eleven on Tuesday morning, Colonel Wentworth came to the conclusion that his men and ordnance were doing so little harm to the Brandon Fort that he might as well send them down to my lord Grandison below Prior's Hill. And while a second day passed in apparently useless volleys and skirmishing, Luciano ground his teeth and wondered whether he had been foolish to stay.

But by mid-afternoon the various comings and goings took on a new air of urgency and Selim, mingling companionably with the common soldiery, came back with the news that rumour predicted a general assault. Two hours later this was confirmed by Francis Langley who said negligently, 'An assault? Yes. At dawn tomorrow. *Aren't* you glad you waited?'

'Ecstatic. Will it work?'

'It's no use asking a mere lieutenant.' Francis smiled annoyingly. 'All I know is that we're all required to get hot and sweaty, rushing about with bits of greenery in our hats and screaming the word "Oxford". *So* tedious!'

Bernard de Gomme having been called to a briefing with the Prince at Redland, and Selim having gone off fraternising again, Luciano ate a solitary and unappetising meal and then sat outside the tent, staring unseeing into the deepening dusk. The sound of firing still tore the air – occasionally punctuated with the odd explosion – but, with his mind tuned to what lay ahead of him in Bristol, Luciano found it less disturbing than usual. And then, without warning, Cyrus Winter was before him.

It was the first time they had met since that memorable

evening at Whitehall eighteen months ago – for one could not count the more recent episode at Thorne Ash. Gazing enigmatically up at the striking, silver-haired figure, Luciano wondered whether Winter even knew he'd been there at that time; and then concluded that, gossip within the army being what it was, he probably did. In which case the instinctive and wholly mutual dislike that eddied and flowed between them had found a reasonable cause at last.

Luciano neither moved nor spoke and finally Cyrus Winter said softly, 'I heard that you were here – and ought, I suppose, to have known better than be surprised at your effrontery.'

'Oh, quite,' came the bored reply. 'Deformed and low-bred as I am, colossal nerve is an absolute necessity. Did you want something?'

'Aside from giving you a lesson in manners? Yes. I wished to remark that your presence amongst us is becoming a little too coincidental. Suspiciously so, in fact. I believe we can dispense with it.'

'Or you'll have me taken for a spy? But if you could do that, we wouldn't be here discussing it, would we? And perhaps you should consider the fact that, without access to my purse, His Majesty might delve a little deeper into yours.'

'But if what one hears is true, your purse – like your loyalty – is offered both ways.'

His loan to the Parliament ought not to be common knowledge; but because civil war is by nature incestuous, Luciano saw no reason for undue concern. Instead, he came slowly to his feet, a smile spreading over his face and said, 'Dear me. I know what it is. You're still peeved because Mistress Kate and I made your men dance. But you mustn't worry. I haven't told a soul how foolish they looked. And experience, as they say, is never bought cheaply.'

The storming of Bristol began somewhat prematurely when, still fermenting with confidence from their victory over Waller, the Cornishmen fell to on the Somerset side at a little before three in the morning. Prince Rupert immediately drew up the various regiments of Horse in places where they might best assist the work of the Foot, and then issued the order for the general assault – after which the dawn broke over six-pronged pandemonium.

The key lay in finding some exploitable weakness. Lord Grandison began by testing the line on either side of Prior's Hill, while Major Sanders brought his men within push of pike of the enemy at a ravelin some little way further east. On the other side, Prince Maurice and Lord Hertford led the Cornish over the worst of the ground, and Colonels Wentworth and Washington attacked the works between Brandon Fort and the Windmill. Lord Grandison was shot in the leg; Major Sanders lost twenty men in just over an hour; and the Cornish, attacking without the faggots that would have helped them cross the ditch, suffered heavy losses and retired in disorder. Colonel Washington's dragoons, on the other hand, advanced successfully into the dead ground directly below the enemy, from where they were able to clear the Roundheads from their lines with grenadoes and fire-pikes and thus force the first breach.

Armed to the teeth and with Selim at his shoulder, Luciano had taken up a position as close as possible to the Prince's staff. Rupert himself, of course, was no more than an energetic blur as he galloped hither and thither, encouraging, reforming and steadying his men. But that did not matter. The command-post was the centre for all news and Luciano was determined to keep it under his eye.

He did not, as it turned out, have that long to wait. Word of Washington's breach was brought to Colonel Legge, along with a request for someone to bring up a fresh mount for His Highness to replace the one that had just been shot from under him. Luciano eavesdropped attentively to the messenger's description of progress so far and then murmured thoughtfully, 'I wonder . . . I wonder if we might risk moving a little closer.'

'Closer,' asked Selim, 'to what?'

'The way in. What else?'

The Turk eyed his master uneasily. Better than anybody,

he knew Luciano's single, pursuing weakness; and better than anybody he knew what the response was likely to be if he mentioned it. He said cautiously, 'Is it not a little soon? The man said they are still fighting their way into the suburbs.'

'Quite. But the man also said they have Fiennes' cavalry in retreat ahead of them.' The lean mouth curled in a brilliant, impersonal smile. 'Come on. I promise I won't faint. And with practice, I may even learn not to be sick.'

The breach was easily found and even easier crossed since they were able to do it in the wake of Colonel Bellasyse's relief force. Inside, however, was the kind of shambles that reminded Luciano nastily of Powick Bridge and forced him to control his stomach. It was the smell that was his chief enemy. With a little care, it was possible to avoid seeing the worst of the butchery: the torn and burnt flesh, the sightless eyes and mangled limbs. But the odour of fresh blood came with every breath, inescapable and instantly cathartic. Luciano let his lungs empty and then forced himself to reinflate them. He was here, after all, to test himself. And one couldn't remain twelve years old forever.

Afterwards, he was never very sure how he survived the hours that followed. When your formal education ends abruptly at the age of ten and the rest of your youth is spent acquiring unrivalled excellence in a back-street workshop, you used your moments of leisure and the time when other people slept to snatch whatever learning you could. And then, since books were expensive, you studied geography and languages with the sailors at the dockside, mathematics amidst your uncle's ledgers, and self-defence, both physical and verbal, from every lout who called you a hunchback. True, you emerged with an education of sorts – the kind, at any rate, that you needed. But music was denied you; and poetry and philosophy and history. All the gentler, apparently useless arts that appealed to you. And one more which did not appeal at all but which was, unfortunately, necessary. The use of arms.

His knowledge of swordplay had mostly come from a one-eyed Venetian mercenary-turned-knife-grinder and, never having fought in earnest, he had no idea how effective it would be. He felt more comfortable with firearms, for marksmanship was easier to practise and accuracy came naturally to him; but then again, perhaps it was different shooting at a live target. At any rate, he would soon know.

There was rapid firing ahead. The Cavaliers, feverishly trying to fill in a traverse ditch so their Horse might pass, were being methodically picked off from roofs and windows. Finding suitable cover and coolly instructing Selim to reload for him, Luciano selected a target, took aim and fired. A man dropped neatly from a roof-top. His next shot took out a musketeer from an upstairs window and his third, a red-faced fellow perched uncomfortably on a gable-end. It also brought a near-lethal retort whizzing past Luciano's ear.

Selim, who preferred to trust in his knife, swore.

Time passed, redolent with noise and confusion. The next stage of the advance took Colonel Bellasyse to the Frome Gate and some of the day's worst carnage, while Colonel Wentworth, with Luciano and Selim grimly following, fought his way towards College Green and the cathedral. Ahead of them, an inner fort known as the Essex-work was taken by accident when its defenders mistook a party of Royalists fleeing from a cavalry charge for a concerted attack and decided to run for it. Far away at the back of his mind, Luciano knew how they felt. For himself and Selim, however, grimly advancing behind Wentworth's men and coming under increasingly heavy fire from the Brandon Fort, there was no turning back. And in the mêlée that followed, he ceased to think of it – or, in fact, of anything at all.

They took the cathedral and pressed on to the quay. Any experienced soldier would have called the resistance weak, but Luciano did not know that. He merely obeyed the impulse to survive and, drawing his sword, used it.

Wentworth sent to the Prince for permission to fire the ships on the quay and was refused it. His Highness, it seemed, was intent on the minimum of destruction. But petards had been sent for to blow the gates of the Brandon Fort, and the Cornish were preparing to reinforce them; and Colonel Bellasyse, they were told, had taken the Frome Gate. In short, the day was almost theirs.

More than almost. High in the castle, Nathaniel Fiennes was facing both the folly of trying to hold a not entirely sympathetic city once its defences were breached, and the fact that his losses were already heavy. It was time to save what he could. His mouth full of bitter aloes, he ordered a drummer out to ask Rupert for a ceasefire and parley.

It was over. Bristol had fallen.

Luciano sat on the quayside, his hands loose and not quite steady between his knees. The silence, now that the guns had stopped, seemed less peaceful than uncanny – or as if one had gone suddenly deaf.

Selim watched him for a moment and then, holding out the shining ribbon of his sword, said, 'Take it. It is clean now.'

Luciano looked at the slender blade. As Selim said, it was clean. Gripping the nausea hard inside him, he held out his hands to receive it.

Everyone said the terms of surrender contained no surprises. Colonel Fiennes lost his artillery, ammunition and colours, and all the usual clauses were inserted for the protection of the city's inhabitants. Nothing out of the ordinary . . . and nothing to account for the colonel choosing to march his men out a good two hours before the appointed time on Thursday morning and before the Royalist officers were present to restrain their men from jeering and plunder.

'Where were thou at Runaway Hill – and where art thou now, O Lord?' came the impiously mocking cry as fights erupted over sundry articles.

'Stragglers and sharks,' remarked de Gomme, emerging at Luciano's elbow. 'And some, perhaps, of our boys that were ill used at Reading.'

Luciano said nothing but merely waited in silence until Rupert and Maurice arrived to restore order with the flat of their blades so that the exodus could proceed with dignity. Then, leaving the Cavaliers to enjoy their conquest, he slipped discreetly into the heart of the city.

Wealthy, respected and secure, Alderman Ahiram Webb was by no means sorry to see Colonel Fiennes kicked out of Bristol. Not that this meant his sympathies lay with the King – for Ahiram was a Puritan, of sorts. It was good for business and made it unnecessary for his wife and daughters to squander a fortune on furbelows. He'd decided that there was a lot to be said for Puritanism – provided one didn't carry it too far. And therefore he would have felt more comfortable actively supporting the Parliament, had it not been for the indisputable fact that the Parliament's occupation of Bristol hadn't done much for trade.

In addition to owning the largest soap-works in the city, Ahiram also had two fine new merchant-ships in the Kingsroad harbour. He was grateful to the Robber Prince for not burning them. He'd be even more grateful if the King – who, lacking London, needed the good city of Bristol very much indeed – were to show his appreciation with a little commercial encouragement. Such as a monopoly on the manufacture of soap, for example. And so, with this winsome possibility in mind, it wasn't hard to put a smile on his face and join the Common Council in welcoming the victors to the city. Indeed, the only thing he wouldn't do was have soldiers billeted in his house. After all, he had two young daughters to think of – and his sons had yet to learn the art of flexible Puritanism.

July became August while Rupert and Lord Hertford squabbled over the governorship of Bristol. Then, amidst bells, bonfires and banquets, King Charles arrived in person for a state visit. And though he didn't fulfil Ahiram's dreams on the subject of soap, he did something almost as good. He issued a charter making Bristol the staple port for the Levant, Eastland and Russia Companies instead of London. Ahiram was ecstatic. He pored over charts and ledgers and went about his daily business, both public and private, with increased confidence and vigour. He did not notice the discreet, hawk-nosed individual who shadowed his every step. There was, of course, no reason why he should.

He first encountered the man del Santi at a meeting with certain other merchants who, like himself, were eager to link their fortunes to the great companies. Ahiram began by wondering who had invited him, and then ceased to care. The Italian, like a gift from God, was precisely the expert they needed. Clearly and concisely, he expounded on cargoes, routes and charter arrangements, and ended by recommending an approach to the Levant Company for the sake of its lower risk potential and the substantial profits to be made in silk, spices and cedar-wood.

Before leaving the gathering for a very different sort of appointment near the docks, Ahiram invited the signor to sup with him the following evening, and was pleased when the fellow accepted. It would do no harm to steal a bit of a march on the others, after all – and who knew what might not come of it?

What came of it was that the Italian spent the evening charming Ahiram's wife and daughters, listening attentively to his sons' maunderings on the intricacies of soap-making, and admiring the size and style of their home. On the matter of trading in the Levant, however, he proved maddeningly elusive. And when, at the end of the evening, Ahiram tried to force the issue, the signor said blandly, 'Forgive me, but I never mix business with pleasure or embark on a new venture without first getting to know my potential partner. I'm sure you understand.' He paused, the dark eyes pleasantly inscrutable. 'But perhaps you'd care to dine with me at my inn one evening next week. Shall we say Thursday?'

'Well?' demanded Luciano crisply when, much later that night, Selim returned from a certain house on the quay-side. 'Is it a brothel?'

Selim spat hard and accurately into the empty grate. 'Yes. And more.'

'What, then? Opium?'

'Opium – bhang – hashish. And children.' There was a

409

long, significant silence as black eyes locked with black. Then, 'The soap-maker,' finished Selim, with contempt, 'likes young boys.'

'How young?'

'Nine – ten years, perhaps. Everyone in the house knows him. Always, without fail, he goes there on Thursday nights and takes a private upstairs room where a boy and the poppy are awaiting him. Then he leaves, as I have told you, so that he may get home before it is light.'

Luciano loosed a long, noiseless breath. 'That's that, then. You've done well.'

'Is he the one?' asked Selim, hopefully.

'I doubt it. A man stupid enough to dull his wits with opium isn't likely to be bright enough to evolve the kind of tortuous plot that killed my father; moreover, though in certain circles whoring is considered socially acceptable, pederasty is not. So it rather looks as if, like someone before us, we've uncovered friend Webb's dirty little secret.'

'Oh.' Selim was disappointed. 'But you will still punish him?'

'What do you think?' A bitter smile twisted Luciano's mouth. 'Why else am I here?'

While for two men in Bristol the week dragged by on leaden feet, the King proclaimed his devotion to the Protestant religion and offered a free pardon to all those misled by his enemies, with the result that Poole, Portland, Dorchester and Weymouth all promptly surrendered and Royalist risings in Kent took possession of Sevenoaks, Tonbridge and the energetic person of Sir Harry Vane. Mr Pym, meanwhile, added to the gloom in war-shortaged London by putting a purchase tax on goods which he considered did not constitute any of life's necessities; though, since these included beer, wine and sugar, few people applauded his choice. And, then, bowing to the demands of Lord Manchester (and Lord Manchester's importunate but increasingly successful Eastern Association colleague, Oliver Cromwell), he set about raising the seven thousand Horse that would replace those lost by Essex, Waller and Fairfax.

It was probably a smart move – but with the King's army successful just about everywhere and Pym's popularity registering at several points below zero, Richard Maxwell was tempted to wonder if anything could redeem the Parliament's present catastrophic position or mend the ever-widening divisions at Westminster. Essex had followed up his resignation threat with the suggestion that negotiations be reopened with the King which – though it cheered up Lord Holland's Peace Party – annoyed the war extremists into voting Waller an independent command and thus infuriated the sorely tried Essex still further. Why, he demanded, were the needs of his own plague-stricken army continually ignored while the general who had managed to lose an army at Roundway Down was instantly given a new one?

He had a point. But more important as far as Pym was concerned was the need to stop the squabbles and restore confidence in the Lord-General before his support for the Peace Party became any stronger than it already was. Over the torment in his stomach and beginning to suspect how gravely ill he really was, Pym cast about for some means of stabilising his rocking ship – and found it in the extremists' dire mismanagement of the new levies. Within no time at all, Waller was on the wane, Essex back in favour, and the peace proposals narrowly defeated; while, in the City, ministers delivered pro-war sermons and crowds converged on Westminster shouting, 'No peace!' Pym reflected on the fragility of public opinion and was glad that he had other, more substantial irons in the fire.

In Bristol, Luciano del Santi read *Mercurius Aulicus*'s angrily satiric account of Royalist prisoners being held in ships on the Thames prior to being sold as slaves in the Indies, and of the savage dispersal of a group of poor women pleading for peace outside Westminster. Never having had a very high opinion of English justice, it did not surprise him – but neither did it touch him. He had, after all, other fish to fry.

On Thursday evening Alderman Webb presented himself

punctually at the Italian's door and was cordially received. The table, already set for dinner, bristled with the inn's best glassware and pewter and, after a welcoming cup of particularly fine claret, Ahiram found himself sitting down to a well-chosen menu of sea-trout with walnuts, beef and oyster patties and a tenderly roasted goose. Restraining himself admirably through the first course, he waited until the second appeared before launching determinedly into the business which had brought him there; and then was both surprised and gratified by the direct and staggeringly practical answers he received.

His own plans meticulously laid, Luciano ate little, drank even less and was quite content to tell Mr Webb everything he wanted to know whilst keeping his glass unobtrusively filled. On this occasion, the key lay in perfect timing . . . and his initial goal was to get the bastard relaxed but not cup-shot. Then he could begin.

Time passed. Servants cleared the board of all save some fruit and a squat, green bottle of brandy, and Ahiram, filling and lighting a long, clay pipe, embarked confidentially on an equally long tale of certain slightly shady but highly profitable business deals. Luciano listened with apparent interest whilst watching the other man out of hooded eyes. And finally, when the saga drew to a close, he said mildly, 'We all do what we must. The art of success is in relegating sentiment to its proper place and seizing life's opportunities with both hands. I, for example, could put you in contact with a family of Genoese bankers and merchants whose influence and goodwill could prove invaluable to your new ventures . . . but I doubt you would consent to ally yourself with them.' He paused briefly. 'Their name, you see, is Falcieri.'

'Falcieri?' repeated the alderman vaguely. And then, sitting up, '*Falcieri?*'

'Quite. They had, I believe, a kinsman who went to the scaffold here in England on a charge of treason.'

'Did – did they?'

Luciano sighed. 'Let us not play games, Mr Webb. You, of all men, know that they did – for you had a hand in the business yourself, did you not?' A faint smile curled his mouth but left his eyes untouched. 'I'm afraid I took advantage of my position within the Court to gain a brief glimpse of the trial record.'

'I . . . see.' Ahiram looked half blank, half wary. 'So you know all about it, then.'

'More or less.' Luciano absorbed the fact that Webb seemed unaware that the trial record had lain for years in the fat hands of Samuel Fisher and said coolly, 'I haven't, however, mentioned it to the Falcieri – mainly because they care little for the events of so many years ago and also because it is my impression that Signor Alessandro was either a fool, a scapegoat or just plain unlucky. No doubt you – if you felt so inclined – could tell me which.'

Ahiram thought about it. 'Why?' he said. 'Why do you want to know?'

Luciano shrugged slightly. 'My inquisitive nature? A certain curiosity as to how Vittorio Falcieri's brother came to end on the gallows? Or perhaps a simple desire to find out why a man such as yourself should have any part in so unsavoury an affair. Any or all. Take your pick.'

'It was all a very long time ago,' temporised Ahiram. Now that the first shock of hearing that name again had begun to wear off, he found himself feeling pleasantly mellow once more. There was no danger here that he could see. The fellow was just indulging in a little scandal-mongering, that was all . . . coupled probably with a perfectly natural wish to pick up a potentially useful hold on this Genoese banker he'd spoken of. You couldn't blame him for that. Such scraps of knowledge often came in very handy.

Reaching absently for the bottle, Ahiram refilled his glass. There didn't seem any harm in telling del Santi what he wanted to know – or some of it, in any case. After all, who was likely to be interested in a seventeen-year-old trial these days? On the other hand, it would be stupid to break a seventeen-year-old silence unless there was some advantage in it.

Meeting the enigmatic dark eyes across the table, he said slowly, 'This banker-cum-merchant you mentioned –

413

Falcieri's brother, is it? How wide are his interests?'

'Wide enough. In two generations the family's come from the back-streets to owning half of Genoa. Their banking house has offices in Florence and Venice; they have a merchant fleet of some half-dozen ships trading throughout the Levant; and they make jewellery and gold plate for most of the noble houses in Europe – not excluding the Medici and the Vatican.' Luciano smiled meditatively at his untouched glass. 'It's just a pity that the circumstances are so – unfortunate, for my own liaison with Falcieri has been immensely rewarding. However. Naturally one has a care for one's country. And you can't possibly wish to associate with the family of a known traitor – no matter how powerful they may be.' He looked up and met the alderman's eye blandly. 'As I said. A pity.'

It was, as he had known perfectly well, too big a carrot for a man like Webb to resist. Smiling still, he waited.

'All right.' A current of strange excitement ran through Ahiram's veins and he was almost glad he'd been offered the right inducement, for the temptation to tell had been nibbling at him for the last ten minutes. 'All right. But it's to go no further, you understand? If you repeat it outside this room, I'll simply deny the whole thing and it will be your word against mine.'

Luciano's brows rose. 'Of course.'

'Very well, then – I'll tell you.' Ahiram drew a long breath and prepared, all unknowingly, to dive head first into the Italian's web. 'Alessandro Falcieri was no more a traitor than I am. He'd just made one enemy too many – and the wrong one at that. Someone wanted him out of the way without taking the risk of murdering him – so they got the law to do it for them on a false charge.' He leaned back and folded triumphant arms. 'What do you think of that?'

'I don't know,' replied Luciano, gratifyingly amazed. 'I'm tempted to ask if you're sure . . . but since you yourself gave evidence at the trial, one presumes that you must be. It does, however, seem somewhat incredible.'

'I daresay. But it's true enough. As far as the evidence

414

goes, I – well, I was told what to say. And if *I* was, it stands to reason that the others probably were too. Not that I asked, you'll understand. Some things are better left alone.'

'Oh – quite. So . . . you were actually told what to say? By whom?'

'I don't know and never did.'

'Come now, Mr Webb – you surely don't expect me to believe that?' Luciano laughed softly. 'You *must* have known – else how could you have become involved?'

'I – had a letter. An anonymous letter.'

'And blithely perjured yourself on the strength of it? It doesn't sound very likely, does it? Unless . . . unless, of course, you were also very substantially paid. Or being black-mailed.'

Ahiram gave a convulsive twitch and reached for his glass. 'Let's just say I had my reasons,' he said sharply. 'But what I'm telling you is that somebody – perhaps one of the other three – wanted Falcieri dead and had the means to make the rest of us cooperate.' He took another drink. 'The fellow was nothing to me, after all. Just some scurvy money-lender. And you do what you have to, don't you? Said so yourself.'

'Yes. So I did.' Deep within the dark eyes lurked a cold, disquieting gleam, but the beautiful voice remained smooth as ever. 'I'm sure you'll find it worth remembering.'

'Eh?' Ahiram suddenly recognised that he was begin-ning to feel slightly fuddled. He pushed his glass aside and stood up, saying, 'I've done well, you know. Built up my father's soap-works till it's the biggest in the city – expanded into shipping – become a respected figure in the commun-ity. And next year I plan to be mayor.'

'My congratulations.'

'You think I won't do it? I will. I can do anything I set my mind to. Always have.' He peered down at the Italian. 'I'm a rich man, you know. Rich and respected.'

'So you said. But why tell me?'

'So you'll understand. You help me – I'll help you. Simple. And no questions asked on either side. Falcieri's brother may own Genoa – and maybe he *could* do me some good. But I've got Bristol there.' He held out his cupped hand and then closed his fingers hard. 'And if you want to set up in business here, you'll need me. Think about it.'

'Think about it, Mr Webb? I don't need to think about it.' Graceful and deadly as a panther, Luciano came out of his chair. 'I wouldn't trust you to count the loose coins in my pocket.'

'Wh-what?' Ahiram blinked. 'I don't understand.'

'No. You're not very bright, are you?' There was steel, now, beneath the honey. 'Permit me to introduce myself. Luciano Falcieri del Santi. The scurvy money-lender's son.'

Ahiram's skin turned patchily white and, for a moment, he looked as though he might faint. Then he said feebly, 'I – I – what do you want?'

'What do you think? I wanted to hear you confess.'

'You *knew*?' And then, frantically, 'It won't help you. I said I'd deny it and I will. Your word against mine. You can't touch me.'

'I haven't the remotest wish to touch you. You are scum, Mr Webb – and hypocritical scum, at that. But you're right, of course. The law won't help me. And you need not fear the assassin's knife – for, if that were my way, you would already be dead.' As swiftly as he had arisen, he dropped neatly back into his seat. 'Get out.'

Ahiram reached for his hat and then stopped nervously, as if fearing some catch. He said, 'You're letting me go?'

'Before you turn my stomach. Yes.' The implacable, derisive black eyes burned through him. 'Go. We shan't meet again. But I think you will remember me.'

Standing at his window, Luciano watched Webb emerge into the street below; and then waited until another figure appeared in his wake. Precisely as arranged, Selim looked up to receive his master's signal and, on being given it, set off noiselessly to follow the alderman. Luciano sat down by the hearth and prepared to wait.

Twenty-five minutes later the door swung open on the Turk, faintly breathless but charged with satisfaction.

'Well?' said Luciano. 'Did he go?'

'He went – and is there now,' came the simple reply.

Luciano closed his eyes for a moment. It had been the only possible flaw; the one thing outside his control. But he'd gambled that, after his own revelations, Webb would want the opium quite badly . . . and apparently he'd won.

Opening his eyes again, he said flatly, 'On to Phase Two, then. And remember what I said. It's to look worse than it is. More alarm than destruction. Then get back to the quay to arrange matters there.'

'Everything is taken care of, *hakim*. It's no problem,' said Selim. And with a rare, immensely cheerful smile, went out.

Luciano remained by the hearth. He looked at the brandy but did not touch it. It wasn't time. Later perhaps, if all went well. He thought of Webb, saving his skin at the expense of another's and admitting it without a trace of shame; proclaiming his respectability while he debauched small boys in secret. Then, his eyes open, he looked back down the years on the things he himself had done and wondered, cynically, how much further he could go before arriving at the point where he was no better.

'*Vengeance is mine, sayeth the Lord*. But there again, the Lord helps those who help themselves. So who am I to judge? Am I better than those I seek? Perhaps . . . perhaps not. But at least my motives are worthier.'

He could hear the sound of feet on the stairs and then a fist hammered urgently on his door. Drawing a long breath, Luciano rose from his place and coolly bade his visitors enter.

Three men tumbled into the room. He surveyed them impassively. Both of Webb's sons and another merchant of the Common Council. It was even better than he had expected. Selim had done well.

He said in a tone of courteous surprise, 'I appreciate the honour, gentlemen – but am at a loss to account for it. Is there something I may do for you?'

'My father,' said the older Webb boy baldly. 'He was

417

supposed to be dining with you, wasn't he? Where is he?'

'Gone. As you can see.'

'But he *was* here?' It was Webb's friend, Joseph Wood, who spoke. 'When did he leave?'

'More than an hour ago,' replied Luciano. 'Forgive me for asking – but is there some difficulty?'

'The manufactory's on fire,' blurted out the younger boy. He was no more than sixteen years old and his name, so far as Luciano could remember, was something like Ezekiel. 'The office is ablaze – all the ledgers and order-books and so on. It's being put out but Father ought to be there. *Where is he?*'

'I believe – at a certain establishment near the quay.'

'Do you know the address?'

Luciano smiled soothingly. 'Why, yes,' he said. 'As it happens, I do.' And softly, in as few words as possible, he gave it to them.

Nine

On an unseasonably cold day towards the end of
the month, Luciano rode back into London and found
people looking more cheerful than he'd expected – considering Parliament's recent defeats and the shortages of
cheese, grain and vegetables. He also found, on entering
his own premises on Cheapside, that the house was full of
whores.

'Well, what did you expect?' demanded Gwynneth.
'London's no place for a brothel these days, let alone one
as cosmopolitan as ours. I'm sick of having the windows
broken and things thrown at me in the street. What's more
– with trade so poor – the girls are sick of it too.'

Luciano looked for a vacant chair and failed to find one.
He said, 'I'd no idea things were that bad. You should have
told me.'

'And how was I to do that? I haven't clapped eyes on
you for the best part of five months – and the last time I
did, you were moving so fast that the dust didn't settle for
a week. So I've taken matters into my own hands and shut
up shop.'

'And here you all are. How nice. Giacomo must have
thought it was his birthday. And Gino . . . and Felix. Oh
God. Where *is* Felix?'

'I haven't the remotest idea,' said Gwynneth irritably.
'And we only came yesterday. You'll also notice, if you take
the trouble to look, that Zorah, Firuze and Christina are
missing.'

'Are they?' Luciano looked round at the five other
exquisite faces inhabiting his parlour and felt the first

quiverings of hysteria. 'It seems a shame to break up the set. What happened to them?'

'They had other offers.'

'Lucky girls. And the rest?'

'Have their own plans. *Why are you laughing?*'

'I'm sorry,' he gasped. 'I was just wondering how I'm going to explain this to Richard if he should happen to call. Or perhaps he'd l-like to put in a bid. Then again we might use the situation to boost business downstairs. Buy a brooch for your wife and get a free—' He stopped and raised a brimming gaze to Gwynneth's disapproving one. Then, drawing a long breath, 'All right. It's not funny. So tell me what you want me to do?'

'Take Bridie, Ghislaine, Marie-Claude and Elena to Oxford. They want to set up their own house there.'

'I commend their enterprise. But why do *I* have to take them?'

'Because,' answered Gwynneth patiently, 'they need an escort. And you're the only man we know who seems to have the freedom of every town in the land.'

'Ah.' This, unfortunately, made sense and finally killed any desire to laugh. He'd only just arrived back from Bristol and, aside from the mountain of work that he knew would be waiting for him – and the need to earn some money – there were various other matters he had to attend to. A trip to Oxford, therefore, was the very last thing he needed. He said crisply, 'All right. I take your point. But what about Aysha – and yourself?'

For the first time since he'd came in, Gwynneth looked less than composed. She said, 'Aysha wants to stay with Selim. As for myself, I – I'm open to suggestions.'

Or to one in particular, thought Luciano grimly. And recognised that, if she hadn't allowed herself to become overfond of him, he probably wouldn't have been averse to making it for the sake, just sometimes, of not being alone. As it was, however, it seemed hardly fair.

'I'm sure Selim will be delighted,' he replied at length. 'And regarding your own future – I'm sure if we put our heads together that we'll come up with something.' He looked at the four bright, interested faces. 'Very well, ladies. Pack up your perfumes and saddle the camels. We'll leave for Oxford in the morning.'

Felix drifted back part-way through the evening and admitted to having taken leave of absence to visit his sister and brother-in-law. He was completely unabashed and even faintly accusing.

'I was sick of kicking my heels,' he said. 'There's scarcely any work and you're never here. I'm never going to learn anything at this rate. And now I suppose you'll be taking the girls to Oxford?'

'With regret – yes.' Luciano looked at him. 'Disappointed?'

'Not especially, although the Irish one is quite nice. I just want to know whether, when you come back, you might find the time to instruct me in the art of enamelling. If, of course, it's no trouble.'

There was a look in the clear grey eyes that reminded the Italian sharply of Kate. He sighed, assured his apprentice in caustic tones that he would be happy to do his poor best, and then decided to cut his losses and go to bed.

Gwynneth was in it, her dark hair loose against the alabaster-pale skin of her shoulders.

Luciano stopped dead and then closed the door with a click. 'Don't tell me,' he said gently. 'What else did I expect?'

She looked at him gravely and let the sheet slip a few inches. 'Do you want me to go?'

'Where to? Giacomo?' He advanced to the foot of the bed. The candlelight accentuated the hollows at the base of her throat and bathed the soft curves of her breasts. He supposed, vaguely, that he oughtn't to offer any encouragement. On the other hand, it had been a long time; and once more couldn't make much difference. 'Or perhaps he's already suited?'

'Elena,' she replied, her voice as calm as infinite care could make it. If he knew how much she wanted him, he would go. 'This was the only bed I could find. And I rather hoped that – without prejudice and just for tonight – you wouldn't mind sharing it.'

'I see.' Thoughtfully and without haste, he moved to her side. 'And is that all?'

'That would depend. What else did you have in mind?'

'This,' said Luciano, cupping her warm flesh in his palms. 'And this . . . and this.'

Gwynneth took her time about replying. Then, as lightly as she was able, she said, 'It's an idea, I suppose.'

'I thought you'd like it.'

His hands were visiting her skin with exquisite artistry. She had never known him less than courteous. She only wished she knew the way to bind him to her. Before her breathing became completely disrupted, she said, 'There is, however, just one thing you might do for me.'

'And that is?'

'Take off your boots,' she said. And had the satisfaction of having him come to her laughing.

In the end, because of the unlikelihood of one man conveying four inviting armfuls unmolested to Oxford or anywhere else in these troubled times, Luciano decided to separate Selim temporarily from Aysha and take him with him. Then, on the brink of departure, Felix presented himself booted and cloaked on the doorstep and announced that – having nothing better to do – he'd quite like to go along for the ride.

'Why not?' responded Luciano sardonically. 'Let's all go. Let's take some cakes and ale and plenty of *joie de vivre*. Does anybody know any jolly songs?'

The journey was neither better nor worse than he expected. The roads were fairly empty of traffic but they were challenged three times in the last ten miles. Rupert – or at least, one assumed it was Rupert – was plainly giving security a high priority, but with Rupert's safe-conduct in one's pocket, it did not present a problem.

The city was heaving with people. Luciano sighed and then applied himself to finding beds for seven people. It was, not surprisingly, impossible. He eventually found the girls a pair of rooms from which a gentleman whose credit had finally run out was in process of being evicted, and then resigned himself to sharing with Selim and Felix a squalid attic in an equally squalid tavern. The girls professed themselves perfectly suited and accepted the purse he gave them with becoming reluctance. Luciano bade them a graceful farewell, told Selim to show Felix the city without letting him out of his sight, and then spent three fruitless hours searching for Liam Aherne.

He eventually learned that Ivo Courtenay had returned to Ireland alone and that Aherne was probably somewhere about – though no one seemed to know where; and, after drawing a blank in a dozen likely locations, Luciano came to the inevitable conclusion that the fellow wasn't in Oxford at all just at present. He was probably – if what Richard had told him back in June was anything to go by – at Thorne Ash visiting Gianetta.

Well, if that were the case, it would just have to wait. Right now, Luciano's most pressing need was to attend to his business – from which, as Felix had quite rightly pointed out, he had been absent far too long of late and which would require some adroit handling if he were not to find himself unable to meet next spring's obligation in Genoa. He therefore returned unenthusiastically to his attic, listened with surprising patience to Felix's animated description of the swordfight he and Selim had witnessed in Magdalen Grove, and then lay down to sleep – fully dressed in the feeble hope of escaping the fleas.

They arrived back in Cheapside the following evening to find the door bolted against them. Luciano frowned a little and instructed Selim to hammer on it with his fist.

'While the cat's away,' grinned Felix. 'They're all having a holiday of their own.'

Luciano did not reply. Gino's face appeared briefly at an upper window and, in due course, they heard the sound of bolts being withdrawn. Then the door swung wide.

Except where it was marked with cuts and bruises, Gino's face was ghastly white and there was evidence of bandaging about his ribs.

'Thank God,' he breathed in Italian. 'Thank God you have come.'

'What's happened?' Luciano was over the threshold in two strides. 'Where's Giacomo?'

'Upstairs. We've had . . . there was a burglary.'

'God's teeth!' remarked Felix, impressed. 'If this is what you look like, I'd hate to see the other fellow.' And then, differently, 'The workshop. What have they taken?'

Luciano was already half-way up the stairs with Selim in hot pursuit. The door to the parlour stood wide and, for the space of a breath, Luciano hesitated. Then he stepped into the shambles within.

The furniture was too solid to have been reduced to matchwood, but there wasn't a piece of it left undamaged and someone appeared to have taken an axe to his desk. Cushions had been split open, papers scattered, glasses smashed; and in the midst of it, Giacomo lay propped on a half-splintered settle with Aysha in close attendance and one hand to the blood-soaked bandages at his shoulder.

Aysha looked up, her face streaked and swollen with crying and hurtled across the room to cast herself on Selim's chest. Luciano dropped on one knee beside Giacomo and said quietly, 'Tell me.'

'They – they came in the night.' Wincing and grey-faced, Giacomo replied in his own language. 'Three of them. Gino and I, we did what we could – but they were too much for us.' He paused and then, with an effort, went on. 'I don't know what they have taken. A little money, perhaps. You can see what they did to the desk. But it is worse than that.' Another pause. 'I don't know how to tell you.'

'As quickly and simply as possible.'

Giacomo closed his eyes. 'Gwynneth,' he said, baldly. 'She's dead.'

It was the very last thing Luciano had expected. His insides turned suddenly very cold and the air seared his lungs. Then, in a voice that seemed to come from a long way off, he said, 'Where is she?'

'In – in the spare bedchamber. Gino carried her up. I – we thought that was the best place.' There were shining

424

rivers on the contorted face. 'She tried to go for help and they pushed her down the stairs. They pushed her downstairs, the bastards. There was no need for that.'

Gwynneth lay, silent and cold, on the red-covered bed. Someone had combed her hair and arranged her robe in decorous folds and laid coins on her eyes. She was unmarked, for a broken neck doesn't show. She looked like a stranger.

Luciano stood by the curtained window, looking at her. His veins were frozen and his nerves raw. But for him, she wouldn't have been there. But for him, she wouldn't have died.

Alerted by Felix, Richard came. He said simply, 'I'm sorry. I barely knew her, of course – but I know how you must feel.'

'Do you?' Luciano looked through him in the manner which, in less than twenty-four hours, the other members of his household were already finding hideously familiar. 'I wish I did.'

Richard contemplated Luciano in silence for a moment. He looked alarmingly fine-drawn and remote . . . and something else that Richard found he didn't particularly care for. He said, 'Violence of this kind is never acceptable – but unfortunately these things happen. So what is it you're not telling me?'

Luciano's skin became, if possible, even more colourless, and for the first time the dark eyes focused on Richard's face. Then he said flatly, 'They didn't take anything. Not even a piece of gold wire. Gwynneth died for nothing.'

'Are you sure?'

'Perfectly. What's more – since they chose the night the house was at its emptiest – it seems that the thing was quite carefully planned.'

'You're suggesting,' said Richard slowly, 'that these weren't any ordinary thieves.'

'That is precisely what I'm suggesting.'

Richard thought about it. Then, 'What happened in Bristol?'

'Ahiram Webb was caught in bed with a ten-year-old boy and a quantity of raw opium – thus becoming the city's latest scandal. And before you ask,' said Luciano, 'I didn't arrange the scenario – just the manner of its exposure. But I doubt Mr Webb will get to be mayor after all.'

'Could he have been behind this?' Richard gestured to the superficially tidied but ruined parlour.

'It's possible but unlikely. His story was the same as that of Ferrars. Someone blackmailed him – presumably about his dubious personal habits.'

'So where does that leave you?'

Luciano shrugged to hide the fact that he was shivering. 'Precisely where I was before. In search of Robert Brandon. Who else is there?'

'Samuel Fisher? Oh – I don't mean that he had your house ransacked. But he sold you the trial record for – what? A few hundred?'

'Not quite. A particularly fine emerald ring of mine. You may recall it.'

Richard did and his brows rose.

'All right. So it wasn't cheap. But what he sold to you, he may equally have sold to someone else.'

'Who'd want it? The only ones who care are those who know anyway,' said Luciano. 'To my mind, there are only two possibilities. Either Brandon is the man who blackmailed the other three and is now understandably anxious to stop me getting to him; or there's a fifth man whose identity I can't even begin to guess at, who isn't sure how much I know. In either case, the only way to find out is to see Brandon.'

'You don't,' suggested Richard, 'foresee a small snag?'

'I foresee half a dozen,' came the edgy reply. 'If Brandon knows what I'm doing, I'm unlikely to learn anything from him – even if I knew where to find him – which, of course, I don't. And if there's an unknown *deus ex machina* watching over me, my first move towards Brandon could occasion either his death or mine.' He stopped and looked at Richard out of cold, purposeful eyes. 'But forewarned is forearmed, as they say. And what choice do I have? I can't stop now.'

They buried Gwynneth on a cold, wet day when, all over London, bells were ringing to celebrate Lord Essex's successful relief of poor besieged Gloucester. It was, of course, the need to save Gloucester that had inspired the new cheerfulness and determination – and now both were gloriously vindicated. To Luciano, however, the general rejoicing seemed almost a personal affront. He went straight from the graveside to lock himself in the workshop for three hours, refusing both to open the door and to speak to anyone through it. Then he came out and started setting up the lines of inquiry which he hoped would eventually lead to Robert Brandon.

By the middle of September he had managed to collect most of the previous quarter's interest payments, terminated a few old bonds and accepted certain new ones from gentlemen who were willing and able to leave items of value in his keeping by way of security. He had also begun making a small but select collection of intricately crafted pieces which would find a ready market in France and Italy next spring. Felix was overjoyed. Luciano was glad that somebody was.

The Brandon trails started leading to the usual brick walls. There was a Robert Brandon in Sussex who turned out to be at least ten years too young, and a Robert Brandon in Kent who had spent the whole of 1626 fighting in the Low Countries. Luciano stifled his impatience and had Selim follow up each possible clue. He also took every precaution he could think of to guard his own back. And finally, in reluctant desperation, he crossed the river to Lambeth and tried to see Samuel Fisher.

He was denied entry. Whatever the state of the house inside, the front door was solid – and locked. Eventually, however, the same slatternly maidservant who'd admitted him before stuck her head out of an upper casement and delivered the information that the Justice wasn't receiving visitors.

'Not even,' said Luciano, 'ones who bring him gold?'

The girl's head vanished and was replaced by that of the Justice himself, swollen and pendulous as ever.

'Oh – it's you, is it? The hunchback. Well, you can take yourself off. I've nothing to say to you.'

Luciano stood amongst the weeds, looking up. Stuck incongruously half-way down Mr Fisher's left little finger, his own emerald winked mockingly back at him. He said, carefully, 'Five minutes of your time, on a matter of contractual law. And you'll be well paid.'

'With that piddling little purse you're holding?' wheezed the old man. 'Forget it. You've got nothing I want. Now clear off and don't come back.'

The window slammed shut. For a moment Luciano considered the wisdom of attempting to break in, and then decided against it. It hadn't come to that yet . . . and it wouldn't help him to be taken up for housebreaking.

He was half-way home again before it occurred to him that Justice Fisher hadn't just refused his purse out of scorn for its size. He'd refused it because he was frightened.

Two days later Richard came to see him and, without any kind of preamble, said, 'I've found a Robert Brandon for you – though whether he's the one you want remains to be seen. He sat in the 1629 Parliament – which might make him roughly the right sort of age – and he lives in Yorkshire.'

Too accustomed to false trails, Luciano remained supremely unexcited. '*Where* in Yorkshire?'

'Ah. Well, that's the problem. I can't find anyone who knew him well enough to say.'

There was a small, telling silence. Then Luciano said gently, 'I don't want to appear ungrateful, Richard, but Yorkshire is one of the largest counties in England.'

'I know.'

'And one of the most remote.'

'I know that too.'

'Added to which – having freedom from arrest – members of the House don't usually need to exterminate those they owe money to.'

'Quite.' A smile lurked somewhere at the back of

428

Richard's eyes. 'So, all in all, it's just as well you can't travel north just yet.'

Luciano looked at him. 'I can't?'

'No. You,' announced Richard, 'have got to go to Thorne Ash.'

Silence. Then, 'It doesn't,' remarked Luciano at length, 'sound very likely.'

'Then I can only assume that Gianetta's stopped writing to you.'

'Oh – that.' Luciano dropped neatly into a chair. 'Hardly. There were two effusions waiting for me when I got back from Bristol and another's arrived since. They all say basically the same thing. The sun shines out of Liam Aherne's backside and she's determined to marry him. I've heard it all before. And though I realise I'll have to meet the fellow sooner or later and either prise them apart or give my blessing, the matter's hardly urgent, is it? Unless Mistress Dorothy is tired of having him underfoot?'

'It's not that. Dolly writes that his behaviour is impeccable and she never saw two people better suited. No. It's rather more serious than that. The Earl of Ormonde has made a truce with the rebel Irish.'

'Hell.' Luciano sat up. 'So Mr Aherne will want to go home and Gianetta will want to go with him.'

'And you,' nodded Richard, 'are going to Thorne Ash. But don't worry. If Kate attacks you with a meat-cleaver, I promise to stand by you.'

The dark brows rose. 'You're absenting yourself from the House?'

'And giving myself time to decide whether or not to return,' came the calm and wholly astonishing reply.

The silence this time reached epic proportions. Then, 'Why?' asked Luciano.

'Because I'm not at all sure I'm prepared to take the Covenant,' said Richard. All traces of levity had vanished. 'But perhaps I'd better start at the beginning?'

'Perhaps you had.' Luciano rose and reached for the wine-jug. 'I take it the House is proposing an alliance with the Scots?'

'Yes. Small wonder, is it? Our high command is full of bickering and back-biting and, aside from managing to hold on to Gloucester, our armies have had no successes worth mentioning since the end of May. Until yesterday, that is; and yesterday – so the House was told this morning – we won our first major field engagement in over three months at Newbury. But by then, of course, Pym was already in negotiation with the Scots.'

Luciano handed him a cup of wine. 'All's fair in love and war? If the King can raise Irish troops, Parliament can raise Scottish ones?'

'Partly. There are other factors, too. The fact that the war has already dragged on for a year and could last another; the defeat of Fairfax in the North; the recent call for peace from the Lords; and the divisive nature of the various factions that are beginning to rear their ugly heads.' Richard paused and took a pull at his wine. 'In practical terms, the alliance makes perfect sense. But what troubles me is the price the Scots are putting on it and the direction in which it's leading us. It's not that long since the Scots went to war with the King for trying to force Laud's prayer book on them. Now we – and everyone who holds a command under the Parliament – are required to sign a document that is essentially Presbyterian. And I, for one, can't see where the difference lies.'

Luciano stirred thoughtfully. 'What does the Covenant actually say?'

'"That we shall defend our religion and resist all those contrary errors and corruptions according to our vocation and to the utmost power that God hath put into our hands",' quoted Richard dryly. 'But it's not what it says that matters. It's the fact that we're cluttering what ought to be a purely political treaty with religion – and at the same time opening the way for Presbyterianism to be rammed down our throats by allowing a clause that binds us to bringing the churches of the Three Kingdoms into conformity.'

'Ah. Now that *could* be a mistake.'

'Exactly. So I'm taking a well-earned holiday in order to give the matter some thought. And you are coming with me to pronounce judgement on your sister's Irishman . . . and Felix is coming too so I can keep him under my eye.' Richard rose and drained his cup. 'I thought – unless you've any objections – that we might leave in the morning.'

At Thorne Ash, the first person to hear from sources of her own of the Royalist disaster at Newbury was Celia. She said nothing of it, however, and the rest of the household was left, as usual, to hear the news from Nathan. Dorothy tolerated his sanctimonious gloating over the heavy losses inflicted on the Cavaliers until, in precisely the same vein, he happened to mention that one of the lives lost had been that of Viscount Falkland. Then she rounded on him with suddenly open disgust and sent him off with the suggestion that next time he saw fit to exhort the Almighty he should ask for something he sorely needed: namely compassion.

It seemed no time at all since those bright, lazy days at Far Flamstead; yet now the house itself lay under threat of sequestration and, of those gathered there that summer, poor Suckling was dead and Lord Brooke – and now gentle Lucius Cary whose wife had been so kind to Eden. A small total, perhaps, when set against the national loss. But after a year of bloodshed, Dorothy found that you started to mourn only the people you knew, such as Kit Clifford and the tenants who had gone off to war with Eden but would never come back. And all the time, you wondered how many more . . . how many more before it ended?

Fortunately – before depression had time to get hold of her – Richard's arrival provided precisely the tonic she needed; and that he should have brought Felix with him was almost overwhelming.

'Oh, my dears – my dears!' She tried and nearly succeeded in hugging them both at once. 'I can't believe it. Why didn't you send us word?'

'I knew it,' said Richard gloomily. 'Our beds aren't made and there's only turnips for supper.' He looked around him. 'So much for the welcoming committee, as well. Where *is* everyone?'

'Celia's gone to Far Flamstead, Kate is in the garden, and Felicity is cosseting her beloved hens.'

'Hens?' said Felix, with interest. 'Excuse me.' And vanished.

'Some things,' said Dorothy with gratitude, watching him go, 'never change.' And then, remaining in the circle of her husband's arm, she looked challengingly at Luciano del Santi and said, 'As for Gianetta, I'm afraid she's out riding with Liam. Chaperoned by her groom, of course.'

'Of course,' he agreed with the glimmer of a smile. 'I gather that you approve of the gentleman?'

'Wholeheartedly, as it happens. But if you *really* want my opinion, it's that you've left it a bit late to form one of your own. He wants to leave for Ireland on Wednesday.'

'Accompanied, one presumes, by Gianetta.' The dark eyes surveyed her thoughtfully. 'One wonders what he was going to do if I hadn't arrived in the nick of time, as it were. Elope?'

'Well, you'd only have had yourself to blame if he had,' said Dorothy. 'Goodness only knows Gianetta has written to you often enough. Fortunately, however, Liam's principles won't permit him to run off with a girl he's not married to.'

The last words, for some reason, caused Richard and Luciano to exchange a mutually knowing glance.

'Dolly, my heart,' said Richard gently. 'What is it you're not telling us?'

She looked up at him with a suspicion of rueful laughter and said virtuously, 'I'm not sure it's for me to say.'

'Oh, I think it is,' grinned her husband. 'What have you done?'

There was a brief pause; then, 'Agreed to a wedding,' came the faintly despairing confession. 'I didn't seem to have much choice with Gianetta swearing she'd go anyway. Liam's hot on the heels of an understandably elusive Jesuit – and we sent a messenger to you, yesterday,' she finished, looking at Luciano whose expression had become somewhat strained. 'I'm sorry if you don't like it – but, as I said, you should have come before. And, quite honestly, I'd like to see you do any better.'

The amusement which had been threatening to consume Richard finally did so. He gasped, 'So would I, my love. So would I. And if he tries to tell you what a shock it's all been – don't believe him. We met your messenger on the road.'

Gardening had become Kate's latest passion. It was a pleasant change from helping Jacob with the farm and handling the estate's finances and it gave her the sometimes welcome chance to be alone. Just now she was tying up those flowers that had been dashed by the recent heavy rain and inwardly lamenting the damage done to her precious roses. She hoped they would pick up again before Liam found his priest or Gianetta might have to make do with a posy of Michaelmas daisies.

A shadow fell across her and she felt a familiar rush of irritation. Without turning her head, she said, 'Go away. I don't want to talk and I doubt if the plants will do any better for being prayed over.'

'God forbid,' responded a pleasant voice, 'that I should volunteer for the first or presume to the last. But I'll confess that I'm disappointed about the middle one.'

Kate froze and her nerves snarled into a painful tangle. She had known, ever since they sent the messenger, that he would probably come – but he was at least two days too early. Not that it should matter. She'd already had eleven months in which to plan this meeting. On the other hand, she hadn't bargained for being caught on her knees or mistakenly assuming him to be Nathan. Rising slowly, she turned to face him and felt the cord tighten. Nothing had changed; but her task, now more than ever, was not to let him see it. She said smoothly, 'Dear me. Big brother at last. Gianetta *will* be pleased.'

'And Mr Aherne?'

'Is unlikely to be intimidated. But I'll enjoy seeing you try.'

'Is that what you think I've come for?'

'Isn't it?'

433

'Not necessarily.' He paused, eyeing her reflectively. She might be dressed for gardening but her lashes were still artfully darkened and her posture was pure Whitehall. Smiling faintly, he decided to test the water. 'Are we going to continue quarrelling? Or would you not prefer – like me – to settle our differences in private?'

'You've come to offer me an apology?' marvelled Kate. 'Good heavens! But they do say, of course, that one mellows with age. Did Gianetta tell you about Kit?'

'Yes. What do you want me to say? That it made me feel worse than I already did? All right – I admit it.' He drew a short, impatient breath. 'Kate – my second sight being no better than most other people's – I did what seemed right to me at the time. If I miscalculated, I can only ask you to remember that it had been a hell of a day.'

She stared at him. He knew very well he hadn't miscalculated . . . but he was actually apologising. And for the first time that she could remember. Damn. She'd been doing so well at maintaining her guard, too. But if he thought she was going to spoil it all now, he was wrong. She summoned a gracious smile and said, 'I haven't forgotten. Very well, then. Let's cry a truce. If we're careful, we may even manage to maintain it.' She paused artistically. And then, 'I suppose Mother's told you about the wedding. Have you really not come to forbid it?'

'Not unless you're about to tell me that Mr Aherne's only after the pearls?'

If he expected her to laugh, he was disappointed. She merely shook her head and said, 'They're still buried behind the hen-coop. I suppose we ought to think of digging them up – but, truth to tell, we've had more serious things on our minds. Like how to get the priest here – and, of course, away again – without Nathan finding out. We've been unable to decide between sending him on a suitably long errand and a few poppy-seeds in his cherry cordial. But now you're here, I suppose we could just get Selim to sit on him.'

Something altered in Luciano's expression but he said only, 'You're asking if I've brought him? I haven't. He's

434

keeping an eye on things in London. Giacomo is . . . unwell.'

'Oh. I'm sorry. Not seriously, I hope?'

'He'll live,' said Luciano, rather more significantly than she realised. And then, partly in response to an earlier thought and partly to divert her, 'Have you had any problems with the Royalists in Banbury?'

'Not really. They take a percentage of our rents, of course – though not such a large one as they think they do.' Her mouth curled a little. 'They also prevent Nathan and his canting friends from getting above themselves – which has to be an advantage. And, aside from that, they leave us pretty much alone.' She tilted her chin to examine him. 'I understand that you were at the siege of Bristol. Was Francis there?'

'Yes. And survived, as far as I am aware, without a scratch.' He wondered how deep her apparently unassailable composure went. She was treating him much as a society hostess might treat a little-known guest. He found that he didn't particularly like it . . . but saw the sense, reluctantly, in not trying to change it. 'Have you seen Eden at all?'

'Not since the spring – though he wrote to Celia after Roundway Down so at least we know he was safe then.' Kate saw no reason to mention the fact that they all hoped Celia's pregnancy might bring him home quite soon. She said lightly, 'How's Felix? I don't suppose you've brought any letters from him – or Father?'

He smiled at her then and, as usual, her bones dissolved. 'No. But if you were to go into the house, I don't think you'd be disappointed.'

It took her a moment to work this out. Then, incredulously, 'They're both here with you? Truly? Then why didn't you say so in the first place?'

'Probably,' replied Luciano doucely, 'because I was waiting to be asked.'

The initial meeting of Luciano del Santi and Liam Aherne was conducted along exquisitely formal lines which gave nobody any clues about whether or not they were likely to take to one another. Then they repaired to the privacy of Richard's book-room for over an hour before inviting a distinctly frayed Gianetta to join them.

'Well?' she demanded challengingly from the door. 'Are the two of you reconciled to becoming brothers?'

From across the room, Liam gave his rare smile. 'Let's just say we understand each other, alannah. Better, perhaps, than either one of us expected.'

Gianetta looked at her brother. 'So we may be married?'

'Would you take any notice if I said no?' Luciano asked.

'Not a bit.'

'That's what I thought.' He exchanged an almost imperceptible smile with Liam. 'So it's just as well that I approve of your choice, isn't it?'

The impact of her gratitude all but overset him. Then, when she was safely established at Liam's side, he said in a rather different tone, 'I can't pretend I'm exactly ecstatic at the prospect of you taking up residence in Ireland at this time, but I'm not going to waste my breath trying to dissuade you – especially as Mr Aherne has already spent a considerable amount of time assuring me that, should the need arise, he and his followers can protect you more than adequately.' He paused and looked from the Irishman to Gianetta. 'There is, however, something else which we probably ought to talk about before you go. It concerns our father.'

Without giving any hint that he already knew that his love's late parent had gone to the scaffold, Liam said, 'Would you like me to go?'

'No,' said Gianetta, holding fast to his hand.

And, 'No,' said Luciano, a shade grimly. 'If you're going to join the family, you've a right to hear it, because it may one day concern you. All I ask is your absolute discretion.'

'It's yours.'

'Thank you.' The Italian bent his head over his hands and then looked up at his sister. He said, 'You once asked me what I was doing. And now, because it may be my last opportunity, I propose to tell you – but only so that you may know. There is no room – and nor will there ever be – for discussion.'

It was Felix who provided Kate with some of the details deliberately withheld by Luciano, when a casual inquiry into the state of Giacomo's health caused him to remark that, despite having lost so much blood and still being confined to bed, he appeared to be on the mend.

'Blood?' echoed Kate, sharply.

'From the stabbing,' nodded Felix. And then, lifting his gaze from the piece of paper on which capered a number of small figures, 'We were burgled. Didn't you know?'

'No.' Kate sat down at the other side of the table and rested her chin on her hands. 'Supposing you tell me?'

So – in as few words as possible and not forgetting to notice her expression when he spoke of Gwynneth – he did. And at the end of it all, added thoughtfully, 'It's a funny thing, though. Why break into a goldsmith's shop and then waste your time on the owner's writing desk instead of heading for the valuables? It doesn't make sense.'

There was a very peculiar look in Kate's eye and it was a long time before she spoke. Then she said slowly, 'Felix, has it ever occurred to you to wonder why Signor del Santi spends so much time running around the country?'

'Well, of course – but he's hardly likely to tell me, is he? And neither are Giacomo or Selim – or even Father, for that matter.'

'Father knows?'

'And has for ages. Hadn't you guessed?'

'Yes,' said Kate simply. 'I just wasn't sure if you knew.'

'It'd be difficult not to with the two of 'em obviously thick as thieves,' he retorted. 'I know something else, too. You may have been wondering *why* Luciano travels about so much – but I've been wondering *how*. And now I think I know.' He grinned at her. 'He's got a Royalist pass. I saw it when we went to Oxford.'

Kate's eyes widened. 'That must come in handy. Do you suppose he's got a parliamentary one as well?'

'I shouldn't be surprised. If it were anyone else, it would

be tempting to start thinking in terms of espionage . . . but Sir, of course, doesn't give a tinker's curse who wins the war.'

'So what *is* he doing?'

Felix shrugged. 'At the moment, making a few rather nice pieces to sell on his way to Genoa next spring – and looking for some fellow called Brandon.'

There was another long silence. Then Kate said calmly, 'Felix – I could murder you. How do you know?'

'I overheard something Selim said.' He addressed himself once more to his drawing. 'And I can't honestly see that it's very much help. After all, we don't know *why* he wants to find him, do we? It may just be business.'

Yes. The same sort that took him to Worcester and Oxford and Bristol, thought Kate cynically. But said only, 'You're right, I suppose. It's just very difficult not to be a bit curious.' And then, looking down at what he was doing, 'What's that?'

'Oh – nothing much.' Felix rose and picked up his paper. 'I was just passing the time, you know.'

Something clicked in Kate's brain. She said, 'It reminds me of those political cartoons we've been seeing such a lot of. Felicity's got a whole collection of them.'

'Has she?' he responded negligently. 'Funny girl. But I suppose everyone's entitled to a pastime.'

The wedding of Gianetta Caterina Falcieri del Santi and Liam Patrick Aherne took place discreetly two evenings later beneath *The Fall of Lucifer* in Thorne Ash's chapel. Nathan, with Adam Woodley to keep an eye on him, had been despatched on a seemingly vital mission to Warwick, and Celia, informed of the event at the last possible moment, unsurprisingly declined to attend. The bride, wearing a gown of her favourite cherry silk and attended by Mistresses Kate and Felicity Maxwell, elected to dazzle her bridegroom with every one of her newly exhumed jewels, and the bride's brother performed his part with what, to one pair of eyes, appeared to be a cross between resignation and relief.

438

Back in the house and with the Jesuit safely on his way, they all sat down to what, in certain respects, was less a wedding-breakfast than a last supper – for it had been arranged that Gianetta and Liam would leave on the following morning for the coast. Kate pushed her food around her plate, drank three glasses of wine and contributed little to the general air of festivity. She was occupied with the knowledge that Signor del Santi would in all probability leave the house within an hour of his sister, and therefore that, if she was going to present him with any information she might have on the Brandons, it had better be done tonight. The only question, of course, was how.

She was still debating this point when the party transferred to the parlour and Luciano himself emerged at her elbow to say softly, 'Something on your mind, Kate?'

She encompassed him in a repressive green gaze. 'Such as what, for example?'

'Such as wondering if it will ever be your turn?'

Kate opened her mouth on a suitably blighting rejoinder and then closed it again as an idea occurred to her. 'No,' she said mildly. 'As a matter of fact I was thinking about Venetia – Kit's sister, you know. I don't suppose you saw her while you were in Oxford, did you?'

'No. I didn't.' A frown gathered behind his eyes. 'Felix has a big mouth. I must remember to speak to him about it.'

Kate kept her smile purposefully vague and pressed on before she found herself on very dangerous ground indeed. 'She used to write to me before Kit and I . . . well, you know. And I was wondering if she and Ellis were married yet.' She stopped, as if struck by a gladsome thought. 'Actually, if you've been consorting with the King's army, you may have met him. His name is Brandon. Ellis Brandon.'

Even watching as carefully as she was, Kate could detect no change in his expression; but he was so long about replying that she had to remind herself to breathe. Then he said gently, 'I don't think so. The name is not familiar.'

'Oh.' It was impossible, as usual, to tell whether or not

he was lying, especially as Felix had been unable to provide her with a forename. Kate swallowed her frustration, kept her eyes wide and innocent and shot her last bolt. 'That's a shame. You were my only hope. The last I heard he was with George Goring . . . but I suppose he may have thought better of it and gone back to Yorkshire.' She shrugged. 'Not, from what I saw of him, that I can imagine him joining forces with his father. He always managed to give the impression that the two of them disagreed on just about everything almost as a matter of principle.'

This time there was a change in Luciano's expression but not one that she cared to interpret. In a voice as bland as butter, he said softly, 'His father is a Parliament man?'

'Sir Robert? Yes. I believe he used to sit in the Commons – possibly in the last Parliament.' Kate could feel the air starting to dwindle in her lungs and thought weakly, *Bull's-eye!* Then, before her resolution failed completely, she said baldly, 'His estate marches with that of Venetia's father. Brandon Lacey. Near Knaresborough.'

Silence stretched out on invisible threads. And then, in a tone she had never heard before, Luciano said, ' All right, Kate. I won't ask what you know – or even how. I'll just give you one piece of very sound advice. Stay out of it in future.'

'I might,' she said, wistfully, 'if I knew what I was staying *out* of.'

If he was relieved, it didn't show, and his smile was far from comforting. 'Be grateful. That's the only fact in Felix's favour. Or yours.'

'Aside, of course, from my having told you something you wanted to know.'

His brows rose. 'And what, dear Kate, makes you think that you have?'

The departure of Gianetta and Liam took place amidst a welter of emotions and promises to write. Gianetta, having embraced each of the Maxwells in turn, spent her last minutes rather desperately hugging her brother . . . and then it was time to go.

Everyone gathered to wave them off. And when they were almost out of sight, Luciano said quietly to Richard, 'It will come as no surprise that I, too, am leaving.'

'For London?'

'No. For a place called Knaresborough. In Yorkshire. It might be better, however, if you didn't tell Kate that.'

Richard's head turned sharply. 'Kate? What's she got to do with this?'

'Nothing – I hope.' Luciano met his gaze with wry candour. 'I just thought you ought to know that, but for her, I still wouldn't know where to look.'

Ten

It was a long ride to Yorkshire and, since the weather remained unsettled throughout, not an especially pleasant one. It took three days to reach Stamford and a further two to Newark – by which time Luciano had run into numerous small bodies of cavalry and lost count of the number of times he'd got wet. His safe-conducts, as he moved continuously in and out of opposing districts, had proved beyond price . . . but his hat and cloak would never be the same again and his backside was growing decidedly saddle-sore.

Onwards ever onwards, along the seemingly endless Great North Road, through country he had never expected to see again and dialects he could at times barely understand. And finally, on the ninth day of his odyssey, he rode into the small market town of Knaresborough with its neat, gabled houses and imposing castle perched high above the River Nidd.

It was a pretty place, but Luciano did not waste time admiring it. He bespoke a comfortable bed, a good dinner and a large tub of hot water at the Red Bear behind the market-place; he established that the castle was being held for the King; and he learned, without any difficulty at all, the precise location of the manor named Brandon Lacey.

He also discovered what would probably prove to be the fly in the ointment. Sir Robert, he was informed, was a strong Parliament man – and because he lived in a largely Royalist area, he had fortified and garrisoned his house to the point where not even a mouse could get in unchallenged. Or so people said. At any rate – having failed to take the

442

place by storm – the King's men had apparently decided that it wasn't important enough to warrant a full-blown siege and thus resigned themselves to doing without Sir Robert's taxes.

Luciano's problem was less how to get in than how to deal with matters once he had done so. And even after an hour's meditation in a relaxing bath, he found he was still no nearer to finding an answer. It began to look as if – unless he wanted to spend weeks over the business – his only real option might be the direct approach. He sighed and sank deeper into the water. It was all very unsatisfactory . . . and still more so was the fact that, since Sir Robert had reputedly not left home in the last six months, he was unlikely to have been responsible for the events which had led to Gwynneth's death. In one sense, thought Luciano, it was comforting to know that he wasn't about to put his head in the lion's mouth; but in another it was sheer disaster. For if Brandon, like Ferrars and Webb before him, turned out to be yet another pawn, the hand that had placed them all on the board seemed likely to remain forever anonymous.

Brandon Lacey lay off the road to Boroughbridge, close by the village of Staveley, and was situated on a slight rise in the ground. As Luciano had been told, it was walled and ditched and positively bristling with small artillery, and by the time he arrived at a point some thirty feet before the main gate, there were at least six muskets trained on him. It was all very impressive – and a downright, bloody nuisance.

He presented – or rather bellowed – his name up to the captain of the guard, waved his parliamentary pass and asked to see Sir Robert. Five minutes later he was admitted to the gatehouse and courteously parted from his weapons while the bars and bolts were shot once more behind him. Then, overlooked from above by two sentries, he was escorted across the small, orderly courtyard, through a second gate and thence to the house. The message was clear, thought Luciano. Put a foot wrong in this place and you haven't a snowball-in-hell's chance of getting out again.

The room into which he was eventually shown was

tapestried rather than panelled and had probably once formed part of a Great Hall until somebody had very sensibly decided to divide it. A huge fire blazed in the hearth, the furniture dated from the last century; and seated at a table beside the window was a vigorous-looking man in his early fifties. The man, presumably, that Luciano had travelled almost two hundred miles to see.

In the brief silence that followed, Luciano realised two things. First, that the captain of the guard had entered the room with him and now stood just inside the closed door; and second, that his own scrutiny was being met with another equally searching. Removing his hat, he bowed slightly and said, 'Sir Robert?'

'Yes.' Brandon rose but remained where he was, his fingers resting lightly on the table-top.

'I am obliged to you for receiving me.' Luciano advanced to within a few feet of the window. 'No doubt the good captain here has given you my name?'

'He's given me *a* name,' agreed Sir Robert, slowly. And then, with an unexpectedness that took Luciano like a blow to the stomach, 'But I don't somehow think it's yours. Is it?'

Luciano kept his face expressionless and, with an effort equally invisible, controlled his breathing. He said, 'Now why, I wonder, should you suppose that?'

A strange smile twisted the older man's mouth. 'That shoulder of yours gives you away.'

The dark brows rose. 'We've met before?'

'Yes . . . long ago. And I, of course, have very good reasons for remembering it.' There was a pause; and then, with a sort of detached irony, Brandon said, 'You'd be surprised, I daresay, at how often I've wondered if this day would ever come. But I suppose the question now is whether you're here to talk . . . or kill.'

Luciano felt rather than heard the slight hiatus which afflicted the guardian at the door. It was, of course, nothing compared to the one afflicting him; but he disguised it by remaining perfectly still while he waited for the words he needed to hear.

'Well, Signor Falcieri? Which is it?'

Luciano drew a long breath and then loosed it. The air was thick with tension. He said softly, 'As far as I can see, I don't have a choice – unless, of course, I'm happy to commit suicide. Fortunately, however, I don't consider assassination to be particularly apt. Given the right circumstances, I may ruin you; but I can safely promise not to murder you. Is that what you wanted to hear?'

There was another yawning silence broken only by the sound of a log shifting in the grate. Distantly, Luciano wondered which of them was more out of his depth. Then Brandon gave his answer. He dismissed the man at the door.

'But, sir!' protested the fellow, horrified. 'If you think that he – well, that he has reason to want to kill you, you can't just take his word for it that he won't!'

'Yes I can. But, if it makes you any happier, you may check that I am alive and well before letting this gentleman leave. Now go.'

Reluctantly, the captain went. And when the door had closed behind him, Brandon said stiffly, 'I ought to know where to start, but I don't. Except, of course, that we need to talk. Perhaps we could begin by sitting down?'

Wordlessly, Luciano accepted the chair he was offered.

Brandon remained standing, still visibly at a loss. After a moment, he said, 'Will you take wine?'

'I think not.'

'No.' Again that faint, bitter smile. 'I can't say that I blame you. But I hope you don't mind if I do?'

'Not in the least – if you feel you need it.'

'Wouldn't you?' Sir Robert filled a glass on the dresser and then returned to his chair. Then he said, 'I think it might be best if you were to tell me what you already know – after which I'll add what I can. How did you find me?'

Somewhere deep inside himself, Luciano was aware of a slight worrying tremor. Keeping eyes and voice equally impassive, however, he said that he had seen the trial record.

'Ah.' Brandon nodded and then proceeded to produce his second bombshell of the day. 'But which one?'

'Both.' Luciano stared at him. 'You knew the original had been removed? How?'

'It was while I was a member of the Commons. I . . . exerted a little pressure on the right people. I thought that if I was able to read the entire transcript it might tell me something. But what I eventually got, of course, was a completely useless forgery that wouldn't have deceived a child.' Sir Robert paused and then said, 'You say you've seen them both. Who has the original?'

'I hope and believe that I do – now. I bought it from Justice Samuel Fisher. I have also found and interviewed Thomas Ferrars and Ahiram Webb.' A chilly, impersonal smile curled his mouth. 'You will wish, I feel sure, to know what became of them. Ferrars is dead by his own hand, and Webb is disgraced and exiled.' The smile grew. 'Neither of them, you see, was disposed to be particularly helpful.'

Abruptly, Sir Robert drained his glass and then rose to refill it. Remaining on his feet he said, 'You don't need to show me the scourge – nor even the lure. I have had this matter on my conscience for seventeen long years – and you are possibly the only man to whom I can confess it. So I am waiting with honest impatience to do just that.'

Since he had first walked into the room, thought Luciano, nothing had gone as expected. Either Brandon was entirely unlike the others . . . or he was playing a very clever game indeed. It would be interesting to discover which. He said sardonically, 'Then do so. I am all attention.'

Sir Robert sat down again and set his glass on the table. Then, keeping his eyes on his hands, he said. 'Thirty-two years ago, I fell in love. I was twenty . . . and she slightly younger. She was the daughter of one of the noblest houses in England; and on the day I first saw her was being married to a man whose rank and fortune matched her own.' He hesitated briefly and, when he spoke again, his voice was noticeably harder. 'Her husband was one of the old King's intimates – and no different to the rest of them. If . . . if he'd cared for his wife or shown her the least consideration, things might have been different. As it was he preferred to spend a good deal of his time in travel. Sometimes he was away for as much as a year.' He looked up and met Luciano's eyes. 'You can probably guess with what result.'

'The obvious one,' came the inimical response.

'Yes. We were so happy it didn't even seem wrong. And then the unthinkable happened. She became pregnant.' Sir Robert reached for his glass but made no move to drink. 'It wasn't possible to pass the child off as that of her husband . . . and, even if it had been, I don't think we would have done it. So, it was necessary to arrange for the baby to be born in secret.'

'Go on.'

'The details don't matter; except, perhaps, for the stupendous cost of it all – mostly in bribes. My father was still alive at that time and I had very little money, so of course I ran into debt. But that didn't matter then.' For the first time a real smile touched Brandon's face. 'You see, we had our son. And even though he had to be brought up by others, we were able to see him sometimes – so long as we were careful and went separately. He's thirty now and a professional soldier fighting for the Parliament – but he still doesn't know who his mother was. And that, until he reached the age of thirteen, was my only regret.'

'Ah.' His gaze unreadable, Luciano leaned back in his chair. 'Don't tell me. Someone found out.'

'Yes. I still don't know how. We'd been so careful . . . and we were no longer even lovers. That had ended ten years before when my father died and I myself was married. So by 1626 we had every reason to believe ourselves safe. She had children by her husband and I a son by my wife. As for our boy, he was still in Shoreditch and knew nothing. But someone – a servant, perhaps – must have talked. And the result was a letter, threatening to expose everything if I didn't do what it said.'

'And naturally you couldn't take the risk,' remarked Luciano caustically. 'After all, what's a man's life compared to your domestic harmony?'

Lines of strain were becoming apparent on Brandon's face and he closed his eyes for a moment. Then, opening them, he said, 'It wasn't myself I had to protect. Exposure would have meant little to me. My marriage was one of convenience, not love; and, since the affair pre-dated it, Margaret – my wife – would scarcely have cared. No. The one who would suffer most from disclosure was my mistress.' He spread his hands in a gesture half-helpless, half-appealing. 'I don't know if you've ever loved a woman to the exclusion of all else; loved her so much that you would do anything for her sake. But that's how it was for me. And I couldn't stand by and let her be ruined. Can you understand that?'

'Perhaps. But I also understand that there are a variety of ways of dealing with threats.'

'You think I don't know that?' asked Brandon bitterly. 'I tried quite hard to get free, believe me. The letter said that someone would come for my answer in two days. I used those days to warn my mistress and send Margaret and Ellis back here to Brandon Lacey. I visited Shoreditch and told Gabriel that he was my son. And then I collected together as much money as I could lay my hands on.' He picked up his glass and drained it. 'The man who came was an obvious hireling. I named the highest price I could afford and told him to put it to his master. Then, when he left, I set a man of my own to follow him.'

'And?' prompted Luciano.

'It didn't work. My servant was found clubbed half to death in an alleyway not five hundred yards from my door. And when the next letter came, it said that silence could only be bought by compliance to the original orders. Furthermore, if I made any more attempts to trace the writer or was foolish enough to try and warn your father, my legitimate son would die and the threat of exposure would still stand.' Sir Robert drew a long, weary breath. 'I gave in. There didn't seem to be anything else I could do. Aside from that, I have no excuses.'

For a long time, Luciano stared thoughtfully down at his lightly laced fingers. Then, without moving, he said, 'It is almost certainly a silly question . . . but can you prove any of this?'

'Yes,' said Brandon simply. And was immediately impaled

on a bright, obsidian gaze. 'I have both the letters.'

The shock of it drove the blood from Luciano's skin. He said raggedly, 'You kept them?'

'Oh yes,' came the grim reply. 'I kept them. I hoped that one day they might lead me to the evil bastard who wrote them.'

In one smooth, explosive movement, Luciano left his chair for the window embrasure and stood staring blindly through the small panes while he attempted to control his breathing. And finally, in a fair semblance of his usual tone, he said, 'I'll drink to that. If, that is, the offer's still open?'

It was Brandon's turn to be silenced by simple relief at being believed. Crossing to the dresser, he filled a second glass – spilling a little because his hands were less than steady. Then, passing it to the Italian, he said abruptly, 'Under the circumstances, an apology is a useless thing. But before we go any further I have to at least try to tell you how bitterly I regret what happened to your father and my own part in it.'

Thor's hammer started to beat in Luciano's skull.

'You want absolution?' he asked. 'I can't give it. I believe, however, that I'm beginning to arrive at some degree of understanding.' He took the glass and drank. Then, 'You said you saw me as a child. How did that come about?'

'Your father made a diamond pendant for my wife. You were there on the day I collected it.'

The sculpted face was turned very slowly towards him. 'A tear-drop diamond surrounded by small sapphires in a filigree setting?'

Brandon nodded. 'You remember it?'

'Vividly. It was one of the last pieces I saw him make.' Luciano paused and then, with a visible effort, said, 'I don't suppose your wife would consider selling it?'

'My wife has been dead for three years, Signor Falcieri. If you want the pendant, it's yours. And no,' he added quickly, as Luciano would have spoken. 'That's an attempt neither to placate my own conscience nor make reparation. Both are impossible and the second would be nothing short of an insult.'

'I am glad,' remarked Luciano, 'that you realise it.' There was no hostility in his voice; only an incredible weariness. He supposed, somewhat distantly, that he ought to thank the fellow, but it seemed too great an effort. Then, as he opened his mouth to try, the door opened and a woman came in.

She was on the shady side of forty and draped in numerous scarves and shawls, one of which had escaped to trail along the floor. Ignoring Luciano completely, she said with gentle anxiety, 'Robert, dear . . . you haven't seen Moppet, have you? I can't find her anywhere – and the kittens are due any day now, you know.'

'Oh God,' breathed Sir Robert. And then, patiently, 'No, Sophy – I haven't seen her. And if she gives birth on my bed again, I'll—'

'Of course!' came the pleased response. 'Your room. How could I have forgotten that? I'll go and look there immediately.'

'By all means, do. And pick up that shawl before you break your neck.'

'What?' She hunted vaguely about for the offending article and finally succeeded in looping it over one elbow. Then, with a sweet, myopic smile in Luciano's direction, she said, 'I'll have Baxter bring some food. The young man looks as though he needs it.' And wafted irresolutely back through the door, leaving it open behind her.

Brandon looked across at his visitor with a sort of desperate calm. 'My sister,' he said. 'If she finds the cat, she *may* remember the food. . . but I wouldn't like to rely on it.'

'No,' agreed Luciano weakly. He was aware of finding it funnier than it actually was and had to fight a dangerous impulse to laugh. If he once started, he might not be able to stop. On the other hand, Mistress Sophia had cut through the tension like a knife. He said unsteadily, 'And that would be a shame . . . because I, for one, am all out of lofty principles.'

'Well, thank God for that,' came the honest reply. 'I, of course, never had any. Or not when it comes to food. So sit down and finish your wine. I'll be back in five minutes.'

Over a simple meal of bread and cold meat, they spoke only of the war and the likelihood of either side being able to bring it to a successful conclusion. Then, when they had finished eating, Sir Robert silently passed Luciano two much-folded and slightly yellowing pieces of parchment.

Handling them with controlled distaste, Luciano read and reread both of them. The handwriting was ornate and completely unknown to him; the contents, exactly as Brandon had described. At length he placed them on the table in front of him and looking up said flatly, 'As you say, an evil bastard.'

Brandon sighed. 'It's no help, is it?'

'Except for the unlikely event of either one of us seeing a hand that exactly matches this – none.' As he had been doing for the last two hours, Luciano tried to shut out the thought that he appeared to have arrived at the ultimate brick wall; that he had spent the best part of seven years and a small fortune in order to destroy two men who were nothing more than cogs in the wheel; that there was quite plainly a fifth man who was the only one who really counted, and to whose identity he had no clues at all. He said slowly, 'Giles Langley died of a broken neck. I wonder if he knew something?'

'And was murdered because of it? Possibly. But what good is that?'

Luciano shrugged slightly and picked up his glass. 'Just that it would be nice to think that whoever began all this isn't absolutely foolproof.'

Sir Robert grunted and then said, 'Of course, we'll never be sure that it wasn't Langley himself.'

'On the contrary. We know that it wasn't – for the simple reason that, less than a month ago, just after I dealt with Webb, someone took the trouble to have my house searched.' A wry smile touched the hard mouth. 'I was rather hoping that it might have been you. As it is, another great theory bites the dust. And all we're left with is Samuel Fisher.'

'You think it may have been him?'

'No. He is already precisely aware both of what I know and how much use it's likely to be.' Luciano sipped his wine, frowning a little. 'But he must have had some reason for appropriating the trial record . . . aside, let us assume, from simple kleptomania or the fear that someone might one day recognise it for the travesty that it was. And he knew that the evidence was a tissue of lies. In fact, it's beginning to look as if he may know a damned sight more than I'd thought possible.'

Brandon drew a long breath and then loosed it. He said, 'You know where to find him?'

'Yes. And that, I might add, is the only thing keeping me from climbing the walls at my own stupidity. I was expecting four names and Fisher provided me with four names. When Thomas Ferrars told me he'd been blackmailed, I just presumed the culprit must be one of the other three; and when Webb said the same, I still thought it had to be either Langley or you. Or no. That's not strictly accurate. I was counting on it being you, since Langley is beyond my reach. Only then my house was broken into.' He stopped for a moment, trying to curb the rush of anger. 'That cost another life. And all because I've been too bloody inept to look beyond the end of my nose.'

Sir Robert Brandon closed his teeth on all the futile words that sprang to mind. Finally he said simply, 'I've a stake in this too. I'd like to come with you.'

'No,' snapped Luciano irascibly. 'Haven't you realised yet that, since the day I found Webb, the only thing keeping you alive has been your ignorance? The man who wrote those letters is clever and ruthless and *still alive*. He's also, at the very least, beginning to guess what I'm doing. So do you really think that, had he not known how little you could tell me, I'd have been allowed to reach you?'

Brandon took his time about replying. Then he said, 'In which case – if Fisher *does* know something – the first move you make towards him will sign either his death warrant or yours.'

'Not necessarily. The very fact that he's still alive suggests that he's either kept his information to himself or arranged his own protection. And as for me, I ought to be safe enough provided I take adequate precautions against being followed. At any rate, I'll take my chances.'

'And four or five of my men,' said Sir Robert calmly. 'Just to be on the safe side.'

Luciano eyed him with irritation, slowly giving way to wry amusement. 'All right. If and when I find our friend, you want to know about it. Understood. But you don't need to make yourself responsible for my safety.'

'I do. It's a long way back to London – especially if, as you suspect, you're being watched. I'd as soon you didn't die before you're able to talk to Fisher.'

'Thank you. For myself, I'd as soon not die at all.'

'Quite. So you'll take my men?'

'If you insist – and they're quite happy to masquerade as my servants. But only as far as my own door. After that, I'll make my own arrangements.' Luciano stared down into his glass, the momentary levity dying from his face. Then, meeting the older man's gaze, he said reflectively, 'It's odd, isn't it, how things turn out? Life is full of surprises.'

Brandon allowed his understanding to show but let it lie unspoken. Then, reaching into his pocket, he drew out the delicate diamond pendant that Alessandro Falcieri had made for him eighteen years before and placed it carefully in front of Alessandro's son. Then he said quietly, 'God moves in mysterious ways. And at least your father was fortunate in his heir. There are a good many men – myself amongst them – who would envy him that.'

It took eleven days to get back to Cheapside, by which time Luciano was as heartily sick of his frigidly efficient companions as they apparently were of him. If they were followed, it was done with consistently flawless discretion; and they met with no violence at all: a fact which Captain Harper seemed to find regrettable as well as unsurprising. Neither did he take kindly to passing himself and his troopers off as Royalists; indeed, had it not been that the alternative was probably spending the rest of the war in prison, he would almost certainly have refused. But at least the news was good. The Scots, having signed a treaty with the Parliament, were preparing to cross the border . . . and, on the edge of the Lincolnshire Wolds, Lord Manchester and Colonel Cromwell had routed a Royalist force from Newark and taken eight hundred prisoners. Filled with circumspect elation, the captain was able to face the road ahead with greater equanimity and looked blithely forward to saying goodbye to his charge. Luciano looked forward to it as well and, when they finally arrived outside his door, bade the captain and his men a suitably acidic farewell and directed them to a nearby hostelry. Then he went thankfully inside to create untold relief in the bosoms of Selim and Giacomo.

There had been no further trouble during his absence and he devoutly hoped he could visit Fisher without causing any. He therefore spent the best part of the evening discussing with Selim the various routes and times that might enable him to get to Lambeth unobserved; and this done, threw himself into bed and attempted to get a few hours' sleep.

He left the house again swathed in a dark cloak a couple of hours before dawn, with Selim following at a sensible distance: near enough to help should help be needed, but far enough behind to pick up any signs of other pursuit. In this way – and sticking to a prearranged and highly tortuous route – they successfully reached the river and found a boat to take them across. No other craft, so far as they could see, set out after them. And, in due course, Luciano found himself once more amidst the weeds of Samuel Fisher's garden.

Dawn was breaking – a fact which he found himself rather glad of. He had no especial objection to confronting the old man in bed, but he would rather not do it by the light of no more than a candle. Aware that Selim had arrived at his elbow, he said softly, 'All right. Let's find a window.'

The one they chose was at the side of the house: well hidden from the gaze of local early-risers; its frame so rotten that it was but the work of a moment for Selim to force it. Then they were inside.

The room, so far as they could tell in the gloom, was

virtually empty of furniture but thickly carpeted with dust. Luciano led the way across to the door, opened it as quietly as possible and stepped into the familiar territory of the hall.

The smell, this time, had nothing to do with cabbage or fish and was infinitely worse than either. Luciano's first breath nearly choked him and even Selim came to an abrupt halt, one hand clamped hard over his mouth. But then, Selim had a good excuse. He knew what it was.

Closing his other hand on his master's arm, he said rapidly, 'We should go. There is nothing here for you.'

His lungs full of the sickly, cloying odour, Luciano peered back at him through the near-darkness. Then he understood.

'Oh bloody hell,' he breathed desperately. And, tearing his arm free, took the stairs two at a time.

Selim swore and followed him.

Luciano checked for a moment outside Fisher's room, as if trying to summon all his resources. Then, with every muscle rigidly controlled, he pressed the latch and let the door swing wide.

Light, filtering dimly from the uncurtained windows, fell on overturned furniture, yawning cupboards and ripped-out panelling. Someone had conducted something that was less a search than a systematic dismantling. Even the floor had not escaped attention. And the stench was overpowering.

Luciano stepped inside, his eyes raking the cluttered floor. And then he saw it: a foot protruding from behind the great, toppled chair. Slowly and without hesitation, he forced himself to advance towards it until he could see the bloated, sprawling body of Samuel Fisher. It had been stabbed, very messily, a number of times. It had also been dead for several days. But the thing that finally shattered all Luciano's careful self-discipline was the sight of the old man's left hand . . . from which someone, presumably for the sake of his own emerald, had hacked the little finger.

It was too much. Luciano's stomach rose into his throat and, reeling clumsily away from the corpse, he vomited into the nearest corner. It was both painful and disgusting, but it was better, he already knew, than facing the only fact that mattered.

With Fisher dead, there was nowhere else to go. It had all been for nothing. Stalemate.

It wasn't until much later that he thought of some of the things that were already worrying Selim. Such as whether, for example, Samuel Fisher would be the only one to end up being murdered.

'His Majesty hath now no way left to preserve his posterity, kingdom and nobility but by a treaty. I believe it a more prudent way to retain something than to lose all.'

Rupert of the Rhine

Let Chaos Reign

January 1644 to November 1645

Through regions farr devided
  And tedious tracts of tyme,
By my misfortune guided,
  Make absence thought a cryme;
Though wee weare set a sunder
  As far, as East from West,
Love still would worke this wonder,
  Thou shouldst be in my breast.

Aurelian Townsend

One

By the time they took Arundel Castle, Eden was heartily sick of rain and mud. He was also sick of having his major – whom he liked and respected – tell him that he could not possibly be released from duty.

'Don't even think of it,' advised Gabriel, crisply. 'Quite apart from the fact that I can't spare you, we've already got enough trouble keeping our fellows together without them getting wind of an officer taking leave to attend his wife's confinement. Every man-jack would turn into an expectant father overnight. And winter is no time for recruiting.'

It was all too aggravatingly true. Back in November, after they'd failed once again to take the great stronghold of Basing House, virtually all the London boys had marched off home through the driving rain, leaving the rest of the army – equally wet and unpaid and also hamstrung for lack of numbers – to seek shelter at Farnham. Eden sometimes wondered if the other generals – Lord Manchester and the Fairfaxes, for example – suffered as much from desertion as Waller and his arch-rival Essex did; or whether, cynically, they'd found some magic formula for getting clothes and pay and munitions out of Westminster.

It had been a mixed year since he'd transferred to Waller. Roundway Down, of course, had been an unmitigated disaster. He still carried the mark of it across his left cheek – and would for the rest of his life. But some things had gone right, such as taking Alton from that silly fellow Crawford who'd sent to Waller asking for some wine in exchange for an ox. Eden and Ralph had delivered the wine personally, taken a good look at the Royalist dispositions – and returned with the impudent message that Sir William should have his ox if he cared to fetch it. Well, they'd fetched it, all right; and taken five hundred prisoners into the bargain – some of whom had re-enlisted under Waller. So much, as Ralph said, for relying on amateurs. And now, after four days of sitting in the mud, they'd also succeeded in forcing Sir Ralph Hopton – who was not an amateur at all – out of Arundel.

As far as progress elsewhere was concerned, everyone agreed that it was very hard to judge. After a glorious summer, the Royalists had taken Newport Pagnell only to lose it again, and were now reputedly squabbling nearly as much as Essex and Waller; Colonel Cromwell's cavalry had made its mark at Winceby, and Meldrum had put an end to Lord Newcastle's attempt to reduce Hull; and while the King was expecting troops out of Ireland, some twenty thousand Scots were preparing to cross the border in aid of the Parliament. But if either side were about to win the war, nobody Eden knew was keen to put money on it.

In fact, the most momentous event of the last three months had not happened in the field at all but on a quiet bed in London when, racked with pain and wasted to a skeletal thinness, John Pym had finally relinquished his hold on life. 'Eaten by worms', had been the immediate and gleeful Cavalier verdict . . . and the Scots whom Pym had worked so hard to befriend condemned his funeral rites as Popish and refused to attend. But there were others left to speak for him and note that 'what he was, was only to promote the public good; in and for this he lived; in and by this he died'. And everywhere, as was natural, people speculated on who would succeed him.

After that, the second Christmas of the war came and went more or less unnoticed – mainly because, in deference to the Scots Commissioners, Parliament decreed that it was to be treated as an ordinary working day. This, as Ralph pointed out, was probably not such a good idea. With no bear-baiting or plays, a fast-day every Wednesday and only the occasional hanging or parade of prisoners to break the monotony, people were getting pretty tired of the miserable remnant left at Westminster. And now the King was offering a free pardon to any members who'd like to exchange their seat in London for one in the Parliament he planned to open in Oxford, there was bound to be trouble.

Eden didn't doubt it but was more concerned with his own problems for once. Within days of Arundel, the mud and rain he'd so deplored was replaced with a week's continuous snow as the winter closed in with a vengeance. The baby, so far as he could calculate, must be due any day now, and yet here he was kicking his heels in the modest Royalist household at Farnham that Gabriel had appropriated as a billet. This – what with Mistress Maynard's glacial courtesy and her two children's implacable hostility – was strain enough; but when it was also the very last place one wanted to be just now, the effect was well-nigh intolerable.

The snow eventually ceased, leaving the whole country smothered under a blanket of white and the Scots army marooned at Berwick. Nothing moved on the roads and when Eden stepped outside the front door into the nicely timed avalanche delivered by Robin and Jessica Maynard from above, he began to feel his sense of humour deserting him.

'I'll murder those two,' he said shortly to Gabriel later.

'No you won't,' came the arid reply. 'You won't be here.'

Eden stared at him. 'How do you work that out?'

'Because Sir William wants some letters and despatches sent to London – and I've arranged for you to take them. You'll have to wait for the thaw, of course. But, with the weather as it is, no one will be particularly surprised if the round trip takes a bit longer than usual. Or even quite a lot longer, I should imagine.'

'You're saying,' said Eden slowly, 'that I can go home?'

'No,' sighed Gabriel. 'I'm not. I'm just pointing out that once you're away from here, what you do is your own business. Provided, that is, that you use some common sense.'

461

He paused, a glimmer of amusement dawning behind his eyes. 'Ah yes. And while you're about it, you might deliver my other sword to a fellow named Jack Morrell in Shoreditch. The hilt needs some repair work.'

'Mr Morrell is an armourer?'

'The best,' said Gabriel. And then, almost as an afterthought, 'He's also my foster-brother.'

With only Tom Tripp for company, Eden made it from Farnham to London in four days – which, considering the quagmire of slush that lay between, wasn't at all bad. Discharging his errand in Westminster took a further three, during the course of which he visited Amy, Felix and the major's foster-family, avoided Luciano del Santi and learned something about his father that he hadn't expected to hear. Then, with the Parliament's replies to Sir William tucked safely in his pocket, he set off north towards Thorne Ash before the rapidly expanding flood-water could make his passage impossible.

He arrived, mud-spattered and monumentally weary, just as the family were rising from supper. For a moment there was stunned silence and then, as always, his mother reached him first.

'*Eden!* Oh my dear – my dear!' Dolly embraced him, half laughing and half crying; then, her fingers tracing the thin, pale pink line on his cheek, 'But your poor face. How – ? No. That's silly. I should just be thanking God you're alive.'

'Scars,' remarked Kate unsteadily from a distance, 'are often held to lend distinction. Ralph is probably quite jealous. Unless he's got one too?'

'Not where it shows,' responded Eden. And then they were all on him; all, that is, save for one.

Presently, when the worst of the tumult was over, he said painfully, 'Celia?'

'Safe and well,' Dorothy assured him quickly. And then, smiling, 'Go up. There is someone you should meet.'

'The – the baby?'

'Yes. Born a month ago and doing beautifully. You've

462

nothing to worry about, you see? So go – before your father breaks all the rules and tells you whether you've a son or a daughter. And then, when you're ready, there will be food waiting for you.' Which was fairly noble – considering she couldn't be sure how Celia would receive him and would, in any case, have much preferred to sit him down by the fire with a cup of mulled wine.

Somewhere between the parlour and his wife's door, Eden found time to discard his sword and buff-coat. Then, drawing a slightly unsteady breath, he rapped lightly on the dark panels and set his hand to the latch.

Celia sat by the hearth. Her hair was loose and she was wearing a wide-sleeved chamber-robe that glimmered dully in the firelight. She looked stunning . . . but it was not that which stopped Eden's breath. The baby lay in her lap. It was a picture he had never seen before. And then, in the time it took for his heart to resume its usual pattern, she rose and said sharply, 'My God. How did *you* get here?'

Typically, it was not the welcome he had hoped for . . . but it was necessary, he realised, to allow for shock.

'With extreme difficulty,' he smiled, moving towards her. 'But surely you've been expecting me? My letters must have told you that much at least.'

Pulling herself together, Celia grasped the easy option without even thinking. She said, 'Oh yes. But you're a little late, don't you think?' And then, before he could answer her, 'However, now that you're finally here, I suppose you'd better meet Viola Mary.'

'Viola Mary?' queried Eden, cautiously. He came to rest in front of her, his eyes on the sleeping infant in her arms.

'It's her name,' came the impatient response. 'You chose Jude – so I felt it was my turn. And besides, how was I to know how long it would be before you found the time to visit us? So I decided upon Mary for Her Majesty the Queen; and Viola because she was born on Twelfth Night. It's from Shakespeare, you know.'

Eden, whose acquaintance with Shakespeare was no better now than it had ever been, didn't know. But intent only on avoiding the challenge in her voice, he said merely,

'I see. It's charming . . . and so, as far as I can tell, is she. Can I hold her?'

'If you like,' began Celia ungraciously. And then as, turning to receive the baby, his left cheek came for the first time within reach of the light, 'Merciful heaven! Where did you come by *that*?'

'At Roundway Down,' he replied, settling Viola Mary competently on his arm. 'I'm sorry. I suppose I ought to have warned you.'

'Yes. Well . . . it certainly doesn't do much for your looks, does it?' she retorted carelessly. Then, with a small brittle laugh, 'Roundway Down. Wasn't that the battle everybody calls Runaway Hill?'

'The Cavaliers called it that,' he said quietly. 'It would be nice, however, if my wife felt able to be a bit more tactful. Celia, why are you so angry?'

'Angry? I'm not especially. I just don't feel inclined to fall on your neck, that's all. You should try remembering that I've only laid eyes on you once in the last eighteen months and that I disagree with everything you're doing; so if we've become strangers, you've only yourself to blame.'

An all-too-familiar pain gathered around Eden's heart. Frowning a little, he said, 'To an extent, I suppose that is true. But a little effort on both our parts could overcome that, surely? And I love you no less than I have ever done. I . . . I don't ask you to meet me half-way. But couldn't you at least be patient a little longer and – and accept what I bring you in the brief time we can be together?'

'And what, exactly, is that?' she asked, coolly deciding that now was as good a time as any to come to the point. 'You rushed here last year and went off again without a backward glance, leaving me pregnant. Were you thinking of doing the same again? Because, if so, you will have to pardon me if I tell you that's not what I want. Nor, I am afraid, what I will have.'

The pain grew. Eden stared down at the small, puckered face in his arms and said wearily, 'You're saying you won't sleep with me?'

'Precisely. What did you expect?'

'Some discussion, perhaps. Will you have your woman take the baby to the nursery so that we can talk?'

'No,' said Celia. 'I don't think I will. We can talk tomorrow if you wish, but right now I'm rather tired. So why don't *you* take Viola to the nursery? That way you can also look in on Jude – and I can get some rest.'

The hazel eyes rose slowly to encompass her face and it was a long time before Eden spoke. Then he said tonelessly, 'It rather seems, does it not, that you no longer love me?'

'Probably not,' returned Celia, with sudden deadly bitterness. 'But what difference does that make? We're married, aren't we?'

It was hard to go downstairs with a smile on his face and enthuse about his baby daughter as though his wife had not said what she had just said. It was even harder to appear to do justice to the food his mother put before him whilst answering Father's and Kate's questions about the war and Felicity's light-hearted ones about Ralph. But he did it and gradually his mind recovered its tone so that he was eventually able to look non-committally at Richard and say, 'I hear that you've quit your seat. Why?'

'Because I preferred not to take the oath that would have let me keep it,' came the calm reply.

'The Covenant?' Eden looked vaguely surprised. He and Ralph and Gabriel and the others had taken it in a somewhat jaundiced vein and, being rather busy at the time, without overmuch thought. 'I agree that the Scots are overstepping themselves by insisting on it – but there's no real harm, is there?'

'Probably not. I just found myself reluctant to pander to them any further. After all, their divines now sit in the Westminster Assembly, Archbishop Laud's impeachment has been resumed and we're all supposed to be strenuously removing anything decorative from our churches. We're even denied Christmas. It seems to me that ought to be enough.'

'True,' sighed Eden. 'But the devil of it is that we need them.'

'In order to beat the King?' asked Richard. 'Perhaps we do. But if the cost of their help is turning England Presbyterian, I doubt if I'll be the only one asking if it's worth it.' He paused and then said abruptly, 'Do you *know* how many members are left in the Commons? Two hundred out of six. And as for the Lords, I doubt if they can raise a total strength of more than twenty. The King has called Parliament a remnant of rebels but it's worse than that. It's a farce. And now Pym is dead it will fall into the hands of that young fanatic Harry Vane and Solicitor-General St John – who's nothing but a mouthpiece for Oliver Cromwell and his godly clutch of Anabaptists. Leave matters up to such as *him* and you could find your next order is to get yourself baptised again. Probably,' finished Richard with a sudden grin, 'under a name like Repent-and-be-Saved.'

Felicity giggled.

'Nathan says one of his Banbury friends has called his son Jerusalem. He thinks it most s-suitable. In fact, he was rather hoping that Celia might be persuaded to have poor little Viola christened Purity instead – only of course she wouldn't.'

'And who shall blame her?' remarked Dorothy, wondering if the shadow in Eden's eyes was to do with Celia's choice of name or something infinitely more serious. Since she couldn't ask, however, she merely said, 'You look appallingly tired, my dear. How long can you stay?'

'Not long. I'm not really supposed to be here at all,' he replied wryly. 'Fortunately, I've a sympathetic major. But in order not to try credulity too far, I'd better be off again the day after tomorrow.'

Kate's brows rose. 'It's to be hoped, then, that you don't mind swimming.'

'Needs must,' he shrugged. 'I've got to return via London to pick up Gabriel's sword – and then it's back to the hell-born babes.'

'Gabriel?' asked Kate.

And, 'Hell-born babes?' echoed Felicity.

Eden managed a grin and stood up, stretching. 'Gabriel is my sympathetic major; and the brats – by name, Robin and Jessica – are the unholy offspring of the Royalist gentleman whose house we are currently occupying. It's their mission in life to remind us daily of our intrusion.'

'Well, you can't blame them for that,' said Felicity. 'In their position, I'd be doing the same thing myself.'

'I know you would,' replied Eden, yawning. 'And I'm just thankful that, dreadful as they are, they don't quite aspire to your levels of invention. Yet.'

On the following morning, Kate noticed two things. The first was that Tom Tripp had managed to find his way into the nursery at a time when Meg was absent from it and was sitting on the floor, playing an intricate game of building bricks with Jude and Eve. Kate crossed her fingers and whisked herself past the open doorway before he should see her. If a reconciliation was in the air, she had no mind to spoil it. And that was why, when she met her brother coming out of the room which adjoined the one he shared with Celia, she grabbed his hand and bundled him back inside.

'What's the matter?' asked Eden a shade irritably. He had spent the last hour trying to recreate some kind of rapport with Celia, only to find that every turn brought him back to where he had been last night. 'I was going to the nursery.'

'Yes. That's what I thought,' grinned Kate. 'But now is not a good time. Tom's in there.'

'So?'

'So if he's taking an interest in Eve, it may be because – despite everything – he still cares for Eve's mother.'

'He does,' said Eden flatly. 'But I doubt it will come to anything. She betrayed him with another man, Kate – and has a child to show for it. You can't just forgive and forget a thing like that.'

Kate sighed. 'No . . . perhaps not. But Eve's two now and the image of Meg – so I just hoped that Tom might have got over his hurt. It seems a shame to let one piece of foolishness blight your whole life. And what's going to happen to Eve? She's being brought up as if she were Jude and Viola's sister, but she's not and everyone knows it. The poor child will end up not knowing *what* she is.'

'Very likely. But that's not Tom's problem, is it? And even if it were,' finished Eden bitterly, 'he'd have to be sixpence short of a shilling to marry Meg before the war ends.'

'I realise that. But it doesn't alter the fact that he's sitting on the nursery floor with Eve at his knee. Do you *have* to be so discouraging?' asked Kate. And then was struck by her second discovery of the morning. Eden looked even more fatigued than he had last night . . . and the unmade truckle-bed in the corner explained why. She drew a long breath and said cautiously, 'You look terrible. Do you want to talk about it?'

His brows soared. '*To you?*'

'Unless you'd rather worry Mother – yes. But I take your point. Would you believe me if I promised not to snipe?'

Eden turned away to the window and leaned his hands on the ledge, staring out into the wintry garden. He said remotely, 'Let's put it to the test, shall we? Tell me – simply and without unnecessary elaboration – how Celia's been since I was last here.'

'Until about the middle of October, absolutely fine. Happy, even. Then the weather turned unpleasant and her condition made riding difficult so it seemed quite natural that she should be a little less cheerful.' Kate gave it some thought and then said, 'That's probably what ails her now. She's tired of being cooped up. So am I, come to that.'

'And the baby . . . how has she been with her?'

'A bit more interested, perhaps, than she was in Jude – though still not overly enthusiastic. I think we just have to accept that she's not an immensely maternal person.'

'My God!' said Eden, swivelling caustically to face her. 'If you struggle to be any fairer, you'll do yourself a mischief.'

Kate stared back at him, temporarily silenced by the look in his eyes. Finally, she said quietly, 'Eden . . . what has she said to you?'

'What do you think?' he retorted, gesturing to the state of the room. 'I'm surprised that you're bothering to ask.'

'But it can't just be that, surely? It – it's still a little soon after the baby, isn't it? And I should have thought you'd have understood that.'

'Yes. I would have understood it – had that been how it was put to me.' He paused briefly. 'Would you say Celia has seemed angry with me for not being here when Viola was born?'

'No, I don't think so. Or not that I've noticed, anyway.'

Eden's expression altered subtly and it was a long time before he spoke. Then, in a voice she did not recognise, he said, 'I see. Well . . . that appears to cover all the possibilities, doesn't it? And now – Tom or no Tom – I'm going to see my children.'

He devoted the afternoon to remedying the fact that his three-year-old son did not know him and divided the evening between reassuring his mother of his own well-being and discussing wider issues with his father. Throughout it all, he strove to treat Celia exactly as usual, avoided Kate's eye and made sure no one asked any questions he wasn't prepared to answer. Then, on the following morning, he said his goodbyes and rode off into the ghostly pre-dawn light, taking Tom Tripp with him.

Dorothy stood on the gatehouse with Richard, silently watching until he was out of sight. Then she said, 'There's trouble between him and Celia. I can smell it.'

'So can I,' agreed Richard. 'But that's hardly new, is it? And I daresay it will blow over.'

'It might – if he were here. Or then again, perhaps not. He still hasn't learned, has he?'

'Learned what?'

'That the more he tries to please her, the worse she behaves.'

Richard looked down at her with a sort of rueful amusement. 'What are you saying? That he should beat her?'

'No. No – of course not. But I do wish he'd do something to shake her out of her goddamned complacency,' she replied with a spurt of unusual violence. Then, sighing,

'I'm sorry. It's just that he struggled here through hell and high water and his visit should have been a happy one. Only it wasn't, was it?'

'No.' Richard folded her lightly in his arms. 'No, I don't think it was. But this isn't something we can help him with – except perhaps by being here.'

'I know. But it's hard, sometimes, to stay meekly by the hearth.'

'Tell me something new,' said Richard grimly. 'You would like to sort out Eden's marriage – and I, the bungled affairs of the nation. But neither would be welcome. And neither would work.'

Throughout the rest of February, people spoke mostly of the weather, the opening of the King's Parliament in Oxford and the convening, in Westminster, of something called the Committee of Both Kingdoms which was to be composed of Scots and English and replace the old Council of War. It was this last which interested Richard most; and when he heard that Vane, St John and Cromwell had all been voted seats on it but that Denzil Holles had not, he was moved to a brief, sardonic laugh.

'It's funny?' asked Dorothy.

'Not if you happen to be Robert Deveraux, Earl of Essex,' he replied. 'Holles was the only friend he had. The rest of them are committed to getting rid of him – probably, for the time being at least, in favour of Waller.'

'But why? What's he done?'

'Made two big mistakes. Failed to win the war and allied himself too clearly with the Peace Party. Ah yes – and I almost forgot,' added Richard with a twisted smile. 'The Scots know he doesn't like them.'

Word from the North said that Irish troops had begun pouring in through Chester for the King's service and that neither the parliamentary fleet nor Sir Thomas Fairfax seemed able to stop them. The Scots had got as far as Newcastle and were busily but unsuccessfully besieging it, and Sir John Meldrum was having similar difficulties driving the Royalists out of Newark. The King seemed still to hold the advantage; and the Committee of Both Kingdoms, sitting amongst His Majesty's purloined tapestries in Derby House, were at a loss to know what to do about it.

March brought no signal improvement in the weather. It did, however, bring Colonel Cromwell, who – whilst guarding a convoy from Warwick to Gloucester – ran into a Cavalier raiding party from Banbury and drove it smartly back into the castle. He and his little army then lingered in the town whilst he sent to Northampton for artillery and would undoubtedly have settled down for a siege had not a force under Prince Rupert entered the vicinity and proved a more tempting target. Colonel Cromwell promptly set off in hot pursuit . . . and Hugo Verney arrived at Thorne Ash to collect the quarter's rents.

With her father absent about the farm, Kate had the captain escorted to the book-room and proceeded to deal with the matter herself. As usual, she neither welcomed him nor invited him to sit – a ploy which she found expedited the business no end – and in less than ten minutes he was being shown to the door again. It was then, however, that she found he had dropped one of his exquisitely embroidered gloves.

Kate picked it up, sighing. If it wasn't returned, he would call again to retrieve it. Without wasting time summoning a maid, she shot across the hall, through the front door and out into the courtyard.

She caught up with him in the shadows of the gatehouse and had already said, 'Captain Verney? Your glove,' before she realised he was not alone. Then, looking from his dismayed face to Celia's flushed one, she simply raised inquiring brows and remained silent.

Hugo took his glove, saying, 'Thank you. But how careless of me to put you to such trouble.'

'Not at all,' replied Kate coolly. 'I'm glad I caught you.'

'I'm sure you are,' remarked Celia sweetly. 'But don't let your imagination run riot, Kate. I was merely asking Hugo to try and get a message to my father. Far Flamstead's going to rack and ruin in his absence and I can't be expected to deal with quite *everything* myself. Although, if the weather remains dry, I really must try and get over there tomorrow.' She paused and turned back to the captain with a slight shrug. 'However. You won't forget, will you, Hugo? It distresses me that the house has been empty for so long.'

Looking at him, Kate thought she detected a rather desperate look in Captain Verney's eye. Then it was gone and he said smoothly, 'I'll do my best not to disappoint you. It shouldn't be too difficult. And now I'm afraid I should be going. We've a number of errands to complete this morning.'

Celia watched him leave and then walked past Kate with a taunting smile and a swish of violet satin. Neither of them spoke. There was, after all, nothing that either of them could usefully say.

A week later, Luciano del Santi arrived with Felix in tow.

'Well, well,' said Richard, by way of greeting. He had not seen or heard from Felix since he'd returned to London in early January . . . and the Italian had been silent even longer. 'Wonders will never cease. Has Cheapside been washed away – or is this merely a social call?'

Felix, looking faintly subdued, kept his mouth shut.

'Neither,' said Luciano sourly. 'We're here because I'd like to leave for Genoa without wondering if your son has managed to get himself clapped up again – and returning him to you seemed the best way to do it.'

'*What?*' asked Dorothy.

'Oh Lord!' muttered Felicity, looking at her twin out of wide, gloomy eyes. 'I *told* you to be more careful.'

Richard, Dorothy and Kate all turned to stare at her.

'You knew?' snapped Luciano del Santi. And when she nodded, 'Then why the devil didn't you tell someone?'

'I couldn't,' replied Felicity simply. 'Felix and I don't break promises to each other. And I promised to keep it a secret.'

Richard lifted his eyes to the ceiling. 'Will someone please tell me what all this is about?'

'Cartoons,' said Luciano, succinctly. 'Political cartoons,

472

to be precise. Felix draws them, Geoffrey Cox captions them and they both print and distribute them. Or did, until they were caught and arrested for running an illicit press. Show him, Felix.'

Wordlessly, Felix pulled a broadsheet from his pocket and handed it to his father. In a neatly executed drawing, the King, backed by Prince Rupert, Edward Hyde and a handful of other notable faces all perfectly recognisable, faced Sir Harry Vane, Oliver St John, Colonel Cromwell and a quantity of tartan-clad Scots; and hovering irresolute between the two, my lords Essex and Manchester were saying plaintively, 'O Lord, show us thy will? Shall we be Papist or Presbyterian?'

Richard scrutinised it at some length and then passed it to his wife. If he felt like laughing, there was no sign of it. He said flatly, 'You're a fool, Felix. And so, apparently, is Geoffrey. What happened?'

'We got caught running the last batch through the press,' said Felix simply. 'Someone must have informed on us. I'm not surprised. The Committee of Examinations is trying to stamp out unlicensed printing and its spies are everywhere. Anyway, four pursuivants came and dragged us off to the Gatehouse. We were there nearly a week.'

'And are monumentally lucky,' said the Italian caustically, 'that you're not there still. They were not at all eager to let you out.'

'But you persuaded them,' said Richard. It was not a question. 'How much did it cost you?'

'Too much. But don't worry. I recouped it from your enterprising son-in-law. It seemed only fair. No profit without risk of loss, you know,' finished Luciano. And smiled.

By means of a little stealth and cunning, Kate managed to isolate him in the parlour shortly before supper – and, knowing she did not have much time, came straight to the point.

'Did you find him?' she asked.

Luciano raised faintly baffled brows. 'I beg your pardon?'

'Robert Brandon. Did you find him?' And then, when

he didn't answer, 'You did, didn't you? Was he the right man?'

There was a long silence. Then, 'I rather thought,' he said gently, 'that I told you to stay out of it. This is not your affair, Kate – nor will it ever be. And I have a morbid dislike of childish prying.'

'Oh it's worse than that,' Kate assured him, disposing herself gracefully on the window-seat. 'You're so secretive, I doubt your right hand knows what your left is doing half of the time.'

'And you,' he returned blandly, 'have a number of characteristics generally attributed to ferrets. Now, does that conclude the compliments? – or have you anything you'd like to add?'

Able to think of at least three smart answers, Kate opened her mouth on the best of them – and then shut it again as the door opened and her mother walked in.

'Check,' said Luciano softly, laughter lighting his face. 'Company manners, Kate.'

'Well, at least I have some,' she returned, equally softly and with restrained enjoyment. 'But what are *you* going to do?'

Late that night, when the rest of the family had retired, Luciano faced Richard across the hearth and said thoughtfully, 'So you've stuck to your guns and stayed at home. Doesn't it irk you?'

'Every hour of every day,' came the honest reply. 'But there's no room in the House now for men like myself . . . and so the best I can do is to stay out of it and look to my own.' Richard handed his friend a glass of brandy and sat down, staring meditatively into his own. 'Is it true there's a certain disappointment in the air over our Scottish allies?'

'You could put it that way. It's been a long, cold winter and people are tired of felling trees while they wait for the Scots to take Newcastle so they can have some coal. As for the City, the last forced loan nearly broke it.'

'How much was asked for?'

'Seventy thousand – on top of the thirty thousand advanced by the Merchant Adventurers. With Royalist pirates, Dunkirk pirates and increased competition from Bristol, these kind of demands just can't continue being met. And if the rumblings within the Worshipful Company of Goldsmiths is any indication, the Parliament's going to find itself going to the well once too often.'

'In which case the Scots will doubtless withdraw their services. I don't see them assisting Parliament for love, do you?' Richard leaned back in his chair and sipped his brandy. Then he said, 'That cartoon Felix drew . . . *are* people saying the Earl of Manchester's joining the Peace Party?'

'Not that I've heard. They do, however, say he's less than happy in his partnership with Oliver Cromwell.'

'Then he should find plenty of sympathisers. As I understand it, there's a feeling within the Commons that Colonel Cromwell is useful for fighting the war but could become a problem when it's won.'

'*If* it's won,' said Luciano sardonically. 'At the moment, there's scant sign of it – though I would agree that the longer it drags on, the less chance there is of victory going to the King. The divisions within his high command may not be so well publicised as that between Waller and Essex, but they're there none the less. After Lord Falkland died at Newbury, George Digby became Secretary of State; and he and the Queen oppose Rupert over nearly everything, which means that policy changes as soon as the Prince turns his back.' He paused to drink and then gave a short laugh. 'And if that feels as though he's banging his head against the wall, I can only say that I know the sensation well.'

'Ah,' said Richard. 'At last. I wondered how long it would be before we got to more personal matters. From your silence I rather assumed that you didn't find Brandon after all.'

'That's not what Kate thinks.'

'*Kate?* Hell. I thought she'd forgotten all about it.'

'As far as I can see,' came the acid response, 'she never forgets anything. She's also too damned shrewd.'

'Shrewd enough – with what she's picked up from Felix and Gianetta – to work out the whole story?' asked Richard. 'Yes. It's what I've thought myself. Fortunately, she also knows how to keep her mouth shut.'

Luciano's expression said that this was a matter of opinion.

Richard grinned. 'You know what I mean,' he said.

'I think so. But if you're suggesting that I take her into my confidence, I can only say I'd need a better reason than merely to stop her asking questions.' He drew a long breath and then said, 'I found Brandon. He's not like the others. He actually went to some trouble to find another way out that didn't involve my father. It wasn't his fault he failed. But, to cut a long story short, we discussed the matter in some detail and, at the end of it all, I went back to Samuel Fisher . . . mainly because there was nowhere else left to go.' Luciano stopped to take a drink and let the silence gather around them before he finally said baldly, 'He was dead when I found him – and had been for a week or more.'

'Of natural causes?' asked Richard sharply.

'Hardly. He'd been stabbed. Someone had also ripped the house apart, looking for something. And, if it was there at all, I assume they found it.'

'You didn't search the place yourself, then?'

'Without knowing what I was looking for and on the heels of a remarkably thorough person who obviously did, there seemed little point. Besides, the stench was intolerable.' He paused again. 'However. The point is that it looks as though Fisher knew who was behind the whole thing and was killed because of it. But what I can't understand is – why now? Why *now*, when it stands to reason that he must have been sitting on the information for years?'

'The Chief Bastard didn't know he knew?' suggested Richard. 'Or he had some written proof tucked away as insurance?'

'Which the Chief Bastard has now taken.'

'Yes. That would fit, wouldn't it? And didn't you say that you tried to speak to Fisher last autumn? That might account for the sudden need to silence him. After all, if you're right about the raid on your house, you're in the picture too.'

Luciano looked sick. He said, 'Christ. Do you still want me to tell Kate all about it?'

'No. It's getting messy. And dangerous.'

'I think I may truthfully be said to have noticed that.'

'Then let the thing drop.'

'And sit back waiting for him to kill me?'

'He probably won't if you stop trying to trace him.'

'You'll pardon me,' observed Luciano caustically, 'if I say it's a gamble I don't particularly like. Not, unfortunately, that it seems I have too much choice. Giles Langley is dead – and Ferrars and Fisher; Brandon has told me all he knows and Webb's gone abroad. Aside from two rather frail clues, I haven't the remotest idea where to look.'

Richard's gaze sharpened. 'Clues?'

'Brandon furnished me with a sample of our friend's handwriting – for all the use that's likely to be,' came the flat reply. 'And whoever murdered Fisher has my emerald ring – unless, of course, they've sold it. It depends, I suppose, on whether Fisher was killed by hired ruffians or by the man himself. All I know is that whoever did it knew a fine stone when he saw it, and wanted that ring badly enough to hack off the old man's finger to get it.'

A spasm of pure revulsion contorted Richard's face and he said, 'God's teeth! And you still can't see the sense in letting the matter drop? How many times do I have to say it? *He knows who you are.*'

'Yes. And therein lies my only hope,' came the mild reply. 'That one day he'll come for me himself.'

Richard shut his eyes and let his head drop back. He said, 'You've got a death-wish. You must have.'

The Italian smiled a little. 'Far from it. I just don't like giving up. And this is important to me.'

'So you'll die for it.' The grey eyes opened again on an expression of grim exasperation. 'Make no mistake, Luciano – you're not up to dealing with this man. Could *you* have mutilated someone's hand for the sake of a ring?'

'You're making an assumption.'

'But not, I suspect, an unreasonable one. Well?'

Luciano stared down at his glass for a moment. Then he said slowly, 'No. I had good reason to hate Fisher . . . but I couldn't have done that.'

'Then how do you expect to fare with the man who did?'

The dark gaze rose, filled with chilly determination. 'Only give me the chance and you'd be surprised how quickly I'd learn,' he said. And then, 'Stop worrying, Richard. It's not your problem.'

'No? And I suppose if I suddenly decided to hurl myself from the roof, it wouldn't be your problem either?' came the biting retort. 'Or perhaps that's another bloody assumption?'

'No. Not at all.' Luciano smiled crookedly. 'But then *I'd* have an ulterior motive. You see, you're the only friend I have.'

Two

For those at Thorne Ash, Rupert of the Rhine's brilliantly executed relief of the besieged town of Newark fell into almost instant eclipse when Sir William Waller (assisted, no doubt, by Captain Eden Maxwell) successfully thrashed the Royalists at Alresford. Then, as April drifted into May, attention was torn between the deliberate drowning by a parliamentary sea-captain of a number of Irish troops destined for the King, and the combining outside the city of York of the Scots and the Fairfaxes. The first left a nasty taste in a lot of people's mouths; the second, because it necessitated Rupert's absence from Oxford, was eventually responsible for the King making Lord Essex a gift of Reading and Abingdon by evacuating his own forces from them.

Essex's delight at having Oxford helpless before him caused him temporarily to bury the hatchet with Waller, and in no time at all the pair of them were menacing the city from three sides – while, belatedly recognising his mistake, the King very sensibly winnowed both himself and his cavalry out to safety in Worcester. If there was some strategy behind these moves of His Majesty's, Richard Maxwell was not the only one who found it hard to comprehend – for, should Oxford fall, the Royal cause was unlikely to recover. For a couple of days it was tempting to wonder if the end might not be in sight, but then Essex took it into his head to march off and save Lyme from the marauding hands of Prince Maurice, and Waller was left with little alternative but to go and play grandmother's footsteps with the King. So much, thought Richard irritably, for making the most of your opportunities. At this rate the war could last another decade.

While Rupert took Stockport, Bolton, Wigan and Liverpool, brother Maurice abandoned Lyme and the Earl of Manchester added his Eastern Association troops to those already besieging York. And, at Thorne Ash, Felix Maxwell waged his own private campaign to be allowed to return to London – to which, for reasons of his own, his father was finally persuaded to give in.

'Who do you think you're fooling?' asked Dorothy when he told her. 'You just want an excuse to go to London and get the news first-hand. Isn't that so? You want to visit your friends and discover exactly what's happening in Westminster and put the world to rights over a cup or two of wine with Luciano del Santi – assuming he's back from his travels.

'Never say,' she finished with a smile, 'that I don't understand you.'

'I wouldn't dare! But can I also take it that you've no objections? I shouldn't be gone much above two weeks.'

'Oh? Well . . . no doubt Kate and I can just about manage to hold things together for that long.'

'Vixen,' murmured Richard appreciatively. And then, pulling her into his arms, 'All right. I know you can cope . . . but some small reluctance to let me go would be nice. Or I might get the idea that you won't miss me.'

'No you won't.' She tilted her head back to look at him. 'You know I'll miss you – and you know how much. But I've been expecting this. You've been itching to go for weeks, haven't you?'

'The thought has occasionally crossed my mind.'

'Of course it has. If I'd spent as long enmeshed in the affairs of the nation as you have, I think *I'd* find it a struggle to return to purely domestic pursuits. So off you go and enjoy yourself.'

Richard kissed her. 'You're a wonderful woman. Do you know that?'

'Yes,' laughed Dorothy. 'So it's fortunate, isn't it, that you deserve me?'

480

Observing a modicum of care, Richard and Felix arrived in London without mishap on 20 June to find that Luciano del Santi had still not returned from Genoa. Felix found this surprising. Richard, understanding the difficulties faced by shipping around England's coast, did not. He merely said calmly, 'He could be here any day, Felix. So possess your soul in patience and keep away from Geoffrey's presses. If you get yourself arrested again, I'll be very tempted to let them keep you.'

Felix gave a rueful grin. 'Don't worry. Sir's threatened me with worse than that. If I get in trouble again, he'll terminate my indentures and send me home.'

'God forbid! And you believe him?'

'Oh yes. When he says he'll do something, he does it. Haven't you noticed? And he also knows precisely how much I want my own attempts at filigree to start resembling his. At the moment it's like putting an iron griddle next to a spider's web. So, as I said, you've got nothing to worry about. Nothing at all.'

Put like that – and knowing his son – Richard was content to believe it and was therefore able to set off on the round of calls he had set himself with a clear conscience. He went first to deliver a few strictures into the suitably abashed ear of Geoffrey Cox and afterwards spent a pleasant, if not exactly stimulating, hour with Amy. Then he went back to Cheapside and bore Felix off to sup with him at the Bear.

Four days later – and still with no sign of the Italian – Richard was beginning to find that the erstwhile colleagues who had all been so happy to see him, had ulterior motives. They wanted him to return to the House.

'There'd be no difficulty,' said Henry Cox. 'With numbers so badly reduced and no chance of new elections, I doubt if anyone would stand on ceremony – and, if they did, you could always plead ill-health to account for your absence. So what do you say?'

'Exactly what I said before,' replied Richard. 'I don't feel inclined to take the Covenant. And if you're about to quote John Selden to me and say that such oaths, like pills, are better swallowed without chewing – I can only remark that I consider that singularly pointless.'

'No more pointless than giving up and going home,' muttered Denzil Holles. 'The rest of us may have had to put our tongues very firmly in our cheeks, but at least we still retain our seats.'

'And what good,' asked Richard directly, 'has it done you? Whether you like it or not, policy is being shaped by Vane and St John and the rest of them – while you've been relegated to the position of a lone voice crying in the wilderness. That can't, surely, be what you want.'

Holles fell silent and stared gloomily into space. They were sitting in a small tavern just outside the precincts of Westminster and, save for two other men talking in low-voiced murmurs on the far side of the room, they had it to themselves. Henry Cox stirred and said, 'If the Scots take York, it'll make the whole thing seem more worthwhile.'

'*If* they do,' said Holles. 'God knows three armies ought to be able to take a town. But I wouldn't wager a groat on the Robber Prince not turning up before they do.'

'Neither would I. And it seems to me that three armies is two too many,' asserted Mr Cox. 'It just leads to commanders squabbling amongst themselves. If Oliver Cromwell can spare the time from bickering with Lord Manchester, he's probably at it tooth and nail with Tom Fairfax or old Leven by now. No. One army – one commander-in-chief. That's what we need – eh, Richard?'

'What?' Richard's attention had become fixed on the men in the corner – for no better reason than that he recognised one of them and had the annoying feeling that he also ought to be able to name the other. 'Henry . . . isn't that Samuel Luke over there?'

Mr Cox peered across the room. 'Couldn't say. Never seen him before.'

'The scoutmaster-general?' Denzil Holles sat up. 'So it is. I wonder what he's doing here?'

'The same thing he does elsewhere, I imagine.' Richard

continued to stare at Sir Samuel's companion and wondered why he had a peculiar suspicion that the two somehow didn't belong together. Then the naggingly familiar gentleman rose to go and stood for a moment leaning negligently against the settle with one tapering hand resting against its back; and quite suddenly Richard had it. Lowering his voice, he said, 'Surely that fellow with Luke is a King's man? Denzil – or no. You weren't there. But you, Henry – you'd remember him. The day His Majesty came to the House to arrest our friend here, the doors of the chamber were kept open by two men. One was Roxburgh – and the other, unless I'm much mistaken, was that man there. Well?'

Mr Cox scratched his head. 'Could have been, I suppose. I can't say I took much notice. But what if it was him? He won't have been the first to change sides – and I don't imagine he'll be the last.'

'No. No, I suppose not,' sighed Richard. He felt faintly and unreasonably cheated, as if something important was eluding him; which it might well be if the fellow was one of Sir Samuel Luke's spies. Not, it had to be admitted, that he looked like a spy. Richard took in the exquisite lace collar, the gold-embroidered baldrick and the jewel flashing green fire on the supple, white hand. No. One tended to assume that spies presented a less affluent appearance . . . or, at the very least, a less striking one. Still frowning a little, Richard drained his tankard and absently accepted Henry's invitation to dine at his home on Ludgate Hill.

He never got there. Half-way between his lodging and St Paul's, he suddenly realised precisely what it was about Sir Samuel Luke's friend that had been troubling him. His stomach gave an unpleasant lurch and he stopped dead in the street, thinking furiously. It was nothing to do with where he had seen the fellow before, of course. It was the thrice-blasted ring on his left hand, the bloody, great emerald that Richard now cursed himself for not getting a better look at. He drew a long breath and told himself not to get too excited. The world must be full of emeralds, but of that size and cut – visible even at such a distance? Unlikely. Damn. He wished he could be sure. He wished he'd made the connection five hours ago. But that was futile. The question now was what – if anything – could still be done about it.

Richard stared unseeingly into a haberdasher's window, debating various possibilities. Then, giving a small boy sixpence to carry his apologies to Henry, he walked quickly down to Queenhithe and found a boat that would take him to Westminster, where he hoped to find someone who would be able to direct him to Sir Samuel Luke.

The following morning found him hammering on Luciano del Santi's door before Giacomo had opened up for the day. Then, when he was finally admitted, he said briskly, 'Is he back?'

Giacomo shook his head. 'No. But soon, I think.'

'Soon's not good enough.' Richard eyed the little man calmly. 'All right. How deep are you in your master's confidence?'

Giacomo thought about it. Then, smiling wryly, 'As deep as you, signor. You want I should give him a message?'

'Yes. Tell him . . . just tell him I've gone off following a ring I saw yesterday. And that, if I find it and it turns out to be the right one, I'll try and bring him its owner's signature.'

Giacomo's smile evaporated and was replaced by a look of uncharacteristic grimness. He said simply, 'You have a name?'

'Yes. But I'll keep it to myself until I'm sure.'

'Monsignor will not like it. I think is better you tell me.'

'No doubt you do. But if monsignor doesn't like it, he'll just have to do the other thing. And, in the meantime, I'm leaving you with other problems. I want you to get Felix back to Thorne Ash,' said Richard flatly. 'He won't like it, of course, but if my mission prospers, Luciano is hardly likely to be devoting the next few weeks to Felix's filigree-work, is he? And if these premises are going to become the target of someone's unfriendly attentions, I'd rather my son wasn't here. Do I make myself clear?'

'Very clear, signor,' came the gloomy reply.

'Good. Then I'd best be off. Don't take any nonsense from Felix – or let Luciano's impatience gather momentum,' said Richard, heading for the door. Then, turning, 'Oh – and Giacomo?'

'Signor?'

'Give them both my love.'

Kate wasn't sure precisely when and why her prevailing sense of unease about Celia's frequent visits to Far Flamstead finally crystallised into dark suspicion – only that it was so. It had begun, of course, on the day she'd caught her loitering in the shadows of the gatehouse with Hugo Verney: less on account of Celia's presence there than for the glibness of her excuses. And after that had come the noticeable diminution in the twice-weekly excursions that had lasted only as long as Waller's army was known to be outside Oxford, and returned to normal as soon as it drew off in the wake of the King. Just as if, thought Kate unhappily, the possibility of Eden arriving home unexpectedly made it necessary to take a few extra precautions. But that was pure speculation and certainly not sufficient to warrant an accusation of adultery – neither to Celia herself nor, indeed, to anyone at all.

To do her justice, Kate desperately hoped she was wrong. The difficulty was in knowing how best to go about finding out. Her own relationship with Celia made it impossible to offer to ride to Far Flamstead with her; and when Felicity had quite innocently asked if she might accompany her one day, the response had been a crushing snub. All that was left, therefore, was the unpleasant process of spying; and after a good deal of soul-searching, Kate came to the reluctant conclusion that it behoved her to undertake it. After all, if she was lucky, Celia's visits to Far Flamstead might prove completely innocuous; and if not . . . well, at least there might be some small chance of putting an end to the affair before Eden was destroyed by it.

She finally steeled herself to make the attempt ten days after Richard left for London with Felix. There were rumours that, far from being somewhere in the vicinity of Worcester, the King's army was in fact a good deal nearer at hand: that it had recently been in Buckingham and was now no further away than Brackley. If this was true, it made riding around the countryside – even if only to Far Flamstead – a somewhat risky business in Kate's opinion, and she could not help hoping that Celia would think so too and choose to stay at home. But either Celia was made of sterner stuff, or she had better sources of information, for she set off, with no apparent concern, exactly as usual. And after hovering irresolutely in the stables for the best part of ten minutes, Kate simply told herself that it was now or never – and set off after her.

There was no need to keep Celia within sight. It was enough to ride slowly along the lanes which led to the village of Farnborough and Lord Wroxton's manor . . . and then, leaving the carriage-drive, to make her way unseen through the park to the west wing of the house.

Two horses were tethered outside. Celia's bay mare . . . and a powerful-looking black that Kate knew only too well and which made it unnecessary to go peering through windows or keyholes. Hugo Verney was in there with Celia – and not, presumably, for the first time. Kate shivered. Apart from the latter part of her pregnancy during the winter, and those few days in May when Eden was close by, Celia had been 'keeping an eye on Far Flamstead' for over a year. Since well before little Viola could have been conceived, in fact. And that, of course, was the most frightening thought of all.

Weighed down with sick anger, Kate remained hidden amongst the trees and waited. She did not know how long it was, but finally Celia and Hugo came out of the house and walked, hand in hand, to the horses. They were talking but she could not hear what they said. She could, however, see the transparent happiness on Celia's face and the way she nestled close to Hugo while her fingers busied themselves retying his collar. And then, as if that were not enough, she saw them melt into each other's arms and exchange a long, desperate kiss.

Kate turned away and pressed her clenched hands against the bark of an oak in an attempt to overlay one pain with another. It didn't work. The hurt was too severe. For it wasn't only Celia and Hugo and the mess they were making of Eden's life; it was her own blind, searing need for Luciano . . . and the terrible void it was making of her own.

Kate arrived home half an hour after Celia with no memory of having got there, then spent the evening alone in her room, nursing a very real headache. And on the following morning, still with no completely satisfactory plan of how to deal with Celia, she rose to the news that the King and Sir William Waller had apparently spent the night facing each other across the River Cherwell just outside Banbury.

A bubble of faint hysteria formed in Kate's chest. Didn't they say it never rained but it poured? She only hoped Captain Verney got court-martialled for dereliction of duty or whatever it was called. No. That was silly. What she *ought* to be hoping for was that Eden got no closer to His Majesty than the other bank of the river. Anything else didn't bear thinking about.

The morning passed without news, rather as it had done on that fateful day the October before last when Edgehill had been fought. And then, at around noon, a tenant from one of the outlying farms arrived breathlessly at the gate to inform them that both armies were on the move again. Colonel Sir William Waller had left Banbury by the Southam road and was now on top of Bourton Hill . . . and the King had taken the Daventry road as far as Wardington.

'Oh God,' said Dorothy, dully. 'They must be within sight of each other – and have been all the way.'

'But still with the river between them,' said Felicity quickly, with intent to comfort. 'It'll be all right. If they were going to fight, they'd have done it by now, wouldn't they?'

'Not,' replied Kate remotely, 'without a bridge to cross. And where's the bridge nearest to both of them right now?'

Felicity thought about it and then turned rather pale. 'Cropredy?' she said feebly.

'Cropredy,' agreed Kate. And said nothing more. There was, after all, no need . . . for the village of Cropredy lay less than four miles down the lane from Thorne Ash.

They heard it begin an hour later – first with indistinct shouting and then with volley upon volley of musket-fire. Along with the rest of the household, Kate stood silently above the gatehouse and listened, without knowing quite what she expected the distant noise to tell her. Celia, she noticed coldly, looked as tense as any of them. Kate wondered if she had finally realised that Eden was out there fighting for his life and was prey to well-deserved remorse . . . but came to the conclusion that it was improbable. She was more likely to be worrying about Hugo Verney. 'Only let this day pass safely,' Kate told herself grimly, 'and I swear I'll cook her goose for her if it's the last thing I do.'

It was then that she realised that Dorothy was missing – and why. Leaving the others to their vigil, Kate walked slowly to the chapel to sit at her mother's side and hold her hand through the long afternoon.

They spoke only once.

Dorothy said, 'When it's over, Eden will surely come home, won't he?'

'If his sympathetic major will let him,' replied Kate steadily, 'I'm sure he will. But it may not be straight away.'

And then they fell silent till the guns at Cropredy stopped.

Eden did not come that night – but he did send Tom Tripp with the message that he was safe and would come if and when he could. Dorothy shed a few thankful tears and then instructed Goodwife Flossing to see that a hot meal would be ready to serve at a moment's notice. Celia remained cool to the point of indifference and only smiled when Tom gruffly admitted that victory at Cropredy Bridge had gone to the King. Their own army, he said, had lost colours, light artillery and men – though as yet no one knew exactly how bad the numbers were.

Since the two armies spent Sunday staring each other out and indulging in sporadic sniping between Bourton and Cropredy, Kate decided that it wasn't really a good time to tackle Celia on the thorny question of adultery.

She therefore let the day drift by without saying anything and worked hard at behaving normally. Then, at around four in the afternoon, while she was helping her mother repair some of Jude's clothes, Dorothy gave a tiny shiver and said oddly, 'Is there a draught in here – or am I just showing my advanced years?'

'Neither,' said Kate. 'You're just thoroughly on edge and won't be happy until you've seen Eden with your own eyes.'

'No. No, I won't. I just wish he'd hurry up and—' She stopped and sat up very straight, her eyes brightening. 'And get here. There's a horse in the yard.'

'Yes.' Kate grinned. 'Perfect timing, wouldn't you say?'

'Perfect,' agreed Dorothy. And then they were both skimming out into the hall.

It wasn't Eden. It was Felix. Dorothy and Kate stopped dead and stared at him.

'Don't blame me,' said Felix bitterly. 'Father's orders, apparently. It seems that, with him chasing off God-knows-where and Mr Santi still not back from Genoa, I'm not to be trusted with nobody but Giacomo to keep me out of trouble. And no – I didn't travel here alone. I rode with a couple of merchants on their way to Birmingham. They've gone on.'

Kate shut her mouth and waited for Dorothy to give her brother a hug. Then she said, 'Did you say *Father* has gone off somewhere?'

'Yes,' he snapped. And, on a long fulminating breath, 'I just wish people would start remembering I'm seventeen – not seven!'

'When you give them cause to remember it, I daresay they will,' observed his mother absently. 'But what's this about your father? Where is he?'

'I haven't the faintest idea. All I know is that he went off to see somebody or other and said he'd be back in a few days.' Felix shrugged. 'It's probably something to do with the House. He's been seeing a lot of Geoffrey's father and Denzil Holles.'

'How very odd,' murmured Dorothy. And then, smiling, 'Ah well. I suppose you're hungry?'

'Starving,' he agreed, rather more cheerfully. 'I could eat an ox whole.'

'We're saving it for Eden,' said Kate. 'But I imagine we might find you a crust or two. And while we look, you can explain how you managed to get here past two armies. Come on, I'm listening.' And she bore him away to the kitchen.

Neither that evening nor the following morning brought any sign of Eden, and when they heard that the King's army was moving away towards Aynho, Dorothy's nerves began to show distinct signs of wear. Kate, as usual, combated anxiety with activity and spent the early part of the afternoon energetically weeding the garden and snipping spent blooms from her precious roses. And that was why it was past three o'clock before she learned from Felicity that Celia had taken her horse and gone out.

'Did she say where she was going?' asked Kate sharply.

'Not to me. But I expect she's at Far Flamstead.' Felicity eyed her sister with puzzled inquiry. 'You look very odd. What's the matter?'

'I – nothing. I just can't believe she'd go off like this, knowing Eden could be here at any moment.'

'Well, he didn't come yesterday and she's probably thinking there's no guarantee he'll come today,' came the reasonable reply. 'Besides, it's Monday. She always goes to Far Flamstead on Mondays. And if Sir William's decided to follow the King, it seems to me that Eden may not get here at all.'

'Which only goes to prove how wrong you can be.' Kate's gaze was fixed on some point beyond Felicity, through the open window. 'He's here now. Look.'

Felicity looked and then was off, with a pleased exclamation, in the direction of the stairs. Kate followed more slowly, an unpleasant sinking sensation taking place somewhere behind her ribs.

By the time they got downstairs, Dorothy already had Eden in her arms and was bubbling over with questions. Then, seeing Felix and his sisters, Eden set her gently aside and said tonelessly, 'I think we should all go into the parlour. I have something to tell you.'

Kate stared at him. His face was like carved ivory. A terrible fear that had nothing to do with her worries about Celia invaded her body, but she quelled it and wordlessly drew Felix and Felicity through the parlour door. Behind them, she heard her mother saying, 'Eden . . . what is it? You look so ill.' And was aware that Eden did not answer.

Once in the parlour, however, he settled his mother in a chair and, still holding her hands, dropped to his knees in front of her. Then, as if the effort of speaking was almost beyond him, he said, 'You must be brave. There is no easy way to say this – so I'll be quick. It's Father. He – he's dead.'

The world turned dark and there was no air. Felicity made a tiny mewing sound and then stifled it with her fingers. Felix turned perfectly white and Kate sat like a stone. For a long moment, no one spoke. Then, in a voice of thread-like courtesy, Dorothy said, 'It isn't possible. You're mistaken.'

'No.' Eden's hands tightened their grip and his chest heaved. 'I'm afraid not. I only wish I was.'

'What happened?' It was Kate who spoke, dry-eyed and shaking. 'Did he . . . was it the battle?'

'The day after. Yesterday.' Still watching his mother, Eden assembled his words with care. 'I don't know how it can have come about – but he seems to have arrived in the King's camp yesterday morning. There was still some skirmishing going on, so perhaps . . . but I can't be sure. Indeed, had it not been for Ralph, I probably wouldn't have—' He stopped abruptly and then said unsteadily, 'Mother, you have to believe me. I – I've seen him.'

A convulsive shudder passed through Dorothy's frame and her eyes grew wide and dark. She felt numb from head to foot; and behind the numbness lay horror.

Eden turned his head to look helplessly at Kate. He said, 'What shall I do?'

'Tell her the rest quickly,' came the flat reply. 'None of us can stand much more of this.'

Felicity was already sobbing silently in Felix's arms and Kate looked as though she wanted to be sick. Turning back to Dorothy, Eden said rapidly, 'Ralph was taken prisoner during the battle and exchanged along with some others this afternoon. He – he told me he'd seen Father's body. So between us, we managed to arrange for the Cavaliers to release it to us . . . and Ralph and Tom will be bringing him home in a short while.'

Cruel, excoriating silence stretched out into every corner of the room. And finally Dorothy used every ounce of her strength to say painfully, 'How? How did he die?'

Eden swallowed hard. 'He was shot. Through the heart.'

It had been necessary. He knew it had been necessary . . . but he found he could no longer bear the sight of his mother slowly disintegrating before his eyes. He dropped his head upon his hands and hers; and then the storm broke . . . and Kate was there to bear it with him.

Later, while Dorothy was being put to bed and dosed with the strongest opiate Kate could find in the house, Eden was left alone with the twins. Felicity continued to cry as if her heart would break; but Felix – though still the colour of parchment – clung grimly to the shreds of his self-control. Eden said simply, 'I thank God you're here, Felix. Mother's going to need you.'

A peculiar tremor touched the boy's face and when he spoke, his voice was raw. He said, 'I can't believe this is happening. Why was he with the King? *Why?*'

'I don't know. It doesn't make any sense. But it will do us no good to think of that now. We – we have to make ready to receive his body. And I must tell Celia. Where is she?'

'At Far Flamstead,' said Felix. And then, with suppressed violence, 'Do you think she'll care?'

Every bone in Eden's body ached as if it had been savagely clubbed and he was too weary to argue. He said, 'I don't know. I hope so. Either way, she still has to know. I'd better go and fetch her.'

'Fetch who?' demanded Kate from the doorway.

Eden turned to face her. 'Celia.'

'There's no need. She'll come herself presently.'

'And arrive at the same time as – as Father? I can't let that happen.'

'*Why not?*' thought Kate bitterly. There had been no time yet for her own emotions and still wasn't – on top of which she had somehow to stop Eden going to Far Flamstead. To be subtle as well was more than she could manage. She said harshly, 'What difference does it make? And you've other duties which require your presence here.'

'I know. And therefore the sooner I go, the sooner I'll be back.'

He was already moving towards her. Kate blocked the doorway and said explosively, 'All right. God in heaven – *all right*! If you're so set on it – let me go. Or Felix.'

'No. You should be with Mother – and telling Celia is my job, not Felix's.' Eden stared down at his sister out of frowning, intolerant eyes. 'Stand aside, Kate.'

She shook her head and watched the fuse of tension ignite.

'Then you leave me no choice,' he said. And, grasping her shoulders in a bruising grip, he moved her from his path and strode out.

Short of screaming out the truth before the twins, there was no way of holding him. Kate leant weakly against the wall, her arms clamped tight about the pain that was beginning to rip her apart.

'Please God,' she prayed, silent and despairing. 'Don't let it happen. Not today. Or how shall we bear it?'

Eden rode to Far Flamstead as fast as he dared. Like Kate before him, he found two horses already tethered under the trees outside . . . but, unlike Kate, he recognised only Celia's bay. Preoccupied and grey with strain, he ran up the shallow steps and, opening the door, walked once more into his wife's old home.

There was no time for memories. The elegant, impersonal hall was chilly and lightly mantled with dust, its few pieces of furniture shrouded beneath white sheets. Eden

493

took a deep preparatory breath and harnessed his dwindling resources.

'Celia?'

His voice echoed hollowly on the still air. Then, nothing. Eden set his foot on the ornately carved staircase and started to climb, empty of everything except for a deathly, dragging tiredness. At the top, he opened his mouth to call again, and then closed it as a small sound reached him. The sound of low, husky laughter. A little ahead and to his right, a door stood slightly ajar. Eden started instinctively towards it.

Nothing warned him to turn back. And, because the normal processes of thought had deserted him, he did not even check his pace. He simply arrived at the door and pushed it wide.

A fire burned low in the grate and on a small table before it were the remains of a simple meal. Reposing neatly on a chair, a blue silk gown contrasted oddly with the impatient tangle of other clothing that was strewn across the floor. And in the velvet-hung bed, frozen into stunned immobility, Celia lay entangled in Hugo Verney's arms.

It was like a moment trapped in time. Eden did not know how long he stood there, vacantly observing every tiny detail of the scene in front of him, or how long he waited for the desert inside him to be imprinted with thought. But it eventually came; irritation at his own stupidity for not being able to understand and react to the significance of what he was seeing and standing, instead, like some doltish half-wit in the doorway. Then the tableau dissolved and the spell shattered.

Celia sat up, clutching the sheet over her breasts – an instinct which Eden dimly recognised as being cripplingly ironic; and Captain Verney shot out of the far side of the bed, dragging the coverlet with him. In a play, it might have been funny; in one's own life and on this of all days, it was cataclysmic.

Petrified by something in his face, Celia stammered, 'Eden – d-don't do anything s-silly! You- you've got to listen.'

'Listen? To what? To you trying to convince me it isn't

494

as it seems?' he asked gratingly. 'But there again – why not? It will pass the time while your lover dresses.'

White-faced and decidedly disadvantaged, Hugo stepped round to the foot of the bed. He said quietly, 'I'll fight, of course. But I think you should know that—'

'Keep your mouth shut or I won't wait.' A pulse hammered in Eden's jaw and his fingers were already lingering on the hilt of his sword. Though not yet at their peak, the pain and anger within him needed to be exorcised; and since the means was to hand, he did not even try to resist it. He said, 'Just put your clothes on. You too.'

Unable to believe he meant it, Celia stared at him and opened her mouth on a word of protest.

'*Do it.*' The words cracked like a pistol shot. 'I haven't much time. But you don't know about that yet, do you?'

'Kn-know what?' she asked. She had struggled into her shift and her teeth were chattering with fright.

'About Father.' Eden let the pause build while he watched her tying her petticoats and searching for her stockings. His eyes were cold and hard and at no time did he permit them to stray to Hugo Verney. Then he said baldly, 'He's dead.'

Hugo froze in the act of fastening his shirt and stared at Celia's husband, recognising that his own death-sentence lay in those words. His skin prickled and he wondered, distantly, how good Eden Maxwell was with a sword. Very good, probably . . . whereas he himself was no more than mediocre. But then *he* hadn't spent the best part of two years at Angers. Stiffly, his fingers resumed their task. Then, not bothering to put on his coat, he reached for his sword and said expressionlessly, 'I am at your disposal. Where do you want to settle this?'

'Downstairs in the hall,' replied Eden briefly. And then, to Celia who was still struggling awkwardly with the laces of her gown, 'If you want to watch, you'll have to hurry. I'd like to be at home when they bring back Father's body.'

He turned back through the door and, as he did so, Celia flung herself at Hugo crying, 'Don't go! Tell him you won't fight. He won't kill you in cold blood.'

'Not normally, perhaps.' Hugo held her briefly, then

stepped back with a small twisted smile. 'But today is not normal, is it? And I don't think he could be blamed if he did.' And, dropping a swift, hard kiss on her lips, he strode off in Eden's wake.

Except in battle, most fights begin cautiously while you test your opponent's skill. This one opened with a furious onslaught that jarred the bones in Hugo's wrist and drove him back across almost the entire width of the hall. His heart was in his mouth and his only hope was that Eden's haste might make him careless. Without knowing how he did it, he managed to halt his retreat and engage the ferocious blade in a couple of moves that were not purely defensive. His nerves started to settle.

Celia clung to the banister half-way down the stairs, petrified as much by the grim intent in Eden's face as by the dreadful echoing clamour of steel ringing on steel. Hugo was being beaten back again and the times when he was able to stand his ground seemed to come less and less often. And all the time the swords chimed and hissed and slithered till she thought her head would burst.

Having let off a little of his murderous rage, Eden felt cold reason start to return. He stopped pushing Verney around the floor and concentrated on finding just the right opening. It wouldn't do to make a mess of it – and he had already wasted enough time. And then, as he began the series of moves that would bring him what he wanted, he suddenly realised something. Killing Verney wouldn't solve anything. It wouldn't even make him feel better. The only man he wanted to kill was the one who had shot Richard. And, as for Celia, he already knew he could never live with her again after this. Nor did he want to. *None of which was Hugo Verney's fault.*

The moment he had been working towards arrived and he sent Verney's sword spinning from his hand. Then, with swift, relentless precision, he drove his own blade deep into the other man's shoulder.

Hugo crumpled and fell, a flood of bright crimson staining the whiteness of his shirt . . . and, with a tiny, strangled cry, Celia came hurtling down the stairs to kneel at his side.

Eden stared motionlessly down at them for a second; and then absently wiped and sheathed his sword.

Finally, in a tone drained of everything except fatigue, he said, 'Get up, Celia. We're leaving.'

She looked up at him, her face bathed in tears. 'You think I'd go with you? He could *die!*'

'He won't. And you *will* come with me. Whether you like it or not, you'll come back to Thorne Ash and say nothing of any of this . . . and behave like my wife until we've given my father a decent burial.' Eden paused and then said bitingly, 'After that, you may go where you like and with whom you like. Personally speaking, I never want to see you again.'

Three

On the day that Richard Maxwell was laid to rest in the family vault, Dorothy suffered a nerve-storm and Kate thought that life had finally reached its nadir.

She was wrong.

The following morning saw Eden depart – still grimly uncommunicative and with a worried Ralph in tow – to rejoin Waller's reputedly fast-dwindling army; then, forty-eight hours later, Celia abandoned the threadbare performance which had carried her through the funeral and simply disappeared without a word. Three days after that a strange new captain arrived to collect the quarter's rents in place of Hugo Verney.

Kate accepted the yoke and continued to contain her own grief. To spare both herself and him, she let Eden leave without asking what had happened at Far Flamstead . . . and when Celia vanished overnight, she made up a story to account for it. This worked with Dorothy – who was too frighteningly apathetic to care – and, to a degree, with the household servants, whose sole aim was to ease Kate's burden. But Felix and Felicity saw through it and had to be told the truth . . . or, at least, what Kate suspected was the truth. They were not surprised.

'Good riddance,' said Felix. 'I hope she never comes back.'

And, 'Thank God she didn't take the children,' said Felicity. 'Jude is the only one who can make Mother speak.'

This was undeniably true – and the only ray of hope Kate had. Like the twins, she spent what hours she could spare sitting in Dorothy's room, trying to pierce her cocoon of frozen detachment with talk. She talked of the tenants, the rapidly approaching harvest, the raspberry stains on Felix's best shirt; and, when all else failed, she tried the news from outside, telling how Prince Rupert had apparently succeeded in relieving the besieged city of York only to be immediately defeated in an enormous battle just outside it at a place called Marston Moor. Kate talked till she was hoarse – but to no avail. Dorothy was simply not interested. The only thing that seemed to stir her at all was when Jude climbed on to her lap.

So even before Captain Ambrose put in an appearance, Kate's days were already a constant battle and she could have done without his particular brand of crisp efficiency. When asked, he told her that Captain Verney had sustained a shoulder-wound and been allowed to recuperate in Oxford – thus confirming all Kate's darkest suspicions. And then he proceeded to ask a stream of questions of his own about the estate's tenants and the yields and acreages of the various farms . . . from which she sickeningly deduced that he was both less embarrassed by his errand and a good deal more knowledgeable than Hugo Verney had been. Kate covered her tracks as best she could but was unable, at the end of the day, to prevent him taking the ledgers away for further study. He promised to call again to return them. Kate hoped he fell off his horse and broke his leg.

For a long time after he had gone, she continued to sit at Richard's desk and stare gloomily into space while she tried to decide what to do if Captain Ambrose spotted their deception. And then, almost absently, her fingers reached for the small drawer in which Eden had placed the contents of Father's pockets.

Everything was there, just as she had last left it. All those small, precious items that her mother was as yet too fragile to receive. A handkerchief, a tortoiseshell comb, a small purse with a handful of sovereigns in it . . . and something else. A brief letter in an unfamiliar, flowing hand, addressed to someone named Samuel and signed with a single initial, so confidently convoluted as to be completely indecipherable.

Kate frowned at it. Was it a G . . . or perhaps an L or a J? She couldn't make it out. More importantly, she couldn't work out what it had been doing in Father's pocket.

The door opened and Nathan came in, smiling his unctuous smile. There was something, he said, which – after long hours of prayer and soul-searching – he wished to discuss with her. Kate repressed a sigh. It was probably the purification of the chapel again. At any rate, it would take him twenty minutes to come to the point. She let her gaze drift back to the puzzling letter in her hand, and for perhaps the hundredth time found herself searching for a solution to the most vexing question of all. *Why had Father left London to go to the King?*

Something Nathan was saying suddenly achieved a stranglehold on her wandering attention. Kate came abruptly to her feet and, cutting across his measured tones, said incredulously, 'What? *What* did you say?'

Nathan maintained his smile and suppressed a spasm of annoyance. Without a hint of diffidence, he said patiently, 'I said, dearest Kate, that you cannot go on shouldering responsibilities too heavy for an unmarried girl – and that God has shown me how best I may relieve you of them. In short, I would wed you.'

It was a long time before Kate could bring herself to speak. Then she said unsteadily, 'Are you out of your mind?'

'On the contrary, my dear. I am proposing the only sensible solution. Of course, I realise that the notion comes as a shock. But I am sure you will soon come to recognise the manifold advantages of it.'

'Will I?'

'If you allow yourself a period of calm reflection – yes.' He moved towards her, exuding patronising persuasion. 'Think, Kate. With your father at peace in God and Eden away prosecuting the war and your poor, grieving mother no longer able to help you – how long can you go on alone?'

'As long as I have to,' she said frigidly. 'And I think you've said enough.'

'That is because you are prone to be overly impulsive,' observed Nathan indulgently. 'You require a helpmeet, Kate – and more than that. You need a husband. You are twenty-one years old, and it is not God's wish that you should die a maid. Of that I am convinced. You should have a man to care for and children at your knee. Don't you feel this yourself?' His hands grasped hers. 'Doesn't your womanhood *demand* it?'

A gust of pure temper washed over Kate and she freed her hands with one violent jerk. 'My – my womanhood demands a good many things,' she responded furiously. 'First and foremost, that you should refrain from touching me. And in case that's not plain enough for you – let me put it another way. I wouldn't marry you if you were the last man on earth.'

Nathan's smile evaporated and something shifted in the pale lightless eyes. He said, 'Such sentiments do you no credit, cousin. But I shall try to overlook them and pray that God will pardon your ingratitude.'

'Don't bother,' snapped Kate. 'I'm sure God understands my feelings only too well. Did you *really* think I'd let you get your sanctimonious hands on Thorne Ash? Or that Eden would welcome you as a brother-in-law?'

'Eden isn't here – and nor, since his whoring wife ran off, is he likely to be,' came the suddenly vicious reply. Then, smiling again, 'Oh yes, dear Kate. I've guessed why she's gone. Your lies might have fooled Goodwife Flossing and the rest but they didn't delude me. I've always known *exactly* what Mistress Celia was. No. Eden won't be back. And I don't think that your poor deranged mother will—'

The words ended in a cry of pain as Kate hit him hard across his mouth.

'Get out,' she said fiercely. 'Get out of this room and out of this house. Now. Today. And if you ever show your face here again – as God is my witness, I swear I'll set the dogs on you.'

Her hand-print red against the whiteness of his face, Nathan reached out as though to take hold of her again, but Kate did not give him the chance. Snatching up a small paper-knife from the desk, she said, 'Touch me and I'll use this. Now go. I want you away from here within the hour.'

'You can't do this!'

'I can.' Still holding the knife, she forced him to retreat before her to the door. 'And one more thing. My mother is not mad. If I ever hear that you've told anyone she is, I'll tell Eden of it. And Eden will probably kill you.'

Nathan felt the wood at his back and fumbled blindly for the door-latch. He couldn't quite believe that this was happening. But Kate looked capable of murder, so he opened the door and backed cautiously round it into the hall – and the arms of Luciano del Santi.

It was hard to say who was more surprised. Nathan, who gibbered and achieved a nimble, swivelling twist to one side; or Kate, who simply stopped breathing and let the knife fall from suddenly nerveless fingers. For a few seconds, there was silence. Then, stooping unhurriedly to retrieve the knife and weighing it thoughtfully in his hand, Luciano said, 'The door was open so I took the liberty of letting myself in. Problems, Kate?'

'No,' she said shortly. And, struggling to reinflate her lungs, 'No. Mr Cresswell is leaving. Permanently.'

'Ah.' Amused dark eyes took in the red mark over the tutor's mouth. 'Then we shouldn't delay him.'

Nathan looked from one to the other of them and recognised defeat. There was nothing he could say and, though Kate needed to be taught a lesson in humility, now was not the time. Without a word, he stalked to the stairs and went up to his room to pack.

From the moment Luciano had returned from Genoa to hear what Giacomo had to say, he'd been bristling with cheerful vitality – and it showed. Smiling, he jerked his head in the direction taken by Nathan and said, 'Let me guess. He made an assault on your virtue?'

'Not quite – though it amounts to the same thing. He asked me to marry him.'

'So you threw him out at knife-point?' He started to laugh.

'Don't you think that's a trifle drastic? And what is your father going to say?'

The ground shifted under Kate's feet and she placed a hand against the door-frame to steady herself. Then she said flatly, 'You don't know.'

'Know what?' A faint frown touched his brows and he was suddenly struck by the unrelieved black gown and the fine-drawn pallor of her face. 'Something's happened.'

'Yes.' She turned wearily back towards the book-room. 'You'd better come in.'

He followed her, closing the door behind him. And then, when she merely stood with her hands resting on Richard's desk, he said, 'Kate? Quickly is best. Is it Eden?'

'No.' Drawing a long breath, she turned to look at him. 'No, it isn't Eden. It's Father. He's dead.'

With some disembodied part of her mind, she watched the blood drain slowly from his skin and his eyes turn to pools of obsidian before he swung violently away to the window. Then, for the first time in all the years she had known him, he said exactly what she expected him to say.

'*How?*'

So, draggingly and without expression, she told him what she knew . . . and, when it was done, said vaguely, 'It – it's been two weeks now, but I still – I still can't believe it.'

His hand clenched hard against the stone of the window, Luciano said abruptly, 'What – do you know what he was doing with the King's army?'

'No. I only wish we did. It . . . it might make it easier to bear.' She paused and then added wryly, 'Or then again – maybe not.'

A horrible grinding fear lay at the back of Luciano's mind and he was aware that he was shaking. 'You said there was still some skirmishing going on after the battle. Is that how Eden said it happened?'

'He thought so. There's no other explanation, is there? But I don't suppose we'll ever be sure. Ralph couldn't find anyone who saw what happened, and neither he nor Eden could well go round the Cavaliers asking questions.'

'No. I suppose not.' His stomach knotted with cramp, Luciano continued to stare unseeingly through the window. Richard had followed the ring to the King's army; *ergo* – but for himself, Richard wouldn't have died. That was crippling enough and already more than he could bear. But what if the shot that killed him had *not* been fired in the skirmish but by— No. Don't think of it. Later, perhaps – but not now. If he thought of it now he'd be ill, and he owed Kate something more than that. Turning a little, he said, 'I'm sorry. You can't want to go through all this again.'

'It's all right,' replied Kate automatically. It wasn't, of course, but one got used to saying so. 'I understand.'

He hesitated for a moment, trying to find something he could safely say. Then, 'How are things with you? Are you coping?'

'Barely.' He was the first person to have asked and it nearly undid her. 'Mother is still in a state of shock. She won't leave her room and scarcely eats or speaks. Eden went back to Waller immediately after the funeral. And Celia . . . well, everyone except Felix and Felicity thinks Celia's gone to her mother – but she hasn't. Unless I'm very much mistaken, she's run off with Hugo Verney.' She stopped and met his gaze with the travesty of a smile. 'Quite. It's a mess, isn't it?'

'Yes.' Luciano regarded her sombrely. 'Does Eden know?'

'I imagine so. It's why he wouldn't stay. I think . . . I rather think he caught them in bed together at Far Flamstead on the day he came to tell us about Father, you see.'

'Christ. And no one's dead?'

'No. But Hugo's left Banbury to recover from a shoulder-wound, so there was probably a fight. As for Celia, I suspect Eden only brought her back here for the look of things and to save himself explanations. And now she's gone.'

'In which case there's surely nothing to stop Eden coming back to share your load for a while, is there?'

'It – it depends.' Kate stared miserably down at her hands.

'On what?'

'On whether or not he's worked out that Viola may not be his child,' she said tonelessly. Then, steeling herself to look at him, 'If he has, he may never come back. And I don't know how I'm going to explain it to Mother.'

'Oh *Kate*.' She looked so solitary, there was only one thing he could do. Crossing the room to fold her in steady, passionless arms, he said, 'You don't deserve this. And I don't know how I can help.'

'You can't.' She leaned her forehead against him. 'You can't. But I'm glad you're here.'

And suddenly, against all expectation, the flood-gates burst open and she was sobbing all her grief and anxiety and bitterness into his velvet-covered shoulder.

Luciano laid one hand on her hair and stared blankly over her head, but made no move to hurry the process. She was not aware – nor could he tell her – that he had his own demons to fight; demons that whispered a possibility more terrible than anything he had known since the day his own father had died. And as yet it was all he could do not to break down himself.

At length Kate lifted her head and said unevenly, 'I'm sorry. I d-don't know what came over me. I haven't cried b-before.'

'Then it was time you did.' He released her to give her his handkerchief. 'And at least it seems I've done something right.'

'What do you mean?' Kate mopped her face and then turned the dampened cambric over and over between her hands. 'None of this is your fault.'

He didn't answer. He wasn't even looking at her . . . and the quality of his stillness was suddenly alarming. She said, 'What is it? What's wrong?'

Luciano did not hear her. He simply stared like a sleep-walker at the litter of objects and papers on Richard's desk. His body was racked with pulses and he had no more colour to lose. A perfect match to the letters given to him by Robert Brandon, the flowing black script before him burned into his skull; and finally, in a voice that

505

seemed to come from a long way off, he said, 'That letter. Where did you get it?'

'This?' Following his gaze, Kate reached out and picked it up. 'It was in Father's pocket. Do you recognise the hand?'

There was a long, blistering silence. Then Luciano twisted away to drop into the nearest chair and drive his face into his spread fingers.

Kate waited, fear and suspicion feathering the back of her neck. Then she said slowly, 'You know who wrote it. Don't you?'

Very, very carefully, as though an unwary movement might result in irreparable damage, he uncovered his face and let his hands lie loose. They were hopelessly unsteady. Keeping his eyes fixed on them, he put every skill he possessed into saying evenly, 'No, Kate. I don't. But I think – I'm fairly sure – it's what took Richard to Cropredy.'

Kate shivered. 'Why?'

More than anything, he wanted to be sick . . . but if he was to make Kate believe him, it wasn't a release he could allow himself. Yet. He swallowed, tried to force his brain to work and said remotely, 'He was doing me a favour. I – I gathered as much from something Giacomo told me when I got back . . . but I wasn't sure until I saw that letter.'

'Go on.' Kate's nails were biting into her palms.

'Someone had – cheated me. The details don't matter. It's sufficient to say that, though I'd seen the fellow's hand-writing, I didn't know his real name. Richard must have found something out and decided to follow him. He – he'd have been bringing the letter back to me as proof.'

'I see.' The green eyes were suddenly inimical. 'But without Father to tell you who wrote it, it's no use to you is it? What a shame. No wonder you're so upset.'

'Is that what you think?'

'I don't know. What *should* I think?' She flung the words at him and then stopped. He looked ill. 'Oh God. No. Probably not. But you're saying it's your fault he was there.'

With a visible effort, Luciano rose from the chair and stood looking at her. His voice raw with strain, he said, 'Yes. And I'm sorry. So very, very sorry.'

The room seemed airless and Kate's chest ached with the mere effort of breathing. Every day, a fresh disaster. She did not know how much more she could bear. She said dully, 'I know you are, but I can't talk to you now. It – it's all too much. Later, though . . . if you're staying?'

'That's for you to say.' Distantly, he wondered how much longer he could control his insides. 'I couldn't blame you for asking me to leave.'

There was another yawning silence.

'No. But Father would,' said Kate. And fled before the look in his eyes.

Dinner was a tense affair. Kate told the twins about Nathan's eviction, though not what had in truth caused her to do it, and then watched Felix wrestling silently with a desire he felt barred from expressing. Felicity tried to fill one of the many silences by speaking of the ecstatic and long-delayed letter she had recently received from Gianetta; and Luciano let his food congeal in front of him and said virtually nothing.

In the end, it was left to Kate to say baldly, 'Felix. If you want Signor del Santi to take you back to London with him, why not ask?'

'Because I can't possibly go,' he replied shortly. 'You and Felicity need me. You know you do.'

'I don't deny it. But it won't last. Mother will soon start feeling better – and we have some good friends amongst our servants and tenants. And the war can't last forever, so Eden will come home.' She paused briefly but avoided Luciano's eye. 'We managed before and we can again. But this is your future we're talking about. If your apprenticeship still means anything to you, then you must go.'

Felix concentrated on reducing a piece of bread to crumbs. 'It means as much as ever it did. But I can't be that selfish.'

'It's not being selfish, it's being practical. And how will Felicity and I feel if you give up three years' work for us?'

Felix sighed and looked across at the Italian. 'What do you think, sir?'

'That I don't envy you your choice,' came the unhelpful reply. And then, catching the expression on Kate's face, 'I'm sorry. I can't advise you, Felix. All I can tell you is that Kate wouldn't tell you to go if she didn't mean it – which you already know. And that you've a talent for gold that isn't given to many – which perhaps you didn't know. But the decision has to be yours. You may return to your work with me whenever you wish.' He rose from his seat. 'And now, if you will all excuse me, I'll say goodnight.'

'But you haven't eaten anything,' objected Kate without thinking.

'No,' he agreed flatly. 'No I haven't. I'm afraid I couldn't face it. In which,' glancing around the table, 'it appears I am not alone.'

The night was hot and humid – and sleep, for other reasons entirely, was a sheer impossibility. Kate sat at her window, staring down into the darkened garden, and tried to put what Luciano had told her into perspective. He couldn't, after all, have known what Father would do – or even, from a point somewhere between Genoa and London, have stopped him doing it. So it was unreasonable to blame him – and unnecessary, since he clearly already blamed himself.

She pressed the heels of her hands over her hot eyes. It had helped to cry but one couldn't go on doing it and it didn't mend the pain. Nothing did that. All you could do was to struggle on from day to day, burying the hurt in all the trivial and not-so-trivial tasks which still had to be done even though their meaning had gone. And when things threatened to overwhelm you, you still had to carry on because there was no one else; and it was what Father would have wanted.

She lifted her head and drew a long breath of the night air. Enough. It was time to pull herself together. Self-pity didn't solve anything.

Below in the garden, a glimmer of white caught her eye. She froze for a moment and then relaxed. Of course. She should have known. Tonight, the curse of sleeplessness did not belong only to her; and tonight she need not bear it alone.

Brandy bottle in one hand and a pewter goblet in the other, Luciano leaned against an ash tree and watched her come towards him. In some way he did not even try to understand, he realised he had known she would come. And why. What he had not anticipated – but probably should have done – was that she would come barefoot, with her hair unbound and wearing nothing but a long, flowing night-rail. Under the circumstances, this ought not to be a problem, but Luciano, with no guidelines left to him, knew already that it was. For tonight was the one night he could neither dissemble nor deceive her with pretended rejection. And, truth to tell, he did not even want to.

He waited till she arrived before him, then poured a measure of brandy into the cup and handed it to her.

'Welcome,' he said dryly, 'to the banks of Lethe. I fear I am a little ahead of you – but I'm sure we can soon remedy that. And don't worry. I promise I'll see you safely back to your door.'

Wordlessly, Kate took the goblet and drank. Her throat burned and warmth invaded her body. Then, taking her time, she said steadily, 'I came to tell you that I don't blame you. And that you shouldn't blame yourself.'

'Generous – but untrue. I thought we'd already established that.'

'No. But if you want to convince me, you could always try telling me the truth. The *whole* truth – not that half-and-half version you gave me earlier.'

His face, in the darkness, was hard to read, yet still he took the precaution of turning away from her. 'There's nothing more to tell. Forgive me . . . but if you insist on speaking of this, I'm going to break all my good intentions and get very drunk, very fast.'

'That isn't very fair, is it?'

'No. But then life isn't. Hadn't you noticed?'

This was too close to the bone. Kate took another gulp of brandy and thought for a moment. Then, 'Tell me something. Are we friends, you and I?'

His shoulders tensed, and his voice when he spoke held

a note she could not interpret. 'We've always been friends. Didn't you know it?'

'How could I, when you spend so much time shutting me out?'

'I shut everyone out. It's safer.' He raised the bottle to his mouth, then set it securely in a fork of the tree and turned back to her. The air was still and curiously charged. Link by link, he could feel the chain slowly tightening and drawing him further from the path he had followed for so long, so that at length he said abruptly, 'Think for a moment. How many times have you told yourself it would have been better if we'd never met? Several hundred? A thousand, perhaps?'

'Something like that.' She drained the goblet and then, taking a momentous decision, stared wryly down at it. 'I think I've said it to myself nearly every day we've spent apart . . . and sometimes I almost believed it. But the pity of it – so you would say – is that it was never true.'

His breath snared and he said quickly, 'Careful, Kate. You must know where this is leading us.'

'Of course. Why else am I here?' Her eyes rose to meet his. 'You know that I love you. You've known it for a long time.'

He was alone in the wilderness without a compass and the effort of not moving was fast growing beyond his control. It was as if all the hours of his life had been leading to this one moment . . . yet still he had to give her another chance to turn aside. He said raggedly, 'I should warn you that the façade is quite thin and may crack at any second. Unless it's what you want, I think you should go. Or I may be driven to something we shall both regret.'

'Speak for yourself.' Kate's heart turned over and she could feel herself shaking. She could not believe he was letting her come this close, or that he would not still raise the barricade against her. Expecting to be rejected but praying she was not, she took one diffident step towards him and said simply, 'I'm not asking you for any great declaration, Luciano. But if you have any kindness for me or any small need of comfort for yourself, now is the time to show it.'

'Oh Christ!' Beyond every thought save one, Luciano closed the remaining space between them and removed the goblet from her unresisting grasp. Then, tossing it carelessly aside, he said, 'This is nothing to do with either kindness or comfort. Don't you know it, even now? But though it can only be ours for a night, still I can't resist it. Or you.' And, gathering her to him with light, unsteady hands, he finally sought her mouth.

Neither knowing nor caring what his words meant, and hardly daring to breathe in case he changed his mind, Kate melted against him. Although she had been wiser than to let herself hope, it was for this that she had left her room . . . and the joy of suddenly being given what she had always wanted was terrifying in its intensity. She let her hands slide slowly up his chest and on through the crisp, night-dark hair, to clasp themselves around his neck; and felt the tremor that passed through him. He had kissed her once before and it had been sweet. But not like this. Never, surely, like this, with a passion and hunger that outstripped even her own and sent bubbles of honeyed expectancy spinning through her veins. If he let her go now, she would shatter like glass. And then he drew her closer still and she shattered anyway.

When he finally released her mouth it was to feather tiny kisses across her jaw and down the curve of her throat to the hollows beneath. One hand cradled her skull while, through the thin stuff of her night-robe, the other moved lingeringly over her back. As he had said, he lacked the resolution that would make him leave her, but he hoped he still commanded other resources. For at long, long last, the girl in his arms was the only one he wanted. And though some warped piece of logic denied him the right to say words that might bind her, he could and would use every art he possessed to ensure that she did not miss them. For Kate, this night must be an amber chalice. It was her right – and his pleasure.

The honey in her blood had turned to wild-fire and he knew it. Holding her gaze with his own and smiling a little, he drew her past the ash tree to a place where they were hidden from the house and the grass was soft and sweet. Then, taking his time, he loosed the ribbons of her robe until it slithered slowly from her shoulders to lie in a pool at her feet.

The air evaporated in his lungs.

Under the moon, her skin glowed translucent as pearl and every exquisite inch of her was in perfect, delicate proportion. Luciano looked at her: from the untrammelled copper hair and wide, luminous eyes to the arches of her slender feet. And finally, he drew a long, stricken breath and said simply, '*Sabrina fair* . . . I am blinded.'

'And I,' replied Kate shakily, reaching out to him, 'am alone.'

He merely smiled and, spreading his hands in a gesture of surrender, stood quite still while she unlaced his shirt. Then, when she had done, he swiftly shed the rest of his clothing and, entirely without haste, placed a kiss that was half-humble, half-enticing in her palm. For a moment, he remained quite still. Then, lacing her fingers with his own, he drew her slowly into his arms. Skin met skin and Kate gasped, electrified from head to foot; and when his mouth once more found hers, the world swung on its axis.

Down, down into an endless vortex of pleasure . . . down on to the scented grass that was to be their bed. Gently but with growing urgency, Luciano explored every line and curve of her body, treasuring each quiver of response; and Kate, her bones melting and her senses on fire, embarked on her own voyage of discovery as the lean hardness of his limbs, the slight imperfection of his shoulders and the texture of his skin all imprinted themselves on her light, questing fingers.

The warm summer night closed around them, bathing them in its faint music. With seductive, tantalising grace, Luciano led Kate unhurriedly through the labyrinth towards the delight that was at its core. And only when he was sure beyond every possible doubt that her hunger matched his own did he bring his patient courtship to its exquisite end by joining his starving flesh to hers.

Amber and gold, flame and silk, poetry and counterpoint; time frozen in a crystal. And then the magic was in them and of them and around them . . . and the garden exploded, taking them with it.

It was a long time before Luciano stirred and, propping himself on one elbow, looked down on Kate's quiet face. Her breathing was still light and rapid, and her lashes lay motionless on her cheeks, but there was no doubt that she was smiling. Then her eyes opened full on his . . . and he knew. The course which, in his madness, he had thought he could follow was not possible and never had been. Because she was who she was – and because of what had just passed between them – he could not simply rise up and go, leaving them both with this one jewelled memory. It was too late.

Reality returned with a vengeance. The only fitting end to this interlude was to do what he wanted – and what Richard had wanted. But now, more than ever, that was to place her in jeopardy. His self-imposed mission of revenge had already killed Richard – as yet he dared not contemplate how directly; and, after being so careful for so long, he was not about to expose Kate to the same danger. Therefore he had to obey the same constraints as before, only with different methods.

Kate smiled up at him and then nestled closer, her face buried against his chest. She said softly, 'Experienced in all things. I might have known.'

'Quite. But there was also,' he replied, responding to the faint note of laughter, 'some natural talent involved. On both sides.'

Her body was still bathed in delicious languor and his fingers were once more moving lightly over her hip, but she managed to take up her cue with creditable pertness. 'A compliment after all these years. I can't believe it.'

'You can't have been attending either – if you think that's the first,' he retorted. And felt rather than heard the tiny gurgle that rippled through her.

After a time, her voice muffled against his shoulder, she said diffidently, 'I know I probably shouldn't ask . . . but is it always like that?'

'No.' Warning bells rang in his head and he thought, *And that's enough of that. Stop her before she has you admitting that, in all the vast experience she thinks you've got, it's never been like this. Or even come close.* He said carefully, 'Kate . . . it will be dawn soon and you need to get back to your room before the house begins to stir. But first, if you can bear it, we should talk. And I suspect we'll do it more successfully with some clothes on.'

She sighed and twined her arms about his neck. 'Oh. Must we?'

'Yes.' Unable to resist the lure, he held her close for one last, lingering kiss and then, gently disengaging himself, reached out and handed her her night-rail. 'Put it on. Or how do you expect me to concentrate? And this is important.'

Something in his tone permeated Kate's delectable lassitude and, very reluctantly, she sat up. Then, slipping the robe over her head, she waited quietly while her lover threw on his own clothes with rather more haste than care.

His shirt still unlaced and his face slightly grim, Luciano sat beside her again and stared thoughtfully down at his hands for a moment. Then, looking up, he said abruptly, 'Have you realised yet that you and I have just committed the single, most monumentally stupid act of our entire lives?'

Her breath caught and the last of her languor promptly evaporated. 'You regret it?'

'No. I haven't that much sense. But *you* might.'

'Don't worry.' Relaxing again, Kate smiled at him. 'You're wondering how to take your leave – and if I'll let you go. But there's no need for concern. None at all. It . . . it was just this one night. I understand that. It was all I asked for and all you were offering. You made that perfectly clear.'

'And you didn't pray to be saved from the lunatic?'

'No. Should I have done?'

'Yes. Oh yes.' He gave the merest ghost of a laugh. Then, sternly repressing the impulse to touch her, he said austerely, 'It won't do, Kate – and if you were less remarkable than you undoubtedly are, you would know it.'

'I'm sorry.' Her brow wrinkled in puzzlement. 'I'm sorry, but I haven't the remotest idea what you're getting at.'

'No? Then let me put it plainly.' His fingers gripped each other hard around his upraised knee and he drew a long, steadying breath. 'I am not looking for a gracious exit line because there can be no such thing. Quite simply, the notion that this night could somehow exist in beautiful isolation was insane . . . and I can think of only one way to mend matters. I want you to marry me.'

It was the very last thing Kate had ever expected to hear him say and sheer incredulity froze her to the marrow. For a long, airless minute, she was completely incapable of speech; then she said painfully, 'I think you had better tell me why.'

'Isn't it obvious? For one thing, there may be a child.'

'And then again, there may not. What else?'

'I'm not in the habit of seducing virgins.'

'But you didn't.' Some very peculiar sensations were taking place behind Kate's ribs but she managed to say calmly, 'In case you've forgotten, it was I who came out here to you. And I didn't do it in order to put a chain round your neck.'

'I know that, damn it!'

'Then you'll also know that I won't marry you on the strength of what you've said so far.' She paused and met his eyes with wry candour. 'I'm satisfied with what I've had, Luciano – and I'm not about to let you sacrifice yourself. Mainly because there's no need – but also because, if I did, you'd hate me for it one day.'

Luciano could feel the ground being cut rapidly from beneath him and was, for once, powerless to stop it. He could remark that while she was refusing to sacrifice him, she was forcing him to sacrifice her – but that wouldn't help. Or he could tell her the simple truth: that there was no question of sacrifice between them because she was his soul, his life-blood, the other half of him. But that would create more problems than it cured; for once she knew that, there would be no way in which he could relegate her to the safe edges of his life whilst he sorted out the mess he had made of it. So, at length, he opened his mouth on the one thing he could think of that might possibly work and said, 'Since you're so busy setting me free, martyrdom hardly comes into it, does it? However. If you want a reason for marrying me, I suppose I'd better give you one.'

Kate said nothing but merely eyed him warily and waited for him to continue. And finally he said crisply, 'The idea is not new, Kate – and neither is it a bad one. In short, though I doubt if he'd be happy with the precise way it has come about, it's what your father wanted.'

Kate discovered that she felt slightly faint. She said feebly, 'He – he *said* so to you?'

'Yes. A long time ago when you were loosely tied to Kit Clifford. You know how little Richard liked that situation – and that was one of the reasons I felt I had to end it; but what you may *not* know is that, rightly or wrongly, he also considered me a . . . a worthy replacement.' He paused, watching her carefully. 'Of course, I can't prove it.'

Kate's mind slid back to an afternoon ride almost two years ago. 'You might find my views on a suitable match something of a revelation,' Father had said. Shivering a little, she said, 'Go on.'

'What?' he asked, mildly taken aback.

'I asked you to go on. I – I think I can believe that Father may have suggested such a thing, but it's obvious you didn't agree or something would have been said before now. So what answer did you give?'

Whether he liked it or not, Luciano recognised that the moment was upon him and that he couldn't afford any more mistakes. Smoothly blending truth and fiction, and with a flawless appearance of candour, he said, 'I told him that my personal circumstances, coupled with my financial obligations, made marriage out of the question – and to a lesser degree, that is still true. The fact is that I owe my uncle in Genoa a spectacularly large sum of money but that I now have more chance of repaying it than I did two years ago. As for the rest, my life is no less chaotic than it was then – though I hope this, too, may soon mend. And so, although the timing is far from ideal, I am offering you, if not marriage, at least a marriage-ring. It's not much, I know. But if you will be patient and can bring yourself to bear with me, I hope to do better in time.'

Kate could feel herself trembling. She needed to ask him if he loved her but she had promised not to make him say it. And so, instead, she said remotely, 'I think, in fairness, you must tell me one other thing. Would you be offering me anything at all if we hadn't made love just now?'

'Eventually – but not yet.' Luciano surged to his feet. '*Cara*, it's getting light and we've argued enough. Will you marry me or not?'

Her vision blurred. *Cara*. An easy, careless endearment, or something more? And if he meant it, why could he not say so? She said helplessly, 'I don't *know*! I – I want to but—'

'Then you will.' His voice altering subtly, he employed his last weapon. 'Kate – if you say no, I can't come here again. Surely you can see that? What happened tonight can't ever be repeated – and neither can it simply be forgotten. Things have changed between us. And we must either adapt or part.'

For a long time Kate merely stared back at him out of wide, stark eyes. Then, with a small crooked smile, she said wryly, 'And that, of course, is the one argument I can't fight. I'd willingly settle for half a loaf because I never expected any more . . . but I can't afford to lose you completely. And you know it perfectly well.'

The dark gaze remained hooded and unreadable, giving no sign of the turmoil within. 'So?'

She rose to face him, her nerves vibrating like plucked wires. 'So I'll marry you – if you're sure that's what you want.'

'It is.' There was a small glow of warmth somewhere in the turbulence of his mind, as though light had appeared at the end of the tunnel. He knew he shouldn't risk her getting caught up in his affairs but, if she would accept the half-measure he had in mind, he ought to be able to protect her. And then, once he'd found and dealt with the bastard

517

who had arranged his father's death and also probably murdered Richard, he would be able to say all the things he dared not say to her now; and she would find she had a whole loaf after all – and always had done. But all that was for the future and the present moment still required caution so he said calmly, 'For the time being, however – and for reasons I don't intend to give you – I'd like it kept quiet. Tell the family, but no one else. And don't have the banns read. I'll leave for London today and return after the harvest. I'll also make sure Felix stays here until we're married because I imagine you're going to need him. How does that sound?'

'Efficient,' said Kate acidly. 'And peculiar. Typical of you, in fact.'

He smiled at her then with all his customary, devastating effect and took her hand in light, comforting fingers. 'I know. Some things never change, do they? But cheer up. Better the devil you know, after all. And at least you can't say you didn't know what you were getting.'

Four

Felix and Felicity received the news of Kate's forthcoming marriage with a remarkable absence of surprise and a certain circumspect pleasure. Dorothy, on the other hand, was finally shocked out of her long apathy.

'You're going to do *what*?' she snapped.

Kate stared at her, desperately praying that this time the key would turn. 'Marry Luciano del Santi. I love him. I always have.'

Dorothy stood up and the unopened book on her knee slid unheeded to the floor. She said urgently, 'Kate, you can't! He hasn't even told you his real name, let alone what dangerous games he's playing.'

Her daughter's green eyes widened thoughtfully. 'His real name?'

'It's Falcieri – not del Santi. After all Gianetta's obstinacy on the subject, did you never suspect it?'

'The thought had occurred to me, yes.'

'And has it also occurred to you to wonder *why*? Or do you seriously believe he's only been hiding his identity all this time because – justly or otherwise – his father went to the gallows for treason?'

'No.' Kate drew a long breath and then loosed it. 'I think he's done it because, like Gianetta, he believes his father was innocent. And he's trying to prove it.'

For a moment there was silence. Then Dorothy said impatiently, 'Face facts, Kate. That's not all and you know it.'

'I *know* nothing. All I can do is guess.'

'Then do it.'

519

'All right – *all right*!' She dug her nails into her palms and forced herself to voice the suspicion which had grown up almost without her knowing it and which she'd so far refused to name, even to herself. 'It's possible he's looking for revenge. Is that what you wanted to hear me say?'

'Yes. And knowing that, you can still contemplate marrying him?'

'I've told you. I love him.' Kate hesitated briefly and then took the first resolute step into the quagmire. 'And Father liked him. You know he did.'

A strange quiver passed over Dorothy's face and one hand moved as though to ward off a blow. 'Don't. I'm not sure I can bear it.'

'You *must* bear it. Can't you see? It's time. Father knew exactly what Luciano is doing, didn't he? *Didn't he?*'

'Yes.' It was no more than a sighing breath.

'And liked him in spite of it. So it stands to reason that it can't be so very terrible, can it? Or Father wouldn't have . . .' She paused again and then, gritting her teeth, went on flatly, 'Or Father wouldn't have told him he'd rather see me married to Luciano himself than to Kit.'

Dorothy crumpled slowly back into her chair, her face torn apart with pain. 'Stop it, Kate. What are you trying to do?'

'Make you understand. Last night I lay with the man you say I don't know – and later, when I wouldn't agree to marry him, he finally told me that Father had wanted it. And I believed him.' Shivering a little, Kate prepared the *coup de grâce* in her mind and then ruthlessly delivered it. 'At such a time and on such a subject, he wouldn't lie. And if you'd seen his face when I told him of Father's death, you'd be as sure of that as I am.'

A silent deluge began to cascade down the pale face, and for a moment Kate thought she had misjudged it. Then, chokingly and with hands outstretched, Dorothy spoke her name.

Kate discovered that her own lashes were wet. Her progress across the room, too, was less than graceful. But when she felt Dorothy's arms close about her she knew that she had won . . . that the long withdrawal was over and the process of grieving about to begin. And that tomorrow, God willing, she might be able to tell her mother the truth about Eden's marriage.

While Dorothy slowly picked up the threads of her life and tried – with only moderate success – to come to terms with the prospect of acquiring Luciano Falcieri del Santi as a son-in-law, the Queen fled abroad to avoid being captured by Lord Essex, eleven hundred Irish under Alastair M'Coll Keitach landed in Scotland, and Sir William Waller failed to take Oxford. The first brought the King's army down about the earl's ears, forcing him to surrender Fowey and escape by sea, and the second, though no one as yet suspected it, marked the beginning of a quite spectacular year in His Majesty's fortunes north of the border. But it was Waller's sulky withdrawal to Farnham that had the greatest, if indirect, effect on Thorne Ash; and the first sign of it was that Captain Ambrose failed to reappear with the accounts ledgers.

Kate's reaction to this progressed from cowardly relief to faint alarm and finally, by the time they were ready to start harvesting, to downright annoyance. The fellow might, and obviously did, suspect that they weren't declaring their entire revenue – but he couldn't possibly prove it from the accounts she'd given him.

She chewed her nails for a further three days before coming to a decision. Then she donned her second-best riding habit and told Felix that she needed him to escort her to Banbury. She did not, however, explain *why* until they were half-way there.

'You're joking!' he said at length. 'You're going to ride up to the castle, bold as brass, and demand our ledgers back?'

'Why not? And I'm not about to be fobbed off or bullied – so if your nerves aren't up to supporting me, you might as well go home now.'

'After four years of your newly betrothed, I think you'll find my nerves are up to pretty well anything,' he replied sweetly. 'Speaking of which, there's something I've been wanting to ask you. If you're not going to announce your marriage and you intend to go on living at home after the ceremony, why are you doing it at all?'

There were a number of answers to this: some truthful, some less so, and none of them very convincing. Kate assumed her most astringent tone and said, 'Why do you think? At my age you have to take what you can get.'

Felix eyed her meditatively. Then he said laconically, 'You're saying the whole thing's Luciano's idea. I thought as much.' And rode peacefully on, happy in the knowledge that he had deprived her of breath.

Banbury turned out to be surprisingly busy considering that it wasn't market-day, and Kate, who had been there only rarely since the war had begun, surveyed the bustle with a perplexity that verged on mild foreboding. North Bar was thronged with carts and barrows and Parson's Lane was little better. Carefully avoiding both the Cuttle Brook and scurrying pedestrians, she led the way past the Reindeer Inn and Mistress Welchman's cake-shop to the lighter, clearer air of Cornhill. And all the time a small voice at the back of her mind whispered that something was wrong.

Felix obviously thought so too and, dropping a light hand on Kate's bridle before they turned out of the market-place to approach the castle, he paused beside a fellow who appeared to be removing half the contents of his house and asked precisely what was going on.

'Haven't you heard?' came the grim reply. 'They say the Parliament's coming to take the castle. The town could be full of soldiers in no time. And we all know what *that* means – for one lot's as bad as another. What one side don't steal, the other will like as not set fire to.'

Kate and Felix looked at each other. And finally Kate said weakly, 'Well, well, that explains everything, doesn't it? And if the threat of a parliamentary army is having this much effect on the town, I can't wait to see what it's doing to the Royalists. Come on.'

The pair of troopers who challenged them at the gate looked more than a little harassed and Kate's request to see Captain Ambrose did nothing to dispel this. It therefore took a good deal of insistence and the presence of an officer with only one arm, one Will Tirwhitt, before she and Felix were permitted to enter and taken under escort to the duty-room.

The outer bailey was a hive of activity. A variety of cannon were being systematically greased and reassembled; a troop of green-jacketed infantry were being ruthlessly drilled in musket practice; and numerous cheeses and sacks of flour were being unloaded from their respective carts. Kate directed an expressive glance at Felix but said nothing and continued to tread meekly in the wake of their guide.

It was quieter in the inner courtyard but the room into which they were presently shown was full of miscellaneous clutter and looked as though it had recently been used for everything except sleeping. There was, however, only one inhabitant: a dark-haired man who looked up from the sheaf of lists in front of him to gaze inquiringly at the trooper.

'Visitors for Captain Ambrose, sir. Only he's not back yet so Captain Tirwhitt said I was to bring them here to wait for him.'

'The chamber over the gatehouse being full to overflowing, I suppose?' came the gently satiric reply.

'Couldn't say, Captain Vaughan, sir.'

'No. Of course you couldn't. Oh, never mind. Get back to your post, man. I'll deal with this.' And then, when the fellow had thankfully removed himself, the captain looked at his unlooked-for guests and rising, said courteously, 'I'm afraid your visit is somewhat ill timed. Captain Ambrose is at present concluding some business in the town and I'm not entirely sure how long he'll be. Is there anything that *I* can do for you?'

'Perhaps.' Kate impaled him on a jewel-green stare. 'My brother and I are Maxwells of Thorne Ash – and we've come to reclaim our accounts ledgers.'

'Ah.' Hugh Vaughan removed two half-eaten platters of bread and meat from a settle and indicated that they should be seated. 'Yes. I believe he said something of it and, though concerned at the delay, was rather anxious to return them personally. The trouble is, of course, that we've all been rather busy.'

'So I see.' Kate cast a withering eye over the disorder. 'But equally *you* must see that we can't be forever awaiting Captain Ambrose's convenience. So if you'd have the ledgers brought from wherever he has left them, we should be glad of it.'

'I daresay – but I can't do it. It really wouldn't be proper of me to dispose of them without his knowledge.'

'Why not?' Felix decided that it was time he too entered the fray. 'They don't belong to him and he's had them too damned long already.'

'Quite possibly. And I sympathise with you. But—'

'That's your trouble, Hugh,' said a crisp voice from the door. 'Always too sympathetic by half. Now I, on the other hand, have but little sympathy at the best of times – and none at all when I suspect I'm being gulled.'

Kate rose and faced her errant quarry. She thought he looked rather pleased with himself. Then, before she could speak, he strolled forward, casually stripping off his gloves and continued smoothly, 'Mistress Maxwell, you shall have my undivided attention in just one moment. Hugh, I'm sorry to ask but one of us ought to see that cloth safely bestowed; and it doesn't look as if it will be me.'

Captain Vaughan grinned. 'You got it, then?'

'Well, of course. It's all in the timing. With dear Jonas away at a meeting of the Common Council, I was bound to be served by the minions.' He smiled suddenly. 'He'll come back having changed his mind about supplying us and find it's too late. I only hope the Almighty is ready for the subsequent tirade.'

Kate shut her mouth and swallowed. 'Jonas?' she said. 'You persuaded *Jonas Radford* to sell you some cloth?'

'In a weak moment. I fear his profits are down.' Captain Ambrose examined her beneath raised brows. 'You obviously know him.'

'Mostly,' she replied, thinking of Nathan's eulogies, 'by repute. And of course his sisters have done some sewing for us from time to time. But why do you think he'll change his mind after the meeting?'

'Because he'll have learned that there are parliamentary forces as close as Broughton and Warkworth. Hugh – are you going or not?'

'On my way,' said Captain Vaughan, heading for the door. 'Oh – and Justin?'

'Well?'

'Don't let your morning's achievements go to your head. And spare a thought for the unfortunate minions.' And he was gone.

Justin Ambrose surprised Kate by laughing. Then, dropping himself negligently on the corner of a table, he said, 'And now to business. You presumably want your ledgers back, and *I* want to know why your farm rents are incompatible with the various acreages. Well?'

Kate opened her eyes guilelessly wide. '*Are* they? I had no idea. As far as I know, those are the rents that have always been paid and I understand nothing of acreages. You see, I've never had to deal with such things before. My father and second cousin Nathan saw to all that. But Nathan's left us now and – Father died just six weeks ago.'

Precisely as she had intended, Captain Ambrose found the wind taken out of his sails. He had been about to observe that it was a nice try but that he didn't believe a word of it . . . but that was scarcely appropriate now she'd dragged her father's demise into it. And though he was absolutely sure she was deliberately acting the part of the helpless female, he couldn't prove it . . . any more than he could prove those accounts were fraudulent. *Damn.*

Trying a different tack, he looked at Felix and said dryly, 'And what about you? Are you similarly ignorant?'

'Oh – even more so, I should think,' responded Felix cheerfully. 'The trouble is that I'm rarely at home. But it's extremely good of you to tell us that we could be taking more in rents. We can't really increase them now, of course; but once the war's over it will be a big help to Mother and the girls.'

'I am delighted to have been of service,' came the

sardonic reply. 'But what of your elder brother? You *do* have another brother, I believe? Currently fighting for the Parliament?'

'Yes.' Kate's smile was tinged with acid. 'But Father's death would probably have changed that, had it not been for your predecessor.'

The captain looked back at her with wary exasperation. 'Hugo Verney? What has he to do with it?'

She took her time and allowed each syllable to arrive bathed in bitter honey. 'He ran off with our brother's wife. It's how he came by his shoulder-wound and why he wanted to go to Oxford. Didn't you know? And now, of course, Eden has nothing to come home for.'

For a moment she wasn't sure it had worked. Then, hoisting himself off the table, Justin Ambrose said abruptly, 'All right. You don't need to labour the point. It is well taken. Better, probably, than you might believe. You may have your ledgers. You may also – if the parliamentary presence in the district amounts to anything – look forward to gathering your harvest without me arriving to count every cornstalk. I trust that takes care of any moral obligation on our part?'

'It's certainly a start,' replied Kate, skilfully concealing the fact that she would have given a great deal to know what had made him give in so easily. 'But you'll have to forgive me if I don't wish you well in your coming ordeal. If, of course, there *is* an ordeal – for after waiting so long, I can't see why the Parliament should choose to dispossess you now.'

'Can't you?' A disquieting gleam lit the clear grey eyes. 'It's a simple case of Oxford not falling while Banbury flourishes. Ask Sir William Waller.'

Early in the morning of 25 August, the Roundheads invested Banbury, and two days later the castle refused Colonel John Fiennes' summons to surrender. The great siege had begun, and at Thorne Ash everyone took enormous interest in its progress, whilst simultaneously throwing themselves into the business of getting the harvest in.

The shortage of men around the estate being so acute, Kate was glad to take on a pair of itinerant workers who presented themselves one day in the yard. Both claimed to have served in the army, but were reluctant to say precisely *which*, and since one lacked an eye and the other two fingers from his right hand, it was not hard to understand why they were now reduced to seeking work door to door. Such injuries – and worse – were becoming commonplace, and Kate grimly supposed that they would probably become more so. She installed the brothers Carter in Tom Tripp's old quarters above the stables, saw to it that they had a decent meal, and privately decided to keep them on if they acquitted themselves adequately.

In spite of the increased activity, her mind continued to return, hour by hour, to that exquisitely confusing night beneath the ash tree. She found she could make sense neither of Luciano's reasons for allowing it to happen at all nor the feelings that had motivated him to say what he'd said afterwards. She herself, on the other hand, existed in a limbo of joy for what had been and terror of what was to come; for though marriage was the greatest gift he could offer her, there would be nothing but ashes for either of them if he gave it for the wrong reasons. And that, she discovered, was a more truly frightening possibility than any other she could think of.

News from outside came and went bringing little impact. Plans to make Prince Rupert *generalissimo* of the King's forces apparently ground to a halt when it was learned that his elder brother, Charles Louis, had settled cosily in amongst the enemy at Westminster – and George Goring inherited command of the Western Royalists when Wilmot was arrested for an alleged conspiracy with Essex. Oliver Cromwell and the Earl of Manchester laid their escalating disagreement over the increasing presence of religious sectaries within the army before the Committee of Both Kingdoms; and while John Goodwin preached that Essex had been defeated because God was not a Presbyterian, those members of the Commons who *were* furiously denounced Milton's *Doctrine and Discipline of Divorce* along with Roger William's defence of Jews, Turks and Papists. The Scots continued their dogged siege of Newcastle, unaware that the Marquis of Montrose and Alastair M'Coll Keitach had successfully taken Perth; and, in Banbury, Colonel John Fiennes gave up hope of tunnelling his way into the castle and prepared a massive assault.

By the time Thorne Ash heard about the latter the harvesting was all but over, and Felix decided to award himself a well-earned half-holiday in order to see the sights at first-hand. He found the excursion well worth his while – for, quite apart from the simple entertainment to be got from watching Fiennes' men busily constructing scaling ladders whilst indulging in a sporadic exchange of artillery shot and insults with the Cavaliers, he also went home with two interesting snippets of information. The first was that the Parliament had finally succeeded in enforcing the sequestration order it had long since placed on Far Flamstead, and the second, that – far from returning to the bosom of his family – Nathan Cresswell had somehow attached himself to the slightly less than grateful besiegers as a sort of unofficial lay-preacher.

'My God!' said Kate acidly. 'Only think how much he must be enjoying himself.'

'But for how long?' Felix grinned. 'You know what he's like. It's not so much that he's an arch-Puritan. It's his air of sanctimonious self-righteousness that really sticks in your throat. And if he doesn't watch his step, somebody's likely to seal him up in one of those useless bloody tunnels. Not everyone,' he finished cheerfully, 'is as tolerant as we are.'

Colonel Fiennes' grand assault was an utter failure and left him in the ignominious position of having to choose between letting his dead lie where they were or yielding to Will Compton's conditions in order to reclaim them. He chose the latter and ground his teeth in private. It began to look as though Banbury Castle would never fall.

Equally beset and even more determined to hide it, Kate Maxwell lived through the last days of September in a maelstrom of nerves. After the harvest, Luciano had said; but that had been three long months ago, during which there had been no word at all to indicate whether he was still of the same mind or had changed it completely. And when one did not know whether one was still to be married or not and whether – if one was not – this was a well-disguised blessing or a catastrophe, it made the daily remarks and questions of one's family particularly hard to bear.

The natural result of all this was that when Luciano finally arrived towards the end of the first week in October, she greeted him with a furious, 'Have you *no* consideration? Where the devil have you been till now?'

And Luciano snapped back, 'Busy. What's the matter? You're not pregnant, are you?'

There was a long, blistering silence during which Felicity ducked smartly back inside the parlour door and informed her mother and brother that the groom had indeed arrived – but in the sort of mood that would probably have the bride throwing him out again. In the hall Kate said frigidly, 'No. As it happens, I'm not. So you've no need to sacrifice either your person or your time and may take yourself back to London with a clear conscience, if you like. After all, none of this was *my* idea.'

Sparks flared in Luciano's eyes and for a moment she thought he was going to reply in kind. Then, dropping his hat on the chest in which she kept the firearms, he said tiredly, 'Christ, Kate, what do you expect if you go for my throat before I'm properly over the threshold? It's a long ride, you know.'

'Quite. Is that an apology?'

'If that's what it takes to earn me a chair and a glass of wine – yes. Well?'

Kate's own flash of temper evaporated, leaving her suddenly ashamed of the childishness of it and she said abruptly, 'I'm sorry – I'm sorry. I don't know what came over me. It's just that these last months have been more difficult than you can perhaps imagine.'

For very good reasons, Luciano took his time about

replying. In the last eight weeks he'd been regularly hauled in and out of Westminster on suspicion of carrying messages between the King and various foreign governments. He'd been forced to answer endless stupid questions, had his house searched and all his paperwork examined, and finally resorted to buying his way out of trouble with a hefty donation to the Parliament's war effort. Then, as soon as the danger of being clapped in gaol appeared to be over, there had been a mysterious fire in the shop which only Giacomo's sharp nose had enabled them to catch in time and, two days later, they'd all got up to find the kitchen unaccountably swarming with rats. By then, of course, it was perfectly plain to Luciano that the *deus ex machina* was once more at work, and so it came as no surprise at all when he was set upon in the tavern one evening and given a thorough kicking on account of supposedly being a Papist agent.

It had taken nearly two weeks for the bruises to fade from his face and hands so that he could present himself apparently unscathed at Thorne Ash. His ribs, on the other hand, were still tightly strapped and exceedingly painful, but that was something Kate need know nothing about provided he was careful. At length he said lightly, 'I think I can appreciate the awkwardness you've been facing. But if the family's speculation is beginning to wear you down, by all means let us go and put an end to it.'

'Presently.' Despite the fact that he looked worn to the bone and very much in need of the wine he had asked for, Kate was determined not to allow him into the parlour just yet. Keeping her head high and her voice level, she said, 'Since, as I said, I'm not pregnant, there's still time for you to change your mind about this marriage. I assure you that I'll understand. But you must decide now – for once you go in to Mother and the twins, you'll be committed.'

An odd expression crossed his face and then vanished. He said quietly, 'But I'm already committed. Why else am I here?'

'I wish I knew!'

'You do know. Kate, we've had this conversation before

and there's really no more to be said. Right now what I ought to be doing is seeking your mother's permission – if, that is, she's well enough to receive me?'

'Oh, she's well enough,' came the grim reply. 'Just don't be surprised if she reminds you that marriage under an assumed name tends to be regarded as illegal.'

His hand closed on her wrist. 'What?'

Kate looked at him with faint exasperation. 'Look. I'm trying very hard not to ask too many questions. But you really can't be surprised that we've guessed certain things – or that Mother's apparently known all along that your name is Falcieri. And she's bound to want to know more.'

'A general airing of my personal concerns? I think not.' His fingers released her and, for the first time that she could recall, he offered her his arm. 'But by all means let us go and see what she has in mind.'

What Dorothy had in mind was not instantly obvious. She received both Luciano and his condolences politely but with a complete absence of warmth, directed Felicity to pour him a cup of wine, and allowed Felix to take charge of the conversation. And only when the barest demands of hospitality had been met did she calmly despatch Felicity to the hen-house, Felix to inspect a leaking roof, and Kate to the nursery – with the uncompromising addition that she did not wish to see any of them for at least an hour.

Kate met her betrothed's enigmatic gaze with a perfectly expressionless one of her own and debated the wisdom of pointing out that she had a certain right to attend the coming interview. Then, recognising her presence might do more harm than good, she rose and shepherded the twins smoothly from the room. It was time Luciano and her mother cleared away the debris . . . and for that they needed to be left alone.

The door closed behind them and Luciano remained quite still, waiting for Dorothy to speak. Finally she said flatly, 'You were Richard's friend. I won't pretend I ever really understood why, but I know he had a high regard for you.'

'It was mutual.'

'Quite. And for that reason I am prepared to do what he would have done and treat this conversation in complete confidence. I am not, however, prepared to be kept in the dark. If you want to marry Kate, you're first going to have to tell me exactly what it is that you're trying to achieve with regard to the death of your father. Well?'

There was silence, broken only by the crackling of the fire in the hearth. Then, drawing a long breath, Luciano said slowly, 'I question neither your word nor your right to ask . . . and if you insist on my telling you, then I will. But it would be better for all our sakes if you did not know.'

'Why?' she asked.

'Because the whole business has become much more dangerous than I had thought possible. And I would prefer that the only life in jeopardy was my own.' He paused, frowning down at his hands. And then, meeting her eyes, 'Richard could have told you everything you want to know. That he never did was as much out of concern for your safety as my own insistence on secrecy. In short, what you don't know can't hurt you.'

'And Kate?' Dorothy stared at him witheringly. 'What about her? Won't marriage to you put her squarely in the firing line whether she knows or not? Or – if you're in as much danger as you say – is she likely to find herself a widow almost before she's a wife?' Rising, she swept away to the window in a swish of black damask before turning to say sharply, 'It doesn't seem to me that ignorance is much defence against these things. And that being so, what in God's name do you think you were about to make this marriage necessary by seducing her?'

The merest suggestion of colour touched Luciano's cheekbones and he said bleakly, 'I have no excuses for that. And you can't possibly blame me any more than I blame myself.'

'I daresay. But what use is that? And I'm not looking for excuses. What I want is a *reason*.'

It took him a long time to reply. And finally, as if the words were being dragged out of him he said simply, 'Is love a reason? I'm not sure. All I can say is that I've known for a long time that she loves me . . . and, for almost as long, that I wanted no one but her.' He stopped for a moment, then added raggedly, 'But the tragedy is that if I'm to keep her safely out of my affairs, I can't ever tell her. And if you know a greater punishment than that, I'd be glad to hear it.'

Entirely without warning, Dorothy found herself experiencing again the same unfamiliar mixture of sympathy and reluctant liking that she'd felt for him the night he'd described the battle of Edgehill. But although it was stronger now than it had been then, it was still not enough . . . so at length she said, 'I can't begin to comprehend this mess. So I think you'd better start at the beginning – telling me only what you feel you can. And then you can try convincing me that Kate shouldn't know.'

A wry smile twisted his mouth. 'That's the easy part. If Kate knew how much . . . how much I love her, she wouldn't rest until she also knew what I was about. And having found *that* out, she'd refuse to stay out of it.'

'And that would put her at risk.'

'Yes.' No longer troubling to veil his expression, Luciano looked straight into Dorothy's eyes. He said, 'There is a man whose name I don't know but who I can prove arranged the conviction of my father. Unfortunately, he now knows precisely who I am and what I'm doing. And that is where the danger lies.'

She frowned a little. 'You're sure of this?'

'Oh yes. At present he is merely toying with me. A series of sadistic little games intended to cause damage and disruption. But he could tire of that at any moment; and when he does he'll go for the kill. Unless, of course, I can get to him first.' He waited, continuing to hold her gaze, and then said bitterly, 'This is the point where – if you have any sense at all – you will tell me to go away and not come back. I'm a foreigner and a usurer and I'm deeply in debt to my uncle in Genoa . . . on top of which I've somehow got to live long enough to kill a man who will otherwise kill me. Not very good, is it?'

'It's disastrous,' said Dorothy frankly while, against her will, a small bud of respect slowly started to open. 'But more calamitous still is the fact that Kate loves you.'

'Yes.' The strain was beginning to manifest itself on his face. 'You probably won't believe it, but I tried quite hard to prevent that.' He hesitated and then added vaguely, 'Another of my great successes.'

'So I see. And yet, despite all of these things, Richard would have countenanced a match between you.'

This time Luciano said nothing, merely bending his head over his hands. A minute passed and then two. And finally Dorothy said carefully, 'I never knew him to be wrong about a person's character and, that being so, it seems unlikely that he would have made his first mistake in you. I also . . . I also know what it is to love someone in the way I am beginning to believe you love Kate. And therefore I suppose we'd best discuss how this wedding is to be managed.'

Very, very slowly, his eyes rose to meet hers. In a tone of complete surprise, he said, 'You're sure?'

'No. But that's something I'll just have to live with – just as *you* will have to find a way of sorting out your affairs as quickly as possible so that you can start offering Kate a normal life. Then – if you succeed in doing that – I may feel justified in welcoming you to the family.'

Luciano rose to face her. 'But not before?'

'Well – be reasonable,' said Dorothy. 'What would *you* do?'

They eventually agreed to send Felix discreetly for Parson Fletcher so that the wedding might take place as privately as possible in the chapel. And thus it was that, less than three hours later, Kate found herself dressing for the occasion in something of a daze.

'What are you doing?' demanded Felicity when she saw the gown her sister had chosen. 'You can't get married in black. It's the very last thing Father would have wanted. Find something else.'

'Such as what?' asked Kate. Her fingers were frozen and

her mind felt numb. 'I've nothing in white or even grey. And it doesn't seem right to be wearing colours.'

'Why not? I shall – and so, for this one night, will Mother.' Then, when Kate continued to stand irresolutely in the middle of the floor, 'For heaven's sake – this is your *wedding*! Spare a thought for Luciano at least!'

A faint grin touched the still face. 'That's no argument. He'll wear black himself.'

'So?' Felicity dived head-first into the clothes chest. 'You're going to the altar looking like a bride if I have to dress you myself. Ah! The very thing!'

Kate stared at the bronze and amber gown that had been given to her by Queen Henrietta Maria. Its elbow-length sleeves were trimmed with lavish falls of gold lace, its full skirt ended in a sweeping demi-train and, in place of the usual pearls, it was girdled with topazes. So far, so good . . . and of course the colours were undeniably becoming. But the wide square neckline which barely clung to the points of her shoulders and framed the gentle swell of her breasts was one of the most décolleté Kate had ever seen, and revealed a good deal more of her than seemed quite proper. She said weakly, 'I can't wear that. It's barely decent.'

'Nonsense!' Felicity laid the bodice tenderly on the bed and turned her attention to shaking out the skirt. 'Anyway – he's seen you in it before and will soon be seeing you in a good deal less. If,' innocently, 'he hasn't already?' Upon which masterly note she set about readying the blushing and silenced bride for her nuptials.

The chapel was ablaze with candles and someone had apparently found time to raid the garden for the last of the roses. There was no music and, with her hand on Felix's arm and Felicity two paces behind, Kate walked down the aisle to the echo of her own footsteps. But Mother was there in her best emerald silk – and Meg Bennet and her father, along with Goodwife Flossing and the Woodley brothers; and, a little apart from the others and turning slowly to look at her, Luciano.

Without quite meaning to or even being fully aware of

it, Kate stopped walking and took the time to glance from the sculpted Renaissance face of her bridegroom to the painted one gazing down on her from the chapel ceiling – Lucifer the beautiful and splendid, being hurled from grace. Then, looking back at Luciano, she met the shock of his laughter, silent, inviting and impossible to resist; and with the warmth of it flooding her heart, she took the last few steps to his side.

The ceremony, kept deliberately simple, was soon over. In his usual enigmatic tone, Luciano promised to love, honour and keep her, forsaking all others; and Kate, wondering somewhat distantly at the back of her mind how far he meant it, found herself suddenly transformed into Katharine Elinor Falcieri del Santi. She did not think she would ever get used to it.

'Kate del Santi,' murmured her husband as he formally saluted her on both cheeks. 'And then only to those you trust.'

'How much trouble are you in?' she whispered back, testing what her new status would do for her.

'Trouble? What trouble? I'll have you know I'm a respectable married man,' came the calm reply. And, laying her fingers on his black velvet sleeve, he led her unhurriedly back up the aisle to the door and the congratulations of her family.

Although, with so little time in which to prepare it, the bridal supper was by no means lavish, Goodwife Flossing had worked wonders to produce a succulent side of beef served with oyster sauce, jugged pigeons, stuffed turbot and a variety of creams, custards and candied fruit. And though the spectres of Richard and Eden were in everyone's minds, they did not colour the festival by sitting at the board. In fact, between wine, ale and good food, the party grew surprisingly merry; and Kate was treated to the novel sight of Signor del Santi setting out to amuse . . . and, as was his habit, succeeding.

From time to time Kate's eyes strayed involuntarily to the gold band he had placed on her hand. It was slightly wider than the wedding rings she was accustomed to seeing and intricately engraved with a design of leaves and flowers. It was also, amazingly, a perfect fit.

'I hope you like it,' said Luciano softly.

She had discovered in the last hour that, no matter what he appeared to be doing, his attention never totally strayed from her. Something else she had not expected. She said, 'It's beautiful.'

'So I should hope. I made it myself.' Tearing his eyes from the delicacy of her wrists, he refilled her glass and said casually, 'I've something else for you, too – but I'll require a favour first.'

Feeling her colour rise, Kate turned to meet a smile that was half sardonic, half not. 'Oh?'

'Yes. I'd be grateful if you could see to it that we're spared the circus.'

And, smiling back, she said, 'It's done. Did you think I wouldn't remember? And with only Felix and Felicity, it wouldn't have been much of a circus anyway, would it?'

Although entirely unaware of it, she glowed with anticipation of the night ahead; and to Luciano's own very real regret that it was not to be, was added concern. At best she was going to be disappointed – at worst, hurt. But unless he was prepared to risk explaining the multi-coloured state of his rib-cage, there wasn't a damned thing he could do about it.

Her pride, however, was quite another matter. So he continued to make flippant conversation and bathe her in the full extent of his charm until the moment arrived when he could spirit her discreetly away to her chamber.

The bed had been given fresh hangings, a flagon of wine stood on the chest and a fire crackled cheerfully in the hearth. Suddenly shy, Kate stared round her and said breathlessly, 'My goodness. Someone has been busy.'

Luciano said nothing. Alone in this room and with his senses awash with her, it was going to be even harder than he had thought. There were words he must not speak and a growing need to take her in his arms that he did not know whether or not he dared give way to. And most treacherous of all was the fact that if he did not do something sensible very quickly, he might no longer have a choice in the matter.

Contemplating and then mentally rejecting the wine, he pulled a small box from his pocket and offered it to her. 'I am about to say something you won't like. I'm hoping, however, that this will soften the blow. Open it.'

Very slowly, she lifted the lid. From its nest of blue velvet, a tear-drop diamond surrounded by tiny sapphires and set in fragile filigree winked back at her. For several seconds Kate simply stared at it. Then, raising her eyes to his, she said, 'It's exquisite. Did you make it yourself?'

'No. But I watched its creation many years ago by – by a man who once taught me. And it's the only example of his work I possess.'

The air evaporated in Kate's lungs. His father. He was talking about his father. And he was giving her the only souvenir he had of him. Tears stung her eyes but, before she could speak, Luciano said abruptly, 'Sit down, Kate. You seem to have understood rather more than I intended – but that's where it must stop. And there are other, more pressing things to be said.'

A trifle shakily, Kate took the stool beside the fire and watched him drop neatly to the rug at her feet. Then, frowning a little, he said, 'There's no diplomatic way to put this – so I'll come straight to the point. I am not staying.'

The words took a long time to sink in. But finally she said, 'You mean you're going back to London tomorrow?'

'Yes.' A pause. 'I also mean that I'm not going to sleep with you tonight.'

A strange and not very pleasant plummeting sensation took place behind Kate's ribs. She said, 'If – if that's a joke, it's not very funny.'

'You think I don't know that?' Holding every nerve and muscle under rigid control, he looked sombrely up at her. 'It's for your own good, Kate. I don't know how long I'm going to be away this time . . . and I never take the same risk twice. In short, I'm making sure I don't leave you pregnant.'

'Does that matter so very much?' she asked wistfully.

'To me – yes.'

'I see.' She thought about it and then, striving for lightness, said, 'Well, that's very chivalrous of you. But aren't we supposed to consummate our marriage?'

'We did that three months ago,' came the flat reply. 'Please try to understand. It's not that I don't *want* to stay—'

'Then stay.' Continuing to hold his gaze and resolutely squashing her pride, Kate said, 'We – we don't have to make love, if you'd rather not. But, if you're to be away for months on end, at least we could be together for this one night.'

'Kate – no!' Without thinking what he was doing, he reached out to grasp her hands and pull her down beside him. 'It wouldn't work – can't you see?'

'Why *not*?'

'Because I'm not a bloody machine!' snapped Luciano. And, powerless to resist the impulse this time, drew her hard against his chest and kissed her.

Aeons later – or perhaps it was only minutes – he slowly released her to look into her eyes. His breathing was as disturbed as hers and he knew that if he did not go now, he was lost. Letting his hands slide quietly from her, he moved a little away and said, 'You see? No self-discipline whatsoever. And that's why I have to go. Will you forgive me . . . and perhaps also be patient?'

Kate watched him get to his feet and discovered that she was shaking. She said, 'You know – you know you need not ask. But you must promise me that you will take care. I am afraid for you.'

'Don't be. There's no need.' He smiled at her and hoped it was reassuring. 'Or if you *must* worry, let it be because I promise I'll live to plague you. That ought to be enough to put the fear of God into anyone.' And, bending to drop one last, light kiss on her hand, he was gone.

539

Five

Luciano left for London taking Felix with him, and Thorne Ash seemed suddenly very empty indeed. The loss of Richard was still an open wound and the absence of Eden, Gianetta and Felix was not calculated to make matters any better. Felicity bemoaned the eternal quiet; Dorothy tried to fill her days with the rearing of Eden's children; and Kate, shouldering the burden of estate-management with increasing ease, wondered how long she must wait for the man she had married to allow her to be his wife.

The suddenness of his departure was a source of piercing disappointment, and his absence a steadily growing wound. People said you didn't miss what you'd never had . . . but Kate knew it for a lie. She'd never had Luciano's company on a daily basis, but she missed him at every step – from the second she awoke each morning, to the time she lay sleepless on her pillow at night. And no matter how busy she kept herself, nothing seemed to mend it.

Then, five days after Luciano's departure, half the sheep in the upper pasture fell violently sick and died within twenty-four hours. It was Kate's first farming crisis and she dealt with it as best she could, spending almost the whole night out in the byre helping Jacob Bennet and John and James Carter dose the dying beasts. Then, chilled to the bone and thoroughly depressed, she went in to break the news to her mother.

'I don't know how it happened. The rest of the flock is down in Meadow Bottom, apparently perfectly healthy, so it doesn't look like something contagious or more of them would be coming down with it. And if it's something they ate – which is what I first thought – how come only half of them were affected? It doesn't make sense.' She took a cautious sip of the hot posset Dorothy had placed in her hands and then frowned irritably. 'And I thought I'd got everything so nicely under control, too. Serves me right, doesn't it?'

'Not at all,' came the calm reply. 'You can't blame yourself, Kate. These things happen from time to time. Call it Nature or Fate – or just plain bad luck. All farms have the occasional disaster. It's part of life.'

A week later, one of the outlying barns caught fire, illuminating the countryside for miles around and reducing two hundred bales of hay to ashes before anyone could do more than fill a few buckets.

'*More* bad luck?' thought Kate, staring moodily at the smoking debris in the cold dawn light. 'Or a sudden plague of carelessness? And if Flossie's right and these things always come in threes, what misfortune will beset us next? Flood? Famine? Or will we be lucky and just get the frogs?'

But as the days became weeks and no fresh catastrophe struck, it began to seem that she'd panicked too soon. Life slid back into its usual uneventful groove and they were all able to take more of an interest in outside affairs – such as enjoying the irony of the Scots finally taking Newcastle while, behind them, Montrose and his Irish tore their way through Aberdeen. Closer to home and slightly less amusing was the arrival on 25 October of a Royalist relief-force in Banbury which put a summary end to the castle garrison's twelve-week ordeal – just in time, so rumour said, to prevent the last two horses being turned into collops. And not amusing at all, because Eden had presumably been there, was a second large-scale battle in Newbury between His Majesty and the combined forces of Waller, Essex and Cromwell – apparently brought about when Sir John Hurry changed sides again and informed the parliamentary generals that the King had just sent fifteen hundred cavalry north to Banbury. *Mercurius Britanicus* enthusiastically reported a huge parliamentary victory; *Mercurius Aulicus* preferred to dwell on my lord Manchester's increasing disenchantment with the war in general, and Oliver Cromwell in particular.

November brought a lonely old man back to the public eye when the Commons decided to encourage its Scots allies by hauling Archbishop Laud from his cell in the Tower and putting him on trial. And while the Committee of Both Kingdoms sat down to consider reorganising the army, a new peace delegation was sent to the King – only to return with the inevitable flea in its ear.

Throughout all this, word came from neither Eden nor Luciano and Kate did not know which of the silences annoyed or worried her more. If anything had happened to Eden, they would doubtless have heard by now; and if not, she felt he might at least have a care for their mother's peace of mind and send some message. As for Luciano, she spoke of her fears to no one and only gave way to them when she was alone in her room at night. Often she even sat foolishly in the dark, trying to find him with her mind . . . but either she did not have the gift or he was deliberately shutting her out. Either way the answer was always the same. A blank.

The month slid by on leaden feet and the weather began to turn seasonally murky. Cromwell accused Manchester of neglecting his opportunities and being backward in prosecuting the war, and Manchester called Cromwell a man of dangerous ideas. Essex and Denzil Holles continued to support the Scottish alliance whilst worrying about possible sectarian riots following a rumour that the House of Lords was trying to save Archbishop Laud's neck. And at Thorne Ash, the first week of December brought a recurrence of small accidents.

Wheels fell off carts, depositing produce in the mud; gaps appeared in fences allowing livestock to wander; milk curdled and the hens stopped laying. Kate started to dread the sight of Jacob Bennet appearing grim-faced on the doorstep, and Dorothy, with the words 'damage and disruption' ringing unpleasantly in her ears, found herself becoming more than a little frightened.

It was not, however, until Jude went missing that she

finally screamed her fears into Kate's and Felicity's at first uncomprehending ears.

'He'll be hiding,' Kate had said, on hearing the news. 'I'll go and alert the servants. We'll soon find him.'

And taking hold of her daughter's shoulders in a biting grip, Dorothy had shouted back, 'We *won't*! Someone's taken him – can't you see? It's all of a piece with everything else that's happened since you married that thrice-damned Italian!'

Suddenly very still, Kate stared at her. 'What are you talking about?'

'Sabotage,' came the uneven reply. 'Sadistic games, he called it. And now we've become a target, too. But we're wasting time. The important thing is to find Jude. He was in the yard with Meg and Eve – only then Eve fell over and Meg brought her in to Flossie and, when she went out again, Jude had vanished.'

'And you think someone's taken him?' said Felicity, still without really believing it.

'Yes! God in heaven – how many more times must I say it? Get everyone you can find and let's go and look for him. It's been barely twenty minutes – so he can't be far away yet. *Move!*'

With the aid of all the servants and every tenant Kate could reach, they combed the house and garden and outbuildings, the orchard, the lanes and every cottage within a three-mile radius – all without finding a trace of Eden's small son. Incredible as it seemed, it began to appear that Dorothy was right . . . and by the middle of the afternoon, everyone was sick with fear.

'It will be dark in a couple of hours,' said Kate numbly to Adam Woodley. And then, with agonised violence, 'He's not quite four years old! How could anyone *do* such a thing?'

'Don't know, Miss Kate,' came the flat reply. 'But if I get my hands on the evil bugger, I'll break his bloody neck. Meantime, I think it's best if some of us look a bit further afield. As far as the main road, maybe. I'll get Jack and Mr Bennet.'

Another hour wore by. Kate made her mother return to the house before she dropped with fatigue and anxiety, and then set out again herself with one-eyed John Carter to search the woods for the second time.

The light started to fade and her voice grew hoarse with calling – and still they found nothing.

'Better go back, mistress,' said Carter. 'We can't do nothing in the dark.'

'We can,' snapped Kate. 'We can get torches and search all night if necessary. And if food and rest mean more to you than the life of a little boy, you can seek employment elsewhere.' And without further ado, she led the way smartly back in the direction of the house with Mr Carter trailing sullenly behind.

Then, as they rejoined the lane, Kate saw four horse-men approaching through the dusk. Three she recognised as the Woodley brothers and Jacob Bennet . . . and the fourth, with his cloak wrapped securely about the drowsy form of her small nephew, became gradually and surprisingly identifiable as Ralph Cochrane.

With an odd little choking sound, Kate slid recklessly from the saddle to hurl herself at Ralph's horse. 'Thank God – oh, thank God! Where did you find him?'

'On the Southam road,' replied Ralph grimly. 'Damned nearly ran over him, poor little chap. He was frightened to death and half frozen. Then I met your fellows here and they told me you suspect somebody of making off with him. Is that true?'

'Yes.' She reached up to touch Jude's cheek. 'But that can wait. Right now he needs to be got into the house before he catches his death. I – I don't know how to thank you, Ralph. Mother will be so *relieved*.'

Mere relief in no way described Dorothy's feelings – which, for one perilous second, threatened to completely overset her. Then, summoning Meg and Goodwife Floss-ing, she became suddenly and intensely practical and Jude was whisked away to hot milk and a warm bed without even opening his eyes.

It was an hour or more before Dorothy once more reap-

peared down the stairs, by which time Kate had called off
the various searches and Felicity had installed Mr Cochrane
in the best spare bedchamber with a tankard of mulled ale
and a jug of hot water for washing. Then, when they were
all assembled in the parlour, Dorothy said baldly, 'I was
right. Jude says a man took him for a ride on his horse to
see the baby foxes and then left him.'

'Who?' asked Kate. 'Someone he knew?'

'Yes, though not by name,' came the bitter reply. 'A man
with a funny hand, he said. In short, James Carter.'

'Carter?' echoed Felicity. 'But why?'

'Presumably because he was paid.' Kate rose. 'Excuse
me. I'm just going to part Adam Woodley from his supper
and give him the chance he's been praying for.'

'Wait,' said Ralph. 'I don't know what's going on, but
it seems a few answers are needed before Mr Woodley
pulverises the fellow. So, unless you've any objections, it
might be as well if I went along too. Well?'

'Go,' invited Dorothy. 'You'll find Adam in the kitchen.'
And, when the door had closed behind him, 'It's a pity
that Eden can't be bothered to be here himself, but at least
we can thank God for Ralph. I suppose he's come with a
message?'

'I haven't asked.' Kate remained on her feet, staring
tensely at her mother. 'Now Jude is safe, all I care about
is hearing why you feel our problems are somehow Luciano's
fault. What, for example, is all this about "sadistic games"?'

Dorothy closed her eyes for a moment and then opened
them. 'It's what he said himself. The trouble is that he
doesn't know who's playing them – only that it's the man
he's looking for in connection with his father's death.' She
paused and then added wearily, 'I wasn't supposed to tell
you. He's afraid any knowledge you acquire – or just the
mere fact of your marriage – may put you in danger. And
it seems he's right.'

Kate sat down on the nearest stool, her mind working
furiously. Finally she said acidly, 'And of course it occurred
to neither of you that forewarned is forearmed? Or that it
was just possible – if I'd known all this – that I might

conceivably have been a little more cautious about employing casual labour? *God's teeth!* Do neither of you think I've got a brain?' She stopped, forcing back the sudden burst of temper. Then, 'However. Having confessed this much, you may as well tell me the rest. What sort of disasters has Luciano been facing?'

'He didn't say. My goodness, Kate, you know what he's like! He'd rather have bled to death than tell me the little he did.'

'But somehow you persuaded him.' It was not a question.

'Not quite. I simply made it plain that, if he expected to marry you, he didn't have any choice,' replied Dorothy. And then, hurriedly, so that she wouldn't find herself in the position of having to disclose any of the other things Luciano had said, 'And frankly, if I'd known what was going to come of it, I'd have refused my consent and told him to come back when he'd put his house in order.'

Chin on hands and eyes wide with interest, Felicity said, 'I wish somebody would explain why this man's making trouble for Luciano – and us.'

'Because he appears to have arranged the death of Luciano's father and knows that Luciano is looking for him,' said Dorothy, her gaze still fixed on her elder daughter. 'And now – forget that you know anything about it. *Both* of you.'

Kate's brows rose. 'Rather a tall order when the person at the centre of all this happens to be my husband,' she began. And then broke off as the door opened again on Ralph.

Frowning, he moved forward under three expectant pairs of eyes and said tersely, 'We were too late. The fellow's already dead.'

Kate swallowed. 'How?'

'Murdered by the other one, at a guess, since that one-eyed so-called brother of his is nowhere to be found.' Ralph considered the matter and then, deciding there was no harm to be done, added, 'If you really want to know, his skull was split like an apple. I've left Adam and Jack Woodley digging a hole to bury him in.'

Dorothy looked faintly sick. 'Can we *do* that?'

'Only thing *to* do, in my opinion,' came the prosaic reply. 'It will save a lot of explanations. And you can't deny that the bas— that the fellow deserved it.'

'Quite.' Kate rose and went to pour Ralph some wine. 'But what I can't understand is why John killed him. After all, they must surely have been in it together.'

'Looks like it.' Ralph accepted the glass and sat down. 'But the dead one proved unreliable and had to go. Or that's how I view it, anyway. You see, I don't think Jude was supposed to be found.'

There was a long, chilling silence. Then Felicity said chokingly, 'That's *horrible*!'

'Yes. Yes it is,' agreed Kate weakly, her eyes locked with her mother's. 'And so we'd all better take extra special care that nothing like it can happen again.'

Ralph looked from one to the other of them. 'I don't suppose anybody would like to tell me about it?'

'No,' said Kate quickly. And then, 'In fact, there's nothing to tell, except that I should never have taken the Carters on in the first place since I knew nothing about them.'

'But a little earlier you spoke of them being paid by someone else to do what they did.'

'Did I?' Kate's brow creased in a fair assumption of perplexity. 'But that was just a guess, you know. And James's death puts a whole different complexion on things. No. We've nothing to worry about now – and are just overwhelmingly grateful to you for all you've done.'

'Think nothing of it.' He did not believe a word but knew he was being told not to press the matter. 'I was just in the right place at the right time.'

'You certainly were,' said Dorothy warmly. 'And, as far as I can make out, none of us has yet asked you why – and whether you were actually on your way here to visit us.'

For the first time, Ralph looked slightly uncomfortable. He said slowly, 'Well, yes. I was. To be absolutely plain with you, it seemed to me that if Eden wouldn't come himself – or at least write – then somebody ought to come and tell you why.'

Kate watched the disappointment darken her mother's eyes and said dryly, 'We know why. It's because of Celia, isn't it?'

'You knew?'

'Enough to draw certain conclusions. Is Eden aware that she's no longer here?'

Ralph nodded. 'Francis got a message to him. If it hadn't been for that, I probably wouldn't have known anything about it myself – because Eden's closed up like a clam.' He paused and then said bluntly, 'Apparently she's living openly with some fellow called Verney in Oxford. Francis is livid.'

'That's nice,' said Dorothy bleakly. 'And Eden?'

Ralph took a large gulp of wine and wondered how you told someone that their son had changed out of all recognition – and not for the better. That he shunned even the simplest companionship and had acquired an edge like a razor; that in order to find out even the smallest part of what troubled him, you first had to provoke him into attacking you and then use the basic persuasion of your fists. But it wasn't possible to tell Dorothy any of that so instead he said cautiously, 'He's bitter, of course. And he doesn't want to lay eyes on Celia again.'

'That's understandable. But since he knows she's not here, it can't be why he doesn't want to come home,' said Dorothy. 'Well?'

'No.' Ralph drew a long breath and prepared to say the one thing that could not be omitted. 'It's worse than that. He . . . he doesn't want to see the children. Particularly the little girl. He says . . . he says she's not his.'

Kate sat like a stone and watched her mother turn perfectly ashen. It had, after all, been a hellish day and none of them was up to coping with this as well – not even she herself who, seemingly alone of them all, had already guessed it. Rising, she said sharply, ' "Sufficient unto the day is the evil thereof." I'm going to ask Flossie to serve supper.'

'*Food?*' Dorothy shuddered. 'I don't think I could.'

'Possibly not. But Ralph must be ravenous,' retorted Kate. 'And even if he's not – life has to go on and it's the little things that help it to do so. I thought we'd already learned that.'

With Christmas a mere week away and Waller's army firmly entrenched in its winter quarters at Farnham, Ralph was easily coaxed into staying to spend the festive season at Thorne Ash.

'Except that it won't be very festive,' said Kate candidly. 'With so few of us here and this worry over Eden and, more important than anything else, having so recently lost Father, we wouldn't be celebrating much even if Westminster *hadn't* decided to abolish the holiday.'

'You can blame the Scots for that,' muttered Ralph. 'Blasted sour-faced killjoys!'

'You've obviously less sympathy with them than you once had,' she grinned. 'But never mind. At least you can count on being well fed here – and we'll certainly appreciate your company. Particularly Felicity.' And she drifted away leaving him to wonder precisely how random that parting remark had been.

The truth was that he was finding himself increasingly drawn to Eden's youngest sister but had no idea whether or not it was mutual. Because of his lack of prospects except as a soldier, he tried to believe that it would be better if she held him in nothing more than simple friendship. But still he could not help seeking her out and, in time, telling her more about himself and about Eden's current state of mind than he would ever have admitted to Kate or Dorothy.

Felicity listened and responded to his talk and was aware of nothing save a feeling of deep pleasure in his company. She discovered that it was possible to say anything to Ralph and have complete faith in his discretion. And that was why, when a mud-spattered courier arrived on Christmas Eve with a packet for Kate from London, she pulled him unobtrusively into the parlour so that Kate could be alone and said quietly, 'It's from Luciano del Santi. They were married in October and she's been waiting for some word ever since.'

Ralph stared at her 'Married? My God! Does Eden know?'

'No. And, at the moment, there's no reason why he should. The truth is that Luciano's engaged in some business he'd rather Kate wasn't connected with, so they're keeping their marriage quiet until it's concluded. Eden might not understand that. And I don't think he's ever liked Luciano much, anyway.'

'I can't say that I blame him,' replied Ralph. 'And rich as del Santi undoubtedly is, it's not everyone who wants an Italian leech in the family.'

Felicity's gaze became disconcertingly direct. 'Possibly not. But in *this* one, we tend to accept people for who they are, not what they do for a living. And if Eden's forgotten that, he must have changed even more than you've said.'

Alone in her room, Kate read the brief, impersonal note that told her nothing at all about her husband's activities and looked for a long time at the lovely, antique cameo he had sent her. Then she washed the tearstains from her face, composed her expression, and went downstairs to join the others. He was alive and had not forgotten her; and that, it seemed, was the only knowledge she was to be allowed.

Christmas passed quietly with nothing more than church and the good food Kate had promised to mark it from other days. And when gifts had been exchanged and Goodwife Flossing's goose both cooked and eaten, the talk drifted back – as it had tended to do throughout Ralph's visit – to Parliament's attempts to reorganise the army through something called the Self-Denying Ordinance. This, explained Ralph, would prohibit members of either House from holding military office and thus enable the Committee of Both Kingdoms to elect a single supreme commander. That it would also force the resignation of Essex, Manchester, Cromwell and Sir William Waller was something that no one at Westminster appeared to be worrying about too much.

Dorothy didn't worry about it either, since whatever the

Parliament did with the army was unlikely to bring Eden home. But on the night before Ralph's departure, she drew him to one side and said, 'I'm aware that you've tried to be tactful – and I thank you for it. But I've heard from Felicity a little of what Eden is suffering and how concerned you are about him, and I'd like you to tell him this from me. I understand his absence and recognise that only time can soften the pain of what has happened. But none of it is little Viola's fault – and he should also remember that she may be his daughter after all. *Or why did Celia not take her?*'

The year of our Lord sixteen hundred and forty-five opened with the execution of Archbishop Laud and more abortive peace talks, this time at Uxbridge. In Oxford, Prince Rupert had finally been made *generalissimo* of all the King's forces and a terrible fire had devastated part of the town. North of the border, Montrose and his Irish vanished into the fastness of a Scottish winter; at Westminster, leadership of the Commons veered between Harry Vane and Richard's friend, Denzil Holles – while the Lords refused to pass the Self-Denying Ordinance; and at Derby House, the Committee of Both Kingdoms started laying plans for their New Model Army.

Throughout all of this the weather was less than kind and Kate, whilst attending meticulously to each and every one of her daily duties, began to strain at the leash that kept her from Luciano. With James Carter discreetly buried in the orchard and one-eyed John having apparently disappeared into thin air, no fresh disasters struck either farm or household and, though they were all a little more wary than they had been before, the sense of incipient cataclysm swiftly evaporated. Consequently, Kate's desperate desire to see Luciano boiled to fever pitch and, by the middle of February, would have carried her south to London in the teeth of everybody's opposition, had not the state of the roads prevented her.

It was not until the end of the month that Justin Ambrose finally put in a belated appearance to claim the previous quarter's rents and Kate, with a sardonic quip already hovering on her tongue, found herself stricken into silence by the sight of him. He described his condition, with irony, as having been slightly singed . . . and only the look in his eyes prevented Kate asking questions. Like everyone else in the district, she had heard all about the garrison's recent attempt to repossess Lord Northampton's family home of Compton Wynyates – and how forty of them had been roasted alive as a result. Then, because she did not think she had ever seen anyone look so ill, but hadn't the slightest wish to feel sorry for him, she offered him first a chair and then a glass of wine . . . and finally, darkly suspecting that the burns hidden by his gloves far outstripped those she could see on his face, a pot of Mother's salve. He accepted the first two but declined the last with a flick of one eyebrow and a cryptic remark about the number of Roundheads whose sisters seemed to want to restore him to health. Then he took the purse that Kate gave him and left, leaving her to wonder precisely which of the daughters of Banbury had formed an attachment for him.

March brought a slight improvement in the state of the roads and a backlog of news-sheets – from which they learned that Sir Philip Skippon was to be major-general of the New Model Army and Sir Thomas Fairfax its commander-in-chief. No mention was made of Waller or Cromwell, but it was noticed that no one had as yet been appointed to take charge of the cavalry; all of which was very interesting but, as far as Kate was concerned, paled into insignificance beside the news that the City of London (aided no doubt by Luciano del Santi) had been asked for a mere eighty thousand pounds to help pay for new uniforms and the like.

But the next news from the outside world was more momentous still. A letter arrived from Geoffrey Cox announcing that Amy was pregnant – thus providing Kate with the perfect excuse for travelling to London. Without wasting a moment, she said brightly, 'One of us ought to go and see her, don't you think? I mean, I know she has Geoffrey's mother and sisters to look after her, but it's been a long time since she saw any of *us*. And Geoffrey admits she seems a trifle homesick just at present.'

Dorothy eyed her with faint foreboding and said, 'Let me guess. You're about to offer to go yourself in order to see that absentee husband of yours. Am I right?'

'Yes. Can you blame me? If I sit meekly by the hearth much longer without a word to tell me how he's faring, I think I shall go mad. I have to satisfy myself that he's still alive and well – and if I'm not quick, he'll be half-way to Genoa.'

'Oh, *Kate*. I understand it all, believe me. But he said you were to stay out of it and we've been given adequate proof of the sense of that. So even if I were happy to let you go – which I'm not – do you really think he'd offer you any kind of welcome?'

'Not at all. He's more likely to completely lose his temper. But that's a chance I'll just have to take, because I can't go on as I am. I love him, you see; so much that not being able even to lay eyes on him is like dying of slow starvation. And I can't bear it any longer.' She paused and managed a small, crooked smile. 'Mother, I'm sorry – but I *have* to go even though I know you can't really spare me. And I promise I'll take every care. I'll wear my wedding-ring on a chain round my neck and travel as Kate Maxwell and take both my maid and Adam Woodley for escort. I'll even do no more than simply call on Luciano as if I were just going to see Felix. But please don't ask me to stay away. I can't do it.'

She arrived on Amy's doorstep four days later, bone-weary and liberally spattered with mud. The maidservant who opened the door seemed in two minds whether or not to admit her . . . and whatever pleasure Amy felt on seeing her was well hidden behind a series of critical remarks on her appearance. Kate, however, could not have cared less. Luciano was no more than half a mile away and tomorrow, God willing, she would see him. So it was easy to smile affectionately at Amy and suggest she be allowed to wash and change instead of sullying the parlour in her present state; and, when that was done, to sit down with her sister over a mug of spiced wine and inquire with perfect sincerity about her health.

'I'm no worse than is to be expected, I suppose,' came the slightly pettish reply. 'But the least little thing tires me and I have to rest a good deal.'

'Yes. Mother said that might be the case – and has sent you some of her special cordial,' said Kate neutrally. Privately she thought that Amy looked very well indeed, aside from having gained a little extra weight . . . and that probably had more to do with the dish of apricot tartlets at her elbow than her pregnancy – which was as yet completely disguised by the fullness of her skirts. 'She's written to you, too – pages of good advice, I'm sure. She wanted to come herself, of course. But with Celia gone . . . ah. Felix told you about that, I suppose?'

'Yes. And I can't say I'm surprised. I expect *you* were glad.'

Kate stared at her. '*Glad?* No. Not really. Coming on top of Father's death as it did—'

'Don't.' Unexpectedly, Amy's lip trembled. 'I don't want to speak of it. I – I still can't believe he's gone.'

'No.' Kate swallowed hard and concentrated on keeping her voice level. 'No. Neither can I.' She fell silent for a moment and then said hearteningly, 'Geoffrey must be ecstatic about the baby.'

'He is.' As ever, Amy was easily diverted. 'He brings me a present almost every day and spends much less time with those horrid presses of his. His parents are thrilled, too,' she added smugly. 'It will be their first grandchild.'

'And what about you?' asked Kate. 'Are *you* happy about it?'

'Well, of course! Having children gives one much more standing, you know – which is something you ought to think of yourself. After all, you're not getting any younger, are you? And if you don't find a husband soon, you probably never will.'

Kate continued to smile and said nothing. Then, gently turning the subject, she asked if Amy saw much of Felix.

'Oh, now and then. He comes to dine occasionally when Geoffrey invites him.'

'You don't visit him in Cheapside, then?'

'And risk being seen entering a money-lender's establishment? Certainly not! Besides, simply looking at that dreadful Italian makes me shudder. I hate deformity.'

For one breath-stopping moment, Kate felt again the smooth, warm skin of that slightly raised but otherwise perfectly formed shoulder – and then it was gone. Digging her nails into her palms so that she should not give herself away, she said negligently, 'Oh? That's a shame – for I was thinking that we might perhaps call there tomorrow to surprise Felix.'

'*You* can do whatever you wish,' shrugged Amy, reaching for another tartlet. 'I have an appointment with my dressmaker. Ah, and while I think about it, I suppose I ought to apologise for the fact of there being no fire in your bedchamber. You may not know of it but we've had a coal-shortage here – and even though the Scots are supposed to have taken Newcastle, things don't seem to have got any better. So we only heat the main rooms – and *my* chamber, of course, because of my condition.' Polishing off the tart, she brushed the crumbs from her fingers and smiled sweetly. 'But if you're cold, don't hesitate to say. I'll be happy to lend you a shawl.'

On the following morning Geoffrey Cox, who had appeared rather more pleased to see Kate than she had expected, discovered her intention to visit Cheapside and offered to escort her. Graciously but with complete finality, Kate declined his offer. Since she didn't know how matters would turn out, the only witness to possible embarrassment she was prepared to tolerate was her maid, Jenny Platt. She therefore saw Adam Woodley off on the return journey to Thorne Ash, put the finishing touches to an extremely careful toilette and set forth with a quaking heart to see her husband.

She arrived to find that none of the speeches she had prepared were of the least use – and for one very simple reason. Luciano was standing in the shop with Giacomo.

She froze on the threshold and watched something that might have been gladness flare in his eyes before it was replaced by the shuttered look she knew so well. Then Giacomo surged forward, rounder than ever and wreathed in smiles.

'Signorina Kate! What a surprise you give us!'

Grateful for the little man's warmth, Kate allowed herself to be embraced and, in an effort to take the wind out of Luciano's sails, said, 'Yes – I couldn't resist it. I'm staying with my sister in Fleet Street but Felix doesn't know yet, so . . . well, here I am.'

'Here you are,' agreed Luciano coolly. 'Unfortunately, however, Felix *isn't* just at present. Perhaps you'd care to join me in the parlour while you wait? I am sure Giacomo will be delighted to entertain your maid.'

It was precisely what she had wanted but somehow it didn't feel like a victory. With a feeble 'Thank you', Kate let him usher her silently up the stairs and, when the parlour door closed behind them, waited resignedly for the storm to break.

'So.' Luciano eyed her broodingly over folded arms. 'You're staying with Amy, are you? Why?'

'Because she's pregnant.'

'Ah. And the sisterly affection between you being so strong, she couldn't bear to go through the experience without you. Is that it?'

'No. You know it isn't.'

'Precisely. I know it isn't. So let's start again, shall we? You came to see me. You probably also have some muddled notion of settling here in connubial bliss. The first was a mistake – and the second is little short of lunacy.'

'I know. Or, at least, I knew you'd say so.' Drawing a long fortifying breath, Kate decided to take the bull by the horns. 'Personally, however, I can't see the point. Your nasty friend knows all about us, anyway.'

Luciano became very still. 'Explain,' he said softly.

'Do you want the minutiae or will the bare bones do? Half a flock of sheep poisoned, a barn full of hay reduced to ashes and a stream of other minor irritations. You must know the kind of thing. Mother tells me you've been having similar difficulties yourself. And no – she didn't break your confidence lightly. But when your friend's hirelings made off with Jude it was time to stop being coy.'

'Oh Christ.' The blood drained slowly from Luciano's skin. 'You'd better sit down and tell me.'

So she did; and at the end said flatly, 'Since this man obviously knows – if not that we're married – at least that there is some connection between us, I can't see any use in further pretence. More important still, I think it's time you told me the whole story. You must by now have realised that I know most of it anyway . . . and if I'm to join you in the firing line, I think I've a right to know why . . . Well?'

Still standing beside the table, Luciano laid his fingers lightly along its polished edge and frowned thoughtfully down at them. Finally he said remotely, 'The whole story? I'm not even sure what that is. But if I am to tell you anything at all, you must promise me one thing; that, *no matter what happens*, you will never, ever involve yourself in it. Make no mistake about it, Kate – this man you persist in calling my friend is dangerous. He has killed at least once that I know of – and if you get in his way or betray even the smallest sign of knowing what he is about, he won't hesitate to brush you from his path . . . or, worse still, use you as a pawn in his game. Do I make myself quite clear?'

'Yes.' Kate felt rather sick. 'You're saying that one day he'll kill you.'

'He'll almost certainly try. But what I'm actually trying to say is much worse than that.' He paused and summoned every ounce of strength. 'I can't be sure . . . I may never be sure . . . but I suspect him of murdering your father.'

Silence stretched out on invisible threads. And then Kate said carefully, 'Yes. I rather thought you did. But I wasn't sure if you'd bring yourself to tell me.' She waited for a moment, watching his fingers whiten against the dark wood of the table and, when he still did not speak, said, 'I've had a long time in which to think of it – and after

Jude was taken and Mother told me that this man you're looking for knows who you are and why you want to find him, everything else started to fall into place. I – I couldn't help but wonder if he wasn't the same person Father followed to Cropredy. And if he *was* . . . well, the conclusions were pretty obvious.'

Very slowly, Luciano left the table and crossed the room to sit beside her. He was extremely pale and his eyes held a look that was more worrying than anything he had said. 'As you say, you know nearly all of it,' he remarked, folding her hand in a light clasp of his own. 'So I suppose it behoves me to tell you the rest. And I will – when you've first given me the promise I asked for.'

Since there was nothing else for it, Kate promised; and then sat perfectly still while with a complete absence of emotion, he unfolded the tale from its beginning. And when it was done he said aridly, 'So there you have it. Unless I can somehow lure him into coming for me himself, I am facing a blank wall . . . and the advantages are all on his side. I know that he is a King's man and that – since it was what drew Richard to him – he is wearing my ring, which in turn means that he presumably killed Samuel Fisher himself. I can also recognise his handwriting. But none of that is enough. And unless God sends me a miracle, I'm never going to be free of him.'

Kate's cheeks were wet. She said unevenly, 'Can't you stop? He must know you can't trace him. If you stop, surely he'll leave you alone?'

'Everybody's favourite theory,' came the wry response. 'And my answer has always been that it's too great a risk. But heavier persuasions have been laid in the balance since then. I began this thing because I felt it was something I owed my father – and that is still true. But the last two years have taught me that the world will be a nicer place when this particular bastard is no longer in it. Also, if he murdered Richard, I want his head. So I won't stop until I either get it – or lose my own in the attempt.' He paused and managed a twisted smile. 'This is where you're supposed to damn me for marrying you.'

She drew a long, shuddering breath. 'I can't. You know I can't.'

'No? Well, that's comforting, because it brings me to the only thing I haven't yet told you.' His hand tightened on hers and his voice gathered a note she had heard only once before. 'You should know that I didn't make love to you out of simple lust, or marry you through guilt. I have never said it; indeed, I have fought very hard *against* saying it . . . but both of these things happened because I love you. And will until death.'

As always, it was the last thing she had expected. But the truth of it was in his eyes and in the stillness of his waiting; so that at length she said, 'And I you. But you know that.'

'Yes.'

The channel of understanding moved very slowly and she was still drowning in the wonder of what he had said. 'Why are you telling me this now?'

His smile liquefied her bones.

'Because the reason for my silence has been removed; because if the worst happens, I don't want my last regret to be that I never told you that you are my soul. And because, with the greatest reluctance in the world, I am leaving tomorrow for Genoa.'

Delight faded as swiftly as it had come and she drew a sharply ragged breath. 'You – you *can't*!'

'I must. Call it a whim of my uncle's, but a personal appearance each April to pay the interest is part of the contract; and if I fail to make it, I'm ruined,' he said matter-of-factly. 'I'd call that one catastrophe too many – wouldn't you?'

Kate opened her mouth on the first words that occurred to her. 'Then let me come with you.'

'No.' His tone was gentle but utterly final. 'One day, perhaps – but not yet. Thanks to the war, it's getting more and more difficult to find a ship, and just getting out of the Channel is a dangerous business, not to mention the squalor of the accommodation. No. But don't worry. I'm not going to leave you behind to become prime target without any defence. Selim will take care of you.'

'While you travel alone?' she snapped, pulling her hand free and coming abruptly to her feet. 'Do you think that's going to make me feel any better?'

'Probably not. But it will certainly increase *my* peace of mind,' came the calm reply. Then, rising to face her, 'You might as well save your breath and start thinking up a convincing lie to account for Selim's presence to your sister – because, whether you like it or not, he's going with you when you leave here. And then, as soon as it's possible, I want you to go back to Thorne Ash.' He smiled again and touched her cheek with light, insubstantial fingers. '*Cara* . . . are we really going to spend these last few minutes together arguing? Or do you think we might not give ourselves something a little more pleasant to remember instead?'

He was taking an unfair advantage and they both knew it. But still she could not damn him for it, any more than she could find the willpower to resist. Silently and with neither haste nor hesitation, she moved into the waiting circle of his arms . . . and was given her reward.

Six

He was gone and she knew she should leave for Thorne Ash: not just because he had told her to go but because that, if anywhere, was where she was needed. Yet somehow she could not quite bring herself to go and, as the days grew into weeks, was able to find perfectly logical reasons for staying. After an easy start to her pregnancy, Amy had suddenly become subject to prolonged fits of the megrims which Geoffrey was only too glad to let Kate handle; and if Dorothy's last letter was to be believed, Felicity and Jacob were running the estate so efficiently that her own presence could easily be dispensed with for a little while longer. But more vital than either of these was her determination to be here in London when Luciano returned – which, when coupled with the thorny question of passes for travelling, made it much more sensible to stay where she was.

She had explained Selim's presence to Amy and Geoffrey by saying that Luciano had asked her to give the fellow employment while he was abroad and that, since she herself would presently need an escort home, the idea had seemed a reasonable one. Geoffrey had been perfectly happy with the arrangement and immediately allotted Selim a room in the attics; Amy had remarked that if any of her maids fell pregnant, she would know whom to blame.

And so the days passed. At first, the news was all of Cromwell and Waller's exploits in Dorset and the Royalists' problems in the West, where George Goring was said to be permanently roaring drunk. Then a nine-day wonder was produced by the discovery that the Marquis of Montrose had not simply vanished into the highland mist but had managed to cross the Grampians in the dead of winter to descend on the Clan Campbell at Inverlochy. And barely had this nebulous excitement died down than the Earls of Essex and Manchester resigned their commissions exactly twenty-four hours before the Lords finally passed the Ordinance which would have forced them to do so. Oliver Cromwell, it was said, was being allowed to continue in the field on a temporary basis. Within a few weeks he was confirmed as general of the Horse.

Kate read the news-sheets and listened to the gossip but felt herself to be growing more and more distanced from it all. If the end was in sight, she could not see it . . . and the longer the conflict went on, the more diverse and complex it seemed to become. Religious pamphlets poured off every press in London; Presbyterians and Independents harangued each other from every pulpit; and the death of Archbishop Laud had been but one of a series of such executions – and seemed all of a piece with the Parliament's vindictive declaration that every Catholic or Irish prisoner taken was to be immediately shot. In short, it rather looked as though they were all engaged in a war which one side or the other would eventually claim to have won. But the unpleasant truth was that, with this new ruthlessness in the air, the old life was gone forever and any victory now could not be anything other than Pyrrhic.

All of this, however, occupied but a small corner of her mind. Her main preoccupation was with the exquisite, incredible fact that Luciano loved her and the simultaneous fear of what horrible danger might even now be stalking him on his lone pilgrimage to Genoa. It was also fairly plain from Selim's grim-faced demeanour that he strongly resented being left to care for Kate when he should have been guarding his master's back . . . a point of view with which Kate found herself in total sympathy but which he somehow never allowed her to express. He simply sat sulkily in the kitchen when she was in the house and trod a dogged two paces behind her every time she set foot outside it – which very soon irritated Amy beyond bearing.

'Does that heathen creature *have* to follow you everywhere you go?' she demanded crossly as she and Kate strolled about the half-deserted labyrinth of the Exchange one morning. 'The way everyone stares at him, I feel as though I'm part of a peep-show!'

Kate sighed and was just about to observe that there were precious few people *to* stare, when a tall familiar figure detached itself from a shop doorway and began sauntering elegantly towards them. With no time to think of anything better, Kate swung Amy forcibly round to stare at a pitifully lacklustre display of ribbons and trimmings – but too late. She had been recognised; and before Amy was properly launched on her dislike of being manhandled, a drawling voice from behind said softly, 'Why, Mistress Kate! What a delightful surprise. And here was I thinking London sadly devoid of quite all its former attractions.'

Kate turned very slowly and met the silvery eyes of Cyrus Winter. 'And seeing me has changed all that?' she asked coolly. 'I'm afraid I find it very difficult to believe.'

His teeth gleamed. 'Direct as ever, I see. Or does that little attempt I made to call upon you after Edgehill still rankle?'

'Not at all. I try never to let a person's failures count against them. But if all you wanted was a glass of blackberry wine, you should have said so. I'm sure we could have come to some arrangement.'

The smile lingered and he said suavely, 'Perhaps we still can. But where are my manners? Won't you introduce me to your charming companion?'

It was the very last thing Kate wanted but there seemed no choice. 'My sister, Mistress Cox,' she said shortly. And then, 'Amy – allow me to present Mr Winter.'

Amy dimpled and held out her hand. Kate was obviously not going to tell her, but she rather suspected that this fashionable gentleman must be an acquaintance from Whitehall; and that being so, Amy had no intention of letting him pass on unimpressed. Gazing limpidly into the stranger's undoubtedly appreciative eyes, she said, 'I'm very happy to know you, sir – and consider you quite right. London *is* insupportably dull these days.'

'At this moment,' returned Cyrus Winter gallantly, 'there is nowhere I would rather be.'

'Even though – for safety's sake – it's the last place you *ought* to be?' offered Kate sweetly. 'You must pardon me for mentioning it, but I thought you were a Cavalier?'

'And so I was,' came the unperturbed reply. 'But times change, you know – and the wise man with them.'

The green eyes widened. 'You're saying you've changed sides?'

'Well, of course. Ah . . . I see that shocks you. But really, my dear, it's a great deal more commonplace than you might think. And only a fool allows himself to end up on the losing side when there are steps he can take to prevent it.'

He was still smiling and Kate rather wished he wouldn't. She found it was setting her teeth on edge. Then, before she could speak, he said, 'But tell me of yourself. How come I find *you* here? And why – if I may ask it – are you wearing mourning? Not, surely, for the late lamented Mr Clifford?'

Inside her gloves, Kate's fingers curled into claws. She really did not like this man and she could not understand why she had ever had anything to do with him.

'And why should you assume that?' she snapped. 'Kit—'

'Dear me, no!' cut in Amy, tired of being ignored. And then, allowing her eyes to fill with tears, 'It – it's our father. He was killed at the battle of Cropredy Bridge last summer.'

'Your father? I'm sorry. I had no idea.' His tone expressed exactly the correct degree of shocked sympathy. His eyes, so far as Kate could see, didn't change at all. 'Please forgive my clumsiness and accept my sincere condolences. His death must have been a sad blow to you both.'

'It was,' said Kate curtly. 'And now, if you'll forgive us, we promised to call on Amy's sisters-in-law and are already late.' She held out her hand. 'Goodbye.'

This, fortunately, had the merit of being true and so, although Amy pouted a little, she extended her fingers once more and said, 'It's been *so* nice to meet you. And if you're to be in London for some time, I hope you'll call and take

564

a glass of wine with us.'

'That,' he bowed, 'is more than kind of you.'

'Fleet Street,' said Amy, struggling against Kate's propelling arm. 'Opposite the Scrivener's Arms. Don't forget.' And then, in a furious undervoice, 'Kate, what *is* the matter with you? And will you please let go of my wrist!'

Since they were now several yards away, Kate released her and said, 'Do you realise who that was? He's the man Celia wouldn't marry.'

'*Is* he? But of course – I should have known. My goodness! Celia must have been mad. Isn't he dreadfully rich?'

'Couldn't you tell? The gold embroidery on his gloves probably cost more than everything I'm wearing,' replied Kate caustically. 'But that's beside the point. What you ought to be remembering is that he was considered the worst philanderer at Whitehall and that he's old enough to be your father.'

'Oh – stuff!' said Amy. 'I think he's charming – and very much hope he calls. All my friends will be green with envy!'

May was well advanced by the time Cyrus Winter visited the house in Fleet Street and, as luck would have it, Kate was out at the time. Unfortunately, however, it wasn't possible to be wholeheartedly glad of this because Amy was so plainly entranced that it seemed someone would have to keep an eye on her during future visits.

'And that someone,' said Kate gloomily to Felix the following day when she visited him in Cheapside, 'will probably have to be me. Damn! I just wish that, once in a while, Amy would see sense.'

'When has she ever?' he grinned. 'But what exactly are you worried about? That he'll seduce her?'

'I don't know. Possibly. But how can you trust anyone who trims their coat as he's just done?'

'Well, as to that, I don't like it any better than you. But he's hardly the first, is he? What about that fellow Hurry who changed over to the King and then back again? Or

George Goring holding Portsmouth for the Parliament and then rushing off to declare allegiance to His Majesty?'

'That was different. It was right at the beginning of the war – and everyone with any sense knew where Goring's loyalties lay,' said Kate, frowning. 'No. Cyrus Winter *hasn't* any loyalty – or morals either. And if he sets his sights on Amy, she'll fall into his lap like a ripe plum.'

'Is he going to see her again?'

'Next Tuesday, she says. She's invited him to dine with her at noon – and Geoffrey is never home much before five.'

'So you'll make sure you're there to sit bodkin between them.' Felix laughed. 'God! I wish I could see it!'

'You can,' she replied without thinking. And then, 'Of course! The perfect answer. She can't send you away – and we'll turn her little tryst into a family party.' She smiled winsomely at him. 'You will come, won't you?'

He made her wait for a moment and then laughed. 'Why not? It will be worth it just to see the look on Amy's face.'

Felix was not disappointed. He and Kate made their entrance with perfect timing, just minutes before Cyrus Winter was announced, and Amy was left with no alternative but to pin a brittle smile on her face and make the best of it. Felix sensibly avoided Kate's eye and, in between the quail's eggs and the cream darioles, came to the interesting conclusion that, if the butter-smooth Mr Winter had his eye on anyone, it certainly wasn't Amy. This intrigued him so much that they had discussed the King's recent foray into Leicestershire along with Fairfax's chances of taking Oxford and were well into an idle dissection of the various organisational problems facing the New Model Army before something even more peculiar struck him. Felix lapsed into silence and pondered the matter. The answer would come to him. He knew it would.

He left the house in Cyrus Winter's wake in order to miss the storm that was plainly brewing in Amy's eyes and it was therefore several days before he saw Kate again. But when Giacomo summoned him from the work-room one afternoon with the intelligence that his sister was awaiting him in the parlour, he strolled in on her with a cheerful, 'You're still alive, then. I rather thought Amy might have taken a meat-cleaver to you.'

'Well, it's no thanks to you that she didn't, is it?' retorted Kate. 'I never saw anyone disappear so fast in my life.'

'Can you blame me? I only promised to attend the feast, not stay for the battle royal that was bound to follow it.' He perched on the arm of a chair and grinned at her. 'I suppose she was a bit put out?'

'You could put it that way. She threw a dish of nuts at my head,' she replied. And then, 'What did you make of Cyrus Winter?'

Felix shrugged. 'He's just your everyday silver-tongued gallant with a liking for the power his money gives him. On the other hand, I'd say he's far from stupid. For one thing, it's not Amy he fancies – it's you.'

'Yes. I've started to wonder about that myself – and could more or less stop worrying if Amy wasn't so determined to throw herself at him.'

'So why not let her? A rebuff would do her no harm at all.' Felix slid into the chair, leaving one leg dangling idly over its arm. Then, yawning, he said, 'To be absolutely honest, the only thing I find the least bit interesting about your Mr Winter is how he comes to be wearing Sir's emerald.'

For a brief, unpleasant moment the parlour seemed to dissolve around Kate, leaving her blind and dumb. Then, through the roaring in her ears, she managed to say, 'What? *What* was that?'

'That enormous square-cut emerald on his left hand. Surely you can't have failed to notice it?'

'No. I mean, I saw it – yes.'

'Well, it's Luciano's – or at least, it was. He used to wear it all the time,' said Felix. And then, looking at her, 'What's the matter? You've gone as white as a sheet.'

The air seared her lungs and her skin hurt. Finally she said unevenly, 'Are you sure? Are you *sure* it's the same ring?'

'Well, of course I am! What do you think I've been

doing for the last four years – playing football? And no one could mistake that stone. I doubt there are two like it in the world.' He stopped again, then said, 'There's no need to look so sick. Luciano probably sold it to him. It's worth a fortune after all – and if anyone could afford to buy it, Cyrus Winter could.'

Except that he didn't, thought Kate; but had the sense not to say it aloud.

It was necessary to think fast but the difficulty was in knowing where to start. If Felix was right, Luciano's anonymous enemy was none other than Cyrus Winter – though *why* this should be so was something she could not begin to guess. But what was instantly obvious was that he had re-entered her life knowing of her links with Luciano – and perhaps even of their marriage. He must also have recognised Selim that day at the Exchange and know that Felix was Luciano's apprentice. Altogether, thought Kate grimly, he knew too damned much for comfort. So the questions to be answered were whether she dared try using the one weak weapon in her armoury – and whether or not to share her discovery with Felix and Selim and Giacomo. She had a fair idea of what Luciano's answer would have been . . . but then, Luciano wasn't there. Drawing a long, steadying breath, she said, 'Felix – get Selim and Giacomo up here. There's something we need to talk about.'

His brows rose but, sensing the urgency in her, he forbore to argue and disappeared from the room. Five minutes later, they were all assembled and, without preamble, Kate said, 'Selim, Giacomo – I've called you in so that we may protect ourselves – and hopefully also Luciano – from a man who has been at some pains to destroy us all. But for Felix's sake, I think it's best to start at the beginning – mainly because, having just handed me the key to the whole business, he can't be kept in the dark any longer and remain safe.'

Giacomo shook his head doubtfully. 'Monsignor will not like it.'

568

'Monsignor doesn't know what I know,' returned Kate, crisply. 'Listen.'

Swiftly and without elaboration, she went through it all – detailing the facts as far as she knew them and revealing for the first time the previous autumn's events at Thorne Ash.

'Christ!' said Felix, angrily. 'Why didn't I hear of this before?'

'Because you didn't need to know it before,' replied Kate.

'It has been like this here also,' remarked Selim thoughtfully. And he told of the fire, rats, Luciano's fight against being imprisoned as a royal courier and, finally, the kicking he'd received in the tavern. Then, looking full into Kate's overbright eyes, he said simply, 'Much is now clear to me. I did not know he had married you – and was only angry that he had left me behind. You will understand this.'

'Yes. And, like you, I wish he hadn't done it,' she said.

'No. It is very proper. Also, the man Winter is here in London. We know this.'

'But he doesn't do things himself – can't you see?' cried Kate. 'And we don't know he hasn't sent someone after Luciano.'

Silence fell. Then Felix said abruptly, 'Why is Winter turning his attention to Thorne Ash all of a sudden? He can't surely be putting in all this effort just because you and Luciano are married?'

'He's not.' Kate swallowed hard. 'Like you, Father also recognised the ring – and followed it to Cropredy. I think . . . I think Cyrus Winter killed him.'

Without a word, Felix erupted from his chair and strode over to the window. For a long time no one spoke; but at length, Kate said flatly, 'Put it aside, Felix. You must put it aside for the present, as I have done. The question that must be faced now is, knowing what we know, what are we going to do?'

'But that is easy.' It was Selim who spoke. 'I will kill him.'

569

'And I,' snapped Felix, breathing hard, 'will help.'

Kate looked at Giacomo. She said, 'And what do you think?'

'Me?' The little man shook his head sadly. 'I also think killing would be best. But we cannot do it. This man's life, it does not belong to us. And Luciano will never forgive us if we end it before he can ask why his father died.'

Felix spun round on a brief, derisive laugh, but before he could speak Kate said quietly, 'I'd wondered about that myself – and fortunately there's another way. We now hold one of the cards, so let's see what we can do with it. Cyrus Winter doesn't know the ring gives him away or he wouldn't be wearing it. Therefore, he also doesn't know that we know who he is.'

'What are you saying?' asked Felix.

'I'm saying that we – or more particularly *I* – should try luring him into a false sense of security and holding him here in London until Luciano gets back. Then we shall hopefully see an end to the business.'

Selim shook his head. 'I do not think I like this plan.'

'I don't like it much myself,' responded Kate tartly. 'But have you a better idea? And now we know where the danger lies, it shouldn't be too difficult – provided, of course, that we're careful. *Your* job is to watch both me and Cyrus Winter whilst also making sure no one drives a knife in your own back; Giacomo and Felix have the task of going on exactly as normal. And I . . . I, God help me, have got to let Mr Winter think that I don't dislike him quite as much as I'd have him believe.' She paused and achieved a small, sardonic smile. 'In the last twenty years, friend Cyrus has dug himself an amazingly deep pit. Don't any of you want to see if we can push him in?'

'Make no mistake about it – this man is dangerous,' Luciano had said; and, in the days that followed, Kate made sure that she never forgot it for an instant. The game was to continue being cool to the point of rudeness whilst simultaneously allowing the odd swiftly repressed glimpse of some reluctant pleasure in his company – a process both arduous

and naturally slow. At the end of two weeks, Kate had run through every trick she could think of and, aside from the fact that Cyrus Winter's visits to Amy's house had increased in frequency, still had no idea at all whether or not she was succeeding. Then came the inevitable day when he caught her alone . . . and with a fast-beating heart she allowed the maid to admit him, in order to see what, if anything, would come of it.

He came in, imperturbably elegant as ever and she said coolly, 'I'm afraid your luck is out. My sister is a trifle indisposed today and will not leave her room.'

'Then my luck, dear Kate, is most assuredly *in*.' He tossed his hat on to a table and advanced, smiling. 'It's not your sister that I come here to see.'

'Oh?' Feigning disinterest, Kate bent her head once more over her tambour-frame. 'You'll be saying next that you come to see me.'

He dropped lazily into the seat at her side. 'Is that so hard to believe?'

'Not hard – impossible. You know perfectly well that I don't like you very much, and I've always fancied that it was mutual.'

'Then you were mistaken. I could like you very well indeed, my dear.' Without giving her time to read his intention, he twitched the tambour-frame from her hands and tilted her chin up towards him. 'And – correct me if I'm wrong – but I think you are beginning to find yourself attracted to me. Reluctantly, perhaps – but attracted none the less. Isn't that so?'

'No!' Twisting herself nimbly from his grasp, Kate fled to the other side of the hearth. 'No it isn't. And only an overweening conceit like yours could imagine that it was.'

He stayed where he was and she thanked God for it. His touch made her skin crawl. Laughing a little, he said, 'What's the matter? Don't you like plain speaking – or are you afraid that the truth may come out? Either way I'm surprised at you. I thought you favoured the direct approach. And you can't go on fooling yourself for ever.'

'What makes you think I'm fooling myself at all? And

why can't you simply accept that you really don't interest me?'

'Experience, dear heart.' The silver-grey eyes were full of amused indulgence. 'I'm afraid your powers of concealment are not all you would like to think them. Then again, even in those far-off days at Whitehall, it was obvious that life wasn't offering you the things you wanted – and that is still true. But there is a difference. At Whitehall you were much younger and too inexperienced to know the right opportunity when you saw it. *Now*, however, you are aware that your life is slipping away down a channel of mediocrity and would give anything to stop it. You don't want to waste your youth in domestic tedium and increasingly irksome chastity. You want to *live*. Am I not right?'

Kate took her time about answering. Quite apart from marvelling at his effrontery, she was beginning to realise that the game had unforeseen pitfalls. Say the wrong thing now and she could either end up quietly murdered or suffer a fate worse than death in Cyrus Winter's bed. Neither was a pleasant thought. Fortunately, however – if she was willing to gamble on the fact that he was very far from being seriously interested in her except as a pawn – she already saw her way clear to a rather daring countermove. Allowing her gaze to drop and speaking as though the words were being torn from her, she said, 'Perhaps. Oh – yes. I suppose at least part of what you say is true. But there are other things. Things you know nothing of. And I can't speak of them.'

There was a pause; and then, on a note of gentle invitation, he said, 'Are you sure? Think well, Kate. Think how much I understand you and how rarely one is offered a second chance.' He waited and then, when she merely stood tugging restlessly at her handkerchief, said softly, 'You are referring to some other involvement. Isn't that so?'

'Yes.' She made it no more than an unwilling whisper. 'Yes . . . there is someone. Someone I thought I c-cared for. But it was a mistake.'

'A mistake? My dear, we all make those. There's no need for you to look so tragic.'

572

'But there is!' she replied with sudden violent desperation. The half-shredded handkerchief fell to the floor and she looked at him out of anguished eyes. 'There *is*. Can't you understand? *I married him!*'

She let her hands creep to her mouth and remained quite still, scarcely daring to breathe while she searched his face without appearing to do so. His brows rose a little and she thought she detected a hint of satisfaction in his eyes. Then he drawled, 'Married? But how can this be when your sister makes continual fun of your single state?'

'She doesn't know,' admitted Kate suffocatingly. 'Very few people do. So please don't speak of it – and don't ask me his name. I can't tell you. Not you, of all people.'

'Dear me! Is it as bad as that?'

'Worse. But what can I do? His pride will never allow him to let me go.'

This time the silence stretched out on invisible threads. Then he said smoothly, 'All this is very confusing. But if you are tied to a man you don't want, you can do the same as every other woman in your situation. Take a lover.'

'You?' asked Kate, as if both mesmerised and terrified.

'Why not? I don't think I need tell you that you could do very much worse.' Rising, he crossed unhurriedly to her side and Kate had to force herself to stay passive as he took her expertly in his arms and kissed her. Then, looking tauntingly down into her eyes, he said, 'But you're not ready, are you? So perhaps it's just as well I've to leave London for a while. It will give you time to make your choice.'

'Leave London?' she echoed faintly. She wished he would let her go. The sudden rush of relief his words had brought was the only thing stopping her from being sick. 'Where are you going?'

'That, dear Kate, is my business.' His hands slid lingeringly from her body and he turned to pick up his hat. 'But I'll return in a week or so . . . by which time you'd better have decided whether you wish to cling to your virtuous, sterile marriage, or take what happiness you can outside it.' He smiled at her. 'Goodbye, sweetheart. Try not to miss me too much.' And he was gone.

Kate stood absolutely still until she was sure he had left the house and then fled incontinently to the privy. Everyone had their limitations, after all; and she had just discovered her own.

She relayed the gist of the meeting to Felix, Selim and Giacomo and fell back into a palsy of waiting. Her twenty-second birthday came and went, the King took Leicester and May became June. Of Luciano there was no sign at all and the week of Cyrus Winter's absence turned into a fortnight. Kate began quietly to panic. Then, in the middle of the month, London went wild with joy at news of a parliamentary victory over the King at a place called Naseby; Selim was arrested on a charge of assault; and Cyrus Winter reappeared wearing the uniform of the New Model Army.

As soon as Kate saw him, the terrible suspicion that had afflicted her ever since Selim had been taken crystallised into certainty. But it was vital not to show it, so she swept across the room past Amy, saying urgently, 'Thank God you've come back! Now perhaps we can get something done at last.'

He accepted her hands and surveyed her with half-startled mockery. 'My dear – what a welcome! I am quite overcome. But what exactly is it you're expecting of me?'

'It's my servant,' she explained tersely. 'He's in the Gatehouse for common assault – though I can't understand *how*, since he was here in the kitchen on the night in question. However. Geoffrey has done his level best but all to no avail and––'

'And I, for one, am not at all sorry,' cut in Amy waspishly. 'I never liked the fellow and can't understand why you didn't leave him with that horrid Italian.'

'Italian?' queried Cyrus Winter. And waited.

'L-Luciano del Santi,' admitted Kate reluctantly. 'But what Amy doesn't know is that Selim left of his own volition after a – a disagreement and offered his services to me. Naturally I took him on. We all know how hard it is to find good servants these days.'

Amy snorted. 'The only thing that one's good for is getting maids with child!'

'Oh, do be quiet!' snapped Kate. And then, to Cyrus Winter, 'Please – won't you see what you can do? I'm sure people will listen to *you* . . . and I would be so grateful.'

'Would you?' His smile was slow and tinged with purposeful satisfaction. 'Then how can I refuse?'

Having made sure, via Felix, that Selim knew what story he was supposed to comply with, Kate settled uncomfortably back on her knife-edge to await developments. In the week that followed, Cyrus Winter called three times but never with any progress to report, and Kate was able to ensure that she never received him alone. Then, on 21 June, he arrived on the doorstep just as she and Amy were setting out on a shopping expedition and immediately offered his escort. Kate's heart sank. Unless she was very careful indeed, it would be all too easy for him to speak to her privately – and that was the last thing she wanted. There was, however, very little hope of Amy seconding any attempt to send him away and, by the time he'd explained that the four thousand prisoners taken at Naseby were even now being marched into London, none at all.

'Oh do let's go and watch!' exclaimed Amy. 'There are so few processions these days and this will be quite a big one.'

'Big – but not necessarily pleasant,' objected Kate.

'I don't care. I want to go and I will!'

Kate hesitated and then, because Cyrus Winter was saying absolutely nothing, allowed herself to be overborne. If she turned on her heel and went back into the house, she couldn't be sure he would not go with her. So she irritably resigned herself to watching four thousand poor wretches being turned into a side-show and set about selecting a suitable excuse for when Major Winter asked her to go to bed with him.

The streets were thronged with people all out to enjoy the spectacle but, in his New Model red, Cyrus Winter had no difficulty at all in commanding an advantageous viewpoint for his ladies. Kate thanked him sourly and wondered if Eden also possessed a coat like that – and whether, if he had, he'd been home to show it to Mother.

The procession was headed with the bright silks of fifty captured standards and Kate listened glacially while Major Winter identified them for her.

'You don't think,' she said abruptly, 'that your presence here today is in somewhat dubious taste?'

'Not at all,' came the amused reply. 'Half of these will turn their coats fast enough if it gets them out of prison. I simply made my choice a little sooner.'

Kate stared stonily at the columns of men passing in front of her. Somewhat surprisingly, most of them were far from being the poor wretches of her imagination but, on the contrary, looked to be in perfect health. And then, just as she was coming to the conclusion that perhaps the sight wasn't going to be quite as insupportable as she'd feared, a familiar face hove into view.

Without stopping to think, Kate hurled herself forward. *'Francis!'*

Behind the dirt and fatigue of the worst fight he'd ever known, followed by a long and gruelling march, Francis Langley managed something approaching a smile. 'Kate? A friendly face at last! What are you doing here?'

'Visiting Amy,' she replied, clutching his arm to keep pace with the column. 'Where are they taking you?'

'Tothill Fields. Not that it matters. I rather think my goose is cooked this time.'

'No! Francis, no – they'll ask you to re-enlist.'

'And you think I'd do it?' The blue eyes were hard as sapphires. 'Not me. I haven't come this far to change sides now. And, in truth, I doubt I'll be asked. They'll find they have too many other counts against me.' He paused and then, giving her a swift hug, 'Go back to Amy, Kate. It's best you don't become involved. Just give my love to Eden when you see him – and tell him I'm sincerely sorry about Celia. He deserved better.'

Because there was little alternative, Kate pressed his hand and then stood back, watching him march away. Moments later, Cyrus Winter materialised at her elbow and she said distantly, 'It was Francis. Francis Langley.'

'Ah. The fair Celia's brother.'

'And Lady Wroxton's only son,' returned Kate, pointedly.

His brows rose. 'You're not about to demand another mercy mission, are you?' And then, when she remained silent, 'Well, well. I see that you are. But not, if you are wise, on behalf of the once-delectable Mary. No. If you wish to ask a second favour of me, I'm very much afraid that it must be for yourself.'

Damningly and too late, Kate recognised that her pose of appearing helpless and ignorant was swiftly getting out of hand, but that she dared not jeopardise it before Luciano returned. Over the pain in her chest, she said, 'And if I do?'

'Why then, dear heart, you must be willing to pay the price,' he smiled. 'Or perhaps you are more attached to this mysterious husband of yours than you would have me believe?'

Seven

Three days later, Luciano walked into his parlour to find Felix, Giacomo and Gino all talking at once whilst apparently arming themselves to the teeth.

'What the devil's going on here?' he demanded; and was accorded instant and total silence. 'Well?'

Felix finished buckling on his sword and, in as few words as possible, told him.

'The man who killed your father and mine is Cyrus Winter. In an hour's time, Kate has an assignation with him – the purpose of which is to get Selim released from prison. And *my* job—'

'Kate has *what*?' Luciano's voice cracked like a pistol shot.

'You heard,' returned Felix curtly. 'And I haven't got time to argue about it with you. As I was about to say, my job – flanked by your friends here – is to make sure that nothing untoward comes of it by bursting in on a tide of brotherly outrage. And now, if you don't mind, we ought to be off.'

Luciano's hand closed like a vice round his arm. 'But I do mind. You say the man I've been looking for is Cyrus Winter. Are you sure of that?'

'Well, he's wearing your bloody emerald,' snapped Felix. 'How much more proof do you need?'

Luciano was extremely pale and his breathing had become rather erratic but his fingers maintained their grip. 'Does he know you recognised it?'

'Don't be stupid. If he knew that, Kate would have more to worry about than just staying out of his bed, wouldn't she?' And then, wincing, 'What are you trying to do – break my damned arm?'

'No – though it's no more than you deserve for not putting a stop to this insane scheme.' Releasing him, Luciano turned back towards the door. 'Go to the rendezvous if you wish – but Kate won't be there.'

'Think you can stop her, do you?' called Felix caustically.

'Yes,' came the swiftly diminishing reply. 'And you, for one, ought to thank God for it.'

Luciano met Kate less than a hundred yards from Amy's door and, without giving her time either to speak or even get over her shock, said flatly, 'Forget it, Kate. You're not going.'

Since he obviously knew everything and time was of the essence, there was no point in denial. She said rather shakily, 'You don't understand, I *must*. He's leaving tomorrow to join the New Model and had promised to secure Selim's release before he goes if I – if I . . .'

'If you what?' Tucking her hand firmly into his arm, Luciano led her out of Fleet Street and on up Ludgate Hill. 'Lie with him?'

'*No!* It wouldn't have come to that. We had it all planned.'

'Ah yes. Felix to the rescue. And precisely what do you think that would have achieved – except possibly getting Felix killed and leaving you open to rape? Or did you think Winter would baulk at that? If so, think again. It's more likely to make his day. And at the end of it all, did you seriously suppose he'd free Selim?' Every cadence of the beautiful voice indicated rising temper. 'Mother of God! I don't understand how any of this has come about – but do you *still* not understand what we're dealing with here? And what happened to your promise to stay out of it?'

'I didn't forget it,' she protested vehemently. 'But I had the chance to convince him that none of us knew anything – so I took it. And if putting up with his determination to seduce me means that he's spent the last few weeks concentrating on humiliating you rather than sticking a knife in your back, I'd say it was undoubtedly worth it.' She drew a short ragged breath. 'I was trying to help – and everything was quite straightforward until he decided to force the issue by having Selim arrested. But I s-still wouldn't have slept with him – not even if he'd sworn to get Francis out as well.'

'Francis?' The dark eyes instantly impaled her. 'Francis Langley? What the hell's he got to do with it?'

Kate sighed and, with a sinking heart, told him. When she had finished, there was a long brooding silence before Luciano said blightingly, 'Have you completely lost your mind? No one is going to execute Francis. Much though it may hurt him to admit it, he's just not important enough. No – don't say any more! I think I'd prefer to hear the rest when I can lose my temper in private.'

Back in Cheapside, Felix and Giacomo were anxiously waiting. Both questioned Kate with their eyes but remained wisely silent. Luciano, on the other hand, had no such inhibitions. 'Sit down,' he invited grimly. 'Now we're all assembled, I'd like the whole story from the beginning. Kate?'

She thought for a moment and then began. It was necessary to make what they had done in his absence sound not only logical but safe . . . and fortunately Felix knew it too. So, between them, the tale of the last few weeks unfolded under Luciano's forbidding gaze.

'And if the ring isn't proof enough for you, you'd better take a look at this,' concluded Kate at length, handing him a folded piece of paper.

Luciano examined it. It stated only the time and place for that afternoon's meeting with Kate, but it was written in the same ornate hand he'd seen twice before and signed with a single, convoluted initial. And finally, of course, it all made sense. Cyrus Winter – who'd been in Oxford when Ferrars blew his brains out and in Bristol when Webb became the subject of a public scandal. Cyrus Winter – to whom two apparently random events had not been random at all – but sufficient to arouse his suspicions of Luciano's real identity and order the ransacking of his house.

Very slowly, Luciano's eyes rose to encompass his wife.

He said, 'So now we know. But the only thing I can think of is the unforgivable risk you ran by staying here to let the bastard court you. Quite honestly, I don't think I've ever been so frightened in my life as I was this afternoon when Felix told me what you were up to. And if nothing I can say will persuade you to have a care for your own safety, you might occasionally think of me.' He paused and then added, 'I've too many lives on my conscience already, Kate. And if something happened to you, I don't think I could bear it.'

A hint of colour stained her cheeks and she said, 'I'm sorry. I didn't . . . I never looked at it that way.'

'Then I'd be grateful if you'd start doing so.' He rose again and somewhat wearily picked up his hat. 'And now I suppose I'd better go and do something about Selim – after which it might be as well if we were to put our heads together and come up with a plan of campaign. Preferably – if it's not too much trouble – over a meal?' Upon which gently sardonic note, he was gone.

By the time he returned nearly four hours later, Kate had been introduced to Aysha and assisted her in preparing a hearty supper. Then Luciano and Selim strolled in and she was edified by the sight of the Turkish girl throwing herself on Selim's neck while Luciano looked on with a faint smile.

'Heavens!' Kate grinned and wiped her floury hands on a cloth. 'How on earth did you do it?'

'The usual way,' replied Luciano negligently. 'Bribery and corruption. I've become quite expert in knowing which palms to grease. Ought I to mention that you've got a smut on your nose?' He removed it with the tip of one finger and then dropped a fleeting kiss on her lips. 'That's better. Ah yes . . . and doubtless you'll also be glad to hear that you can stop worrying about Mr Langley.'

Faintly flushed and sternly repressing a reprehensible desire to fling herself on him in the manner of Aysha, she said feebly, 'Francis? You don't mean you found time to free him as well?'

'Not exactly. But I have discovered that both the French and Spanish residents have received permission to do some recruiting at Tothill Fields amongst those Royalists who won't enlist in the New Model – and the Frenchman is an acquaintance of mine. If Francis will agree to fight under the fleur-de-lys, Sabran is willing to offer him a captaincy.' He smiled, shrugging slightly. 'It may not be what you had in mind, but it offers Francis the chance to leave England without making any promises he'd rather not. And that, *cara*, is the best I can do.'

Kate gave up trying to be circumspect and flung her arms round his neck.

'And about time too,' grumbled Luciano, catching her in a hard embrace. 'I'd have thought a three-month separation was enough to provoke some sort of welcome – without having to perform the labours of Hercules as well.'

Supper – due to the twin reliefs of having Luciano and Selim safely back in the fold and knowing that Cyrus Winter would be leaving London on the following morning – was a pleasanter meal than might have been expected. Then, when it was over and Aysha had disappeared to the kitchen, Luciano leaned his elbows on the board and, looking round at Kate, Felix, Selim and Giacomo, said, 'And now to business. Thanks to Felix, we are finally aware that our quarry is Cyrus Winter – and Kate has told us that, for the next few weeks at least, he can be found with the army. This, I need not tell you, is the miracle I had given up hoping for. But it doesn't mean that we can count ourselves safe. Far from it, in fact.'

'You'll follow him?' asked Felix.

'In due course and when I can see my way clear to achieving my ends – yes. First, however, I think there is something else we might find it profitable to consider.' Luciano let them wait for a moment and then said simply, 'You tell me that Cyrus Winter has gone over to the Parliament. I am not sure that I believe it.'

Kate's brows rose. 'Why not? It's all of a piece with everything else we know of him, after all – and I've seen his New Model uniform with my own eyes. Why *shouldn't* you believe it?'

'For a whole battery of reasons,' replied Luciano calmly.

'Can you see a man with Cyrus Winter's wealth and reputation slotting happily in amongst the Covenanters, the Puritans and Cromwell's sectarian friends? I can't. And then we come to the other things we know about him. This is a man of quite incredibly tortuous mind. Think of the way he chose to get rid of my father. All right, I'll allow that we don't yet know *why* he needed to be rid of him. But if you want someone dead, the simplest means is a knife on a dark night, not a complicated scenario involving four other people. And what has he been doing recently with regard to me? He knows he intends to kill me – but, instead of doing it, he indulges himself by trying to make my life a misery first. This,' said Luciano meeting Kate's eyes, 'isn't a man who does anything straightforwardly. And my opinion, for what it's worth, is that he's either spying for the King or playing a double game. The only question is – which?'

The silence that greeted this pronouncement was positively electric. Then Selim said, 'If this is so, we have him.'

'Wait a minute,' frowned Felix. 'That's a pretty big assumption to make on sheer guess-work. And unless you've a shred or two of evidence to support it, who's going to believe you?'

'No one,' said Luciano. 'But then – after the doubts Winter has been so busy placing about me in so many quarters – no one would believe me anyway.'

'So what use can we make of it?' asked Kate. 'Even if you're right, it's no good unless we can tell somebody.'

'Quite. Which is why we're not just going to tell one person, or even two. We, beloved, are going to tell the world.' Luciano leaned back, smiling and allowed his eyes to travel to Felix. 'I never thought to hear myself say this, but I think it's time you and Mr Cox went back into the cartoon business. A series of six, let us say: some for distribution in Royalist districts which indicate disloyalty to the King, and others to be circulated here in London and throughout the ranks of the New Model, suggesting the exact opposite.' The smile grew. 'Let's put friend Winter in the public pillory and see how he likes it. And then, when we've damaged both his reputation and his influence . . . *then* it will be time for the final move. Check and mate in one.'

In the wake of the disaster of Naseby, Prince Rupert marched pessimistically to secure Bristol and defend the West, and his royal uncle's correspondence fell under the delighted scrutiny of the Commons. It had been seized at the late battle and, since it covered more than two years, revealed the King's efforts to get men and money from Denmark, France and Holland – along with his plans to import the forces of the Irish Confederacy. It was, of course, too damning a weapon not to be fully exploited and within a month the letters were published. *The King's Cabinet Opened* promoted distrust even amongst His Majesty's closest friends; and, following hard on the heels of his greatest and most total defeat, dealt a heavier blow to his cause than he yet realised.

For possibly the first time, remarked Luciano dispassionately, the Parliament could count itself firmly in the ascendancy. The Marquis of Montrose might still be scoring victory upon Royalist victory in Scotland, but that was of little use to the King when his English troops were achieving almost nothing and Goring (sober for once) had just had two thousand of his men taken prisoner at Langport. In short, unless His Majesty had an ace up his sleeve or was determined to fight on to the bitter end, it was probably time he started considering negotiation.

Kate could see the sense in this but, after three long years of hostility and so many false predictions, found it hard to accept. She also had more important things to think about – such as Luciano's constant pressure to get her to go home to Thorne Ash, and the little excursions he and Felix and Selim were making to distribute bundles of illicit cartoons. But the cartoons themselves, she had to admit, were works of art . . . each one brilliantly conceived and captioned by Luciano and flawlessly executed by Felix. It had taken a ruthless exposure of Amy's infatuation with Cyrus Winter to persuade Geoffrey to court trouble with a second round of nefarious printing, but Kate had done it without a qualm. After all, the end justified the means. And if their efforts made life just a tithe less comfortable for Major Winter, it would undoubtedly have been worth it.

The only difficulty was that, due to Luciano's ridiculous obstinacy on the subject, Kate found herself condemned to continuing to live under Amy's roof – and a situation which had never been precisely comfortable now became well-nigh intolerable.

'Why can't I simply tell her we're married and come here to live with you?' she asked Luciano for possibly the twentieth time, on a day when Amy had given way to another fit of temper. 'Since Cyrus Winter knows we're married, I can't see why everyone else shouldn't know as well. And I'm getting sick and tired of Amy's tantrums.'

'Then go back to Thorne Ash,' came the unsympathetic reply. 'You know very well it's what I want – and your mother too, come to that. As for why you can't live here, God knows we've been through it often enough. When the inevitable gossip starts to bite, Winter will know exactly who to blame – and this house will be the first target of any repercussions.'

'You can't be sure of that,' argued Kate. And then, with cunning, 'Besides . . . only think how much better you could protect me if I was constantly under your eye.'

'And how much less I'd get done with you under my feet,' he retorted with a sudden smile. 'No, Kate. You're not taking up residence beneath my roof-tree until I can be sure it's not going to collapse on your head. And that is quite final.'

July moved slowly towards August. The King lost Carlisle, Pomfret and Scarborough and had his forces in Pembrokeshire scattered by Rowland Laugharne; the yeomen of Dorset and Somerset attacked troops from either side with increasing venom; and, so gradually that no one was able to say exactly when it began, Cyrus Winter became one of the most talked-of men in the kingdom.

In Oxford, as in London, the first faint whispers grew steadily in a crescendo of speculation. Sardonic insertions began to appear in *Mercurius Aulicus* and, with its usual originality, *Britanicus* observed that there was no smoke without fire. Luciano settled back to wait, his satisfaction imperceptibly charged with tension. They were approaching the point where, if anything was going to happen, it would happen very soon – and it was therefore sensible to take a few extra precautions. He despatched the last batch of cartoons westwards by carrier, organised a round-the-clock guard on the Cheapside shop, and forbade any of his little family to go anywhere unaccompanied. Then he set about liquefying his assets and investments, called in numerous loans and spent long hours in the workshop with Felix and Gino, completing every outstanding commission. In short, though only Giacomo was aware of it, he was paving the way to leave London at a moment's notice – with every penny he owned sewn neatly into his coat lining in the form of a banker's draft.

Kate, meanwhile, was beginning to find the waiting irksome – mainly because, though she spent long hours in Cheapside, she rarely saw Luciano for more than ten minutes together.

'Why doesn't something *happen*?' she asked restlessly. 'Or do you think it's at all possible that Mr Winter has grown tired of the game?'

'Not,' said Luciano succinctly, 'unless he's on his deathbed. And even then he'd find a way to leave a parting gift.'

Kate fell silent. It was a pleasant August evening and, with darkness just falling and Selim shadowing their steps, Luciano was escorting her back to Fleet Street. Though the Presbyterians and sectaries ranted as much as usual, London was once more in jubilant mood owing to Sir Thomas Fairfax's capture of Sherborne Castle and Cromwell's taming of the Clubmen . . . but any optimistic stirrings Kate had wanted to cherish withered before Luciano's words. For what he was really saying was that the trail could only end in a death: Cyrus Winter's, or his own.

Shivering a little, she said, 'Then what is he waiting for? He must have seen the cartoons by now. Unless, of course, he doesn't realise who he has to thank for them?'

586

'He'll realise it. He'll know, you see, that Felix and Geoffrey were arrested for this once before. No. The only doubt in his mind will be over whether I'm doing it out of simple jealousy – or because I know who he is.' He paused and met her eyes. 'And, since he can't risk assuming it's the former, he'll have to move in for the kill.'

'Oh God,' said Kate weakly. 'Why didn't I just let Selim cut his throat while I had the chance?'

'You know the answer to that. It's because I have to know why my father had to die. If I don't discover that, everything I have done will count for nothing; and Richard will have died in vain.'

A lump formed in Kate's throat and she swallowed hard. It had been more than a year now but still the pain did not lessen. Then, before she could speak, Selim's voice came softly from behind them. *'Efendim?* We are being followed.'

Luciano's arm tensed beneath Kate's hand. Without turning, he said, 'How many?'

'Two.'

'And you're sure they're following?'

'Yes. I saw them first as we turned from Friday Street.'

'Then I think we'd better assume that there are others.' With the massive bulk of St Paul's blocking out what remained of the light, the darkness was almost total. Luciano eased his sword free and took hold of Kate's hand. 'It's probably nothing. But just in case someone's lying in wait, we'd better make a little detour – and quietly. Ready?' And without giving her time to reply, he swerved abruptly through a narrow passageway to their left, secure in the knowledge that, where he led, Selim would unerringly follow.

The passage became a small courtyard and then, after some searching, a passage again. Over the pounding of her own heart, Kate could hear footfalls running behind them. She wondered how many were chasing them . . . and then, since there was only one way to find out, decided that she would rather not know.

They emerged in front of the Wardrobe and immediately

plunged past it into Doctor's Commons before pausing for a moment to listen. The sounds of pursuit had disappeared.

'They've gone,' whispered Kate hopefully. 'Given up?'

'Perhaps.' Luciano looked past her to Selim and, keeping his voice low, said, 'If this is an attack, they'll know where we're going. And that being so, they'll realise we have to cross the Fleet and will try to beat us to the only places we can do it.'

Selim nodded. 'And so?'

'The bridge in Bridewell,' came the rapid reply. 'And *hurry*!'

The noisome alleyways of Bridewell had previously lain completely outside Kate's experience and, in no time at all, she was wishing they might have remained so. There was an all-pervading odour of rotting refuse and she dared not think what was squelching and sliding under her feet. Not that it would have done much good if she *had* thought of it, for this was scarcely a time for being choosy about where one was treading, and the pace Luciano was setting did not allow for it anyway. *He*, it was perfectly plain, knew exactly where he was going – ploughing erratically but persistently eastwards and leaving Kate with no alternative but to hoist her skirts as far clear of the filth as she could and struggle to keep up.

When they were nearly upon their goal and realising that the bridge lay less than thirty feet past the next bend, Luciano halted again in the shadows and softly invited Selim to reconnoitre. The Turk grunted and the long knife glimmered in his hand. Then he was gone.

Luciano filled the time by kissing his wife. If asked, he would probably have said this was purely in order to give Kate new heart whilst simultaneously keeping her quiet. It would, of course, have been a lie.

Suddenly, the silence was broken by a rush of feet and the sound of scraping metal. Releasing Kate and drawing his sword in the same instantaneous movement, he said, '*Stay here!*' and was off in Selim's wake.

He moved fast but with caution, keeping as close to the

wall as he could. Then, from out of the dark ahead of him came a choking cry and the unmistakable sound of a body hitting the ground. Luciano threw caution to the winds and ran.

There were three of them – in addition to the inert heap on the cobbles – and all were circling just out of range of Selim's knife. Without stopping to think, Luciano took the one nearest to him with a rush and felt his blade connect with flesh and bone. Howling, the fellow dropped his cudgel to grasp his own shoulder and fell back. Selim grinned.

'Welcome, *efendim*,' he said. And then, 'May it be easy.'

Luciano was too busy to reply. Of the two remaining assailants, only one held a sword and he had already launched his attack with a ringing blow that jarred Luciano's arm from wrist to shoulder.

'Don't be afraid,' said the fellow viciously. 'By the time I've finished with you, death will be a relief.'

'Then you'll have to try harder.' Luciano found himself suddenly gripped by cold, hard anger. 'But if you survive tonight, you can tell Cyrus Winter that I'm still waiting for him to come in person.' And, summoning every ounce of strength and skill he possessed, opened a relentless attack.

Selim stopped playfully sidestepping and slicing at his own opponent. Sending the threatening cudgel flying with a well-placed kick, he closed in and drove his knife expertly between neck and shoulder. The fellow died with a choking gurgle and blood pumped out over the cobbles but Selim did not see it. He had eyes only for his master.

Kate was watching too. Though the whole business could have taken no more than three minutes so far, she had not waited where Luciano had left her but instead crept forward in the shadow of the houses to a place from which she could see what was happening. She had not previously known whether or not Luciano knew how to use a sword; now she saw that he undoubtedly did. It ought to have made her less afraid but somehow it didn't – even though he was driving the would-be murderer back and back towards where she stood. A discarded club lay at her feet and, heart in mouth, Kate picked it up. Then, sensibly waiting for the right moment, she stepped out into the lane and brought it down hard on the villain's head.

He dropped like a stone, leaving Luciano staring at her with a mixture of disbelief and unwilling laughter. Then he knelt swiftly beside the fallen man and, after a second, said, 'Well done, *cara*. I thought for a moment you'd killed him. And what price my message to Cyrus Winter then?' He rose, turning. 'Selim? The wounded one got away and may be bringing reinforcements down from Ludgate, so let's go. They'll assume we've crossed the bridge. Fortunately for us, they'll be wrong. Come on.'

'But where?' asked Kate, stumbling blindly after him back the way they had come. Then, as the warmth of his hand began to banish the shakiness that had afflicted her, '*Not* back to Cheapside?'

'No. Nor anywhere else Winter's minions are likely to think of.'

'Blackfriars,' said Selim simply and with bountiful satisfaction. 'Of course. It is well.'

'I'm glad you approve,' responded Luciano sardonically. 'And now, if you don't mind, we'll save our breath for running.'

Due to almost two years of emptiness and neglect, the Heart and Coin was no longer the neat, well-cared-for place it had once been. Bars had been nailed across doors and windows, and weeds grew in Gwynneth's cherished flower-troughs. But the sign was still there, hanging askew from one hinge, and it was that which finally told Kate where she was.

The brothel. He had brought her, out of necessity, to the house that had once been run by his mistress; the white-skinned Welsh woman who, according to Felix, had been pushed to her death by another of Cyrus Winter's hired bravos. Kate's breath caught and, turning, she met Luciano's eyes. They were carefully blank.

Selim, meanwhile, had wrenched the bars from the back door and forced it open. Inside was a smell of dust and mildew. Kate waited in the pitch-dark for someone to make a light and, in time, Luciano appeared shading the flame of a candle with one hand. His face, in the fitful shifting light, was that of a stranger, but his voice robbed the illusion of its potency. 'Welcome,' he said blandly, 'to my secret hovel. It won't be the most comfortable night you've ever spent – but what's a little squalor between friends? And at least it's safe – as far as we know.'

'I'm glad to hear it.' Pulling herself together, Kate matched her tone to his. 'So – instead of bemoaning the mess – why don't we see what can be done to make it a bit more habitable? There must, for example, be other candles.'

'There are.' Luciano shepherded her further into the large room which, aside from the kitchen, was the only accommodation below stairs. 'There is also a small stock of firewood, which will enable me to demonstrate yet another of my skills. And while I do, no doubt Selim will be good enough to see if there's anything left in the cellar.'

Selim departed without a word. And when Kate had lit more candles from the one he held and he was able to set about building a fire, Luciano said quietly, 'You knew about this place?'

She nodded. 'Felix told me.'

'And . . . Gwynneth?'

'Yes.' Her throat felt raw. 'She was one of the . . . one of the lives you referred to, wasn't she?'

'Yes.' He kept his eyes on his task and his voice strictly neutral. 'But that is another matter. The reason we are having this conversation is so that I may tell you what Gwynneth herself always knew. I never loved her – nor even pretended to.' The kindling began to crackle and there was a spurt of flame. 'Perhaps it doesn't matter. But I knew you would never ask.'

Kate slid on to her knees beside him and turned his face gently towards her with one light palm. 'Everything matters,' she said simply. 'Only not always in the way we think.'

The shuttered expression faded and his fingers found, then entwined themselves with hers. His gaze caressed her mouth, causing her to sway towards him. And then Selim reappeared with a bottle of wine in each hand.

Later, when they each held a cup of claret and were sitting around the cheerful blaze, Kate said, 'What happens now?'

'Until it's light, nothing. Then you go back to Fleet Street and I go back to Cheapside and we pack.'

Her brows rose. 'We're going somewhere?'

'In a manner of speaking. You – accompanied by Felix, Giacomo and Gino – are setting out immediately for Thorne Ash; I, along with Selim here, am going in search of Cyrus Winter.' He smiled at her. 'You're about to argue. Don't. It's time to clear the stage of spectators and set the scene for the last act. Everything is in train for me to shut up the house in Cheapside in the next day or two – and by that time you'll be half-way home.'

Kate knew that tone as the one against which it was never any use protesting. Quelling a furious impulse to hurl her cup into the fire, she said, 'I see you've got it all worked out.'

'Yes. And not before time, don't you think? After all, I've devoted the last ten years of my life to this business.'

'And what if that becomes literally true? Do you still not think I've some right to be with you?'

'No. I don't. I want you safely out of harm's way – and after tonight, it must be perfectly obvious why,' he replied flatly. 'So pack your bags and tell Amy you're going home. Felix and the others will collect you around noon.'

On top of a sleepless night during which he'd thought of little except the twin impossibilities of risking leaving his wife pregnant – and after making love to her in the brothel once run by his mistress – Luciano was not in the mood to be tactful when Felix and Giacomo also objected to the plans he had made. He therefore resorted to a blighting speech of epic proportions before pointing out that he was depending on them to care for Kate in his absence and to deliver Aysha safely to her erstwhile colleagues in Oxford. And finally, thankfully, they agreed to go.

With a myriad small things still to be done, he had fixed

his own departure for the next day. He spent the afternoon alternately burning papers or storing them in iron-bound boxes and, by the early evening, was engaged in clearing out the workshop.

Very little remained of the stock he had amassed in earlier days – either of his own making or that which he had bought at the beginning of the war. But there were a number of enamelled chains and quantities of loose stones: rubies from India, topaz from Brazil and Persian lapis. And, along with various bracelets and necklaces of his own creating, lay the pride of his collection. Antique cameos such as the one he had sent Kate: Byzantine, Roman and Egyptian. For a long time, he stared meditatively down on the perfectly carved face of Cleopatra. Then, carefully and with precision, he set about packing every piece and stone into a wooden chest.

He had his precious banker's draft and a fair amount of loose coin. It would be stupid to take the jewels too. But the question, with time pressing, was what to do with them instead. Shrugging slightly, Luciano picked up the box and carried it down into the cellar where the floor was of beaten earth. It wasn't the best of solutions but it was all he was left with. He found a spade, took off his coat and started to dig.

An hour later, hot and decidedly grubby, he opened the parlour door and stopped as if he had walked into a wall.

'Life is full of small surprises, isn't it?' asked Kate sympathetically. 'As you can see, I sent Felix and the others on without me. And since they're now well on their way to Oxford and I've quarrelled so successfully with Amy that she's told me never to darken her door again, you're left with a choice between taking me with you or leaving me to follow on my own.' She paused and directed a sweetly confident smile into the night-dark eyes. 'But one thing is quite certain. Come hell or high water, I intend to be with you. And there is nothing – absolutely nothing – that you can do to stop me.'

Eight

While Sir Thomas Fairfax laid siege to Bristol, Kate sat in the window of a small country inn some seven miles further east and made contented repairs to one of her husband's shirts. It was 9 September and they had been there for over a week while Luciano kept a weather eye on events and waited to see if Prince Rupert would defend the city more successfully than Nat Fiennes had done – or whether the might of the New Model would prove too great to withstand. But whatever the outcome, he himself would make no attempt to close in on Cyrus Winter until a more suitable and less public opportunity presented itself; and Kate was heartily glad of it.

She was glad of other things, too. For, once he had come to terms both with her unshakeable determination to travel with him, and the fact that she had left him with no alternative but to let her do so, Luciano had finally and surprisingly removed all the barriers he had hitherto placed between them and allowed her to take her place as his wife. The result was that the last twelve, precious days since leaving London had, in an odd sort of way – and despite their other anxieties – become a honeymoon; and Kate, at least, found that she would have wanted no other. By day, while Luciano and Selim went out and about in various guises seeking information, she occupied her time with the small things which had suddenly regained their meaning, and stayed close to the inn as ordered. And by night, she lay in Luciano's arms, learning the secrets of her body and his – and was simply and gloriously happy.

The sewing lay forgotten in her lap and, for perhaps the

hundredth time, she gazed hopefully down the quiet lane. They had gone out today disguised as cabbage sellers, with a loaded cart purchased from a passing pedlar, and the impudent notion of offering their wares to the besieging army. Kate only hoped it had worked and that they weren't, even now, under close arrest for spying. But no. Surely that was the sound of wheels rumbling up the lane? Tense and expectant, she waited a few more moments until the rickety vehicle with its two disreputable-looking occupants trundled into view and then, tossing the shirt unceremoniously to one side, surged to the door.

Smiling at her from beneath his filthy hood, Luciano vaulted neatly from the cart and left Selim to drive it out of sight round the back of the inn. Then he took her in his arms.

'*Ugh!*' grimaced Kate, laughing and pushing him away. 'You smell quite disgusting!'

'It's only cabbage,' came the mock-hurt reply. And then, feverishly scratching, 'Or then again, maybe not. But what's a bit of dirt and the odd louse between friends? Or doesn't an honest day's toil deserve a kiss?'

'Not until you've shed those clothes,' she said, nimbly evading his hands. 'And you probably need a wash too. I'll go and ask them to send up some hot water. Now for heaven's sake get inside before the landlord sees you and has us evicted.'

Ten minutes later she was back in the parlour, setting the finishing touches to Luciano's shirt and waiting for him to come down and tell her about his day, when the door was virtually kicked open by an officer in New Model red. Startled, Kate looked up and then felt the air rush from her lungs.

'Jesus Christ!' said Eden, with flat incredulity. '*You!*'

Kate rose, reinflated her lungs and said weakly, 'Who were you expecting?'

'I imagine you know that perfectly well. Thanks to Tom, I recognised your crooked Italian friend and his damned servant skulking about the fringes of the army – selling cabbages, of all things. If it hadn't been for Felix, I'd have had the pair of them clapped up on the spot. As it is, I've

595

had to waste time I could ill afford following them in order to find out what the bloody hell they think they're up to.' He paused and regarded her out of eyes filled with scornful hostility. 'And what do I find? My own sister, cosily ensconced in a sordid little love-nest. Not that I ought to be surprised. You've always wanted him, haven't you? And all women are whores at heart.'

Rather pale and feeling as though she had been kicked in the stomach, Kate stared back at him. Ralph had said he had changed . . . but nothing had prepared her for this. The harsh voice and intemperate language, the bitter eyes and mouth, the hard face with its thin white scar all belonged to a stranger. She said tonelessly, 'You are under a misapprehension, Eden. Luciano and I are married.'

'*Married!*' He gave a venomously derisive laugh. 'I thought you said you couldn't be that stupid? No – don't bother to explain it to me. I understand only too well. And, married or not, you're still prostituting yourself.' He stripped off his gloves and threw them on the table. 'But that's your affair – and not what I came for. Where *is* the devious bastard?'

'Here.' Clad only in shirt and breeches and with a towel still in his hands from drying his hair, Luciano stepped through the door and pushed it shut behind him. Across the room, his eyes sought Kate's and then, looking thoughtfully at Eden, he said, 'You may insult me in whatever way you please. What you will *not* do, however, is treat your sister with anything less than respect. And if you've forgotten how that is done, I'll be forced to remind you.'

'Try it,' advised Eden, coldly smiling, 'and I'll paste you to the walls. But in the meantime, I'll say what I choose – and I don't accord respect where it's not deserved.'

Luciano moved and, seeing it, Kate hurled herself across the floor to grasp his arms. 'Don't! It's what he wants – can't you see? And it won't achieve anything. Just let him say what he came for and go.'

Carefully neutral black eyes met bleak green ones. Then, shrugging slightly, Luciano said, 'As you wish. But it might be better if you waited upstairs.'

'No. Despite all appearances to the contrary, he's my brother,' she replied acidly. 'And that being so, I think I'd prefer to stay.'

'Afraid he'll need protection, Kate?' taunted Eden.

'No. Only that he may not find words simple enough to penetrate that warped brain of yours and explain what we're doing here,' she snapped, whirling round to face him. 'Or perhaps you don't really care for the truth and are only intent on making trouble?'

'If that's what I wanted, your Papist lover would already be behind bars.'

'He's my *husband*!'

'So you say – though personally I doubt it and don't give a tinker's curse what he is.'

'This,' remarked Luciano crisply, 'isn't getting us anywhere. I presume you followed me back here in order to ask what I was doing today. Fortunately, I have no objections to telling you. I was trying to find out whether you and your colleagues intend to take Bristol or merely sit looking at it for another month or so. And my sole reason for doing so is that I'm awaiting a chance to catch up with Cyrus Winter, preferably not under the eyes of the whole New Model.'

'My God, not you as well!' Eden's brows rose and his tone grew markedly scathing. 'No one talks of anything else these days – though, if he's a spy, it's more than anyone's managed to prove.'

'Have they tried?' asked Luciano.

'Well, of course they've bloody tried! You didn't think that, after the flood of publicity he's received, he'd be simply left alone to wreak havoc at will, do you? His duties have been restricted, somebody shadows his every step and he's been hauled in for questioning both in the Army and at Westminster – none of which has produced a shred of evidence that he's done anything except change sides. Not,' he added caustically, 'that I should think you care whether he's a spy or not. After all, this isn't your war, is it? So what do you want with him – aside from asking how he's enjoyed being in the pillory?'

There was a brief silence. Then Luciano said deliberately, 'Since it was I who put him there, what else *would* I want?'

For a moment Eden looked frankly stunned and then his mouth curled in an unpleasant smile.

'Well, well. Never say the pair of you are *still* trying to beat each other to my undiscriminating mother-in-law's door?'

Kate made a small choking sound and closed one hand hard over the other. She said raggedly, 'If – if that was said for my benefit, it's missed its mark. I've known for years. I just didn't know that *you* did.'

'Of course he knew.' The white shade bracketing Luciano's mouth indicated temper barely held in check. 'It's why he's never liked me. But we're straying from the point again.' He paused and fixed Eden with an implacable stare. 'I didn't bring Cyrus Winter to the public notice out of spite – or any other trivial reason. I did it because everything I know of him points to the accusation being true. In short, the man is an artist of destruction. And if he finds out that Kate and I are here, neither of our lives will be worth a groat.'

The hazel eyes narrowed a little and then Eden shrugged dismissively. 'Theatrical rubbish!'

'No it isn't!' cried Kate. 'Oh – why won't you *listen*?'

'Because I've more important things to do.'

'More important things than hearing how close Cyrus Winter came to killing—'

'Kate.' Luciano's voice checked her and his gaze held hers. 'It's too long a story and, since he's not ready to hear it, it would do more harm than good. All we want is his word that he won't betray us.' He looked at Eden. 'Well? I'm asking you not to speak of our whereabouts to anyone. Will you do it?'

'You think I'd *want* anyone to know that my sister is living with a brothel-keeping bloodsucker?' came the withering retort. And then, 'But if I catch you or that servant of yours creeping around my men again, I won't vouch for my actions. As for Cyrus Winter, you won't get near him.

And if he's as dangerous as you say, you'd be better employed getting Kate right away from here.'

'I'm more than aware of that. Unfortunately, she won't go.'

'Doing your breathing for you, is she? I can't say I'm surprised. But that's your problem. Mine is that we're launching an assault on Bristol at first light tomorrow – and I've wasted enough time already by coming here, without wasting yet more wondering what you may be up to.'

'Don't worry. You've made your point,' said Luciano. 'But do you expect Bristol to fall?'

'Probably.' Eden picked up his gloves and put them on. 'And then we'll see, won't we, whether Rupert gets court-martialled for surrendering as Nat Fiennes did?' His eyes returned bleakly to Kate. 'I won't say it's been a pleasure. It hasn't. But at least you know now why I'm not fit to go home.' And, turning on his heel, he strode out of the room, slamming the door behind him.

For a long moment, Kate looked helplessly at Luciano. Then she said violently, 'He's my brother – but I don't know him any more. I could *kill* Celia!'

'I know.' He enclosed her in warm, steady arms and drew her head against his shoulder. 'And I'm sorry I couldn't let you tell him about Jude. But you understand why, don't you?'

'A little knowledge is a dangerous thing? Yes. And I doubt if he'd have believed it, anyway.' She sighed and then, at length, said, 'If Cyrus Winter really is under surveillance, the fall of Bristol won't be much help to you, will it?'

'Probably not. Fortunately, however, I have infinite patience.'

She lifted her head to look up at him. 'So you'll go on watching and waiting?'

'For as long as it takes,' he replied, smiling a little. 'And it cuts both ways, you know. For if *I* can't reach *him* – then, by the same token, *he* can't reach *me*. And it would be a shame to ruin the game by rushing it now, wouldn't it?'

***

With plague, discontent in the town, and only fifteen hundred Cavaliers to span its five miles of defences, the fate of Bristol was never in doubt. Fairfax began his assault at two in the morning and, by five, had broken through in two places on the Avon side and taken Prior's Hill Fort. Like Nathaniel Fiennes before him, Rupert was forced to withdraw his forces to the castle, and by eight o'clock was appealing for terms in order to save his remaining men from ruthless annihilation. As once he had taken Bristol, so now he lost it; and because that was quite bad enough, it was fortunate he didn't yet know that his uncle's regard, his command and his reputation had gone with it.

While Fairfax, with his customary civility, permitted the Prince to march away under safe conduct to Oxford with all his colours, drums, swords and pikes, Luciano waited to see what would happen next – and within a couple of days had his answer. Fairfax led half the army north towards Gloucestershire, and Lieutenant-General Oliver Cromwell, with Eden Maxwell and Cyrus Winter somewhere in his train, took the other half off to reduce Devizes.

'And that,' said Luciano to Kate later that same evening, 'has got to be good news. Firstly, because the haystack is now much smaller – and secondly because we ought to be able to remain where we are for the present at least. Although with so much military activity around us and no way of knowing which way Cromwell will choose to move next, I think the time is fast approaching when we could do with a safer haven than a common inn.'

'You mean you'd like *me* to have a safer haven,' she replied peaceably, her fingers continuing to trace lazy patterns on his chest. 'Forget it. And anyway, where could be safer than this? It's like being shut away in our own little world.'

'An illusion, *cara* – and you know it.' He smiled and pulled her down on top of him. 'But I, for one, am not complaining.'

Kate's breath caught and she said severely, 'You, sir, are insatiable.'

His mind and hands being busy with other things,

Luciano took his time about replying. Then, 'And you're not?' he said.

It was harder, now that Eden was looking out for him, for Luciano to get close enough to the army to ask the questions that needed to be asked – but not entirely impossible. A week after the fall of Bristol, and with the collapse of Devizes expected daily, Luciano finally learned that the next town to receive Cromwell's personal attention would be Winchester – and the discovery caused him to decide on a course of action which he had been contemplating for some time.

If Cromwell – as seemed to be the case – was intent on mopping up every Royalist garrison in the whole of Wiltshire and Hampshire, the chances of Kate and himself finding themselves caught in the cross-fire grew stronger every day. And though *he* had no choice but to continue playing grandmother's footsteps with the army until Fate placed Cyrus Winter on the right square, it was time to put Kate in the one strategically placed stronghold where she would be safe.

'*Basing House?*' she echoed incredulously when he told her. 'But it's already under siege – and has been for weeks!'

'By a Dutch engineer who hasn't enough men to throw a ring round it,' nodded Luciano. 'I know. But it's the greatest house in England, Kate, and said to be impregnable. It's come under attack at least twice before by Waller; and I don't see a mere engineer succeeding where he failed – do you?'

'I wouldn't know. But what I *do* know is that Lord Winchester is said to be nourishing none but Catholics – so even if you could get me inside the place, it's not very likely he'd let me stay.' She stopped and then, reading his face, said bitterly, 'Oh God. Don't tell me. The lord Marquis is a bosom friend of yours.'

'We've met,' agreed Luciano with a faint smile. 'And, because I'm Italian by birth, he'll not only assume that I am a good Catholic, but that you are one too. Unless, of course, you're determined to tell him otherwise.'

'Brilliant. You'll be garlanding me with a crucifix and rosary beads next. But before you regale me with any more details of your wonderful plan, just tell me one thing. What will *you* be doing while I'm snug as a bug with the Jesuits?'

'Following the army to Winchester,' came the wry response. 'But that means I won't be far from Basing and we needn't be parted for long. So —'

'We won't be parted at all. I'm not leaving you.'

'I'm afraid,' he told her quietly but with utter finality, 'that you are. You're only here at all because you left me with no alternative, but from this point on, the terms are mine.' He took her shoulders in a firm clasp and held her eyes with his own. 'The honeymoon is over, *cara* – and the reason is a very simple one. I can dodge Eden, lurk wraith-like in the tail of the army and face up to Cyrus Winter; but I can't do all those things and protect you properly as well. So it's time to take other measures . . . and I'd be glad, just this once, if you'd make it easy for me.'

The turrets and spires of the greatest house in England peered coyly over a massive wall of dark Tudor brick. Home and fortress of John Paulet, fifth Marquis of Winchester, Basing House was more truthfully two mansions in one and it sprawled over some fourteen acres. An ancient motte-and-bailey structure fronted by a hugely solid four-storey gatehouse glared balefully at its newer, more luxurious three-hundred-and-eighty-roomed neighbour; and about and between both lay courtyards, sentry-walks, barns and fish-stews. Kate had expected it to be big; what she had not expected was that it would be both more complex and more crowded than Whitehall.

With a little help from Selim, Luciano had no difficulty at all in spiriting the three of them inside – mainly because the Parliament's Dutch engineer was focusing all his attention on one precise point of the Old House. And once within the walls, they were warmly welcomed by the courtly, jovial-faced marquis – and Kate found herself speedily installed in a chamber with three other ladies. Wisely perhaps, Luciano gave her time to do little more than exchange a last kiss and beg him to be careful. Then he was gone again, leaving her alone in a sea of strange faces.

The house was bursting with Royalist refugees, every one of whom was Catholic. Inigo Jones the architect was there, and the engraver Wenceslas Hollar, and no less than seven priests. Sensing pitfalls ahead, Kate feigned shyness, introduced herself as Mistress del Santi and was grateful when the name caused a degree of lofty withdrawal. But more worrying than any mistakes she herself might make in this company was the discovery that the marquis had dismissed his Protestant military governor, Colonel Rawdon – along with five hundred of his men. Kate didn't know how good the colonel had been at his job or whether the remaining garrison was so large that the men he had taken wouldn't be missed. But with Mynheer Dalbier about to open fire, she couldn't help but feel that it would have been nice to know there was a professional in charge.

The expected cannonade began the following morning and, to begin with at least, few of the other inmates did more than complain gaily about the infernal noise. Kate did her best to share their confidence. After all, most of them had much more experience of siege-warfare than she did, so perhaps they were right when they said that Basing would not fall. But two days later the great tower against which the guns had been consistently blazing crumbled spectacularly into a heap of rubble – and Colonel Dalbier turned his attention to the New House. Cannons were trained on the huge corner turret, horrible fumes from burning straw impregnated with arsenic and brimstone filled the house, and Kate watched the hitherto carefree atmosphere turn to one of discreet concern.

On the day that the first gaping, serpentine fissure appeared in the walls, she took a long thoughtful look at Lord Winchester's exquisite house with its gilding, its moulded plaster-work and its lovely, elegant windows, each with the motto '*Aimez Loyauté*' engraved upon it. Part palace, part fortress, there was no doubt that the place was strong. But impregnable? Kate wondered. And prayed that Luciano would come back before she was forced to find out.

Devizes fell before the end of the month; Cromwell led his forces off to Winchester; and Luciano, despite his much-vaunted patience, began to get very tired of biding his time. News from elsewhere said that Fairfax had taken Berkeley Castle and the King, having dismissed Rupert and watched his northern cavalry being routed from the walls of Chester, had taken himself off to Newark to wait for Montrose to lead his all-conquering army southwards. But for Luciano, nothing existed outside the apparent impossibility of isolating Cyrus Winter from his fellows so that the business might be ended one way or another. And, as day followed day, he found himself growing increasingly short-tempered and reckless.

When Cromwell forced his way into Winchester, and its garrison shut themselves up in the castle, Luciano gave up worrying about Captain Eden Maxwell's views on the subject and slid unobtrusively into the city. For several days, he watched and listened as the guns of the New Model destroyed towers and created breaches. Then, just as it became obvious that the castle must be on the point of surrender, Selim disappeared.

It wasn't, as it happened, his fault. One minute he'd been pouring ale down the willing throat of a red-faced sergeant for the sake of picking up a few scraps of information, and the next he'd found himself looking down the barrel of Tom Tripp's pistol.

'Got you,' said Tom, neatly and cheerfully appropriating the nasty heathen knife. And then, tutting reprovingly, 'You didn't ought to have come back spying again. Mr Eden told you that, didn't he? And now I reckon he's going to have quite a few things to say to that slippery master of yours – when we find him. So get up. You're coming along with me.'

Back in their squalid lodgings, Luciano did not become seriously worried until much later in the afternoon; then it took a further two hours before he eventually found someone who had seen Selim marched off under close arrest. And after that, of course, there was naturally only one thing he could do.

Having got past the troopers at the door, he found Captain Maxwell buckling on his sword whilst receiving a series of crisp orders from his superior. Luciano did not know that the dark-haired major was the man whose illegitimacy had helped send his own father to the scaffold – and, even if he had, would still have said curtly, 'I believe you have my servant.'

'What did you expect?' returned Eden. And then, to the major, 'I apologise for the interruption – but this fellow and his groom have been creeping about asking questions ever since Bristol. So I thought it was time to pull them both in.'

'Quite right.' Gabriel Brandon pulled on his gloves and looked fleetingly at Luciano. 'But you haven't time to attend to that now.'

'I know.' Smiling coldly, Eden summoned the men at the door and then said, 'You were warned, I believe. But what have you done with your so-called wife?'

'She's safe,' snapped Luciano. Then, 'Don't play games, Eden. You don't know what you're meddling with.'

'Don't I? Then it will be up to you to tell me, won't it? Tomorrow.' And, signalling to the troopers, 'Put him in the cellar with the other one and stay on watch. If they escape, I'll hold you personally responsible.'

The cellar was dark, damp, and not made any more comfortable by the results of his stupid attempts at resistance or Selim's determination to apologise every second or third word. Luciano bore it as long as he could and then, forcefully and in the vernacular, told the Turk to be quiet. Time passed . . . how long, he did not know. Outside in the town, the great guns fell silent; and then, much later, came the faint sound of voices and jingling of harnesses followed by a great many hooves. Icy fear began to settle in Luciano's chest. And finally, more than twenty-four hours after it had been locked, the door swung open again.

605

It was very early morning and, blinking in the light, Luciano and Selim were taken at swordpoint to the room once more occupied by Eden Maxwell. He was sitting on a table, gently swinging one booted foot and, when the door closed behind his prisoners, he said crisply, 'I asked you once before – and I think this time you'd better tell me. Where's Kate?'

'Why should you care?' retorted Luciano.

'Because, with the exception of my own regiment, the rest of the army's already on the move and I'd like to be sure you haven't left her in its path. Now. *Where is she?*'

'Your concern overwhelms me,' came the sardonic reply. 'But you needn't worry. She's at Basing House.'

Eden froze. '*What?*'

Luciano felt his heart stop. For a long, airless moment, hazel eyes met black and then Eden said furiously, 'You bloody madman! Do you know what you've done?'

Luciano had turned perfectly white. He said, 'I'm beginning to guess. How long ago did Cromwell leave?'

'Last evening. He'll be marching on Basing from Alresford just about now. And when he gets there . . . *Christ!* He's got six thousand men and a full artillery train, including a cannon royal! Do you know what that can do? This time Basing will fall.'

'And Cromwell won't show much mercy to a nest of Papists – of which Kate will be assumed to be one. Quite. You don't need to paint a picture.' Luciano drew a long breath. 'You've got to let me go. I may not be in time to get her out – but at least I can be with her.'

'And what good will that do?'

'On its own, not much perhaps – though you'll know that no one will touch Kate while Selim and I are alive to prevent it. But the outcome really depends on how much other help you're prepared to give me. And we haven't the time to argue over it. Well?'

Eden hesitated and then swung himself from the table. 'Go on,' he said frigidly. 'I'm listening.'

Once more armed with their own weapons and on horses

of Eden's providing, Luciano and Selim covered the twenty, seemingly endless miles to Basingstoke at break-neck speed, only to find the town already swarming with the Army's advance guard. Luciano swore but did not waste time investigating further – and another twenty minutes brought Basing House into view.

Dalbier's guns could be heard firing on the far side of the mansion and, even though he could not see what damage they were inflicting, Luciano discovered that he felt rather sick. But now was no time to hesitate. Following the same cunning route they had used before, he led Selim up to the walls and sought admittance. Then they were inside and being taken directly to the marquis.

He listened gravely while Luciano described the parliamentary forces about to descend on him and then said, 'It seems we're about to face our sorest test. I had best alert the garrison.'

'You'd also,' replied Luciano tersely, 'better consider how to answer Lieutenant-General Cromwell's summons when it comes.'

'I don't need to consider it. My house's other name is "Loyalty". And once His Majesty knows that we are *in extremis*, he will almost certainly send help.'

'He's none to send. His armies are in disarray everywhere and rumour has it that even Montrose has been defeated.'

'Then we are in God's hands,' came the gentle reply. And then, as the door opened, 'Ah. Your charming wife. I will leave you to be reunited in private.'

Her hand frozen on the door-latch, Kate neither curtsied to nor even saw the marquis as he passed her. She merely drowned in her husband's eyes until he said wryly, 'Forgive me, *cara*. I came to take you away . . . but I am very much afraid that it is already too late.' And then, half-blinded by thankful tears, she flew across the room into his arms; and thought was suspended for both of them.

Nine

'Tomorrow,' said Luciano finally and with certainty. 'For good or ill, it will end tomorrow.'

It was Monday 13 October and the forces of the New Model had been outside for six days: arriving within an hour of Luciano himself to take up positions in the park, towards Hackwood and on Cowdrays Down, and effectively crushing any hopes of a discreet exit. Then they had begun siting their guns and the inmates of Basing House had watched in silence as the great cannon royal was heaved majestically into place, ready to fire its murderous sixty-three-pound shots. One look at it had been enough to convince the marquis that other, non-defensive measures were now called for, with the result that Luciano had spent the next three days melting down quantities of plate and transforming it – for want of more suitable casts – into a herd of small, golden stags, which his lordship had then promptly and privately hidden.

The long-awaited summons to surrender had eventually come on the afternoon of the 11th and contained an unsurprising warning from Cromwell that the house could look for no mercy if it continued to stand against him. Equally unsurprisingly, the marquis sent back a flat refusal. And, on the morning of the 12th, the Lieutenant-General's guns opened fire.

For two days the house was subjected to a heavy, ceaseless bombardment until, by the evening of the 13th, the walls had been severely breached in at least two places. And that was when Luciano looked grimly at Kate and said, 'Tomorrow.'

Her nerves frayed by forty-eight hours of deafening noise and tooth-rattling vibration, she took her time about answering. Then, 'Have we *no* hope of holding out?'

'With a garrison of only three hundred against seven thousand? None. They'll take this place by storm – probably in a matter of hours.'

'And when they do?'

'All hell will break loose – in more ways than one,' he replied deliberately. 'Because when they come, Cyrus Winter will come with them. And it is time we met.'

Veiling her fear as best she could, Kate lifted her eyes to meet his. She said carefully, 'So this is it, then.'

'Yes.' His hands lightly clasping her waist, he suddenly smiled with all the old, wickedly enticing charm. 'This is it. And you are thinking precisely what I am thinking.'

'I am?'

'Certainly you are. You're thinking that – no matter what tomorrow may bring – we still have tonight. And you're wondering just where, in this magnificent, overcrowded hen-coop, we can find the privacy to spend it together. Fortunately, however, I have the answer.'

'Of course you have,' said Kate, somewhere between tears and laughter. 'It's a habit with you.'

'Are you complaining?'

'Yes. I'd like to know why you didn't address this problem six days ago. Unless, of course, you *like* sleeping with Selim?'

'And Viscount Stavely and his man,' he nodded, cheerfully leading her away towards the back stairs. 'The bonhomie in our garret is frankly crippling. But enough is enough and I believe I can bear to miss it for once.'

Maintaining this gentle flow of eloquence all the way to their destination, he finally threw open a door in one of the less frequented corridors and said, 'There! Never say I don't know what's due to a lady.'

It was a small, windowless store-room, piled high with old tapestries, balding rugs and moth-eaten furs. It was also, as he had said, wonderfully private.

'It's beautiful,' she said. And meant it.

'I thought you'd like it. And see – the door is even equipped with a key.' He turned it in the lock, and producing candle and tinder from his pocket, made a light. 'What more could we possibly want?'

'Nothing.' She moved, dream-like, into the waiting circle of his arms. 'Nothing. It's all here.'

He kissed her slowly and with tantalising lightness before gathering her closer still. Her fingers wove their way through the long, night-dark hair at his nape, and her mouth opened like a flower under his. Then he began the leisurely and entirely pleasurable process of disrobing her.

Her body aflame at the exquisite mastery of his hands, Kate smoothed the shirt from his shoulders and murmured ragged endearments against the column of his throat . . . until desire, inextricably laced with desperation, flowed between them like a rushing stream and bore them down upon their makeshift bed of furs.

Urgency overcame artistry but could not dim what lay behind it. Love and delicacy and tenderness, all gleaming like so many golden coins in the torrent and lighting the darkness long after the candle had guttered and gone out.

The following morning dawned chill and grey. Together with Selim, Kate and Luciano stood high on a turret watching the mist swirl in from Loddon Marsh and waiting for the light to show them what, if anything, was happening out there beyond the walls. It was a little past five o'clock and, for the first time in days, the silence was broken only by the steady tramp of the sentries' feet. Luciano frowned, wondering if he'd guessed wrongly . . . or, if he hadn't, why the whole garrison wasn't already standing to arms. Then, because there are times when you have to accept that, with the best will in the world, you can't control everything, he looked down on Kate and said, 'It's time we considered our own personal strategy. Once Cromwell's fellows get past the breaches, they'll overrun the house in no time and there will be a good deal of general unpleasantness. So since there's no one outside Selim and myself to whom I can confidently entrust your safety once the chaos starts – and I'm not prepared to run the risk of you being hauled out of some priest's hole or other – the only thing we can do is to stay close together.'

'You know me.' Kate surveyed him out of eyes that were at distinct variance with the apparent levity in her voice. '*I am a kind of burr; I shall stick.*'

'See that you do. And if we're to stand any chance of coming out of this alive, you'd also better make sure you follow my instructions to the letter,' he returned grimly. 'And now we come to the best bit. I told you that Eden has rediscovered some brotherly concern for you – enough, at least, to let Selim and myself out of his cellar. What I haven't yet told you is that – unless he's thought better of it – we also came to a small arrangement.' And with brisk and faintly caustic satisfaction, he explained.

At six o'clock the pall of silence was briefly shattered by a single, thunderous roar of cannon-fire; and from out of the gloom, rank upon rank of the New Model Army began their relentless advance on Basing House. The breath of each man smoked on the early morning air, and the only sound was that of their footfalls, coupled with the metallic rasp of arms on armour. On they came for God and the Parliament . . . on and on, across the soft, wet grass of the park, like the well-honed fighting machine they were. And finally, half-way to their goal and far, far too late, they were seen from the walls.

A confused cry of, 'To arms – they are upon us!' arose from within and alarm drums began frantically beating. With the mechanical ease of two long years' practice, the garrison swarmed to their posts and down into the cavernous breaches which they had somehow to defend against the oncoming flood . . . while, with no further use for stealth, Cromwell's forces bellowed a great, seven-thousand-strong chorus and hurled themselves in a massive red tide on both sides of the house at once.

Pandemonium erupted. Musket-fire tore the air and created a kind of savage counterpoint with the drums; swords chimed and hissed and slithered; men shouted in triumph, howled with pain and died, screaming. With glorious, hopeless courage, Lord Winchester's men attempted to stem the furious onslaught by selling their lives at the highest possible cost; and, maimed, bleeding or dying, men dropped where they stood and were trampled underfoot. For there was no way of stopping the wild, rushing cataract that poured endlessly in upon them, and in no time at all the breaches were full of Roundheads.

Knowing already that they would not be granted quarter and therefore determined to resist to the bitter end, the remaining members of the garrison retreated to the houses to pepper their attackers with grenadoes – but with little useful result. Some of the enemy had already taken the Norman bailey and were preparing to storm the huge gatehouse, while others were streaming in through the windows of the New House. Now that the day was unalterably theirs, the tumult of violence soared to fever-pitch and the previously spasmodic battle-cries became a single, bloodthirsty howl of 'Down with the Papists!'

Disputed to the last bullet and broken blade, the Old House finally fell and was immediately turned into a charnel-house as every Cavalier found alive inside it was ruthlessly butchered – some, like Major Robinson, in the very act of surrender. In happier days he had made Drury Lane audiences rock with laughter; now, he attempted to hand his sword to one of Cromwell's fanatical officers and was promptly shot in the head.

Flown with victory and the promise of rich Papist spoils, the army cheerfully indulged itself with a little cold-blooded murder. And, freed for once from Fairfax's scrupulous, restraining hand, the lieutenant-general did nothing to stop it.

As yet, Kate had seen mercifully little of the untrammelled horrors taking place outside. The very moment that the garrison drums first began signalling the assault had seen her hurtling down to a prearranged destination in the New House with her hand clamped firmly in Luciano's and Selim pounding dutifully at their heels.

The corridors and stairways were awash with rising fear

as ladies and gentlemen – not all of whom were as yet fully dressed – ran first this way and then that. Doors slammed, wild-eyed servants rushed by clutching bags and coffers, feet pounded towards secret hiding places; and everywhere there arose a jumbled cry of 'What's happening? Are they past the walls? Tell us what to do!'

Without ever slackening his pace, Luciano hurled back the information that the Roundheads would be in soon enough and that the Royalists should look to saving themselves rather than their goods. It was all he could do. His own task was to keep Kate, Selim and himself safe from the invading hordes long enough for Eden's promised protection to arrive; then, if Fate placed itself in his hands, he had to finish what he had started. Neither was simple and both could easily end in disaster; so today, as always, was for his own concerns – and the rest must shift for themselves.

They reached the library and found it mercifully empty. No one, obviously, had as yet had the idea of hiding, rescuing or purloining the fortune in books that lined his lordship's shelves. While Selim locked the door and stationed himself in front of it, Kate looked vaguely around her and said, 'Why here?'

'Two reasons,' replied Luciano briefly. 'It's on the first floor – so we needn't worry about attack from the windows; and the only other door is the sole means of entry to the marquis's private office.'

'And you think Cyrus Winter will try to go there?'

'It depends on where his loyalties lie and what he has reason to believe may be in there. But yes – I hope so.' Turning away from the window, outside which the noise of battle was rapidly escalating, he said, 'Selim – help me move some of this furniture down towards the inner door. If all goes well, we'll need space . . . and a barrier we can shelter behind may not come amiss. Kate, my heart – we've four pistols between us. Check they're properly loaded and then bring them down to this table.'

Glad of something to do, Kate carried the weapons to a place which afforded an oblique view of the courtyard.

Members of the garrison were already flying across it, apparently in full retreat and, seconds later, a wave of pursuing red-coats appeared in their wake. Then the rattle of musket-fire was drowned in a series of loud explosions. Mechanically checking the last pistol with shaking fingers, Kate peered down through the smoke and said sharply, 'They're getting in downstairs.'

'All right. Don't worry.' Luciano materialised at her side and picked up two of the guns. 'Come and sit on the floor behind this desk and make ready to reload for Selim and me if the need arises. With luck, we shouldn't have to hold out for long. Eden promises to have a couple of his own men from Thorne Ash come straight to this room – and it will be your job to recognise them. I don't want Selim shooting our friends by mistake.'

'From what I kn-know of him,' responded Kate grimly from between chattering teeth, 'he couldn't hit a barn door at ten paces. So, if it's all the same to you, I think it will be b-better if *I* do the shooting.'

'Much better,' agreed Selim, joining them behind the hastily constructed barricade. 'I trust only my knife. But I do not mind reloading if you wish it.'

'That's good of you,' retorted Luciano with a faint, crooked grin. And then they all fell silent, listening.

The clamour of swords, crack of pistols and din of shouting voices was much closer now, and ominously punctuated by the sound of exploding locks and splintering wood. Feet stampeded on the stairs and cries of, 'Down with the Papists!' could be distantly heard through the library door. His face pale and set, Luciano cocked his pistol.

The commotion reached the passageway outside. The heavy brass latch clattered under someone's hand and the stout oak door shuddered in response to an almighty blow. Her breathing light and shallow, Kate strained her ears for the sound of particular voices but was defeated by the general mêlée. The door withstood a second assault – then a third. And finally there was a deafening bang as someone fired a pistol into the lock at point-blank range.

The door burst open, revealing Cyrus Winter with three

iron-helmeted troopers at his back. The gun in his hand was still smoking, his coat was streaked with dirt and, for once, he wasn't smiling.

'*At last!*' breathed Luciano.

One of the soldiers kicked the door shut and Kate caught her breath . . . and the utter incredulity in Winter's light grey eyes was slowly replaced with cruel satisfaction. Then, 'My God! The gutter-bred crookback and his jade of a wife, no less. How utterly perfect. But don't you ever get anything right?'

'You'd be surprised.' His tone as smooth as silk, Luciano stood perfectly still, a pistol steady in either hand. 'Just now, for example, your way to Lord Winchester's private papers lies through me.'

'And you think that will stop me?' came the contemptuous reply. Then, to the silent trio behind him, '*Kill them.*'

Nothing happened.

'You heard what I said!' he snapped, half turning. 'What the devil are you waiting for?'

'A better order than that one,' grunted Tom Tripp, sourly. And then, 'Are you all right, Miss Kate?'

'Better than all right,' she said unsteadily. 'I've never been so glad to see anyone in my life!'

'Nor I,' began Luciano. Then, as Tom was forced to side-step a vicious blow to his head from the butt of the major's spent pistol, 'Stand – or I'll put a bullet through your elbow!'

Cyrus Winter froze, his face contorted with fury, and Kate said quickly, 'Tom – we need time to talk to this – this *gentleman*. Can you and Robert and Abel stop anyone else from coming in while we do it?'

'We can try. With half the army running wild after plunder, it won't be what you'd call easy. But I suppose we can always say Old Noll's in here. That ought to hold 'em.' He directed a laconic stare at the seething major. 'If you want to see me court-martialled, you'd better not lay a hand on Miss Kate – or you won't live long enough.' And, with a jerk of his head for the other two, he was gone.

The ruined door closed behind them, leaving Cyrus

Winter alone in the middle of the floor, his gaze resting narrowly on Luciano. From elsewhere in the house the sounds of pillage and destruction raged like a swelling tide; but inside the room the currents of violence were marked only by ugly, voiceless hatred until, at length, Winter said coolly, 'So. Here we are at last. You seem to have gone to some trouble.'

Luciano's brows rose over an expression of purposeful restraint. 'None worth mentioning. And at least you don't need to ask why.'

'Hardly – unless you wish to ask if I enjoyed your wife? But no. We're presumably here to discuss your tediously unimportant father.'

The fingers of his right hand tightening on the cocked pistol, Luciano said, 'Just in case the perils of your present situation have somehow failed to strike you, allow me to point out that a small modicum of diplomacy is called for.' A slow, cold smile dawned. 'Of course, I don't intend to let you leave this room alive . . . but you may continue to hope for a rescue party as long as I don't pull this trigger. Or then again, you might regret it if I were provoked into shattering your tediously unimportant ankle.'

There was another long, poisonous silence. Kate dug her nails into her palms and prayed she wouldn't be sick.

'And now,' continued Luciano, 'we will begin. Selim – a chair for the major; position yourself between it and the door. Kate – I suggest you go through to his lordship's office and wait there till this is done.'

'I can't.' Her throat was raw and aching. 'You know I can't. Not yet. Not till I know about Father.'

Harsh, savagely amused laughter scored the air like a razor and, dropping carelessly into the chair Selim brought him, Winter said, 'Your father? He saw me talking to the Parliament's scoutmaster-general and came blundering after me to Cropredy at a time when I was fairly busy. Naturally, I had to get rid of him. Is that what you wanted to hear?'

Luciano cast a brief, worried glance over his shoulder at his wife. She was ashen and her eyes were stark with distress. To spare her the need to ask, he said quickly, 'You're saying you killed Richard Maxwell because he found out that you were betraying the King?'

'Why else?'

Kate gave a small choke of hysteria, swiftly checked.

'And now?' pursued Luciano.

'Oh – now I'm "betraying" the Parliament, as you so picturesquely put it. But surely you knew that – unless those cartoons weren't your work after all? No. The only thing this war means to me is what profit I can make out of it. You see? I don't mind admitting it to you – for neither you nor anyone else will ever prove it. But then, having already tried, you know that too. Don't you?'

'You make an awful lot of assumptions,' remarked Luciano, strolling across the floor to within four feet of him. 'The cartoons were merely inspired guess-work. A small repayment in kind, designed to tell you that your anonymity was over. And Richard Maxwell didn't follow you because you were a spy, but because he knew you for a cold-blooded killer.'

'Did he? Dear me! Can it be that I underestimated him?' For the first time, the silver eyes exhibited something other than mocking boredom. 'And how, precisely, could he have done that?'

'The same way that I do.' Taking his time, Luciano allowed each syllable to arrive in crystals of ice. 'You made the mistake of wearing the ring you cut from Samuel Fisher's hand. It was once mine.'

The words echoed on into the four corners of the room and this time there was no mistaking the naked malevolence on Cyrus Winter's face. Screams and raucous calls came from beyond the door, but the air inside it was charged with something infinitely worse. Kate clung grimly to the shreds of her self-control and wondered why Luciano did not make an end. He must know, as she did, that it was dangerous to linger . . . and that the man in the chair knew it too and was playing for time.

Then, 'Yours?' grated Winter, in voice suddenly stripped

of all pretence. 'Then take it, you poor, ill-formed bastard! *Take it!*' And dragging the emerald from his hand, he hurled it straight at Luciano's face.

Luciano stepped neatly from its path and heard it strike the wall behind him. It was almost time to ask the only question that mattered; almost but not quite. And so, without once moving his eyes from the other man's face, he waited.

'Fisher – that filthy, stinking old goat!' spat Winter. 'Yes. I killed him – and enjoyed doing it. But why should you care?'

'I don't,' replied Luciano softly. 'Or less, perhaps, than I care for the deaths of my father and Richard Maxwell – or the woman your cut-throats murdered in my house. But you can tell me why Fisher had to die, if you like. After all, we've very little else left to say to one another, have we?'

'Enough, I think, to stop you from touching me,' came the swift, savage taunt. 'But by all means let us talk about Fisher. He knew, you see. Did you never suspect it? He knew that it was I who had orchestrated both the indictment against your father and the evidence that would convict him. He discovered it after the trial when he tried to put the squeeze on Giles Langley.'

Luciano drew a long, slightly ragged breath. '*Langley* told him?'

'You really don't know very much, do you? Of course Langley told him. He was my go-between, the weak link in my chain – and the only one holding an incriminating document with my name on it. But for that, I'd probably have done away with him sooner. As it was, I had to wait. Only then, of course, he gave the bloody thing to Fisher in lieu of money – thus enabling the old fox to blackmail me instead.'

'So you broke Langley's neck.' Luciano could feel cramp beginning to stir in the hand that held the pistol and was distantly grateful that his nerves had so far remained steady. 'And then, once you'd worked out who I was, you murdered Fisher before he could be tempted by a higher price than the one you were paying him.' He thought for a moment. 'Tell me . . . do you sleep at nights?'

'Better than I imagine *you* have done these past two years,' retorted Winter, with a short abrasive laugh. 'How did you like knowing yourself at my mercy, I wonder? Did you enjoy the kickings, the fires, the arrests and the abduction of your brother-in-law's brat? Were your gutless dealings with Ferrars and Webb worth the cost of bringing yourself to my attention? I doubt it. For I knew everything about you, my pathetic misshapen cretin. And I could have killed you at any time.'

'Then it is your misfortune that you didn't, isn't it?' observed Luciano. He let the pause develop until it lapped the edges of the room. Then at long last he said carefully, 'And now . . . now you will tell me why you destroyed my father.'

Thank God, thought Kate. Every bone and muscle in her body burned with tension and she was resting heavily against the makeshift barricade. *Thank God.*

Cyrus Winter leaned back in his chair and folded his arms. 'Oh no,' he said with soft derision. 'No, I don't think I will. For that's the only thing you want to know, isn't it? So telling you would be tantamount to cutting my own throat. And that would be a pity – because, from the noise outside, I'd say your friends won't be able to hold the door for much longer.'

It was unfortunately true. A miscellany of thuds and angry, shouting voices emanated from the other side of the oak panels, followed by the clash of swords and, finally, a shot. Luciano's steely calm, however, did not waver by so much as a hair's breadth. He said, 'Perhaps – perhaps not. But if you think that will help you, I fear you are misreading the situation. And in the meantime, my servant is an artist with a knife. You'd be quite surprised at the amount of damage he can inflict without in the least endangering your life. So I'll ask just once more. *Why did you destroy my father?*'

Abruptly abandoning his careless pose, Winter sat up and twisted his head as Selim approached, smiling. 'You're bluffing!'

Luciano merely shrugged and, without turning round, said, 'Kate. Go into the other room. Now.'

His tone told her that he meant it. Fortunately, it told Cyrus Winter so too and for the first time a flicker of real fear appeared in his face. Without taking his eyes from the bright, wickedly advancing blade, he said sharply, 'All right — all right! I'll tell you.'

'I thought you might.' Luciano sent Selim back to the door with an almost imperceptible movement of his head. 'Well? I'm listening. And you'd better make it quick. It all began with money, I suppose?'

'How else? You don't suppose I associate with Papist bloodsuckers for the pleasure of their company, do you?'

'Stick to the point!'

'The point? *The point* is that I'd gone through one fortune and needed to found another in order to maintain my position at Court,' came the bitter response. 'So I borrowed twenty thousand pounds from Alessandro Falcieri and invested it in Irish land.'

Luciano's breath leaked away. 'Oh Christ,' he murmured. And then, 'Go on. Or no. I think perhaps I can guess. My father found out how you were using his money and recalled it.'

'Well, well . . . some small showing of intelligence at last,' sneered Winter. 'Yes. That is precisely what happened. More than that — he even had the insolence to lecture me on what he called the "shocking evils of profiteering and exploitation". He drew a long and harrowing picture of what I and others like me were doing to the Irish — casting the poor Papist bogtrotters off their land to starve. And then he threatened to ruin me if I didn't restore every acre I'd bought to its former owner.'

'Yes. He would.' The last hour was beginning to take its toll and Luciano's voice had grown curiously remote. He thought about Gianetta and Liam and the sudden ironic aptness of it all. Then, pulling himself together, he said, 'Only of course you didn't. There was too much money to be made. So you decided to do away with both your debt and my father in one move. Except that it

620

wasn't one move, was it? It was a whole five-act bloody drama.'

'Which – on top of having the desired effect at the time – has taken you half your life to unravel,' replied Cyrus Winter, an unpleasant smile curling his mouth. 'If you don't admire the neatness of it, you must surely applaud my ingenuity?'

'It may come as a surprise – but I neither admire nor applaud anything about you.'

'No? Then I shall have to see if I can mend that.' The chaos outside the door had increased in volume and, raising his voice over it, Winter said, 'I see you're wearing a sword – and assume that you've left me mine for some purpose. So let's end this, shall we?'

Luciano took his time about replying and, long before he spoke, the expression in his eyes warned Cyrus Winter of his final, catastrophic miscalculation. Then, at last, Luciano said coldly, 'Yes. It's time. But not that way. Not in honourable, gentlemanly combat. For you have no honour and I am no gentleman; and this is not a duel. It is an extermination.' He paused, putting every resource he possessed under iron control and watching the rising panic in his enemy's face. 'I told you that you would never leave this room alive; and even if I pitted my blade against yours, that would still be true – for if I don't kill you, Selim or Kate quite certainly will. And that is not a task I will lay upon either of them. So if you want to pray, pray now – for mine is the last face you will see in this life.' Ashen but resolute, he levelled the pistol in an unfaltering grip. 'Kate – for the love of God, look away!'

It was a nightmare but one she had to share with him. Knowing he would not now turn to check, she gave him the affirmative he needed and then remained frozen to the spot, while, seeing his death approaching, Cyrus Winter sent the chair crashing over as he surged to his feet shouting.

'No – wait! It doesn't have to be this way! Just listen to me for a moment and—'

'No. I've already heard more than enough,' came the

flat, lethal response. 'Because of the damage your careless greed may have done both sides in the war and the needless distress you have inflicted upon the Maxwells and upon Robert Brandon . . . but, above all, for the lives of my father and mother, of Richard and Gwynneth . . . I claim reparation.' And gently, deliberately, in the suddenly ominous silence, he pulled the trigger.

The room blurred in a fountain of red and the door burst open.

'Bloody hell!' said Eden. Then, looking around in more detail, 'Oh Christ.'

Nothing remained of Cyrus Winter's face and close by, colourless and frowning in a cloud of acrid smoke, Luciano stood staring motionlessly down at him. Equally pale and still, Kate gazed out from behind a jumble of heaped-up furniture, while Selim had swung to meet the invasion, knife in hand; there was blood everywhere.

It flowed sluggishly from Winter's smashed head, forming a pool on the polished floor and dyeing the silver hair crimson; it spattered the book-lined walls, the glass of the windows – even Kate's collar. And Luciano was quite literally covered with it.

'*Hell*,' said Eden again. And then, turning abruptly on the stunned, curious faces thronging the doorway, 'Robert, Abel – send the spectators away and guard the door. Tom – find something to throw over the major.' He hesitated briefly. Luciano still hadn't moved and the dark eyes were peculiarly empty. Eden shrugged and said, 'Kate? Are you all right?'

'Yes.' Her voice was thread-like but composed and her gaze had shifted from Cyrus Winter's corpse to her husband's rigid back.

Something in the charged atmosphere of the room lifted the hairs on Eden's neck. He said, 'What the devil happened here?'

'Justice was done,' replied Kate. And, laying down her loaded pistol, she made her way to Luciano's side.

The blood was drying on his clothes and skin and, though the unspeakable thing on the floor was now decently covered with a curtain, he continued to stare at it. Like Selim, Kate waited without speaking. And finally, like one awaking from a long sleep, Luciano looked down on his bloodstained hands before turning his head towards his wife. Expression returned slowly to both green eyes and black, bringing a quiet, perfect understanding in which words had no part. Then, in his own time, Luciano said simply, 'It's over – and this is no longer any place for us. Let's go.'

From all around and as far away as London, merchants came to barter with the soldiers for the rich spoils of Basing House. Meats, cheeses, wines, elegant furnishings, vibrant tapestries and fine gowns – some literally stripped from the backs of their owners – all changed hands at bargain prices. The sale would probably have gone on for days, had not the house burst suddenly and inexplicably into flames.

It could probably have been put out if anyone had wanted to try. But it was a Papist stronghold and so the crowd fell back and watched avidly while it burned. Fire engulfed the walls, heat shattered the windows and lead poured in a molten flood from the roof. And only then, when it was too late, did the New Model remember the prisoners it had consigned to the cellars.

Twenty hours later, the horrible screams had dwindled into a pall of silence and there was nothing left but blackened walls and charred, smouldering wreckage. Completely and irretrievably gutted, with six of the priests and half its garrison dead and its lord gaoled in Basingstoke, the house sometimes known as 'Loyalty' had paid the ultimate price.

Handfast and silent, Kate and Luciano took one last, long look before leaving the place forever. Then, turning from it to gaze deep into his wife's eyes, Luciano said, 'This is not an end – it's a beginning. And though the debt I owe my uncle will take every penny I have, we shall still be rich in the only things that truly matter. For I love you beyond life . . . and together we can do anything.' He paused and then, smiling, said, 'Let's go home.'

Kate drew a long, purifying breath and nodded. With sure, tender hands he helped her to the saddle and vaulted lightly to his own. Then, with Selim as ever in their wake, they turned their horses' heads towards Thorne Ash . . . and did not look back.

Genoa

April 1646

'Give me but one firm spot on which to stand and I will move the earth.'

Archimedes

Epilogue

Despite all Luciano's descriptions of it, Kate found that nothing had prepared her for Genoa. It was a living tapestry of gleaming white marble, soft black slate and glowing terracotta whose colours constantly veered and shifted with the changing light; a regal city of palaces, churches and turreted ramparts, all squeezed between the mountains and the sea. There were richly painted cloisters, porticoed villas, bustling quaysides; and in the narrow, winding alleyways like the one in which Luciano had spent eight years learning his trade, hundreds of small, niched Madonnas gazed serenely down upon the squalor.

The intervening months had been passed at Thorne Ash, in talk and laughter and simple, daily companionship. And while the war shuddered to its inevitable, inglorious conclusion, and Ralph Cochrane arrived, disillusioned from the fray, to slip gradually into the role of general factotum, Luciano perfected Kate's sketchy Italian, told her the grim unvarnished tale of his early life, and spoke for the first time of the Black Madonna. Then, in the spring, he took her with him on the last stage of a journey which would end – as it had begun, ten full years before – at the Villa Falcieri.

The vast frescoed salon was still exactly as it had been a decade ago. It was only Vittorio, sitting alone amidst the splendour in his great carved chair, who had changed. Ill health and the strain of protecting his empire almost single-handed had drained the vigour from his frame and the spark from his eye. He looked old – and worse still, he felt it.

Broodingly, he surveyed the young couple in front of

him. At thirty, Luciano was no longer the gaunt, worryingly self-possessed child he'd tried to reject – nor even the impersonal, shabby youth he'd only been able to keep by means of a massive loan. He was a man at the height of his powers . . . a man whose true calibre and potential could as yet only be guessed at; and the red-haired girl at his side looked as though she was worthy of him. Vittorio thought fleetingly of his own good-for-nothing sons and the chattering magpies they had all married. Then, drawing a long breath, he opened the channel that would lead to decision.

'Well? Is it done?'

'It's done,' replied Luciano. And with one ironically lifted brow, 'Did you think I would fail?'

Vittorio ignored the provocation. 'And the money?'

'Here.' Releasing Kate's hand, he walked unhurriedly forward to lay a stained and crumpled piece of paper before his uncle. 'I apologise for the state of it. But, as you can see, it's been through rather a lot.'

The fingers that reached out to pick it up were less than steady and, for a moment, there was silence. The amount was exact to the last florin. Vittorio looked up from it and said slowly, 'There's blood on it. Whose?'

'That of the man who murdered your brother. It didn't get there intentionally – but I thought perhaps you wouldn't object to seeing it.' Luciano paused and, turning, held out his arm to Kate. Then, when she was once more at his side, he said, 'It's a long story. But we could tell it, if you wish.'

A long-forgotten feeling stirred in Vittorio's chest, but because he no longer knew how to express it, he merely said, 'Then you'd better help yourself to wine and sit down. This floor is hard on the feet – and I wouldn't like your lady wife to think me lacking in courtesy.'

Kate grinned. 'Mother always said one should be wary of making hasty judgements – particularly in the family.'

And Vittorio, without quite knowing how it happened, found himself smiling back.

As Luciano had said, the tale took time. But by the end of it there was colour in Vittorio's cheeks and he felt more alive than he had in years. He said reflectively, 'So . . . you've done what you set out to do and managed to settle with me as well. But how has all this left you placed?'

'Financially?' Luciano exchanged a small, private smile with his wife and then shrugged. 'We still own a shop in Cheapside – to which we're not especially eager to return; Kate has her dowry and I the skill of my hands. It's not much, but it's enough to enable us to start again and hopefully build something for our children.'

Kate smiled back but said nothing. The last few days had given them reason to believe that she was pregnant, but it was still a little early to be sure.

Vittorio saw the look and drew his own conclusions. Pulling open a drawer of his desk, he laid two items beside the banker's draft. One was a scrolled document . . . and the other was the Madonna. His fingers lingering on its smooth curves, he said, 'Under the terms of our agreement, you also have this. Take it.'

Luciano enclosed the lady in a light, cool clasp. Since the day he had given her up, this was the first time he had seen her. A faint smile touched his mouth. So small and plain an object to have achieved so much; so unlikely a tool to bring about a man's destruction. He looked at Kate and received her understanding of what this moment must mean to him. Then, with a complete absence of drama, he placed the Madonna back on the polished surface in front of his uncle and said, 'I can wait. Hold her in trust for me.'

The unexpectedness of it caught Vittorio by the throat and it was a long time before he spoke. Then he said unevenly, 'You are – generous.'

'No. Let us just say that, for the present, your need is greater than mine.' Luciano rose. 'And now, with the obligations on both sides satisfactorily fulfilled, I think it's time we left you to rest.'

'*No!*' Some of the old vitality returned to Vittorio's voice. 'You'll go when I tell you and not before. You may be used to doing as you please – but I'm still your uncle, God damn it!'

629

'So?' came the deliberately infuriating reply.

'So read that,' snapped Vittorio, shoving the scroll at him. And almost but not quite under his breath, 'Arrogant puppy!'

Laughter sprang to Luciano's eyes, only to evaporate as soon as he glanced at the document in his hands. 'This is your Will,' he frowned.

'I know that! Now do as you're bid and read it.'

Subsiding slowly back into his chair, Luciano did so; and Kate watched with some concern as his face grew steadily paler and more austere. Then, finally, he looked up at Vittorio and said flatly, 'You can't mean this.'

'Can't I? Why do you think I insisted on you coming here in person all these years, if not because it was my only way of keeping track of you,' rumbled Vittorio. And then bitterly, 'Do I have to say it? You know as well as I do what my own sons are worth. And, much though I hate to admit it, I've grown . . . fond of you.' He scowled forbiddingly and hunched one shoulder. 'But don't run away with the idea that I'm doing this for your benefit. I'm not. And things would have been very different if you'd failed. Now. Tell your wife what we're talking about and let's make an end.'

Very, very slowly, Luciano turned a strangely dilated gaze on Kate. Then he said dryly, 'Do you need to be told? My uncle – as I'm sure you've gathered – is offering us a future that is rather different to the one we had in mind.'

Kate slid her hand into his. 'What, precisely?'

'Wealth and commercial power,' he replied. 'His sons, my cousins, are to get this house and all it contains, along with Vittorio's personal fortune. But I am to inherit all the Falcieri interests in banking, shipping and gold.'

Kate's eyes widened and then turned to Vittorio. 'Why?' she asked baldly.

'Because I don't want the work of two generations reduced to nothing – and my three would milk the business dry inside a year to finance their own pleasures,' he responded. 'Luciano, on the other hand, is the only one of the four who could build it into something greater. And if his father hadn't run off to England, he'd have had at least half of it anyway.'

'It's basically a matter of there being no room for sentiment in business,' remarked Luciano in something not quite his normal tone. 'But what *you* have to consider is whether you want to live here in Genoa.'

Her fingers tightening on his, Kate said, 'It's the perfect vehicle for your talents. Are you saying you'd give it all up for me?'

'Something like that.'

'And you think I'd *let* you?'

Wicked amusement hovered at the corners of his mouth. 'Now that you come to mention it – no. But never let it be said that I don't consult you. And you know what they say. Whether a woman accepts or refuses, she is always glad to have been asked.'

Author's Note

In 1912, the collection of cameos, loose stones and early seventeenth-century Italianate jewellery known as the Cheapside Hoard* was discovered in the precise location I have given for Luciano's shop. I do not, however, say that my version of how it came to be there is the true one; I merely suggest it as one of many ways in which it *may* have happened.

The Marquis of Winchester's golden stags, on the other hand, belong more properly to legend – since, if they really existed, it seems unlikely that his lordship would have continued to live in reduced circumstances after the Restoration.

And finally . . . although Luciano and the Maxwells are purely my invention, I've tried to give an accurate picture of the complex times in which they lived. I have therefore read numerous books and would like to pay particular tribute to the following: *Love Loyalty* by Wilfred Emberton; *The Storm of Bristol* by Bernard de Gomme, Raider Games of Leeds; and C.V. Wedgwood's *The King's Peace* and *The King's War*, William Collins & Sons.

Stella Riley

*Now on display in the Museum of London.

RUTH NICHOLS

The Burning of the Rose

A
compelling
fifteenth
century
love story

In the Florence of the Medicis and the Renaissance painters, Claire Tarleton, beautiful and talented musician, artists' model and scholar, is brought up by the foster parents who have cared for her since her real parents died in the plague of London.

Despite her elegant surroundings and protected upbringing, Claire is conscious that she lives in a world of adventure and danger, born into the knowledge that war is permanent. Even as the Hundred Years' War is ending, the Turks are advancing on Italy and Claire and her family flee to Normandy. For Claire the move from a city of beauty and culture to a grey coastal village proves traumatic . . .

Here, English by birth but French by nurture, Claire discovers half-denied questions about her true parentage, and about where her own future lies. Trapped within the violently divided loyalties of the community, she betrays and is betrayed by the man she loves . . .

FICTION/HISTORICAL   0 7472 3512 0

A selection of bestsellers from Headline

FICTION

WINDSONG	Unity Hall	£5.99 ☐
HIGH WATER	Peter Ling	£4.99 ☐
HALLMARK	Elizabeth Walker	£5.99 ☐
DARK MOUNTAIN	Richard Laymon	£4.99 ☐
THE RED SWASTIKA	Martin L Gross	£4.99 ☐
THE PALACE AFFAIR	Una-Mary Parker	£4.99 ☐
POLLY OF PENN'S PLACE	Dee Williams	£4.99 ☐
THE PIRATE QUEEN	Diana Norman	£5.99 ☐
GAMES OF THE HANGMAN	Victor O'Reilly	£5.99 ☐
GLEAM OF GOLD	Tessa Barclay	£5.99 ☐
A GARLAND OF VOWS	Harriet Smart	£5.99 ☐

NON-FICTION

THE QUEEN	John Parker	£6.99 ☐
TRAVELLING PLAYER	Michael York	£6.99 ☐
GINGER: MY STORY	Ginger Rogers	£6.99 ☐
LES ANGLAIS	Philippe Daudy	£7.99 ☐

SCIENCE FICTION AND FANTASY

GUARD AGAINST DISHONOUR	Simon R Green	£4.50 ☐
THE ULTIMATE FRANKENSTEIN	Byron Preiss (Ed)	£4.99 ☐

All Headline books are available at your local bookshop or newsagent, or can be ordered direct from the publisher. Just tick the titles you want and fill in the form below. Prices and availability subject to change without notice.

Headline Book Publishing PLC, Cash Sales Department, PO Box 11, Falmouth, Cornwall, TR10 9EN, England.

Please enclose a cheque or postal order to the value of the cover price and allow the following for postage and packing:
UK & BFPO: £1.00 for the first book, 50p for the second book and 30p for each additional book ordered up to a maximum charge of £3.00.
OVERSEAS & EIRE: £2.00 for the first book, £1.00 for the second book and 50p for each additional book.

Name ....

Address ....

....

....